A full-time professional writer since 1969, BILL PRONZINI has published more than 30 novels, including a dozen in the 'Nameless Detective' series; 275 short stories, articles, and essays in a wide variety of fields; and some 35 anthologies, including several in co-editorship with Martin H. Greenberg. *Hoodwink*, a 'Nameless Detective' novel, won Pronzini the PWA (Private Eye Writers of America) Best Novel Award for 1981. His fiction has been translated into 17 languages and published in two dozen countries around the world.

MARTIN H. GREENBERG, who has been called 'the king of anthologists,' now has some 115 of them to his credit. Greenberg is professor of regional analysis and political science at the University of Wisconsin - Green Bay, where he also teaches a course in the history of science fiction. With Isaac Asimov and Charles G. Waugh, Greenberg is co-editor of *The Mammoth Book of Classic Science Fiction*.

The Mammoth Book of
PRIVATE EYE
Stories

The Mammoth Book of
PRIVATE EYE
Stories

Edited by Bill Pronzini
and Martin H. Greenberg

Robinson Publishing
London

Robinson Publishing
11 Shepherd House
Shepherd Street
London W1Y 7LD

First published 1988

ISBN 0 948164 81 6

Typset by Grassroots, London
Printed by Wm. Collins & Sons Ltd., Glasgow

CONTENTS

viii

ACKNOWLEDGMENTS

'The Pencil' (also known as 'Wrong Pigeon') by Raymond Chandler. From *The Midnight Raymond Chandler* by Raymond Chandler. Copyright © 1971 by Helga Greene, Executrix. Reprinted by permission of Houghton Mifflin Company.

'Suicide is Scandalous' by Henry Kane. Copyright © 1947, 1948 by Henry Kane. Reprinted by permission of the Scott Meredith Literary Agency, Inc., 845 Third Avenue, New York, NY 10022.

'Wanted–Dead and Alive' by Stephen Marlowe. Copyright © 1963 by Flying Eagle Publications Inc. Reprinted by permission of the Scott Meredith Literary Agency, Inc., 845 Third Avenue, New York NY 10022.

'Dead Giveaway' by Richard S. Prather. Copyright © 1957 by Fawcett Publications, Inc. Reprinted by permission of Richard Curtis Associates, Inc.

'So Dark for April' by Howard Browne. Copyright 1953; renewed © 1981 by Howard Browne. Reprinted by permission of the author.

'Before She Kills' by Fredric Brown. Copyright © 1961 by Pocket Books, Inc. Reprinted by permission of the Scott Meredith Literary Agency, Inc., 845 Third Avenue, New York, NY 10022, and Roberta Pryor, Inc.

'Death Flight' by Ed McBain. Copyright 1954; renewed © 1982 by Evan Hunter. Reprinted by permission of the author and John Farquharson, Ltd.

'Guilt-Edged Blonde' by Ross Macdonald. Copyright 1953 by Kenneth Millar; Copyright renewed 1981 by the Margaret Millar Survivor's Trust u/a 4/12/82. Reprinted by permission of Harold Ober Associates Inc.

INTRODUCTION

The private eye story is an acclaimed sub-genre of crime fiction, important for its high entertainment value, the contributions of its best writers, and its influences on other aspects of popular culture (films, radio and television drama). The P.I.'s antecedents may be traced all the way back to Sherlock Holmes, himself a 'private inquiry agent', although it was in the pages of the pioneering pulp magazine *Black Mask* in the 1920s that the modern realist school of American private detective fiction was established by Carroll John Daly and, far more importantly, by Dashiell Hammett.

During the past sixty-odd years there have been thousands of novels and stories featuring the tough, often cynical, and sometimes hard-drinking loner who, in Raymond Chandler's now-famous phrase, walks 'the mean streets' of such urban centers as New York, Los Angeles, Chicago, and San Francisco. ('. . . But down these mean streets a man must go who is not himself mean – who is neither tarnished nor afraid . . .') Many of these novels and stories have been very good; many more have been very bad or (cardinal sin!) indifferent. Yet there has been no waning of the private eye's popularity, as evidenced by the number of writers successfully producing this type of detective story today, and the enthusiasm with which their work is received.

There is no question that the most influential producers of private eye fiction over the past six decades have been Hammett, Chandler, and Ross Macdonald. Hammett virtually invented the modern 'hard-boiled' school with his tales of the Continental Op and Sam Spade; Chandler with Philip Marlowe and Macdonald with Lew Archer each refined it in a different way. But these three writers are by no means the only important ones in P.I. literature. Many others have added dimension and scope to the form; have shaped it in the past and are reshaping it for the future.

None of these other important writers is a strict and slavish imitator of the 'Big Three'. Each has his own style, his own quirks and embellishments and innovative ideas. Robert Leslie Bellem, for instance, delighted a generation of pulp magazine readers with his wonderfully slangy, campy Dan Turner stories; these spawned a number of his own imitators, and attracted the attention of humorist S.J. Perelman, whose *New Yorker* essay on Bellem and Turner, 'Somewhere a Roscoe...', 'is a minor classic. Richard S. Prather injected a strong element of sexy, farcical humor into his Shell Scott series, a combination that sold millions of paperbacks in the 1950s and 1960s and also begat a host of imitators. Stephen Marlowe took his P.I., Chet Drum, out of a strictly American milieu and embroiled him in adventures in such far-flung locales as Berlin, Greece, South America, and Iceland. William Campbell Gault and Thomas B. Dewey imbued their investigators with human instead of super-human qualities and thereby paved the way for a new type of private eye novel, one which emphasizes the detective's private life and the short and long-range effects his walks down the mean streets have on *him*, as well as on those whose paths he crosses. Writers such as Joseph Hansen, Michael Collins, and Lawrence Block have proven that a detective who is 'different' is just as effective as his more orthodox counterparts: Hansen's Dave Brandstetter is a practicing homosexual, Collins's Dan Fortune is a one-armed intellectual, Block's Matt Scudder is a hard-core (later recovered) alcoholic with a tragic past. And Marcia Muller, Sue Grafton, and Sara Paretsky, among others, have entered what was previously the all-but-exclusive domain of men by establishing significant female private eyes of their own–not merely reflections of their male counterparts, but realistic and fully realized women who happen to be private investigators.

The twenty-six stories in this book represent some of the finest short private eye fiction of the past half century, by most of the writers above, and others who have helped define and are in the process of redefining P.I. literature. To paraphrase Chandler: Down all these mean streets men and women go who are not themselves mean, who are neither tarnished nor afraid–and in whose company you'll find hours of reading enjoyment.

Bill Pronzini and
Martin H. Greenberg

RAYMOND CHANDLER
(1888-1959)

Wrong Pigeon
(Philip Marlowe)

He was a slightly fat man with a dishonest smile that pulled the corners of his mouth out half an inch leaving the thick lips tight and his eyes bleak. For a fattish man he had a slow walk. Most fat men are brisk and light on their feet. He wore a gray herringbone suit and a hand-painted tie with part of a diving girl visible on it. His shirt was clean, which comforted me, and his brown loafers, as wrong as the tie for his suit, shone from a recent polishing.

He sidled past me as I held the door between the waiting room and my thinking parlor. Once inside, he took a quick look around. I'd have placed him as a mobster, second grade, if I had been asked. For once I was right. If he carried a gun, it was inside his pants. His coat was too tight to hide the bulge of an underarm holster.

He sat down carefully and I sat opposite and we looked at each other. His face had a sort of foxy eagerness. He was sweating a little. The expression on my face was meant to be interested but not clubby. I reached for a pipe and the leather humidor in which I kept my Pearce's tobacco. I pushed cigarettes at him.

"I don't smoke." He had a rusty voice. I didn't like it any more than I liked his clothes, or his face. While I filled the pipe he reached inside his coat, prowled in a pocket, came out with a bill, glanced at it and dropped it across the desk in front of me. It was a nice bill and clean and new. One thousand dollars.

"Ever save a guy's life?"

"Once in a while, maybe."

"Save mine."

"What goes?"

"I heard you levelled with the customers, Marlowe."

"That's why I stay poor."

"I still got two friends. You make it three and you'll be out of the red. You got five grand coming if you pry me loose."

"From what?"

"You're talkative as hell this morning. Don't you pipe who I am?"

"Nope."

"Never been east, huh?"

"Sure–but I wasn't in your set."

"What set would that be?"

I was getting tired of it. "Stop being so goddam cagey or pick up your grand and be missing."

"I'm Ikky Rosenstein. I'll be missing but good unless you can figure some out. Guess."

"I've already guessed. You tell me and tell me quick. I don't have all day to watch you feeding me with an eye-dropper."

"I ran out on the Outfit. The high boys don't go for that. To them it means you got info you figure you can peddle, or you got independent ideas, or you lost your moxie. Me, I lost my moxie. I had it up to here." He touched his Adam's apple with the forefinger of a stretched hand. "I done bad things. I scared and hurt guys. I never killed nobody. That's nothing to the Outfit. I'm out of line. So they pick up the pencil and they draw a line. I got the word. The operators are on the way. I made a bad mistake. I tried to hole up in Vegas. I figured they'd never expect me to lie up in their own joint. They outfigured me. What I did's been done before, but I didn't know it. When I took the plane to LA there must have been somebody on it. They know where I live."

"Move."

"No good now. I'm covered." I knew he was right.

"Why haven't they taken care of you already?"

"They don't do it that way. Always specialists. Don't you know how it works?"

"More or less. A guy with a nice hardware store in Buffalo. A guy with a small dairy in KC. Always a good front. They report back to New York or somewhere. When they mount the plane west or wherever they're going, they have guns in their briefcases. They're quiet and well-dressed, and they don't sit together. They could be a couple of lawyers or income tax sharpies–anything at all that's well-mannered and inconspicuous. All sorts of people carry briefcases. Including women."

"Correct as hell. And when they land they'll be steered to me, but not from the airfield. They got ways. If I go to the cops, somebody will know about me. They could have a couple Mafia boys right on the City Council for all I know. It's been done. The cops will give me twenty-fours to leave town. No use. Mexico? Worse than here. Canada? Better but still no good. Connections there too."

"Australia?"

"Can't get a passport. I been here twenty-five years–illegal. They can't deport me unless they can prove a crime on me. The Outfit would see they didn't. Suppose I got tossed into the freezer. I'm out on a writ in twenty-four hours. And my nice friends got a car waiting to take me home–only not home."

I had my pipe lit and going well. I frowned down at the grand note. I could use it very nicely. My checking account could kiss the sidewalk without stooping.

"Let's stop horsing," I said. "Suppose–just suppose–I could figure an out for you. What's your next move?"

"I know a place–if I could get there without bein' tailed. I'd leave my car here and take a rent car. I'd turn it in just short of the county line and buy a secondhand job. Halfway to where I'm going I trade it on a new last's model, a leftover. This is just the right time of year. Good discount, new models out soon. Not to save money–less show off. Where I'd go is a good-sized place but still pretty clean."

"Uh-huh," I said. "Wichita, last I heard. But it may have changed."

He scowled at me. "Get smart, Marlowe, but not too damn smart."

"I'll get as smart as I want to. Don't try to make rules for me. If I take this on, there aren't any rules. I take it for this grand and the rest if I bring it off. Don't cross me. I might leak information. If I get knocked off, put just one red rose on my grave. I don't like cut flowers. I like to see them growing. But I could take one, because you're such a sweet character. When's the plane in?"

"Sometime today. It's nine hours from New York. Probably come in about 5:30 p.m."

"Might come by San Diego and switch or by San Francisco and switch. A lot of planes from Dago and Frisco. I need a helper."

"Goddam you, Marlowe–"

"Hold it. I know a girl. Daughter of a chief of police who got broken for honesty. She wouldn't leak under torture."

"You got no right to risk her," Ikky said angrily.

I was so astonished my jaw hung halfway to my waist. I closed it slowly and swallowed.

"Good God, the man's got a heart."

"Women ain't built for the rough stuff," he said, grudgingly.

I picked up the thousand dollar note and snapped it. "Sorry. No receipt," I said. "I can't have my name in your pocket. And there won't be any rough stuff if I'm lucky. They'd have me outclassed.

There's only one way to work it. Now give me your address and all the dope you can think of, names, descriptions of any operators you have ever seen in the flesh."

He did. He was a pretty good observer. Trouble was the Outfit would know what he had seen. The operators would be strangers to him.

He got up silently and put his hand out. I had to shake it, but what he had said about women made it easier. His hand was moist. Mine would have been in his spot. He nodded and went out silently.

It was a quiet street in Bay City, if there are any quiet streets in this beatnik generation when you can't get through a meal without some male or female stomach singer belching out a kind of love that is as old-fashioned as a bustle or some Hammond organ jazzing it up in the customer's soup.

The little one story house was as neat as a fresh pinafore. The front lawn was cut lovingly and very green. The smooth composition driveway was free of grease spots from standing cars, and the hedge that bordered it looked as though the barber came every day.

The white door had a knocker with a tiger's head, a go-to-hell window and a dingus that let someone inside talk to someone outside without even opening the little window.

I'd have given a mortgage on my left leg to live in a house like that. I didn't think I ever would.

The bell chimed inside and after a while she opened the door in a pale blue sports shirt and white shorts that were short enough to be friendly. She had gray-blue eyes, dark red hair and fine bones in her face. There was usually a trace of bitterness in the gray-blue eyes. She couldn't forget that her father's life had been destroyed by the crooked power of a gambling ship mobster, that her mother had died too. She was able to suppress the bitterness when she wrote nonsense about young love for the shiny magazines, but this wasn't her life. She didn't really have a life. She had an existence without much pain and enough oil money to make it safe. But in a tight spot she was as cool and resourceful as a good cop. Her name was Anne Riordan.

She stood to one side and I passed her pretty close. But I have rules too. She shut the door and parked herself on a davenport and went through the cigarette routine, and here was one doll who had the strength to light her own cigarette.

I stood looking around. There were a few changes, not many.

"I need your help," I said.

"That's the only time I ever see you."

"I've got a client who is an ex-hood; used to be a trouble-shooter for the Outfit, the Syndicate, the big mob, or whatever name you want to use for it. You know damn well it exists and is as rich as

Rockefeller. You can't beat it because not enough people want to, especially the million-a-year lawyers that work for it, and the bar associations that seem more anxious to protect other lawyers than their own country."

"My God, are you running for office somewhere? I never knew you to sound so pure."

She moved her legs around, not provocatively–she wasn't the type–but it made it difficult for me to think straight just the same.

"Stop moving your legs around," I said. "Or else put a pair of slacks on."

"Damn you, Marlowe. Can't you think of anything else?"

"I'll try. I like to think that I know at least one pretty and charming female who doesn't have round heels." I swallowed and went on. "The man's name is Ikky Rosenstein. He's not beautiful and he's not anything that I like–except one. He got mad when I said I needed a girl helper. He said women were not made for the rough stuff. That's why I took the job. To a real mobster, a woman means no more than a sack of flour. They use women in the usual way, but if it's advisable to get rid of them, they do it without a second thought."

"So far you've told me a whole lot of nothing. Perhaps you need a cup of coffee or a drink."

"You're sweet but I don't in the morning–except sometimes and this isn't one of them. Coffee later. Ikky has been pencilled."

"Now what's that?"

"You have a list. You draw a line through a name with a pencil. The guy is as good as dead. The Outfit has reasons. They don't do it just for kicks any more. They don't get any kick. It's just book-keeping to them."

"What on earth can I do? I might even have said, what can *you* do?"

"I can try. What you can do is help me spot their plane and see where they go–the operators assigned to the job."

"How can you do anything?"

"I said I could try. If they took a night plane they are already here. If they took a morning plane they can't be here before five or so. Plenty of time to get set. You know what they look like."

"Oh sure. I meet killers everyday. I have them in for whiskey sours and caviare on hot toast." She grinned. While she was grinning I took four long steps across the tan figured rug and lifted her and put a kiss on her mouth. She didn't fight me but she didn't go all trembly either. I went back and sat down.

"They'll look like anybody who's in a quiet well-run business or profession. They'll have quiet clothes and they'll be polite–when they want to be. They'll have briefcases with guns in them that have changed hands so often they can't possibly be traced. When and if they do the job, they'll drop the guns. They'll probably use revolvers, but they could use automatics. They won't use silencers because silencers can jam a gun and the weight makes it hard to shoot accurately. They won't sit together on the plane, but once off of it they may pretend to know each other and simply not have noticed during the flight. They may shake hands with appropriate smiles and walk away and get in the same taxi. I think they'll go to a hotel first. But very soon they will move into something from which they can watch Ikky's movements and get used to his schedule. They won't be in a hurry unless Ikky makes a move. That would tip them off that Ikky has been tipped off. He has a couple of friends left–he says."

"Will they shoot him from this room or apartment across the street–assuming there is one?"

"No. They'll shoot him from three feet away. They'll walk up behind him and say, 'Hello, Ikky.' He'll either freeze or turn. They'll fill him with lead, drop the guns, and hop into the car they have waiting. Then they'll follow the crash car off the scene."

"Who'll drive the crash car?"

"Some well-fixed and blameless citizen who hasn't been rapped. He'll drive his own car. He'll clear the way, even if he has to accidentally on purpose crash somebody, even a police car. He'll be so goddam sorry he'll cry all the way down his monogrammed shirt. And the killers will be long gone."

"Good heavens," Anne said. "How can you stand your life? If you did bring it off, they'll send operators to you."

"I don't think so. They don't kill a legit. The blame will go to the operators. Remember, these top mobsters are businessmen. They want lots and lots of money. They only get really tough when they figure they have to get rid of somebody, and they don't crave that. There's always a chance of a slip-up. Not much of a chance. No gang killing has ever been solved here or anywhere else except two or three times. Lepke Buchalter fried. Remember Anastasia? He was awful big and awful tough. Too big, too tough. Pencil."

She shuddered a little. "I think I need a drink myself."

I grinned at her. "You're right in the atmosphere, darling. I'll weaken."

She brought a couple of Scotch highballs. When we were drinking them I said: "If you spot them or think you spot them, follow to where they go–if you can do it safely. Not otherwise. If it's a hotel–and ten to one it will be–check in and keep calling me until you get me."

She knew my office number and I was still on Yucca Avenue. She knew that too.

"You're the damnedest guy," she said. "Women do anything you want them to. How come I'm still a virgin at twenty-eight?"

"We need a few like you. Why don't you get married?"

"To what? Some cynical chaser who has nothing left but technique? I don't know any really nice men–except you. I'm no pushover for white teeth and a gaudy smile."

I went over and pulled her to her feet. I kissed her long and hard. "I'm honest," I almost whispered. "That's something. But I'm too shop-soiled for a girl like you. I've thought of you. I've wanted you, but that sweet clear look in your eyes tells me to lay off."

"Take me," she said softly. "I have dreams too."

"I couldn't. It's not the first time it's happened to me. I've had too many women to deserve one like you. We have to save a man's life. I'm going."

She stood up and watched me leave with a grave face.

The women you get and the women you don't get–they live in different worlds. I don't sneer at either world. I live in both myself.

At Los Angeles International Airport you can't get close to the planes unless you're leaving on one. You see them land, if you happen to be in the right place, but you have to wait at a barrier to get a look at the passengers. The airport buildings don't make it any easier. They are strung out from here to breakfast time, and you can get calluses walking from TWA to American.

I copied an arrival schedule off the boards and prowled around like a dog that has forgotten where he put his bone. Planes came in, planes took off, porters carried luggage, passengers sweated and scurried, children whined, the loudspeaker overrode all the other noises.

I passed Anne a number of times. She took no notice of me.

At 5:45 they must have come.

Anne disappeared. I gave it half an hour, just in case she had some other reason for fading. No. She was gone for good. I went out to my car and drove some long crowded miles to Hollywood and my office. I had a drink and sat. At 6:45 the phone rang.

"I think so," she said. "Beverly-Western Hotel. Room 410. I couldn't get any names. You know the clerks don't leave registration cards lying around these days. I didn't like to ask any questions. But I rode up in the elevator with them and spotted their room. I walked right on past them when the bellman put a key in their door, and walked down to the mezzanine and then downstairs with a bunch of women from the tea room. I didn't bother to take a room."

"What were they like?"

"They came up the ramp together but I didn't hear them speak. Both had briefcases, both wore quiet suits, nothing flashy. White shirts, starched, one blue tie, one black striped with gray. Black shoes. A couple of businessmen from the East Coast. They could be publishers, lawyers, doctors, account executives–no, cut the last; they weren't gaudy enough. You wouldn't look at them twice."

"Look at them twice. Faces."

"Both medium brown hair, one a bit darker than the other. Smooth faces, rather expressionless. One had gray eyes; the one with the lighter hair had blue eyes. Their eyes were interesting. Very quick to move, very observant, watching everything near them. That might have been wrong. They should have been a bit preoccupied with what they came out for or interested in California. They seemed more occupied with faces. It's a good thing I spotted them and not you. You don't look like a cop, but you don't look like a man who is not a cop. You have marks on you."

"Phooey. I'm a damn good looking heart wrecker."

"Their features were strictly assembly line. Neither looked Italian. Each picked up a flight suitcase. One suitcase was gray with two red and white stripes up and down, about six or seven inches from the ends, the other a blue and white tartan. I didn't know there was such a tartan."

"There is, but I forget the name of it."

"I thought you knew everything."

"Just almost everything. Run along home now."

"Do I get a dinner and maybe a kiss?"

"Later, and if you're not careful you'll get more than you want."

"A rapist, eh? I'll carry a gun. You'll take over and follow them?"

"If they're the right men, they'll follow me. I already took an apartmen across the street from Ikky. That block on Poynter and the two on each side of it have about six lowlife apartment houses to the block. I'll bet the incidence of chippies is very high."

"It's high everywhere these days."

"So long, Anne. See you."

"When you need help."

She hung up. I hung up. She puzzled me. Too wise to be so nice. I guess all nice women are wise too. I called Ikky. He was out. I had a drink from the office bottle, smoked for half an hour and called again. This time I got him.

I told him the score up to then, and said I hoped Anne had picked the right men. I told him about the apartment I had taken.

"Do I get expenses?" I asked.

"Five grand ought to cover the lot."

"If I earn it and get it. I heard you had a quarter of a million," I said at a wild venture.

"Could be, pal; but how do I get at it? The high boys know where it is. It'll have to cool a long time."

I said that was all right. I had cooled a long time myself. Of course I didn't expect to get the four thousand, even if I brought the job off. Men like Ikky Rosenstein would steal their mother's gold teeth. There seemed to be a little good in him somewhere–but little was the operative word.

I spent the next half hour trying to think of a plan. I couldn't think of one that looked promising. It was almost eight o'clock and I needed food. I didn't think the boys would move that night. Next morning they would drive past Ikky's place and scout the neighborhood.

I was ready to leave the office when the buzzer sounded from the door of my waiting room. I opened the communicating door. A small tight-looking man was standing in the middle of the floor rocking on his heels with his hands behind his back. He smiled at me, but he wasn't good at it. He walked towards me.

"You Marlowe?"

"Who else? What can I do for you?"

He was close now. He brought his right hand around fast with a gun in it. He stuck the gun in my stomach.

"You can lay off Ikky Rosenstein," he said in a voice that matched his face, "or you can get your belly full of lead."

He was an amateur. If he had stayed four feet away, he might have had something. I reached up and took the cigarette out of my mouth and held it carelessly.

"What makes you think I know any Ikky Rosenstein?"

He laughed a high-pitched laugh and pushed his gun into my stomach.

"Wouldn't you like to know?" The cheap sneer, the empty triumph of power when you hold a fat gun in a small hand.

"It would be fair to tell me."

As his mouth opened for another crack, I dropped the cigarette and swept a hand. I can be fast when I have to. There are boys that are faster, but they don't stick guns in your stomach. I got my thumb behind the trigger and my hand over his. I kneed him in the groin. He bent over with a whimper. I twisted his arm to the right and I had his gun. I hooked a heel behind his heel and he was on the floor. He lay there blinking with surprise and pain, his knees drawn up against his stomach. He rolled from side to side groaning. I reached down and grabbed his left hand and yanked him to his feet. I had six inches and forty pounds on him. They ought to have sent a bigger, better trained messenger.

"Let's go into my thinking parlor," I said. "We could have a chat and you could have a drink to pick you up. Next time don't get near enough to a prospect for him to get your gun hand. I'll just see if you have any more iron on you."

He hadn't. I pushed him through the door and into a chair. His breath wasn't quite so rasping. He grabbed out a handkerchief and mopped at his face.

"Next time," he said between his teeth. "Next time."

"Don't be an optimist. You don't look the part."

I poured him a drink of Scotch in a paper cup, set it down in front of him. I broke his 38 and dumped the cartridges into the desk drawer. I clicked the chamber back and laid the gun down.

"You can have it when you leave—if you leave."

"That's a dirty way to fight," he said, still gasping.

"Sure. Shooting a man is so much cleaner. Now, how did you get here?"

"Screw yourself."

"Don't be a crumb. I have friends. Not many, but some. I can get you for armed assault, and you know what would happen then. You'd be out on a writ or on bail and that's the last anyone would hear of you. The biggies don't go for failures. Now who sent you and how did you know where to come?"

"Ikky was covered," he said sullenly. "He's dumb. I trailed him here without no trouble at all. Why would he go see a private eye? People want to know."

"More."

"Go to hell."

"Come to think of it, I don't have to get you for armed assault. I can smash it out of you right here and now."

I got up from the chair and he put a flat hand out.

"If I get knocked about, a couple of real tough monkeys will drop around. If I don't report back, same thing. You ain't holding no real high cards. They just look high," he said.

"You haven't anything to tell. If this Ikky guy came to see me, you don't know why, nor whether I took him on. If he's a mobster, he's not my type of client."

"He come to get you to try to save his hide."

"Who from?"

"That'd be talking."

"Go right ahead. Your mouth seems to work fine. And tell the boys any time I front for a hood, that will be the day."

You have to lie a little once in a while in my business. I was lying a little. "What's Ikky done to get himself disliked? Or would that be talking?"

"You think you're a lot of man," he sneered, rubbing the place where I had kneed him. "In my league you wouldn't make pinch runner."

I laughed in his face. Then I grabbed his right wrist and twisted it behind his back. He began to squawk. I reached into his breast pocket with my left hand and hauled out a wallet. I let him go. He reached for his gun on the desk and I bisected his upper arm with a hard cut. He fell into the customer's chair and grunted.

"You can have your gun," I told him. "When I give it to you. Now be good or I'll have to bounce you just to amuse myself."

In the wallet I found a driver's license made out to Charles Hickon. It did me no good at all. Punks of his type always have slangy pseudonyms. They probably called him Tiny, or Slim, or Marbles, or even just 'you'. I tossed the wallet back to him. It fell to the floor. He couldn't even catch it.

"Hell," I said, "there must be an economy campaign on, if they sent you to do more than pick up cigarette butts."

"Screw yourself."

"All right, mug. Beat it back to the laundry. Here's your gun."

He took it, made a business of shoving it into his waistband, stood up, gave me as dirty a look as he had in stock, and strolled to the door, nonchalant as a hustler with a new mink stole. He turned at the door and gave me the beady eye.

"Stay clean, tinhorn. Tin bends easy."

With this blinding piece of repartee he opened the door and drifted out.

After a little while I locked my other door, cut the buzzer, made the office dark, and left. I saw no one who looked like a lifetaker. I drove to my house, packed a suitcase, drove to a service station where they were almost fond of me, stored my car and picked up a Hertz Chevrolet. I drove this to Poynter Street, dumped my suitcase in the sleazy apartment I had rented early in the afternoon, and went to dinner at Victor's. It was nine o'clock, too late to drive to Bay City and take Anne to dinner. She'd have cooked her own long ago.

I ordered a double Gibson with fresh limes and drank it, and I was as hungry as a schoolboy.

On the way back to Poynter Street I did a good deal of weaving in and out and circling blocks and stopping, with a gun on the seat beside me. As far as I could tell, no one was trying to tail me.

I stopped on Sunset at a service station and made two calls from the box. I caught Bernie Ohls just as he was leaving to go home.

"This is Marlowe, Bernie. We haven't had a fight in years. I'm getting lonely."

"Well, get married. I'm chief investigator for the Sheriff's Office now. I rank acting-captain until I pass the exam. I don't hardly speak to private eyes."

"Speak to this one. I could need help. I'm on a ticklish job where I could get killed."

"And you expect me to interfere with the course of nature?"

"Come off it, Bernie. I haven't been a bad guy. I'm trying to save an ex-mobster from a couple of executioners."

"The more they mow each other down, the better I like it."

"Yeah. If I call you, come running or send a couple of good boys.

You'll have had time to teach them."

We exchanged a couple of mild insults and hung up. I dialed Ikky Rosenstein. His rather unpleasant voice said: "Okay, talk."

"Marlowe. Be ready to move out about midnight. We've spotted your boy friends and they are holed up at the Beverly-Western. They won't move to your street tonight. Remember, they don't know you've been tipped."

"Sounds chancy."

"Good God, it wasn't meant to be a Sunday School picnic. You've been careless, Ikky. You were followed to my office. That cuts the time we have."

He was silent for a moment. I heard him breathing. "Who by?" he asked.

"Some little tweezer who stuck a gun in my be'ly and gave me the trouble of taking it away from him. I can only figure why they sent a punk on the theory that they don't want me to know too much, in case I don't know it already."

"You're in for trouble, friend."

"When not? I'll come over to your place about midnight. Be ready. Where's your car?"

"Out front."

"Get it on a side street and make a business of locking it up. Where's the back door of your flop?"

"In back. Where would it be? On the alley."

"Leave your suitcase there. We walk out together and go to your car. We drive the alley and pick up the suitcase or cases."

"Suppose some guy steals them?"

"Yeah. Suppose you get dead. Which do you like better?"

"Okay," he grunted. "I'm waiting. But we're taking big chances."

"So do race drivers. Does that stop them? There's no way to get out but fast. Douse your lights about ten and rumple the bed well. It would be good if you could leave some baggage behind. Wouldn't look so planned."

He grunted another okay and I hung up. The telephone box was well lighted outside. They usually are, at service stations. I took a good long gander around while I pawed over the collection of give away maps inside the station. I saw nothing to worry me. I took a map of San Diego just for the hell of it and got into my rent car.

On Poynter I parked around the corner and went up to my second floor sleazy apartment and sat in the dark watching from my window. I saw nothing to worry about. A couple of medium-class chippies came out of Ikky's apartment house and were picked up in a late model car. A man about Ikky's height and build went into the apartment house. Various people came and went. The street was fairly quiet. Since they put in the Hollywood Freeway nobody much uses the off-the-boulevard streets unless they live in the neighborhood.

It was a nice fall night–or as nice as they get in Los Angeles' spoiled climate–clearish but not even crisp. I don't know what's happened to the weather in our overcrowded city but it's not the weather I knew when I came to it.

It seemed like a long time to midnight. I couldn't spot anybody watching anything, and no couple of quiet-suited men paged any of the six apartment houses available. I was pretty sure they'd try mine first when they came, and if Anne had picked the right men, and if anybody had come at all, and if the tweezer's message back to his bosses had done me any good or otherwise. In spite of the hundred ways Anne could be wrong, I had a hunch she was right. The killers had no reason to be cagey if they didn't know Ikky had been warned. No reason but one. He had come to my office and been tailed there. But the Outfit, with all its arrogance of power, might laugh at the idea he had been tipped off or come to me for help. I was so small they would hardly be able to see me.

At midnight I left the apartment, walked two blocks watching for a tail, crossed the street and went into Ikky's dive. There was no locked door, and no elevator. I climbed steps to the third floor and looked for his apartment. I knocked lightly. He opened the door with a gun in his hand. He probably looked scared.

There were two suitcases by the door and another against the far wall. I went over and lifted it. It was heavy enough. I opened it. It was unlocked.

"You don't have to worry," he said. "It's got everything a guy could need for three-four nights, and nothing except some clothes that I couldn't glom off in any ready to wear place."

I picked up one of the other suitcases. "Let's stash this by the back door."

"We can leave by the alley too."

"We leave by the front door. Just in case we're covered–though I don't think so–we're just two guys going out together. Just one thing. Keep both hands in your coat pockets and the gun in your right. If anybody calls out your name behind you, turn fast and shoot. Nobody but a lifetaker will do it. I'll do the same."

"I'm scared," he said in his rusty voice.

"Me too, if it helps any. But we have to do it. If you're braced, they'll have guns in their hands. Don't bother asking them questions. They wouldn't answer in words. If it's just my small friend, we'll cool him and dump him inside the door. Got it?"

He nodded, licking his lips. We carried the suitcases down and put them outside the back door. I looked along the alley. Nobody, and only a short distance to the side street. We went back in and along the hall to the front. We walked out on Poynter Street with all the casualness of a wife buying her husband a birthday tie.

Nobody made a move. The street was empty. We walked around the corner to Ikky's rent car. He unlocked it. I went back with him for the suitcases. Not a stir. We put the suitcases in the car and started up and drove to the next street.

A traffic light not working, a boulevard stop or two, the entrance to the Freeway. There was plenty of traffic on it even at midnight. California is loaded with people going places and making speed to get there. If you don't drive eighty miles an hour, everybody passes you. If you do, you have to watch the rear-view mirror for highway patrol cars. It's the rat race of rat races.

Ikky did a quiet seventy. We reached the junction to Route 66 and he took it. So far nothing. I stayed with him to Pomona.

"This is far enough for me," I said. "I'll grab a bus back if there is one, or park myself in a motor court. Drive to a service station and we'll ask for the bus stop. It should be close to the Freeway. Take us towards the business section."

He did that and stopped midway of a block. He reached out his pocketbook, and held out four thousand-dollar bills to me.

"I don't really feel I've earned all that. It was too easy."

He laughed with a kind of wry amusement on his pudgy face. "Don't be a sap. I have it made. You didn't know what you was walking into. What's more, your troubles are just beginning. The Outfit has eyes and ears everywhere. Perhaps I'm safe if I'm damn careful. Perhaps I ain't as safe as I think I am. Either way, you did what I asked. Take the dough. I got plenty."

I took it and put it away. He drove to an all-night service station and we were told where to find the bus stop. "There's a cross-country Greyhound at 2:25 a.m.," the attendant said, looking at a schedule. "They'll take you, if they got room."

Ikky drove to the bus stop. We shook hands and he went gunning down the road towards the Freeway. I looked at my watch and found a liquor store still open and bought a pint of Scotch. Then I found a bar and ordered a double with water.

My troubles were just beginning, Ikky had said. He was so right.

I got off at the Hollywood bus station, grabbed a taxi and drove to my office. I asked the driver to wait a few moments. At that time of night he was glad to. The colored night man let me into the building.

"You work late, Mr. Marlowe. But you always did, didn't you?"

"It's that sort of a business," I said. "Thanks, Jasper."

Up in my office I pawed the floor for mail and found nothing but a longish narrowish box, Special Delivery, with a Glendale postmark.

I opened it. It contained nothing at all but a new freshly-sharpened yellow pencil, the mobster's mark of death.

I didn't take it too hard. When they mean it, they don't send it to you. I took it as a sharp warning to lay off. There might be a beating arranged. From their point of view, that would be good discipline. "When we pencil a guy, any guy that tries to help him is in for a smashing." That could be the message.

I thought of going to my house on Yucca Avenue. Too lonely. I thought of going to Anne's place in Bay City. Worse. If they got wise to her, real hoods would think nothing of raping her and then beating her up.

It was the Poynter Street flop for me. Easily the safest place now. I went down to the waiting taxi and had him drive me to within three blocks of the so-called apartment house. I went upstairs, undressed and slept raw. Nothing bothered me but a broken spring. That bothered my back. I lay until 3:30 pondering the situation with my massive brain. I went to sleep with a gun under the pillow, which is a bad place to keep a gun when you have one pillow as thick and soft as a typewriter pad. It bothered me so I transferred it to my right hand. Practice had taught me to keep it there even in sleep.

I woke up with the sun shining. I felt like a piece of spoiled meat. I struggled into the bathroom and doused myself with cold water and wiped off with a towel you couldn't have seen if you held it sideways. This was a really gorgeous apartment. All it needed was a set of Chippendale furniture to graduate it into the slum class.

There was nothing to eat and if I went out, Miss-Nothing Marlowe might miss something. I had a pint of whiskey. I looked at it and smelled it, but I couldn't take it for breakfast, on an empty stomach, even if I could reach my stomach, which was floating around near the ceiling. I looked into the closets in case a previous tenant might have left a crust of bread in a hasty departure. Nope. I wouldn't have liked it anyhow, not even with whiskey on it. So I sat at the window. An hour of that and I was ready to bite a piece off a bellhop.

I dressed and went around the corner to the rent car and drove to an eatery. The waitress was sore too. She swept a cloth over the counter in front of me and let me have the last customer's crumbs in my lap.

"Look, sweetness," I said, "don't be so generous. Save the crumbs for a rainy day. All I want is two eggs three minutes—no more—a slice of your famous concrete toast, a tall glass of tomato juice with a dash of Lee and Perrins, a big happy smile, and don't give anybody else any coffee. I might need it all."

"I got a cold," she said. "Don't push me around. I might crack you one on the kisser."

"I had a rough night too."

She gave me a half-smile and went through the swing door sideways. It showed more of her curves, which were ample, even excessive. But

I got the eggs the way I liked them. The toast had been painted with melted butter past its bloom.

"No Lee and Perrins," she said, putting down the tomato juice. "How about a little Tabasco? We're fresh out of arsenic too."

I used two drops of Tabasco, swallowed the eggs, drank two cups of coffee and was about to leave the toast for a tip, but I went soft and left a quarter instead. That really brightened her. It was a joint where you left a dime or nothing. Mostly nothing.

Back on Poynter nothing had changed. I got to my window again and sat. At about 8:30 the man I had seen go into the apartment house across the way–the one with the same sort of height and build as Ikky–came out with a small briefcase and turned east. Two men got out of a dark blue sedan. They were of the same height and very quietly dressed and had soft hats pulled low over their foreheads. Each jerked out a revolver.

"Hey, Ikky!" one of them called out.

The man turned. "So long, Ikky," the other man said. Gunfire racketed between the houses. The man crumpled and lay motionless. The two men rushed for their car and were off, going west. Halfway down the block I saw a Caddy pull out and start ahead of them.

In no time at all they were completely gone.

It was a nice swift clean job. The only thing wrong with it was that they hadn't given it enough time for preparation.

They had shot the wrong man.

I got out of there fast, almost as fast as the two killers. There was a smallish crowd grouped around the dead man. I didn't have to look at him to know he was dead–the boys were pros. Where he lay on the sidewalk on the other side of the street I couldn't see him; people were in the way. But I knew just how he would look and I already heard sirens in the distance. It could have been just the routine shrieking from Sunset, but it wasn't. So somebody had telephoned. It was too early for the cops to be going to lunch.

I strolled around the corner with my suitcase and jammed into the rent car and went away from there. The neighborhood was not my piece of shortcake any more. I could imagine the questions.

"Just what took you over there, Marlowe? You got a flop of your own, ain't you?"

"I was hired by an ex-mobster in trouble with the Outfit. They'd sent killers after him."

"Don't tell us he was trying to go straight."

"I don't know. But I liked his money."

"Didn't do much to earn it, did you?"

"I got him away last night. I don't know where he is now. I don't want to know."

"You got him away?"

"That's what I said."

"Yeah—only he's in the morgue with multiple bullet wounds. Try something better. Or somebody's in the morgue."

And on and on. Policeman's dialogue. It comes out of an old shoe box. What they say doesn't mean anything, what they ask doesn't mean anything. They just keep boring in until you are so exhausted you flip on some detail. Then they smile happily and rub their hands, and say: "Kind of careless there, weren't you? Let's start all over again."

The less I had of that, the better. I parked in my usual parking slot and went up to the office. It was full of nothing but stale air. Every time I went into the dump it felt more and more tired. Why the hell hadn't I got myself a government job ten years ago? Make it fifteen years. I had brains enough to get a mail-order law degree. The country's full of lawyers that couldn't write a complaint without the book.

So I sat in my office chair and disadmired myself. After a while I remembered the pencil. I made certain arrangements with a forty-five gun, more gun than I ever carry—too much weight. I dialed the Sheriff's Office and asked for Bernie Ohls. I got him. His voice was sour.

"Marlowe. I'm in trouble—real trouble."

"Why tell me?" he growled. "You must be used to it by now."

"This kind of trouble you don't get used to. I'd like to come over and tell you."

"You in the same office?"

"The same."

"Have to go over that way. I'll drop in."

He hung up. I opened two windows. The gentle breeze wafted a smell of coffee and stale fat to me from Joe's Eats next door. I hated it. I hated myself. I hated everything.

Ohls didn't bother with my elegant waiting room. He rapped on my own door and I let him in. He scowled his way to the customer's chair.

"Okay. Give."

"Ever hear of a character named Ikky Rosenstein?"

"Why would I? Record?"

"An ex-mobster who got disliked by the mob. They put a pencil through his name and sent the usual two tough boys on a plane. He got tipped and hired me to help him get away."

"Nice clean work."

"Cut it out, Bernie." I lit a cigarette and blew smoke in his face. In retaliation he began to chew a cigarette. He never lit one.

"Look," I went on. "Suppose the man wants to go straight and suppose he doesn't. He's entitled to his life as long as he hasn't killed anyone. He told me he hadn't."

"And you believed the hood, huh? When do you start teaching Sunday School?"

"I neither believed him nor disbelieved him. I took him on. There was no reason not to. A girl I know and I watched the planes yesterday. She spotted the boys and tailed them to a hotel. She was sure of what they were. They looked it right down to their black shoes. They got off the plane separately and then pretended to know each other and not to have noticed on the plane. This girl–"

"Would she have a name?"

"Only for you."

"I'll buy, if she hasn't cracked any laws."

"Her name is Anne Riordan. She lives in Bay City. Her father was once Chief of Police there. And don't say that makes him a crook, because he wasn't."

"Uh-huh. Let's have the rest. Make a little time too."

"I took an apartment opposite Ikky. The killers were still at the hotel. At midnight I got Ikky out and drove with him as far as Pomona. He went on in his rent car and I came back by Greyhound. I moved into the apartment on Poynter Street, right across from his dump."

"Why–if he was already gone?"

I opened the middle desk drawer and took out the nice sharp pencil. I wrote my name on a piece of paper and ran the pencil through it.

"Because someone sent me this. I didn't think they'd kill me, but I thought they planned to give me enough of a beating to warn me off any more pranks."

"They knew you were in on it?"

"Ikky was tailed here by a little squirt who later came around and stuck a gun in my stomach. I knocked him around a bit, but I had to let him go. I thought Poynter Street was safer after that. I live lonely."

"I get around," Bernie Ohls said. "I hear reports. So they gunned the wrong guy."

"Same height, same build, same general appearance. I saw them gun him. I couldn't tell if it was the two guys from the Beverly-Western. I'd never seen them. It was just two guys in dark suits with hats pulled down. They jumped into a blue Pontiac sedan, about two years old, and lammed off, with a big Caddy running crash for them."

Bernie stood up and stared at me for a long moment. "I don't think they'll bother with you now," he said. "They've hit the wrong guy. The mob will be very quiet for a while. You know something? This town is getting to be almost as lousy as New York, Brooklyn and

Chicago. We could end up real corrupt."

"We've made a hell of a good start."

"You haven't told me anything that makes me take action, Phil. I'll talk to the city homicide boys. I don't guess you're in any trouble. But you saw the shooting. They'll want that."

"I couldn't identify anybody, Bernie. I didn't know the man who was shot. How did *you* know it was the wrong man?"

"You told me, stupid."

"I thought perhaps the city boys had a make on him."

"They wouldn't tell me, if they had. Besides, they ain't hardly had time to go out for breakfast. He's just a stiff in the morgue to them until the ID comes up with something. But they'll want to talk to you, Phil. They just love their tape recorders."

He went out and the door whooshed shut behind him. I sat there wondering whether I had been a dope to talk to him. Or to take Ikky's troubles on. Five thousand green men said no. But they can be wrong too.

Somebody banged on my door. It was a uniform holding a telegram. I receipted for it and tore it loose.

It said: "On my way to Flagstaff. Mirador Motor Court. Think I've been spotted. Come fast."

I tore the wire into small pieces and burned them in my big ash tray. I called Anne Riordan.

"Funny thing happened," I told her, and told her about the funny thing.

"I don't like the pencil," she said. "And I don't like the wrong man being killed, probably some poor bookkeeper in a cheap business or he wouldn't be living in that neighborhood. You should never have touched it, Phil."

"Ikky had a life. Where he's going he might make himself decent. He can change his name. He must be loaded or he wouldn't have paid me so much."

"I said I didn't like the pencil. You'd better come down here for a while. You can have your mail re-addressed—if you get any mail. You don't have to work right away anyhow. And LA is oozing with private eyes."

"You don't get the point. I'm not through with the job. The city dicks have to know where I am, and if they do, all the crime beat reporters will know too. The cops might even decide to make me a suspect. Nobody who saw the shooting is going to put out a description that means anything. The American people know better than to be witnesses to gang killings."

"All right, loud brain. But my offer stands."

The buzzer sounded in the outside room. I told Anne I had to hang up. I opened the communicating door and a well-dressed—I might say elegantly dressed–middle-aged man stood six feet inside the outer door. He had a pleasantly dishonest smile on his face. He wore a white Stetson and one of those narrow ties that go through an ornamental buckle. His cream-colored flannel suit was beautifully tailored.

He lit a cigarette with a gold lighter and looked at me over the first puff of smoke.

"Mr. Marlowe?"

I nodded.

"I'm Foster Grimes from Las Vegas. I run the Rancho Esperanza on South Fifth. I hear you got a little involved with a man named Ikky Rosenstein."

"Won't you come in?"

He strolled past me into my office. His appearance told me nothing. A prosperous man who liked or felt it good business to look a bit western. You see them by the dozen in the Palm Springs winter season. His accent told me he was an eastener, but not New England. New York or Baltimore, likely. Long Island, the Berkshires–no, too far from the city.

I showed him the customer's chair with a flick of the wrist and sat down in my antique swivel-squeaker. I waited.

"Where is Ikky now, if you know?"

"I don't know, Mr. Grimes."

"How come you messed with him?"

"Money."

"A damned good reason." he smiled. "How far did it go?"

"I helped him leave town. I'm telling you this, although I don't know who the hell you are, because I've already told an old friend-enemy of mine, a top man in the Sheriff's Office."

"What's a friend-enemy?"

"Law men don't go around kissing me, but I've known him for years, and we are as much friends as a private star can be with a law man."

"I told you who I was. We have a unique set-up in Vegas. We own the place except for one lousy newspaper editor who keeps climbing our backs and the backs of our friends. We let him live because letting him live makes us look better than knocking him off. Killings are not good business any more."

"Like Ikky Rosenstein."

"That's not a killing. It's an execution. Ikky got out of line."

"So your gun boys had to rub the wrong guy. They could have hung around a little to make sure."

"They would have, if you'd kept your nose where it belonged. They hurried. We don't appreciate that. We want cool efficiency."

"Who's this great big fat 'we' you keep talking about?"

"Don't go juvenile on me, Marlowe."

"Okay. Let's say I know."

"Here's what we want." He reached into his pocket and drew out a loose bill. He put it on the desk on his side. "Find Ikky and tell him to get back in line and everything is oke. With an innocent bystander gunned, we don't want any trouble or any extra publicity. It's that simple. You get this now," he nodded at the bill. It was a grand. Probably the smallest bill they had. "And another when you find Ikky and give him the message. If he holds out—curtains."

"Suppose I say take you goddam grand and blow your nose with it?"

"That would be unwise." He flipped out a Colt Woodsman with a short silencer on it. A Colt Woodsman will take one without jamming. He was fast too, fast and smooth. The genial expression on his face didn't change.

"I never left Vegas," he said calmly . "I can prove it. You're dead in your office chair and nobody knows anything. Just another private eye that tried the wrong pitch. Put your hands on the desk and think a little. Incidentally, I'm a crack shot even with this damned silencer."

"Just to sink a little lower in the social scale, Mr. Grimes, I ain't putting no hands on no desk. But tell me about this."

I flipped the nicely sharpened pencil across to him. He grabbed for it after a swift change of the gun to his left hand—very swift. He held the pencil up so that he could look at it without taking his eyes off me.

I said: "It came to me by Special Delivery mail. No message, no return address. Just the pencil. Think I've never heard about the pencil, Mr. Grimes?"

He frowned and tossed the pencil down. Before he could shift his long lithe gun back to his right hand I dropped mine under the desk and grabbed the butt of the .45 and put my finger hard on the trigger.

"Look under the desk, Mr. Grimes. You'll see a .45 in an open-end holster. It's fixed there and it's pointing at your belly. Even if you could shoot me through the heart the .45 would still go off from a convulsive movement of my hand. And your belly would be hanging by a shred and you would be knocked out of that chair. A .45 slug can throw you back six feet. Even the movies learned that at last.

"Looks like a Mexican stand-off," he said quietly. He holstered his gun. He grinned. "Nice smooth work, Marlowe. We could use you. But it's a long long time for you and no time at all to us. Find Ikky and don't be a drip. He'll listen to reason. He doesn't really want to be on the run for the rest of his life. We'd trace him eventually."

"Tell me something, Mr. Grimes. Why pick on me? Apart from Ikky, what did I ever do to make you dislike me?"

Not moving, he thought a moment, or pretended to. "The Larsen case. You helped send one of our boys to the gas chamber. That we don't forget. We had you in mind as a fall guy for Ikky. You'll always be a fall guy, unless you play it our way. Something will hit you when you least expect it."

"A man in my business is always a fall guy Mr. Grimes. Pick up your grand and drift out quietly. I might decide to do it your way, but I have to think. As for the Larsen case, the cops did all the work. I just happened to know where he was. I don't guess you miss him terribly."

"We don't like interference." He stood up. He put the grand note casually back in his pocket. While he was doing it I let go of the .45 and jerked out my Smith and Wesson five-inch .38.

He looked at it contemptuously. "I'll be in Vegas, Marlowe. In fact I never left Vegas. You can catch me at the Esperanza. No, we don't give a damn about Larsen personally. Just another gun handler. They come in gross lots. We *do* give a damn that some punk private eye fingered him."

He nodded and went out by my office door.

I did some pondering. I knew Ikky wouldn't go back to the Outfit. He wouldn't trust them enough if he got the chance. But there was another reason now. I called Anne Riordan again.

"I'm going to look for Ikky. I have to. If I don't call you in three days, get hold of Bernie Ohls. I'm going to Flagstaff, Arizona. Ikky says he will be there."

"You're a fool," she wailed. "It's some sort of trap."

"A Mr. Grimes of Vegas visited me with a silenced gun. I beat him to the punch, but I won't always be that lucky. If I find Ikky and report to Grimes, the mob will let me alone."

"You'd condemn a man to death?" Her voice was sharp and incredulous.

"No. He won't be there when I report. He'll have to hop a plane to Montreal, buy forged papers–Montreal is almost as crooked as we are–and plane to Europe. He may be fairly safe there. But the Outfit has long arms and Ikky will have a damned dull life staying alive. He hasn't any choice. For him it's either hide or get the pencil."

"So clever of you, darling. What about your own pencil?"

"If they meant it, they wouldn't have sent it. Just a bit of scare technique."

"And you don't scare, you wonderful handsome brute."

"I scare. But it doesn't paralyze me. So long. Don't take any lovers until I get back."

"Damn you, Marlowe!"

She hung up on me. I hung up on myself.

Saying the wrong thing is one of my specialties.

I beat it out of town before the homicide boys could hear about me. It would take them quite a while to get a lead. And Bernie Ohls wouldn't give a city dick a used paper bag. The Sheriff's men and the City Police co-operate about as much as two tomcats on a fence.

I made Phoenix by evening and parked myself in a motor court on the outskirts. Phoenix was damned hot. The motor court had a dining room so I had dinner. I collected some quarters and dimes from the cashier and shut myself in a phone booth and started to call the Mirador in Flagstaff. How silly could I get? Ikky might be registered under any name from Cohen to Cordileone, from Watson to Woichehovski. I called anyway and got nothing but as much of a smile as you can get on the phone. So I asked for a room the following night. Not a chance unless someone checked out, but they would put me down for a cancellation or something. Flagstaff is too near the Grand Canyon. Ikky must have arranged in advance. That was something to ponder too.

I bought a paperback and read it. I set my alarm watch for 6:30. The paperback scared me so badly that I put two guns under my pillow. It was about a guy who bucked the hoodlum boss of Milwaukee and got beaten up every fifteen minutes. I figured that his head and face would be nothing but a piece of bone with a strip of skin hanging from it. But in the next chapter he was as gay as a meadow lark. Then I asked myself why I was reading this drivel when I could have been memorizing The Brothers Karamasov. Not knowing any good answers, I turned the light out and went to sleep. At 6.30 I shaved and showered and had breakfast and took off for Flagstaff. I got there by lunchtime, and there was Ikky in the reastaurant eating mountain trout. I sat down across from him. He looked surprised to see me.

I ordered mountain trout and ate it from the outside in, which is the proper way. Boning spoils it a little.

"What gives?" he asked me with his mouth full. A delicate eater.

"You read the papers?"

"Just the sporting section."

"Let's go to your room and talk about it. There's more than that."

We paid for our lunches and went along to a nice double. The motor courts are getting so good that they make a lot of hotels look cheap. We sat down and lit cigarettes.

"The two hoods got up too early and went over to Poynter Street. They parked outside your apartment house. They hadn't been briefed carefully enough. They shot a guy who looked a little like you."

"That's a hot one," he grinned. "But the cops will find out, and the Outfit will find out. So the tag for me stays on."

"You must think I'm dumb," I said. "I am."

"I thought you did a first class job, Marlowe. What's dumb about that?"

"What job did I do?"

"You got me out of there pretty slick."

"Anything about it you couldn't have done yourself?"

"With luck–no. But it's nice to have a helper."

"You mean sucker."

His face tightened. And his rusty voice growled. "I don't catch. And give me back some of that five grand, will you? I'm shorter than I thought."

"I'll give it back to you when you find a hummingbird in a salt shaker."

"Don't be like that," he almost sighed, and flicked a gun into his hand. I didn't have to flick. I was holding one in my side pocket.

"I oughtn't to have boobed off," I said. "Put the heater away. It doesn't pay any more than a Vegas slot machine."

"Wrong. Them machines pay the jackpot every so often. Otherwise–no customers."

"Every so seldom, you mean. Listen, and listen good."

He grinned, His dentist was tired waiting for him.

"The set-up intrigued me," I went on, debonair as Milo Vance in a Van Dyne story and a lot brighter in the head. "First off, could it be done? Second, if it could be done, where would I be? But gradually I saw the little touches that flaw the picture. Why would you come to me at all? The Outfit isn't that naive. Why would they send a little punk like this Charles Hickon or whatever name he uses on Thursdays? Why would an old hand like you let anybody trail you to a dangerous connection?"

"You slay me, Marlowe. You're so bright I could find you in the dark. You're so dumb you couldn't see a red white and blue giraffe. I bet you were back there in your unbrain emporium playing with that five grand like a cat with a bag of catnip. I bet you were kissing the notes."

"Not after you handled them. They why the pencil that was sent to me? Big dangerous threat. It re-inforced the rest. But like I told your choir boy from Vegas, they don't send them when they mean them. By the way, he had a gun too. A Woodsman .22 with a silencer. I had to make him put it away. He was nice about that. He started waving grands at me to find out where you were and tell him. A well-dressed, nice looking front man for a pack of dirty rats. The Women's Christian Temperance Association and some bootlicking politicians gave them the money to be big, and they learned how to use it and make it grow. Now they're pretty well unstoppable. But they're still a pack of dirty rats. And they're always where they can't make a mistake. That's inhuman. Any man has a right to a few mistakes. Not the rats. They have to be perfect all the time. Or else they get stuck with *you*."

"I don't know what the hell you're talking about. I just know it's too long."

"Well, allow me to put it in English. Some poor jerk from the East Side gets involved with the lower echelons of a mob. You know what an echelon is, Ikky?"

"I been in the Army," he sneered.

"He grows up in the mob, but he's not all rotten. He's not rotten enough. So he tries to break loose. He comes out here and gets himself a cheap job of some sort and changes his name or names and lives quietly in a cheap apartment house. But the mob by now has agents in many places. Somebody spots him and recognizes him. It might be a pusher, a front man for a bookie joint, a night girl, even a cop that's on the take. So the mob, or call them the Outfit, say through their cigar smoke: 'Ikky can't do this to us. It's a small operation because he's small. But it annoys us. Bad for discipline. Call a couple of boys and have them pencil him." But what boys do they call? A couple they're tired of. Been around too long. Might make a mistake or get chilly toes. Perhaps they like killing. That's bad too. That makes recklessness. The best boys are the ones that don't care either way. So although they don't know it, the boys they call are on their way out. But it would be kind of cute to frame a guy they already don't like, for fingering a hood named Larsen. One of these puny little jokes the Outfit takes big. "Look guys, we even got time to play footies with a private eye. Jesus, we can do anything. We could even suck our thumbs.' So they send a ringer."

"The Torri brothers ain't ringers. They're real hard boys. They proved it—even if they did make a mistake."

Mistake nothing. They got Ikky Rosenstein. You're just a singing commercial in this deal. And as of now you're under arrest for murder. You're worse off than that. The Outfit will habeas corpus you out of the clink and blow you down. You've served your purpose and you failed to finger me into a patsy."

His finger tightened on the trigger. I shot the gun out of his hand. My gun in my coat pocket was small, but at that distance accurate. And it was one of my days to be accurate myself.

He made a faint moaning sound and sucked at his hand. I went over and kicked him hard in the chest. Being nice to killers is not part of my repertoire. He went over backwards and sideways and stumbled four or five steps. I picked up his gun and held it on him while I tapped all the places—not just pockets or holsters—where a man could stash a second gun. He was clean—that way anyhow.

"What are you trying to do to me?" he said whiningly. "I paid you. You're clear. I paid you damn well."

"We both have problems there. Yours is to stay alive." I took a pair of cuffs out of my pocket and wrestled his hands behind him and snapped them on. His hand was bleeding. I tied his show handkerchief around it. I went to the telephone.

Flagstaff was big enough to have a police force. The DA might even have his office there. This was Arizona, a poor state, relatively. The cops might even be honest.

I had to stick around for a few days, but I didn't mind that as long as I could have trout caught eight or nine thousand feet up. I called Anne and Bernie Ohls. I called my answering service. The Arizona DA was a young keen-eyed man and the Chief of Police was one of the biggest men I ever saw.

I got back to LA in time and took Anne to Romanoff's for dinner and champagne.

"What I can't see," she said over a third glass of bubbly, "is why they dragged you into it, why they set up the fake Ikky Rosenstein. Why didn't they just let the two lifetakers do their job?"

"I couldn't really say. Unless the big boys feel so safe they're developing a sense of humor. And unless this Larsen guy that went to the gas chamber was bigger than he seemed to be. Only three or four important mobsters have made the electric chair or the rope or the gas chamber. None that I know of in the life-imprisonment states like Michigan. If Larsen was bigger than anyone thought, they might have had my name on a waiting list."

"But why wait?" she asked me. "They'd go after you quickly."

"They can afford to wait. Who's going to bother them—Kefauver? He did his best, but do you notice any change in the set-up—except when they make one themselves?"

"Costello?"

"Income tax rap—like Capone. Capone may have had several hundred men killed, and killed a few of them himself, personally. But it took the Internal Revenue boys to get him. The Outfit won't make that mistake often."

"What I like about you, apart from your enormous personal charm is that when you don't know an answer you make one up."

"The money worries me," I said. "Five grand of their dirty money.

What do I do with it?"

"Don't be a jerk all your life. You earned the money and you risked your life for it. You can buy Series E Bonds. They'll make the money clean. And to me that would be part of the joke."

"*You* tell *me* one good reason why they pulled the switch."

"You have more of a reputation than you realize. And how would it be if the false Ikky pulled the switch? He sounds like one of these overclever types that can't do anything simple."

"The Outfit will get him for making his own plans–if you're right."

"If the DA doesn't. And I couldn't care less about what happens to him. More champagne, please."

They extradited "Ikky" and he broke under pressure and named the two gunmen–after I had already named them, the Torri brothers. But nobody could find them. They never went home. And you can't prove conspiracy on one man. The law couldn't even get him for accessory after the fact. They couldn't prove he knew the real Ikky had been gunned.

They could have got him for some trifle, but they had a better idea. They left him to his friends. They turned him loose.

Where is he now? My hunch says nowhere.

Anne Riordan was glad it was all over and I was safe. Safe–that isn't a word you use in my trade.

CARROLL JOHN DALY
(1889-1958)

Not My Corpse
(Race Williams)

1
DEATH COMES TWICE

There may be likeable crooks and there may even be likeable killers, but Jake O'Hara was not one of them. He curried favor with everyone who needed currying. He was rubbing his hands when he came into my office.

"Well, what do you want?" I demanded.

"I don't know, Race," he said. "That's a fact." He opened his wallet and placed two century notes on my desk. "I'll pay that to find out."

"I don't like anything about you, Jake," I told him. "Beat it."

"But," he insisted, "you're a private eye, aren't you? I got trouble. We've never crossed."

I shrugged. "You don't cross anyone in the open. You do your shooting from behind garbage cans and the corners of buildings." And when his eyes widened, "I understand you even peddle the stuff."

Jake didn't get mad. "I never sold a dime's worth of the stuff."

"Okay, Jake. I hear you can't make a dame unless you feed her the stuff. It all adds up to the same. I don't like you."

"We can't like everyone." Jake stood there and agreed with me.

"Remember the dirty little man in the dirty little room?"

"Harvey Rath?" I was startled. "I never believed that myth, Jake–and he's been dead, anyhow out of circulation, for a long time."

"He ain't out now." O'Hara laid a card on the desk before me. On it was printed:

THERE'S A DIRTY LITTLE MAN IN A
DIRTY LITTLE ROOM

"Would you like to get a card like that?" Jake asked me.

"I wouldn't mind," I told him.

But I was curious. I noticed that there was a nervous twitching to his fingers and that his usually ruddy face was pale.

"Go back a couple of years. Race." He wet his lips. "Guys were being shook down, bumped for no reason at all. Tough Tony walked into Eddie Smart's place. Eddie was behind the bar. Him and Tony were friends, see. Tony pulled out a gun and shot him through the head. 'That,' said Tony, 'is straight from a dirty little guy in a dirty little room.' Tony was hopped up, all right. What more he might have said we don't know. Milligan was in the bar and he pulled out a rod and blew Tony apart."

"Jake," I said, shoving the two Cs back into his hand, "I'll give you some free advice. I think someone is trying to scare you to death." I opened the door. "On your way, Jake."

"It isn't me so much as my girl," Jake whimpered as I let him out of the office.

Five minutes later Jerry, my boy, came in.

"Boss," he said, "wasn't that Jake O'Hara who just left you a little while ago?"

"Yes," I said. "So what?"

"So I know something about him you don't know. He's lying dead in the gutter. Two doors down the street. Someone stopped a car, called him over and shot him."

"Where do you get your information?"

"Clarice–on the newsstand downstairs. She buzzed me. I know it was O'Hara. I put the glasses on him out the window."

They were moving the body and the crowd, too, when I put my six-power glasses on the street below. I guessed Jake O'Hara wasn't worrying so much now. I shrugged–and gulped. What of the girl?

"Has Jake got a girl?" I hollered to Jerry. "And do you know where she lives?"

"A dame called Sissy Pierson," he said. "She slipped down from the upper crust. Does a number in one of the night spots. I'll get her address for you."

Jerry was efficient that way. In five minutes he had her address, on Ninety-second Street.

"If she's got a phone," he said, "it's a secret."

I went out and took a taxi to Ninety-second Street to a small walk-up apartment.

Sissy Pierson's card in the mail box read "4D." I pressed the bell and held my hand on the door, waiting for the latch to click. There was no click. Perhaps she wasn't in. Perhaps she *was* in danger and Jake had told her not to answer the bell.

I pressed the buzzer of a ground-floor apartment and got service. I was in the door fast and on the stairs before 2A could get a look at me. Though you can always apologize. On the fourth floor I found 4D, and it didn't take too much of a keen eye to see that the door latch wasn't caught. Someone could do that going out quietly: someone could do it door open and walk into a lot of trouble. A burst of gunfire or a tap on the head from someone behind a door. I gave the bell a ring, heard it plainly back in the apartment. No response.

I thought I'd go in and wait for Sissy Pierson. I was there to do her a favor. Most normal people don't like getting themselves killed, that's quite certain.

The hall was fairly dark, so I swung my gun into my right hand, crouched low, hoping that if it was gunfire, they'd shoot high, or that I'd shoot first, and started to push the door, to put the squeeze on anyone hiding behind it.

Nothing stirred. I got the door back as far as it would go. I looked down a long straight hall and into a living room with curtains drawn back from the windows. I had plenty of light now.

I stepped in, closed the door and with my gun still in my hand, walked slowly down the hall. A kitchen loomed up to my right, and I took a look-see–empty–so I went to the living room. The furniture was comfortable, expensive and in good taste.

Living room empty. No dining room. The door to the room down the side hall was closed. I raised my gun slightly and pushed this door open.

I didn't even have to enter the room. I was looking straight at the bed and the girl that was huddled on it–a dead girl. Despite the rope that bound her feet to the foot of the bed and her hands to the head of it, she was curled up, half turned on her side.

Her lips were torn, and the skin on either side of her mouth was raw with little bits of whitish linen still clinging to it. Strips of adhesive tape lay on the floor, evidently tossed there as they had been stripped from the lips they sealed.

She was fully dressed, but her feet were bare–and blistered and burned, and many burned matches and cigarette butts were in the deep ashtray.

Someone had tied that girl on the bed and before killing her had tortured her for information. Whether he'd got it or not, I didn't know.

There are times for lads in my business to get from under. This was not one of the times. I lifted the phone by the bed, dialed headquarters and got Sergeant O'Rourke.

"I've walked in on a body, O'Rourke," I said. "It's murder." I gave him the address and the apartment number. "I'll give you the setup, and don't bring Inspector Nelson with you."

"He's Homicide, Race," O'Rourke said easily. "He's got to come along."

Which was true enough.

I took a quick look-see in the bathroom, then sat down in the living room and took a smoke. I guessed the dame was Sissy Pierson, all right. Her picture was around the place enough, in all sorts of poses—mostly costume stuff or lack of costume stuff.

How had she died? I thought off-hand, from the marks of her throat, that she'd been choked to death. How long had she been dead? Not long—her body was still warm. I didn't question further. She was not my corpse. She belonged to the police department.

I went into the kitchen and looked for a bottle of whisky. I've seen a lot of mean killings. I can take them, but that doesn't mean you ever get exactly used to them. She hadn't been a bad-looking kid. I took a stiff drink.

She couldn't have been a day over twenty-three. I took another hooker, went back in the living room and sat down to wait. I was thinking she would not mind about the whisky.

Pretty soon they came—O'Rourke, the same friendly cop as ever, and Inspector Nelson. O'Rourke was only a sergeant in rank, but he was close to Commissioner Porter. He could have been an inspector a long time ago, but as he said, and meant it, a copper learns more when he keeps close to his men.

Inspector Nelson acted with his usual belligerency, as if he had just found me after I'd murdered the woman. He disliked all private dicks and me in particular. But I wouldn't be shoved around like other private eyes, and he knew it.

2
DAUGHTER OF WEALTH

Our assistant medical examiner, Dr. Spear, came on the heels of the boys who were setting up cameras and going over the place. Dr. Spear was not the public's idea of a big city medical examiner. He never complained that he was pulled away from his dinner, never made flippant remarks about the corpse, never kidded with the police or permitted levity from them. It was a hard, cold and serious business with the assistant medical examiner.

I was wrong about the choking to death. She had been stabbed. Right through the heart. No knife was found. The time of death he set within the hour. That made Nelson look at me sharply.

"I suppose, Williams," he said, loud enough for the cops in the living room to hear, "you can account for your time?"

He gave me a look that showed how he felt about private eyes.

"Sure," I said just as loud. "I was out looking for the Malone brothers."

Which held Nelson. The Malone brothers had disappeared a couple of years ago, not five minutes before Nelson had dropped down on them. Nelson had had an anonymous tip and the evidence that would convict them of murder for more than four hours. But he had checked up before even trying to make an arrest. The story still went over big–if you wanted to get under Nelson's skin–which you often did.

The girl might have been killed in anger at not getting the information the murderer wanted. But it was Dr. Spear's opinion that the torture had gone on for some time.

One thing more. A card had been thrust down the girl's blouse. I didn't need to see it to know what was printed on it.

"Come around to my office and I'll match that card for you," I said to O'Rourke.

He showed the card to me then. Of course it read:

A DIRTY LITTLE MAN IN A DIRTY
LITTLE ROOM

O'Rourke came around, and I told him all about O'Hara's visit.

"A dirty little man in a dirty little room," he thought aloud. "Remember Harvey Rath? He was a fence for over forty years. He lived back of his pawn-shop–yes, in a dirty little room, and he was a little man, not overly clean. There were hints that he started to cash in on some of his knowledge. Tough Tony blurted it out before he died. But we never found out anything. Rath disappeared–we never found his body...O'Hara say anything else to you?"

"Not a word."

"And you never saw the girl before?"

"Not until I saw her on the bed dead. No skin off your nose, O'Rourke–another cheap gangster and his dame."

O'Rourke looked at me steadily. "She had a scrapbook in her apartment, Race. She was Daniel Pierson's daughter. The stockbroker. Plenty of money and society, though he was rather pushed out of it a few years back when he was divorced. A mess. His daughter blew up and got a job singing in a Chicago night club. Made pretty good money at first. Then she met O'Hara. Doc Spear said she needled herself."

I nodded. "O'Hara would get his girls that way. I told him so. I guess he deserved the dose."

Only Foster of the *Journal* put me into the morning papers–a line about O'Hara taking the dose "almost immediately after leaving the office of a private detective." Evidently the advertising department wouldn't let him put my name in.

The wages of sin and hints at the sins of the parents and so on were played up good. O'Hara and the dope were pushed down as if the divorce had everything to do with it.

There were pictures of the girl when a child, and at an exclusive girls' school, and the information that last summer she had done a song-and-dance act at the invitation of the Junior League up in Maine for a new hospital opening on Moosehead Lake.

O'Rourke trotted into my office several times to see if I had heard anything, and it was surprising the things he knew about that girl– alive–and how little he knew about her dead.

"A couple of guys were making a play for her," he told me about a week after the murder, "and in spite of the dope, O'Hara was having a tough time keeping her in line. If O'Hara hadn't come to you, Race, I'd think he threatened the wrong man in a jealous rage and got himself knocked over."

"And the card–the dirty little man?"

"Just a red herring of O'Hara's."

"So the guy gets rid of O'Hara because he wants the girl, then tortures and kills her because she won't tell him what she saw in O'Hara. How does Nelson cater to that idea?"

"Nelson," said O'Rourke, "has it all sewed up. He liked the idea of the lover killing O'Hara and explains it that the girl has a new boy friend. O'Hara tortures the girl to find out his name. She won't talk, so O'Hara kills her. The boy friend walks in on the body, goes after O'Hara and pops him off. The time element makes it possible."

"And I suppose I was to help alibi O'Hara."

"Could be." O'Rourke shrugged. "Anyway, a lot of guys liked her, and O'Hara wasn't one to scare a man much."

"No." I shook my head. "O'Hara was scared himself."

Jerry came in then.

"I've plugged it in here." He nodded toward the phone then at O'Rourke, who took it and listened.

"Sure," he said. "I know where it is. Loft building. Body, huh? She was—" O'Rourke straightened. This was not simply another body to him. He said, "Like that, eh?" and dropped the phone back in the cradle and walked toward the door.

"It's a dead girl," he said slowly. "Tortured, too—burnt matches and butts."

"And a card?" I asked.

"Yes—and a card." His lips set tightly. "And if you ask me what was on it, I'll bash your teeth down your throat. Want to come along? We're traveling fast."

I went. And I didn't need to ask him what was on the card.

I knew.

The Loft building was in the Bronx. We made time in a police car.

Nelson was already there. The homicide boys had set up their cameras, the place was being dusted for fingerprints, and Dr. Spear was finishing up his job. I got a look at the girl lying on a dilapidated couch, an old chair beside her, a tin box full of butts and matches, and the torn lips and scarred face where the adhesive tape had been torn off repeatedly as the girl evidently had been given a chance to talk.

That was all I did see. Nelson wanted no part of me, and O'Rourke didn't try to buck him.

Nelson was within his rights, so I went out into the hall and talked to the reporters.

The girl was identified two hours later at the city morgue, and the papers had a field day. She was not simply a child of wealth and respectability and society. There was no personal blot on her character and certainly no family scandal back of her.

She was Elsa Ames, daughter of Otis Ames, the real estate man, and Mrs. Ames, the former Constance Barrow of the Barrow Chemical Works and the Barrow fortune. Those two names, Ames and Barrow, meant plenty of dough, and the Barrow name took care of the society, back a few generations.

The card made the papers this time. The speculations were most anything you wished to name.

What's more, the Ames girl had disappeared in broad daylight. She had been shopping in a well-known Fifth Avenue shop and had walked out onto the avenue–or at least walked toward the door. The store wanted her all the way out, but O'Rourke told me the girl had last been seen walking toward the Fifth Avenue entrance by a saleslady who knew her.

That was at half-past eleven in the morning. She was not seen again until four in the afternoon. Then she was dead. Some kids playing in a condemned building had found her.

The underworld of New York–the dives and the gambling houses came in for a bad time. Even night clubs were investigated.

I went around personally and couldn't find anything. In one of the big uptown clubs Bill Cruthers, who owned the place, came over and sat down.

"It's a rotten racket, Race," he said. "Look at this club. Of course, we have shady customers." He waved a hand. "They're all missing tonight. It's the same in the big hotels. Lads who can't stand being questioned. They've run. Not a bit of harm in–well, ninety per cent of them."

"What do you think, Bill?" I said. "You've been around a long time."

"Off the record?" He grinned at me and I nodded. "Understand, Race, it's only my opinion–not anything I've heard. But the bad boys of the city are scared. There is a sort of code in the underworld of self-preservation. They keep their quarrels and their wars among themselves. They don't murder respected citizens any more than they kill cops if they can avoid it. It's bad for business–from the pickpocket in the subway to the lad at the roulette wheel. Look what it does to the night life–a respectable place like this, too, almost deserted."

"Why don't you chuck it up? There's nothing to hold you–nothing shady."

He put that nice smile on me. "Perhaps the dough I brought along in the beginning and put into different spots wasn't made by the sweat of my brow. But how many big business men would not say the same thing if they told the truth? I don't let myself get pushed around and I don't push too much myself. But I'm not a sucker."

"And your idea?"

"Well–" He rubbed his clean-shaven chin. "I don't take too much stock in that card business. I never knew Harvey Rath, but I think he did use the threat of disclosing things to get a few enemies bumped off. Then someone got to him. I think, Race, the cops have a tough job. I think someone is trying to cover something."

"How?"

"Well," he said, "it's hard to connect up the two murders. I don't think O'Hara counts too much. He was only in the way. The girls had met, I suppose, and that would make it appear like a link to the police. But I think a certain guy wants to do in a certain girl and that these are preliminaries."

"So it will look like the work of a maniac?"

"Sure." He grinned. "Maybe I read too many detective stories—but maybe the killer did, too."

"But the torture business," I said.

"Why not?" He shrugged. "It's got to look macabre."

"But a man couldn't work it alone," I said. "Remember the death car and O'Hara."

"Don't spoil a good story, Race." He got up from the table. "Here's news for you. I've sold out my interest in the night spots to some A Number One lads—Harry Long, Spencer Clarke, Malcolm Drew. They're forming a syndicate and pulling in bank money from outside. But I'll stick around a bit and see this through. The cops are running roughshod through the night. It would be something, Race, if you broke this case. If I hear anything—it's yours for a little bit of quiet when I blossom out as a gentleman, maybe a financier."

He gripped my hand again and was gone.

I liked Bill Cruthers. Never saw anything bad about him, though I heard plenty—but then, I heard the same things about myself. Still, I knew he'd be a mean man to cross. He was like me.

He wouldn't be shoved around.

3
THE NEXT VICTIM

The next day Mr. Otis Ames made several statements. One of them was that his daughter had never been in a night club in her life. The best one was that it was quite possible that his daughter had met Sissy Pierson, since they were both up at Moosehead Lake in Maine on the occasion of the opening of the hospital.

The police were raising the roof through the underworld, and men were talking who had never talked before. The general feeling was that Harvey Rath was alive and had returned, that he had passed the word along that certain people must be killed, and that these killings included not only the two girls but Jake O'Hara as well, and anyone else whose death could not be satisfactorily explained.

When two gunmen were fished out from under a wrecked car alongside the reservoir by Kensico Dam above White Plains, the word traveled fast that these were the birds who had picked up the Ames girl and spirited her to Harvey Rath up in the warehouse in the Bronx.

O'Rourke was too busy to have any talks with me.

Then things broke wide open. A girl named Dorothy Sears Briggs, of the Johnson Briggs clan, not yet twenty-one, received a message during a late dinner at a smart night spot. There were eight in her party. Every one of the eight, including her escort, the idiotic but extremely wealthy Mortimer Chase, saw her read the note carefully before excusing herself. Two of the party were sure she carried the note from the room with her.

That was the end of Dorothy Sears Briggs. At 1:20 the following morning they found her body behind some bushes in Central Park. There were no burnt matches, but her bare feet showed signs of the use of fire. Her face and lips were torn like those of the other two girls, though the tape was missing. Fingers that had gripped her smooth white throat had finished the job.

O'Rourke came to see me again. Even his voice was tired.

"I want to check my thinking with yours, Race," he said. "You can lie in bed and do your thinking."

"Well," I told him, "I think each of these girls knew something. Maybe the first victim told them."

"Yes, yes. We figured on that, but it doesn't jell. The Pierson girl, yes. She might have been afraid to talk, for in a way she was one of the mob. But the others—why should they keep a secret, one so terrible to the murderer that he would kill to prevent its being known? And O'Hara—and the two thugs who were picked up, and—"

"Wait a minute, O'Rourke," I said. "Did these last two girls know each other—and did they know Sissy Pierson?"

"They knew each other socially. Dorothy Sears Briggs was a nice kid, and so was Elsa Ames, but she wasn't as far up the ladder. They met at social affairs but weren't chummy if that's what you mean."

"Well," I said, "someone knows something and won't or can't talk."

I asked him what the department was doing.

"Plenty," O'Rourke told me. "Since the Briggs girl was found dead Nelson has got the names of nearly every young girl who is in the social set or trying to get in. He's got the name of everyone who knew

Dorothy Briggs personally, and a few who knew Sissy Pierson. He's interviewed most of them."

"And the results?" I wanted to know.

"Irate papas, and friends of irate papas, and lawyers of irate papas have been calling the commissioner. But Nelson's not backing down."

"What did he find out?"

"That the daughters of the rich have their secrets as well as the daughters of the poor–and that some of their so-called friends are about as willing to talk about it. But the killer's hot. Some day he'll make someone talk–say exactly what he wants to hear."

"I'm lucky to be out of it," I told him.

"But you're not out of it." He looked straight at me. "No citizen is out of it–no decent citizen. The alert is on for eight million people in New York. Someone is sure to talk. Something is sure to break any minute. No, Race, you're not out of it."

The shock came exactly one week after the death of Dorothy Sears Briggs. And it jarred me like an explosion.

I got a phone call to meet a man named Riley. He was a familiar figure to be seen strolling along Broadway. A dapper old guy, though not as old as he'd like you to think. He had come up from the gutter but wasn't going back into it–not alive. He had been a pickpocket, a common stick-up and a con man, but all that was years ago. Riley had slipped from one thing to another so fast that the cops had never been able to put the finger on him. Then suddenly he went in for high-class literature and poetry, and could misquote most any authority you named.

But he did get around and he did know what was going on. Now he was the go-between for so many things, and stepped on so few toes doing it, that he was taken for granted around the underworld when anything diplomatic had to be pulled off. So he had his nose in everything.

I got his secret call–everything about Riley was secret. He wanted me to have dinner with him in a delicatessen-restaurant in Brooklyn. I wondered who thought I was after his hide and wanted Riley to sound me out on what Riley always called "a meeting of the minds."

This cheap but large restaurant was doing a big business. But they had booths for two and poor lighting in the back. It was in one of the booths that I found Riley.

"I know how fastidious you are, Race," he said as I sat down, "so I ate my dinner before you came. We haven't got more than a moment to give to each other, but it's a moment of some importance."

There was a note of excitement in his voice–strange to Riley–and a trembling to his hand and a furtiveness in the way he looked around. It was all the more strange because Riley had always had a direct look, an honest, steady handclasp and a voice of assurance.

"Important to me or you?" I grinned at him.

"To me," he said. "There is ten thousand cash in it." Riley never said "grand" any more. "For you, as much as you can make the traffic bear above that. Maybe a small fortune." He leaned across the table. "And maybe death."

Riley could always be melodramtic. Then he went into swearing me to secrecy, insisting on my solemn oath that I would not divulge the source of my information.

I gave him all the assurance he needed. "Since the thing is big and it will take time," I said, "get talking. What have you got that's worth ten thousand dollars?"

He coughed and prepared to give me his usual spiel about how he served mankind. Then he suddenly thought better of it and said in a hoarse, unnatural voice, "I've got the name of the next victim of the dirty little man in the dirty little room."

"What!"

The dishes rattled on the table. If Riley had wanted to throw me, he certainly had. He hushed me to silence.

"That's it," he said, his voice hardly a whisper. "The name of the next—shall I say intended victim?"

"What do you mean, intended?" I said.

"You might gather a large fortune preventing it."

"And who will pay you this ten thousand? You don't think I have it."

"I think you could get it," he told me. "Her father should pay. He's worth enough."

I wanted to tell him he was crazy. But Riley was not crazy. When Riley gave, or rather sold, information, it was good information. You got all you paid for.

"Look," he was saying. "I only want your word that the ten thousand is mine. Then I'll give you the name of the girl. Then you'll send me the ten thousand. I'll be out of the city until the vicious fiend is dead, the girl is dead, or you are dead. Don't you see, Race, the chance I'm taking—for a measly ten thousand?"

"I'm to go to the girl's father and ask him for ten thousand dollars to tell him his daughter is the next victim. Why he'll know it as soon as I peep the request for money." I thought a moment. "I see. You give me the name. I'm to collect the money. He'd run to the phone and the police would be in. Give me the name, Riley. Maybe I can work something. Certainly you'll be entitled to a reward after–"

"No. Listen, Race. If I was as young as you, as quick with a gun as you, as willing to die as you are–and as much of a fool as you are– I'd work it myself. This guy's millions. I'm risking my life."

I shook my head and felt my jaw harden.

"Riley," I said slowly, "you're risking your life more right now by not telling me. When I think of the way those girls died–and that another is to die horribly if you don't speak–why I'd choke the truth out of you for a lead nickel." I looked around the crowded restaurant. "If the place wasn't so crowded, I'd start now."

"It does you credit." Riley was more himself now. "I thought of that when I picked this crowded haven of hungry mortals. No, Race. I must have the money–and I have a plan."

"In the meantime, a girl dies."

"I think not."

"Riley–" I was recovering now– "you can't know. If the money was obtained and then–the girl–well, we'd want her to live, of course."

"Of course. And for once I'll break my rule and tell you how I know. Tiny Prague–you know him?" I nodded. "He used to be a bad boy. He did his stretch, and I guess he was lucky he didn't sit down on a chair for murder. He's been straight since. Has charge of the bar at the Golden Eagle. I think Cruthers gave him his chance. Big, handsome fellow, Tiny Prague.

"Well, I was at the Golden Eagle and Tiny took a phone call in the booth. I happened to be in the next one and heard him curse and then swear that if he fried, he wouldn't do it. Then he mentioned a girl's name, and there was horror in his voice. 'I'll go to the police,' he said. 'I'll go to Bill Cruthers!' Then I heard the girl's name again, and when he came out of the booth, he was white. Perspiration was running down his face. He doesn't drink, but he did then, and put on his hat and coat and went out."

"Anything else?"

"Yes. He muttered over the phone like he was repeating what he heard–'A dirty little man in a dirty little room.'"

I looked carefully at Riley. "Well, Bill–"

"He won't go to Cruthers," Riley was saying. "Tiny's dead, Race. Stabbed in his own apartment–through the back. And no card, Race." He paused. "That's significant, isn't it?"

"Could be." But I couldn't think of anything significant about it.

"So," said Riley, "ten thousand is dirt cheap. Listen how you can work it. Of course, you don't go to the girl's father. You go see–" And Riley talked . . .

I had done some work for the Second National Bank. In a way I knew the president. He had bowed stiffly when the others had shaken my hand at that board meeting. But he hadn't liked my methods and my ethics, though he congratulated me grudgingly on behalf of the stockholders and the depositors.

"I'll be satisfied with what he says, Race," Riley went on. "If you don't get the money–" he shrugged– "I've done my duty. But I expect you to get the money."

"I don't like it, Riley," I told him, "but I'll play it your way. If it doesn't pan out and you don't give me the girl's name, or go to the police with it, I'll get the information out of you."

Riley smiled as we both stood up.

"You'll mail me the money, Race–in cash–or you won't find me."

4
BODY BLOW

To walk in at night and call on J. Fletcher Logan, president of the Second National Bank, for a private conference–as Riley wanted me to do–was something. I had to pull a few fast ones to do it.

I decided to work through Frank Rainer, playboy with plenty to play with. Not that he'd have any influence with J. Fletcher Logan, but his eccentric aunt would. She was both society and money, and even J. Fletcher Logan would respect her wishes.

It took me a couple of precious hours to work it. Enough to say that "a gentleman would call on J. Fletcher Logan on a matter of the gravest importance." The gentleman was me. Rainer insisted on it that way, since anything less wouldn't impress his aunt.

At that, I guess it wasn't the first secret visit J. Fletcher had ever had. His secretary met me in the alley of his Fifth Avenue home, at the door. He was a bald-headed, horse-faced individual with eyes like a ferret and he knew me at once.

"Mr. Logan will see you briefly in his upstairs study," he said. "The hour is late. You will understand that."

I said I would and followed him along a dim narrow hall to a small elevator. It shot up like a snail.

J. Fletcher Logan was a formidable looking as his name and position in the financial and social world indicated he would be. He was in a dark purple dressing gown. His white hair was neatly combed and parted in the middle with mathematical precision.

He was standing behind a desk, tall and rather on the thin side, and with a slight stoop. There were two pairs of glasses on his desk, the nose type and spectacles. His eyes were blue, not bright and pleasant, but steady.

"Mr. Williams–with a message of the gravest importance," he said simply.

I looked at the secretary who closed the door and stood by it, and he got the point and said, "My secretary, Mr. Norman Hilton, has been with me twenty years. You may proceed."

I proceeded. His dark eyebrows went up when I broke into the society murder cases, but although I didn't like the man, I'll admit he heard me through, even to details. His face expressed nothing when I came to the ten-thousand-dollar part. I finished with the final crack that I believed in my informant, that he had never misled me, and that he wanted to know if Mr. J. Fletcher Logan would advise the father of the girl to pay the money–even before he knew the father's name.

"A close personal friend of yours, who accepts your advice always," I finished, just as Riley had put it.

J. Fletcher Logan spoke then. "Mr. Williams, this girl's father, whom your informant has in mind, is quite evidently a personal friend of mine or one who is in a position or in the habit of seeking my advice and reasonably certain of acting on that advice. Would I advise him to then place in the hands of this doubtful character the sum of ten thousand dollars for information of a most tragic and horrifying nature, affecting the welfare of his home, actually, as you believe, the life or death of his daughter? Now suppose that this informant, being as you frankly state of an unsavory character, made the same offer to a dozen different men at the same time through different intermediaries."

"Mr. Logan," I interrupted, "I have stated the case to the best of my ability. I want a yes or a no."

"Really. Then–"

"If I may suggest," the secretary cut in, "we have had dealings with Mr. Williams before, Mr. Logan. Perhaps we might–compromise on a small amount in advance and later–"

"With a girl's life in the balance and every moment precious? I said. "If the price was low enough, I'd pay it myself. I wouldn't be here."

"How low?" Mr. Logan's voice was soft now.

"I can raise five thousand," I told him. "I found that out tonight. And it's from people you wouldn't even meet."

"Very well, Mr. Williams," Mr. Logan said. "The bank will lend you the other five. I'll go on your note myself."

He bowed stiffly and was about to dismiss me when I saw a phone across the room and asked to use it. When he nodded, I lifted the phone and dialed my number. I heard Riley answer as Logan was rebuking his secretary in a soft voice for bringing me so neatly into making my offer.

"All right," I said to Riley. "The money goes to you at the opening of the bank tomorrow. Never mind congratulating me. I don't want congratulations. The girl's name!...What?" I guess my voice went up. "And her father is–her–"

I dropped the phone in her cradle, turned and faced J. Fletcher Logan.

"You look a little stunned." For the first time he actually smiled. "I hope you found your investment–satisfactory.

I couldn't speak. I simply looked at him. When I did speak, my voice sounded far off. "Not satisfactory at all, Mr. Logan–not at all."

"Well, I won't question you. You have your ethics, or so you told me once. Our little talk will be confidential, and the bank will take care of you in the morning. I am not to know the girl's name, of course."

"But you are to know it." A hundred ways to break it to him were dashing through my muddled brain. Then I tossed it out. "The girl's your daughter." And when his face remained the same, "Your daughter Martha. Martha Logan."

People have taken blows before too heavy for the mind to accept at once, and I thought that was what had happened to Logan. I guess the secretary did, too, for he came over and took his arms.

"It's true, Mr. Logan," he said. "Somehow I knew the moment Mr. Williams spoke, yet he couldn't have guessed it."

No, I hadn't guessed it. Maybe I should have. Later I knew I shouldn't have. Not J. Fletcher Logan's daughter. Not Riley actually sending me to the father.

I'll say this for J. Fletcher Logan. He could take it–plenty. He opened his mouth to speak, but no words came. But he didn't let his mouth hang open. He closed it firmly and leaned on the desk, not gripping it for support exactly, or at least, not giving me that impression. Logan had faced crises before, though not like this, and he was gathering his mental strength to face this one.

His secretary suggested a brandy and that he sit down. Logan waved him aside.

"No, Norman," he said. "I like to take things standing–a little brandy perhaps in a moment." Then looking at me: "I recall your doing some work for us at the bank. I did not approve your methods, yet I did not question your integrity. Now–is it possible that your information is erroneous?"

"Anything is possible," I told him, "but I'd say that the odds were twenty to one that my information is correct."

"There is nothing from my point of view to substantiate this–this horror. I am thinking."

Logan waited a full minute, took the brandy Norman offered him.

"Nothing strange about Martha's actions lately," he murmured. "Not even little things. She is an especially level-headed girl, Williams. The police must be notified at once."

"I wonder, sir." Norman was in it now. "The police are capable, honest, and without doubt anxious to protect you and yours. But you know yourself, Mr. Logan, that things leak out."

"Leak out!" Logan's voice raised. This strong man of finance was using all that strength now to fight hysteria. "What does it matter? A cordon of police day and night! I'll call the commissioner."

I broke in hurriedly. "Where is Miss Logan now?"

"Ah!" He swung then. "Norman, she's in bed, isn't she? Mr. Williams, you think–"

"I don't know," I told him. "Who knows where she is? The thing to do is to find her at once." As he moved toward the phone, I said, "I don't know if your phone is tapped or not, but a call to the police might bring immediate and disastrous action. I want to find her."

"Her maid–Walters," Norman said, and pressed a button. "But I think Miss Martha is out of town."

Walters came. She was not a frivolous young French maid but rather stout, motherly and dependable looking.

Martha Logan had gone up to Westchester to a party, she said. But she was not staying the night. "Her work at the hospital, you know." Her train would arrive at 11:27. Thomas, the chauffeur, was to meet her at the Roosevelt Hotel. Yes, the maid thought she was returning alone.

I got a good description of how Martha Logan was dressed before the maid left us.

5
A GUN ROARS

I guess the same thought entered the minds of all three of us at the same time. The thought was that there was a long underground tunnel, the passage from Grand Central station to the Roosevelt Hotel.

I walked over to the desk and lifted a small picture from it.

"Miss Logan?" I asked and when both men nodded, I shoved it into my pocket, grabbed up my hat and went to the door.

"Better let me out as quietly and quickly as possible," I said to Norman. "The house might be watched."

"Yes—yes." Logan was still beside the telephone. "Norman will see you down. Williams, don't hesitate to protect Martha in any way necessary."

"In the way perhaps that you objected to when I worked for the bank last year?"

He faced me squarely.

"I was a narrow-minded man then. Perhaps I am a narrow-minded man now." His lips set grimly. "Strike without mercy. Kill, if it is necessary. My name, my money and my lawyers will stand behind you."

"I don't think it will come to that yet, Mr. Logan," I said. "I've got plenty of time to reach the station. Wait until I contact your daughter before using that phone."

As I left the room, J. Fletcher Logan called after me, "Are you armed?"

I grinned and swung a gun into my hand from a shoulder holster so fast that Norman jumped. I stepped into the elevator with him and crawled down three floors. If I had had an acetylene torch, I'd have burned the cable and dropped the car.

Norman said as he let me out the back. "Think nothing of that ten thousand, Mr. Williams. I'll have the check ready for you as soon as you return."

The long tunnel that runs from Grand Central Station to the Roosevelt Hotel is hardly ever full of people at eleven-thirty at night. As a matter of fact, I've seen it deserted sometimes at seven P.M.

A good place for a murder, but not too hot for a kidnaping. The girl would scream if conscious, and if unconscious, would have to be carried out. That would be my meat. At least, this three-time murderer of young girls had to get his prey alone where he could torture information out of them.

I was thinking it over as I got out of the taxi and walked into Grand Central Station, coming down the ramp from Forty-second Street. I still had seven minutes before the train came in. I'd had a good look at the girl's picture and I had liked what I had seen. A little on the ritzy side maybe, but good.

She held her head as if she were somebody, and I guess she was, at that. Her features were sharply defined, but not too sharply cut. There was a delicate fineness to her face, like that in old-time paintings, with a little firmness tossed in. A hands-off sort of look.

She was a blonde and her eyes were blue. Best of all, I had a full description of what she was wearing.

I got up to the gate where the train came in but not too close. I couldn't spot anyone in the theater crowd returning to Westchester who looked too out of place.

Thomas had already left with her car, but my idea was to introduce myself to Martha Logan, preferably after she left the tunnel and came up in the Roosevelt Hotel. I'd take her home in a taxi in case this was the pay-off and an accident had been arranged for the Logan car.

The station was pretty crowded. There was quite a mob around the gate where she would arrive.

The train came in. The gates opened, and people poured through. The train must have come from well upstate because it was pretty crowded and a lot of people were coming through and a lot more were meeting them—and I saw the girl.

If you didn't know there was great wealth and family behind her, you'd fall for her right away. She walked like a thoroughbred. It was only knowing about the dough that gave you the idea she might be snooty.

Blonde hair peeped out from a little hat. The weather was still cold, but she carried her coat over her arm. A plain coat, a plain tailor-made suit—but I expect it cost heavy dough. It fitted her perfectly, or she fitted it perfectly. Fine straight body, quick walk, nice blue eyes.

I turned in after her when she was in the thickest part of the crowd.

I was closing in to get on her heels when I saw the man. Short, stocky, well-dressed, nothing loud. I didn't know him, but he didn't give me a pleasant impression. He walked through the crowd, got close to the girl, and I saw his hand come out of his overcoat pocket. There was a gun in it.

A place like that seemed no place to intimidate a girl and make her walk quietly to the nearest exit and disappear into the night. Certainly the gun was jammed close to her. One woman saw it, for she cried out—and my right hand swung up under my left armpit. A man alongside me was jarred back by my sudden movement. Maybe I could have shot the gun out of that fellow's hand under ordinary circumstances. But heads were bobbing in and out between me and the girl.

There was the man's body. There's was the man's face. There was the man's gun—and I read death in that face. Death for the girl. In that hard, cold evil face of a killer. For an instant his face was clear, his eyes were clear, his gun was clear and raised close to the girl's head. All clear–and I squeezed lead once.

The roar of the gun. A woman alongside me, looking at me and folding up and fainting. The screams of another. The–yes, the gunman going down amid the small jammed-up crowd.

I moved fast then. I knew the man was dead. You don't lay a .45 into a man's head at twenty-five or thirty feet and not get results. Hysteria took the crowd as I reached Martha Logan. Women were screaming. Men were shoving and yelling, and that inevitable man in every crowd who can handle things was shouting orders to stand back and give the man air, and "Where the devil did that shot come from anyway?" As many people were trying to break into that circle that held death as were trying to get out.

"This way, Miss Logan." I had her by the arm and steered her along quickly. "I'm from your father," I told her, weaving in and out. "Keep your head now. Remember the notoriety if you get into the papers. Take it easy–this way."

I steered her toward the restaurant, twisted right, joined those who were going up the ramp and avoided those who were coming down asking what had happened.

It wasn't hard to get away. The gun-man had figured that. People who were close to that shooting were fighting to get away from it. Those who weren't close were running toward the excitement.

The ride to the Logan house in the taxi was something. A lot of class was sitting beside me needing protection–a few million dollars' worth of class. Also she was asking questions, and I was avoiding them and telling her to ask her father. I handed her one of my cards which she made out in flashing lights.

"Race Williams, isn't it?" she said. "Yes, Race Williams, the detective."

I liked the way she put "the detective."

But I wasn't talking.

When we reached the house, I hustled her in. The place was already overrun by the law. O'Rourke was there, and Commissioner Porter himself. Logan, telling Norman to give me a check, was tossing his arms around his daughter. She wanted an explanation. Logan told her that there had been trouble at the bank and hustled her off to her rooms. But before she went she tossed a parting shot that hit the bull's-eye.

"The bank?" she said. "But, Father, if it has anything to do with–with these awful murders, I want that man there." She pointed at me, smiled. "Yes. I mean Race Williams. I like him."

She was gone up the stairs then, and they were all questioning me. Had I told her? What had I told her? To my surprise, I got the drift of what Logan was saying–that he was dismissing me, handing me a check.

"Norman considers it my duty," he said. "Ten thousand dollars for the man who furnished you with such information." He bowed slightly toward the commissioner. "Of course, Williams, I realized after you had left the impossibility of my daughter actually being involved in such a sordid–" He choked that off. "I am inclined to agree with the commissioner that you yourself were taken in and had nothing to do with the–extortion."

I looked at the check. It was for ten thousand, all right. I looked at the commissioner and at O'Rourke. They knew nothing about the shooting at the station. Then I turned to Logan, but I didn't throw in his face the suggestion that I kill if necessary, that his lawyer would stand back of me.

"The ten thousand, Mr. Logan, is simply expense money," I said. "There is a small fee for escorting your daughter home from the station. I get twenty-five dollars an hour or for any part of an hour."

"Very well," Logan said, but the commissioner's eyebrows went up, and O'Rourke grinned. "Norman, make Mr.–this man–out another check for twenty-five dollars."

"One moment." I was calm but I was good and mad. "There is a small extra charge for additional service. I don't know what the other agencies charge, but I always demand three dollars and seventy-five cents extra when I kill a man in protecting the life of my clients' daughters. If you think it too high, why mail me what you think it's worth." I turned then and started toward the door–just in time to bump into Inspector Nelson.

"So," said Nelson, grabbing me by the shoulder, "you shot somebody–just like that."

"Just like that," I repeated. "So what?"

Ten minutes later we were all in the upstairs study. All but the girl. Intended victim Number Four–Miss Martha Logan.

6
RACE HAS A THEORY

Commissioner Porter was quiet and composed. Nelson was pacing the room and talking. O'Rourke was standing beside the door, and J. Fletcher Logan was sitting uncomfortably in the big chair by the flat desk, Norman beside him as if ready to take notes but without his usual secretary's pencil and notebook.

"If this is a pinch, say so," I said, "and I'll get my lawyer. Not yours." I looked at J. Fletcher Logan who had made no remark.

"Come, come." Commissioner Porter was poring the oil around. He was a good commissioner and he was a good politician, too. "Let's have it all, Williams. Tell us what happened at the station."

So I told it. The killer's face, the gun in his hand, death in his eyes.

"It was a split second or death for Miss Logan," I said. "A wound would only have jarred him, and he'd have fired. So I shot to kill—and he died."

"Like that." Nelson stopped walking and glared at me. "You know these girls have never been killed on sight. They've been kidnaped or lured away and tortured before they died. Don't say you didn't think of that. You claim to think of everything."

"Sure," I said. "I thought of it. I thought, too, that maybe the murderer could have changed the pattern. All right, Nelson." I glared back at him now. "If you were there, you'd wait and see what his plans were—is that it?"

"I'm asking the questions." Nelson pulled the iron jaw on me.

"You're not asking this one, Nelson. I'm asking it." I turned to J. Fletcher Logan. "What would you expect from the police? A wait-and-see game? I had an instant decision to make."

"Why—er—" J. Fletcher sort of stiffened. "Under the circumstances—"

"You'd prefer the newspaper to carry a story about how quick-acting Inspector Nelson wounds murderer five seconds *after* brutal slaying? How would it read to you—the girl's father?"

"Come—come," said the commissioner. "The inspector is merely questioning whether your action was necessary. Let us presume it was necessary. I think perhaps the least publicity given to the whole affair in the station, the better for all concerned. We must assume that this was a hired assassin who misunderstood his orders. It's about

I told them all except Riley's name.

"Well, well," said the commissioner, "I think Williams has perhaps performed a commendable action. What do you say, O'Rourke?"

"I know Williams," said O'Rourke. "He calls them as he sees them. No man can do better than that, Commissioner"

I'll give all of them credit for respecting my position and not trying to get Riley's name out of me. Nelson, no doubt, because the commissioner hamstrung him a bit.

"You feel certain you got all the information available from your–informer, Williams?" the commissioner asked.

"I'd have wrung his neck for what I got if he hadn't made that impossible. And I'd have paid him myself. Ask Mr. Logan about that."

"Yes, yes," said the commissioner. "I am quite aware of the dramatic denouement in naming his daughter. Now, Williams, you are to understand that in a case of this importance your protection alone would hardly be satisfactory. Miss Logan must have complete protection. I would request your silence. Leave this entirely in our hands. And be so kind as to give us your opinion on the matter."

"For free?" I asked.

"For the benefit of the citizens of New York," he said slowly. "I know you too well to offer you money from the public funds."

"Nicely put."

The commissioner was a smooth lad. He didn't like my methods. But he was honest in that dislike. He had never hounded me. Cautioned me at times, yes. Maybe threatened me once or twice. But he was no hard-driving, bull-headed Nelson.

He knew there would be nothing in it for him if he started driving me for killing a man in saving the life of Martha Logan. Logan–like it or not–would have to stand behind me, or the newspapers would make him. I had a story and it was a beaut.

"Well," I said, and this was my big moment, for I'd had this in my mind ever since the last girl was killed, "all of these victims held a secret–a secret of a crime–and each one who knew that secret must die."

"And the torture?" The commissioner was interested.

"The murderer knew the name of one girl who held the secret in the beginning, but he knew that there were others. He tortured Sissy Pierson to get the names of the others and got only one name. Let's say Sissy Pierson knew only one name–Elsa Ames. So he tortured Elsa Ames to get the other names, and she knew but one name. He got that name and tortured the third victim, Dorothy Sears Briggs, to get the other names—and got only one name—Martha Logan."

"Would girls like that keep a secret that was so important?" said Nelson. "You're out of your mind. We had that idea, but it wouldn't fit after the second death and certainly not after the third girl died. Now there's Martha Logan. None of these girls showed any fright, or the least apprehension even, at any time before they were killed."

"These girls didn't know what the secret they held was," I said. "Martha Logan doesn't know it now. Can't you see? All of them were at the scene of some crime. All of them saw the murderer's face. Not one of them even knew a crime was committed."

"Then why trouble to kill them?"

"Because," I said, "all of them saw the murderer. That must be the only solution. They saw the murderer, no doubt fresh from his crime, but they didn't know he was a murderer because they didn't know a crime had been committed."

"Then why would the murderer kill them?"

"Because the murderer knows that sooner or later they *will* know a crime was committed and will remember him. Now, my suggestion for solving the case, if you're interested—"

"Yes," said the commissioner. "We would be interested in that."

"Well," I said, "make a list of every unsolved murder committed in New York within the last year, or out of New York at any time Martha Logan was out of the city. Try to place her at the scene of any of those crimes. Martha Logan has seen this murderer smack at the scene of his crime, but she doesn't know it, because she never heard of the crime. Good night, gentlemen."

I turned and walked out of the room. And out of the house. Cops were all over the place...

The next night I went down to the Bright Spot, a small new night club that was coming along. The talent was not expensive, but it was good. Boys and girls got a chance to show their stuff there and make names. They had a fine talent scout combing the city. It was like a proving ground for some of the big clubs.

I wasn't there to be entertained. I wanted to see what I could pick up. Big shots dropped in there, and not-so-big shots, too—lads who would be barred when café society discovered it.

I guess I wasn't the only one who hoped to get some information. Lieutenant Hogan from the Broadway squad was sitting at a table, looking for all the world like an old-time matinee idol. A plainclothesman named Cohen was with him, dolled up for the sporting mob.

Joey Paleno, the manager, came over and flopped into a chair beside me.

"Business not so good," I said.

"Bad." he said. "I've been asked a dozen times already if the regulars were all here last night, and when they left or if they acted nervous–and I don't know who are regulars and who aren't any more. They all got up and left last night at about the same time, except a few."

"A telephone call tipped them off that something was wrong?"

"Just nothing, Race." Paleno spread his hands. "You know how those things are. Everyone knew something at once. I was out at the bar, and Fingers Levine is drinking alone. Suddenly he puts his half-drunk glass down and walks straight out of the place. It was a double whisky sour, at that. Talk about mental telepathy. Duke University should do its experimenting here. It's uncanny. I've seen it hundreds of times. They were all out by midnight when the cops were on the prowl."

He got up as Lieutenant Hogan went by and beckoned to him.

"See?" Paleno tossed out those expressive hands again. "Now it'll be what time some of the drunks got to playing musical chairs."

I watched the show. The girl who was on had talent. "Feather" Falon they billed her as. And I appreciated the club a little more. Her old man had been shot to death in a gang war when she was a kid. Feather was tough. Feather was afraid of nothing.

Feather looked like a million dollars. Maybe two million, for that was the first time it struck me that Feather looked like Martha Logan. Or was it simply that the Logan girl was on my brain? No. She looked like her, all right. Not that they were twins. Just a likeness in height, color of hair, fair skin.

I saw Bill Cruthers. I gave him the hand as he passed and he came over and sat down at the table beside me.

"They'll have me down at headquarters, Race, for associating with you," he said. "It'll be my first trip, too."

"What are you doing down here?" I asked him.

"Getting around. The Bright Spot is part of the syndicate, but it won't be known until we branch out and welcome the big money. I'm trying to smooth the rough spots. The cops are at it again."

"So Joe told me. Another big crime?"

Bill Cruthers had a nice smile. "Don't be coy, Race," he said. "A shot was fired, and everyone who should know knows. The cops go into a panic and start raiding again." He leaned forward. "How deep are you in it?"

I ignored that.

"What are are you doing down here?" I asked him again. "You've got bigger business."

"Well," he said and he was serious, "it isn't known and I wouldn't like a guy who started guessing. When this panic clears up, I'm going to marry Feather Falon and take her out of this business."

"Feather Falon?" I was surprised.

"She's the cutest, straightest little shooter that ever trod the avenue. Anyway, I'm for her whether she likes it or not. She'll take a chance on anything for money and she's ambitious, so I guess I'm set. I'll take her to South America–abroad if things are right–to the West Coast, and I won't be back until they've forgotten–if then. Then maybe I'll star her on Broadway. The truth is–"

"Yes?" I waited.

"I'm in love with her, Race."

Then he went on to talk about his age. Thirty-eight not being so old. That he'd make it up to her in many ways. He'd run straight for years. Her old man had been no good, but the kid was straight. Loyal.

"Bill," I told him, "you don't have to cry all over your face to me. It will be a real break for her. She's getting a swell guy." I shook his hand. "I wish you luck and I'll send you a present."

He hesitated moment before he spoke. "You might do something for me now," he said. "I don't want to mix my name up with hers or I'd do it myself. Inspector Nelson is buzzing her backstage. Every once in a while they drag her in because of her old man. But the girl's straight as a die–I know that. I thought maybe you'd slip back and break it up. I've got to toddle. Nelson would forget anything to jump on you. Give him the Malone brothers gag."

I didn't like it, but I did wander backstage. I'd had no idea that Bill Cruthers was gone on Feather Falcon, but it explained how she had got her chance at the club.

I didn't cross Nelson and I didn't see Feather Falon. I found out enough to know that she had gone off with Nelson, but if he had dragged her down for questioning, I couldn't tell. The watchman backstage said he didn't know.

"Cops are like that," he said, adding that Feather had a temper but she hadn't been using it. "Believe me, son," he said, "she ain't tongue-tied, either. He must have offered a few bucks. That kid will do anything for money."

So I left without any information, except the item of Bill Cruthers' heart throb that any gossip columnist would give his right eye to have.

7
A DIFFERENT PATTERN

A late edition of the paper had not a word about Martha Logan, nor had I been mentioned yet in the Grand Central Station shooting. The commissioner was soft-pedaling things until he got the breaks.

I wondered. Three girls had never got the breaks. Martha Logan— I rather liked the kid. At least, she'd had a break the other girls hadn't had. The police knew for certain that her number was up.

Did that give her safety? It should, for a while. Surely they'd toss enough police around her. She would have an escort every place she went, if they let her go any place. No. It looked as if she would have to stay in her own house until she–or the killer–died.

The next day I liked her better. I went down to the *Times* and went through some old papers with the help of a doll who knew the society angle. Martha Logan had done her stuff. She held a record for war bond sales and not to the millionaire set, either. She had gone out and done her part at public gatherings. Sold them on her personality, too, without benefit of identification.

She had been a nurse's aid. None of this stuff of running around in a pretty uniform and meeting important visitors to the hospital. She had done more than straighten flowers and hand over vases to be filled with water by someone else. She had worked. Seven o'clock in the morning stuff–six days a week, and sometimes seven.

What's more, she hadn't simply waved the flag and folded it up when the war folded. She had kept right on at the hospital. More work and less pictures in the papers than any girl in the city, was the way the superintendent of the hospital put it.

I felt a little proud. I had given her a chance to carry on, and now the police were watching her, so she couldn't carry on until the thing was settled...

O'Rourke came in to see me the next day before I had breakfast. He still looked worried, but he looked as though he'd had more sleep. He had some type-written data in his hand.

"Here," he said, "is a list of every murder for the past two years in the city of New York, and out of it, on the dates we can fix the Logan girl as out of town. She has never been near most of the places at any time. The Central Park killing–well, she rides in the park once in a while but never at the right time to have been near when a killing was pulled off. Besides, she's never had the other three girls riding with her. She's sure of that."

"Has she ever been with them? I mean all at once."

"She doubts it," said O'Rourke. "Sissy Pierson she remembers meeting–but she doesn't know where. She identified her from the picture. Both the other girls she knows. The first one to die after Sissy–Elsa Ames–she didn't know too well, but had met her around. The third one she knew better. That was Dorothy Sears Briggs. But only met her at parties."

"Have you ever placed the four together?"

"Yes," said O'Rourke. "At the Plaza in April of Forty-four and Madison Square Garden in December of Forty-five. Uptown at the Armory on New Year's Eve of the same year. A lawn fete on the old Untermeyer estate up in Yonkers last May. There may have been other affairs, but we can't be sure. Like the docking of a troop ship in Forty-four. Sissy Pierson is hard to place always. The last Labor Day up in Maine on Moosehead Lake." When I looked up at him, he said, "There were one hundred and thirty-seven guests that came from New York. At the other affairs, all but the Plaza, there were over a hundred, at the Garden nearly two hundred–and no one was killed at the Plaza or the other places."

"She's not keeping anything back?"

No," said O'Rourke. "It's a wonder she remembers as much as she does. All she did was entertain, sell bonds, and work at the hospitals. Half the time she didn't know where she was going, even when the time came. Says she met a lot of people a lot of places. I was out early this morning, talking to all the girls she knows well. Boy, are they a suspicious lot! I didn't mention her name in particular. I let them think I was asking her questions, too. They remember a lot of the damnedest things and make up a lot of the damnedest things. For my money, I'd bury the Logan girl in the Tombs until we clear up this thing."

"You showed her pictures, I suppose."

O'Rourke chuckled and shrugged.

"Practically moved the rogues' gallery up into her sitting room." He shook his head then. "She recognized one guy for us. Said she didn't know where she had seen him but remembered his face. Nelson hit the ceiling and had every cop in the city after him–picked him up in twenty-seven minutes. He has a record, yes, but the fact was he served the Logan girl at a luncheon in a midtown hotel two years ago. She's got a memory, all right. Nelson wanted to pin something on the bird, but as soon as he spoke of that luncheon, the girl recalled him. Said he had served the soup cold."

"Had he?"

"Well, he–" O'Rourke stopped. "What the devil are you talking about? You're not serious? Cold soup."

"No," I said, "I'm not serious about that. Why tell me all this?"

"Old friends, Race. The police have their place and you have yours. There are a lot of things you can do we can't do."

I asked O'Rourke about Harvey Rath.

"We showed her pictures of him, but she said she had never seen him. Of course, she couldn't be sure from the pictures. I knew Rath well."

"Tell me about him–his character." And when O'Rourke's eyebrows went up, "We all have character, O'Rourke, good or bad."

"His," said O'Rourke, "was just bad. He fenced things in a small way for years. Then he went in for bigger stuff. We never could lay the finger on him after he hit the high-priced stuff. Suddenly he got real smart. We were sure some big stuff went through him, but we couldn't prove a thing."

"Used blackmail, put the finger on big-shot crooks, too," I said and when O'Rourke nodded: "That's dangerous stuff."

"There was talk he had a little book and that it would go to the cops if he was ever knocked over. I guess it was only talk. He disappeared suddenly. Two, three years ago. He's dead, of course."

"Why of course? No body."

"It is easier to hide a dead body than a live one. Racketeers, politicians, far bigger lads than Harvey Rath have died and their bodies have never been found. I come in to pump you, and you start pumping me. I'll have to be on my way, Race. I'm worrying about the chances this killer will take."

"He can't get through a real police block, O'Rourke," I told him seriously. "But it is a desperate situation for the killer. I think Miss Logan is the last of his victims. So this time it has only to be a quick and sudden death, and no doubt soon. Look at how the other deaths followed one upon the other."

"But we didn't know then," said O'Rourke. "We know now. We've taken every precaution possible without letting the press in on it. The girl has seen pictures of everyone worth seeing." O'Rourke grinned. "She's recognized a few big-shot racketeers, a couple spotted for black market stuff, but nothing to remember about them. Just one." His smile was a tired one. "A pick-pocket at the Plaza two years back. He was acting odd. We'll get some small stuff back through it. What a memory that girl has got!"

"That's what the murderer is thinking, O'Rourke. That's what he fears. Four girls saw something that will stand out in their minds when it is forced back into conscious memory through something startling, no doubt. Something that is going to happen soon. Take care of the little lady, O'Rourke. She's got lots on the ball."

"Don't you worry," O'Rourke said with great confidence, but he was still worrying his head off when he left me . . .

Four days later, what happened knocked the opening of *Aida* with the newly discovered young opera star right onto Page Five. A woman looking out a window saw it. She didn't report it right away. She didn't have a phone and was afraid to go out to telephone.

Early in the morning, along about three, she saw a car come down the side street past a brownstone front that had been turned into a rooming house. She saw the door open, saw something pushed into the street. Saw it roll over and lie in the gutter. And that's all it did, lie there.

She hadn't been able to get to sleep and was sitting at the window. She sat there for quite a long time staring, fascinated. Then she woke up the girl across the hall in the back. It was almost a full hour, though, before the landlady called the police. Yep, the body lay there, undiscovered, right in the city of New York.

The man had been shot dead only a few hours before they found him. He hadn't been identified when Jerry brought me the early editions of the afternoon papers. But there had been a neatly typed card pinned on his chest—not the same terrifying note that had startled millions and struck terror to those who had daughters. It was not the same simple message that had sent the underworld into a panic. It read a little bit differently. It said:

THIS IS FOR YOU
YOU DIRTY LITTLE MAN IN A DIRTY
LITTLE GUTTER

O'Rourke fairly breezed in to see me. His eyes were bright, the wrinkles gone out of his forehead.

"You were right, Race." He patted me on the back, chuckled. "It was Harvey Rath. I knew him well. Been hiding out, all right. What Martha Logan knew about him will never be known now."

"Did she see the body?"

"Her old man hit the ceiling at the very idea. And to tell you the truth, Race, I was timid about taking her down to the morgue." In a matter-of-fact voice he added, "But he wasn't mussed up any. A bullet hole in his heart. We had some mighty good pictures made and sent up for her to look at. She said she had never seen him."

"That wonderful memory!" I took a silent laugh. "So Rath had all his trouble for nothing. Got anything on his killing?"

"No." O'Rourke looked at me steadily. "This Norman lad, the Logan secretary. He hasn't been in touch with you, has he?"

"Not a peep. What's on your chest?" I inquired.

"The pattern. The bullet hole in Rath's chest. Sort of different. Not true to form. Like Grand Central Station."

I came to my feet.

"You think I killed him!" Then I laughed. "The pattern is all right, O'Rourke, for remember, this is a different pattern. This is someone that Rath put the finger on to do some killing for him–out of the book maybe. And this guy–well, he was big or he was mad or he knew where the book was, and he plugged Rath." I nodded. "I'll admit that card on the body was a classic and worthy of me. Was it Nelson's idea?"

"Well–" O'Rourke scratched his head– "don't blamed Nelson too much. I was wondering. What's so strange or insulting about it? It's like you, isn't it? Nelson thought maybe Logan had his secretary send you around some dough, too, for the job."

"I'm flattered, not insulted," I told O'Rourke. "And if you never find the lad who dished it out to Harvey Rath, you can give me the credit."

O'Rourke put cowlike eyes on me and went out chuckling. He was in a rare good humor.

8
SITTING DUCK

Of course I thought that was the end of it. The papers thought so, too. The boys of the press surmised and conjectured and went all out according to their imaginations. They made a lot out of Nelson's ambiguous statement. But never once was the name of Martha Logan brought into the story.

The following day I saw her pictures in the society columns. She was among those who would attend the opera *Aida*.

My first thought was that the police were finally convinced that all danger was past for Martha. Then I saw the point, or thought I did. Dislike Nelson or not dislike him, he was a good cop and a careful one–at least with a name like J. Fletcher Logan. He'd have cops watching that girl at the opera. At that, it seemed like he was setting her out to see if there would be any attempt on her life.

Well, I'd probably never see Martha Logan again, unless I went to the opera to get a peek at her. And that I wouldn't do for any woman.

Logan had sent me a check for twenty-five hundred, so I had made a few bucks out of it.

That night I went to Johnny Swan's Grill to eat. It was surprising the food he could dig out of his vest pocket if you had the money to pay for it. It was surprising, too, the people you could dig up there, and this night was no exception. As I passed through the grill an important voice spoke up.

"Mr. Williams, sir," it said, "the tables are crowded. I dislike dining alone. Be my guest, please."

A dapper little man was on his feet, half bowing from the waist. I tried to keep the surprise out of my voice, but I knew, or thought I knew then, that Martha Logan's peril was a thing of the past. Riley was back in the city.

"Sit down, sir." He waited for me to fall into the chair across from him. "You've missed me, I see. Well, I went up to northern Michigan for a bit of shooting. Or was it fishing, or was it even Michigan?" He smiled pleasantly as he beckoned to a waiter. "A little business transaction called me back. A deal that came through quite handsomely." He lowered his voice. "No doubt you read about it in the papers." And, with a little bow, "Let me thank you for your promptness in our little deal."

When the waiter had brought my steak and gone, Riley started in again.

"It's like this, Race." He lit up an expensive cigar. "I like to look after my friends. There's a man now, an upright, wealthy, and distinguished gentleman who could use your services. Worked hard, you know, and played a bit too hard. A doctor has kept his body in good shape, but even a psychiatrist can't help his mental condition. You and I can–at a handsome figure."

I looked at him. "And I'm to buy back the letters. I don't like blackmails."

His sharp eyes appraised me. "If I didn't expect to live to a ripe old age, I'd manage you, Race," he said. "Say twenty per cent, and I'd be a millionaire in a couple of years. I don't object to your swaggering in and out of places daring guys to take a shot at you, but I'd see that you got big money for each swagger–plenty of swag! I'll bet you didn't drag down what I got in our little deal."

"I didn't," I told him. "And I wouldn't have wanted to drag down what you would have got that night if we'd been alone...What's the trouble at the bar?"

Riley was out of his seat at once. If there was anything he could cash in on, he wanted to have that nose of his in it first. While others were digesting what had happened, Riley would be at a phone to see what was in it for him. When I reached the door, I saw him disappearing out the side entrance.

Small knots of men were talking. Other little knots were breaking up and leaving the place. Then I heard an excited guy blubbering what the commotion was all about.

"I saw it, I tell you! The car came down the street right behind the big Caddie. They poured tons of lead into it. The Caddie hit a pole but didn't turn over. And of all things, a police car shot after that black Packard and dumped it over at the next corner. But she was dead. Her face shot away almost. Conley of the *News* was there. Got pictures."

Things were sort of swimming. I don't think I heard someone asking questions, but I heard the little guy answer them.

"Sure, it was the financier's daughter, Martha Logan. There were cops in her car with her, going to the opera, too."

For the first time in my life my stomach went back on me. I went into the men's room and was violently sick. I must have thought a lot of that girl. And what I thought of Nelson! A sitting duck–a trial ballon to see if things were all right! Harvey Rath. All a plant to get the girl out in the open. A dead man planted to kill a live girl!

Those thoughts came later. At the time, only words were going through my head : Martha Logan's face shot half away. Conley of the *News* had pictures. Cops in the car. Following the car. The killers turned over. Martha Logan.

I had the boy bring me three whisky sours before I got one to stay down. I gave him a five-dollar bill and told him to keep the change, then smacked him such a wallop with my open hand that he sat down on the floor. Why did I smack him? He'd started to tell me the story of the shooting because he thought I'd been out of the café so long I hadn't heard. I slapped him down and went out onto the sidewalk.

An extra was on the street by now. I got a copy, walked into a strange dump, and read it. Not a thing new. It seemed everyone had been killed until you read the big print over again. And there was nothing but big print. Only one thing seemed to be certain–that was that Martha Logan was dead. Cops had been riding in the car with her, and another police car was following along behind. But you couldn't tell from the newspaper story whether the police car was there by accident or design.

I knew that it had been planted. And Martha had hardly left her house before the gunfire had broken loose. Two machine guns had peppered the Logan's big Cadillac.

If the *News* had pictures, they would be in a later edition, so I didn't buy it. Martha Logan's picture covered what part of the front page was free from black print. The print read:

FINANCIER'S DAUGHTER DIES IN CAR AS POLICE BATTLE THUGS

So that was the end. I'd go out and get gloriously drunk.

That wasn't my usual line. Too many people want my hide, and if I were caught staggering or caught reaching slowly for a gun, it would be my last drunk.

Anyway, the stuff went down bad, so I spent my time walking up and down side streets. I didn't want to hear any more details. I simply walked. Not thinking; only walking.

Finally I shrugged and headed for home. After all, it wasn't as though I'd had a client shot from under me. She was a girl I had seen only one night. Ten to one I'd never have seen her again, anyway. I'd go home, sleep it off. If I could sleep.

I have a nice apartment. Nice guys work there. It wasn't yet twelve o'clock. The doorman was still on the job. He was just about to go off duty. He looked at me, shook his head.

"Bad business," he said.

I nodded and walked back to the automatic elevators and took myself upstairs. I shoved my key in the lock, pushed the door and got no results. So Jerry had heard, hadn't gone home yet, and was guessing how things would be. Jerry was like a dog. He knew if things weren't right, if they weren't going to be right.

I gave the buzzer a couple of shorts and one long and got action. Not that I heard his feet. The walls and the door are too thick for that. I like my joint built well. I like quiet for myself and like quiet for the other tenants if I intend to be noisy.

The bolt clicked off, the door opened the length of the chain.

"Okay, Boss," Jerry said. "Okay."

I remembered my instructions in case I ever walked up to my door with a gun in my back.

"Hunkery dorey," I told him. Sounds silly–but you don't live like I do.

"I know," I told him when he let me in. "You've been reading the papers."

He grinned. "I've been listening to the radio and I'm—"

"I don't want to hear anything about it," I cut in and walked past him into the living room.

He was saying something about a visitor when I turned, half facing him, half facing the bedroom door that was slowly opening.

When it opened wide, I was knocked into a tailspin. If you had put a hand grenade into my mitt and told me it was an apple, and asked me to take a bite and I did, I couldn't have been more surprised.

Standing in that doorway was Martha Logan, or a reasonable facsimile thereof. And me? I stood there with my mouth open.

"Boy," Jerry was saying, "like a play, isn't it?"

The girl ran over and took both my hands. She was real, all right, and her hands were little and soft; and all that stuff on the radio about smooth, soft hands that had sounded like hooey was suddenly true.

"I-I thought—" I said and let it go at that.

"I know," she said. "You thought I was dead. But didn't you hear? It was on the radio after—after what happened."

"Sure," Jerry chimed in. "I tried to tell you, Boss. There was another girl in that car. But it isn't explained yet how she got there. Miss Logan, here, come in and wanted to wait for you, and I seen the society page you folded to—"

"That's enough, Jerry," I told him. "Beat it into the kitchen. Close the door and don't try to listen."

Jerry went, and I turned to the girl.

"You shouldn't have come here. Don't you know you're in danger?"

"That isn't like the Race Williams I've been hearing about—from Norman, of course. They don't know I'm here, Race. No one can know. If they wanted to kill me, they think I'm dead. I slipped out. Even the servants watched the other girl go. I climbed out the window. How terrible! How terrible! I don't care what she was paid, I didn't want her to *die* for me! I came to engage you—to have you take me off some place." She stepped back and looked at me. Her smile was something. "Why, Race Williams," she said, "I believe you are really glad to see me!"

I put my hands on her shoulders and shook her up a bit. Like she was a kid. I was glad and relieved and even my stomach felt better.

"I was never more glad to see anyone in my life," I told her and meant it. "But still you shouldn't have come."

"I had to. I couldn't be cooped up there any longer. They hired this girl, Race—maybe a not too nice girl, for her face was hard—but she didn't want to die. They wanted to take her out before that man Rath was found, but I wouldn't let them. Then when it seemed all over, they did take her tonight, and she was killed. I feel to blame."

"You needn't," I said. "How much did they tell you? The police, I mean?"

"They tried to tell me very little, but I guessed the truth. I had to look at pictures–nothing but pictures. They wanted to know if I kept a diary, but I didn't have one. I had a date book, and they went back over everything." And when I would have questioned her, she said quickly. "Don't, Race–don't. I've thought and thought and thought. I've never seen a murder committed, never been near any place where a murder was committed. It's all a horrible mistake!"

9
THE REGULAR ROUTINE

Just as if I believed Martha Logan, I nodded, but I knew it wasn't any mistake. I went down the hall and put the chain on the door. I tried all the windows, but Jerry had locked them.

"You can't stay here," I said to the girl, "and on the level, I'm afraid to take you out alone."

"But I won't go back. I can't stand it! If I get up in the night, there's a rap on the door and a policeman wants to know, 'Are you all right, miss?'"

"Look." I was thinking it over. "I don't like running away. You are too well-known. The safest place for you is home with the cops."

"Race–" she came close to me–"my place is in the hospital, but if that may endanger the patients, I won't go. I saw the truth of that when that understanding Sergeant O'Rourke spoke to me."

The phone rang. I picked it up. I didn't recognize the voice at first, then I knew it was Bill Cruthers.

"You wanted information, Race," he said, and his voice was hard, determined. "I'll give it to you tonight. I want to come around and see you now."

"How much do you know?" I asked.

"Enough to give you a chance to burn this fiend down. And you are the one to do it. Can I get into your apartment without being seen by anyone–anyone, understand? I'm a block away."

I hesitated, then gave him the dope. "The rear door. Jerry, my boy, will have it open." When he objected strenuously, I told him, "It's pitch dark. Jerry will stand there with his back to you, and you can slip into the elevator."

I told him how to reach that door.

Then he began to holler about Jerry. Being seen might mean his life. Girls had been tortured and had talked, and so would Jerry. I saw his point of view and explained how Jerry simply stood downstairs by the automatic elevator that the superintendent had dropped into the basement for my private use. Jerry stood by the door so clients wouldn't make a mistake–his back to my visitors.

"No worry, Bill," I told him. "I've worked it a long time. A hundred guys have come in that way. Big shots in the rackets. Little punks. Millionaire playboys. A couple of society women even, to say nothing of a well-known broker. They didn't want to be seen by anyone but me, either. They never were."

After a pause he said, "Your word, Race, that this Jerry won't see my face or body?"

"My word," I told him, and that word meant something in the underworld. "Just run the car up to the seventh floor. I'll be watching for you."

"Ten minutes," he said. "Exactly."

I was puzzled. Why would Bill Cruthers risk his life to give me a break?

"This may be the big moment," I told Martha Logan. "A lad is coming up to empty his chest." And then, offhand, "This girl who took your place in the car–what did she look like?"

"Oh, about my build and size. And my carriage and features, that inspector said. Feather Falon they called her . . . What's the matter, Race?"

"Nothing," I said after I rocked back on my toes again.

I knew now why Nelson had been in the Bright Spot the other night. This case was a series of jolts. I knew now why Bill Cruthers was coming over to spill it all. Feather Falon! The girl he was going to marry. The girl he was going to star. The girl he was going to build up and–

Had Bill Cruthers known the truth of these murders for some time? He must have had something to go on. But he wouldn't have talked before. After all, he was of the night. Those of the night who talked, died. Now, Cruthers would even chance that. He must have thought a lot of the Falon girl.

I dragged Jerry out of the kitchen and gave him his instructions.

"Usual thing," he said. "No peeking even a little bit?"

"Not even a little bit, Jerry." I was deadly serious. Bill Cruthers was a swell guy, but anyone knew he wasn't a lad to fool with. "We play this always on the level."

After Jerry had gone, I said, "Listen, Martha. I want you to go in that bedroom. I'll lock the door, and you stay there until I tell you to come out. A visitor–maybe a break on the case."

She went without a word. There was no fire escape on that window. I was seven floors up, so she was in no danger from intruders. Then I went to the front door, held it open slightly, and dropped my gun into my right hand.

Bill came quickly, his coat collar turned up, his fedora pulled well down over his face. He was breathing heavily when I let him in, closed the door, put on the chain.

I was seeing a new Bill Cruthers–nothing calm and suave about him now.

"You know why I came," he said and preceded me into the living room.

"Yes," I said. "Feather. Feather Falon. You didn't know she took the job?"

"I never suspected. That devil Nelson!"

He flopped into a chair, got up almost at once, walked to the kitchen, the bathroom, down the hall, tried the closet door, looked inside. All slowly and deliberately. Then he went to the bedroom door, tried the knob, turned and looked at me.

"Your word of honor, Race, that there is no one in the apartment."

I hesitated. He swung on me almost viciously.

"Okay, Bill," I told him. "I have the key. It's a–well a woman."

"I see." He seemed relieved. "All right, Race. I'm not going to waste time. Pick up that telephone book. I'm giving you the name, the telephone number–and the truth."

I started to turn to the phone book, my back half to Cruthers.

Something was wrong. Something was missing from the picture. I swung back, and my gun was in my hand. It didn't seem to make sense. But my hand was steady, and my eyes were straight, and my finger was on the trigger.

I couldn't have shot him to death like that. So he had time to aim and fire and put me out smack through the head if he had waited a second longer.

He must have seen my right hand jerk up under my left armpit as I swung. and he was afraid to wait. He fired as he stood, and it took me high in the chest, spun me around a fraction of a second faster than I would have made it.

No, I didn't have the same chance Bill Cruthers had. The cards were dealt, and he held all the aces. I saw his body as I staggered back and I pumped lead into it. He had lifted his gun for my head.

But my head wasn't there. It wasn't there because his shot in my chest had knocked me down and taken my head out of the picture. His bullet cracked against the wall, and I heard the picture crash and I remembered in a dull sort of way that it had cost me seven dollars and fifty cents–and wasn't worth it.

I didn't understand it all when the shooting ended. I simply knew that I was on my feet again and that Cruthers wasn't. He was on his knees and holding his stomach and was bent over like the dying gladiator, only not looking so noble about it.

My vision wasn't too good but it was clearing now, and I heard a woman screaming. Not a hysterical girl pounding on the door. A woman had her head out of a window some place and was shouting into the night.

Cruthers wasn't taking it too well. But who would, full of lead? I leaned down and took his gun from his hand. He rolled slightly and turned his agonized face up at me. Then he went all the way over and stretched himself out on the floor. It was almost too theatrical to be real–but it was real, terribly real. He was unconscious now, and his face wasn't agonized. It looked sort of drawn, but his eyes were closed, and he was white.

No sound from the bedroom. I leaned down and gave Cruthers a quick search. No other gun. But there was a knife. it might have been the knife that–

I jerked erect, felt the sharp pain up by my shoulder. I got my hand in my pocket and went to the bedroom door. My stomach was bad again. But not from the shot. Things were too quiet behind the door. I hoped she hadn't fainted, but she didn't seem the fainting kind. Could she have jumped from the window? But she wouldn't be the jumping kind either.

I swung open the door, and she stood by the open window, holding her throat.

"It's you–you–" she said. "Then I shouldn't have screamed, but I thought that–"

"Stay here," I told her. "I've got to use the phone."

Then I was buzzing around, trying to locate O'Rourke and did get his friend, Detective Kahn. I got my message through, too.

By that time people were pounding at the door. I started toward it. Martha stopped me. Her voice was sort of uncertain, then it wasn't. She was looking straight down at Bill Cruthers. He opened his eyes.

"I know that man," she said. "I saw him. Why, we flashed the searchlight from the boat right on his face. He was kneeling on the dock, or just getting up from it, of something. I remember asking him what he was doing on the dock. It was Dorothy Briggs's boat."

"I was right," Cruthers groaned. "I knew one of them would remember, and it *would* be the last one." Then he passed out again.

When I swung open the apartment door, a tenant who had wanted in jumped back ten feet, and several others crowded behind him made for the stairs. Funny how people will demand entrance and then wish they hadn't.

The cops came, all right–lots of them. I came around and hollered about Jerry. They wouldn't let me out, but they found him in the elevator and brought him in.

"What a skull the kid must have," the doctor said in admiration. "The wallop he took with a gun, I think, should have cracked it like an egg shell. But he'll be all right."

Jerry opened his eyes and winked once at me.

"The regular routine," he said. "You killed the guy, I hope."

"He killed him, all right," said the doctor. "Sort of on the installment plan, but he won't last another twelve hours."

10
END OF A LOVE LIFE

Lead I had taken had gone in high up in my chest and far over to the left side and didn't give me much trouble. I was at the hospital when Bill Cruthers made his ante-mortem statement. He was willing to talk, insisted only that I should be there.

Cruthers said it started in Pittsburgh when he was little more than a kid. A few drinks, kidding around at a dance hall with a girl because some tough guy didn't like it, a street fight later, his grabbing the gun from the thug's hand. Cruthers killed him.

"I'd have got a few years at the most," he said, "but I was young and I was scared, and Harvey Rath took care of me. That was when he first put the hooks into me.

"And here's something no one knew. Harvey Rath had a daughter who lived in Pittsburgh. He kept her out of the picture entirely. She was a devil, all right. Don't ask me how I knew about her–I married her. And I had to visit her once a month, too.

"Why? Well, Rath said to me some ten years back when I was beginning to make the night clubs pay–his clubs, 'I've treated you like a son, Bill, and now I'm going to make you really my son. I'm going to give you my daughter.' He put those ratlike eyes on me then. 'I could turn you in for murder, but you're smart—my child loves you. Shall we say the wedding will take place on Saturday?'

"There wasn't a decent thing about that she-devil, except that she thought I was heaven's gift to this earth. She was the only thing in the world Rath cared about, the only person he really trusted. There was money in those night spots, and none but his daughter and I knew he had a hand in it. I ran everything, and he took the money. No matter how much he made he lived in the same dirty little room alone back of the pawnshop, and some place there was that yellow folder in which he kept everything about me, everything about others. Most people thought it was a book, but it was a folder. He had fenced more stuff than any man in the city. Then when the night club business wasn't too good he began to shake down the boys themselves. When he fenced things, he knew if murder went with it."

Cruthers did a bit of coughing but refused a drink of water. He seemed anxious to spill it all.

"So Rath started to run roughshod over the boys. Then he went too far. He got the Malone brothers to knock over a rival fence in the Bronx with the promise of big money, but paid them nothing—simply threatened them with what he knew about them. He had affidavits and all. Both the Malone boys were hard, but it worked once. Rath tried it a second time, and there are still a couple of bullet holes in his bed to show how much they disliked it.

"He sent the information about them to the police, even planned to have them at a certain spot so the cops could pick them up—all anonymous. But the Malones sensed the trap, got from under, and disappeared. After that Rath was nearly killed twice. He had no threats to hold over their heads now. They were fugitives from the electric chair, and Rath believed—and he was right—that their one mission in life was to get him. That's why he disappeared—hiding until they were caught by the police or he could have them traced. I was to help him." With a grimace that was meant for a smile, he added, "I didn't."

"That was over two years ago. Rath hid out in Pittsburgh. Then he didn't like the way I treated his daughter. Treat her? It was a wonder I didn't crush her skull long ago. Then I met Feather. After that there was one girl only for me—Feather Falon."

"Then you didn't plant her on the cops—on Nelson?" I came in quick with that one.

"No!" he almost shouted the words. "They killed her! On my orders and with the money I paid them and with the threat I pretended came from Harvey Rath. I arranged it all on the phone, but I thought it was the Logan girl."

Cruthers seemed to have difficulty in breathing. The doctor shook his head at Nelson.

"We're not interested in your love life, Cruthers," Nelson said brutally. "Why did you kill those three girls?"

"My wife stole that hidden yellow folder from her father and gave it to me," Cruthers went on slowly. "It helped me to get men to bring those girls to me–they thought they were doing it for Harvey Rath. They never saw me. Those girls had seen me up in Maine on a dock at Moosehead Lake. They were coming from some hospital dance, but I thought they had all reached the dock and gone when a big boat dissembarked dozens of them twenty-five minutes earlier. Four girls came in the speed boat later. I couldn't see their faces, but they could see me. Their spotlight lit right on my face."

"What were you doing?" O'Rourke asked.

"Sinking my wife. I drove her up to Maine, strangled her in the car and sank her by the dock. No one knew Rath had a daughter. No one knew I had a wife. I don't know how Williams finally suspected. I was pretty clever."

"Very smart," I cut in. "But what made you kill the girls? What made you think they'd know you again, and would suspect you of anything?"

Cruthers gave an odd little gurgling laugh that brought the doctor half erect. Cruthers said:

"I haven't any conscience and I never believed in this subconscious mind business. But it exists. One killing–a gun battle years back, a short stretch would have been all I got–and it all came from that. Sissy Pierson was the first. O'Hara introduced me to her one night, and she tried to remember where she had met me. I knew where and knew she would, too, later. I got a couple of guys to knock over O'Hara in case she had told him anything.

"I went to see Sissy. She swore up and down she knew only one of the girls on the dock that night–and as soon as I mentioned the dock, she knew where she had seen me. I taped her mouth to stop her screaming and put her through the works for more information. I had to kill her.

"The second girl–not too difficult. I got a couple of boys to snatch her and bring her to the loft. They never saw me. And she remembered the name of only one other in the boat! I got that other later with a simple telephone call. The last name came up. Logan's daughter.

"You know the rest. Somehow Logan was tipped off, and Williams killed the guy who had the girl in Grand Central Station. I was almost free–and the police all around the house, and time running short."

"What do you mean short?" I asked.

"The ice would be breaking up in Moosehead Lake. They'd find the body. It would be spread all over the papers. The police were questioning society girls, and the Logan girl might see me and remember. She wouldn't if there was no body. That's that sub-conscious mind you read about."

"But why would they find the body?" I asked. "You weighted it down, must have picked a deep spot."

"Deep–yes, good and deep, and plenty of weight. But don't you read the papers about Maine? The place belonged to the father of the Ames girl. He sold it for a quarry, no less, wanted deep water. They were going to dredge when the ice broke up. They'd find the body."

"How did you know that Martha Logan was at my place?" Me again.

"I saw her leave her house. I thought she was a maid. She slipped out a window. I could have killed her then–easy. But I thought she was dead in the car. When I learned different, I guessed where she would go, but I made sure she was at your apartment by asking for your word that no one was there. I wouldn't have tried to kill you if you hadn't admitted a woman was there.

"I had intended to toss Rath's body into the picture after the Logan girl was dead so all the blame could rest on him. But with half the cops in the city guarding Martha Logan I had to act. I hoped to con-vince them that the show was over by dumping Rath into the street. But the cops were still timid and hired Feather Falon to ride in the death car. Feather–well, she gave me my chance to see you, Williams. It would seem natural that I'd talk."

Bill Cruthers stopped then, and his pain was apparent, his face con-torted. It was to me he spoke now, or rather, gasped.

"I planned it all, Race–carefully. I don't know how I could have slipped up. I didn't even take a chance that Jerry didn't take a look at visitors. I cracked him because I wanted to be sure he didn't get a look at me. How could you have suspected–and turned shooting like that? How–did you know it was–me?"

Nelson looked at me then. O'Rourke too. I heard Logan breathing heavily from where he stood against the closed door. I almost blurted it out. But I didn't.

The doctor looked up at me, shrugged white-coated shoulders which said quite plainly, "It won't be long now."

Cruthers half lifted a hand. There was a plea in the gesture, in his eyes, in his voice.

"I've known you a long time, Race. We—you always liked me. I'm going out. I want to know. I got to know. It will help me go easier."

"Hurry, sir," the doctor said, and when I didn't speak: "He went through torment last night. Five shots in his stomach. If you can ease things, do it in the name of humanity."

I guess I laughed, but I didn't feel like laughing. I was thinking of the girls who had died, and how they had died—not the attempt to kill me. I was thinking, too, of the load of lead he had had dumped into the machine and which was meant for Martha Logan.

"Ease things?" I shot the words at them. "Let the dirty rat go out with the lead in his insides." and when Cruthers made an agonized twist, I growled, "So you don't like it now. All right—take this with you. You were a fool. I knew it. It all fitted. It couldn't be anyone, but you. You rotten—"

He cried out once, and died. Logan took off his hat. O'Rourke hesitated, put up his hand, dropped it, raised it again and lifting his hat off, held it at his side. Nelson and I stood looking down. Nelson maybe because he didn't know any better. Me—well, I had had a lot of respect for Cruthers living, because I hadn't known any better. But I knew better now, and I didn't have any respect for him dead. My hat stayed on.

The doctor tossed a sheet over Cruthers' head. We turned and left the room. Nelson wanted to know all I knew. Logan wanted to pay. He did, and plenty. I took the check and I told Nelson that if he was half a cop, he would have known the answers long ago. With a wink at O'Rourke I invited him up to my place for a drink.

"It was mighty clever work, Race," said O'Rourke over his whisky—the third, by the way. "The newspapers will get the whole story. I understand Miss Logan is making a hero out of you, so any hush-hush is off the books. Listen, Race, I always knew you had a head, but I never thought you'd bother to use it. Cruthers made a mistake some place, and you caught on. We boys either didn't recognize it or didn't have your chance to see it."

"Yes," I said, "he made a mistake. And my solution and how and when I solved the crime is strictly off the record—and for your ears alone."

"Not for the papers?"

"Not unless I can think up a better story than the truth. I'm still a man of action, O'Rourke."

"Yes, I know." O'Rourke nodded. "You turned your back and gave him a chance to use his gun, and he damn near killed you. What was his first mistake?"

"He made only one," I told O'Rourke. "Otherwise he could have walked in here, shot me through the back of the head and killed me, then shot the girl dead, walked upstairs, straddled a few low walls from roof to roof, and have been as free as the air."

"Yes, I know that. Come on."

"Well," I said, "it was Jerry. You heard Cruthers say that he didn't quite swallow that stuff about Jerry not seeing visitors. He should have believed it because it's true. Jerry does leave the rear door open and lean against the elevator my secret visitors are to enter. It's hard enough to get people to trust me without asking them to trust him. Cruthers thought Jerry might watch, give me some signal. So he flattened him. and that, O'Rourke, was my signal."

"How?" O'Rourke stiffened.

I laughed a little at his puzzlement. "We have a routine," I said. "When the client is in the elevator, Jerry goes out and sees that our meal ticket wasn't shadowed. If things are right, he gives me a buzz. It's a protection I furnish my clients. If Jerry doesn't telephone me, I know that things are all wrong. Well, he didn't buzz. Cruthers had made his one mistake."

"Yet you turned your back and went for the phone book."

"Sure." I grinned. "I never suspected Cruthers. It never entered my head until he put it there. He said for me to take a look at the telephone book. That was to get my back to him. I wasn't suspicious. I was facing him with my hands at my sides. He had every chance to draw and kill me. But he was too careful, had planned things too well. Also, he was a bit afraid of that shooting hand of mine. I turned to the book, saw the phone, missed Jerry's ring–and it was that subconscious stuff that Cruthers was talking about. If Cruthers had waited a breath of time, he could have shot me through the head. I wasn't shooting as I swung, but he thought the swing meant death to him." I poured O'Rourke another drink and said, "And it did."

O'Rourke downed the drink.

"Sometimes," I told him, "one hunk of lead is worth all the thought in the world. You never saw a fighter think himself out of one of Joe Louis's fights. Cruthers had a sight better head than I have, but I'll be using what I got a lot longer."

"I'll be hanged," said O'Rourke.

Then the phone rang.

"I'll be hanged," said O'Rourke again, when I put the phone down and told him I'd have to give him the air, for I was having lunch with society–Martha Logan herself.

"I'm paying for the lunch, too," I told O'Rourke, "but she says she's needed so badly at the hospital she can only give me forty-five minutes. Blamed if I don't like that girl!"

ROBERT LESLIE BELLEM
(1902-68)

Diamonds of Death
(Dan Turner)

I grinned at Mitzi Madison. "Nix, hon I've been a private gumshoe here in Hollywood too many years to go for a corny gag like that. It wears whiskers."

Mitzi was a gorgeous little taffy-haired morsel, dainty as a Dresden doll in a combed wool ensemble. It was about ten-thirty at night when she ankled into my apartment, making with the moans regarding an alleged fortune in sparklers which she said had been glommed from her dressing bungalow on the Supertone lot. Now, as I slipped her the brush-off, her blue glims puddled with brine.

"Y-you think I'm lying?" she faltered.

"If you'll pardon my warty exterior, yes."

"But why would I—?"

I said: "Look, sis. You're the hottest star on the Supertone roster. You already rate more headlines in one month than most actresses get in a lifetime. Right?"

She nodded.

"So it's silly to try crashing the front pages with a phony jewel heist," I said. "That's been done so often the newspapers would giggle in your teeth, toss your story in the handiest spittoon."

She looked plaintive. "But I don't *want* publicity!"

"Sure. It would be a deep, dark secret between you and your press agent. And presently every gossip columnist in town would be ribbing me. Dan Turner, movie hawkshaw, falls for stolen gem routine. Mitzi Madison slips snoop the hotfoot."

Her shoulders sagged wearily. "You're wrong. I don't suppose I can convince you, but my d-diamonds really were stolen. Almost sixty thousand dollars' worth, right off my dressing table while I was playing a scene on the sound stage."

"You should have reported it to the cops," I said.

She reddened. "Do you know Max Murphy?"

"Of course. He's the Supertone producer in charge of your pix. What's he got to do with it?"

"Everything," she said. "Max gave me most of the stones. He and I were engaged until yesterday. Then we quarreled and he demanded them back. That was why I took them with me to the studio this evening. I had some late retakes scheduled, with a thirty minute break for supper. When the supper break came, I discovered the diamonds were g-gone."

"So what?"

"So I'm afraid he'll say I faked this robbery to keep from giving him back his jewelry," she made a woeful mouth.

That sounded screwy. "Nuts," I grunted. "Max would be dopey to smear you with any such charge. You're Supertone's most valuable box office property."

"You don't know him as well as I do. He hates me for breaking our engagement. He'd do anything to get even. He threatened to k-kill...well, he said some ugly things."

"Vindictive, huh?"

"I never realized how vindictive until we quarreled. Then I saw his true colors. Please, Mr. Turner, won't you try to locate those diamonds? I've got money to make a deal with the thief if I can get them back in time to return them to Max."

I fastened the speculative focus on her; wondered if she was leveling or feeding me a line of waffle batter. She met my gaze steadily enough, but that might not mean anything. An actress as talented as Mitzi could register honesty without even generating a slight sweat.

The more I thought about it, the less I believed what she'd told me. Parts of it rang as wrong as a counterfeit dime, especially Max Murphy's supposed nastiness. Max happened to be a guy I liked, and when she called him vindictive, she was as haywire as hailstones in Havana. He had the most amiable disposition on the West Coast; wouldn't willingly harm a kitten. As for threatening to croak somebody, that was plain idiotic.

I was on the verge of saying so when my phone jingled. I unforked the receiver; came near gulping my gasper, fire and all, as I tabbed the voice that crackled over the wire. "Philo? This is Max Murphy."

"Well, speak of the devil," I said.

He sounded too excited to savvy this remark. "Can you rush over here to the studio right away? I'm in a jam. We've just had a theft, but that's only part of it. It's something I can't let the police know about. Not now, anyhow. I need a private shamus and you're it."

I said: "Okay, bub," and rang off; turned to the Madison filly. "That was your ex-sweetie reporting a robbery."

She went pale around the fringes.

"You m-mean he's found out about the d-diamonds?"

"He didn't say." I stood up. "Would you have your chariot with you by any chance, babe?"

"Y-yes. I'll give you a lift to the lot."

We barged downstairs to her bucket, a sleek blue-and-chrome Cad with patent leather upholstery. Mitzi took the wheel and I settled beside her. "What, no chauffeur?"

She darted a glance at me as we nosed into the thin line of late traffic. "I have a chauffeur. Kettridge. He drove me to the studio this evening but I couldn't find him at supper time when I discovered my jewelry missing." Sudden suspicion tinctured her voice. "Why did you ask that question?"

"No reason. Just manufacturing small talk, is all."

"Maybe you were trying to be clever," she said. "Pumping me about Kettridge."

"Why should I?"

She flushed in the glow from the streamlined instruments panel. "Because he's the reason I quarreled with Max Murphy."

"Jealousy?"

"Yes. Max accused me of...of..."

"Any truth in it?"

"Certainly not!" she said hotly. "Kettridge is a nice, clean young man. He deserves more than a chauffeur job. I tried to get him a screen test, and Max thought...oh, skip it." Whereupon she clammed up from there to the main Supertone gateway. The way she froze me, you'd have thought I had leprosy.

Not that it mattered. I thanked her for the buggy ride, told her I'd let her know later if I decided to hunt her missing baubles. Then I made for the executive office building, where lights gleamed in the Murphy sanctum.

Max hopped from behind his desk, grabbed my flipper. "Well, Sherlock, am I glad to see you!"

He was a chunky, sawed-off bozo, square as a block of marble and just about as hard. He'd been a stunt man in the early silent days and he still had stunting muscles now, although he was nudging up to forty. He had more than muscles, too. It takes brains to work your way to a producer's berth without benefit of powerful relatives.

Under sandy thickets of eyebrows his optics were warm, brown, friendly–but worried. I recaptured my mitt, rubbed the fingers back in shape where he'd squeezed them into pretzels. "What cooks, Max?"

"Trouble. Bad trouble. Come along, I'll show you." He led me outdoors, across to one of the vast sound stage buildings. There was a Hindu doing sentry duty at the side entrance; or at least I tabbed him for a Hindu until I got closer. Then I saw he was a lanky guy in overalls, wearing a bandage on his conk. It was the bandage that fooled me. It looked like a turban.

He whispered: "Nobody's been here, Mr. Murphy."

"Okay, Steve." Then Max turned to me. "Steve's our head prop man. Steve Welch, Dan Turner. Let's go in."

We ankled over the threshold into solid darkness; closed the door after us. Max snapped a switch and a big dangling incandescent showered raw white light on the surroundings. Dead ahead you could pipe what appeared to be a partially dressed gambling hall set strewn with dice layouts, roulette tables and a scattering of chuck-a-luck cages, silent and ghostlike in the harsh overhead glare.

I copped an appreciative gander. "Nice. A few slot machines would make it perfect."

Murphy uttered a stricken noise in his gullet. "So you guessed!"

"Guessed what?" I glued the puzzled glimpse on him.

"The jam I'm in," he rasped. "Look. Gambling's illegal here in Los Angeles County. You know what the D.A.'s office does whenever a joint opens."

I said: "Yeah. Knock it over and confiscate the equipment."

He waved at the set. "This stuff is all confiscated apparatus. We borrowed it from the cops for a western opus I'm putting into production. I had to stand personally responsible for every item, including eight slot machines."

"I don't see any," I said.

"That's because they've been hijacked from under my very nose. Stolen right out of this sound stage!" His voice got shrill. "Can you imagine where that puts me with the district attorney? He may think I rigged the whole thing; accuse me of being tied in with a gambling syndicate that needed the machines–"

I said: "Not necessarily. Not if you explain it."

"Explain it!" his kisser twisted. "Did you ever try to explain a murder to a county prosecutor who's building himself a political reputation?"

And then he showed me the corpse.

The defunct ginzo lay sprawled behind a big wheel-of-fortune on the far side of the set, where you wouldn't notice him unless he was pointed out to you. He was tall, youthful, almost too handsome in tailored whipcord livery and shiny patent leather puttees; or anyhow he'd been handsome until some sharp disciple caved in his cranium with a blunt instrument. Now his scalp was messy with shattered bones and coagulated gravy, and he was deader than canceled postage.

I blurted: "What the–!" and sensed my clockworks fluttering like a bucket full of drunken butterflies. "How did this happen? Who was the guy? Who croaked him and why?"

A visible shudder rippled through the producer's chunky form from north to south. He gulped, licked his lips, started to say something. He never got the words out, though. Somebody beat him to the answer.

It was a frigid she-male voice behind us that said: "Better confess, Max. Make a clean breast of it before I put a bullet in your murderous heart."

There was deadly menace in this unexpected remark. It was delivered in a flat monotone that dripped icicles loaded with hate, crammed with unadulterated venom. I pivoted, hung the flabbergasted focus on a taffy-haired cupcake embellished in a combed wool ensemble.

She was Mitzi Madison, and she had a gat in her duke the size of a fowling piece.

I recovered from my befuddlement, took a tentative step toward her. "Hey!"

"Stay where you are. Don't make me do something I might regret. Max is the one I'm after, not you." Her finger was taut on the roscoe's trigger.

Murphy's peepers popped like squeezed oysters. "Mitzi, honey, surely you don't think I –"

"Quiet!" she snapped. Then, to me: "Phone the police, Mr. Turner. I want this rat arrested for murder."

I held my tone steady. "On what grounds, sweet stuff?"

"Isn't it obvious? I drove you to the studio, thinking you'd hunt my missing diamonds. Naturally I wondered if Max knew they'd been stolen, since he also had called you about a theft. When he brought you to this sound stage I followed, eavesdropped."

I said: "You didn't hear anything that would implicate him in the bump-off, though."

"That's where you're wrong," she grated between her clenched grinders. "Can't you guess who the dead boy is?"

Then it hit me. "Oh-oh. Your chauffeur. Kettridge."

"Yes. The youngster Max was jealous of; the innocent cause of our quarrel, our broken engagement. Now he's been k-killed. I wonder if you remember, back in your apartment, when I started to mention a murder threat Max had made?"

"Yeah, only you didn't give me the details."

"I will now," she said. "It was Kettridge he threatened." She glared at the sawed-off producer. "You heel."

His optics looked reproachful. "So you're trying to pin it on me because of something I said in a moment of anger."

"I'm going to send you to the lethal chamber, yes."

He made a reluctant gesture. "Take her, Steve."

Until that instant I'd forgotten Steve Welch, the lanky prop man with the Hindu bandage on his noggin. This was understandable, because Welch had moved into the shadows behind a crap table when the Madison quail first showed herself on the set. Now the bandaged bozo emerged from the darkness and dived at Mitzi's back.

The blur of action that followed reminded me of a movie reel being unspooled too fast. The taffy-haired jane whirled, lamped Welch hurtling toward her. She raised her roscoe to ward him off. Max Murphy catapulted in her direction like a chunky spring uncoiling, as if frantically seeking to keep her from plugging the lanky guy.

Max took a wild swat at the wren's rod. Maybe she actually hadn't intended to discharge it, but the impact of Murphy's mitt made her trigger finger jerk. The cannon sneezed: *KaChow!* and a tongue of flame licked at the prop man, a bright orange flash of fire that streaked across the set and stabbed him in the thigh. He staggered and went down in a writhing heap.

For a second I was paralyzed by the suddenness of all these shenanigans. I goggled at the carnage; tried to get my frozen reflexes thawed. The Madison quail was staring at Steve Welch and moaning: "I've killed him. I've k-killed him . . . !" Her heater dropped to the floor, cluttering.

Max glued the grab on her. "Run, Mitzi. For heaven's sake–get out of here! I'll take care of everything!"

That snapped me out of my trance. "Run, my nostril!" I roared. "The dame stays here and takes the consequences. I'm holding her for the bulls." And I whisked out my nippers, sprinted around a roulette layout to head her off as she lammed.

The Murphy bozo intercepted me. "Lay off her, Sherlock. This is none of your affair." Then he festooned an uppercut smack on my chinstrap; a poke that packed all the power of his stunt man's muscles. It rocked my conk so far back I could count the rafters overhead. They merged into a jumble as my glimmers went cock-eyed. Then Max corked me again.

All my fuses short-circuited and I became useless.

When I woke up, I thought I was drowning. Some dope had fetched a big red fire-bucket full of water onto the stage and was engaged in the maniacal pastime of dunking my profile like a cruller. I strangled, choked, sputtered, and snapped to my senses just as I was going down for the third time. "Hey, what the gloobsh is the idea?"

Then I pinned the groggy swivel on the beefy lug who was render-ing me the drastic first aid. He was my friend Dave Donaldson of the homicide squad, and the consternation on his map turned to relief when he realized I was not deceased. He said: "Gosh, Hawkshaw, I thought you were a goner."

"Two more dips in the drink and I would have been," I snarled. "Where did you come from and what are you doing in this vicinity?"

"Telephone tip," he told me. "Some anonymous jessie called a bleat to headquarters."

The anonymous jessie would be Mitzi Madison, of course. "How much did she spill?"

Dave shrugged. "She said we'd find two stiffs here, one shot, one blackjacked. She called the turn on the blackjacked guy," he glanced over to where some of his minions were loading the earthly remnants of Kettridge, the chauffeur, into a meat basket. "But she was wrong about the one with the bullet in him. He's not dead; just got a hunk nipped out of his thigh."

I followed the direction of Dave's stare; piped an ambulance interne vulcanizing the lanky prop man, Steve Welch. Now the poor slob wore a bandage around his gam as well as on his dome. He resembled a battle casualty.

When I looked for Max Murphy, though, I couldn't find a trace of him. I lurched upright, shook the water off my mush, set fire to a gasper. "Listen, Dave. Did you run across a chunky character when you arrived? A bozo built like a block of granite?"

"If you mean Max Murphy, no."

I blinked. "How did you know who I meant?"

"The dame that phoned said he was the killer."

Hearing this, Steve Welch limped toward us. "That's a lie!" he yowled. "Max didn't shoot me. Miss Madison did. You know that as well as I do, Mr. Turner. You saw it happen."

I said: "Yeah, at least the rod was in her mitt at the time, although it didn't blast until Max took a swat at it. So now she tries to blame him for croaking you–not realizing you're still alive to contradict her."

While this chinfest was going on, Donaldson kept scribbling in his notebook. "Mitzi Madison, huh? Now I've got two suspects, begahd!"

"Not on the Kettridge kill," I objected. "Why would she cool her own chauffeur?"

Steve Welch rubbed his bandaged skull. "I can think of one possible reason," he said. "Maybe she knew Kettridge was the guy who'd stolen her diamonds. Maybe she tried to make him give them back; used a length of lead pipe as a persuader and accidentally hit him too hard."

For an instant I stared at Welch as if he'd spoken in Cherokee. Then I regained control of my vocal chords. "How in purple blazes did you know Mitzi's rocks had been glommed?"

"She mentioned it right here on the set, just before she put that slug in me. Remember? She said she'd hired you trace the missing jewelry."

"Yeah, that's right," I admitted. "She did mention it. Even so, I don't savvy your suspicions of Kettridge as the thief–if there ever was a theft."

The prop man made a sour mouth. "I just put two and two together, is all. It adds up to four and explains a lot of things, including my busted head." He rubbed the bandaged place again; winced when he touched it. "If you're interested, I'll tell you what happened."

"Cockeyed right we're interested!" Dave Donaldson yeeped in strangling accents. "Start singing, pal."

Welch said: "Just before the supper break tonight I noticed Kettridge leaving Miss Madison's dressing bungalow and sneaking into this sound stage building. He was carrying a small package. I didn't pay much attention at the time, except to wonder why he acted so funny–like he was scared of being watched. It wasn't any of my business, though."

"Okay, go on," Dave rumbled.

"Well, I went on about my own affairs. Maybe thirty minutes later I saw a big moving van backed up to the sound stage door; one of our own Supertone studio trucks. A couple of guys seemed to be hauling things out of the building, but it was so dark I couldn't see their faces or what they were moving."

I said: "Come to the point."

"All right. I'm in charge of all props, and I hadn't ordered anything moved. So I knew something was wrong, and I braced the two guys on the moving van. When I got close to them, I saw they were wearing masks. That's about all I did see."

"They maced you?"

He grinned ruefully. "Plenty. It felt like the roof fell down on my head. I was out stiff. When I woke up I was here on the set. Kettridge's corpse was nearby, and all our borrowed slot machines were gone."

Donaldson buried his puss in his palms and emitted plaintive groans. "For Pete's sake, why don't I turn in my badge and raise rabbits or something? First it's stolen sparklers, then it's slot machines. What is this, a murder case or a merry-go-round?" And he called on heaven to witness that he didn't savvy whether he was afoot or a-horseback.

I took time out to explain the slot machine angle to him, and then I turned back to Steve Welch. "You think the masked thugs got away with the machines in the moving van, eh?"

"Sure. And at first I also thought they must have killed Kettridge by slugging him the way they did me. Now I'm not so positive it happened that way."

"What's your theory?"

"Well, I've really got two of them. They both start with Kettridge stealing Miss Madison's jewels and hiding the package here on the gambling set. She follows him, see? They get into a brawl and she hits him over the head–too hard. He dies. She rushes to you, hires your services as a private dick. That's to give herself an alibi. Later she tries to pin the kill on Max Murphy."

"What about the slot machines?"

"That's where I've got two possible theories. First, the two masked guys are working with Kettridge on the diamond robbery; a deal where he's to meet them here on the stage and slip them the loot. But when they arrive, he's dead; can't tell them where he hid the stones. So they make the best of a bad bargain by stealing some gambling equipment."

"And your second idea?" I said.

He lifted a shoulder. "The thugs had nothing to do with Kettridge or the diamonds. They just came here to steal the machines, and by coincidence they found a corpse."

I turned to Donaldson. "There's a third angle, Dave. What if Kettridge and the two hoods were partners in the jewel heist, and they bumped him to keep from splitting the swag three ways? Then, after frisking him for the rocks, they decided to glom the slot machines as a sort of bonus."

Dave presented me with an embittered sneer. "Yah. Max Murphy chilled Kettridge. Mitzi Madison chilled Kettridge. Two masked guys chilled Kettridge." All of a sudden he blew his top with a loud roar. "Maybe the chief of police chilled Kettridge. Or Santa Claus. Or a pack of gremlins. Maybe Kettridge isn't even dead. Maybe I'm having delirium tremens. Get the hell away from me! Leave me alone with my nervous breakdown!" And he went staggering across the stage with froth foaming out of his kisser like a baby chewing soap.

I felt sorry for him, but not sorry enough to invite him to weep in my clean handkerchief.

Instead, I wheeled, made for the exit, took myself a powder into the misty night.

That was when Max Murphy loomed out of the shadows in front of me and said: "Okay, shamus. This is it."

With the midnight fog from Santa Monica blowing in and drifting around him, he looked like a spectral gorilla; his chin was hunched down between shoulders as wide as a barn and his dangling arms reached to knee-length, ending in fists that could hit like the kick of a mule. His mitts were open, thought; the fingers limber and relaxed to match his voice.

Maybe he wasn't planning to paste a haymaker on my dimple; I couldn't tell. But I remembered the last dose of knuckle tonic he'd doled me; my bridgework still ached from it, all the way to the shoestrings. On a lug like Max you couldn't afford to take chances. I feinted with my left; brought a right cross to his button with all the weight of my hundred and ninety pounds steaming behind the punch.

His gams turned to rubber and he started to sag; reached out as if to grab me and support himself. "Just...wanted to...surrender and...confess the...kill..."

I nailed him with another bash on the jowls; drove the words back down his gullet. He dropped on the grass and rolled over, as cold as an iced codfish. I gave him a light kick on the dandruff to make certain he wasn't playing 'possum; then I hefted him on my back, toted him across the lot.

Toward the rear of the layout there was a somber, unlighted building marked *Property Warehouse No. 1, Supertone Pictures*. I piped a side door, saw it was locked, dug out my ring of master keys, and burgled the bolt open. Lugging Murphy past the threshold, I risked a ray from my pencil flash; sprayed a pale beam through darkness three degrees thicker than the inside of a brunette cow. A pallid, waxen face leered towards my peepers, dead ahead and vacantly grinning.

It was only a clothing dummy, but I nearly jumped out of my rind before I realized this. And when I broomed the joint with my torch, I saw other things so crazy they gave me the drizzling meemies. There were ancient torture racks, an Egyptian sarcophagus, dusty Russian droshkies stored against coffins and guns and pipe-organs covered with spiderwebs. In brief, the entire place was overflowing with props used in previous pix and waiting to be used again in future ones. The air smelled musty.

I hauled my inert burden to an empty mahogany casket; deposited him in its satin lining and used his belt to tie his ankles. His necktie served for his wrists; made an effective binding when I drew the knot tight. For gagging purposes I removed his right shoe, peeled off the sock, wadded it and crammed it in his yapper. It probably didn't taste very good, though. Or anyhow it wouldn't when he woke up and discovered what it was.

But that was the least of my worries. My chief concern now was to locate Mitzi Madison and give her a psychological test. Two answers were what I craved; and I knew they'd better be the correct ones or my own hips would be in a nasty sling. I was skating on illegal ice from this point onward, and if I made one haywire move, Dave Donaldson would have my private license jerked so fast it would curl my toenails.

Imprisoning Max Murphy in a property coffin would alone be grounds for disbarring me. The guy had actually confessed murdering that chauffeur, Kettridge; had been on the brink of giving himself up to the bulls. I'd stopped him, for reasons of my own; but Golly help me if those reasons were wrong!

I snapped off my flash, groped back to the door, barged outside. Around on the studio parking lot I spotted Mitzi Madison's sleek blue-and-chrome Cad. Its very presence made me feel better. It told me something I wanted to know.

Since I hadn't brought my own jalopy, I decided to use Mitzi's. I slid my pistol pockets across the patent leather upholstery, reached for the ignition switch; cursed when my fingers found no key in the lock. That meant I had to bridge the wires, a job that cost me four precious minutes I couldn't afford. Presently I got the motor purring and headed for the main gates.

A uniformed guard swung the wrought-iron portals open when I drew up. I said. "Thanks, cousin," and gave him a flash at my badge. "Can you tell me if Miss Madison and Mr. Murphy went out of here together some while ago?"

Yes, sir. In Mr. Murphy's coupe. He came back later, though. By himself. Within the past five or ten minutes."

"I know," I said. "By the way, have any studio trucks or vans left the lot since supper time?"

He thought it over. "One, I think. Riding light."

"Much obliged." And I gunned my cylinders, whammed forth on squealing treads. Time was what counted now. I swung hard to starboard under forced draft, aiming toward Melrose in a shower of sparks.

Seven minutes later I drew up before a neat little cottage partially hidden by heavy shrubbery. I loped to the porch, thumbed the bell, kept jingling until the door opened.

Then I said: "Hiya, toots," and glued the grab on Mitzi Madison's shoulders.

The taffy-haired cupcake gasped as she recognized me; tried to squirm free. "G-get your hands off me! What's the idea?" Then, as I shoved her inside and followed her, she added: "How d-did you f-find me?"

I grinned. "That's my business, finding people. I remember Max Murphy owned this little stash, kept it as a sort of hideout when he wanted to elude the Hollywood-Beverly social crowd and commune with his soul. I've been here with him a few times on private drinking jousts."

"But wh-what made you think I might have c-come here?"

"Several things," I said. "He was fronting for you, there on the sound stage. Even after you accused him of creaming the Kettridge punk, he was concerned only for your safety. When you accidentally shot Steve Welch, it was Max who biffed me unconscious so you could escape."

Her complexion went pasty. "Welch...that prop man...tell me, is he...d-dead?"

"No. Merely perforated through the thigh."

Her breath rose and fell swiftly in a sigh of relief. "Th-thank heaven for that!"

"Yeah," I said. "Thank Max, too. He deflected your aim. And then he helped you lam away from the spot you were in. He didn't want you punished for assault and shootery, and he didn't want you involved in the Kettridge kill. The minute I piped your Cad on the parking lot I figured you'd powdered with Max. The cop on the main gate told me I was right; so it was just a matter of logic that brought me to this igloo."

Her tempting crimson kisser drooped miserably. "And you came to arrest me?"

"That depends. After all, I'm in the private skulking racket for the dough. I'm trying to save up a retirement fund in Security Bonds."

"Are you hinting you'd t-take a bribe?"

"No, but I'm open for a legitimate deal. You claimed your diamonds were lifted and you asked me to find them; offered to pay full value. Does that offer still stand?"

She hesitated. "I don't think it does. True, I'd like to get them back; but it's not as important as it was earlier tonight. I mean–"

This was the answer I'd been hoping for. My psychological experiment had panned out, told me something I yearned to know. I said: "In other words, the cash loss in those sparklers never did bother you. Money didn't count, but the stones themselves did. As long as you were on the outs with Max Murphy you were anxious to recover the rocks and return them to him."

"That's right."

"But now it doesn't matter," I said. "Which proves two things. First, there really was a jewel theft; and second, you've made up with Max."

Her cheeks turned a delishful pink. "Yes, we're engaged again. I realize, now, how absurd our quarrel was; how much he actually cares for me. I'll never forgive myself for accusing him of...of murdering Kettridge, now that I know he was innocent."

"You're taking a lot for granted," I said.

"What d-do you mean? Max didn't kill him! He convinced me of that. If he were guilty, he wouldn't dare risk doing what he's going to do."

"And just what is he going to do, babe?"

"Lay the whole story before the police; clear me and see that the real murderer is caught."

I said: "Yeah, he's already squared the beef. He gave himself up and confessed the croaking."

Her hand flew to her throat and her glims walled back. Then she swooned in my arms.

I couldn't be bothered by that; probably it was a help. I toted her out to the blue Cad. Propping her in the front seat, I almost regretted what I had to do.

But murder is murder no matter how thin you peel it, and California has a law against committing killery. I kicked the Cad's motor into motion; made knots in the direction of Supertone lot. Halfway there, the Madison cookie opened her glims and drifted back to life. "Wh-wha-what–how–wh-where are we going?" she moaned as she suddenly realized she was being ferried through the fog at a maniac clip.

"To the studio, kitten." Then I fired the sixty-four dollar question at her. "Tell me, what was Kettridge's job before he began chauffeuring for you?"

"Why, I–I picked him up from a gambling place in Las Vegas. He was a house man, making change for the customers. You know. He wore one of those funny short aprons with a big wide pocket full of dimes and quarters and halves and silver dollars. I was there with a unit on location and went into this place to try my luck at the machines, and–" her voice trailed away, then sharpened. "What's that got to do with Max confessing he killed him? Does it matter if I hired a gambling house employee to drive for me? What are you trying to say?"

I grunted: "Nothing, sis. I'll let the facts speak for themselves." Then the Supertone gates showed directly ahead, swinging open to let a sedan roll out. The sedan's headlights were white blobs in the fog.

I swung across their path, blocking them; bounced out and sprinted forward. The car was an official police chariot, with Dave Donaldson at the rudder and three of his underlings jammed in the tonneau. "Hey, Dave!"

He fastened the sour scrutiny on me, like a guy with stomach ulcers contemplating a dill pickle. "Move that circus wagon out of my way, dope. I'm going back to headquarters. We're all through here."

"That's what you think. You're wrong, as usual. Get the lead out of your elbow and I'll clean up this Kettridge bump for you. It's in the bag." I kept my fingers crossed when I said this, however. I was playing a long shot.

Donaldson erupted from his buggy faster than a glob of lava bubbling out of a volcano. "What's that you uttered?"

"You heard me." And I pointed to the Cadillac. "There's one of your suspects. Mitzi Madison."

He swelled up as if somebody had suddenly pumped him full of helium gas. "Mitzi Madison? Come on, boys!" He charged through the gateway with his minions panting at his heel; yanked the sleek blue bucket's door open and fastened the clutch on the taffy-haired gazelle. She squealed as she was hauled forth; clawed an assortment of fingernail furrows down Dave's apoplectic lineaments. Then, as he snapped nippers on her wrists, she squirmed around to me.

"You dirty double-crossing creep!" she caterwauled.

I said: "Sorry, kiddo. Is it my fault that cops haven't got any manners? Quiet down. Everything will be over in a jiffy. Our next job is to see about Max Murphy."

Donaldson's jaw sagged. "Don't tell me you've got *him* under wraps, too!"

"Yeah, in the property warehouse building. At least that was where I left him. Let's go check. Leave Mitzi here with your henchmen. You and I can handle the payoff."

He grunted an order to the plainclothes heroes, then tailed me as I hotfooted toward the rear of the sprawling lot. Bye and bye we gained the warehouse, and again I burgled the lock; but this time I didn't need my pocket torch when we tiptoed inside. There was a dim light burning somewhere in the depths of the cavernous storage joint, with just enough pallid reflection to keep me from stumbling over assorted suits of armor and similar miscellaneous junk.

Dave shivered. "Lord, what a museum of horrors! Where did you leave Murphy?"

"Sh-h-h-h!" I whispered. "Listen."

Faintly in the distance you could hear metallic sounds, undertoned by fervent oaths. First there would be a tinny tinkle, then a *ker-blunk* noise following by the whirring of cog-wheels and gears against ratchets. This would end in a *ping!* and sometimes you'd hear a faint clatter-clatter-clatter afterwards, but not too often. Generally the *ping!* drew forth nothing but voluble damns from some unseen bozo who seemed as sore as a lanced boil.

I pinched a blister on Donaldson's forearm; warned him silent and drew him forward through a maze of cluttered aisles, heading toward the source of light and sound. Abruptly we skirted a pile of automobile bodies, pool tables, and birchbark canoes; came to a recessed alcove where a weak electric bulb glowed dismally. Under the yellows rays I piped eight boxlike metal gadgets, each on its individual iron stand. The contraptions were garishly decorated in pressed steel designs, the face-plates blank and solid. On the right side of each box there was an armlike lever protruding like a vertical pump handle, with a coin slot nearby. Toward the bottom, directly under the slot, there was a spillway.

"Max Murphy's eight stolen slot machines!" I hissed below my breath. "And cop a gander at who's playing them!"

Dave stared along my pointing finger. A guy was slipping nickels and dimes into the various contrivances; yanking the levers and swearing as the wheels revolved. Occasionally one of the machines would stop on two cherries or three plums and spit out a few slugs, but mostly they came up lemons, meaning no pay-out to player.

I yanked my .32 automatic from the shoulder holster where I always carry it; snapped off the safety. My quarry was so busy pumping those metal arms that he didn't hear the click. I drew a bead on the turbanlike bandage he wore around his conk. "*Okay, Steve Welch!*" I rasped.

The lanky Supertone prop man straightened up, whirled, lamped my roscoe and turned six shades of pale. "Wh-what-?"

I moved toward him. "You're under arrest for murder."

"Me? M-murder? You must be c-crazy!"

I said: "Crazy like a fox, bub. You're the louse that bumped young Kettridge. We've got the deadwood on you."

"Th-that's ridiculous!"

"You won't think so when they give you a whiff of cyanide in the

San Quentin smoke-house," I growled. "The way I tab it, your story was a mixture of truth and lies a while ago. And the lies tripped you up."

"I d-don't g-get you."

"So I'll draw you a picture. It was true that Kettridge glommed Mitzi Madison's sparklers out of her dressing bungalow this evening. For all his handsome pan he was a crooked young jerk; a thief. You were leveling when you said you saw him sneak across the lot to that sound stage, toting a bundle. From there on, however, you lied."

He bared his uppers and lowers. "Did I?"

"Yeah. In reality, you followed him onto the gambling hall set. You knew he'd stolen something and you decided to help yourself to the swag. You crushed his skull with a spanner and then frisked him; one burglar searching another. But the diamonds weren't on the corpse. Kettridge had stashed them somewhere, just before you rendered him extinct.

"Having croaked him, you then prowled the set for the hidden rocks. They weren't in sight. There was only one possible place Kettridge could have cached them. You guessed it when you remembered how he had once been a house man in a gambling joint up at Las Vegas; a change-maker. On that job he had learned all about automatic gaming devices; how to open them and extract the coins. So you figured he must have hidden Mitzi Madison's gems in one of these slot machines.

"The trouble was, you didn't know which one. Also, being unfamiliar with the gadgets, you didn't know how to open them from the back and get at the coin receptables. And you couldn't risk taking the time to experiment with eight machines. They were like so many steel safes and you didn't have the combinations.

"So you got a hand truck and wheeled the slot machines, one by one, over here to this warehouse. Even if anybody saw you, it wouldn't matter; you probably had them covered with tarpaulins, and a prop man is always moving props. As it happened, you weren't seen. You now had the gadgets safely stored away where you could work on them later.

"To alibi yourself, you then went back to the gambling set and doled yourself a bop on the attic, pretending to be knocked senseless. Afterward you went to Max Murphy and reported a phony yarn about two masked thugs in a moving van who'd swiped eight pieces of borrowed gaming equipment. When I arrived, you told me the same malarkey—and that's when I began to suspect you. Part of it didn't ring true."

He lifted a blustery lip: "What part?"

"The masked guys in the moving van," I said. "All trucks have to be checked past the gate; that's a studio rule. If a loaded van had gone off the lot tonight, its contents would have been inspected for okay. I asked the gate guard and he said only one truck had rolled out since before supper–and it had been running light. In other words, empty.

"So nobody had hauled any slot machines off the grounds. I knew, then, that they must still be on the lot somewhere; and you, as chief prop man, were the only person who could have moved them without attracting suspicion. From then on it was just a question of making sure Miss Madison's sparklers really had been pilfered; and when she told me Kettridge used to be a gambling joint attendant, I tabbed the whole score."

"Very neat," he sneered. "But how can you prove it?"

I said: "Finding you here trying to work these slot machines is proof enough. You still haven't found the diamonds, though, have you?"

"No.–Er, that is, I mean–"

"Okay. You gave yourself away that time. Keep him covered, Dave, and I'll show you a little trick." Whereupon I ankled past the row of mechanical coin-grabbers until I spotted one with an extra large slot; a silver dollar machine that would take nothing smaller than a cartwheel. Since it was constructed for big round iron men, it would have an oversized money receptacle in its innards; which would be the obvious place for Kettridge to have hidden his loot.

I reached behind the gadget, unfastened its back plate, did certain things to the gears and locking cogs. Then, tripping the release, I yanked down on the outside lever as if I had just played a buck.

The lever went *ker-blunk*, followed by the whirring of ratchets ending in a deep *ping!* Instead of lemons or cherries or plums showing under the glass window, three black bars fell into line. That dumped the jackpot–and a double fistful of diamonds came tumbling from the lower sluice into my waiting palms: solitaires, earrings, pendants and a necklace.

"Mitzi Madison's rocks," I said.

Steve Welch goggled at the baubles and suddenly went off his chump. "You stinking snoop, I corpsed a guy for those diamonds! Now I'm gonna have them!" He leaped at me.

A thunderous bellow flashed from Dave Donaldson's service .38, full at the prop man's elly-bay. Welch gasped like a leaky flue, hugged his punctured tripes, and slowly doubled over, fell flat on his smeller. A bullet can give a man a terrific case of indigestion, frequently ending in a trip to the bone yard. That's how it turned out with Steve Welch, thereby saving the cost of a murder trial.

I ankled away from the gory scene. "Much obliged, Dave. Now comes the part I regret."

"What's that?" He stared at me.

"Releasing Max Murphy from his coffin confinement and giving him into the embrace of his ever-loving sweetie, the Madison cupcake. I sort of fell for that taffy-haired babe. If she weren't going to marry Murphy, I'd make a play for her myself."

Donaldson favored me with a supercilious leer. "Maybe Max'll let you kiss the bride. Then at least you'll have your memories laid away in lavender and old Scotch. Come on, Casanova, let's go call the meat wagon and then get plastered."

It sounded like a very nice idea.

FREDRIC BROWN
(1906-72)

Before She Kills
(Ed and Am Hunter)

The door was that of an office in an old building on State Street near Chicago Avenue, on the near north side, and the lettering on it read HUNTER & HUNTER DETECTIVE AGENCY. I opened it and went in. Why not? I'm one of the Hunters; my name is Ed. The other Hunter is my uncle, Ambrose Hunter.

The door to the inner office was open and I could see Uncle Am playing solitaire at his desk in there. He's shortish, fattish and smartish, with a straggly brown mustache. I waved at him and headed for my desk in the outer office. I'd had my lunch–we take turns–and he'd be leaving now.

Except that he wasn't. He swept the cards together and stacked them but he said, "Come on in, Ed. Something to talk over with you."

I went in and pulled up a chair. It was a hot day and two big flies were droning in circles around the room. I reached for the fly swatter and held it, waiting for one or both of them to light somewhere. "We ought to get a bomb," I said.

"Huh? Who do we want to blow up?"

"A bug bomb," I said. "One of these aerosol deals, so we can get flies on the wing."

"Not sporting, kid. Like shooting a sitting duck, only the opposite. Got to give the flies a chance."

"All right," I said, swatting one of them as it landed on a corner of the desk. "What did you want to talk about?"

"A case, maybe. A client, or a potential one, came in while you were feeding your face. Offered us a job, but I'm not sure about taking it. Anyway, it's one you'd have to handle, and I wanted to talk it over with you first."

The other fly landed and died, and the wind of the swat that killed it blew a small rectangular paper off the desk onto the floor. I picked it up and saw that it was a check made out to Hunter & Hunter and signed Oliver R. Bookman–a name I didn't recognize. It was for five hundred dollars.

We could use it. Business had been slow for a month or so. I said, "Looks like you took the job already. Not that I blame you." I put the check back on the desk. "That's a pretty strong argument."

"No, I didn't take it. Ollie Bookman had the check already made out when he came, and put it down while we were talking. But I told him we weren't taking the case till I'd talked to you."

"Ollie? Do you know him, Uncle Am?"

"No, but he told me to call him that, and it comes natural. He's that kind of guy. Nice, I mean."

I took his word for it. My uncle is a nice guy himself, but he's sharp judge of character and can spot a phony a mile off.

He said, "He thinks his wife is trying to kill him or maybe planning to."

"Interesting." I said. "But what could we do about it–unless she does? And then it's cop business."

"He knows that, but he's not sure enough to do anything drastic about it unless someone backs up his opinion and tells him he's not imagining things. Then he'll decide what to do. He wants you to study things from the inside."

"Like how? And why me?"

"He's got a young half brother living in Seattle whom his wife has never met and whom he hasn't seen for twenty years. Brother's twenty-five years old–and you can pass for that age. He wants you to come to Chicago from Seattle on business and stay with them for a few days. You wouldn't even have to change your first name; you'd be Ed Cartwright and Ollie would brief you on everything you'll be supposed to know."

I thought a moment and then said, "Sounds a little far out to me, but–" I glanced pointedly at the five-hundred-dollar check. "Did you ask how he happened to come to us?"

"Yes. Koslovsky sent him; he's a friend of Kossy's, belongs to a couple of the same clubs." Koslovsky is chief investigator for an insurance company; we've worked for him or with him on several things.

I asked, "Does that mean there's an insurance angle?"

"No, Ollie Bookman carries only a small policy–small relative to what his estate would be–that he took out a long time ago. Currently he's not insurable. Heart trouble."

"Oh. And does Kossy approve this scheme of his for investigating his wife?"

"I was going to suggest we ask Kossy that. Look, Ed, Ollie's coming back for our answer at two o'clock. I'll have time to eat and get back. But I wanted to brief you before I left so you could think it over. You might also call Koslovsky and get a rundown on Ollie, whatever he knows about him."

Uncle Am got up and got the old black slouch hat he insists on wearing despite the season. Kidding him about it does no good.

I said, "One more question before you go. Suppose Bookman's wife meets his half brother, his real one, someday. Isn't it going to be embarrassing?"

"I asked him that. He says it's damned unlikely; he and his brother aren't at all close. He'll never go to Seattle and the chances that his brother will ever come to Chicago are one in a thousand. Well, so long, kid."

I called Koslovsky. Yes, he'd recommended us to Bookman when Bookman had told him what he wanted done and asked–knowing that he, Koslovsky, sometimes hired outside investigators when he and his small staff had a temporary overload of cases–to have an agency recommended to him.

"I don't think too much of his idea," Koslovsky said, "but, hell, it's his money and he can afford it. If he wants to spend some of it that way, you might as well have the job as anyone else."

"Do you think there's any real chance that he's right? About his wife, I mean."

"I wouldn't know, Ed. I've met her a time or two and–well, she struck me as a cold potato, probably, but hardly as a murderess. Still, I don't know her well enough to say."

"How well do you know Bookman? Well enough to know whether he's pretty sane or gets wild ideas?"

"Always struck me as pretty sane. We're not close friends but I've known him fairly well for three or four years."

"Just how well off is he?"

"Not rich, but solvent. If I had to guess, I'd say he could cash out at over one hundred thousand, less than two. Enough to kill him for, I guess."

"What's his racket?"

"Construction business, but he's mostly retired. Not on account of age; he's only in his forties. But he's got angina pectoris, and a year or two ago the medicos told him to take it easy or else."

Uncle Am got back a few minutes before two o'clock and I just had time to tell him about my conversation with Kossy before Ollie Bookman showed up. Bookman was a big man with a round, cheerful face that made you like him at sight. He had a good handshake.

"Hi, Ed," he said. "Glad that's your name because it's what I'll be calling you even if it wasn't. That is, if you'll take on the job for me. Your Uncle Am here wouldn't make it definite. What do you say?"

I told him we could at least talk about it and when we were comfortably seated in the inner office, I said, "Mr. Bookman–" "Call me Ollie," he interrupted, so I said, "All right, Ollie. The only reason I can think of, thus far, for not taking on the job, if we don't, is that even if you're right–if your wife does have any thoughts about murder–the chances seem awfully slight that I could find out about it, and how she intended to do it, in time to stop it."

He nodded. "I understand that, but I want you to try, anyway. You see, Ed, I'll be honest and say that I *may* be imagining things. I want somebody else's opinion–after that somebody has lived with us at least a few days. But if you come to agree with me, or find any positive indications that I'm maybe right, then–well, I'll do something about it. Eve–that's my wife's name–won't give me a divorce or even agree to a separation with maintenance, but damn it, I can always simply leave home and live at the club–better that than get myself killed."

"You have asked her to give you a divorce, then?"

"Yes, I– Let me begin at the beginning. Some of this is going to be embarrassing to tell, but you should know the whole score. I met Eve..."

2

He'd met Eve eight years ago when he was thirty-five and she was twenty-five, or so she claimed. She was a strip-tease dancer who worked in night clubs under the professional name of Eve Eden–her real name had been Eve Packer. She was a statuesque blonde, beautiful. Ollie had fallen for her and started a campaign immediately, a campaign that intensified when he learned that off-stage she was quiet, modest, the exact opposite of what strippers are supposed to be and which some of them really are. By the time he was finally having an affair with her, lust had ripened into respect and he'd been thinking in any case that it was about time he married and settled down.

So he married her, and that was his big mistake. She turned out to be completely, psychopathically frigid. She'd been acting, and doing a good job of acting, during the weeks before marriage, but after marriage, or at least after the honeymoon, she simply saw no reason to keep on acting. She had what she wanted—security and respectability. She hated sex, and that was that. She turned Ollie down flat when he tried to get her to go to a psychoanalyst or even to a marriage consultant, who, he thought, might be able to talk her into going to an analyst. In every other way she was a perfect wife. Beautiful enough to be a showpiece that made all his friends envy him, a charming hostess, even good at handling servants and running the house. For all outsiders could know, it was a perfect marriage. But for a while it drove Ollie Bookman nuts. He offered to let her divorce him and make a generous settlement, either lump sum or alimony. But she had what she wanted, marriage and respectability, and she wasn't going to give them up and become a divorcee, even if doing so wasn't going to affect her scale of living in the slightest. He threatened to divorce her, and she laughed at him. He had, she pointed out, no grounds for divorce that he could prove in court, and she'd never give him any. She'd simply deny the only thing he could say about her, and make a monkey out of him.

It was an impossible situation, especially as Ollie had badly wanted to have children or at least a child, as well as a normal married life. He'd made the best of it by accepting the situation at home as irreparable and settling for staying sane by making at least occasional passes in other directions. Nothing serious, just a normal man wanting to live a normal life and succeeding to a degree.

But eventually the inevitable happened. Three years ago, he had found himself in an affair that turned out to be much more than an affair, the real love of his life—and a reciprocated love. She was a widow, Dorothy Stark, in her early thirties. Her husband had died five years before in Korea; they'd had only a honeymoon together before he'd gone overseas. Ollie wanted so badly to marry her that he offered Eve a financial settlement that would have left him relatively a pauper—this was before the onset of his heart trouble and necessary semiretirement; he looked forward to another twenty years or so of earning capacity—but she refused; never would she consent to become a divorcee, at any price. About this time, he spent a great deal of money on private detectives in the slim hope that her frigidity was toward him only, but the money was wasted. She went out quite a bit but always to bridge parties, teas or, alone or with respectable woman companions, to movies or plays.

Uncle Am interrupted. "You said you used private detectives before, Ollie. Out of curiosity, can I ask why you're not using the same outfit again?"

"Turned out to be crooks, Am. When they and I were finally convinced we couldn't get anything on her legitimately, they offered for a price to frame her for me." He mentioned the name of an agency we'd heard of, and Uncle Am nodded.

Ollie went on with his story. There wasn't much more of it. Dorothy Stark had known that he could never marry her but she also knew that he very badly wanted a child, preferably a son, and had loved him enough to offer to bear one for him. He had agreed–even if he couldn't give the child his name, he wanted one–and two years ago she had borne him a son: Jerry, they'd named him, Jerry Stark. Ollie loved the boy to distraction.

Uncle Am asked if Eve Bookman knew of Jerry's existence and Ollie nodded.

"But she won't do anything about it. What could she do, except divorce me?"

"But if that's the situation," I asked him, "what motive would your wife have to want to kill you? And why now, if the situation has been the same for two years?"

"There's been one change, Ed, very recently. Two years ago, I made out a new will, without telling Eve. You see, with angina pectoris, my doctor tells me it's doubtful if I have more than a few years to live in any case. And I want at least the bulk of my estate to go to Dorothy and to my son. So– Well, I made out a will which leaves a fourth to Eve, a fourth to Dorothy and half, in trust, to Jerry. And I explained, in a preamble, why I was doing it that way–the true story of my marriage to Eve and the fact that it really wasn't one, and why it wasn't. And I admitted paternity of Jerry. You see, Eve could contest that will–but would she? If she fought it, the newspapers would have a field day with its contents and make a big scandal out of it– and her position, her respectability, is the most important thing in the world to Eve. Of course, it would hurt Dorothy, too–but if she won, even in part, she could always move somewhere else and change her name. Jerry, if this happens in the next few years, as it probably will, will be too young to be hurt, or even to know what's going on. You see?"

"Yes," I said. "But if you hate your wife, why not–"

"Why not simply disinherit her completely, leave her nothing? Because then she *would* fight the will, she'd have to. I'm hoping by giving her a fourth, she'll decide she'd rather settle for that and save face than contest the will."

"I see that," I said. "But the situation's been the same for two years now. And you said that something recent–"

"As recent as last night," he interrupted. "I kept that will in a hiding place in my office–which is in my home since I retired–and last night I discovered it was missing. It was there a few days ago. Which means that, however she came to do so, Eve found it. And destroyed it. So if I should die now–she thinks–before I discover the will is gone and make another, I'll die intestate and she'll automatically get everything. She's got well over a hundred thousand dollars' worth of motive for killing me before I find out the will is gone."

Uncle Am asked, "You say 'she thinks.' Wouldn't she?"

"Last night she would have," Ollie said grimly. "But this morning, I went to my lawyer, made out a new will, same provisions, and left it in his hands. Which is what I should have done with the first one. But she doesn't know that, and I don't want her to."

It was my turn to question that. "Why not?" I wanted to know. "If she knows a new will exists, where she can't get at it, she'd know killing you wouldn't accomplish anything for her. Even if she got away with it."

"Right, Ed. But I'm almost hoping she will try, and fail. Then I'd be the happiest man on earth. I *would* have grounds for divorce– attempted murder should be grounds if anything is–and I could marry Dorothy, legitimize my son and leave him with my name. I–well, for the chance of doing that, I'm willing to take the chance of Eve's trying and succeeding. I haven't got much to lose, and everything to gain. How otherwise could I ever marry Dorothy–unless Eve should predecease me, which is damned unlikely. She's healthy as a horse, and younger than I am, besides. And if she should succeed in killing me, but got caught, she'd inherit nothing; Dorothy and Jerry would get it all. That's the law, isn't it? That no one can inherit from someone he's killed, I mean. Well, that's the whole story. Will you take the job, Ed, or do I have to look for someone else? I hope I won't."

I looked at Uncle Am–we never decide anything important without consulting one another–and he said, "Okay by me, kid." So I nodded to Ollie. "All right," I said.

3

We worked out details. He'd already checked plane flights and knew that a Pacific Airlines plane was due in from Seattle at ten fifteen that evening; I'd arrive on that and meanwhile he'd pretend to have received a telegram saying I was coming and would be in Chicago for a few days to a week on business, and asking him to meet the plane if convenient. I went him one better on that by telling him we knew a girl who sometimes did part-time work for us as a female operative and I'd have her phone his place, pretend to be a Western Union operator, and read the telegram to whoever answered the phone. He thought that was a good idea, especially if his wife was the one to take it down. We worked out the telegram itself and then he phoned his place on the pretext of wanting to know if his wife would be there to accept a C.O.D. package. She was, so I phoned the girl I had in mind, had her take down the telegram, and gave her Ollie's number to phone it to. We had the telegram dated from Denver, since the real Ed, if he were to get in that evening, would already be on the plane and would have to send the telegram from a stop en route. I told Ollie I'd work out a plausible explanation as to why I hadn't decided, until en route, to ask him to meet the plane.

Actually, we arranged to meet downtown, in the lobby of the Morrison Hotel an hour before plane time; Ollie lived north and if he were really driving to the airport, it would take him another hour to get there and an hour back as far as the Loop, so we'd have two hours to kill in further planning and briefing. Besides another half hour or so driving to his place when it was time to head there.

That meant he wouldn't have to brief me on family history now; there'd be plenty of time this evening. I did ask what kind of work Ed Cartwright did, so if necessary I could spend the rest of the afternoon picking up at least the vocabulary of whatever kind of work it was. But it turned out he ran a printing shop—which was a lucky break since after high school and before getting with my Uncle Am, I'd spent a couple of years as an apprentice printer myself and knew enough about the trade to talk about it casually.

Just as Ollie was getting ready to leave, the phone rang and it was our girl calling back to say she'd read the telegram to a woman who'd answered the phone and identified herself as Mrs. Oliver Bookman, so we were able to tell Ollie the first step had been taken.

After Ollie had left, Uncle Am looked at me and asked, "What do you think, kid?"

"I don't know," I said. "Except that five hundred bucks is five hundred bucks. Shall I mail the check in for deposit now, since I won't be here tomorrow?"

"Okay. Go out and mail it if you want and take the rest of the day off, since you'll start working tonight."

"All right. With this check in hand, I'm going to pick me up a few things. like a couple shirts and some socks. And how about a good dinner tonight? I'll meet you at Ireland's at six."

He nodded, and I went to my desk in the outer office and was making out a deposit slip and an envelope when he came and sat on the corner of the desk.

"Kid," he said. "This Ollie just *might* be right. We got to assume that he could be, anyway. And I just had a thought. What would be the safest way to kill a man with bad heart trouble, like angina pectoris is? I'd say conning him into having an attack by giving him a shock or by getting him to overexert himself somehow. Or else by substituting sugar pills for whatever he takes–nitroglycerin pills, I think it is–when he gets an attack."

I said, "I've been thinking along those lines myself, Uncle Am. I thought maybe one thing I'd do down in the Loop is have a talk with Doc Kruger." Kruger is our family doctor, sort of. He doesn't get much business from either of us but we use him for an information booth whenever we want to know something about forensic medicine.

"Wait a second," Uncle Am said. "I'll phone him. Maybe he'll let us buy him dinner with us tonight to pay him for picking his brains."

He went in the office and used his phone; I heard him talking to Doc. He came out and said, "It's a deal. Only at seven instead of six. That'll be better for you, anyway, Ed. Bring your suitcase with you and if we take our time at Ireland's, you can go right from there to meet Ollie and do not have to go home again."

So I did my errands, went to our room, cleaned up and dressed, and packed a suitcase. I didn't think anybody would be looking in it to check up on me, but I thought I might as well be as careful as I could. I couldn't provide clothes with Seattle labels but I could and did avoid things with labels that said Chicago or were from well-known Chicago stores. And I avoided anything that was monogrammed, not that I particularly like monograms or have many things with them. Then I doodled around with my trombone until it was time to head for Ireland's.

I got there exactly on time and Doc and Uncle Am were there already. But there were three Martinis on the table; Uncle Am had known I wouldn't be more than a few minutes late, if any, so he'd ordered for me.

Without having to be asked, since Uncle Am had mentioned it over the phone, Doc started telling us about angina pectoris. It was incurable, he said, but a victim of it might live a long time if he took good care of himself. He had to avoid physical exertion like lifting anything heavy or climbing stairs. He had to avoid overtiring himself by doing even light work for a long period. He had to avoid overindulgence in alcohol, although an occasional drink wouldn't hurt him if he was in good physical shape otherwise. He had to avoid violent emotional upsets as far as was possible, and a fit of anger could be as dangerous as running up a flight of stairs.

Yes, nitroglycerin pills were used. Everyone suffering from angina carried them and popped one or two into his mouth any time he felt an attack coming on. They either prevented the attack or made it much lighter than it would have been otherwise. Doc took a little pillbox out of his pocket and showed us some nitro pills. They were white and very tiny.

There was another drug also used to avert or limit attacks that was even more effective than nitroglycerin. It was amyl nitrite and came in glass ampoules. In emergency, you crushed the ampoule and inhaled the contents. But amyl nitrite, Doc told us, was used less frequently than nitroglycerin, and only in very bad cases or for attacks in which nitro didn't seem to be helping, because repeated use of amyl nitrite diminished the effect; the victim built up immunity to it if he used it often.

Doc had really come loaded. He'd brought an amyl nitrite ampoule with him, too, and showed it to us. I asked him if I could have it, just in case. He gave it to me without asking why, and even showed me the best way to hold it and crush it if I ever had to use it.

We had a second cocktail and I asked him a few more questions and got answers to them, and that pretty well covered angina pectoris, and then we ordered. Ireland's is famous for sea food; it's probably the best inland sea-food restaurant in the country, and we all ordered it. Doc Kruger and Uncle Am wrestled with lobsters; me, I'm a coward–I ate royal sole.

4

Doc had to take off after our coffee, but it was still fifteen or twenty minutes too early for me to leave–I'd have to take a taxi to the Morrison on account of having a suitcase; otherwise, I'd have walked and been just right on the timing–so Uncle Am and I had a second coffee apiece and yakked. He said he felt like taking a walk before he turned in, so he'd ride in the taxi with me and then walk home from there.

I fought off a bellboy who tried to take my suitcase away from me and made myself comfortable on one of the overstuffed chairs in the lobby. I'd sat there about five or ten minutes when I heard myself being paged. I stood up and waved to the bellboy who'd been doing the paging and he came over and told me I was wanted on the phone and led me to the phone I was wanted on. I bought him off for four bits and answered the phone. It was Ollie Bookman, as I'd known it would be. Only he and Uncle Am would have known I was here and Uncle Am had left me only ten minutes ago.

"Ed," he said. "Change of plans. Eve wasn't doing anything this evening and decided to come to the airport with me, for the ride. I couldn't tell her no, for no reason. So you'll have to grab a cab and get out there ahead of us."

"Okay," I said. "Where are you now?"

"On the way south, at Division Street. Made an excuse to stop in a drugstore; didn't know how to get in touch with you until the time of our appointment. You can make it ahead of us if you get a cabby to hurry. I'll stall–drive as slow as I can without making Eve wonder. And I can stop for gas, and have my tires checked."

"What do I do at the airport if the plane's late?"

"Don't worry about the plane. You take up a spot near the Pacific Airlines counter; you'll see me come toward it and intercept me. Won't matter if the plane's in yet or not. I'll get us the hell out of there fast before Eve can learn if the plane's in. I'll make sure not to get there *before* arrival time."

"Right," I said. "But, Ollie, I'm not supposed to have seen you for twenty years–and I was five then, or supposed to be. So how would I recognize you? Or, for that matter, you recognize me?"

"No sweat, Ed. We write each other once a year, at Christmas. And several times, including last Christmas, we traded snapshots with our Christmas letters. Remember?"

"Of course," I said. "But didn't your wife see the one I sent you?"

"She may have glanced at it casually. But after seven months she wouldn't remember it. Besides, you and the real Ed Cartwright are about the same physical type, anyway–dark hair, good looking. You'll pass. But don't miss meeting us before we reach the counter or somebody there might tell us the plane's not in yet, if it's not. Well, I better not talk any longer."

I swore a little to myself as I left the Morrison lobby and went to the cab rank. I'd counted on the time Ollie and I would have had together to have him finish my briefing. This way I'd have to let him do most of the talking, at least tonight. Well, he seemed smart enough to handle it. I didn't even know my parents' names, whether either of them was alive, whether I had any other living relatives besides Ollie. I didn't even know whether I was married or not–although I felt reasonably sure Ollie would have mentioned it if I was.

Yes, he'd have to do most of the talking–although I'd better figure out what kind of business I'd come to Chicago to do; I'd be supposed to know that, and Ollie wouldn't know anything about it. Well, I'd figure that out on the cab ride.

Barring accidents, I'd get there well ahead of Ollie, and I didn't want accidents, so I didn't offer the cabby any bribe for speed when I told him to take me to the airport. He'd keep the meter ticking all right, since he made his money by the mile and not by the minute.

I had my cover story ready by the time we got there. It wasn't detailed, but I didn't anticipate being pressed for details, and if I was, I knew more about printing equipment than Eve Bookman would know. I was a good ten minutes ahead of plane time. I found myself a seat near the Pacific Airlines counter and facing in the direction from which the Bookmans would come. Fifteen minutes later–on time, as planes go–the public-address system announced the arrival of my flight from Seattle, and fifteen minutes after that–time for me to have left the plane and even to have collected the suitcase that was by my feet–I saw them coming. That is, I saw Ollie coming, and with him was a beautiful, *soignée* blonde who could only be Eve Bookman, née Eve Eden. Quite a dish. She was, with high heels, just about two inches short of Ollie's height, which made her just about as tall as I, unless she took off her shoes for me. Which, from what Ollie had told me about her, was about the last thing I expected her to do, especially here in the airport.

I got up and walked toward them and–remembering identification was only from snapshot–didn't put too much confidence in my voice when I asked, "Ollie?" and I put out my hand but only tentatively.

Ollie grabbed my hand in his big one and started pumping it. "Ed! Gawdamn if I can believe it, after all these years. When I last saw you, not counting pictures, you looked– Hell, let's get to that later. Meet Eve. Eve, meet Ed."

Eve Bookman gave me a smile but not a hand. "Glad to meet you at last, Edward. Oliver's talked quite a bit about you." I hoped she was just being polite in making the latter statement.

I gave her a smile back. "Hope he didn't say anything bad about me. But maybe he did; I was probably a pretty obstreperous brat when he saw me last. I would have been–let's see–"

"Five," said Ollie. "Well, what are we waiting for? Ed, you want we should go right home? Or should we drop in somewhere on the way and hoist a few? You weren't much of a drinker when I knew you last but maybe by now–"

Eve interrupted him. "Let's go home, Oliver. You'll want a nightcap there in any case, and you know you're not supposed to have more than one or two a day. Did he tell you, Edward, about his heart trouble in any of his letters?"

Ollie saved me again. "No, but it's not important. All right, though. We'll head home and I'll have my daily one or two, or maybe, since this is an occasion, three. Ed, is that your suitcase back by where you were sitting?"

I said it was and went back and got it, then went with them to the parking area and to a beautiful cream-colored Buick convertible with the top down. Ollie opened the door for Eve and then held it open after she got in. "Go on, Ed. We can all sit in the front seat." He grinned. "Eve's got an MG and loves to drive it, but we couldn't bring it tonight. With those damn bucket seats, you can't ride three in the whole car." I got in and he went around and got in the driver's side. I was wishing that I could drive it–I'd never piloted a recent Buick–but I couldn't think of any reasonable excuse for offering.

Half an hour later, I wished that I'd not only offered but had insisted. Ollie Bookman was a poor driver. Not a fast driver or a dangerous one, just sloppy. The way he grated gears made my teeth grate with them and his starts and stops were much too jerky. Besides, he was a lane-straddler and had no sense of timing on making stop lights.

But he was a good talker. He talked almost incessantly, and to good purpose, briefing me, mostly by apparently talking to Eve. "Don't remember if I told you, Eve, how come Ed and I have different last names, but the same father–not the same mother. See, I was Dad's son by his first marriage and Ed by his second–Ed was born Ed Bookman. But Dad died right after Ed was born and Ed's mother, my stepmother, married Wilkes Cartwright a couple years later. Ed was young enough that they changed his name to match his stepfather's, but I was already grown up, through high school anyway, so I didn't change mine. I was on my own by then. Well, both Ed's mother and his stepfather are dead now; he and I are the only survivors. Well. . ." And I listened and filed away facts. Sometimes he'd cut me in by asking me questions, but the questions always cued in their own answers or were ones that wouldn't be give-aways whichever

way I answered them, like, "Ed, the house you were born in, out
north of town—is it still standing, or haven't you been out that way
recently?"

I was fairly well keyed in on family history by the time we got home.

5

Home wasn't as I'd pictured it, a house. It was an apartment, but
a big one—ten rooms, I learned later—on Coleman Boulevard just north
of Howard. It was fourth floor, but there were elevators. Now that
I thought of it, I realized that Ollie, because of his angina, wouldn't
be able to live in a house where he had to climb stairs. But later I
learned they'd been living there ever since they'd married, so he hadn't
had to move there on account of that angle.

It was a fine apartment, nicely furnished and with a living room
big enough to contain a swimming pool. "Come on, Ed," Ollie said
cheerfully. "I'll show you your room and let you get rid of your suitcase, freshen up if you want to—although I imagine we'll all be turning in soon. You must be tired after that long trip. Eve, could we
talk you into making a round of Martinis meanwhile?"

"Yes, Oliver." The perfect wife, she walked toward the small but
well-stocked bar in a corner of the room.

I followed Ollie to the guest room that was to be mine. "Might
as well unpack your suitcase while we talk," he said, after he closed
the door behind us. "Hang your stuff up or put it in the dresser there.
Well, so far, so good. Not a suspicion, and you're doing fine."

"Lots of questions I've still got to ask you, Ollie. We shouldn't
take time to talk much now, but when will we have a chance to?"

"Tomorrow. I'll say I have to go downtown, make up some reasons.
And you've got your excuse already—the business you came to do.
Maybe you can get it over with sooner than you thought—but then
decide, since you've come this far anyway, to stay out the week. That
way you can stick around here as much as you want, or go out only
when I go out."

"Fine. We'll talk that out tomorrow. But about tonight, we'll be
talking, the three of us, and what can I safely talk about? Does she
know anything about the size of my business, or can I improvise freely
and talk about it?"

"Improvise your head off. I've never talked about your business.
Don't know much about it myself."

"Good. Another question. How come, at only twenty-five, I've got a business of my own? Most people are still working for somebody else at that age."

"You inherited it from your step-father, Cartwright. He died three years ago. You were working in the shop and moved to the office and took over. And as far as I know, or Eve, you're doing okay with it."

"Good. And I'm not married?"

"No, but if you want to invent a girl you're thinking about marrying, that's another safe thing you can improvise about."

I put the last of the contents of my suitcase in the dresser drawer and we went back to the living room. Eve had the cocktails made and was waiting for us. We sat around sipping at them, and this time I was able to do most of the talking instead of having to let Ollie filibuster so I wouldn't put my foot into my mouth by saying something wrong.

Ollie suggested a second round but Eve stood up and said that she was tired and that if we'd excuse her, she'd retire. And she gave Ollie a wifely caution about not having more than one more drink. He promised he wouldn't and made a second round for himself and me.

He yawned when he put his down after the first sip. "Guess this will be the last one, Ed. I'm tired, too. And we'll have plenty of time to talk tomorrow."

I wasn't tired, but if he was, that was all right by me. We finished our nightcaps fairly quickly.

"My room's the one next to yours," he told me as he took our glasses back to the bar. "No connecting door, but if you want anything, rap on the wall and I'll hear you. I'm a light sleeper."

"So am I," I told him. "So make it vice versa on the rapping. I'm the one that's supposed to be protecting you, not the other way around."

"And Eve's room is the one on the other side of mine. No connecting door there, either. Not that I'd use it, at this stage, even if it stood wide open with a red carpet running through it."

"She's still a beautiful woman," I said, just to see how he'd answer it.

"Yes. But I guess I'm by nature monogamous. And this may sound corny and be corny, but I consider Dorothy and me married in the sight of God. She's all I'll ever want, she and the boy. Well, come on, and we'll turn in."

I turned in, but I didn't go right to sleep. I lay awake thinking, sorting out my preliminary impressions. Eve Bookman–yes, I believed Ollie's story about their marriage and didn't even think it was exaggerated. Most people would think her sexy as hell to look at her, but I've got a sort of radar when it comes to sexiness. It hadn't registered with a single blip on the screen. And Koslovsky is a much better than average judge of people and what had he said about her? Oh, yes, he'd called her a cold potato.

Some women just naturally hate sex and men–and some of those very women become things like strip teasers because it gives them pleasure to arouse and frustrate men. If one of them breaks down and has an affair with a man, it's because the man has money, as Ollie had, and she thinks she can hook him for a husband, as Eve did Ollie. And once she's got him safely hog-tied, he's on his own and she can be her sweet, frigid self again. True, she's given up the privilege of frustrating men in audience-size groups, but she can torture the hell out of one man, as long as he keeps wanting her, and achieve respectability and even social position while she's doing it.

Oh, she'd been very pleasant to me, very hospitable, and no doubt was pleasant to all of Ollie's friends. And most of them, the ones without radar, probably thought she was a ball of fire in bed and that Ollie was a very lucky guy.

But murder–I was going to take some more convincing on that. It could be Ollie's imagination entirely. The only physical fact he'd come up with to indicate even the possibility of it was the business of the missing will. And she could have taken and destroyed that but still have no intention of killing him before he could make another like it; she could simply be hoping he'd never discover that it was missing.

But I could be wrong, very wrong. I'd met Eve less than three hours ago and Ollie had lived with her eight years. Maybe there was more than met the eye. Well, I'd keep my eyes open and give Ollie a run for his five hundred bucks by not assuming that he was making a murder out of a molehill. I went to sleep and Ollie didn't tap on my wall.

6

I woke at seven but decided that would be too early and that I didn't want to make a nuisance of myself by being up and around before anybody else, so I went back to sleep and it was half past nine when I woke the second time. I got up, showered and shaved–my bedroom had a private bath so all of them must have–dressed and went explor-

ing. I went back to the living room and through it, and found a dining room. The table was set for breakfast for three but no one was
there yet.

A matronly-looking woman who'd be a cook or housekeeper–I later
learned that she was both and her name was Mrs. Ledbetter–appeared
in the doorway that led through a pantry to the kitchen and smiled
at me. "You must be Mr. Bookman's brother," she said. "What would
you like for breakfast?"

"What time do the Bookmans come down for breakfast?" I asked.

"Usually earlier than this. But I guess you talked late last night.
They should be up soon, though."

"Then I won't eat alone, thanks. I'll wait till at least one of them
shows up. And as for what I want–anything; whatever they will be
having. I'm not fussy about breakfasts."

She smiled and disappeared into the kitchen and I disappeared into
the living room. I took a chair with a magazine rack beside it and
was leafing through the latest *Reader's Digest*, just reading the short
items in it, when Ollie came in looking rested and cheerful. "Morning, Ed. Had breakfast?"

I told him I'd been up only a few minutes and had decided to wait
for company. "Come on, then," he said. "We won't wait for Eve.
She might be dressing now, but then again she might sleep till noon."

But she didn't sleep till noon; she came in when we were starting
our coffee, and told Mrs. Ledbetter that she'd just have coffee, as
she had a lunch engagement in only two hours. So the three of us
sat drinking coffee and it was very cozy and you wouldn't have guessed
there was a thing wrong. You wouldn't have guessed it, but you might
have felt it. Anyway, I felt it.

Ollie asked me if I wanted a lift downtown to do the business I'd
come to do, and of course I said that I did. We discussed plans. Mrs.
Ledbetter, I learned, had the afternoon and evening off, starting at
noon, so no dinner would be served that evening. Eve would be gone
all afternoon, playing bridge after her lunch date, and she suggested
we all meet in the Loop and have dinner there. I wasn't supposed
to know Chicago, of course, so I let them pick the place and it came
up the Pump Room at seven.

Ollie and I left and on the way to the garage back of the building,
I asked him if he minded if I drove the Buick. I said I liked driving
and didn't get much chance to.

"Sure, Ed. But you mean you and Am don't have a car?"

I told him we wanted one but hadn't got around to affording it
as yet. The few times we needed one for work, we rented one and
simply got by without one for pleasure.

The Buick handled wonderfully. With me behind the wheel, it shifted smoothly, didn't jerk in starting or stopping; it timed stop lights and didn't straddle lanes. I asked how much it cost and said I hoped we'd be able to afford one like it someday. Except that we'd want a sedan because a convertible is too noticeable to use for a tail job. When we rented cars, we usually got a sedan in some neutral color like gray. Detectives used to use black cars, but nowadays a black car is almost as conspicuous as a red one.

I asked Ollie where he wanted me to drive him and he said he'd like to go to see Dorothy Stark and his son, Jerry. They lived in an apartment on LaSalle near Chicago Avenue. And did I have any plans or would I like to come up to meet them? He said he would like that.

I told him I'd drop up briefly if he wanted me to, but that I had plans. I wanted him to lend me the key to his apartment and I was going back there, after I could be sure both Mrs. Ledbetter and Mrs. Bookman had left. Since it was the former's afternoon off, it would be the best chance I'd have to look around the place in privacy. He said sure, the key was on the ring with the car keys and I might as well keep the keys, car and all, until our dinner date at the Pump Room. It would be only a short cab ride for him to get there from Mrs. Stark's. I asked him if there was any danger that Eve would go back to the apartment after her lunch date and before her bridge game. He was almost sure she wouldn't, but her bridge club broke up about five thirty and she'd probably go back then to dress for dinner. That was all right; I could be gone by then.

When I parked the car on LaSalle, I remembered to ask him who I was supposed to be when I met Mrs. Stark–Ed Hunter or Ed Cartwright. He suggested we stick to the Cartwright story; if he told Dorothy the truth, she'd worry about him being in danger. Anyway, it would be simpler and take less explanation.

I liked Dorothy Stark on sight. She was small and brunette, with a heart-shaped face. Only passably pretty–nowhere near as stunning as Eve–but she was warm and genuine, the real thing. And really in love with Ollie; I didn't need radar to tell me that. And Jerry, age two, was a cute toddler. I can take kids or let them alone, but Ollie was nuts about him.

I stayed only half an hour, breaking away with the excuse of having a business-lunch date in the Loop, but it was a very pleasant half hour, and Ollie was a completely different person here. He was at home in this small apartment, much more so than in the large apartment on Coleman Boulevard. And you had the feeling that Dorothy was his wife, not Eve.

I was only half a dozen blocks from the office and I didn't want to get out to Coleman Boulevard before one o'clock, so I drove over to State Street and went up to see if Uncle Am was there. He was, and I told him what little I'd learned to date and what my plans were.

"Kid," he said, "I'd like a ride in that chariot you're pushing. How about us having an early lunch and then I'll go out with you and help search the joint. Two of us can do twice as good a job."

It was tempting but I thumbed it down. If a wheel did come off and Eve Bookman came back unexpectedly, I could give her a song and dance as to what I was doing there, but Uncle Am would be harder to explain. I said I'd give him the ride, though. We could leave now and he could come with me out as far as Howard Avenue and we'd eat somewhere out there; then he could take the el back south from the Howard station. It would amount only to his taking a two-hour lunch break and we did that any time we felt like it. He liked the idea.

I let him drive the second half of the way and he fell in love with the car, too. After we had lunch, I phoned the apartment from the restaurant and let the phone ring a dozen times to make sure both Mrs. Bookman and Mrs. Ledbetter were gone. Then I drove Uncle Am to the el station and myself to the apartment.

7

I let myself in and put the chain on the door. If Eve came back too soon, that was going to be embarrassing to explain; I'd have to say I'd done it absent-mindedly and it would make me look like a fool. But it would be less embarrassing than to have her walk in and find me rooting in the drawers of her dresser.

First, I decided, I'd take a look at the place as a whole. The living room, dining room, and the guest bedroom were the only rooms I'd been in thus far. I decided to start at the back. I went through the dining room and the pantry into the kitchen. It was a big kitchen and had the works in the way of equipment, even an automatic dishwasher and garbage disposal. A room on one side of it was a service and storage room and on the other side was a bedroom; Mrs. Ledbetter's, of course. I looked around in all three rooms but didn't touch anything. I went back to the dining room and found that a door from it led to a room probably intended as a den or study; there was a desk–an old-fashioned roll-top desk that was really an antique–two file cabinets, a bookcase filled mostly with books on construction and business practice but with a few novels on one shelf, mostly mysteries, a typewriter on a stand, and a dictating machine. This was Ollie's office, from which he conducted whatever business he still did. And the dictating machine meant he must have a part-time secretary, however many days or hours a week. He'd hardly dictate letters and then transcribe them himself.

The roll-top desk was closed but not locked. I opened it and saw a lot of papers and envelopes in pigeon-holes, but I didn't study any of them. Ollie's business was no business of mine. But I wondered if he'd used the "Purloined Letter" method of hiding his missing will by having it in plain sight in one of those pigeon-holes. And if so, what had Eve been looking for when she found it? I made a mental note to ask him about that.

There was a telephone on top of the desk and I looked at the number on it; it wasn't the same number as that on the phone in the living room, which meant it wasn't an extension but a private line.

I closed the desk and went back to the living room and through its side doorway to the hall from which the bedrooms opened. Another door from it turned out to be a linen closet.

Ollie's bedroom was the same size as mine and furnished in the same way. I walked over to the dresser. A little bottle on it contained nitroglycerin pills. It held a hundred and was about half full. Beside it were three glass ampoules of amyl nitrite like the one in my pocket, the one I'd got from Doc Kruger last night at dinner. I looked at the ampoules and decided that they hadn't been tampered with. Couldn't be tampered with, in fact. But I took a couple of the nitro pills out of the bottle and put them in my pocket. If I had a chance to get them to Uncle Am, I'd ask him to take them to a laboratory and have them checked to make sure they were really what the label claimed them to be.

I didn't search the room thoroughly, but I looked through the dresser drawers and the closet. I wasn't sure what I was looking for, unless maybe a gun. If Ollie kept a gun, I wanted to know it. But I didn't find a gun or anything else more dangerous than a nail file.

Eve Bookman's room was, of course, the main object of my search, but I wasn't in any hurry and decided I'd do a little thinking before I tackled it. I went back to the living room and since it occurred to me that if Eve was coming back between lunch and bridge, this would be about the time, I took the chain off the door. It wouldn't matter if I was found here, as long as I was innocently occupied. I could just say that I was unable to see the man I'd come to see until tomorrow. And that Ollie–Oliver to her–had had things to do in the Loop and had lent me his car and his house key.

I made myself a highball at the bar and sat down to sip it and think, but the thinking didn't get me anywhere. I knew one thing I'd be looking for–pills the size and color of nitro pills but that might turn out to be something else. Or a gun or any other lethal weapon, or poison–if it could be identified as such. But that was all and it didn't seem very likely to me that I'd find any of those things, even if Eve did have any designs on her husband's life. One other thing I thought of: I might as well finish my search for a gun by looking for one in Ollie's office. If he had one, I wanted to know it, and he might keep it in his study instead of his bedroom.

I made myself another short drink and did some more thinking without getting any ideas except that if I could reach Ollie by phone at the Stark apartment, I could simply ask him about the gun, and another question or two I'd thought of.

I rinsed out and wiped the glass I'd used and went to the telephone. I checked the book and found a *Stark, Dorothy* on LaSalle Street and called the number. Ollie answered and when I asked him if he could talk freely, he said sure, that Dorothy had gone out shopping and had left him to baby-sit.

I asked him about guns and he said no, he didn't own any.

I told him I'd noticed the ampoules and pills on his dresser and asked him if he carried some of both with him. He said the pills yes, always. But he didn't carry ampoules because the pills always worked for him and the ampoules he just kept on hand at home in case his angina should get worse. He told me the same thing about them the doctor had, that if one used them often they became ineffective. He'd used one only once thus far, and wouldn't again until and unless he had to.

After I'd hung up, I remembered that I'd forgotten to ask him where the will had been hidden in his office, but it didn't seem worth while calling back to ask him. I wanted to know, if only out of curiosity, but there wasn't any hurry and I could find out the next time I talked to him alone.

I put the chain bolt back on the door–I was pretty sure by now that Eve wasn't coming back before her bridge-club session, as it was already after two, but I thought I might as well play safe–and went to her room.

8

It was bigger than any of the other bedrooms–had originally, no doubt, been intended as the master bedroom–and it had a dressing room attached and lots of closet space. It was going to be a lot of territory to cover thoroughly, but if Eve had any secrets, they'd surely be here, not in Ledbetter territory like the kitchen or Ollie's office or neutral territory like the living room. Apparently she spent a lot of time here; besides the usual bedroom furniture and a vanity table, there was a bookcase of novels and a writing desk that looked used. I sighed and pitched in. Two hours later, all I knew that I hadn't known–but might have suspected–before was that a woman can have more clothes and more beauty preparations than a man would think possible.

I'd looked in everything but the writing desk; I'd saved that for last. There were three drawers and the top one contained only raw materials–paper and envelopes, pencils, ink and such. No pens, but she probably used a fountain pen and carried it with her. The middle one contained canceled checks, neatly in order and rubber-banded, used stubs of check-books similarly banded, and bank statements. No current checkbook; she must have had it with her. The bottom drawer was empty except for a dictionary, a Merriam-Webster *Collegiate*. If she corresponded with anyone, beyond sending out checks to pay bills, she must have destroyed letters when she answered them and not owed any at the moment; there was no correspondence at all.

I still had almost an hour of safe time, since her bridge club surely wouldn't break up before five, so for lack of anything else to go through, I started studying the bank statements and the canceled checks. One thing was immediately obvious: this was her personal account, for clothes and other personal expenses. There was one deposit a month for exactly four hundred dollars, never more or never less. None of the checks drawn against this amount would have been for household expenses. Ollie must have handled them, or had his hypothetical part-time secretary (that was another thing I hadn't remembered to ask him about, but again it was nothing I was in a hurry to know) handle them. This account was strictly a personal one. Some of the checks, usually twenty-five- or fifty-dollar ones, were drawn to cash. Others, most of them for odd amounts, were made out to stores. There was one every month to a Howard Avenue Drugstore, no doubt mostly for cosmetics, most of the others were to clothing stores, lingerie shops and the like. Occasional checks to some woman or other for odd amounts up to twenty or thirty dollars were, I decided, probably bridge losses or the like, at times when she didn't have enough cash to pay off. From the bank statements I could see that she lived up to the hilt of her allowance; at the time each four-hundred-dollar check was deposited, always on the first of the month, the balance to which it was added was never over twenty or thirty dollars.

I went through the stack of canceled checks once more. I didn't know what I was looking for, but my sub-conscious must have noticed something my conscious mind had missed. It had. Not many of the checks were over a hundred dollars, but all of the checks to one outfit, Vogue Shops, Inc., were over a hundred and some were over two hundred. At least half of Eve's four hundred dollars a month was being spent in one place. And other checks were dated at different times, but the Vogue checks were all dated the first of the month exactly. Wondering how much they did total, I took paper and pencil and added the amounts of six of them, for the first six months of the previous year. The smallest was $165.50 and the largest $254.25, but the total—it jarred me. The total of the six checks came to $1,200. Exactly. Even. On the head. And so, I knew a minute later, did the six checks for the second half of the year. It certainly couldn't be coincidence, twice.

Eve Bookman was paying somebody an even two hundred bucks a month—and disguising the fact, on the surface at any rate, by making some of the amounts more than that and some less, but making them average out. I turned over some of the checks to look at the endorsements. Each one was rubber-stamped *Vogue shops, Inc.*, and under the rubber stamp was the signature *John L. Littleton*. Rubber stamps under that showed they'd all been deposited or cashed at the Dearborn Branch of the Chicago Second National Bank.

And that, whatever it meant, was all the checks were going to tell me. I rebanded them and put them back as I'd found them, took a final look around the room to see that I was leaving everything else as I'd found it, and went back to the living room. I was going to call Uncle Am at the office—if he wasn't there, I could reach him later at the rooming house—but I took the chain off the door first. If Eve walked in while I was talking on the phone, I'd just have to switch the subject of conversation to printing equipment, and Uncle Am would understand.

He was still at the office. I talked fast and when I finished, he said, "Nice going, kid. You've got something by the tail and I'll find out what it is. You stick with the Bookmans and let me handle everything outside. We've got two lucky breaks on this. One, it's Friday and that bank will be open till six o'clock. Two, one of the tellers is a friend of mine. When I get anything for sure, I'll get in touch with you. Is there an extension on the phone there that somebody could listen in on?"

"No," I said. "There's another phone in Ollie's office, but it's a different line."

"Fine, then I can call openly and ask for you. You can pretend its a business call, if anyone's around, and argue price on a Miehle vertical for your end of the conversation."

"Okay. One other thing." I told him about the two alleged nitro pills I'd appropriated from Ollie's bottle. I told him that on my way into town for dinner, I'd drop them off on his desk at the office and sometime tomorrow he could take them to the lab. Or maybe, if nitro had a distinctive taste, Doc Kruger could tell by touching one of them to his tongue.

9

It was five o'clock when I hung up the phone. I decided that I'd earned a drink and helped myself to a short one at the bar. Then I went to my room, treated myself to a quick shower and a clean shirt for the evening.

I was just about to open the door to leave when it opened from the other side and Eve Bookman came home. She was pleasantly surprised to find me and I told her how I happened to have the house key and Ollie's car, but said I'd been there only half an hour, just to clean up and change shirts for the evening.

She asked why, since it was five thirty already, I didn't stay and drive her in in Ollie's car. That way we wouldn't be stuck, after dinner, with having both the Buick and the MG downtown with us and could all ride home together.

I told her it sounded like an excellent idea. Which it was, except for the fact that I wanted to get the pills to Uncle Am. But there was a way around that. I asked if she could give me a piece of paper, envelope and stamp. She went to her room to get them and after she'd gone back there to dress, I addressed the envelope to Uncle Am at the office, folded the paper around the pills and sealed them in the envelope. All I'd have to do was mail it, on our way in, at the Dearborn Post Office Station and it would get there in the morning delivery.

I made myself comfortable with a magazine to read and Eve surprised me by taking not too long to get ready. And she looked gorgeous, and I told her so, when she came back to the living room. It was only six fifteen and I didn't have to speed to get us to the Pump Room by seven. Ollie wasn't there, but he'd reserved us a table and left word with the maître d' that something had come up and he'd be a bit late.

He was quite a bit late and we were finishing our third round of Martinis when he showed up, very apologetic about being detained. We decided we'd have one more so he could have one with us, and then ate a wonderful meal. As an out-of-town guest who was presuming on their hospitality already, I insisted on grabbing the check. A nice touch, since it would go on Ollie's bill anyway.

We discussed going on to a night club, but Eve said that Ollie looked tired--which he did--and if we went clubbing, would want to drink too much. We could have a drink or two at home--if Ollie would promise to hold to two. He said he would.

Since Ollie admitted that he really was a little tired, I had no trouble talking him into letting me do the driving again. Eve seemed more genuinely friendly than hitherto. Maybe it was the Martinis before dinner or maybe she was getting to like me. But it was an at-a-distance type of friendliness; my radar told me that.

Back home, I offered to do the bartending, but Eve overruled me and made our drinks. We were drinking them and talking about nothing in particular when I saw Ollie suddenly put down his glass and bend forward slightly, putting his right hand under his left arm.

Then he straightened up and saw that we were both looking at him with concern. He said, "Nothing. Just a little twinge, not an attack. But maybe to be on the safe side, I'll take one--"

He took a little gold pillbox out of his pocket and opened it.

"Good Lord," he said, standing up. "Forgot I took my last one just before I got to the Pump Room. Just as well we didn't go nightclubbing, after all. Well, It's okay now. I'll fill it."

"Let me--" I said.

But he looked perfectly well now and waved me away. "I'm, perfectly okay. Don't worry."

And he went into the hallway, walking confidently, and I heard the door of his room open and close so I knew he'd made it all right.

Eve started to make conversation by asking me questions about the girl in Seattle whom I'd talked about, and I was answering and enjoying it, when suddenly I realized Ollie had been gone at least five minutes and maybe ten. A lot longer than it would take to refill a pillbox. Of course he might have decided to go to the john or something while he was there, but just the same, I stood up quickly, excused myself without explaining, headed for his room.

The minute I opened the door, I saw him and thought he was dead. He was lying face down on the rug in front of the dresser and on the dresser there wasn't any little bottle of pills and there weren't any amyl nitrite ampoules, either.

I bent over him, but I didn't waste time trying to find out whether he was dead or not. If he was, the ampoule I'd got from Doc Kruger wasn't going to hurt him. And if he was alive, a fraction of a second might make the difference of whether it would save him or not. I didn't feel for a heartbeat or look at his face. I got hold of a handful of hair and lifted his head a few inches off the floor, reached in under it with my hand and crushed the ampoule right under his nose.

Eve was standing in the doorway and I barked at her to phone for an ambulance, right away quick. She ran back toward the living room.

10

Ollie didn't die, although he certainly would have if I hadn't had the bright idea of appropriating that ampoule from Doc and carrying it with me. But Ollie was in bad shape for a while, and Uncle Am and I didn't get to see him until two days later, Sunday evening.

His face looked gray and drawn and he was having to lie very quiet. But he could talk, and they gave us fifteen minutes with him. And they'd told us he was definitely out of danger, as long as he behaved himself, but he'd still be in the hospital another week or maybe even two.

But bad as he looked, I didn't pull any punches. "Ollie," I said, "it didn't work, your little frame-up. I didn't go to the police and accuse Eve of trying to murder you. On the other hand, I've given you this break, so far. I didn't go to them and tell them you tried to commit suicide in a way to frame her for murder. You must love Dorothy and Jerry awfully much to have planned that."

"I-I do," he said. "What-made you guess, Ed?"

"Your hands, for one thing," I said. "They were dirtier than they'd have been if you'd just fallen. That and the fact that you were lying face down told me how you managed to bring on that attack at just that moment. You were doing push-ups-about as strenuous and concentrated exercise as a man can take. And just kept doing them till you passed out. It *should* have been fatal, all right.

"And you knew the pills and ampoules had been on your dresser that afternoon, and that Eve had been home since I'd seen them and could have taken them. Actually you took them yourself. You came out in a taxi-and we could probably find the taxi if we had to prove this-and got them yourself. You had to wait till you were sure Eve and I would be en route downtown, and that's why you were so late getting to the Pump Room. Now Uncle Am's got news for you—not that you deserve it."

Uncle Am cleared his throat. "You're not married, Ollie. You're a free man because your marriage to Eve Packer wasn't legal. She'd been married before and hadn't got a divorce. Probably because she had no intention of marrying again until you popped the question to her, and then it was too late to get one.

"Her legal husband, who left her ten years ago, is a bartender named Littleton. He found her again somehow and when he learned she'd married you illegally, he started black-mailing her. She's been paying him two hundred a month, half the pin-money allowance you gave her, for three years. They worked out a way she could mail him checks and still have her money seemingly accounted for. The method doesn't matter."

I took over. "We haven't called copper on the bigamy bit, either, because you're not going to prosecute her for it, or tell the cops. We figure you owe her something for having tried to frame her on a murder charge. We've talked to her. She'll leave town quietly, and go to Reno, and in a little while you can let out that you're divorced and free. And marry Dorothy and legitimize Jerry.

"She really will be getting a divorce, incidentally, but from Littleton, not from you. I said you'd finance that and give her a reasonable stake to start out with. Like ten thousand dollars—does that sound reasonable?"

He nodded. His face looked less drawn, less gray now. I had a hunch his improvement would be a lot faster now.

"And you fellows," he said. "How can I ever—?"

"We're even," Uncle Am said. "Your retainer will cover. But don't ever look us up again to do a job for you. A private detective doesn't like to be made a patsy, be put in the spot of helping a frame-up. And that's what you tried to do to us. Don't ever look us up again."

We never saw Ollie again, but we did hear from him once, a few months later. One morning, a Western Union messenger came into our office to deliver a note and a little box. He said he had instructions not to wait and left.

The envelope contained a wedding announcement. One of the after-the-fact kind, not an invitation, of the marriage of Oliver R. Bookman to Dorothy Stark. On the back of it was scribbled a note. "Hope you've forgiven me enough to accept a wedding present in reverse. I've arranged for the dealer to leave it out front. Papers will be in glove compartment. Thanks for everything, including accepting this." And the little box, of course, contained two sets of car keys.

It was, as I'd known it would be, a brand-new Buick sedan, gray, a hell of a car. We stood looking at it, and Uncle Am said, "Well, Ed, have we forgiven him enough?"

"I guess so," I said. "It's a sweet chariot. But somebody got off on his time, either the car dealer or the messenger, and it's been here too long. Look."

I pointed to the parking ticket on the windshield. "Well, shall we take our first ride in it, down to the City Hall to pay the fine and get right with God?"

We did.

HOWARD BROWNE
(b.1908)

So Dark For April
(Paul Pine)

When I got through telling the sergeant at Central Homicide about it, he said to sit tight and not touch anything, that somebody would be right over. I told him I wouldn't even breathe any more than was absolutely necessary and put back the receiver and went into the reception room to take another look at the body.

He was at the far end of the couch, slumped in a sitting position, with his chin on his chest and an arm hanging down. A wick of iron-gray hair made a curve against the waxen skin of a high forehead, his half-open eyes showed far too much white, and a trickle of dark blood had traced a crooked line below one corner of a slack-lipped mouth. His coat hung open, letting me see a circular red stain under the pocket of a soiled white shirt. From the center of the stain protruded the brown bone handle of a switch-blade knife.

I moved over to lean against the window frame and light a cigarette. It was one of those foggy wet mornings we get early in April, with a chill wind off the lake and the sky as dull as a deodorant commercial. Umbrellas blossomed along the walks eight floors below and long lines of cars slithered past with a hooded look.

I stood there breathing smoke and staring at the dead man. He was nobody I had ever seen before. He wore a handsomely tailored suit coat of gray flannel, dirty brown gabardine slacks spattered with green paint and an oil stain across one knee, and brown bench-made shoes.

His shirt was open at the throat, showing a fringe of dark hair, and he wasn't wearing a tie.

The rummage-sale air of those slacks bothered me. This was no Skid Row fugitive. His nails had that cared-for look, his face, even in death, held a vague air of respectability, and they didn't trim hair that way at barber college.

I bent down and turned back the left side of his coat. The edge of a black wallet showed in the inner pocket. That was where I stopped. This was cop business. Let the boys who were paid for it paw the corpse.

A black satin label winked up at me. I put my eyes close enough to read the stitched letters in it. A C G—in a kind of Old English script. The letters seemed too big to be simply a personal monogram, but then there's no accounting for tastes.

I let the lapel drop back to the way I had found it. The dead man didn't seem to care either way. Something glistened palely between the frayed cuffs and the tops of the custom-made shoes. I said, "Huh?" out loud and bent down to make sure.

No mistake. It made no sense but there it was. The pale white shine was naked flesh.

The dead man wasn't wearing socks.

2

Detective sergeant Lund said, "Right smack-dab through the old ticker. He never even had time to clear his throat. Not this guy."

His curiously soft voice held a kind of grim respect. He straightened up and backed away a couple of steps and took off his hat and shook rain water from it onto the carpet and stared thoughtfully at me out of gun-metal eyes.

I moved a shoulder and said nothing. At the wicker table across the room the two plainclothes men were unshipping tape measures and flash-bulbs and fingerprint kits. Rain tapped the glass behind me with icy fingers.

"Your turn, Pine," Lund said in the same soft voice.

"He was like that when I came in," I said promptly. I looked at my strapwatch. "Exactly thirty-two minutes ago."

"How'd he get in here?"

"I usually leave the reception room unlocked, in case I have a client and the client cares to wait."

One corner of his mouth moved up faintly. "Somebody sure wanted this guy to wait, hey?"

I shrugged. He took a turn along the room and back again, hands deep in the pockets of his topcoat. Abruptly he said, "It says on your door you're a private dick. This a client?"

"No. I never saw him before."

"What's his name?"

"I don't know."

"No identification on him?"

"I didn't look. The sergeant at Central said not to."

He seemed mildly astonished. "A man dies in your office and you don't even show a little healthy curiosity? Don't be afraid of me, Pine. I haven't chewed off anybody's arm in over a week."

"I obey the law," I said mildly.

"Well, well," he said. He grinned suddenly, and after a moment I grinned back. Mine was no phonier than his. He snapped a thumb lightly against the point of his narrow chin a time or two while thinking a secret thought, then turned back to the body.

He went through the pockets with the deft delicacy of a professional dip. The blood, the knife handle, the sightless eyes meant about half as much to him as last week's laundry. When he straightened again there was a small neat pile of personal effects on one of the couch pillows and the dead man's pockets were as empty as his eyes.

The wallet was on top. Lund speared it, flipped it open. The transparent identification panels were empty, as was the bill compartment. Shoved into the latter, however, were three or four cards. Lund looked them over slowly and carefully, his thick brows drawn into a lazy V above his long, pointed nose.

"Credit cards on a couple Loop hotels," he said, almost to himself. "Plus one of these identification cards you get with a wallet. According to what it says here, this guy is Franklin Andrus, 5861 Winthrop Avenue. One business card. It calls him a sales representative for the Reliable Amusement Machine Corporation, Dayton, Ohio. No telephone shown and nobody listed to notify. Any of this mean anything to you, Mr. Pine?"

"Sorry."

"Uh-huh. You ain't playing this too close, are you?"

"I'm not even in the game," I said.

"Initials in his coat don't agree with the name on these here cards. That must mean something, hey?"

I stared at the bridge of his nose. "His coat and somebody else's cards. Or his cards and somebody else's coat. Or neither. Or both."

His mouth hardened. "You trying to kid me, mister?"

"I guess that would be pretty hard to do, Sergeant."

He turned on his heel and went through the communicating door to my inner office, still carrying the wallet. He didn't bother to shut it, and through the opening I could see him reach for the phone without sitting down and dial a number with quick hard stabs of a forefinger. What he said when he got his party was too low-voiced for me to catch.

Two minutes later, he was back. He scooped up the stuff from the couch and said, "Let's talk, hey? Let's us try out that nice private office of yours."

I followed him in and drew up the Venetian blind and opened the window a crack to let out the smell of yesterday's cigarettes. On the outer ledge four pigeons were organizing a bombing raid. Lund shoved the phone and ashtray aside, dumped his collection on the desk pad and snapped on the lamp. I sat down behind the desk and watched him pull up the customer's chair across from me.

I got out my cigarettes. He took one, sniffed at it for no reason I knew of and struck a match for us both. He leaned back and hooked an arm over the chair back and put his dull gray eyes on me.

"Nice and cozy," he said. "All the comforts. Too bad they're not all like this."

"I could turn on the radio," I said. "Maybe get a little dance music."

He grunted with mild amusement. All the narrow-eyed suspicion had been tucked out of sight. He drew on his cigarette and blew a long blue plume of smoke at the ceiling. Another minute and he'd have his shoes off.

He let his gaze drift about the dingy office, taking in the Varga calendar, the filing cases, the worn tan linoleum. He said, "The place could stand a little paint, hey?"

"You drumming up business for your day off?" I asked.

That got another grunt out of him. "You sound kind of on the excited side, Pine. Don't be like that. You wouldn't be the first private boy got a customer shot out from under him, so to speak."

I felt my face burn. "He's not a customer. I told you that."

"I guess you did, at that," he said calmly. "It don't mean I have to believe it. Client getting pushed right in your own office don't look so good, hey? What the newshounds call a bad press."

I bit down on my teeth. "You just having fun, Sergeant, or does all this lead somewhere?"

"Why, we're just talking," he said mildly. "Just killing time, you might say, until the coroner shows up. That and looking over the rest of what the guy had on him."

He stuck out an untidy finger and poked at the pile. Besides the wallet, there were several small square transparent envelopes, some loose change, a pocket comb, and a small pair of gold tweezers.

He brought his eyes up to stare coldly at me, his mellow mood gone as quickly as it had arrived. He said harshly, "Let's lay off the clowning around, mister. You were working for him. I want to know doing what."

"I wouldn't bother to lie to you," I said. "I never saw the guy before in my life, I never talked to him on the phone, or got a letter from him. Period."

His sneer was a foot wide. "Jesus, you must think I'm green!"

"I'm not doing any thinking," I said.

"I hope to tell you, you aren't. Listen, I can book you, brother!"

"For what?"

"Obstructing justice, resisting an officer, indecent exposure. What the hell do you care? I'm saying I can book you!"

I didn't say anything. Some of the angry color faded slowly from his high cheeks. Finally he sighed heavily and picked up the necktie and gave it a savage jerk between his square hands and threw it down again.

"Nuts," he said pettishly. "I don't want to fight with you. I'm trying to do a job. All I want is a little cooperation. This guy just don't walk in here blind. You're a private dick, or so your door says. Your job is people in trouble. I say it's too damn big a coincidence him picking your office to get knocked off in. Go on, tell me I'm wrong."

"I'm not saying you're wrong," I said. "I'm saying what I've already said. He's a stranger to me. He could have come in here to get out of the wet or to sell me a slot machine or to just sit down and rest his arches. I admit he might have come here to hire me. It has happened, although not often enough. Maybe somebody didn't want him spilling any touchy secrets to me, and fixed him so he couldn't."

"But you never saw him before?"

"You're beginning to get the idea," I said.

"Go ahead," he said bitterly. "Crack wise. Get out the office bottle and toss off three inches of Scotch without a chaser and spit in my eye. That's the way you private eyes do it on TV eight times a night."

"I don't have an office bottle," I said.

The sound of the reception room door opening and closing cut off what Lund was about to say. A short plump man went past the half-open door of the inner office, carrying a black bag. Lund got up without a word and went out there, leaving me where I sat.

Some time passed. Quite a lot of time. The murmur of voices from the next room went on and on. Flash bulbs made soundless explosions of light and a small vacuum cleaner whirred. I stayed where I was and burned a lot of tobacco and crossed my legs and dangled my foot and listened to the April rain and thought my thoughts.

Thoughts about a man who might still be alive if I hadn't slept an hour later than usual. A man with mismatched clothing and no socks and an empty wallet. A man who would want to go on living, even in an age when living was complicated and not very rewarding. A man who had managed for fifty-odd years to hang on to the only life he'd ever be given to live before a switch-blade knife and a strong hand combined to pinch it off.

I went on sitting. The rain went on falling. It was so dark for April.

After a while the corridor door opened to let in two men in white coats. They carried a long wicker basket between them. They passed my door without looking in. There was more indistinct murmuring, then a young voice said, "Easy with them legs, Eddie," and the basket was taken out again. It was harder to carry the second time.

Sergeant Lund walked in, his face expressionless. He sat down heavily and lighted a cigarette and waved out the match and continued to hold it. He said, "Andrus died between eight-thirty and ten. The elevator man don't recall bringing him up. What time did you get here?"

"Ten-thirty, about. Few minutes either way."

"You wouldn't happen to own a switch-blade knife, hey?"

"With a brown bone handle?" I said.

He bent the used match and dropped it in the general vicinity of the ashtray. "Seven-inch blade," he muttered. "Like a goddam bayonet." He put the cigarette in a corner of his mouth and left it there. "This is a real cute killing, Pine. You notice how Andrus was dressed?"

"No socks," I said.

"That isn't the half of it, brother. New coat, old pants, fancy shoes. No hat and no topcoat. In weather like this? What's the sense?"

I spread my hands. "By me, Sergeant."

"You sure you wasn't work–"

"Don't say it!" I shouted.

The phone rang. A voice like a buzz-saw asked for Lund. He grunted into the mouthpiece, listened stolidly for nearly a full minute, then said, "Yeah," twice and passed back the receiver. I replaced it and watched him drag himself out of the chair, his expression a study in angry frustration.

"I had Rogers Park send a squad over to that Winthrop Avenue address," he growled. "Not only they don't find no trace of a Franklin

Andrus; they don't even find the address! An empty lot, by God! All right. Hell with it. The lab boys will turn up something. Laundry marks, cuff dust, clothing labels. It'll take 'em a day or two, but I can wait. The old routine takes time but it always works.''

"Almost always," I said absently.

He glowered down across the desk at me. "One thing I hope, mister. I hope you been holding out on me and I find it out. That's going to be jake with me.''

He gathered up the dead man's possessions and stalked out. A little later one of the plainclothes men slipped in with his kit and took my fingerprints. He was nice about it, explaining they were only for elimination purposes.

3

By one o'clock I was back from having a sandwich and coffee at the corner drugstore. The reception room was empty, with only a couple of used flash bulbs, some smudges of fingerprint powder here and there and the smell of cheap cigars and damp cloth to remind me of my morning visitor. Without the dead man on it, the couch seemed larger than usual. There were no blood-stains. I looked to make sure.

I walked slowly into the other room and shucked off my trench coat. From the adjoining office came the faint whine of a dentist's drill. A damp breeze crawled in at the window and rattled the cords on the blind. Cars hooted in the street below. Sounds that made the silence around me even more silent. And the rain went on and on.

I sat down behind the desk and emptied the ashtray into the waste-basket and wiped off the glass top. I put away the cloth and got out a cigarette and sat there turning it, unlighted, between a thumb and forefinger.

He had been a nice-looking man. Fifty-five at the most. A man with a problem on his mind. Let's say he wakes up this morning and decides to take his problem to a private detective. So he gets out the classified book and looks under the right heading. There aren't many, not even for a town the size of Chicago. The big agencies he passes up, maybe because he figures he'll have to go through a handful of henna-haired secretaries before reaching the right guy. Then, not too far down the column, he comes across the name Paul Pine. A nice short name. Anybody can pronounce it.

So he takes a cab or a bus and comes on down. He hasn't driven a car; no car keys and no license on him. The waiting room is unlocked but no alert gimlet-eyed private detective around. The detective is home in bed, like a man with a working wife. So this nice-looking man with a problem sits down to wait . . . and somebody walks in and sticks a quarter-pound of steel in him.

That was it. That explained everything. Everything but what his problem was and why he wasn't wearing socks and why his wallet was empty and why his identification showed an address that didn't exist.

I got up and took a couple of turns around the room. This was no skin off my shins. The boys from Homicide would have it all wrapped up in a day or so. The old routine Lund had called it. I didn't owe that nice old man a thing. He hadn't paid me a dime. No connection between us at all.

Except that he had come to me for help and got a mouthful of blood instead.

I sat down again and tried the phone book. No Franklin Andrus listed. No local branch of the Reliable Amusement Machine Corp. I shoved the book away and began to think about the articles that had come out of the dead man's pockets. Gold tweezers, a pocket comb, five small transparent envelopes, seventy-three cents in change, a dark blue necktie. There had been a department store label on the tie–Marshall Field. I knew that because I had looked while Lund was out of the room. But Field's has more neckties than Pabst has bottles. No help there.

Is that all, Pine, I thought to myself. End of the line? You mean you're licked? A nice, clean-necked, broad-shouldered, late-sleeping detective like you?

I walked the floor some more. I went over to the window and leaned my forehead against its coolness. My breath misted the glass and I wrote my name in the mist with the end of my finger. That didn't seem to help any. I went on thinking.

Maybe what *hadn't* come out of his pockets was important. No keys, for instance. Not even to his apartment. Maybe he lived in a hotel. Not even cigarettes or a book of matches. Maybe he didn't smoke. Not even a handkerchief. Maybe he didn't have a cold.

I sat down again. There had been initals in his coat. A C G. No periods and stitched professionally in fancy letters against a square of black satin. Rather large, as I recalled. Too bad I hadn't looked inside the pocket for the tailor's label. Unless . . .

This time I used the classified book. T–for Tailors–Men's. I ran through the columns to the G's. There it was, bright and shining and filled with promise. A. Cullinham Grandfils, Custom Tailor. On Michigan Avenue, in the 600 block. Right in the center of the town's swankiest shopping district.

I closed the window, climbed into my trench coat and hat and locked up. The smell of dime cigars still hung heavy in the outer office. Even the hall seemed full of it.

4

It was made to look like a Greek temple, if you didn't look too close. It had a white limestone front and narrow doorway with a circular hunk of stained glass above that. Off to one side was a single display window about the size of a visiting card. Behind the glass was a slanting pedestal covered with black velvet and on the velvet a small square of gray cloth that looked as though it might be of cheviot. Nothing else. No price tags, no suits, no firm name spelled out in severely stylized letters.

And probably no bargain basement.

I heaved back the heavy glass door and walked into a large room with soft dusty rose walls, a vaulted ceiling, moss green carpeting, and indirect lighting like a benediction. Scattered tastefully about were up-holstered chairs and couches, blond in the wood and square in the lines. A few chrome ashstands, an end table or two, and at the far end a blond desk and a man sitting behind it.

The man stood up as I came in. He floated down the room toward me, a tall slender number in a cut-away coat, striped trousers and a gates-ajar collar. He looked like a high-class undertaker. He had a high reedy voice that said:

"Good afternoon, sir. May I be of service?"

"Are you the high priest?" I said.

His mouth fell open. "I beg your pardon?"

"Maybe I'm in the wrong place," I said. "I'm looking for the tailor shop. No name outside but the number checks."

His backbone got even stiffer although I hadn't thought that possible. "This," he said in a strangled voice, "is A. Cullinham Grandfils. Are you interested in a garment?"

"A what?"

"A garment."

"You mean a suit?"

"Ah—yes, sir."

"I've got a suit," I said. I unbuttoned my coat and showed it to him. All he did was look pained.

"What I came by for," I said, "was to get the address of a customer of yours. I'm not sure but I think his name's Andrus–Franklin Andrus."

He folded his arms and brought up a hand and turned his wrist delicately and rested his chin between his thumb and forefinger. "I'm afraid not. No. Sorry."

"You don't know the name?"

"I'm not referring to the name. What I am attempting to convey to you is that we do not give out information on our people."

I said, "Oh," and went on staring at him. He looked like the type you can bend easy. I dug out the old deputy sheriff's star I carried for emergencies like this and showed it to him, keeping the lettering covered with the ball of my thumb. He jerked down his arms and backed away as though I'd pulled a gun on him.

"This is official," I said in a tough-cop voice. "I'm not here to horse around. Do you cooperate or do we slap you with a subpoena?"

"You'll have to discuss the matter with Mr. Grandfils," he squeaked. "I simply am not–I have no authority to–You'll just have to–"

"Then trot him out, Curly. I don't have all day."

"Mr. Grandfils is in his office. Come this way, please."

We went along the room and through a glass door at the far end and along a short hall to another door: a solid panel of limed oak with the words A. Cullinham Grandfils, Private, on it in raised silver letters. The door was knocked on and a muffled voice came through and I was inside.

A little round man was perched in an enormous leather chair behind an acre of teakwood and glass. His head was as bald as a collection plate on Monday morning. A pair of heavy horn-rimmed glasses straddled a button nose above a tiny mouth and a chin like a ping-pong ball. He blinked owlishly at me and said, "What is it, Marvin?" in a voice so deep I jumped.

"This–ah–gentleman is the police, Mr. Grandfils. He has demanded information I simply haven't the right to–"

"That will be all, Marvin."

I didn't even hear him leave.

"I can't stand that two-bit diplomat," the little man said. "He makes the bottom of my foot itch."

I didn't say anything.

"Unfortunately he happens to be useful," he went on. "The women gush at him and he gushes back. Good for business."

"I thought you only sold men's suits," I said.

"Who do you think picks them out? Take off that coat and sit down. I don't know your name."

I told him my name and got rid of the trench coat and hat and drew up a teakwood chair trimmed in silver and sat on it. He made a quarter-turn in the big chair and his glasses flashed at me in the soft light.

"Police, eh?" he said suddenly. "Well, you've got the build for it. Where did you get that ridiculous suit?"

"This ridiculous suit set me back sixty-five bucks," I said.

"It looks it. What are you after, sir?"

"The address of one of your customers."

"I see. Why should I give it to you?"

"He was murdered. The address on his identification was incorrect."

"Murdered!" His mouth dropped open, causing the glasses to slip down on his nose. "Good heavens! One of my people?"

"He was wearing one of your coats," I said.

He passed a tremulous hand across the top of his head. All it smoothed down was scalp. "What was his name?"

"Andrus. Franklin Andrus."

He shook his head immediately. "No, Mr. Pine. None of my people has that name. You have made a mistake."

"The coat fitted him," I said doggedly. "He belonged in it. I might have the name wrong but not the coat. It was his coat."

He picked a silver paper-knife from the silver trimmed tan desk blotter and rapped it lightly over and over against the knuckles of his left hand. "Perhaps you're right," he said. "My coats are made to fit. Describe this man to me."

I gave the description, right down to the kidney-shaped freckle on the lobe of the left ear. Grandfils heard me out, thought over at length what I'd said, then shook his head slowly.

"In a general way," he said, "I know of a dozen men like that who come to me. The minor touches you've given me are things I never noticed about any of them. I'm not a trained observer and you are. Isn't there something else you can tell me about him? Something you've perhaps inadvertently overlooked?"

It hardly seemed likely but I thought back anyway. I said, "The rest of his clothing was a little unusual. That might mean something to you."

"Try me."

I described the clothing. By the time I was down to where the dead man hadn't been wearing socks, Grandfils had lost interest. He said coldly, "The man was obviously some tramp. None of my people would be seen on the street in such condition. The coat was stolen and the man deserved what happened to him. Frayed slacks! Heavens!"

I said, "Not much in his pockets, but I might as well tell you that too. A dark blue necktie with a Marshall Field label, a pair of gold-plated tweezers, several transparent envelopes about the size of a postage stamp, a pocket comb and some change..."

My voice began to run down. A. Cullinham Grandfils had his mouth open again, but this time there was the light of recognition in his eyes. He said crisply, "The coat was a gray flannel, Mr. Pine?"

"Yeah?"

"Carlton weave?"

"Hunh?"

"Never mind. You wouldn't know that. Quite new?"

"I thought so."

He bent across the desk to move a key on an intercom. "Harry," he snapped into the box. "That gray flannel lounge suit we made for Amos Spain. Was it sent out?"

"A week already," the box said promptly. "Maybe ten days, even. You want I should check exactly?"

"Never mind." Grandfils flipped back the key and leaned into the leather chair and went on tapping his knuckles with the knife. "Those tweezers and envelopes did it, sir. He's an enthusiastic stamp collector. Less than a month ago I saw him sitting in the outer room lifting stamps delicately with those tweezers and putting them in such envelopes while waiting for a fitting."

"Amos Spain is his name?"

"It is."

"He fits the description I gave?"

"Physically, exactly. But not the frayed slacks and dirty shirt. Amos Spain wouldn't be found dead in such clothes."

"You want to bet?"

"...Oh. Of course. I simply can't understand it!"

"How about an address on Spain, Mr. Grandfils?"

He dug a silver-trimmed leather notebook out of a desk drawer and looked inside. "8789 South Shore Drive. Apartment 3C. It doesn't show a telephone, although I'm confident he has one."

"Married?"

He dropped the book back in the drawer and closed it with his foot. "We don't inquire into the private lives of our people, Mr. Pine. It seems to me Mrs. Spain is dead, although I may be wrong. I do know Amos Spain is reasonably wealthy and, I think, retired."

I took down the address and got up and put on my coat and said, "Thanks for your help, Mr. Grandfils." He nodded and I opened the door. As I started out, he said:

"You really should do something about your suits, Mr. Pine."

I looked back at him sitting there like one of those old Michelin tire ads. "How much," I said, "would you charge me for one?"

"I think we could do something quite nice for you at three hundred."

"For that price," I said, "I would expect two pairs of pants."

His chin began to bob and he made a sound like roosters fighting. He was laughing. I closed the door in the middle of it and went on down the hall.

5

The address on South Shore Drive was a long low yellow-brick apartment building of three floors and an English basement. A few cars were parked along a wide sweep of concrete running past the several entrances, and I angled the Plymouth into an open spot almost directly across from 8789.

The rain got in a few licks at me before I could reach the door. Inside was a small neat foyer, complete with bright brass mail boxes and an inner door. The card on the box for 3C showed the name Amos Spain.

I pressed the right button and after a longish moment a woman's voice came down the tube. "Yes?"

That jarred me a little. I hadn't actually expected an answer. I said, "Mrs. Spain?"

"This is Mrs. Monroe," the voice said. "Mr. Spain's daughter. Are you from the post office?"

"Afraid not. I'm an officer, Mrs. Monroe. Want to talk to you."

"An officer? Why, I don't believe...What about?"

"Not from down here, Mrs. Monroe. Ring the buzzer."

"I'll do no such thing! How do I know you're a policeman? For all I know you could be a–a–"

"On a day like this? Don't be silly."

There was some silence and then the lock began to stutter. I went through and on up carpeted steps to the third floor. Halfway along a wide cheerful hallway was a partially open door and a woman in a flowered housecoat looking out at me.

She was under thirty but not very far under. She had wicked eyes. Her hair was reddish brown and there was a lot of it. Her skin was flawless, her cheekbones high, her mouth an insolent curve. She was long and slender in the legs, small in the waist, high in the breasts. She was dynamite.

I was being stared at in a coolly impersonal way. "A policeman you said. I'm fascinated. What is it you want?"

I said, "Do I get invited in or do we entertain the neighbors?"

Her eyes wavered and she bit her lip. She started to look back over her shoulder, thought better of it, then said, "Oh, very well. If you'll be brief."

She stepped back and I followed her across a tiny reception hall and on into an immense living room, with a dinette at one end and the open door to a kitchen beyond that. The living room was paneled, with beautiful leather chairs, a chester-field, lamps with drum shades, a loaded pipe rack, a Governor. Winthrop secretary, a fireplace with a gas log. Not neat, not even overly clean, but the right place for a man who puts comfort ahead of everything else.

I dropped my coat on hassock and sat down on one of the leather chairs. Her lips hardened. "Don't get too comfortable," she said icily. "I was about to leave when you rang."

"It's a little chilly out for a housecoat," I said.

Her jaw hardened. "Just who do you think you are, busting in here and making smart remarks? You say you're a cop. As far as manners go, I believe it. Now I think I'd like to see some real proof"

I shrugged. "No proof, Mrs. Monroe. I said officer, not policeman. A private detective can be called an officer without stretching too far."

"Private–" Her teeth snapped shut and she swallowed almost convulsively. Her face seemed a little pale now but I could have imagined that. "What do you want?" she almost whispered.

"Where's Amos Spain?" I said.

"My . . . father?"

"Uh–huh."

". . . I don't know. He went out early this morning."

"He say where?"

"No." Whatever had shocked her was passing. "Tom and I were still sleeping when he went out."

"Tom?"

"My husband."

"Where's he?"

"Still asleep. We got in late. Why do you want to know where my father is?"

I said, "I think it would be a good idea if you sat down, Mrs.

Monroe. I'm afraid I've brought some bad news."

She didn't move. Her eyes went on watching me. They were a little wild now and not at all wicked. She wet her lips and said, "I haven't the slightest idea what you're talking about. Bad news about what?"

"About your father. He's dead, Mrs. Monroe. Murdered."

"I don't believe it," she said quickly. Almost too quickly.

"He's been identified. Not much chance for a mistake."

She turned away abruptly and walked stiffly over to a lamp table and took a cigarette from a green cloisonné box. Her hand holding the match wavered noticeably but nothing showed in her face. She blew out a long streamer of smoke and came back and perched carelessly on an arm of the couch across from me. The housecoat slipped open slightly, letting me see most of the inner curve of a freshly powdered thigh. I managed to keep from chewing a hole in the rug.

"There's been some mistake, Mr. Pine. Dad never had an enemy in the world. What do you suggest I do?"

I thought back to be sure. Then I was sure. I said, "The body's probably at the morgue by this time and already autopsied. Might be a good idea to send your husband over. Save you from a pretty unpleasant job."

"Of course. I'll wake him right away and tell him about it. You've been very kind. I'm sorry if I was rude."

She hit me with a smile that jarred my back teeth and stood up to let me know the interview was over and I could run along home now and dream about her thigh.

I slid off the chair and picked up my hat and coat. While putting them on I moved over to the row of windows and looked down into the courtyard. Nobody in sight. Not in this weather. Rain blurred the glass and formed widening puddles in thin brown grass that was beginning to turn green.

I turned and said, "I'll be running along, Mrs. Monroe," and took four quick steps and reached for the bedroom door.

There was nothing wrong with her reflexes, I'll say that for her. A silken rustle and the flash of flowered cloth and she was standing between me and the door. We stood there like that, breathing at each other, our faces inches apart. She was lovely and she smelled good and the housecoat was cut plenty low.

And her face was as hard as four anvils.

"I must have made a mistake," I said. "I was looking for the hall door."

"Only two doors," she said between her teeth. "Two doors in the entire apartment. Not counting the bathroom. One that lets you out and one to the bedroom. And you picked the wrong one. Go on. Get out of here before I forget you're not a cop."

On my way out I left the inner door downstairs unlocked. In case.

6

The rain went on and on. I sat there listening to it and wondering if Noah had felt this way along about the thirty-ninth day. Smoke from my fourth cigarette eddied and swirled in the damp air through the no-draft vent.

The Plymouth was still parked across from 8789, and I was in it, knowing suddenly who had killed Amos Spain and why Spain had been wearing what he wore and why he wasn't wearing what he hadn't worn. It was knowledge built piece by piece on what I had seen and heard from the moment I walked in and found the body on the couch. It was the kind of knowledge you can get a conviction with–if you have that one key piece.

The key piece was what I didn't have.

Now and then a car came into the wide driveway and stopped at one of the entrances to let somebody out or to pick somebody up. None of them was for the rat hole to which I was glued. A delivery truck dropped off a dinette set a couple of doors down and I couldn't have cared less.

I lighted another cigarette and crossed my legs the other way and thought about hunting up a telephone and calling Lund and telling him to come out and get the knife artist and sweat that key piece out in the open. Only I didn't want it that way. This was one I wanted to wrap up myself. It had been my office and my couch and almost my client, and I was the one the cops had tromped on. Not that the tromping had amounted to much. But even a small amount of police displeasure is not what you list under assets.

Another twenty minutes floated by. They would still be up there in that apartment wearing a path in the rug. Waiting, sweating blood, hanging on desperately, risking the chance that I had known more than I let on and was already out yelling for the cops.

I would have loved to know what they were waiting for.

When the break did come I almost missed it. An ancient Ford with a pleated front fender wheezed into the curb. A hatless young man in a rained-on gray uniform got out to look at the number over the entrance to 8789. He had a damp-looking cigarette pasted to one corner of his mouth and a white envelope in his left hand. The local post office dropping off a piece of registered mail.

And then I remembered Mrs. Monroe's first question.

I slapped open the glove compartment and got out my gun and shoved it under the band of my trousers while I was reaching for the door. I crossed the roadway at a gallop and barged into the foyer just as the messenger took a not too clean thumb off the button for 3C. I made a point of getting out my keys to keep him from thinking Willie Sutton was loose again.

He never even knew I was in town. He said, "Postoffice; registered letter," into the tube and the buzzer was clattering before he had the last word out. He went through and on up the steps without a backward glance.

The door was off the latch, the way I had left it earlier. By the time the door to 3C opened, I was a few feet away staring vaguely at the closed door to 3B and trying to look like somebody's cousin from Medicine Hat. The uniformed man said, "Amos Spain?" and a deeper voice said, "I'm Mr. Spain," and a signature was written and a long envelope changed hands.

Before the door could close I was over there. I said, "It's me again."

He was a narrow-chested number with a long sallow face, beady eyes, a thin nose that leaned slightly to starboard, and a chin that had given up the struggle. Hair like black moss covered a narrow head. This would be Tom Monroe, the husband.

Terror and anger and indecision were having a field day with his expression. His long neck jerked and his sagging jaw wobbled. He clutched the edge of the door, wanting to slam it but not quite daring to. The silence weighed a ton.

All this was lost on the messenger. He took back his pencil and went off down the hall, his only worry the number of hours until payday. I leaned a hand against the thin chest in front of me and pushed hard enough to get us both into the room. I shut the door with my heel, said, "I'll take that," and yanked the letter out of his paralyzed fingers. It had sealing wax along the flap and enough stamps pasted on the front to pay the national debt.

Across the room the girl in the flowered housecoat was reaching a hand under a couch pillow. I took several long steps and stiff-armed the small of her back and she sat down hard on the floor. I put my empty hand under the pillow and found a snub-nosed Smith & Wesson .32, all chambers filled and dark red nail polish on the sight. I held it loosely along my leg and said, "Well, here we are," in a sprightly voice.

Monroe hadn't moved. He stared at me sullenly, fear still flicker ing in his small nervous eyes. The girl climbed painfully to her feet, not looking at either of us, and dropped down on the edge of a leather chair and put her face in her hands.

The man's restless eyes darted from me to the girl and back to me again. A pale tongue dabbed furtively at lips so narrow they hardly existed. He said hoarsely, "Just what the hell's the bright idea busting in here and grabbing what don't belong to you?"

I flapped the envelope loosely next to my ear. "You mean this? Not yours either, buster."

"It belongs to my father-in-law. I simply signed for it."

"Oh, knock it off," I said wearily. "You went way out of your league on this caper, Tom. You should have known murder isn't for grifters with simple minds."

A sound that was half wail, half sob filtered through the girl's fingers. The man said absently, "Shut up, Cora." His eyes skittered over my face. "Murder? Who's talking about murder? You the one who shoved in here a while ago and told Cora about Amos Spain?"

"I wasn't telling her a thing," I said. "She knew it long before. You told her."

"You might like to try proving that," he said.

"You bet," I said. I put the gun on the couch arm and looked at the envelope. Yesterday's postmark, mailed from New York City. Addressed in a spidery handwriting, with the return address reading: "B. Jones, General Delivery, Radio City Station, New York, N. Y." I ripped open the flap and shook out the contents. A plain sheet of bond paper wrapped around three odd-looking stamps. One was circular with a pale rose background and black letters. The other two were square, one orange and one blue, with the same crude reproduction of Queen Victoria on both. All three wouldn't have carried a postcard across the street.

Monroe was staring at the stamps and chewing his lip. He looked physically ill. The girl was watching me now, her fingers picking at the edge of the housecoat, her face white and drawn and filled with silent fury.

I said, "It would almost have to be stamps. I should have guessed as much two hours ago. How much are they worth?"

"How would I know?" Monroe said sulkily. "They weren't sent to me. I never saw them before."

I slid the stamps back into the envelope and put the envelope in my pocket. "You'd know, brother. If you'd kept a better eye on Amos Spain you might even have gotten away with the whole thing."

"You've got nothing on us. Why don't you just shove off?"

"I've got everything on you," I said. "Not that I deserve any credit.

The Army mule could have done the job. I can give you the State Attorney's case right now."

I picked up the gun and swung it lightly between a thumb and finger and sat on the couch arm. Rain beat against the windows in a muted murmur. From the kitchen came the lurch and whine of the refrigerator motor.

"Somebody named B. Jones," I said, "gets hold of some rare stamps. Illegally. Jones knows there are collectors around who will buy stolen stamps. Amos Spain is such a collector. A deal is made by phone or letter and the stamps are mailed to Spain. In some way you two find out about it. After the stamps are in the mail, perhaps. No point in trying to get them away from Uncle Sam; but there's another way. So the two of you show up here early this morning and force your way in on old Amos, who is still in bed. You tie him up a little, let's say, and gag him, leave him on the bed and come out here in the living room to wait for the postman with the stamps.

"But Amos isn't giving up. He gets loose, dresses and goes down the fire escape. He can't be sure when you're going to open the door and look in on him, so he puts on just enough clothes to keep from being pinched for indecent exposure. That's why he wasn't wearing socks, and why his clothes were mismatched.

"But by the time he's going down the fire escape, you look in. No Amos, and the window is open. You look out, spot him running away without topcoat or hat, and out you go after him. Tackling him on the street wouldn't do at all; your only hope is to nail him in some lonely spot and knock him off. How does it sound so far, neighbor?"

"Like a lot of words," Monroe growled.

"Words," I said, "are man's best friend. They get you fed, married, buried. Shall I tell you some more about words?"

"Go to hell."

I put down the gun and lit a cigarette and smiled. "Like I told you," I said, "you've got a simple mind. But I was telling you a story. I wouldn't want to stop now, so let's get back to Amos. You see, Amos had a big problem at this stage of the game. He couldn't go to the boys in blue and tell them about you and Cora, here. Doing that could bring out the business about the stamps and get him nailed for receiving stolen property. He had to get the two of you thrown out of his apartment before the envelope showed up.

"How to do it?" Hire a strong-arm boy who won't ask questions. Where do you find a strong-arm boy on a moment's notice? The phone book's got half a column of them. Private detectives. Not the big agencies; they might ask too many questions, But one of the smaller outfits might need the business bad enough to do it Amos's way. At least it's worth trying.

"So Amos gets my address out of the phone book, the nearest one to him, and comes up to hire me. He has no idea you're following him, which means he's not too careful about keeping out in the open where nothing can happen to him. He comes up to my office and I'm not in yet. He sits down to wait. You walk in and leave a switch knife in him. But that's only part of your job. You've got to fix it so there'll be a delay in identifying him–enough of a delay, at least, to keep the cops away from here until the mailman comes and goes. Lifting his papers may slow things down, but you want more than that. Being a crook, you make a habit of carrying around phony identification cards. You substitute these for his own. Lift whatever cash Amos had on him, slip out quick and come back here. Right so far?"

The fear had gone out of Monroe's eyes and there was the first faint signs of a smirk to his thin bloodless lips. He said airily, "If this is your idea of a way to kill a rainy afternoon, don't let me stop you. Mind if I sit down?"

"I don't care if you fall down," I said. "There's a little more and then we can all sit around and discuss the election until the cops arrive. A little more, like Cora knowing my name the first time I was here this afternoon. I hadn't told her my name, you see; just that I was a private dick. But to Cora there was only one private detective–the one whose office you'd killed Amos Spain in."

Behind me a quiet voice said, "Raise your hands."

I froze. Cora Monroe's .32 was on the couch arm, no more than six inches from my hand. I could have grabbed for it–and I could get buried for grabbing. I didn't grab.

A slender stoop-shouldered man in his early forties came padding on stocking feet in front of me. He had bushy graying hair, along intelligent face and a capable-looking hand containing a nickel-plated Banker's Special revolver. The quiet voice belonged to him and he used it again, saying, "I won't tell you again. Put up your hands."

I put them up.

He went on pointing the gun at me while knocking the .32 off the couch with a single sweep of his other hand. It bounced along the carpet and hit the wall. He said gently, "I'll take those stamps."

"You will indeed," I said. My tongue felt as stiff as Murphy, the night he fell off the streetcar. "I guess I should have looked in the bedroom after all. I guess I thought two people should be able to lift three little stamps."

"The stamps, Mr. Pine." The voice wasn't as gentle this time.

"Sure," I said. I put my hand in my coat and took out the envelope. I did it nice and slow, showing him I was eager to please. I held it out and he reached for it and I slammed my shoe down on his stocking foot with every pound I could spare.

He screamed like a woman and the gun went off. Behind me a lamp base came apart. I threw a punch, hard, and the gray-haired man threw his hands one way and the gun the other and melted into the rug without a sound.

Monroe was crouched near the side wall, the girl's .32 in his hand and madness in his eyes. While he was still bringing up the gun I jerked the Police Special from under the band of my trousers and fired.

He took a week to fall down. He put his hands together high on his chest and coughed a broken cough and took three wavering steps before he hit the floor with his face and died.

Cora Monroe hadn't moved from the leather chair. She sat stiff as an ice floe off Greenland, her face blank with shock, her nails sunk in her palms. I felt a little sorry for her. I bent down and picked the envelope off the floor and shoved it deep into a side pocket. I said, "How much were they worth, Cora?"

Only the rain answered.

I found the telephone and said what had to be said. Then I came back and sat down to wait.

It was ten minutes before I heard the first wail of distant sirens.

WILLIAM CAMPBELL GAULT
(b.1910)

Stolen Star
(Joe Puma)

I got into the mess late and not by choice. The local papers were giving it more ink than the Japanese surrender and I can imagine it was front page news from coast to coast.

Laura Spain had been kidnapped. Laura wasn't the youngest star in the business but she still had her figure and enough looks to pull all the men over thirty into any theatre showing one of her pictures.

The thing had a bad odor right from the first ransom note. The local police are skeptical about publicity shenanigans; a jewel robbery out here is almost certain to be no more than that. But kidnapping?

It didn't seem logical that a sane citizen would go to that extreme for free ink, but then a sane citizen wouldn't fill a swimming pool with champagne for a party, either. And Laura had done that a few years back.

So the F.B.I. wasn't called in, but on the other hand, the local gendarmes didn't treat it as a gag, either. And woe to Laura, the D.A. was quoted as saying, if she had dreamed it up. She would be prosecuted to the limit.

The thing that made it seem fishy was the modest ransom the kidnappers were asking–twenty-five thousand–and the fact that Laura had been snatched right at her house and had evidently taken a rather complete wardrobe along for the trip. There were three dogs in that house, Dobermans, and two servants, one of them an ex-pug.

Well, it made good bar talk and there were as many opinions as there were people to voice them and nobody was shy about voicing them. It became a farce, almost, and kidnapping is nothing that should ever seem humorous. There are too many crack-pots who get ideas from the kind of spread this thing was getting.

Forty-eight hours after the first news break on the story, Hal Slotkin came to see me. Hal is a divorce and criminal lawyer, about as rich a barrister as this town knows and we had never done business before. And he didn't *send* for me; he *came*. He must have been worried.

"Mr. Puma," he said, "I have known of you for some time, by reputation."

"And I you, sir," I said. "Won't you sit down?"

He took a good look around my inexpensive office before sitting down, as though he'd been searching all the places that might hold a tape recorder.

He sat down and sighed. "Your ethics, I've been told, are unassailable and your courage immense." He was a short, fat man, and his language seemed a little pompous. But I was impressed, nevertheless. In a jungle, he had become king of his tribe.

"My ethics have been stretched from time to time," I told him, "and my courage ebbs with the years." Gawd, now he had me doing it.

He rubbed his fat neck with a pudgy hand and stared wearily at the bamboo shades behind me. Match-stick bamboo, Sears-Roebuck, five bucks a panel. He said, "It's been a hectic two days, hasn't it?"

"Not for me, sir," I said, "but as Miss Spain's attorney, I imagine you've had a busy time of it."

He nodded. "If I had it to do over, I'd have gone in for corporation law." He sighed. "Or probate work. I might have made a few dollars less, but I wouldn't be pampering my ulcers."

I didn't comment. I can never find the proper comment for the wailings of the wealthy. I tried to put some sympathy into my smile.

2

He said suddenly, "How would you like to earn a thousand dollars for two hours work?"

"It would depend upon the work, Mr. Slotkin," I answered.

"Can you guess?" he asked.

"Delivering the ransom money? I thought you'd lost contact with Miss Spain's abductors."

"We had. Until half an hour ago."

"Have you informed the police?"

He shook his head. "I was expressly warned not to."

I said, "Mr. Slotkin, acting as an intermediary in a kidnapping case would not only lose me my license, it could put me in jail."

"Not if you're employed by Hal Slotkin," he said, "not in this town. I could include the Chief in our confidence, if you want me to."

"That puts a different light on it," I said, "but not the whole light. How do I know I don't get bumped? If Miss Spain is dead, the boys who killed her aren't going to hesitate about wiping out one poor private investigator. I might be able to finger them later, they'll realize."

"All right," he said, "I'll make it two thousand dollars." He shrugged. "It's not my money."

I chuckled. "You figure I wouldn't commit suicide for one thousand, but I might for two?"

"Somebody has to deliver the money," he said matter of factly. "If you don't want the job, I'll go elsewhere. If I'm forced to, by your refusal, I'm sure you'll keep this a secret until Miss Spain is safely home again."

"Of course," I said. "Give me a moment to think."

He nodded, and leaned his head back in the chair and closed his eyes. His face was pale and his neck flabby. He didn't look at all like the courtroom tiger of his legend.

I thought about the brake job I needed and the new tires, about the five hundred I owed the bank and the new suit I should have.

"Well?" Slotkin asked.

"Okay," I said. "What's the deal?"

"It's in the desert," he said, "near Canyon Springs. Flat country and they can see if they're being crossed, I suppose. By the way, don't get cute with this, will you? Just deliver the money and pick up Miss Spain."

"Of course," I said. "Why would I get cute with it?"

"I don't know. Maybe to grab a headline. That seems to be a disease in this town." He handed me a slip of paper. "Here's the address." He paused. "Don't deliver the money until you see Miss Spain, *alive.*"

"And if she's not in sight, I still get paid."

"You get paid right now," he said, and took out a checkbook.

He must have been sure they were going to deliver the girl or he never would have paid in advance. Which smelled a little, but it also led me to think I wasn't likely to run into any violence. And yet,

I couldn't believe if the whole thing was a hoax that a man of Hal Slotkin's eminence would be a party to it. He had a reputation as a tricky operator but all his tricks were well within the law.

Any reservations still in my mind were quieted by the slip of paper he handed me next. *Pay to Joseph Puma, two thousand and no/hundredths.*

He told me I was to pick up the ransom money at his office in an hour. It would be a fairly bulky package as they were all small, old bills.

The bank was still open; I went over immediately and deposited the check. And then I phoned Tommy Verch. Slotkin hadn't stipulated I was to go alone, and Tommy could use the business. His office is in Venice and he doesn't get the carriage trade I do.

I said, "How much would you charge me to ride along on a little job tonight?"

"What kind of job?"

"I hate to say over the phone, but it includes delivering some money."

A pause, and then, "A headline story, Joe?"

"That's right."

Another pause, and he said, "You know my rate."

"Yes, but I'm getting two thousand dollars for the job."

"I'll up my rate then. Two hundred all right?"

"That's more than fair."

"You want me armed, Joe."

"Absolutely," I said.

"I'm on the way over," he said.

When he got there, I said, "Maybe you'd better eat, first. I'm going over to pick up the money. When I get back, I'll park in the small lot behind the building here. You climb into the back while I go over to eat. That way, if I'm being watched, nobody will see you get into the back of my car. Once out in the desert, you can sit up again. Clear?"

He nodded. "You looking forward to trouble, Joe?"

I shrugged.

He said, "I'll go and eat." He went out, a stocky man of medium height with a flat and broken nose looking out of place in his thin face.

3

Slotkin wasn't at his office when I got there; I was handed a package by one of his young associates. I'd brought a small grip and I carried the money with me when I went to eat.

The afternoon *Mirror-News* informed me that there were no new developments in the Laura Spain kidnapping. The earlier police skepticism, according to this piece, had disappeared and anxiety about Miss Spain's safety was growing. If nothing new developed by tomorrow morning, the F.B.I. would be called in.

One of Laura's former husbands was quoted as saying he still thought it was a gag. But that could be just the bitter words of a poor loser.

When I got back to the car, I could see that the blanket had been pulled down from the back seat. I got in, started the engine, and asked, "All safe, Tommy?"

"Roll her," he said. "It's the first job I've had in a month."

I rolled her, heading for the Hollywood Freeway which would take me to Highway 99, which would take me to the desert and Canyon Springs. The place I was supposed to make rendezvous was on this end of town. The road leading to it would be visible for miles, and I was supposed to arrive before dusk, *just* before dusk.

Delivery would be made as close to dark as possible, so they could use its cover to get away. But light was necessary for them to be able to watch all the roads. It would require good timing, and I hoped my tires would hold up. A flat would throw the timetable off.

Once off the freeway, I watched to see if any cars persisted in following, slowing and speeding in turn. When I was sure we were unwatched, I told Tommy, "You can sit up now, boy, for a while."

He grunted and came up off the floor, relaxing in the back seat. He said, "Where's the pick-up?"

"Right outside of Canyon Springs."

"Good pick for a desert spot," he commented. "They can go four directions from there. How do you figure it, Joe, a gag?"

I shrugged.

He leaned back. "Well, as long as I'm getting only ten per cent of the money, I hope I only get ten per cent of the lead they throw."

"It was your price, Tommy," I reminded him.

"I know, I know—and very welcome. So starving to death is no easier than being shot. Onward, moneybags."

I looked into the rear-view mirror to see if his comment had meaning, but he looked content and peaceful, his eyes closed. Well, if things went right, I could slip him an extra fifty.

I was doing a steady sixty-five, but traffic went blasting past me. The safest driving in the world should be in the desert, with its unlimited vision, but it had a horrible safety record.

I hit Beaumont at about the proper time and turned south a few miles beyond, down a less traveled road. Nobody followed. To the west and north, the mountains were beginning to show shadows, beginning to take the glare out of the sun.

In the back seat, Tommy stirred, took his .38 from its shoulder holster and spun the cylinder. He replaced it and said, "Maybe I'd better get out of sight again; this road is kind of deserted."

I nodded agreement.

He said, "If you want, you can give me a signal when you see the girl. I guess I could show after that, couldn't I?"

"Why antagonize them?" I asked. "If I need you to come up gunning, I'll holler."

A silence, and then he said, "You nervous, Joe?" I nodded.

"Me, too," he said, and went down below the blanket on the floor.

We were coming to a crossroad now, a two lane asphalt strip that led east to Canyon Springs. A State Patrol car was parked here and I was glad Slotkin had paid me in advance. Because it could easily be a stake-out or a road block. And if it was, the kidnappers would certainly be alerted.

The car was off the road, over on the sand, and both troopers were sitting in the front seat. I slowed, waiting for a signal from them, but none came. I turned east on the crossroad, keeping a careful eye on them in the mirror.

Their car didn't move. I said to Tommy, "Just passed a parked State Patrol car. It might be a coincidence."

"I get my dough either way, remember," he said.

I didn't answer him. Ahead, the first buildings of Canyon Springs were coming into view. Far behind, the police car was still immobile. The purple dusk of the desert was shrouding the harshness of the landscape and one early star was visible in the east. We went over a culvert spanning a dry arroyo and ahead I could see a solitary cactus with a sign pointing toward some buildings to the right. *Air-conditioned cabins*, the sign read.

4

There was a man standing next to the sign and he wore the red jockey cap I was to look for. I slowed, stopped and opened the door on the right side.

"I've brought the money," I called.

He was a thin man, fairly tall, with a long, narrow face and grayish stubble in the black of his week-old beard. He came over and climbed into the seat beside me.

"Up past the cabins," he said.

"There's a State Patrol car back at the turn-off," I told him. "What gives? I don't want to get into trouble."

"It's okay," he said. "Past those cabins, to the end of this road."

The cabins looked deserted as we went by, old-fashioned adobe buildings that probably couldn't compete today. Up the road, now, I could see a solitary, larger cabin, with two cars parked around in back of it. I couldn't read the license plates from here and by the time I got to the cabin, the cars would be out of sight behind it. Well, I wasn't being paid to learn anything.

I said, "I see Miss Spain before you see a nickel. I see her alive."

"Hell, yes." He chuckled. "But what if I told you to go to hell. What could you do?"

"I couldn't tell you right now. I'd have to decide about that when the situation came up."

"You armed, shamus?"

"Always," I told him. "Even on a publicity romp like this, I figured a gun wouldn't hurt."

"I'll take the gun," he said.

"No, you won't. The money's right there, all is small and dirty bills, like you wanted it. When Miss Spain comes with me, that goes with you, and everybody wins."

"The broad isn't here," he said. "Do you think we're crazy? When you hand over the money, we send out the signal and she'll be released. How crazy do you think we are, sitting here in the middle of nowhere with a broad that hot?"

"All right, then, I'll wait until I get word from her attorney that she's safe. Then you get your money. Okay?"

"Hand over your gun," he said, "and stop yacking, or I'll put a hole in you. Get to it, man."

"Okay, Tommy," I said clearly, "Now would be the time."

The man next to me whirled around—just in time for Tommy to

press the barrel of his .38 in the middle of the man's forehead. Tommy said lightly, "Don't even blink, skinny. Don't even breathe heavy. I'm nervous."

The man stared and some obscene muttering came from his thin throat. I had my gun out, now, and I relieved him of the one in his hand. It was an army .45.

I asked, "Is Miss Spain here, or isn't she?"

"No," he said hoarsely. "Look, maybe I talked too rough. She's going to be all right, believe me. And there are plenty of guns in that house; so don't think you can get away with anything."

"I came to deliver the money," I said. "I came in good faith. Now listen carefully–I'm going to let you go up to the house. One of your men can come with me to Canyon Springs, one unarmed man. I'll phone Slotkin from there. The second he hears Miss Spain is released, I'll hand this man this satchel containing twenty-five grand. I'll even give him your gun back. My job was to deliver the money, not you hoodlums, and I'll go through with it. Is that clear?"

His eyes went from me to Tommy and back. "There's Tommy guns in that house; there's sawed-offs."

"And there's you," I pointed out, "sitting here courting a hole in your head. It's a hell of a situation, isn't it? Just because there's no honor among thieves."

Silence all around for a few moments.

Then I said, "I'm going to turn around so we're headed the way we came. I'm going to let you go–unarmed–up to the house and deliver my message. If you're not back in three minutes, with your hands well away from your body and empty, I'm going to go into town and get a lot of law out here." I nodded toward the door on his side. "Get out and go to the house, *now*."

He got out and went trotting toward the house as I turned around and pulled a couple hundred feet down the road from the place. Tommy stayed in the back, watching everything through the rear window.

Without turning around, he said, "Gutty, aren't you? Do you believe him about the fire-power they're holding?"

"No. The rube sees too many movies. Old ones, on TV. Tommy guns, cripes!"

"Maybe, maybe," Tommy said doubtfully. "I still don't like it, Joe."

"It's rougher than I figured," I admitted. "I think I'll give you an extra fifty, Tommy."

"That's white of you," he said. "I wish that bastard would come out again."

"Maybe they'll send somebody else."

"Hell, no. We've already seen *him*; the fewer we can identify later, the better for them."

Tommy was right; in another minute, the same thin and grizzled gent came down the road toward the car, his hands well out from his body. I could see no sign of life from the cabin behind him.

He got in as I opened the door. He said, "I'll go with you. If you try to cross us, those guys will kill you, sure as you're alive this second. They've got your license number and they can find out who you are."

"I'll save them the trouble," I said. "My name's Joe Puma and my office is in Beverly Hills. If everything is okay, the money in that satchel is yours. You can take it out and check it right now."

"Don't worry," he said. "It's there. Or Slotkin will get what I promised you."

"It's my satchel," I said. "When I get the word, you'll get the money, but not the satchel."

He shook his head. "A cheap private eye, worrying about his crummy suitcase. What are you getting for the job, Sherlock, twenty bucks?"

"Fifteen and the gas," I said, "and twenty cents for every shell I have to use."

Tommy said, "Keep a civil tongue in your head, skinny. I don't like lippy hoodlums."

"Go easy on him, Tommy," I said. "The old gent's scared. He's lost his moxie and he's scared."

5

Next to me, the thin man smiled and I thought there was some anticipation in it.

I was back on the two lane asphalt road that led into Canyon Springs and to our right was a modern motel and restaurant with a mammoth parking lot.

I said, "You stay in the car with skinny, Tommy. I'll take the money inside until I get in touch with Slotkin."

"Right," he said. "Park out of view of the highway, though."

I pulled around behind the ell the motel office made and took the ignition keys. It was almost dark now, and all the motel lights were on. I didn't want to bring Skinny into that bright office; just seeing him would make any desk clerk in the country phone for the police.

I had the unlisted number Slotkin had given me and I phoned him collect. He must have been sitting on the phone; he answered immediately.

"Puma," I said. "What's the word?"

"Give them the money," he said. "She phoned me two minutes ago from a drugstore in Hollywood."

I told him okay and hung up. I went out to the car wondering how the police would like this; she had been free and in a public place *before* her abductors had taken delivery of the ransom.

I had an urge to keep the money and turn Skinny over to the local law, but I'd been paid to do a job, not act like a citizen. I wasn't proud of myself as I opened the door of the car.

"Well?" Skinny said.

"The money's yours, boy. Should I leave you here with it, or do you want me to take you back to the house?"

He smiled in the reflected light from the motel office. "Leave me here; you've been followed all the way."

I gave him the money, keeping the grip. He tucked the package under his arm and said, "Drive careful, shamus. There's a lot of desert ahead of you." He climbed out of the car and headed across the parking lot toward the road.

We watched him approach a three-year-old Mercury on the other side of the street. Tommy said, "Ornery bastard, isn't he? I don't think he likes me."

"We'll never see him again, probably," I said. "Want to climb up in front now?"

He shook his head. "I think I'll try to get some shut-eye. I'll curl up on the back seat."

The Merc was still parked at the curb when we headed out of town. It was dark now, and traffic would be light until we got back on 99. The state patrol car was no longer at the corner.

Easy money, I thought. *But if the police swallowed this as a legitimate snatch, I'd have to believe that Slotkin owned the Department. It smelled every way but right. So, what was all that to me? I was paid.*

It continued to bother me.

A half mile past the cut-off, I saw the lights beginning to move up from behind. For no reason at all, I said to Tommy, "What do you think Skinny meant about all that desert ahead of us?"

"Just words," Tommy said drowsily. "He had to sound tough."

"A car turned off back there from the Canyon Springs road," I told him, "and he's catching up. Be careful."

He sat up. "Why? Look, we paid, didn't we?"

"Sure. Both of us could put the finger on Skinny. I don't think he meant it that way. You were along, which he didn't expect. And he's one of those professional tough guys, remember."

Behind, the car's headlights grew closer. Another car was coming from the opposite direction, and I told Tommy, "See if you can get a look at that car behind in the headlights of this one coming. See if it's the Merc."

A few seconds after the car went past, Tommy said, "It's the Merc, all right, Joe. I'm going to lower this back window."

"Don't," I said. "If they shoot at us, it's better to have the windows closed. And don't you do a thing, Tommy, unless they shoot at us."

"I won't shoot unless they do," he said. "But I'm going to lower this window."

"As they start to go by," I said, "I'll hit the brakes. Be ready for that."

The lights grew and now they darted back at me from the rear-vision mirror. I waited until they began to swing out to pass before taking my foot off the accelerator.

I misjudged the speed of the car behind; it was next to us before I could touch the brake. I heard the blast of the sawed-off, and then another shot, but heard no answering shot from the rear seat before the third shot hit my shoulder.

The shock of it made me twist the wheel and the Plymouth went screaming to the right. I almost caught it in time. I would have caught it in time if the arroyo hadn't been there, and the thick concrete wall of the culvert.

The right front wheel caught that wall and we went careening end for end across the road and into the ditch on the other side. The last thing I remember was flying through the air, free of the car, my shoes lost from the impact. *The sand could be soft*, I thought; *the softness of the sand could keep me alive.*

6

I didn't regain consciousness for two days. When I did, I was in a Los angeles hospital and one of Hal Slotkin's associates was sitting in a chair next to the bed.

He smiled at me. "Felling better?"

"I don't know. I don't know how I felt before. Where am I?"

He told me.

I said, "How about Tommy?"

"Tommy? Do you mean Mr. Verch?"

"That's right."

"He's–dead. He died before the car turned over."

I closed my eyes.

The young lawyer said, "Don't worry about a thing, now. All your bills here will be taken care of, and your car's almost all rebuilt by now. That'll be taken care of, too."

"Why?" I asked.

He smiled at me. "Why not?"

"I've a lot of regard from Mr. Slotkin," I said, "but I never for a second confused him with Santa Claus."

The young man smiled knowingly. "Maybe it's not his money. That needn't concern you. Your concern is to get well. Don't worry, now."

It concerned me. Tommy Verch was dead and that had to concern me. But I didn't argue with the young man. I never argue with anyone *before* they pick up the tab.

I'd been brought here from the hospital in Riverside, and I could guess I'd been brought here so it would be convenient for one of the Slotkin young men to remain at my bedside. I relaxed and tried to regain my strength and forget Tommy Verch. The nurse brought me all the papers; that was another expense somebody was shouldering, a private nurse. I had good coverage in all the papers.

And then, as frosting for this expensive cake, I was honored with a visit from Laura Spain. Complete with five photographers, seven reporters, two publicity men and a Slotkin representative. If she was coming to my bedroom as reward, you'd think the least she could have done would be to come alone.

She was certainly a beauty, and her advertised charm was not over-rated. If she had come alone, I think I might have forgotten Tommy Verch.

The morning after her visit, I walked out of the hospital with a Slotkin man, and my car, looking better than ever, was ready for me on the hospital parking lot.

There, the Slotkin man said, "If we can be of any further service, don't hesitate to call on us, will you?"

"I won't," I promised. "Maybe you could give me the West Side Station, huh, for my very own?"

He frowned. "I don't understand, Mr. Puma."

"Yes, you do," I said. "We all understand each other. Take care of yourself, young fellow." I patted his shoulder and got into my car.

He was still standing there, watching me, when I turned into the traffic heading west.

At my office, I checked the week's accumulation of mail and wrote checks for a couple of bills I'd owed for some time. I was writing a letter to my aunt when the phone rang.

It was Hal Slotkin. He said, "I've heard that you're not happy. Would you mind telling me why?"

"This phoney kidnapping rankles in my small soul, I guess, Mr. Slotkin."

"What makes you think it was phoney?"

I gave him all the reasons. The too early release of Miss Spain, Skinny not counting the ransom money and not being worried about the State Police and his not even looking in the back of my car before climbing into it."

"So, maybe he was an amateur."

"Maybe. An *armed* amateur, and a real tough, cool one. I don't think he was an amateur thug, though this may be been his first snatch."

Silence, and then, "Well, I only represented a client. I'm not involved personally. You believe that, don't you?"

"I think I do, Mr. Slotkin."

"So what difference does it make? You got paid and you're not the police."

"In a way, I'm a policeman. I'm licensed by the state. But that isn't important. Mr. Slotkin, the important thing is that a man is dead."

"And that's important to you?"

"Yes. Isn't it to you?"

"It used to be," he said. "I suppose it should be." He sighed. "Well, I guess we have nothing else to say to each other, Mr. Puma."

'I guess not," I said. "Thanks for the business, anyway."

I hung up and sat there, angry for no reason I could isolate, burning. I was no knight; I didn't even have a horse. Why should I burn?"

I phoned Slotkin again, intending to ask for Miss Spain's unlisted phone number. His office girl said Mr. Slotkin was not in and Miss Spain's phone number was never given out to anybody.

Well, I knew where she lived; I went down and climbed into the rebuilt Plymouth.

7

The house was low and probably the architect had tried to give the impression of a sprawling, western ranch house. What emerged from the drawing board was a low, red, shake-roofed home for a Hollywood star who entertains informally.

The maid asked, "Did you have an appointment, Mr. Puma?"

"No, I didn't. I'm just returning Miss Spain's recent visit to me. She didn't have an appointment that day, either."

The maid frowned. "Are you the–the–"

I nodded.

"One moment, please," she said.

In a few minutes, she came back to say, "This way, please."

It was a sunny day; Laura Spain was pool-side in a bikini. Her body belonged to a younger woman, her face was slick with oil.

"Mr. Puma," she said, smiling. "How pleasant."

I stood at the pool's edge and looked down. "Is this where you had the champagne?"

"That's right. Though the story was exaggerated. We only filled it to a depth of three feet."

She was sprawled on a pad; I sat down next to her and said, "I've been thinking about this kidnapping, Miss Spain. The whole business smells of fraudulence."

Her young-old face stiffened. "Really? And why?"

I gave her the same reasons I'd given Slotkin.

She reached out and took a package of cigarettes from a low stand nearby. I lighted one for her. She looked at the water, and said, "I've no idea what the standard operating procedure for kidnappers is. You might be right about their lack of experience. But even if it was a monstrous publicity stunt, why are you concerned?"

I said wearily, "It's a sad civilization that makes me keep explaining that *a man is dead.*"

"Millions are," she said reasonably. "Thousands of men die every day, I imagine."

"Not violently in my car, working for me," I answered. "Don't you feel any responsibility for his death?"

She nodded. "Some. What can I do about it?"

"You could tell me who the men were you hired. I'm sure you didn't expect them to extend their services to murder."

Her face was stone. "I didn't hire any men. It was not a publicity stunt, Mr. Puma. And even if it were, would you actually expect me to implicate myself publicly?"

I took a deep breath. "No. But I had to take the chance." I stood up. "Well, I'll know the man if I ever see him again. And when I do, I'll know how to work the rest of it out of him."

She shook her head. "You sound absurd. You sound like Dick

Tracy. This is 1957, Mr. Puma."

"Of course," I said. "I wasn't thinking of violence. I was thinking of a deal with him."

Her eyes were blank. "You were thinking of violence. That's your kind of operation, I would bet."

I said, "If you're still in touch with them, warn them to stay out of my way."

"I don't know them," she said lightly, "but from what I've seen of them, I can imagine you don't frighten them much. Good day, Mr. Puma. Don't hurry back."

I went out, fully aware that I had learned nothing, but I *had* left a message. And if she were involved and did forward the message, I wouldn't have to look for her abductors. They would find me.

Which was emotional thinking, adolescent thinking, but I wanted to meet Skinny again so bad I could taste it. And Miss Spain had set a wave of violence into motion with her fraudulent stunt; she couldn't escape the responsibility of that. Which absolved me from any concern for what justice might do to her career.

I had a pair of names and two addresses still to check. The first one I went to was a four unit apartment building on Olympic in Santa Monica. This was the address of Laura Spain's second husband. He was an assembler at Douglas Aircraft now, and the manager of the apartment told me he wouldn't be home until 4:30.

Her first husband was undoubtedly also working, but the place he worked wasn't far from here. He was a car salesman for a Venice Ford agency.

He was a big man, almost as big as I am. He wore an Italian silk suit and a hand-painted tie and an air of complete disillusionment. His face was florid, the face of a heavy drinker, but still handsome in a completely virile way. He was on the used-car lot when I drove up.

He said, "I'm due for a coffee break in five minutes. Hang around and we'll go across the street."

Five minutes later, in a crummy greasy spoon on the busiest street in Venice, Jack Dugan, Laura Spain's first husband, gave me the story of that early romance.

She was nineteen when he met her, a refugee from Oklahoma, a thin, tough, very attractive girl whose innocence was at least five years behind her even then.

I said, "I never got that picture from the fan magazines; I had the feeling she came out here clean as new snow and won a beauty contest."

He smiled. "Sure. Not that I'm rapping Laura, understand. She still sends me a buck now and then for auld lang syne and she's bailed me out of some monumental drunks. There's nothing cheap about the girl. It's just that she has this damned driving urge to stay way up there on top."

"We built a civilization on it," I said. "Knowing her, would she have the guts to pull a phoney kidnapping for ink?"

"For publicity," he said, "Laura would arrange to have Eisenhower kidnapped." He shook his head musingly. "And you know, she might get away with it, at that?"

"What was her family like? Did you ever meet them?"

He had. And he told me about them and I wondered why a man who still got a "buck now and then" should go into such detail to hand a private operative a case against his benefactor.

And because I wondered, I asked him. "Why give me all this? How can you benefit from giving me all this?"

"Benefit?" he said. "Look, I'm a drunk and a pitch man and a lot of things that aren't exactly admirable. But I'm still a human being, right?"

"Right," I agreed. "So–?"

"So a man is dead, isn't he? Isn't it important that a man is dead?"

"It always has been to me," I assured him, "but I was beginning to think I was old-fashioned." I smiled at him. "I'll pay for the coffee. And when I need a new car. I'll head this way."

"Do that," he said. "I might even rob you less than the others. Who knows?"

I left him, and went back to the office. I didn't think there was any need to look up Laura's second husband. She'd been young when she had married her first; he had her true story, the story she'd told him before she realized that in Hollywood, backgrounds are invented, not lived. He could be quite possibly the only man in the town who had her true story. Until now.

8

I sat in the quiet office and nothing happened. I went out for lunch and came back and the place was still quiet. I had a hunch now who the skinny man was, and maybe if I sent the hunch out on the grapevine, it would stir up some action. But if I sent it out on the grapevine in this town, the damage would be done but Tommy Verch's killer might still be free.

That blast from the sawed-off had been meant for both of us. He hadn't shot out of pique; he was a pro. He had hoped to kill us both because either of us could identify him.

And if he was a pro, would he come here, into this best-policed town in America, Beverly Hills? There were a number of areas in the county where the police protection is not exceptional; this town would be dangerous hunting grounds. Of course, he didn't lack guts. He had a number of lacks, undoubtedly, but I was sure guts wasn't one.

Why should I sit there burning; solvent, fat and alive? What was Tommy Verch to me? A colleague, a brave and humorous man who lived as honestly as he could in a trade where that wasn't always good business. A man who had been forced to risk his life for two hundred dollars and lose. Tommy Verch was important.

I hadn't put my car on the lot; I'd left it parked right in front of this building so anyone who was interested could see I was in the office. I could have gone home and waited, but I had carpeting on the floor at home and that's harder to clean than the asphalt tile of the office.

The door opened and the hand in my lap stirred. It was Doctor Graves, the young dentist from the office next door. He said, "How about some golf tomorrow afternoon?"

"Maybe. I'll let you know tonight."

"What's the matter?" he asked. "You look nervous."

"I'm still not right. Had a concussion, you know. And a badly strained back."

"Maybe we'd better forget the golf, huh? The back–"

"I'll let you know tonight," I repeated. "How's everything otherwise?"

He yawned. "All right. I'm solvent. I sure get sick of looking into people's dirty mouths, though."

"I get sick of looking into their dirty souls," I said.

He chuckled. "Oi, a philosopher. Two hundred and twenty pounds of thought. You look like you're waiting for Armageddon." He winked. "Call me at home, Joe. Good luck, kid."

I waved my left hand. My right was still in my lap.

My mom had always insisted I had prescience, but my mom had a lot of peasant superstitions, I knew I was more certain than I had a reasonable right to that I'd see Skinny again. I thought I knew who he might be, and if I didn't see him, I would go to the police for help in looking up a picture of the man.

But analyzing what Jack Dugan had told me, it seemed logical that Skinny could be the man I thought the was.

In the windows behind me, the sun was now low and soon the

mountains to the west would cut it from view. On the street below, the going-home traffic was noisy.

I heard footsteps in the hall going past; soon the offices on this second floor would all be vacant, all but this one. I lighted a cigarette and turned on the light. I stood by the window a few seconds, looking down at the traffic, and then came back to sit behind the desk again.

How much did Slotkin know? He was no dummy. Of course, in his business, it wasn't always wise to know too much. His job was leading people through the intricacies of the law, not writing biographies of them. He did his job well and was satisfied to stay within the limits of it.

If Tommy Verch hadn't died, I would have been happy to stay within the limits of my job, which had been to deliver some money.

It was dark now and the light overhead wasn't very bright. From the direction of Wilshire, I heard a siren and a clang of a fire truck.

From the hall outside, I thought I heard a pair of footsteps coming up the stairs. They grew louder, and they were very deliberate footsteps and now they were coming down the hall. I sat where I was.

The door opened slowly and quietly. If I hadn't been facing it, I wouldn't have heard it.

Skinny stood there. Shaved and wearing a cheap dark suit and no longer sporting the red jockey cap. His hair was black, not sprinkled with gray as his beard had been. He had one hand in his jacket pocket.

He came in and closed the door quietly behind him. "You made it, eh? he said. "Tough guy. The way that heap went end for end, I figured you for a goner."

"I'm tough," I said. "Peasant stock. Where's your brother, waiting in the lot behind here, with the engine running?"

His face showed a momentary bewilderment. "Brother–? How'd you guess–" The face went blank again. "You don't know nothing."

"I know there was an Okie named Lorna Spangler who had a couple of no-good brothers," I said evenly. "A couple of punks who thought Dillinger and Nelson and that breed were the greatest Americans of their generation. The girl grew up to become Laura Spain. What happened to the boys? We could find out, I suppose. We could check."

He said nothing, studying me carefully.

'And when Lorna, or Laura, wanted somebody she could trust to pull a cheap publicity stunt, what better pair than these no-good brothers? Man, you've aged a hell of a lot more than she did, haven't you? You didn't take care of yourself like she did, bumming around, knocking off the kind of cheap jobs you're big enough for."

"You're trying to make me hate you, eh?" He looked at me with his head cocked to one side. "Why, shamus? What's your beef? You got paid."

"I'm sick of explaining it," I answered. "Why are you here now?"

"Unfinished business," he said. "You're not much, but you're still a finger."

"I was hoping you'd come," I said. "This thing was getting too personal. It was building into an obsession."

He smiled. "And here I am." In his pocket, his hand moved and came out holding the big .45.

In my lap, my hand moved and my .38 came up swiftly and I just kept pulling the trigger, even though the first shot caught him in the neck.

It's an asphalt tile floor.

His brother was waiting, the engine running, when the local gendarmes put the arm on him. They'd been watching the office, but not looking for a '57 Olds. When they heard the shots, soon after Skinny had come up, they realized the man in the Olds could be their man.

If Skinny hadn't shaved, he would have been picked up downstairs because then they would have seen the gray in his beard. His hair was so black, it didn't seem logical to the men below that his beard could have any gray in it. His hair was touched up, we learned later.

I was glad Skinny had shaved. because though he was guilty of murder and would have been eligible for the gas chamber, there was a possibility he might have avoided that.

There are an awful lot of smart criminal lawyers in this town.

Just look in the phone book.

ROSS MACDONALD
(1915-1983)

Guilt-Edged Blonde
(Lew Archer)

A man was waiting for me at the gate at the edge of the runway. He didn't look like the man I expected to meet. He wore a stained tan wind-breaker, baggy slacks, a hat as squashed and dubious as his face. He must have been forty years old, to judge by the gray in his hair and the lines around his eyes. His eyes were dark and evasive, moving here and there as if to avoid getting hurt. He had been hurt often and badly, I guessed.

"You Archer?"

I said I was. I offered him my hand. He didn't know what to do with it. He regarded it suspiciously, as if I was planning to try a Judo hold on him. He kept his hands in the pockets of his windbreaker.

"I'm Harry Nemo." His voice was a grudging whine. It cost him an effort to give his name away. "My brother told me to come and pick you up. You ready to go?"

"As soon as I get my luggage."

I collected my overnight bag at the counter in the empty waiting room. The bag was very heavy for its size. It contained, besides a toothbrush and spare linen, two guns and the ammunition for them. A .38 special for sudden work, and a .32 automatic as a spare.

Harry Nemo took me outside to his car. It was a new seven-passenger custom job, as long and black as death. The windshield and side windows were very thick, and they had the yellowish tinge of bullet-proof glass.

"Are you expecting to be shot at?"

"Not me." His smile was dismal. "This is Nick's car."

"Why didn't Nick come himself?"

He looked around the deserted field. The plane I had arrived on was a flashing speck in the sky above the red sun. The only human being in sight was the operator in the control tower. But Nemo leaned towards me in the seat, and spoke in a whisper:

"Nick's a scared pigeon. He's scared to leave the house. Ever since this morning."

"What happened this morning?"

"Didn't he tell you? You talked to him on the phone."

"He didn't say very much. He told me he wanted to hire a bodyguard for six days, until his boat sails. He didn't tell me why."

"They're gunning for him, that's why. He went to the beach this morning. He has a private beach along the back of his ranch, and he went down there by himself for his morning dip. Somebody took a shot at him from the top of the bluff. Five or six shots. He was in the water, see, with no gun handy. He told me the slugs were splashing around him like hailstones. He ducked and swam under water out to sea. Lucky for him he's a good swimmer, or he wouldn't of got away. It's no wonder he's scared. It means they caught up with him, see."

"Who are 'they,' or is that a family secret?"

Nemo turned from the wheel to peer into my face. His breath was sour, his look incredulous. "Christ, don't you know who Nick is? Didn't he tell you?"

"He's a lemon-grower, isn't he?"

"He is now."

"What did he used to be?"

The bitter beaten face closed on itself. "I oughtn't to be flapping at the mouth. He can tell you himself if he wants to."

Two hundred horses yanked us away from the curb. I rode with my heavy leather bag on my knees. Nemo drove as if driving was the one thing in life he enjoyed, rapt in silent communion with the engine. It whisked us along the highway, then down a gradual incline between geometrically planted lemon groves. The sunset sea glimmered red at the foot of the slope.

Before we reached it, we turned off the blacktop into a private lane which ran like a straight hair-parting between the dark green trees. Straight for half a mile or more to a low house in a clearing.

The house was flat-roofed, made of concrete and fieldstone, with an attached garage. All of its windows were blinded with heavy draperies. It was surrounded with well-kept shrubbery and lawn, the lawn with a ten-foot wire fence surmounted by barbed wire.

Nemo stopped in front of the closed and padlocked gate, and honked the horn. There was no response. He honked the horn again.

About halfway between the house and the gate, a crawling thing came out of the shrubbery. It was a man, moving very slowly on hands and knees. His head hung down almost to the ground. One side of his head was bright red, as if he had fallen in paint. He left a jagged red trail in the gravel of the driveway.

Harry Nemo said, "Nick!" He scrambled out of the car. "What happened, Nick?"

The crawling man lifted his heavy head and looked at us. Cumbrously, he rose to his feet. He came forward with his legs spraddled and loose, like a huge infant learning to walk. He breathed loudly and horribly, looking at us with a dreadful hopefulness. Then he died on his feet, still walking. I saw the change in his face before it struck the gravel.

Harry Nemo went over the fence like a weary monkey, snagging his slacks on the barbed wire. He knelt beside his brother and turned him over and palmed his chest. He stood up shaking his head.

I had my bag unzipped and my hand on the revolver. I went to the gate. "Open up, Harry."

Harry was saying, "They got him," over and over. He crossed himself several times. "The dirty bastards."

"Open up," I said.

He found a key ring in the dead man's pocket and opened the padlocked gate. Our dragging footsteps crunched the gravel. I looked down at the specks of gravel in Nicky Nemo's eyes, the bullet hole in the temple.

"Who got him, Harry?"

"I dunno. Fats Jordan, or Artie Castola, or Faronese. It must have been one of them."

"The Purple Gang."

"You called it. Nicky was their treasurer back in the thirties. He was the one that didn't get into the papers. He handled the payoff, see. When the heat went on and the gang got busted up, he had some money in a safe deposit box. He was the only one that got away."

"How much money?"

"Nicky never told me. All I know, he come out here before the war and bought a thousand acres of lemon land. It took them fifteen years to catch up with him. He always knew they were gonna, though. He knew it."

"Artie Castola got off the Rock last spring."

"You're telling me. That's when Nicky bought himself the bullet-proof car and put up the fence."

"Are they gunning for you?"

He looked around at the darkening groves and the sky. The sky was streaked with running red, as if the sun had died a violent death.

"I dunno," he answered nervously. "They got no reason to. I'm as clean as soap. I never been in the rackets. Not since I was young, anyway. The wife made me go straight, see?"

I said: "We better get into the house and call the police."

The front door was standing a few inches ajar. I could see at the edge that it was sheathed with quarter-inch steel plate. Harry put my thoughts into words.

"Why in hell would he go outside? He was safe as houses as long as he stayed inside."

"Did he live alone?"

"More or less alone."

"What does that mean?"

He pretended not to hear me, but I got some kind of an answer. Looking through the doorless arch into the living room, I saw a leopard-skin coat folded across the back of the chesterfield. There were redtipped cigarette butts mingled with chair butts in the ash trays.

"Nicky was married?"

"Not exactly."

"You know the woman?"

"Naw," But he was lying.

Somewhere behind the thick walls of the house, there was a creak of springs, a crashing bump, the broken roar of a cold engine, grinding of tires in gravel. I got to the door in time to see a cerise convertible hurtling down the driveway. The top was down, and a yellow-haired girl was small and intent at the wheel. She swerved around Nick's body and got through the gate somehow, with her tires screaming. I aimed at the right rear tire, and missed. Harry came up behind me. He pushed my gun-arm down before I could fire again. The convertible disappeared in the direction of the highway.

"Let her go," he said.

"Who is she?"

He thought about it, his slow brain clicking almost audibly. "I dunno. Some pig that Nicky picked up some place. Her name is Flossie or Florrie or something. She didn't shoot him, if that's what you're worried about."

"You know her pretty well, do you?"

"The hell I do. I don't mess with Nicky's dames." He tried to work up a rage to go with the strong words, but he didn't have the makings. The best he could produce was petulance: "Listen, mister, why should you hang around? The guy that hired you is dead."

"I haven't been paid, for one thing."

"I'll fix that."

He trotted across the lawn to the body and came back with an alligator billfold. It was thick with money.

"How much?"

"A hundred will do it."

He handed me a hundred-dollar bill. "Now how about you amscray, bud, before the law gets here?"

"I need transportation."

"Take Nicky's car. He won't be using it. You can park it at the airport and leave the key with the agent."

"I can, eh?"

"Sure, I'm telling you can."

"Aren't you getting a little free with your brother's property?"

"It's my property now, bud." A bright thought struck him, disorganizing his face. "Incidentally, how would you like to get off my land?"

"I'm staying, Harry. I like this place. I always say it's people that make a place."

The gun was still in my hand. He looked down at it.

"Get on the telephone, Harry. Call the police."

"Who do you think you are, ordering me around? I took my last order from anybody, see?" He glanced over his shoulder at the dark and shapeless object on the gravel, and spat venomously.

"I'm a citizen, working for Nicky. Not for you."

He changed his tune very suddenly. "How much to go to work for me?"

"Depends on the line of work."

He manipulated the alligator wallet. "Here's another hundred. If you got to hang around, keep the lip buttoned down about the dame, eh? Is it a deal?"

I didn't answer, but I took the money. I put it in a separate pocket by itself. Harry telephoned the county sheriff.

He emptied the ash trays before the sheriff's men arrived, and stuffed the leopardskin coat into the woodbox. I sat and watched him.

We spent the next two hours with loud-mouthed deputies. They were angry with the dead man for having the kind of past that attracted bullets. They were angry with Harry for being his brother. They were secretly angry with themselves for being inexperienced and incompetent. They didn't even uncover the leopardskin coat.

Harry Nemo left for the courthouse first. I waited for him to leave, and followed him home, on foot.

Where a leaning palm tree reared its ragged head above the pavements, there was a court lined with jerry-built frame cottages. Harry turned up the walk between them and entered the first cottage. Light flashed on his face from inside. I heard a woman's voice say something to him. Then light and sound were cut off by the closing door.

An old gabled house with boarded-up windows stood opposite the court. I crossed the street and settled down in the shadows of its veranda to watch Harry Nemo's cottage. Three cigarettes later, a tall woman in a dark hat and a light coat came out of the cottage and walked briskly to the corner and out of sight. Two cigarettes after that, she reappeared at the corner on my side of the street, still walking briskly. I noticed that she had a large straw handbag under her arm. Her face long and stony under the streetlight.

Leaving the street, she marched up the broken sidewalk to the veranda where I was leaning against the shadowed wall. The stairs groaned under her decisive footsteps. I put my hand on the gun in my pocket, and waited. With the rigid assurance of a WAC corporal marching at the head of her platoon, she crossed the veranda to me, a thin high-shouldered silhouette against the light from the corner. Her hand was in her straw bag, and the end of the bag was pointed at my stomach. Her shadowed face was a gleam of eyes, a glint of teeth.

"I wouldn't try it if I were you," she said. "I have a gun here, and the safety is off, and I know how to shoot it, mister."

"Congratulations."

"I'm not joking." Her deep contralto rose a notch. "Rapid fire used to be my specialty. So you better take your hands out of your pockets."

I showed her my hands, empty. Moving very quickly, she relieved my pocket of the weight of my gun, and frisked me for other weapons.

"Who are you, mister?" she said as she stepped back. "You can't be Arturo Castola, you're not old enough."

"Are you a policewoman?"

"I'll ask the questions. What are you doing here?"

"Waiting for a friend."

"You're a liar. You've been watching my house for an hour and a half. I tabbed you through the window."

"So you went and bought yourself a gun?"

"I did. You followed Harry home. I'm Mrs. Nemo, and I want to know why."

"Harry's the friend I'm waiting for."

"You're a double liar. Harry's afraid of you. You're no friend of his."

"That depends on Harry. I'm a detective."

She snorted. "Very likely. Where's your buzzer?"

"I'm a private detective," I said. "I have identification in my wallet."

"Show me. And don't try any tricks."

I produced my photostat. She held it up to the light from the street, and handed it back to me. "So you're a detective. You better do something about your tailing technique. It's obvious."

"I didn't know I was dealing with a cop."

"I was a cop," she said. "Not any more."

"Then give me back my .38. It cost me seventy dollars."

"First tell me, what's your interest in my husband? Who hired you?"

"Nick, your brother-in-law. He called me in Los Angeles today, said he needed a bodyguard for a week. Didn't Harry tell you?"

She didn't answer.

"By the time I got to Nick, he didn't need a bodyguard, or anything. But I thought I'd stick around and see what I could find out about his death. He was a client, after all."

"You should pick your clients more carefully."

"What about picking brothers-in-law?"

She took her head stiffly. The hair that escaped from under her hat was almost white. "I'm not responsible for Nick or anything about him. Harry is my responsibility. I met him in line of duty and I straightened him out, understand? I tore him loose from Detroit and the rackets, and I brought him out here. I couldn't cut him off from his brother entirely. But he hasn't been in trouble since I married him. Not once."

"Until now."

"Harry isn't in trouble now."

"Not yet. Not officially."

"What do you mean?"

"Give me my gun, and put yours down. I can't talk into iron."

She hesitated, a grim and anxious woman under pressure. I wondered what quirk of fate or psychology had married her to a hood, and decided it must have been love. Only love would send a woman across a dark street to face down an unknown gunman. Mrs. Nemo was horse-faced and aging and not pretty, but she had courage.

She handed me my gun. Its butt was soothing to the palm of my hand. I dropped in into my pocket. A gang of Negro boys at loose ends went by in the street, hooting and whistling purposelessly.

She leaned towards me, almost as tall as I was. Her voice was a low sibilance forced between her teeth:

"Harry had nothing to do with his brother's death. You're crazy if you think so."

"What makes you so sure, Mrs. Nemo?"

"Harry couldn't, that's all. I know Harry, I can read him like a book. Even if he had the guts, which he hasn't, he wouldn't dare to think of killing Nick. Nick was his older brother, understand, the successful one in the family." Her voice rasped contemptuously. "In spite of everything I could do or say, Harry worshiped Nick right up to the end."

"Those brotherly feelings sometimes cut two ways. And Harry had a lot to gain."

"Not a cent. Nothing."

"He's Nick's heir, isn't he?"

"Not as long as he stays married to me. I wouldn't let him touch a cent of Nick Nemo's filthy money. Is that clear?"

"It's clear to me. But is it clear to Harry?"

"I made it clear to him, many times. Anyway, this is ridiculous. Harry wouldn't lay a finger on that precious brother of his."

"Maybe he didn't do it himself. He could have had it done for him. I know he's covering for somebody."

"Who?"

"A blonde girl left the house after we arrived. She got away in a cherry-colored convertible. Harry recognized her."

"A cherry-colored convertible?"

"Yes. Does that mean something to you?"

"No. Nothing in particular. She must have been one of Nick's girls. He always had girls."

"Why would Harry cover for her?"

"What do you mean, cover for her?"

"She left a leopardskin coat behind. Harry hid it, and paid me not to tell the police."

"Harry did that?"

"Unless I'm having delusions."

"Maybe you are at that. If you think that Harry paid that girl to shoot Nick, or had anything—"

"I know. Don't say it. I'm crazy."

Mrs. Nemo laid a thin hand on my arm. "Anyway, lay off Harry. Please. I have a hard enough time handling him as it is. He's worse than my first husband. The first one was a drunk, believe it or not." She glanced at the lighted cottage across the street, and I saw one half of her bitter smile. "I wonder what makes a woman go for the lame ducks the way I did.'

"I wouldn't know, Mrs. Nemo. Okay, I lay off Harry."

But I had no intention of laying off Harry. When she went back to her cottage, I walked around three-quarters of the block and took up a new position in the doorway of a dry-cleaning establishment. This time I didn't smoke. I didn't even move, except to look at my watch from time to time.

Around eleven o'clock, the lights went out behind the blinds in the Nemo cottage. Shortly before midnight the front door opened and Harry slipped out. He looked up and down the street and began to walk. He passed within six feet of my dark doorway, hustling along in a kind of furtive shuffle.

Working very cautiously, at a distance, I tailed him downtown. He disappeared into the lighted cavern of an all night garage. He came out of the garage a few minutes later, driving a prewar Chevrolet.

My money also talked to the attendant. I drew a prewar Buick which would still do seventy-five. I proved that it would, as soon as I hit the highway. I reached the entrance to Nick Nemo's private lane in time to see Harry's lights approaching the dark ranch house.

I cut my lights and parked at the roadside a hundred yards below the entrance to the lane, and facing it. The Chevrolet reappeared in a few minutes. Harry was still alone in the front seat. I followed it blind as far as the highway before I risked my lights. Then down the highway to the edge of town.

In the middle of the motel and drive-in district he turned off onto a side road and in under a neon sign which spelled out TRAILER COURT across the darkness. The trailers stood along the bank of a dry creek. The Chevrolet stopped in front of one of them, which had a light in the window. Harry got out with a spotted bundle under his arm. He knocked on the door of the trailer.

I u-turned at the next corner and put in more waiting time. The Chevrolet rolled out under the neon sign and turned towards the highway. I let it go.

Leaving my car, I walked along the creek bank to the lighted trailer. The windows were curtained. The cerise convertible was parked on its far side. I tapped on the aluminum door.

"Harry?" a girl's voice said. "Is that you, Harry?"

I muttered something indistinguishable. The door opened, and the yellow-haired girl looked out. She was very young, but her round blue eyes were heavy and sick with hangover, or remorse. She had on a nylon slip, nothing else.

"What is this?"

She tried to shut the door. I held it open.

"Get away from here. Leave me alone. I'll scream."

"All right. Scream."

She opened her mouth. No sound came out. She closed her mouth again. It was small fleshy and defiant. "Who are you? Law?"

"Close enough. I'm coming in."

"Come in then, damn you. I got nothing to hide."

"I can see that."

I brushed in past her. There were dead Martinis on her breath. The little room was a jumble of feminine clothes, silk and cashmere and tweed and gossamer nylon, some of them flung on the floor, others hung up to dry. The leopardskin coat lay on the bunk bed, staring with innumerable bold eyes. She picked it up and covered her shoulders with it. Unconsciously, her nervous hands began to pick the wood-chips out of the fur. I said:

"Harry did you a favor, didn't he?"

"Maybe he did."

"Have you been doing any favors for Harry?"

"Such as?"

"Such as knocking off his brother."

"You're way off the beam, mister. I was very fond of Uncle Nick."

"Why run out on the killing then?"

"I panicked," she said. "It would happen to any girl. I was asleep when he got it, see, passed out if you want the truth. I heard the gun go off. It woke me up, but it took me quite a while to bring myself to and sober up enough to put my clothes on. By the time I made it to the bedroom window, Harry was back, with some guy." She peered into my face. "Were you the guy?"

I nodded.

"I thought so. I thought you were the law at the time. I saw Nick lying there in the driveway, all bloody, and I put two and two together and got trouble. Bad trouble for me, unless I got out. So I got out. It wasn't nice to do, after what Nick meant to me, but it was the only sensible thing. I got my career to think of."

"What career is that?"

"Modeling. Acting. Uncle Nick was gonna send me to school."

"Unless you talk, you'll finish your education at Corona. Who shot Nick?"

A thin edge of terror entered her voice. 'I don't know, I tell you. I was passed out in the bedroom. I didn't see nothing."

"Why did Harry bring you your coat?"

"He didn't want me to get involved. He's my father, after all."

"Harry Nemo is your father?"

"Yes."

"You'll have to do better than that. What's your name?"

"Jeannine. Jeannine Larue."

"Why isn't your name Nemo if Harry is your father? Why do you call him Harry?"

"He's my stepfather, I mean."

"Sure," I said. "And Nick was really your uncle, and you were having a family reunion with him."

"He wasn't any blood relation to me. I always called him uncle, though."

"If Harry's your father, why don't you live with him?"

"I used to. Honest. This is the truth I'm telling you. I had to get out on account of the old lady. The old lady hates my guts. She's a real creep, a square. She can't stand for a girl to have any fun. Just because my old man was a rummy–"

"What's your idea of fun, Jeannine?"

She shook her feathercut hair at me. It exhaled a heavy perfume which was worth its weight in blood. She bared one pearly shoulder and smiled an artificial hustler's smile. "What's yours? Maybe we can get together."

"You mean the way you got together with Nick?"

"You're prettier than him."

"I'm also smarter, I hope. Is Harry really your stepfather?"

"Ask him if you don't believe me. Ask him. He lives in a place on Tule Street–I don't remember the number."

"I know where he lives."

But Harry wasn't at home. I knocked on the door of the frame cottage and got no answer. I turned the knob and found that the door was unlocked. There was a light behind it. The other cottages in the court were dark. It was long past midnight, and the street was deserted. I went into the cottage, preceded by my gun.

A ceiling bulb glared down on sparse and threadbare furniture, a time-eaten rug. Besides the living room, the house contained a cubbyhole of a bedroom and a closet kitchenette. Everything in the poverty-stricken place was pathetically clean. There were moral mottoes on the walls, and one picture. It was a photograph of a tow-headed girls in a teen-age party dress. Jeannine, before she learned that a pretty face and a sleek body could buy her the things she wanted. The things she thought she wanted.

For some reason, I felt sick. I went outside. Somewhere out of sight, an old car-engine muttered. Its muttering grew on the night. Harry Nemo's rented Chevrolet turned the corner under the streetlight. Its front wheels were weaving. One of the wheels climbed the curb in front of the cottage. The Chevrolet came to a halt at a drunken angle.

I crossed the sidewalk and opened the car door. Harry was at the wheel, clinging to it desperately as if he needed it to hold him up. His chest was bloody. His mouth was bright with blood. He spoke through it thickly:

"She got me."

"Who got you, Harry? Jeannine?"

"No. Not her. She was the reason for it, though. We had it coming."

Those were his final words. I caught his body as it fell sideways out of the seat. I laid it out on the sidewalk and left it for the cop on the beat to find.

I drove across town to the trailer court. Jeannine's trailer still had light in it, filtered through the curtains over the windows. I pushed the door open.

The girl was packing a suitcase on the bunk bed. She looked at me over her shoulder, and froze. Her blond head was cocked like a frightened bird's, hypnotized by my gun.

"Where are you off to, kid?"

"Out of this town. I'm getting out."

"You have some talking to do first."

She straightened up. "I told you all I know. You didn't believe me. What's the matter, didn't you get to see Harry?"

"I saw him. Harry's dead. Your whole family is dying like flies." She half-turned and sat down limply on the disordered bed. "Dead? You think I did it?"

"I think you know who did. Harry said before he died that you were the reason for it all."

"Me the reason for it?" Her eyes widened in false naivete, but there was thought behind them, quick and desperate thought. "You mean that Harry got killed on account of me?"

"Harry and Nick both. It was a woman who shot them."

"God," she said. The desperate thought behind her eyes cyrstallized into knowledge. Which I shared.

The aching silence was broken by a big diesel rolling by on the highway. She said above its roar:

"That crazy old bat. So *she* killed Nick."

"You're taking about your mother. Mrs. Nemo."

"Yeah."

"Did you see her shoot him?"

"No. I was blotto like I told you. But I saw her out there this week, keeping an eye on the house. She's always watched me like a hawk."

"Is that why you were getting out of town? Because you knew she killed Nick?"

"Maybe it was. I don't know. I wouldn't let myself think about it."

Her blue gaze shifted from my face to something behind me. I turned. Mrs. Nemo was in the doorway. She was hugging the straw bag to her thin chest.

Her right hand dove into the bag. I shot her in the right arm. She leaned against the doorframe and held her dangling arm with her left hand. Her face was granite in whose crevices her eyes were like live things caught.

The gun she dropped was a cheap .32 revolver, its nickel plating worn and corroded. I spun the cylinder. One shot had been fired from it.

"This accounts for Harry," I said. "You didn't shoot Nick with this gun, not at that distance."

"No." She was looking down at her dripping hand. "I used my old police gun on Nick Nemo. After I killed him, I threw the gun into the sea. I didn't know I'd have further use for a gun. I bought that little suicide gun tonight."

"To use on Harry?"

"To use on you. I thought you were on to me. I didn't know until you told me that Harry knew about Nick and Jeannine."

"Jeannine is your daughter by your first husband?"

"My only daughter." She said to the girl: "I did it for you, Jeannine. I've seen too much-the awful things that can happen."

The girl didn't answer. I said:

"I can understand why you shot Nick. But why did Harry have to die?"

"Nick paid him," she said. "Nick paid him for Jeannine. I found Harry in a bar an hour ago, and he admitted it. I hope I killed him."

"You killed him, Mrs. Nemo. What brought you here? Was Jeannine the third on your list?"

"No. No. She's my own girl. I came to tell her what I did for her. I wanted her to know."

She looked at the girl on the bed. Her eyes were terrible with pain and love. The girl said in a stunned voice:

"Mother. You're hurt. I'm sorry."

"Let's go, Mrs. Nemo," I said.

HENRY KANE
(b.1918)

Suicide is Scandalous
(Peter Chambers)

They sat across from me on the awkward side of the edge-burnt desk: two nice people, a lady and a gentleman, meek as the taste of water. The gentleman was straightaway across the shoulders and dapper, handsome even, in an iron-gray hairdo and a full florid face over a fetching disarray of artistic long loose collar. The lady was little and old, with a wispy smile and cream-white hair and a cockeyed hat in the middle of her head.

I smiled. Reassuringly.

The gentleman hawked in his throat.

The lady's wispy smile widened to sick embarrassed false-toothed grin. But it wasn't grin. It was grimace. It was the stiff spread of silent hysteria. It was a dentured smear of agony. It hung like mirth on a corpse with its lips writhed back.

Then the tears came. "The poor, poor girl..."

It gusted from her, while she bent her head, sobbing into her arm angled on the desk, the cockeyed hat quivering. I looked at the gentleman. The gentleman looked at me. I wondered about the sparkle alongside the spray of kerchief in the showpocket of his jacket. I stood up and I went around the desk to the windows and I looked out into the sunny street. I waited until she stopped crying.

"I'm sorry," she said. I came back and I sat down and I watched her dab at her face with a frail lace handkerchief. "I'm very sorry," she said.

I didn't say anything.

"I'm Mrs. Bentley."

"How do you do?"

"This is Mr. Zetz."

"Glad to know you." ·

He hawked, nodded.

She put the handkerchief away. "The Lieutenant sent us."

"What Lieutenant?"

"The man downtown. The Detective-lieutenant."

"Parker?"

"Yes, sir. Lieutenant Parker."

"A real policeman."

"A fine, good man."

"The best."

"He said this was where to throw it."

"I beg your pardon."

"That's what he said."

"Throw what?"

"My money. That is, if I insisted on throwing it away."

"I *beg* your pardon."

The smile came back, very tired among the faint wrinkles on her face, and it did something to you, no matter you're a cynical wise-guy private richard battened down behind a desk over which too much evil has spewed. It got to you, in a corner inside of you, like "Stardust" on strings in a sawdust saloon after a good many brandies. I grunted.

"How much?"

Her eyebrows peaked. "How much?"

"How much do you insist on throwing away?"

"Oh. He said you were expensive. He also said you were a crook—"

"Look, lady—"

"He was joking, of course. A thousand dollars, perhaps fifteen hundred..."

"Oh." Good-bye Stardust, because business is business, and you have got to have the pretzels for your beer. On the other side of the desk sits your sucker—always; they wouldn't be on the other side of that desk if they didn't need you—badly. Either you squeeze them, or they squeeze you: you learn that early. Always, on one side of the desk sits a sucker. Could be me.

"Two thousand," I said.

She brought up a vast pouch of handbag from off her knees and she took out a checkbook and she wrote a check. "Tell you the truth," she said, "the Lieutenant said you wouldn't handle it for less than five thousand."

So all right. So the sucker rode the good side of the desk. "Why?"

"Because I have recently inherited upwards of fifty thousand dollars."

Then she laughed, howlingly, stood up, holding the edge of the desk with white-knuckled fingers– and fainted away, dead. We got to her, Mr. Zetz and I, and we brought her to the couch and he rubbed her wrists while I went for water. "She's been through a lot," he said. "A helluva lot."

When she came to, she insisted upon going back to her chair. We arranged ourselves again, the three of us. She made a joke. "Put it over on you, didn't I, sir? You were too quick to drive your bargain. But if you help me, Mr. Chambers...I'll pay you the balance. Up to five thousand. As the Lieutenant suggested."

"Sho nuf," I said, real Southern. "Now what's this all about?"

"My daughter. Sally Bentley."

It had been in all of the papers, only a couple of days ago. A suicide in a doll-house on Park Avenue. It had been in all the papers, with pictures. It had been in all of the papers *because* of the pictures. Sally Bentley hadn't been half bad. In fact, from the pictures, Sally Bentley had been gorgeous.

"She didn't kill herself, Mr. Chambers."

"Uh-huh," I said, and I was fairly happy that I had garnered the two thousand. I wasn't ever going to get the balance. Mothers do not believe that daughters kill themselves. Never.

"She didn't?"

"No."

"How do you know?"

"She couldn't."

"Couldn't she?"

"You're smug, Mr. Chambers."

"Listen, lady. Please. It's a big city, New York. I've lived here all my life. A lot of people commit suicide. Every one of them had a mother, positively, but the mothers don't believe it. Not usually. They just don't ever do."

"She didn't, Mr. Chambers."

"All right. She didn't. Why didn't she?"

"Because I was with her the evening before. Saturday night. She is supposed to have shot herself at about eleven o'clock Sunday morning."

Maybe she had something. Most mothers who do not believe their daughters killed themselves at eleven o'clock on Sunday morning weren't in their company on the Saturday night previous. "She didn't kill herself," Mrs. Bentley said. "She had big plans. Look."

Up came the ponderous handbag. Out came an envelope. She handed it across. I opened it. It was a ticket for a one-way passage on the Queen to Southampton. "It's a ticket," I said, bright, "for passage three weeks from today."

"I brought it for her."

"When?"

Early Monday morning. Just before they got word to me."

"Where?"

"In Chicago."

"Why?"

"We live in a small town, Pierceville, near Chicago. On Saturday night, Sally was full of fun and full of large plans. She was to spend a few weeks with me, at home, and then off for a long vacation in Europe. She asked me to arrange for the ticket, to do it from Chicago, that she would pick it up from me when she came home. That was Saturday night. I left her at nine o'clock, an eager young lady, a vibrant happy person. She did not kill herself the next morning, Mr. Chambers. Not Sally."

She pointed a finger at me. Convincingly.

"How come they let you know, the police, on Monday?"

"I stayed with a sister of mine all day Sunday, slept over, then went for the ticket, and when I arrived at home, the telegram was waiting for me."

"Who's he?" I inquired. I meant Mr. Zetz.

"Mr. Zetz."

"Who is Mr. Zetz?"

"Michael Zetz."

"Michael Zetz," I said. "Not *Michael* Zetz. Not Michael Zetz, the author." Nobody said otherwise. I leaned over, and we shook hands. "Well," I said, "Michael Zetz, the whodunit boy. Mr. Zetz, I am one of your devout fans."

"Thank you."

"What do you know?" I said. "Michael Zetz."

Mrs. Bentley said, "The moment I received the wire—"

"Just a minute, please."

She flustered. "Yes, sir?"

"I don't get it."

"What, sir?"

"What's he doing here? Mr. Zetz. You grist?"

"Grist?"

"Grist for his mill? Is he picking up material?"

"Oh, no. The moment I received the wire, arrangements were made for me to fly to New York. The first person I went to see was Mr. Zetz. Mr. Zetz is a good friend, he was Sally's employer for a good many years. She was his secretary. Mr. Zetz took me to see Lieutenant Parker."

"Oh."

Zetz shrugged. "Unfortunate. I don't know what to make of it."

"Suicide?" I asked.

"Apparently. The police are firmly convinced of that. She left a note. I've seen it, the police showed it to us. It seems incontrovertible. Yet, in the light of what Mrs. Bentley tells us, it seems psychologically impossible."

"What were you doing in New York?" I asked her.

"It was a surprise. I came here for one day. To see my daughters."

"Daughters?" I said. "I mean. . .plural?"

"Yes. My other daughter, Delores. She sings at the Cafe Jenz. I spent the afternoon with her, and then I went to Sally's."

I came out from behind the desk and I marched for them, up and down the carpet, like I was practicing for a parade. I scraped the usual knuckle against the usual chin. "All right, what do you want me to do?"

"I want to find out what happened to my daughter."

"Why?"

"*Why?*"

"Why?"

"Because suicide is scandalous. That is why."

"What's murder?"

"I beg your pardon?"

"Murder. She either killed herself, Mrs. Bentley, or someone killed her. I'm asking. If suicide is scandalous, what's murder?"

"Murder, murder—"

"I mean—what is it? Why do people rake it up? You've told me what you've told the police, I'm sure. Is it that you want A Killer To Pay? Something like that. A perfectly competent cop tells you it's suicide. So you go over his head, or under it. . .See what I mean?"

She sobbed, violently, and Zetz, after one punitive glare, went to her, comforting. The thing in his showpocket flashed like sunshine on a drum-majorette.

I kissed off my conscience. Two thousand berries, paid in advance, for a job that would wind up in a statement that policemen know their business, especially when it's suicide—well, that was the way she wanted it. "Okay with me," I said. I stood up straight and pontifical. "I accept the case," I said. For two thousand berries, for nothing, I stand straight and pontifical and I deliver, "I accept the case," with baritone authority.

I shoved a sheet of paper at him. "I want names and addresses, please. Everybody's." Sure enough, the thing in the showpocket was a fountain pen and he did it for me in a thin backhand scrawl with everybody's name and everybody's address, including his own. "Remarkable," I said.

"What?"

"The pen. I've never seen anything like it."

He handed it to me. It had diamonds, one on top and one on bottom, each at least four carats, and in the middle it was all spun gold. "It was made for me," he said, "in Denmark. I have it many years. A gift from royalty. In appreciation of my work."

"Exquisite."

"Thank you."

Mrs. Bentley said: "There's more. I can tell you more—"

"Did you tell the cops?"

"Yes, I did."

"Then don't bother, Madam. No use working yourself up again. I'll do what I can. I'll let you know..."

I got them out of the office, finally, and I sat around and rattled the rocks in my head. I put her check away. I looked at addresses. Distastefully. Like a guy peering through a wrong pair of glasses. Sally had lived at Two Ninety Park and the old lady was staying at the Roosevelt and Zetz lived at Eight East Tenth and the sister, Delores, lived over on West Seventy-ninth.

Delores.

That's a nice name.

I got my hat, and I went to Delores.

Delores wasn't home.

I went downtown to Headquarters.

Detective-lieutenant Parker detected out of a barren third-floor office which he filled amply: Detective-lieutenant Louis Parker, a growl behind a screen of cigar smoke. He was black-haired and square-jawed and grittily genial with a dark rosy face and an expressive cigar amongst strong white teeth. He had a figure like a trimmed-down butter tub, dressed in fashion, and the wedges of stand-up cigars in the vest pocket were part of standard equipment, like blocks for the baby. He was quick as a very rapid cat, upstairs and downstairs; wise, intelligent, practical, incorruptible. So right away he said, "For how much did you do in the poor widow?"

"Widow? Nobody told me."

"How much?"

"Two thousand."

"Thievery."

"With more to come. If I do it her way."

"What's her way?"

"Murder . . . I suppose."

"Why?"

"Who's asking the questions?"

"Me. Right now."

"Oh."

"Why?"

"Because suicide is scandalous."

"*What?*"

"That's what she said."

"She's got a better reason."

"I'm listening, Lieutenant, with both my pretty ears."

He recited for me like Junior exposed to company with his arms stiff in the parlor. Without the curtsy. "I let her spend her money because she's looking for trouble. Understand? Trouble. With you, she'll find it. Plenty. Right where it hurts. In the pocketbook."

"Louis," I said, "please . . ."

"Don't start with the 'please' . . ." He put his feet up on the desk and he put new fire to the diminishing cigar. "She would like it to be murder. She would like it to be this other cookie. This Delores."

"Delores. It's a beautiful name."

"Wait you see the lollipop. You will forget about the name. You, especially. Guy vulnerable as you."

"Vulnerable," I said. "Lieutenant, you're stepping out of character . . ."

Impervious, the Lieutenant said, "She is looking for trouble, the old lady. She is knocking hell out of cops about a simple suicide. And when we don't buy it–after plenty extra checking just to make her happy–then she wants a shamus."

"Because why?"

"Because she likes it–in back of her head."

"Which means what?"

"Which means there's a will."

"Sally Bentley?"

"Who else? Leaves more than a hundred G's. Half to the old lady. Half to the sister, Delores."

"Where'd she get it?"

"Earned it, I suppose."

"So?"

"So, there's a tenet of law, states that if you murder someone, it's not allowed that you inherit out of your own handiwork."

"Tenet," I said. "Lieutenant, you are really making with the words."

"So, if it's murder, and Delores done it, she don't get. See? It goes into the pot, which is called residuary estate, legally. And who gets this residuary estate? The old one, that is who, because then she is the one remaining heir. Catch?"

"I suppose."

"So she comes here and she tells us it's murder because it just can't be suicide, and she tells us about how maybe it's Delores because Delores just hates this Sally, but hates her good and hard, and about the will, and about how Delores knew about the will, and about how Delores could certainly use that dough, as who the hell couldn't."

I dug out cigarettes and I added to the fog hanging off the ceiling. "What about the tickets for Europe? What about the happy good humor of the evening before? And what about—if the old lady is telling exactly the truth, without sordid ulterior motive? Can't it be?"

"Sure it can be. Sordid ulterior motive—now who's shooting with the words. Okay, so she's calling them like she sees them, and no sordid ulterior motive. It makes no difference. We've got a clean suicide, and you can't beat that, and you just can't take the lid off the dead one's head to know what was really operating and why she acted like she did before she knocked herself off."

"How clean?"

"What?"

"The suicide."

"Clean like this. Clean like a bullet in the head, close up, powder burns. Clean like a gun in her hand and a note on the desk and the door locked tight, and it wasn't a snap lock, either. I'm not even handling it. I take care of the hard ones. I don't waste my time." He put a lazy circle of smoke between us.

"Who's handling it?"

"Sergeant Williams."

"May I see him?"

"Why not? And all the exhibits too. I'm no wise-guy. Maybe we don't have it straight, which I doubt. Maybe you can help, which I also doubt. Don't think I like the part about the ticket for Europe, and everybody is gay and carefree the night before."

He took his feet off the desk and he buzzed the box for Williams. "I want you, and all the Bentley things...now...right now." He clicked off. "Smart boy," he said, "that Williams. College boy."

Williams was tall and straight and slim with a pointed nose and an important face. He showed me the exhibits. I saw a picture of a rigid woman with her head sidewise on a desk and her right arm straight down with a gun in its fist. I saw a close-up of a hole in back of her right ear. I saw the gun, a flat and graceful .38 automatic. I read a note in the usual blue-black ink: "I am going to kill myself because I am sick and tired of living. I don't like it. Goodbye and forgive me. Here goes."

"Handwriting?" I asked Parker.

"Hers. Absolutely."

"No signature?"

"A bullet in the head is sufficient signature."

"Behind the ear?"

"Look. Don't carp. A girl writes a note and kills herself. Simple. Nobody wrote it for her. It's not a forgery. We know that. So don't start telling me that behind the ear is not usual. Maybe, for you, we'll arrange it that prospective suicides draw diagrams on themselves first, so we can keep you happy."

"It's sort of reaching around, don't you think?"

"No, I don't think."

"She reached, brother," Williams said. "I checked very careful, because of the old lady's squawk. This case is closed with Mamma's complaint registered right on top of the file. We had them all in. Zetz and the sister and the boy-friend."

"Boy-friend?"

"What," Parker asked, "*do* you know about this case? Anyway? Except that you've got the two thousand."

"Boy-friend," Williams said. "Gino Stark, Five Eighty-eight Lexington. Dancing instructor, when he takes time off from improving the gee-gees over by Belmont. Met her at a dance at the Waldorf about a year ago."

"You check that too?"

"Checked. Zetz introduced them."

"Where did Zetz get to know him?"

"Met him a few years back when Zetz went to Arthur Pallette's to brush up on his Tango, or something."

I heaved off the cigarette. I stood up and I looked down at Parker. "Stinks a little."

"Maybe. But it's still suicide, and that's the only part that's our business."

"How long was she working for Zetz?"

"Six years," Williams said.

"How much she earn?"

"A hundred and fifty a week."

I made eyebrows at Parker. "See what I mean?"

"Sure I see what you mean. You mean how come she's got maybe a hundred G's in the bank, working for a yard and a half a week. Ever hear of party girls?"

"Not the kind that work for a living."

"Well, maybe she partied afterward. Who the hell knows? Maybe Zetz's wife paid her to watch Zetz. She's the former Margot Dinsmore."

"Big society, huh?"

"Biggest and the richest. Out of town right now, she and their two sons. Over by Provincetown."

"Zetz marry her for dough?"

"I wouldn't know, but I'd say no, because Mr. Zetz is a millionaire a couple of times over, mostly by inheritance. I'm sorry, Pete, I just can't make out any of the characters black for you."

"What about her friends?"

"What friends?"

"Out of the address book."

"No good, bright boy. It happens she don't have an address book, not even a diary. Terrible huh? Here's a girl that don't act like the rest of the girls. But she had a lot of letters. Stacks. We went through all of them, checked. Normal people. Just friends."

"Do you have the letters?"

Williams said, "No. They're at the apartment. We had no use for them here any more."

"Can I get to see the apartment?"

Williams looked at Parker and Parker looked back. Parker said, "You still got the key?" Williams said, "Yup."

"Give it to him. What the hell. You got to learn, boy; you got to be friendly with one shamus. One. They're a help, sometimes."

"Oh," Williams said, "there's another exhibit, still over at the lab—"

"Stick it," I said. "I'll take the key."

I took the key and I took my hat and I bid adieu to the Lieutenant and I waved a couple of fingers at the Sergeant, and I got out of there and onto the I.R.T. subway, and I crawled out at Fifty-first, which I figured would be near Five Eighty-eight Lexington, and I didn't figure too badly. I found his name on the brass-plated scoreboard downstairs and I pushed the button and I got a click and I went up one flight and there he was waiting for me in a bathrobe tight around the belly with bulk in the shoulders.

"Mr. Stark?"

"Who wants to know?"

Real pleasant. He was tall, taller than I, maybe six feet four, with a custard-smooth olive complexion and soft sliding eyes. He was

V-shaped in figure and casual with the false poise of a drunk being led to the pie-wagon. He was the long loungy kind of guy that the girlies go for, but bang.

"Peter Chambers," I told him. "I'm checking on the Sally Bentley thing."

He fiddled with the tassel of the robe. "For whom?"

"Confidential, feller. I'm a private detective."

"Oh. One of them guys. No good, bub. I did my talking to the fuzzies. Don't know a thing."

I moved closer to him in the doorway. "But–"

"No but's, bub. It's like I told them. I don't know nothing about it. Don't know a thing."

"Yes, Mr. Stark, but–"

"Don't know nothing from absolutely nothing." He put a wide hand on my chest and he shoved with relish and sharp determination, and the door slapped shut in my face. Mr. Gino Stark got filed away as a handsome young man with a tough-guy complex that needed treatment. Something psychiatric. Like a haymaker.

I took a cab, still rankling along the chest and rumbling around the stomach and trying to engage reasons for administering the treatment for our Gino's complex, all of which is good for the passage of time, because before I knew it I was paying off the hackie in front of Two Ninety Park.

I pushed my hat back and I looked up at the narrow four sandstone stories of a very svelte little pigmy amongst the flat-faced monsters that go to make up our canyon of Park. No doorman. No nothing. Just a silver-grilled ninon-backed glass door with an ivory boundary and a horse's head for a phony knocker and a shining lock. I stuck the key in that Williams had given me and I was in a hallway with enough plush for a lupanar, and a curlicue stairway. Very dandy, but a walk-up, nevertheless. Ah, me, and the rasp of a sigh: your detective trudged, grudgingly, bending over to study nameplates. On the second floor front it said BENTLEY.

She had three sensational rooms, not counting the donicker. She had a living room with two walls papered gold and two walls painted gray and a two-toned diagonal modern carpet and limned-gray furniture, expensive. She had a kitchen, regulation, right up to the latest in drip coffee- makers, and a bedroom that was an invitation to retire. For two. For at least two. It had a double-mattressed circular bed and black-mirrored walls and a miniature stockinged leg for a lightswitch that gave you indirect lighting that called for absinthe and a hazy glow and stifled giggles and a hand to reach out a finger to switch off the lady's leg for darkness. I got out of that bedroom fast.

I was getting ideas about afternoon phone calls. I had work to do.

The kitchen cupboard was stacked with more notable potables than the lockers of a private bottle club and I helped myself to two neat brandies and a slow shake of the head to get over that bedroom. Then I gave the apartment the old one-two. And three. I went over it like an embarrassed Mamma with the fine-comb when Curlyhead gets sent home from school, and the best I could come up with was one box of brand new unsharpened pencils, and a fine typewriter on a carved desk in the living room, and letters. Nothing else. Lots of letters, neatly piled and filed in a tall wooden cabinet with Chinese adornments. I read them all, between skirmishes with the brandy bottle, and they told me nothing except that Sally had had a great many friends who thought she was one hell of a swell girl.

What with the brandy and that bedroom I thought again about Delores, which is a very pretty name, and I hoped that she wasn't one of those hill-billy singers with roped veins in their necks and bandy legs that sometimes the night clubs use. I tidied up, and had another drink on the house, and I got out of there.

I went directly to Delores.

Delores wasn't home.

So I saw a couple of newsreels and let the duck squawk at me out of a couple of special extra shorts, and then I went home and had a shower and a shave and I called the Cafe Jenz. I reserved a table right up front, the evening show was at nine, and I set the alarm clock and I went to sleep. When the thing buzzed, I recollected. I called downtown and I got through very quickly to Parker.

"How come," I said, "you're always in when I call?"

"Nobody's getting killed in New York. I don't knock off till midnight. So I sit and I ponder. What's on your mind?"

"What about the gun?"

"What gun?"

"The tomato with the bedroom. Bentley."

"Thirty-eight automatic."

"I know. Whose?"

"Hers. License and all. Show you I'm a detective."

"Sho nuf."

"She kept it in the end-table back of the desk alongside that turquoise couch. Good, huh?"

"Very good."

"I know because everybody knew. All her friends told me. Anything else, sucker?"

"No thanks."

I dressed in a pin-stripe and a tab collar and I took a lot of care with my moustache. I worked five minutes picking a tie. I gave my military brushes a workout, and I prigged around with all sorts of essentials, like talcum for my face and a switch in ties and some mighty male perfume out of a fancy bottle. That Delores.

The Cafe Jenz bubbled with noise and the clink of eating hardware and the sibilance of half-slammed females. I took my formal table all by myself at the edge of the unspacious square of high-polished dance-floor, and I watched the visiting firemen wag their rumbas at me. I ordered a double brandy with soda and I wrote a note on a napkin for Delores to come see me, and I got a crisp, "Yes, sir," replacing the scowl from the waiter when he glimpsed the ten beside the note I handed up to him.

Then the lights went down and the spot came up and an unseen gentleman on the bandstand lisped along the band-mike about Delores Bentley who was coming on now, folks, to sort of lift you right out of your seats; and vindication dazzled within the rim of the round white spot, vindication for ablutions of mighty male perfume and extra touches with the moustache and indecision amongst ties.

She had auburn hair with glints, and pale high cheekbones under upslanted wide green eyes, and a push-pout of glistening burgundy lips that straightened you out in your night club chair, clutching for your highball. She was tall in a smooth whirl of packed black evening gown that had more cutout than a muffler in Indianapolis, which was all to the good. She was soft-curved with firm shoulders and no bones and her voice was deep and low and soft and lazy. She gave you music like the lap of waves on a hot night by the beach with the sky down near you and lots of stars.

She burned off five terrific numbers and she did things to all of the boys in the appreciative periphery of dimmed-down audience; I do not know about the ladies; and I clapped like the rest of the yokels in a slapping anthem for an encore, and we got a smile and a squeeze of her small tight nose—then lights, and lots of dance music.

I ordered more brandy, and I needed it, because there she was, suddenly, in the seat opposite me, in another black dress with nothing on top except shining white shoulders and a deft cleft of bosom. She looked at me and I looked at her and my hair pinched up on end.

I said, "Drinks?"

She said, "Sure."

I said, "What?"

She said, "Brandy."

I said, "Good."

She said, "Why?"

"Please?" the waiter said.

"Brandy. For the lady."

Mock-toned she said, "Oh, it's good, because you're drinking brandy too. That what you meant?"

"Sho nuf." I had contracted this involuntary sneeze of shonuf from a Copacutie out of New Hampshire by way of a fast two weeks in the land of baseball commissioners–but across from me sat the cure.

The brandy came and the waiter went and she sipped, and she put it down. Her eyes stayed on the pony glass. "The note said you wanted to talk to me about my mother. That a new system?"

"About your mother, *and* about your sister."

Her eyes came off the brandy glass. 'Cop?"

"Yep."

"Not you."

"Well, private cop."

"You look more like a gigolo, well . . . maybe on the interesting beat-up side."

"Like?"

"Tell you the truth–yes. Very much."

"Swell."

"Why?"

"I like you too."

"Sure. Why shouldn't you like. They all like."

"I've seen better, sister, and I haven't liked."

One eyebrow clambered. She made a circle with the bottom of her glass. "Fresh, too. All right, more brandy. Let's have lots more brandy, you and I. Seen better, have you?"

We clicked. Fast. Just like that. We clicked like an abacus in a busy Chinese laundry, and we laughed over brandy and we clinked our glasses and bandied biography and we told our jokes, all the way from rigid right to purple left. We danced, close and warm, and I smelled the salt-sweet smell of her hair and she dug her fingernails into my arm and the trickle of her breath whispered at my ear. We talked about ourselves with sly embellishments. She said, "Let's get out of here."

"Where?"

"Anywhere. I'm not due back till the one o'clock show."

"Sure."

We went to Jackson's, side by side and near on a red leather seat under the dimness of the amber lights, and we listened to the tinkle of the faraway piano. We held hands and we touched knees and I hoped that she wasn't a murderess.

"You've been nice," she said. "Very nice. You're a guy with a lot of kicks. Okay. You've softened me up. Stop being nice. What do you want?"

"I want to help. If I can."

"Whom?"

"You."

"Me?"

"Yes."

"You're nuts."

I took my hand out of hers and I moved my knee away. "Look, lovely, they know you hated her. They also know that she didn't know you hated her. Because she left you all that dough. She wouldn't have done that if she'd have known you hated her, now would she?"

"She was bad. Mean vicious bad. She–"

"Cops are funny people. They'll come awake one day and then you won't lose them, forever. If they figure the old lady is telling the truth, about you and Sally, and maybe they do."

"She told them?"

"She did."

"The old bat."

I made tsk-tsk with the tongue. "Naughty to talk about Mamma like that."

"She's not my mother."

"Once more?"

"Not my mother."

"Sally's?"

"Not Sally's either. Mother died, a long while ago, and Father remarried. Oh, she's been all right, don't get me wrong, she's been a mother, helped like all get-out when Father died. But I didn't expect–"

"She knew how you felt about Sally?"

"Yes. We talked about her often."

"Real bad?"

"Sally? The worst. But you compromise with that sort of thing. You keep away from her, if you can. Look, I, personally, I had nothing against her. It was just . . ."

"You hated her, but you had nothing against her. Good. Real good."

"It's just . . . can you care for something that's loathesome . . . like a spider, or a rattlesnake? Even a pet rattlesnake?"

"I know what you mean."

"That's it."

"Think she killed herself?"

"How would I know?"

"What do you think?"

"She wasn't the type."

"I'm not asking about the type. I'm asking *do you think she killed herself?*"

She opened a slender silver cigarette-case with a bronze Delores in script, and she clipped out a cigarette and tapped it against the table. "No. I don't think she killed herself."

I lit it for her. "Got a candidate?"

"For what?"

"For murder. What else?"

"No."

"Honey, you're a very lovely girl."

"Lovely of you to tell me."

"You're one too many."

"You're real Gertrude Stein, or whatever her name is."

"I mean you're one too many that doesn't think she killed herself. Mamma Bentley's the other one. It leaks out, that sort of thing, what people think. There must be other people that think like that. Miasma of opinion, or something. But coppers smell it out sooner or later. Then *you're* the candidate."

"You trying to frighten me?"

"Natch."

"Why?"

"I want you to open up for me. I want some stuff. Real stuff. It's you, or it's nobody. I mean, for information. If I leave it alone, it's just going to sit around. And if it sits around, it ain't good, honey. Believe me. You'll be number one with them, and the things they can find out when they really go to work."

She was placid scratching out the cigarette, placid picking up the swizzle stick. Then little lumps jumped in her jaw and the swizzle stick broke in her hand and blood crept out along her thumb and she looked at it, moodily. "All right, guy. You've worked me into a corner, and maybe I'm drunk, and maybe I like you, and maybe I'm afraid. Maybe, some damn way, somebody's going to find out that I was there that morning, and maybe that won't play back too good."

"Why didn't you tell them?"

"Whom?"

"Coppers."

"Friend lover, I was afraid to tell them. You don't like to get mixed up in things like that. It's suicide. All right, it's suicide. Why look for trouble?"

"You're telling me."

"I'm telling you. Complete. Because maybe you can work it out. And I'm giving you nothing. Except words. If you bring it to the cops, you made it up, I told you nothing. I deny it. I'm telling you because you've got a way of lousing a person up. With fear."

I smoked, with pleasure. I listened, with eagerness. I'd worked hard for the simmer. Now I got the boil. "I love you," I said, "sister."

She wiped blood from her hand with a napkin and she brought brandy to her mouth, then put it away. Her lips peeled back from her bright teeth and her eyes moved together in a green-glinting squint of indecision. Then she picked up the brandy and finished it. "I had a key to her apartment. For a while, when I first came to New York, I lived with her. She helped, liberally, until I landed my first job. I owed her money, and I paid her, twenty bucks every Sunday morning, after I began to earn it."

"How much money?"

"About twelve hundred dollars."

"Anyone else have a key?"

"What?"

"Key."

"Oh." She looked at the empty brandy glass. I picked up a finger for the waiter. We had more brandy.

"I'm sure," she said. "I'm sure there are others who had a key."

I swiveled with the head. "No. None of that. I mean someone you *know* had a key. That's what I mean."

She snapped her fingers. I waited. She snapped her fingers harder. "Sure. I know one. A guy. Gino Stark." Then she looked like she was sorry she had said it.

"I love that, sister."

"What's that?"

"I said I love it."

"That's what I thought you said. What's the matter with you?"

"Nothing. How do you know?"

"Forget it, will you? Forget I mentioned it."

I started to get up. I upset the glasses on the table. People looked at us. The hell with them. "I'm getting out of here, kid. I'm pouring it right back at you. If that's the way you want it, okay; that's the way you want it."

"Sit down."

"All right. I'm sitting."

She wasn't happy. "I know he had a key, because I had it made for him."

"Why?"

"She asked me to, about a year ago, to have a duplicate of mine made, and she told me, boom, like that, for whom she wanted it, and why. That was Sally."

She had marbles in her throat. That Gino. I changed the subject.

"So you owed her money. So what happened?" The marbles went away. She was back on the beam. "Generally, Sunday mornings she slept late. Generally, I'd just open the door with my key. If she had company, I'd just peek in, leave my check and get out of there. Otherwise, I'd help her over her hangover, make breakfast, that sort of thing."

"Just a minute. This guy Zetz."

"Zetz?"

"The boss guy. What about him?"

"Well, what?"

"Was he ever company?"

"Not that I know of."

"She really work for him?"

"Oh, yes. She liked being a big shot's secretary."

"Was she any good?"

"What do you mean?"

"I mean did she know her business? Did she earn her keep?"

"Yes, I think so. She couldn't take shorthand, I know that, but for a creative writer, that kind of thing, you really don't need shorthand. They think a lot, they go slow; you know, mumble around. But she was a whiz on the typewriter, and she really took over and handled his business all the way along the line. This I can tell you, she was a wonderful secretary for the guy. I know that."

"Where'd she get all the dough?"

She wrinkled her forehead, peering at nothing. "I really don't know. She was very beautiful and very practical and she was full of schemes and she had many friends, many many friends."

"Many many friends," I said. "Anybody special, that she could really hook for a handful?"

"I don't know. I can't say."

"Okay. We go back to Sunday. What happened? Exactly."

"Well, I came in, and there she was, all dressed. She bawled me out for not ringing. That's the way she was, perverse. She told me she had a date with Gino, it was a beautiful day, he was to drive her up to the country."

"His car?"

"Her car. He doesn't have a car."

"Then?"

"Then she talked to someone on the phone. I was in the kitchen."

"Gino?"

"I don't know."

"Incoming call, or out?"

"Incoming. The phone rang and I heard her answer it."

"Did you hear anything? I mean, what?"

"Nothing. That's what. I was in the kitchen. The water was running out of the sink. I wasn't listening."

"Do it careful now, honey. Then what? Exactly."

"Then, exactly, I got out of there." She put her elbows on the table, and put her wrists together, and put her chin on that, and her eyes came down to narrow, recollecting. "I told her I had a date with my agent, with my agent...a spry young guy...for early lunch. I took out my checkbook...I had left my pen at home...I used her pen and I wrote a check for her, which the police found later and asked me about...and then I put the checkbook away and the pen...*oh*!"

She scurried fingers into her pocketbook and she made a small hill of its contents on the table. Then she brought up a fountain pen. "See? I'm telling the truth. Here it is. I put it in my bag by mistake. I took it with me. Now, damn you, do you believe me? The way you've been watching me talk, and cross-examining me..."

She was crying, suddenly.

Softly I said, "Did you kill her, kid?"

"No."

"Let's get out of here. Let's walk."

We walked the cool streets of Madison Avenue and I held her arm and she held the arm close to her. I pushed her into the windy recess of a thin alley between a department store and an apartment house, and I held her and her face tilted up to mine. "Please," she said. "Please, please..." I said, "The hell with that," and I kissed her. I held her and I kissed her, good.

I called a cab and I told him to drive us around, anywhere. He did the curves of Central Park while I bit a fingernail and she made her mouth up. "According to you." I said, "you didn't tell the cops because you were leery. It was straight suicide, and maybe you didn't believe it could happen, but there it was. So you kept your nose clean, because, like most people, and I don't blame you, you're afraid of cops and law and ramifications and the way they can twist things around and it gets to be a mess with lawyers and publicity, and maybe, even, you're stuck, and you can't get out of it. So there it was suicide, so you let it sleep. What did you do with the key?"

"I threw it away. The minute Gino told me."

"*Gino*?"

"The maid found her at twelve o'clock. The police had Gino in for routine questioning. They couldn't reach me. I was out with this boy, my agent. But Gino knows there's a place I like, Courvie's, so he trotted down there, and he told me."

"What'd he do with his key? Do you know?"

"I'd rather not talk about it."

"What'd he do with his key?"

"Just what I did with mine. In fact, he advised me. Not that I didn't agree. I went home alone. There was a policeman waiting for me. He took me downtown. Everybody was polite."

Central Park was all around us and the thousands of lights out of the misty blank buildings made a small broken ice-cube of the pale city moon. A soft wind blew in through the windows and the smell of the park was sweet. I reached for the cabbie. "Roll it up."

"Sure t'ing."

The partition of nothing rose up to a partition of plate glass. I moved close to her. I took her face in my hands. "You're crazy," she said.

"All right," I said. "I'm crazy . . ."

Then she was crying again.

"How much did you hold out?" I asked her.

"Nothing. Nothing about myself. Except about a guy, a man I once thought I loved . . . and Gino . . . I didn't want to involve him . . ."

Oh, that Gino.

"Maybe," she said, "I held out because of Gino."

"You and him? . . ."

"No."

"Then what the hell are you talking about?"

"Look. I'm going to put it in your hand. All of it. In the palm of your hand. If you can use it to show that someone killed her, all right. But if you can't, then throw it away. Will you? Will you?"

"Well . . ."

"Look, guy, there's a lot been happening between you and me, on very short notice. It happens, sometimes. I think I know you. Promise?"

"Okay."

"Mostly because of Gino. Because he's been square with me, more than square. He protected me. I want to protect him. Do you understand?"

"Sure."

"He owed her money."

"How much?"

"Twenty thousand dollars."

"*What*?"

"Twenty."

"That's money."

"She put a clamp on people that way. She could afford it. She owned him, like that. You know?"

"Uh-huh."

"On the other hand, she took a man away from me, a man I thought I was crazy about. And I found out about that only last week. That miserable–"

"My," I said, "How you talk of the dead."

"I'm not talking about her. I'm talking about him. The filthy–"

"Easy, pal."

"Gino knew about it. Gino heard me argue with her. He heard me tell her I'd kill her. But I cooled off. A guy you can lose that simply, a guy like that is nothing. I hated her, but I hate him worse; a guy like that is nothing."

"So?..."

"So Gino, in a sense, was loyal. He didn't talk about it. He told me that he didn't mention it to the cops. He didn't tell them about my having a key, he didn't tell them about what happened between us–"

"Sure he didn't. And you didn't tell about *his* having a key, and about his owing her twenty G's. For a smartened up tomato, a little bit, you're dumb."

She said, "You see it one way, I see it another. I don't want the estate suing him for the money. He earned it, in a way."

"Any proof of the debt?"

"Maybe *I'm* dumb. But Sally wasn't. Sure there's proof of the debt."

"Where is it?"

"I have it."

I looked at her.

"She gave it to me, one time. She didn't want it around the apartment. I kept it for her. She didn't want Gino maybe picking it up. The love affair was finished. Now she had him like she liked him, part escort, part servant, part stallion."

"Where do you keep it?"

"Home."

"Let's go home."

I tapped on the glass. The cabbie rolled it down. The meter showed four bucks and ten cents. "Twenty-two West Seventy-ninth," I told him. The New York cabbie is a Sphinx, a talking Sphinx, a Sphinx that talks but stays a Sphinx. "Sure t'ing," he said.

It was a room and a half with a bed in the wall. It was neat and cozy with quiet lights from two rose-tinted modern lamps. She lifted her hands to a high shelf of books over a writing desk, and the full long immaculate lines of her body heightened in challenge. I moved toward her, warm with the brandy, but her eyes weren't with me; they were murky and preoccupied, dull-shiny-moist, like mud puddles on a wet road. I didn't touch her. She brought down a fat book and she riffled through it and she gave me the envelope. It was dated Rio, three years back, on pale gray linen, and the letter was simple enough in a scrawl of thin backhand, and to the point: "Sally, I love you very much. I miss you very much. I wish you were here. Coochie," but beneath that, in flat wide angry strokes, in a graceful but rigid up-and-down: "I.O.U. From Gino Stark to Sally Bentley. On demand, twenty thousand dollars. Sue me."

"What did he need it for?" I asked.

"He was supposed to open a little dance studio of his own. It never materialized."

"Yeah," I said. "Thanks. I'll be seeing you."

"Where you going?"

"To Gino."

"Be careful."

"Stop kidding."

"And remember what you promised."

"Don't worry." I kissed her, but when you kiss a girl like Delores Bentley, time is on the other side, and it was eleven thirty when I got out of there.

I whisked down a cab and I went to Lexington. I rang his bell downstairs and I rang his bell upstairs and there he was in pajamas, Gino-boy, and I said, "A little talk, you and I. Conversation." I pushed past him and I was inside.

"Out," he said. "I'm sleeping."

"Talk. A little conversation."

He was moving up on me, and I let him. "Mister," he said, "you're a square. Strictly a square."

"Hip," I told him. "You're a real hip kid." I reached up a knee and he grunted, extemporaneously, and his face flowered in front of me. It scraped up rapid landscaping.

He was green, but he was rugged, and he came up off the floor with a surprised look on him, making like a tough-guy out of the side of his mouth. He moved away from the wave of a left fist, and then he ran into the point of a right elbow squash in the socket of his eye. He rasped with screech like chalk edgewise on a blackboard, and he covered up, and then I filled in with a few to the belly and a long one off the floor that sat him down on the scatter-rug, with no mind to get up.

"You had a date with her and you were there. I know that."

"How?–"

"You killed her, you big–"

"No. She was dead when I got there. Please. I tell you, she was dead, just like that, her head on the desk..."

"You hunted around for the note."

"Note?"

"Twenty G's worth of note."

He was truculent, but he stayed sidewise on the floor, blue flesh crowding up around his eye. "Yes, I did. So what?"

"Before or after?"

"Before or after–what?"

"Before or after she was dead?"

"Look..."

Then all of a sudden, it fit. All of it. I swung my hand around and my palm hit me on the forehead, flat-hard.

Pebbly-voiced, Gino said, "Man, I think you're nuts. Get the hell out of here. Puh-lease."

"Get dressed," I told him. "Hurry up, get dressed," but he stayed there on his elbow and I went for him, when a castenet of knuckles rubbed the door. We froze to tableau, the gladiators of Lexington Avenue, the dick with his hand in the suspect's hair, and the suspect reluctant half off the floor, with his mouth open. I dropped him.

"Who's that?"

"Delores."

I opened the door for her.

"I was worried..." Then she saw him.

"Don't worry," I said.

"Uh-huh."

"All right," I told him. "Get dressed. We're going visiting. We're going to have a conference."

"Who?"

"All of us. A coffee-klatch. Where's your phone?"

The phone was in the bedroom. He dressed while I called.

"Parker," I said. "Parker, get the old lady, will you, and meet me down at Zetz's place. What? Yeah. I'll have them all there, the whole damn cast of characters. But characters."

A yellow cab with more bounce than a European waltz took us down to Eight East Tenth, and Mr. Zetz himself opened the door for us, Zetz in a natty blue suit and a flow-collared shirt and a look of disturbed surprise on his face. The look got more disturbed. "Excuse me," I said.

I grabbed at the sparkle with a grasping left, and the right was a straight thump to his throat. He stood stiff and still and courteous, but his eyes weren't blinking. He needed a short right for composure, and he got it. He keeled to the thick-piled mouse-gray carpet and he lay there, spread-eagled, a twitch at his lips and one knee bent, not ungraceful. I put the donation from Denmark by royalty in my jacket pocket, and I closed the door.

"This guy is nuts," Gino said. "But positively."

Delores said, "My God, what's the matter with you? You *must* be drunk." She bent to him.

"Leave him alone," I said, and then Parker was there with Mrs. Bentley.

They brought him to the satin-striped daven-port of the wide-ceilinged rich-furnished room, a flicker coming back to his eyelids, and we all spread out while Delores patted his face. He opened his eyes and he looked at me.

"How's things?" I said. "Coochie."

First his face flamed. A twisted cord of blue vein in his forehead stood out like a plain-jane in Hollywood. Then the vein flattened back and the color drained down and his jowls matched the mouse-gray of the carpet. He was hunched forward, motionless, his hands squeezing his knees, but his eyes were wild chattels in the bleak prison of the locked face. I knew I had him then. I think Parker knew too.

"Everybody," I said, "had their fingerprints around that apartment, I'm sure. But they all belonged there, some time or other, so it didn't make any difference."

"Correct," Parker said.

"All right. I'll tell it. If anybody wants to help, they can fill in. Including you." I pointed a thumb at Zetz.

Parker moved around closer to him.

"Like this," I said. "Mr. Zetz gets a secretary. There's a good title for your next book, if they give you time to write one–Mr. Zetz Gets a Secretary."

"Stop with the grandstand," Parker said.

"All right, they get together. She's his secretary. She's also his sweetheart. She's a wise wise cookie, and this guy's not the most beautiful guy in the world, but look at all the dough he's got. So all right. So after a while she starts taking him. Maybe she threatens a little bit. He's a married man, with kids, and a big society wife. So he pays, and what the hell, but he's drawn himself a losing ticket and he knows it, and he'd like to tear it up."

"Sweeten it," Parker said.

"He's a detective story writer. He thinks about a lot of angles. He wants to get rid of her, but first he tries it kosher. He introduces her to a good-looking lank of boy-friend, and he hopes that she'll fall for him, and marry him, and goodbye sweetheart. That doesn't work."

Parker looked at Gino. Gino looked like he'd just climbed out of a wreck, and wanted to climb back in again. The rest of them looked at me.

"He ponders it, and it comes to him. Finally. Maybe he's tried it a few times, and it hasn't worked, but this particular Sunday–it worked. He calls her on the phone, she's up, and he comes a-visiting. She's sitting at the desk, and, bang, the professor gets a brainstorm– for a short story, for a novel, something. 'Honey,' he says, 'quick. This is something. Take it down.' He puts a sheet of paper in front of her, or maybe there's one there already. She reaches for a pencil. No pencil, only a new box of unsharpened ones. She looks for her pen. That isn't there."

"Why not?–" Parker asked.

"I'll tell you later. He can't wait for her to sharpen pencils. He's got her in position, he's got her all primed, he doesn't want her to get up. He's already sneaked the gun out of the end table. So he gives her his fountain pen, fast, he's excited, and the old genius is working like mad. 'Take it down,' he tells her, 'it's a real beauty, what an idea...' and he starts dictating... She doesn't use shorthand. He knows that. He starts dictating and she starts writing: 'I am going to kill myself because I am sick and tired of living. I don't like it. Goodbye and forgive me. Here goes.' She doesn't suspect, or maybe she just doesn't have time to begin to suspect, or maybe she was good and drunk the night before and the fuzz is still fixed around her brain. He sneaks the gun out and shoves it behind her ear. Bang."

Nobody said anything.

"You know what I mean," I said to Parker. "Behind the ear."

"I know what you mean."

"While she isn't looking. Then he's got it, all done. He wipes the gun, puts it in her hand. There's her suicide note in her own hand-writing in front of her. He has a key to her apartment, as who hasn't. So he first looks through her neat file of letters, and takes out all of his that he wrote in the old heat of early passion, and out he goes, locking the door behind him. Perfect?"

I was waiting for him to move. He didn't move.

"He throws the key away, the dirty–"

"Quiet," Parker said. "We got ladies in the joint."

Now Parker was waiting for his move. He still didn't move. So Parker played it dumb. "How would you know about all this? When'd you get on?"

"Well," I said, "there was one letter of his that wasn't in her apart-ment."

He moved, not much, but he moved. He ran a hand over his hair.

Sweat pasted it down.

"Where was it?" Parker asked.

"Delores had it. Gino here, good Gino, borrowed money from Sally. Sally took a note back. On what? On one of Zetz's letters. Right on the letter, on the bottom part, Gino gives her his I.O.U. Sally doesn't want that I.O.U. around where it can be picked up, so she gives it to Delores for safekeeping."

"Just a minute." Parker made his mouth sour. "Why didn't he heist his letters earlier? He had what they call access to the premises."

"Access to the premises. All right, so he had access to the premises. So then she'd know just who picked them up, and boy, she'd bust out wide with plenty trouble which Zetz couldn't afford. No, sir. It was either that she got married to some guy she loved, and couldn't afford that kind of trouble herself, or else–"

Mrs. Bentley said, "My God, my God..." but Zetz kept right on sitting.

I talked. "She probably knew that Zetz had picked Gino for her, and for what reason. It was her way of showing her contempt for Gino–she made him sign his I.O.U. on a letter from her other lover. That did it. That cooked him, Zetz; that, and the pride that's in him, that's in everybody."

"Don't start with the philosophy," Parker said. "Just shine it up a little."

"I saw the note. I saw the letter on top of it. Out of Rio, three years back. You'll check on that. You'll find he was there. But he had written some addresses for me in my office this morning, and I recognized the handwriting. *A thin scrawl of backhand.* That's when it began to perk."

"No!" Zetz shook his head. "No."

"Yes," I said.

"No. You can't prove any of that. Talk. You want a fall guy. You want to earn an additional fee. Talk, talk, talk. Even if we were lovers, that doesn't mean I killed her." *He knew I had him: he was hoping that I didn't know I had him.*

I talked to Parker. "Like I said, Lieutenant, pride. Pride, twice. Pride in the knowledge that he had committed a murder that couldn't be solved. And pride in a gift from royalty."

His hand scrambled for the showpocket. Right up to then he hadn't known I'd scooped it. Maybe he didn't know, then. Maybe he thought it was lost, somehow, miraculously. His teeth came down over his lip and his face squeezed into a creased mask of constraint. He was shaking.

"You and your Williams," I said to Parker. "Perfect suicide. Did anyone think about the pen that wrote the note? Look, I don't blame Williams. You can't think of everything, not when it's laid out so perfectly. You just don't bother to. It's there, and the small things just get blotted up. But. *There was no pen in the apartment.* Delores had taken it by mistake, that morning. That's when I thought it was Delores; she had the pen and the suicide note was in ink–and then I saw the letter from Rio."

Dryly Parker said, "You know how it is. Cops are stupid. Whose pen?"

"His. A gift from royalty with diamonds. That's what I mean about pride. He threw the key away, but our detective story genius just couldn't know that the sister had taken the pen out of the apartment that morning. He knew the pen could hurt him, but he was so sure he had done it right, he just couldn't part with the pen that royalty had given him in Denmark."

Now I looked at him, straight at him. "Pen marks are as good as fingerprints, or type from a typewriter, and you know it, or you ought to know it. *That's the proof.*" I took it out of my pocket and I waved it at him. I dropped it back before he came at me.

He came fast, in a bull-rush, slobbering at the mouth, but I was expecting him. He got one in the stomach that bent him across to me and then he got all of my shoulder and most of my spine in a crunch to the crockery that left the mark of his bite on my fist for a month. He bounced like a rowboat in a squall. He draped the davenport with his neck over the arm and his face hanging down, and the hasty blood spurted through the quick-swelled lips. Parker brought him back and wiped his mouth and clamped the jangles on him; he shook him up a little and the guy blathered then, he blathered plenty.

"Sure," I said, "the dirty son of a–"

"Quiet," Parker said. "We got ladies in the joint."

And then, later, much later, around a small square table at the one-o'clock show at the Cafe Jenz, with the Detective-lieutenant expansive over rye on the rocks, as my guest, by reason of an additional three thousand dollars honestly earned–and while Delores Bentley was changing from costume–he poked a finger at my shoulder, which agitated a good deal of brand-name brandy. "Don't preen."

"Preen?"

"Preen."

"Oh, preen. I get it. When the private eye does a job, he hears about preen from the flush-faced Lieutenant, he does not hear about thanks."

"Lucky."

"Sure. Lucky. When the private eye does a job–"

"I didn't want to take the shine off of it. In front of the new dolly–"

"Now look, Louis..."

He looked into rye on the rocks. "Remember the exhibit? The one Williams told you was still at the lab, the one you didn't wait to hear about?"

"That college boy? Listen–"

"You listen."

"Don't bother me."

"It was a fountain pen."

"*What*?"

"That's it. Cops and college boys–they're not quite so dumb. Two things, I'll straighten you out about."

"Straighten away, Lieutenant." But my brave words hobbled.

"One. Scratch marks from a pen are *not* conclusive; oh, they'll rule out many pens–*but these fit. The fountain pen we had.*"

"I am a son of a bitch. Underline that, professor."

"Quiet. Two. She must have had *two* pens, because there was this other pen, this exhibit at the lab, which we pick up at the apartment at that time, and the ink fit, too; so both she and Zetz, they evidently filled from the same inkwell. So you see what I mean about lucky?"

I swallowed. Air. "You mean?..."

"I mean we found the pen in the bedroom, in the top bureau drawer. So you *were* right about Zetz not wanting her to get up, once he had her in position. He just handed her *his* pen. Only, we had it figured that she had written the note in the bedroom, put the pen away, put the note on the desk, walked around a little, maybe had a drink, sat down–and did it."

I saw Delores coming and I waved to her. Weakly.

He killed the rye in the old-fashioned glass and he jiggled the ice. "So you barked up the wrong tree, pally, and, if a dumb cop is permitted to rattle up his–uh–figures of what they call speech–you knocked down a ten-strike, regardless. So don't preen. And if I may further mix up what they call–uh–metaphors, again, my bright and my beloved detective, I think, honest, a guy lucky as you, if you should ever happen to fall into a large barrel of–"

"Uh-uh," Delores Bentley admonished. "We got ladies in the joint, Lieutenant. Remember?"

RICHARD S. PRATHER
(b.1921)

Dead Giveaway
(Shell Scott)

She came into my office as if she were backing out of it, a thin, frightened-appearing mouse who looked like the picture taken before the Before picture, and she stared all around the office in a most bewildered way before even looking at me.

"You–are you Mr. Scott? It said on the door–I–oh–"

It says on the door, *Sheldon Scott, Investigations,* but I'd never thought that was anything to crack up about. Not even my appearance–six- two, 205 pounds, stand-up white hair and whitish miniature-boomerang eyebrows, plus a slightly bent nose and a thin slice gone from my left ear–could have done this to her. Life could have. Or jaywalking through the Los Angeles traffic on Broadway one floor below. Or trouble. Well, people come to me when they're in trouble.

"Yes, ma'am, I'm Shell Scott."

I got her seated in the leather chair opposite my desk, then sat down again and waited.

She was about twenty-five years old, possibly less, with muddy brown hair and eyes and complexion. Squint lines of worry etched the skin around her eyes, and the corners of her thin-lipped mouth turned down. Her face was almost expressionless, as if she were trying to keep the features rigid and immobile.

She had been carrying a paper sack in her hand. Now she started to put it on my desk, changed her mind, started again and then let out a little sigh as if she wished she could leave the thing hanging there in the air.

Finally she reached into the sack and took out a bottle of milk. She put the bottle on the edge of my desk, and we both stared at it. I don't know what she was thinking, but I was thinking maybe she was in the wrong office. Next door to me is Dr. Elben Forrest, a consulting psychologist. He's pretty balmy himself, and all sorts of weird characters visit him.

But I didn't say anything except, "What did you want to see me about, ma'am?"

"I–I'm Ilona Cabot," she said. "Mrs. Cabot. I'm married." She paused, her head turned slightly sideways, peering at me from the corners of her eyes. Despite her plainness and drabness, she had a rather sweet look about her. Sweet–but naive, unknowing.

After a pause, she went on, "I've been married four days. And my husband has been–missing since late yesterday afternoon. I hope you can find Johnny. Something bad must have happened to him."

"Johnny's your husband?"

"Yes. Somebody must have hurt him. Maybe he's dead."

Her face didn't change expression, but her eyes, which had appeared shiny as glass, seemed to melt a little, two tears spilling from them and running down her cheeks. They reached her chin and for a second hung oddly from the flesh, like trembling beads, before falling to the dark cloth of her dress.

She went on, "Otherwise, he'd be with me. Maybe whoever's responsible for him being away is–is the same one who's trying to kill us."

"Somebody's tried to kill you?"

"Two nights ago, Sunday night, just about dusk, I was walking to the little store near our place–I live on Robard Street–when the car almost hit me."

"What car was that?"

"Just a car. I can't tell one from another. But it came down the street and, well, it seemed like whoever was driving it tried to hit me."

"Did you see who was driving?"

"No. I jumped and the car just barely missed me. I fell and skinned my leg."

She paused and I nodded encouragingly. I certainly didn't want her to show me her leg. She went on. "At the time I thought–well, that it was just an accident."

"But you don't think so now."

"No." She pointed to the bottle on my desk. "I got the milk from

the porch this morning and before breakfast gave some to Dookie–
my little cat. She died right away."

Without touching the glass, I took the top off the bottle and smelled
the milk. I'm not a poison expert, but with cyanide you don't have
to be an expert. The odor was faint, but it was the smell of peach pits.

"Cyanide," I said. "I'm pretty sure." It appeared that Mrs. Cabot
was in the right office after all.

I found out what I could about her suddenly missing husband.
Oddly enough, she didn't know very much. She'd met Johnny Cabot,
it developed, on the seventeenth of this month, Saturday, exactly ten
days ago.

I said, "You mean that you'd only known each other six days when
you were married?"

She nodded. "It was–all of a sudden." Two more shiny tears oozed
from her eyes. And still there was no real change of expression on
her homely face. It was as if pressure built up inside her head, forcing the tears out like fluid through a pinpoint opening in a mask of
flesh.

"I'm awfully worried about him," she said. "He's all–he's all I've
got."

And right then I moved over onto Ilona's side, not just because
she was about to become a client, or because she seemed to be in
trouble. It was Ilona Cabot's voice when she said "all I've got." Not
the words themselves so much, but the sound of them, the twisted,
aching sound that she seemed to be trying so desperately to control.
The way she said that her husband was all she had it sounded literally
true.

Until ten days ago, Ilona had been Ilona Green, living cheaply and
frugally by herself in a rented house on Robard Street and working
in a secretarial pool at the Grandon Insurance Company on Hill
Street. Usually, after leaving work, she said, she stopped for dinner
at a cafeteria called Hansen's. That Saturday, ten days ago, she'd been
eating when Johnny Cabot joined her at her table. They'd started
talking, and from this casual meeting had gone on to a movie and
arranged to meet the following day. Three days after they'd met he'd
proposed to Ilona, they'd got their blood tests and been married on
Friday, four days ago.

Her husband had gone out after dinner last night, she said, about
seven P.M., and hadn't come back. He had told Ilona he was a
salesman for the Webley Dinnerware Company, but was on vacation; she didn't know where the company was located.

"What about this milk? When is it left at your house?"

"The milkman comes by about five every morning and leaves a

bottle on our porch. Between five and a quarter after, usually."

"Uh-huh. And when did you get it from the porch this morning?"

"It was about six."

"So if somebody poisoned the milk, it was probably between five and six this morning." She nodded and I went on, "Where was Mr. Cabot when you almost got hit by that car?"

"He'd gone out for a walk. That was Sunday."

"Uh-huh." She didn't seem to find anything unusual in the fact that her husband had been nowhere around at the time of both attempts on her life. So I didn't mention it. Instead, I asked her to describe her husband.

Her eyes brightened and a smile touched her lips. She sort of glowed. She beamed. The man she described sounded like a composite of Greek gods and Roman athletes, so I asked her if she had a picture of him. She had brought one along in her purse.

Johnny Cabot even looked a little like a Roman athlete. In the snapshot, he was wearing swim trunks, leaning back on the sand with his elbows under him, sunlight glinting on almost as much muscle as tan. The features were sharp, and pleasant enough. He appeared to be a very well-built, good-looking guy about thirty. The expression was a bit surly, though. The dark eyes under heavy brows seemed angry, or resentful. Take him back a couple of thousand years and put him in a different outfit, and he might well have been a Roman gladiator lying on his back in the arena, glaring up at some egg about to stab him with a trident. He was plenty good-looking, and that puzzled me; he and Ilona Cabot just didn't make a pair.

Ilona gave me their address and their phone number. And in a couple more minutes I was hired, for a minimum fee, to accomplish two things: first find Ilona Cabot's hubby, if he was still alive, and second learn who was trying to kill the Cabots—or kill Ilona; I had a feeling that the poison had been meant solely for her. I told her she'd better move to another address temporarily, but she refused, saying that her husband might come home or try to get in touch with her there. I told her to be extremely careful about answering the door, and that I would phone or come by later in the day. She said that would be fine, and left.

As the door closed behind her, I picked up my phone and dialed police headquarters. I was still talking to Sergeant Prentiss in Missing Persons when the office door opened and my second caller of the morning came in. I didn't even look around for a few seconds, just finished asking Prentiss to let me know if they came up with anything from his bureau or the morgue on John Cabot, then started to hang up, and looked around, and dropped the phone.

This one would have made a pair with Johnny Cabot, gladiator. Or with Caesar. Or, especially, with me. Maybe it was just that she benefited so much by comparison, and that she had entered about fifteen seconds after the dull, drab one had left, but she seemed to have in abundance everything that Ilona had not.

2

This one was bright and sparkling, and her hair was red, fire-engine red, and that was appropriate because she would always be going to a fire. She was about five feet, five inches of spontaneous arson leaning forward on the desk, both hands far apart on its top, and that caused the white blouse she was wearing to fall away from her body far enough to reveal truly remarkable proportions.

"I hope you can help me," she said.

"Help you?" She had great big blue eyes and one of those mouths best described as ripe and red. It was plain asking for it.

She went on breathlessly—but breathing, as I took pains to notice, "Oh, I do hope you can help me."

"I do, too. I—"

"It's men. Men like you. And sex, and all that."

"I—sex?"

"Yes. It's difficult to explain. Perhaps it's because I was so late getting started. I don't know how I could have been so casual about men before. Now I—I just want to hug them and *squeeze*—"

"Hug them and *squeeze*—"

"Like you. I could just hug you! Boy, could I *hug* you! You must be big as a house."

"I'm only six-two. Hardly a house. What the hell—"

"It's nice, but I can't go around like this all the time. Can't you do something to help me, Doctor? Prescribe something?"

"Honey, I know exactly what will...Doctor? What do you mean, Doctor?"

"Aren't you Doctor Forrest?"

"Hell, no," I said disgruntledly. "I'm only Shell Scott."

"Who's Shell Scott?"

"Me. I just told you, I'm Shell Scott—oh, the hell with it."

"What have you done with Doctor Forrest?"

I got up and walked across the room to the bookcase against the wall. I looked at the happy, dumb, multicolored guppies cavorting in their small aquarium atop the book-case. They crowded up at the front of the tank and ogled me, leaping about friskily, expecting me to feed them. But I merely dipped my fingers in the water and put them, cool and wet, on my temples.

When I'd got pretty well calmed down I said, "I haven't done anything to Doctor Forrest. He is right next door, where he belongs. Where you belong. Where, perhaps, I belong."

She laughed, but then got quiet for a moment. "You must mean I'm in the wrong office."

"Now you got it."

She stared at me, then said almost resentfully, "Well, it's a mistake anybody could have made. Especially when I saw that woman leaving here. That proved it."

"Proved what?"

"That this was a psychologist's office. A woman who looked like that would almost have to be coming out of a psychologist's office. What kind of an office is this, anyway?"

"I'm a private detective."

"Gracious. What would a woman like that want with a detective?"

"She wants me to find her husband, among other things."

"Husband!" She looked shocked. "Husband? I–well, who would have thought she'd have a husband?"

"Lady," I said, "this has all been very new and interesting, but it's time to call a halt. I have work to do."

"You must think I'm an awful goof. It's just that I had an appointment with Doctor Forrest and was so worried about telling him. I had to grab my courage with both hands if you know what I mean."

"I think I do."

"I'm really not a goof. Normally I'm quite normal. But–well, I'm sorry. If I need a detective to investigate something I'll get in touch with you, Mr. Scott. All right?"

I grinned. "That would be all right even if you *don't* need a detective to investigate something, miss. Is it Miss?"

She smiled. She was really an interesting, intriguingly fashioned female when she smiled like that. "Miss Carol Austin," she said. "Plaza Hotel, Room Thirty-seven, Mr. Scott."

"I'll remember. And call me Shell."

"Good-bye." She walked to the door, then looked back at me. "Shell." She went out smiling.

I sat behind my desk, smiling. Then my eyes fell on the bottle of milk. Ah, yes; Ilona. I went back to work.

3

It was afternoon before I came up with anything solid. By then I'd had the milk tested–it was loaded with enough potassium cyanide to kill a dozen people–and had located Johnny Cabot's address. At least it had been his address before he'd married Ilona.

At the Hall of Justice I got a copy of the application for marriage license which had been issued ten days before to Johnny Cabot and Ilona Green. He had, automatically, given his parent's true name and address. Mr. and Mrs. Anthony Cabitocchi lived at Pomona, California. When I called them the Cabitocchis knew nothing of their son's marriage, but were able to supply me with the address at which they wrote him. That was Apartment 12 in the Franklin on Sunset Boulevard between L.A. and Hollywood. By five P.M. I was talking to the manager there. After I'd identified myself and explained why I'd like to look over Cabot's room, the manager let me into Apartment 12, and followed me inside.

The room looked as if it had been very recently used. I asked the manager if Cabot were still living in the room. "Far as I know," he said. "Rent's paid up for another month."

In the bureau drawer I found a stack of photographs. There were about twenty of them each different and all of women. Ilona wasn't one of them. In the same drawer were two clippings from newspapers. One of them, yellowed by time, was brief mention of a paternity case that had been tried here in Los Angeles. A man named William Grant, 26, had been accused of fathering the child of one Mary Lassen, 18, but had beaten the case in court. The other clip stated that William J. Grant had died after a long illness and that services for the "well-known local bachelor-millionaire" would be held on the following Thursday.

A paternity case. I wondered why they were never called maternity cases. I also wondered what Johnny Cabot was doing with the two clippings–but then I hit pay dirt. It was a pay voucher, showing that John Cabot had received his salary from the Westlander Theater.

I'd never been to the Westlander, but I knew what and where it was–and I was very soon going to visit it for the first time. The Westlander was a burlesque house, but it was to the burlesque circuit about what Spike Jones is to classical music, or one pair of bloomers is to the Arabian Nights. On occasion newcomers to the game got their start at the Westlander, but usually the game was almost over before an act hit the small theater on Los Angeles Street.

I headed for Los Angeles Street.

The Westlander was showing a twin movie bill–*Dope Hell of the Sadistic Nudists,* and a film about a real negative thinker, *I Even Went Wrong Wrong.* In front of the small theater were stills from the movies, and nearly life-size photos of the burlesque queens currently appearing here. I bought a ticket from the gal in the booth, turned and took a step toward the entrance, then stopped and blinked, and blinked again.

Opposite the box office was the large photo of a large gal, and even though she was a young and shapely creature, especially in contrast to the others pictured here, and even though she was a long lush blonde with equipment which looked like what we might expect on next year's model, that wasn't why I was blinking.

I was blinking at the name printed on the picture's base–Ilona, the Hungarian Hurricane.

Ilona?

Just a few hours earlier I'd been talking to another Ilona, my client, Mrs. Johnny Cabot, who was the only Ilona I'd talked to in months, maybe even years. I looked the picture of this one over carefully, but she was for sure a different Ilona. I went inside.

In a couple minutes I'd located the manager inside his office. He was a pale, cigar-chewing man named Dent. I identified myself and said, "I'm trying to locate Johnny Cabot. He still work for you?"

The manager nodded and said around his long brown cigar, "Yeah. That's funny, y'know? You comin' here."

"How's that?"

"Private detective, I mean. You're the second one been here in the last couple weeks."

"Oh? Who was the last one? What did he want?"

"Guy named–ah, Wells–Welch, that's it, Welch. Wanted to talk to Ilona. She's just started here, new to the business. He talked with her, then left with Johnny."

Johnny Cabot?" Dent nodded and I asked, "What did he want with Cabot?"

"I dunno. I just saw them leavin' together."

"When was that?"

Dent checked some records in his desk. "Fifteenth, it must've been," he said. "Johnny asked off on Saturday the seventeenth, for ten days, and that detective guy was here a couple days before that. Johnny just got back today."

"Back? You mean he's here now?"

"Where'd you expect he'd be? Sure he's here."

"I– Did Cabot say why he wanted time off?"

"Just that something important had come up."

I was remembering that Cabot and Ilona Green had met on Saturday the seventeenth. "Okay if I talk to Cabot?"

"Sure. Have to wait a few minutes. He's my singer."

Dent showed me to a box seat at the side of the stage, briefed me on what remained of the show, and left. The chorus was currently occupying the stage. It consisted of about twenty girls, or rather females, all leaping about with complete disregard of the pit band, shaking to the left and shaking to the right, and backward and forward; but the kindest thing I could say about them was that they were no great shakes.

When they trooped off into the wings, a tall, thin, bony babe trotted listlessly into view, smiling as if it were painful, and proceeded to take her clothes off like a woman preparing to go to bed alone on a freezing night, with only one thin blanket in the house. There just wasn't any joy in it. Her performance didn't make me feel good all over, as the saying goes. It didn't make me feel good anyplace.

Finally it was finished. The chorus trooped back on and began tap dancing to one number while the band played another, and a tall dark guy walked onstage carrying a microphone and its stand. A couple yards in from the wings he stopped, placed the mike before him, spread his arms wide and started singing.

So here, at last, was Johnny Cabot. Somehow I hadn't quite believed Cabot would be there, not until this moment. If the story Ilona Cabot had told me was true, Cabot's being here four days after his marriage, singing in a cheap burlesque house instead of home with his bride, just didn't make good sense to me. Not yet, anyway. But it was the gladiator boy all right. Sharp, good-looking features, heavy eyebrows, thick dark hair. He had that surly look still, I noticed, even though he was smiling most of the time.

But I wasn't smiling. The sounds banging in anguish at my eardrums were coming from Johnny Cabot as if they were escaping. He had a high, squeaky voice that sounded like a musical saw being played in a swamp full of mosquitoes, and his stiff gestures might have been Frankenstein's monster blowing kisses at King Kong.

The girls swung to their right, bent their knees and threw their hands into the air, looking up toward the ceiling, as if they had all seen hairy tarantulas dangling from a crosswalk; then they all spun to the opposite side and did it again, while Johnny cried, "Tem... *tay*... shun!" It wasn't the right song. Nothing would have been the right song, but Johnny made even "Temptation" sound like something midway between rock-and-roll and rack-and-ruin.

At last it was over. Johnny bowed and beamed to a complete absence of applause, then went offstage. The girls trooped out of sight. I got to my feet, ready to go backstage and talk to Cabot, but a voice cut in over the p.a. system, saying that we had reached the climax of the show–Ilona, the Hungarian Hurricane. I watched it all.

The number was *Diane*, played slowly and deliberately, and Ilona was slow and deliberate in her movements, of which there were a great many, and many of them great. She was tall, wearing heels at least four inches high, with a lot of blonde hair and a lot of blonde skin showing, and she seemed to be enjoying herself almost as much as I was.

Let's face it. Men like to watch women take off their clothes. When the day comes when that isn't true any more, then we will have entered the Mental Age and will get our kicks at brain operations. But that day is not yet, so I gleefully ogled the last twitch of tassel, the final flick of bead, and then, when Ilona, the Hungarian Hurricane, bounced and jiggled out of sight, I got up and headed backstage for my first words with Johnny Cabot.

4

I found him in a small room off a hall smelling of powder and perspiration. A stagehand pointed to the room and when I knocked Cabot opened the door and glared out at me. That is, he looked out at me, but the general arrangement of his features made it appear that he was always glaring, or perhaps on the verge of biting somebody.

He was about my height, but slimmer, with thick wavy black hair and light blue eyes. I'm pretty brown myself, but this guy must have made a career of soaking up sun because he made me look anemic by comparison. Those pale blue eyes were startlingly light in his darkly bronzed face.

He was good looking, all right, but to me, anyway, he had the look of those guys who star in pornographic movies. He looked weak, much more physical than mental, not clean-cut, not pleasant. He stood there smiling at me, and while it wasn't a bad smile, I almost wanted to go at it like a mad dentist. Once in a while you meet guys like Cabot. It's as if odorless skunk waves keep coming out from them at you. I wondered how my client had failed to notice it. But maybe he affected women differently.

He had his shirt off, and thick muscles moved on his chest. It seemed incredible that a voice so thin could come out of a chest so thick. "Yeah? What you want?"

"You John Cabot?"

"Yeah. So?"

I flipped open my wallet and flashed the photostat of my license in front of his face. His eyes aimed at it and barely focused on it as I snapped the wallet shut and stuck it back in my coat. Sometimes, if you do that fast enough, people think you're some kind of important official. Like a policeman.

"I'm Scott," I said brusquely. "Mind telling me where you were this morning? Early—say about three to six A.M."

He said slowly, "I had a supper date. You know, real late. From about one till after six."

"Six in the morning?" That seemed like an odd time for a date of any kind. Well, almost any kind.

"Yeah," he said. "Gal didn't get off until after midnight."

"Get off where?"

"Club out on Beverly," Cabot said. "The—Grotto." He paused. "Say, you're not a cop, are you?"

"Nobody said I was. I'm Shell Scott, a private investigator."

He spat out foul words. "Private! Why, you son—"

"Hold it, friend. You can watch your tongue or the ceiling."

He bit off the rest of his words, but said, "What in hell do you want with me? What's the score?"

"I'm checking up on an attempted murder."

He grinned, unpleasantly. "I haven't tried to kill anybody, Scott. If I had tried, I'd have killed him. Who was the victim?"

"The attempt was made on your wife. Matter of fact, she sent me out to find you."

"Ilona? She sent you? How in hell did she know—" He bit it off.

"How'd she know what, Cabot?"

"Beat it."

"Aren't you interested in an attempt on your wife's life? She thought maybe it was an attempt on your life, too, since somebody poisoned the milk and you might have drunk some. I don't see it that way, but—"

"I got no more to say to you."

"What about Welch?" For a stab in the dark it got quite a reaction.

"Huh?" Cabot's face got almost pale. The blood did leave his face for a while, and that tan over pallor made him look sick. Maybe he was sick. "Welch?" he said. "I—I don't know anybody named Welch."

I grinned at him. "No. You always look like this. You know who I mean, Cabitocchi. A detective named Welch."

He stared at me stupidly. His mouth opened and closed. But then he balled up his fists and stepped toward me, anger flushing his features and making him appear normal again.

I thought for a second I was going to get to hit him, but something made him stop. A sort of crafty look appeared in his pale blue eyes. He took a deep breath and let it out, then said levelly, "Out. Out you go, Scott. You're a private dick, and if you bother me any more, I'll–" he grinned nastily– "call a cop."

Then he just stood there and looked at me grinning. He was right, too. A private detective is merely a private citizen, and if I were to let my emotion rule my knuckles, I could very well wind up in the clink. I left.

I had a lot more to puzzle me now than I'd had when I'd come into the Westlander Theater. I'd found Cabot, all right, but the big half of the job was no closer to a solution; I still didn't know who'd tried to kill my client, Ilona.

The thought of one Ilona led logically to thought of the second one. After half a minute and one more question of a stagehand, I was knocking on another dressing-room door. This time it was the dressing room of Ilona, the Hungarian Hurricane. A voice inside said, "Just a minute," with no accent at all except the feminine one. Then the door opened.

The only similarity between this gal's expression and Johnny Cabot's was that she looked as if she were going to bite somebody, too. But gently. With eclat, verve, abandon. "Yes?" she said softly.

"Yes, indeed, I just saw you act–"

"Oh, good. Come in." I went inside and she said, "I'm just learning, you know. Did you like it? My dance?"

"You bet. It was real . . . likable."

"Wonderful!" she cried enthusiastically, and gave a little bump from sheer joy. "Wonderful!"

Ilona was wearing an abbreviated robe which looked a bit like one of those shortie nightgowns and fell down her thighs only about halfway. It was blue, and made a pretty contrast with her white skin.

"I practice all the time," she said. "You know what they say, practice makes perfect."

"That one was pretty near perfect right there."

"*Thank* you," she squealed.

"Uh, my name is Shell Scott." I finally got to tell her I was a detective, and asked her about her co-performer, Cabot. She thought he was real nice. She'd been working here only a little over two weeks, and Cabot had been here the first week only.

So there wasn't much she could tell me about Cabot, but remembering his reaction to detective Welch's name, I asked the Hungarian

Hurricane, "Do you know a man named Welch?"

"No," She was walking around the room, snapping her fingers and everything. "Who is he?"

"Another detective. I understood that he talked to you here a couple weeks ago. About that long back."

"Oh, him. Yes, sure. What about him?"

"Would you mind telling me what he wanted with you?"

She was standing in front of the full-length mirror, leaning slightly back from it and practicing; then she glanced at me and said, "You don't mind if I do this, do you?"

"No." I grinned. "Go right ahead."

"I just want to get the rough edges off this movement. I think I've got most of them off now."

"I'd say so."

"What was it you asked me?"

"I don't remember."

"Oh, yes. About that detective. He just asked me if I'd ever been in the Bunting Orphanage here in Los Angeles, and I told him no, and he thanked me and left." Suddenly she let out a wild, high-pitched noise.

"What was that?" I said. "You all right?" She hadn't even stopped what she was doing.

"Oh, that was just my squeal," she said.

"Your what?"

"Squeal. You know, toward the climax of my act, when I'm all a-frenzy, I squeal. It adds something."

"I see. Yes, it would add something. Bunting Orphanage, huh? What did he want to know that for?"

"I don't know. That was all he asked me, and then he left."

"You ever see him before?"

"No. Nor since."

"Do you know if he was a friend of Johnny Cabot's?"

"I don't know. Johnny asked me what the detective wanted with me, though–right after the detective talked to me."

"He did, huh? What did you tell him?"

"The same thing I just told you."

She described Welch as about five-ten, slim, with a black mustache and black hair, beginning to get gray. She had no idea where Welch lived, but she didn't think he was a Los Angeles detective.

That was about it. She was almost ready to squeal again, anyway, and as a matter of fact so was I, so I thanked her and went out. Not all the way out, though; Johnny Cabot was waiting near Ilona's dressing room for me. He waved a hand at me and I walked over to him.

"Listen, Scott," he said grimly. "Get something through your head. I don't want no more trouble from you."

This guy irritated me like a slap on sunburn, but I kept my voice quiet enough as I said, "If you don't want trouble, you're sure going at it the wrong way, Cabot."

"Yeah? Well, I'm telling you, stay away from my wife, see? And from me, and anybody connected with me. If you snoop around any more, get in my hair any more, I'll bust your skull."

"Quit wiggling your muscles, Cabot. At least you admit you're married."

"So my wife hired you. Well, you're fired."

"I'll wait till I hear it from your wife."

He glared at me. "It's enough if you hear it from me. You're finished; no more job."

"What are you afraid of, friend? You didn't try to knock off your wife, did you?"

He was burning. "If I wanted to kill somebody. I wouldn't use cyanide, I'd use a gun. And a bullet can poke a hole in you just as easy as anybody else, Scott. Remember that."

He spun on his heel and stalked off before I could reply. It was just as well; I had rapidly been reaching the point where my next reply would have been to sock him in the teeth. I went out of the Westlander Theater, found a phone booth in a drugstore, and dialed the number my client had given me this morning.

There wasn't any answer to my ring. I frowned at the phone for a moment, then went back to my Cadillac and drove toward Robard Street.

From my client's house and on past it for perhaps a quarter of a mile, Robard was a one-way street. I parked at the left curb and walked up to the front door. There was no answer to my ring, and I'd started to turn away when I noticed the front door was ajar. I knocked loudly, then went on in.

It was a small, neat place. There wasn't anything unusual about it except that it was empty, and on the kitchen table were some dirty dishes, one of them containing part of a lamb chop and some broccoli. A half-glass of milk sat beside the dish containing the meat. It appeared as if whoever had been eating had left in a hurry.

I lit a cigarette and looked down at the kitchen table, thinking. It seemed fairly clear that Cabot must have immediately phoned Ilona after I'd talked to him at the burlesque theater–before I'd phoned her. One word from him and his bride would naturally have flown to him as fast as she could–not even waiting to finish her lamb chop and broccoli.

I was becoming more and more worried about Ilona Cabot. Somebody had tried twice to murder that mousy, sweetly miserable little gal, and I was pretty sure whoever it was would keep on trying. The thought struck me that I had no proof she was still alive.

I kept thinking about that angle as I got into the Cad and headed on down Robard. The first street at which I could turn off was Garnet, and I swung right there. I'd barely straightened the car out when it happened.

I heard the sound of the shot, but didn't react for a second or so. The slug splatted through the glass and I saw the hole suddenly appear far over on the wind-shield's right side, as the heavy sound of the gunshot reached my ears. For a second or two I looked stupidly at the hole near the windshield's edge, at the white lines radiating from it and spreading like thick cobwebs over the glass. And then I hit the brake pedal so hard that I shoved myself back into the upholstery of the seat behind me.

The power brakes caught and grabbed, tires shrieking on the pavement as the car slid and turned slightly toward the curb. I jerked the steering wheel left, then slapped my foot onto the accelerator again. I straightened the Cad out and let it pick up speed for half a block, then pulled in to the curb and stopped.

I had the door open and was starting through it, right hand under my coat and touching the butt of my .38 Colt, when I stopped. There wasn't much point in charging back down the street like an Olympic sprinter. Whoever had taken that shot at me was almost surely a lot farther away now than he'd been when he let the slug fly at me. Or when she had. A bullet out of the night is anonymous.

But I could count the people who might know that I was going to visit this address on one finger, or two at most if I included Ilona herself. Somebody might conceivably have tailed me from downtown and then waited near the turnoff on Garnet; but it didn't seem likely. So I was extremely anxious to see Johnny Cabot once again.

5

I looked around, but after twenty minutes I hadn't learned anything new. People in a couple of houses admitted hearing the gun-shot, or "backfire," but that was as close as I got. I did use the phone in one of the houses and called the Westlander Theater. When Mr. Dent came on and I asked for Johnny Cabot, he exploded.

"What'd you do to him? What's happening. All of a sudden my star singer's gone. Right after you talked to him he lit out and I ain't seen him since."

I told him I hadn't done anything to Cabot and got him calmed down. Finally he promised to keep it under his hat that I'd called, if Cabot did arrive. I told Dent I'd be phoning him again, then drove into downtown L.A. and spent some more time trying to locate Johnny Cabot or Ilona, without success. I checked again at the Franklin, where Cabot still had his apartment, but he hadn't turned up there. The twenty bucks I left with the desk clerk, however, assured me of the clerk's prompt cooperation if and when Cabot or Ilona showed up.

Cabot had said he'd spent most of last night, or rather this morning, with a gal who worked at the Grotto. If that was true, he couldn't very well have slipped the cyanide into Ilona's milk. I headed for the Grotto.

It was a long, low, gray building on Beverly Boulevard. Shortly before eight P.M. I turned my car over to the parking attendant and went inside. The first thing that caught my eye was a colorful poster in its glass-covered case alongside the checkroom.

It was a large photograph of a busty mermaid resting on her back at what seemed to represent the bottom of the sea. Diving down through the water above her was a muscular male in a pair of bikini-type trunks. The mermaid was, typically, fish from the waist down, but from the waist up there was nothing fishy about her. Long hair streamed through the water like black seaweed, and the whiteness of her skin glowed phosphorescently in the greenish water. A shaft of light fell from above her and touched the white, prominent breasts.

Painted letters that looked like seaweed at the poster's top announced that the Grotto proudly presented "The Neptune Ballet" in the Underseas Room. At the bottom of the big card, more seaweed letters announced that Dan Thrip was the Sea Satyr, and Ilona Betun was "Neptuna, the Venusian Mermaid."

Ilona?

Ilona.

Well, I thought, I'll be damned.

I looked at the shapely mermaid again. If the poster hadn't been a photograph, I might have thought the artist was an advertising man accustomed to ludicrous and enormous exaggeration, but this was a photograph, and this gal was quite obviously not my Ilona, not my client. It is sometimes possible for a reasonably attractive gal to appear uglier than a dead skunk merely by removing all makeup and failing to put up her hair. Add a drab dress and a frown, and the lovely of the night before often becomes the goon of the morning after.

But taking it off is one thing, and putting it on is another. What this mermaid had, gals cannot put on; they have to grow. And grow, and grow.

Almost reluctantly, I turned away from the poster and looked around. Several people sat at the bar and tables, drinking and talking. Near me a young couple was having dinner, thick steaks sizzling on metal platters. A haze of cigarette smoke hung in the air.

I found the manager in his office. He was about five-ten, thin, white-skinned, with receding brown hair and an empty cigarette holder stuck in the side of his mouth.

He was scribbling on a paper before him. "Yeah?"

"My name's Shell Scott. I'm a private detective." I showed him my credentials. "You're the manager?"

"Yeah. Joe Grace. Detective, huh? What you want with me?"

"It's not you personally. I'd like to talk to Ilona Betun."

"Uh-huh. You're the second detective that's been in here wanting to see her. This wouldn't just be a gag to get close to the doll, would it?"

"No. Who was this other detective?"

"Guy named–Welch, I think it was. Like on a bet."

"Do you know what he wanted to see her about?"

Grace shook his head. "Didn't tell me. Went up and talked to her, that's all I know about it." He looked at his watch. "Just about show time now. You want to talk to Ilona, you'll have to wait till after the show." He paused. "Join me at my table in the Underseas Room if you want to. We'll catch the show from there."

I told him okay, and he led me out of his office and into the room I'd noticed earlier. The Underseas Room was dimly lighted, not large, and probably held no more than fifteen tables or so, but every table was occupied. Imitation seaweed hung from the ceiling, and ornamental nets adorned the side walls. The entire wall directly opposite the door was glass, except for about three feet at the wall's base, and as we got closer I could see that the space beyond that glass wall, extending in for six or eight feet, was filled with water. It was like a high, wide, but narrow aquarium, a room of water.

Soft greenish light filled the room-aquarium, fell on seaweed moving slowly as if touched by delicate currents, on the rippled sand that formed the aquarium's floor. Joe Grace's table was almost against the glass wall, over toward its left side. As he sat down I climbed into a chair opposite him and he asked me what I'd like to drink. I told him bourbon and water, and he sent the waiter off for our highballs. The drinks arrived almost before I could get a cigarette lighted, and I had a gulp of the barely watered bourbon as Grace said, "Ah, here we go." Right after his words I heard a soft chord from the band on a small, raised bandstand inside the entrance. A man's voice was saying that we were about to witness the first show of the evening. He told us in hushed, intimate tones that the Sea Satyr and Neptuna would cavort in the Underwater Ballet for our pleasure, and finally finished with, ". . . the Grotto is proud to present the lovely, the luscious, the exciting–Neptuna!"

There was a fanfare from the combo, then sudden silence. In the silence a figure plunged through the water of the tank, trailing silvery bubbles in its descent toward the floor of sand. Music began again, softly, a weird melody unfamiliar to me, and the figure slowed as it neared the sand.

From her waist down, Neptuna wore a closely fitted fish tail, dark green and apparently covered with metallic scales. From the waist up she was nude, her breasts brazenly thrust forward, bare and whitely gleaming.

Neptuna, or Ilona, swam through the water with surprising ease and gracefulness, despite the fact that her legs were held together by the rubber costume. I couldn't guess how tall she might be, but she was beautifully proportioned. The green rubber costume clung tightly to flaring hips, and above them was a sharply indented waist that accentuated both her hips and the heavy breasts. She arched her body slowly, easily, twisting in the water, curling around a black rock and then through the thick grasses.

Two or three times she swept her arms back and rose to the water's surface, then twisted around and swam down again. After the last trip up and down again, as she approached the side of the tank where Joe Grace and I sat, she swam almost touching the glass and I got my first good look at her face.

I had never seen her before, but I was looking forward to seeing her again. It was a very pretty face, and what I could see of the body was sensational, and if the legs were even halfway nice, this was a tomato who could model for lipstick, brassieres, hose, or harems.

What I'd thought a big gray rock lying on the sand turned out to be a giant artificial clam. It opened up as Neptuna swam near it. As she rolled over on her back and neatly maneuvered her tail fin past the edge of the clam's shell, it closed suddenly on her and held her captive.

It was neatly done, and there were even a couple startled or frightened yips from women in the audience. Neptuna twisted and jerked as if in a panic, throwing her body from one side to the other, and her white breasts shivered, rolled on her chest, quivered in the water as she jerked and turned.

Then there was another silvery stream of bubbles as a guy in flesh-colored bikini trunks–the Sea Satyr–dived through the water. His part of the rescue didn't take long, since Neptuna had been holding her breath for quite a while, but he hammed it up for fair in the time he had. I was forced to admit, though, that he looked strong enough to handle a dozen giant clams, even with a couple of sharks and sword-fish thrown in. He knifed the clam, which freed Neptuna, whereupon she zipped to the surface for air, then down alongside the guy again. She swirled around him and rubbed up against him, and the sight of those big white breasts sliding against his sundarkened chest was a good deal more sensual then the pictures in movie magazines.

Then the lips of the two undersea dancers met in a kiss. The lights in the tank went out and it seemed as if the water suddenly turned to ink.

Grace said, "How'd you like it, Scott? Pretty good, huh?"

"Yeah. I'll come in and pay the cover charge next time. Thanks for the vantage point and the drinks, Grace." I got up. "By the way, how do I get up to your star's dressing room? I hope I don't have to swim–"

He interrupted, chuckling, "No. I'd better show you, though." Grace led me to the rear of the club and up wooden stairs to the second floor. Three or four doors opened off a hallway there, and he took me to the third one, where he knocked.

There was the sound of bare feet padding across the floor inside, then the door opened and Neptuna was looking out at us.

Grace said, "This's Shell Scott, honey. Private detective. Help him out if you can. Don't want anybody raiding the joint."

"Sure, Joe." She glanced at him as he turned and left, then looked back at me. "Come on in." The voice was deep, throaty, soft. Even if she were to shout, I thought, that voice would have warm whispers in it.

She stepped aside and I went into her dressing room. As she closed the door behind us I got a glimpse of a big dressing table with a huge mirror over it, a wall closet with its sliding door partly open, a yellow bamboo screen between the dressing table and closet, and the gleam of light reflected from the surface of water at floor level on my left. But then she'd stepped up beside me and I was looking at Ilona–Neptuna–again.

Up close she looked even better than I'd expected. The big eyes were dark, with black brows above them like smears of midnight on her smooth white forehead. The red lips were full, half parted. She wore a thin white robe and held a white towel on top of her head with both hands. The pose did nothing to ruin the robe's appearance, though it pushed it quite a bit out of shape, emphasizing facets of Neptuna's figure that were already quite emphatic. She wasn't a very tall girl, but she had such an abundance of curves that, even if she'd been six feet tall, they would have been enough to stretch out and cover everything most satisfactorily.

"Mr. Scott, is it?" she said pleasantly.

"Shell. No need to be formal."

"Not in this outfit." She smiled. All this time she was rubbing the towel over her hair, presumably to dry it, and that caused quite a commotion in the robe, and quite a commotion in me. Thick clumps of black hair escaped from the towel and hung down on one white-covered shoulder.

"I caught your act," I said. "First time. It was sensational."

"You liked it then?"

"Yes, indeed." I tried a gentle sally. "Any time you need a new partner–"

"I know. You'll start holding your breath." She didn't say it in a sarcastic way, though, but rather as if it were something she'd heard too many times already. She was bored with me.

"I imagine you get a lot of offers from people who can't swim."

"I do." She deftly tied the towel around her head, then cinched the robe's belt more tightly about her waist. She smiled again. "But I turn most of them down."

"Most, huh? How about Johnny Cabot?"

"Johnny? What about him?"

"You do know him, then."

"Sure. Is that why you came up here to see me?"

"One reason. When was the last time you saw Johnny–you don't mind the questions, do you?"

"Certainly not. I saw Johnny last night."

So here it was. Cabot had been telling the truth, or else this lovely was lying, and I didn't like that thought at all. But something was real crazy here; maybe the guy was goofy for Ilonas.

"That would have been after you got off from work?" I said.

"Yes. My last show's at midnight. He picked me up about twelve-thirty and we had something to eat, and talked, you know. Then he dropped me at my apartment at maybe six."

"When did you meet him?"

"Couple weeks ago, about. We went out the night we met, and the next night. But then I didn't see him until last night."

"That's understandable," I said.

"How do you mean?"

"Well, he got married last Friday, and that kept him busy for two or three nights."

I was watching for the reaction, and it came slowly, but it came. It was, however, normal enough for a gal like Ilona Betun, assuming she wasn't really hot for the guy. She frowned, started to speak, then stopped. Slowly she said, "Married? But he–is this a joke?"

"No. He got married four days ago."

"Well... what has he been doing with me–I mean, why did he go out with me?"

"I'm curious about that, myself."

She shook her head. "This is a little too much. I thought... " She paused, then went on, "Well, he's been trying to make me believe he's in love with me."

"I wouldn't be surprised if he is."

She looked at me, frowning again. "That doesn't make sense."

"In a strange way, maybe it does. But it's too complicated to go into now. There's one other thing. Did you recently talk to a man named Welch? Another private investigator?"

She nodded. "Sure, I've even got his card around here somewhere. Isn't it funny–you just asked about Johnny, then about Mr. Welch, and I met them both on the same day."

"That is a little funny." I asked her to describe Welch, and it was the same description I'd got from the Hungarian Hurricane. I said, "What did Welch want to see you about?"

"The funniest thing. He asked me if I'd ever been in some kind of orphan's home. Of course I hadn't, and I told him so. He asked my age and where I was born and I told him." She shrugged. "And he left. What's it all about?"

"I'm not sure. But I'm getting an idea. This orphanage, could it have been the Banting?" I purposely mispronounced it.

"Yes... " She nodded slowly. "That's about–Bunting. That's what it was, Bunting."

"You remember what day it was that Welch came here? And that you met Cabot?"

She thought a minute. "It was either the fifteenth, or not more than a day off either way."

"That's good enough. Johnny knew this Welch, then, huh?"

She looked a little puzzled. "Not that I know of."

"Then you didn't meet them at the same time?"

"No. The detective came here before my first show. And I met Johnny after the last show."

"Welch ever explain why he asked you about the orphanage?"

She shook her head. "He was up here only a couple of minutes.

I had to shoo him out so I could get ready for my act. He did say that I was the wrong Ilona, then he thanked me and left."

So both the Hungarian Hurricane, and Neptuna, had turned out to be the wrong girl, the wrong Ilona. That pretty well told me who the right Ilona was.

6

Now that our interview was about over, I looked around again. Two or three inches below floor level, at the left side of the room, water moved gently. It seemed quite strange to see a room with part of the floor wet and liquid, which was the impression I got. I said to Ilona, "So that's the stage for the floorshow. It looks a good deal different from down below."

"I'll bet it does. You know, I've done that act hundreds of times, but I don't know what it looks like."

"Logical enough. Take my word for it, though–you look gorgeous. The whole act is terrific."

"Such enthusiasm!" She smiled. Then she said, "It's almost two hours until the next show, and I don't usually sit around in *nothing* but a robe." I felt sure that she had purposely emphasized the word "nothing." "So do you mind," she went on, "if I get into something more comfortable?"

"No." I was grinning. "Of course not."

Her own smile was pretty close to a grin as she turned and walked away from me. My hopes were pretty high, but then I remembered the bamboo screen. I remembered because Ilona went behind it, then turned to face me. The top of the screen came just an inch or two below the tops of her shoulders. And now I noted, too, that the strips of bamboo were not right up against each other. That is, there were small spaces between them. I could see little strips of white that were her robe. Then, with one easy movement she pulled the robe from her shoulders and let it fall to the floor behind her.

Before, I had seen little strips of white that were Ilona's robe. Now I could see little strips of white that were Ilona's.

It wasn't an awful lot, but it *moved*. Ilona stepped a short distance to one side and reached for something, then bent down and stepped into it. She reached again and slipped a blouse over her head, then reached once more and stepped into what was obviously a skirt. I counted very carefully, however, and she reached only three times.

Then she stepped out from behind the screen and walked barefoot a few feet from the screen, and even if I had not counted, I would still have known she'd reached only three times. Suddenly Ilona stopped, put her hands on her hips, and looked at me. "Well," she said, "you look like a man who plans to come back for the second show."

That snapped me out of it. "No, ma'am, I have work to do."

She chuckled. "Don't be stuffy. I was hoping you did plan to be here. I thought I might put in one little fin flip just for you."

"It might be your fin, Ilona, but it would be my flip."

She smiled. "That's better."

"Seriously, I do have a lot to do in the next few hours, but–well, a man can't work all the time. Perhaps we could–" I stopped as a thought struck me. "Johnny Cabot isn't planning to pick you up tonight, is he?"

"I should say not! After what you told me? Nothing was said about it last night, anyway. Besides," she added frankly, in music to my ears, "I'd much rather be with you." She paused, then went on slowly, "I'll be around a while after two. Just in case you get all your work done." She smiled widely. "Sometimes, you know, I wait till the club is closed and locked, and nobody but me is here, and I have a little swim all by myself. Practice the new act."

"Swim... by yourself... here?"

She nodded.

"Well, that's–interesting." I changed the subject. "I'd like to talk with this Welch. You know where he lives? Or where his office is?"

"No."

"He a local man?"

"I don't know that for sure, either. But I think he was from out of town. We just had a real short talk, and he didn't tell me much except his name–I remember he said his first name was Harry. Harry Welch."

I thanked her and went out. Downstairs again I hunted up Joe Grace and asked him, "When Welch–the other detective–came in and talked to you, was he alone."

"Let's see. Was when he talked to me. But I think he came in with a younger guy. Yeah, they watched the show and had dinner."

"Do you remember what this other guy looked like?" He shook his head, and I showed him the picture I carried of Johnny Cabot.

"Sure," Grace nodded. "I remember now thinking he was even more tanned than Dan Thrip. And them pale blue eyes–yeah, that's the one it was. What about him?"

"I was just curious. I'm real anxious to see him. Thanks again. I'll send in some customers."

He grinned at me as I left. Well, Cabot had hit the Grotto, then, in the company of Detective Welch. The longer this day lasted, the more puzzled I got. But a ray of light was beginning to filter into my thoughts now. There wasn't anything especially strange about there being three–or even three hundred–gals named Ilona in Los Angeles. But it seemed odd indeed that Johnny Cabot should know all three of them. More–he worked with one, dated another, and was married to the third. My running into one Ilona after another had sort of staggered me for a while, because I'm extremely leery of coincidence. But when I ignored coincidence, the light began to filter.

The reason that Cabot knew three gals named Ilona, obviously, was because he'd made it his business to meet them and get to know them. Two of them, anyway. He'd been working with the Hungarian Hurricane for a while, and that would explain his knowing her. But the other two he had managed to run into on purpose. On the 15th of this month he had met Ilona Betun. On the 17th he had met Ilona Green–whom I now thought of as the "right" Ilona–and on the 23rd he'd married her.

There was food for thought in those items, and mainly it made me anxious to find Cabot and his bride–and Harry Welch. I put in a call to the house on Robard Street, but there was still no answer there. Dent was still fuming at the Westlander. A call to the desk clerk at the Franklin got me the information that Cabot hadn't been in.

Harry Welch wasn't in the L.A. phone book or City Directory. I called half a dozen detective agency heads whom I knew personally, and several other investigators I knew by reputation, but none of them had ever heard of Harry Welch. The Bunting Orphanage, at least, was easy to find. The phone book listed it as at 7230 Orange Drive.

It was only eight-thirty p.m., so I phoned the place and talked to a Mr. Simpson. Judging by his voice, Mr. Simpson was about a hundred and eighty years old, and ready to give up the ghost. It was a voice always on the verge of saying good-by. But Mr. Simpson said, sure, he'd given a detective named Welch some information and yes, it would be all right for me to come out and talk to him.

I parked at the curb and walked up a cement path to steps before the wooden porch. The stairs creaked like rheumatic bones, sighed softly as I walked up on to the porch. At the right of the big door, above the push button of the bell, a small weathered brass sign said, "Bunting Orphanage Home."

Mr. Simpson answered my ring. He was little over five feet tall, with accents of white hair on his pink scalp, and a narrow face, but with brown eyes that were still alert and merry. I told him that I was Shell Scott, the man who had just phoned him, and explained why I was here. Yes, he remembered about the other detective. After a few questions, to get him started, he told me all he knew about Welch and the detective's purpose in visiting the orphanage. It fitted well enough into the pattern that had so far developed.

Welch had told him, Mr. Simpson said, that on April 7th twenty-two years ago, a seven-month-old girl had been turned over to the Bunting Orphanage. The detective wanted to know what had happened to the girl and where he could find her now. Mr. Simpson went on, in his quavering, soft voice, "Well, I checked the records and found the one he was after. Baby was brought here by the mother, Mary Lassen. She killed herself."

"Mary Lassen committed suicide? When was that?"

"About a week after she left the infant here. Baby was born out of wedlock, and the way I figure it, the daddy didn't want nothing to do with either of them. Not then. Must of been somewhat of a strain for the woman. But the funny thing is, the father's the man that set the detective to looking up the girl."

"Who's the father?"

"Well, he's a man named William Grant–that is, he *was*. He's been dead and buried for some weeks." Mr. Simpson went on to say that it was because of Grant's death–he thought, but wasn't sure–that Welch had come looking for the girl. Unfortunately, Simpson said, he hadn't been able to give Welch much help, because some of the orphanage records had been destroyed about ten years ago, and among them were the records of the girl's adoption. Thus Mr. Simpson had been unable to discover the name of the people who had adopted her.

"How about Welch?" I asked. "Did he tell you where he was from? Or where he was staying in town?"

Mr. Simpson shook his head. "Didn't tell me anything."

"Do you remember when he was here?"

"I checked after you called and asked about him. It was the twelfth. That was a Monday, little over two weeks back."

I had just one more question. I knew the answer, of course, but I asked it anyway, for corroboration. "You still haven't told me the girl's name."

"She didn't really have a last name till somebody adopted her. But her first name was Ilona."

7

I got back to my apartment a little after eleven p.m., having tried again, without success, to locate Johnny Cabot or his wife. I parked across North Rossmore from the Spartan Apartment Hotel, crossed the street, went inside, and trotted up the steps to the second floor. And as I reached the top I heard what sounded like somebody else trotting behind me.

I turned around in time to watch Carol Austin bounce up the last few steps. She stopped and looked up at me, panting a little. "Gracious, you move fast," she said.

"Well, hello. What are you doing—"

"You said I could see you. At your office, remember?"

"Yes, but I hardly expected you to show up here. How did you know I lived... " I let it trail off, remembering that this gal might conceivably do almost anything. She still looked as if she were going to a fire; even better, I decided, than she had this morning.

Carol Austin seemed to have dressed with more care, applied her makeup even more expertly, and of course she still had all the items which I had so happily itemized this morning; consequently she was a very tasty-looking dish indeed. So even though I was mentally shaking my head at her, I was lost.

There was a kind of hurt, bewildered look in her wide blue eyes, and she said slowly, "Is something the matter, Mr. Scott? Shouldn't I have come here? I looked you up in the book and got your address, and waited down in the lobby, and you'd said it was all right to come see you even if it wasn't for a case, and I... "

"Oh, that's all right," I said with enthusiasm. "Anything—everything's all right. Why, I'm happy you could make it."

"Oh, good!"

"Well, there's no point in just standing here, is there? My apartment's right down the hall, so why don't we—"

"Oh, that *would* be fun," she said.

The next twenty minutes were, while a bit disjointed, delightful nonetheless. Carol—after a couple of minutes it was Carol—seemed to think mine was a fascinating life, and wanted to know all about my work.

I explained to her that it was well she hadn't come here to hire me, because the case on which I was now engaged was occupying most of my time.

"What case? I didn't know—Oh, you mean that woman who was

leaving your office this morning? You said her name was Ilona Cabot or something, didn't you?"

"Yeah, that's it." We were both sitting on the chocolate-brown divan in my front room. But we were at opposite ends of the divan, so we were yards apart. The divan is big enough to sleep on, or anything.

"Gracious," Carol went on. "Weren't you looking for her husband or something? Did you find him?"

"Yeah, and lost him. But let's not talk shop, Carol."

"Would you think I was awful if I asked if you had anything to drink here?"

I sprang to my feet. "What would you like? Bourbon? Scotch? A Martini, Manhattan–"

"Oh, my, I just meant a Coke or something."

"Nonsense. Though I have Coke."

"Well, all right. A Coke."

"But–"

"With just the teensiest bit of Scotch in it."

"Fine. A Scotch-and-Coke coming right up . . . "

That was such a goofy-sounding drink, like bourbon and beet juice, that it suddenly reminded me of how she'd happened to wind up in my office this morning. I said, "Ah, Carol. How did you make out with Doctor Forrest?"

"Oh, fine. He gave me a pill. You know, to sort of–sort of calm me down."

"And did it calm you down?"

"Uh-huh. I'm fine now. Show me where everything is, and let me mix the drinks. All right? That would be fun."

She got up, took me by the hand and accompanied me to the kitchenette. I watched Carol mix her sticky concoction, then supervised her preparation of a sensible bourbon and water for me. Sensible, that is, except that she managed to slop even more bourbon than I'm accustomed to into my drink.

We got settled again, and I had a glug of my drink and relaxed. There wasn't a great deal of conversation as we finished our drinks, then Carol went alone into the kitchenette to mix a couple more. It seemed to take her quite a while, but I had that much more time to concentrate on problems this case had presented.

When Carol joined me again, I had a small sip of the new highball, then sat it on the coffee table. I was still cudgeling my brain from time to time in the hope of figuring out how I could locate detective Harry Welch. And suddenly I knew.

I'd known all along, if only my memory had functioned. But the salient information had come to me when my mind had not exactly been screwed to the sticking point. I remembered now that while I'd been upstairs in the Grotto, talking to the shapely Neptuna, she'd mentioned that Welch had given her one of his cards. Later she'd said that she had no idea where Welch was staying. But there wouldn't have been any reason for him to leave the card unless his address had been on it. "It's still around here someplace," she said, I remembered now.

I grabbed the phone, looked up the Grotto in the book and dialed. Carol said, "What bit you?"

Joe Grace answered at the Grotto. He told me Ilona was about to dive into her act, but I explained what I wanted and Grace said he'd check with her, if there was time, before the show.

"Thanks, Grace," I said. "I'll be down in a few minutes."

As I put the phone back in its cradle and got to my feet, Carol picked up my drink and walked closer to me. Then she handed me the dark highball and said, "Here. Relax and have your old bourbon."

"Haven't got time. I'm leaving."

"Oh, Shell. You can't ply me with liquor like this and then leave."

"I didn't ply you, you asked for it. Besides, I can feel that first one too much already, and I've got work to do."

"The work can wait, can't it? Please, Shell. I'm enjoying myself."

"Sorry. I'm enjoying myself, too, but–"

"I haven't enjoyed myself so much in a long time. And my pill's wearing off." She stepped close to me, put her arms on my shoulders and looked up at me. I had for a second there thought she probably couldn't get any closer, but I was wrong. She got quite a bit closer. "My pill's wearing off," she said in a low, husky voice. "I can tell."

"I can tell, too. And don't forget, I haven't had any pill."

She was sort of squirming around, and her hands went up behind my neck and traced little paths of cold in my suddenly heated skin, paths like small fire-breaks in the midst of conflagration, and I came very close to weakening.

She said, "I'm so glad I met you, Shell. I don't want to let you go now."

"I'm practically gone. I mean, here I go–I'm–good-by."

The phone rang. I jumped for it and got away from Carol. It was Joe Grace again. "Scott," he said, "I just remembered you mentioning that guy who came in with Welch. The guy with the tan, and the pale blue eyes. I just saw him come in."

"He's there now? Anybody with him?"

"He came in alone. Didn't say boo to me. Went upstairs. Probably to see Ilona, but I figured I'd call you right off, seeing how you said you were anxious–"

There was undoubtedly more, but I didn't hear it. I dropped the phone onto its hook and headed for the door. Carol yelled, "But what'll I *do?* My pill *is* wearing off."

"Take another one," and out the door I went.

8

I left my car in the Grotto's lot, and raced to the club's entrance and inside. The Underseas Room band was playing the weird number which introduced the show. I ran up the back stairs three at a time and as I got to their top and ran down the hallway toward Neptuna's dressing room I saw husky Dan Thrip, in trunks, standing outside her door, apparently waiting for the musical clue that would be his signal to go in and dive into the tank. Cabot wasn't in sight anywhere.

I sprang past Thrip, opening the door and going through as he yelped, "Hey, what duh–" but then I saw Neptuna. Or rather her tail. She had just dived into the pool and was entering the water.

And then I saw Cabot.

He must have been talking to Ilona until the moment she dived, because he was just turning toward me. Those pale blue eyes got about twice as wide as normal in his dark face when he lamped me but then they narrowed again as I jumped toward him. He balled up his fists, stepped toward me, and launched his right hand at me like a brown rock. He didn't have any intention of starting a conversation, he simply wanted to bust my skull.

But I had not been charmed by Cabot, either, so I felt almost gleeful as I pulled my head slightly aside as I got close to him and that brown-rock fist, bent forward a little, and slammed the knuckles of my left hand into his stomach. Or rather, onto his stomach. It felt like I'd busted my hand. That stomach of his was like a piece of corrugated cast iron.

Cabot didn't even grunt, but his fist whispered past my ear without doing any damage. He staggered back a step, then moved around me, lips pressed together. He feinted twice with his left, then slammed his right hand at me–and he was wide open.

I bent my legs and leaned a bit to the side to let that looping right whistle past my face, then straightened up and pivoted, slammed my right fist against the side of his chin. It made a fine, a dandy noise, and he staggered backward, his arms flying up loosely in front of him.

I had him, and knew that just one more punch would settle this alter-
cation if it wasn't already settled. And when Cabot came to, then
I'd ask him all the questions about Welch, and his wife, and the other
Ilonas, and the shot at me, among others.

But that hard-thrown right hand pulled me around a bit, left me
a little off balance, and I moved my left foot back about six inches
to steady myself. That was the wrong thing to do. My foot was resting
on *nothing*.

The horrible realization swept over me even as I flailed my arms
trying to regain my balance. But it was too late. Almost involuntarily
I gave a short hopping movement, and then I was flying backward
into wetness. Wetness, and a sickening realization. My eyes were
closed, but even without looking around I knew where I was. I knew
what I was, too, and it was almost unthinkable, certainly unprintable.

When I opened my eyes I could see quite well, even see the glass
wall of the aquarium in which I was hanging, sort of stunned and
unbelieving. I couldn't see outside, but I could imagine with dull
horror the expressions fixing themselves on customers' faces out there.

Below me was Neptuna, the mermaid. She was swooping through
the water and curling around a rock quite gracefully, entirely unaware
of what dangled here above her head in wet tan slacks and a sopping
brown sports coat. Undoubtedly she had not the slightest suspicion
that anybody–especially me--had yet followed her into the water, and
she was looking happy, almost smiling, as she arched her back down
there and started to glide up through the water.

But she spun slowly around and lamped me and her arms flew up
over her head like springs, her mouth opened wide, and her legs split
through the thin rubber mermaid skin as if it were Kleenex. She froze
in a strained, awkward position, floating there in the water with her
arms and legs akimbo, bent into the approximate shape of a swastika,
and looking very much like an arthritic Balinese dancer engaged in
drowning.

Then she screamed. Bubbles ripped out of her mouth like horrified
silver balloons and popped up past her head. In that moment Ilona
seemed to gather enormous strength from somewhere, and all of a
sudden her arms and legs were moving as if she had six of each. As
she shot past me, I came to my senses and took out after her. My
head popped up past the surface of the pool just as Ilona was clamber-
ing out, inches from me. Only inches. It was a sight that, unfortunately, I couldn't appreciate to the full right at that moment, but
it was often going to flash back into my memory and jangle all my
nervous nerves like pink lightning.

Then she was on her feet and racing away.

"Ilona!" I shouted. "Wait, it's me, Shell Scott. It's me!"

For a second I didn't think my words were likely to have any effect on her, as if the sight of me had drained her of further power to react in any way except running, but then she stopped suddenly and sort of jerked. She quivered slightly like a woman who had stuck her finger into an electrical outlet, and slowly turned. She stabbed me with a strange, anguished gaze as I rose dripping from the water.

"Ilona," I said. "I'm—I—what can I say?"

She stared at me.

"Well," I said a bit pettishly, since I was pretty uncomfortable to begin with, "I didn't do it on purpose, you know."

There was some more silence, and finally I asked, "Did you find the card?"

"Card?" At last she spoke. Her voice was dull. "Yes, I found the card. I didn't know you wanted it so badly." She was still staring at me.

Dan Thrip was staring at me, too. He stood outside in the hall, eyeballing me through the open doorway. His chin was hanging down two or three inches, which was about as far down as it could hang, and his long arms dangled at his sides. He was looking from one of us to the other, with a fixed stupidity of expression, and not a glimmer of understanding in his blank eyes.

His cue had come and gone long ago. He had heard those musical notes that said to him, *Go Into Your Act, Dan*, but somebody had changed the act. Everything was all fouled up. He was bewildered, nonplussed, unsure of himself.

The events of the last minute or so had, understandably, occupied my mind to the exclusion of everything else. Consequently I had forgotten all about Johnny Cabot. But suddenly I remembered that he should be lying without a wiggle on the floor. He wasn't even in sight.

"Dan," I said. "What happened to the guy who was in here?"

It took him a while to answer, but at last in a few, halting phrases, he indicated that a guy had come racing out past him and downstairs, very obviously in a big hurry—which told me that by now Cabot would be about a mile from here. I started to race out after him anyway, but then stopped, knowing that chasing the man now was useless.

I said to Ilona, "What did Cabot want with you? What was he doing here?"

She had practically recovered her senses and poise by now, and she said, "It was about you, Shell. He just came in without knocking or anything and asked if you'd been in to see me. When I told him yes, he seemed real angry, started swearing and all."

Apparently Cabot had remembered telling me he'd been with a girl from the Grotto this morning, and hadn't liked the idea of my coming here. "He say anything else?"

"Yes, he told me if I saw you or heard from you again to deny that I'd been with him or ever met him. He seemed pretty worried about it."

"He would be."

"I'll get that card," Ilona said. "Don't–do anything." Then she looked past me and seemed to notice Dan Thrip for the first time. She slammed the door in his face. It slammed not more than two inches from his nose, but as far as I could tell he didn't move at all.

The recent events had probably put him nearly into a state of shock, but it finally dawned on me that the real push into trauma must have been his first sight of Ilona, the mermaid, without her fishtail, most of which was somewhere in the pool down below. Only wispy segments of it still remained.

Ilona and I both stood there looking at each other and dripping, and then she chuckled. The chuckle turned into a laugh, and after a moment I joined her. When we caught our breath again, we were both back to normal.

I was so back to normal that I had got quite close to her indeed, and she reached up and put both hands on my shoulders. It was about the same movement that Carol had earlier made, but this time it filled me with all sorts of desires, and not one of them was the desire to leave.

It seemed the most natural thing in the world for my arms to go around her, and her fingers to tighten on my shoulders, and her parted lips to get closer to mine, and then meet them eagerly, almost harshly. It was delightful. It was also, there is no doubt, one of the sloppiest kisses in my kissing history.

We mashed together, dripping, squishing, and gurgling. Since she had almost nothing on, I was doing most of the dripping and squishing. But she was gurgling. There was really quite a bit of sound there for a minute or so, like those hi-fi records of heartbeats and joints popping. I even heard a far-off pounding.

Then I realized the pounding wasn't so far off. Somebody was running down the hall. Then I heard Dan Thrip saying, "No! You can't go in. She hasn't got no clothes on."

Ilona leaned back an inch or two and looked up at me. "Why, that's true," she breathed in mock surprise. "How could I have forgotten?" Then she stepped back and said, smiling, "Now, don't peek," and walked slowly, beautifully, artistically, to the bamboo screen and behind it. I felt a bit weak.

In a few seconds she came into view once more, wearing that white robe again, and at almost the same instant the door burst open. Joe Grace leaped into the room, his face livid. He pointed a finger at me. "You!" he shouted hoarsely.

9

Dan Thrip came in and grabbed Grace, who told him he was fired, but then Thrip noted that Ilona was clad in her robe and he calmed down, and Ilona cooed a few words at Joe Grace and said everything would be all right. Her robe fell slightly open as she leaned toward him, but she quickly grabbed it and pulled it together; after that, however, when Ilona asked them to please leave, for just a little moment, they both went out meekly. During all that I managed to elicit the info from Grace that Cabot had gone tearing through the club and outside minutes ago.

As the door closed, Ilona reached into the pocket of her robe and pulled out a small white card. "I found this just before you showed up—Joe said you'd be by. Is this what you wanted?"

"Uh-huh." The name Harold Welch was printed on the card, with the word "Investigator" below the name. That was all, but written across its back was "Rancho Cottages, Cottage 12."

Ilona said, "Shell, maybe if you get all your investigating done real fast, you might get back here before closing."

"A brilliant thought, but highly unlikely."

"Well, you try, anyway. But right now you'd better go—Dan and I still have a show to do."

I shuddered. I looked down at my dripping clothes and shuddered again. A sudden pain rippled through my stomach and I bent slightly forward, wincing. Dizziness swept over me momentarily.

Ilona said, "What's the matter, Shell?"

"I don't know. Must have bent some muscles... "

"You should be sprained all over."

"Maybe Cabot clobbered me when I wasn't looking. No, I understand—I swallowed some water and there wasn't any bourbon in it. The shock shattered my nervous system."

She was smiling, but I wasn't. I had barely noticed similar sensations a couple times in the last few minutes, but in the movement and excitement I'd paid no attention. I did feel a bit dizzy, but that wasn't too unusual. I told Ilona good-by and to put on a sensational act, and left.

Half an hour later, after looking up the Rancho Cottages in the phone book, I'd found the place and was talking to the sleepy owner. At first he'd ogled my wet clothes, but I told him I'd fallen into the lake at MacArthur Park and that seemed to satisfy him. The Rancho was a twelve-unit motel-type spot off Grange Street about five miles from downtown L.A. The owner, a man named Brand, said he remembered Mr. Welch, but he hadn't seen him for over a week; Welch had left word that he wasn't to be disturbed, even for maid service, unless he asked for it.

Mr. Brand went on, "I think he had a babe livin' with him."

"Oh? Who was it, do you know?"

Brand shook his head. "Not even sure there *was* a babe. But that's usually why folks don't want the maid service and all."

The cottages were separate cabins, and Brand took me to Cottage 12. He knocked, but there wasn't any answer. "Don't think he's home," Brand told me. "Like I said, I haven't seen him around. Probably investigating somewhere–detective, you know."

"Yeah."

He looked at me in the glow of the flashlight he held. "Something the matter with you?"

"I'm all right." That sudden pain had caught me several times in the last half hour, but it was now subsiding to a dull ache that stayed with me, along with mild dizziness.

Mr. Brand opened the door, then pressed the light switch on the wall, saying, "I know you're a detective, but I still don't like to . . . Oh, my God!"

Looking past him, I could see the same thing Brand had seen. On our right was the open door to the bathroom, and halfway through it, sprawled on the floor, was a man's body.

I walked to the figure and touched the outflung hand. The arm moved easily, so there wasn't any rigor mortis. I guessed, though, that he'd been killed several days ago; rigor mortis could have set in and then left again, as it will after a few days. I could see the man's face, and it had the distinctively bluish tinge of cyanosis.

The dead man fit the description I had of Harry Welch; he had a lot of dark hair, gray at the temples, and a thin black mustache, but I asked Mr. Brand, "Would you say this is Welch?"

He came a couple steps forward and bent down, peering at the dead man's face, an expression of distaste on his own features. "Yes, but what happened to him? Look at that color; it's . . ." He made a grating sound deep in his throat.

"Cyanosis," I said. "One of the less important effects of cyanide poisoning. You'd better call the police."

Brand went out. I could see that the wrinkled collar of the white dress shirt the dead detective wore was open, and he wore no tie. He had on brown trousers and brown shoes.

It looked as if Welch had been relaxing at night after finishing a day's work. And he had almost surely been poisoned by somebody else. Suicide was such a remote possibility that I ignored it.

There wasn't anything to show that Welch hadn't been living here alone. I looked around for something he might have eaten or drunk from, but there wasn't anything like that in the cottage. In the dresser drawer, however, was the dead man's wallet. I flipped it open with a finger and examined the identification cards behind their transparent windows.

The dead man had been a private detective, all right, licensed by the state of California. His name was Harold M. Welch, and his address was in Fresno, California. So finally I knew where he'd come from.

Looking at the limp body on the floor, I wondered why Welch had been killed. There was one reason, or motive, that fit all facets of the case. But Welch, too, had been poisoned—with cyanide. And there had been cyanide in Ilona Cabot's milk.

I stopped. Remembering, I could hear Johnny Cabot saying to me at the Westlander Theater: "If I wanted to kill anybody, I wouldn't use cyanide, I'd use a gun." How had he known that the would-be murderer of his wife had used cyanide?

I thought about that, and when I remembered that Ilona had been gone by the time I'd arrived at the house on Robard Street, I felt sure I had the answer to that question—and more, including why Welch had been murdered, why there'd been the attempt on Ilona Cabot's life—in fact the whole story, including where Johnny Cabot and his three Ilonas fit in. But I still needed a little more information and a little more proof. And the place to get it was in my apartment, and the method was using the phone to call Fresno.

Carol Austin was still waiting for me in my apartment when I got there. I'd anticipated that, and would have been enormously surprised if she hadn't waited for my return. She didn't anything when I walked in the door, just stared at me.

"Hi," I said. "I wondered if you'd still be here."

Only then did she smile and seem to relax. "You must have known I'd wait. What have you been doing?" Her blue eyes got very wide. "What happened to your clothes? It isn't raining, is it?"

I walked to the divan and sat down, reached for the phone. "No, I fell into a tank of water." She asked some more questions, but instead of answering them I dialed information and asked for the phone number of the Mr. William Grant in Fresno.

Carol got up and said, "I'll mix us something to drink."

"Fine," I told her. "I'd like that."

While she moved about in the kitchenette, I listened to the operator getting in touch with Fresno, then asking for the number of William Grant.

Finally a woman's sleep-dulled voice was saying to me, "Hello."

"Hello, this is Shell Scott in Los Angeles. I wasn't sure I'd reach anyone at this number."

Carol came back and sat on the divan and handed me a dark-brown highball. "Bourbon and water, isn't it?" she whispered.

I nodded. At the other end of the line the woman was saying, "Mr. Grant passed away recently. Perhaps I can help you—I was his personal secretary for many years. I'm Joan Bates."

"What can you tell me about Mr. Harry Welch, a detective."

"Oh?" She hesitated. "I don't feel I should—"

"He's dead," I interrupted. "He was murdered. I'm an investigator, myself." I added, with only slight exaggeration, "I'm working quite closely with the police on this."

And that loosened her tongue. "I see—He's *dead*, then. We hadn't heard anything for several days. How awful! Are you sure he was murdered?"

"There's not any doubt. What can you tell me about him?"

"Well, he was working for the estate. When Mr. Grant's will was read, we learned that he'd left half of all his money to me and his nurse Ann Wilson, and the other half to a friend. But nobody knew where the—friend was living."

"You're referring to his daughter, aren't you?"

She gasped. "Why, how did you—"

"I know all about that, ma'am. Will you excuse me a minute?"

She said she'd hold the line, and I put the phone down on the cushion, then got to my feet, highball in my hand. "Any ice left?" I asked Carol. Or, at least, the lovely I thought of as Carol.

"Yes. Yes, lots. A tray's in the sink. What—"

She started to get up, but I said genially, "Relax, honey. I can do some of the work."

10

In the kitchenette, out of sight of my guest, I made noise getting the ice, rattling the tray in the sink, while I held the highball close to my nose and sniffed. It was obvious, once I looked for it–or smelled for it. The peach-pit odor of potassium cyanide rose even above the strong fumes of bourbon. I poured the drink into the sink, quickly and quietly rinsed my glass and filled it with tap water, plus enough Coca Cola to give it a dark bourbon color, then added a couple more ice cubes and went back into the front room.

Carol hadn't moved. She seemed almost rigid. I beamed at her and said, "I like lots of ice. This conversation may take quite a while." I sat down and picked up the phone, holding my hand over the mouthpiece, then had a sizable gulp of my water-and-Coke. "That's better," I said happily, and then frowned, making a face. "But that's the bitterest bourbon I ever tasted. Carol, next time use the Old Crow–not that cheap stuff."

She nodded silently and smiled. It was a ghastly smile. An hour earlier, I would probably have thought it charming, hot, lovable. But now I could see what it really was, just muscles pulling at lips and cheeks.

Into the phone I said, "Hello again. Would you give me the whole story, please?" She did.

While talking to the woman in Fresno, I sipped occasionally at my drink. When she finished, I thanked her and said I'd get in touch with her again the following day, and hung up.

Carol Austin had her big blue eyes fastened on me like blued steel to a magnet. She couldn't have learned much from the phone conversation, because for the most part I'd been listening, but she said, "Are you getting your case all finished up, Shell?"

"Looks like it."

She raised her highball. "Relax a little. You'll live longer. Bottoms up?"

Live longer, hey? "Bottoms up," I said, and drank the rest of my Coke-and-water. It was fascinating to watch Carol watch me. She didn't even seem to be breathing. I said, "Would you like to hear about the case, honey? About my fascinating life?"

She shrugged, as if that would be as good a way to kill the next minute or two as any. I said, "Some of this I'd already learned, and some of it I got on the phone from Fresno. I was talking to Fresno just now, did you know that?"

"I . . . thought maybe . . . " She stopped. "I mean, I don't know where it was."

"Well, it was Fresno. It seems a man named William J. Grant died up there a little while back, and this Mr. Grant had raked together about four million dollars. About twenty-two years ago, Mr. Grant and a girl named Mary Lassen were, well, let's say in love. Is this interesting to you?"

She gave me one of those pulled-muscle smiles again, as if she had just sprained her face. Carol knew something was very wrong, but she didn't seem sure exactly what it was. Then, too, I was dying rather slowly.

I said, "Well, to boil it down, they had a baby. And they weren't married. The old story; it's happened before, it'll happen again." And right there I stopped. I let what I fondly hoped was a stricken look capture my features. I waggled my face around and bent forward, saying harshly, "Arrggh!"

Carol didn't move an eighth of an inch. She stared at me, and in a voice completely devoid of surprise or even friendly curiosity, asked "What's the matter, Shell?"

"I–a pain. Feel a little dizzy. Something I . . . " After another groan or two I straightened up and shook my head. This time when I looked at Carol there was, oddly enough, an apparently real smile on her face. It was a small, hardly perceptible smile, but after all there wasn't much to laugh about.

"That was strange," I said, and went on. "Well, this guy Grant took a powder, left the Lassen woman and the child in the lurch. The woman turned the kid over to an orphanage and knocked herself off, and by the time Grant learned about that a year or so had passed. He didn't do anything about it. But after another twenty years, he took real sick. He was dying, and his thoughts turned to the girl–his daughter. He was a rich man by then, and he wanted half his fortune to go to the girl. Is this boring you, Carol?"

"What? Oh, no, Shell. This is interesting."

"Fine. There's not much more. I–arrgh!"

I did it all again. Carol really seemed to enjoy this spasm and kept looking at me hopefully. But I recovered and continued, although in a weak voice.

"Well, Grant died, and the executors of the estate, in accordance with his wishes, hired a detective named Welch to find the missing daughter. All they could tell the detective was the name of the orphans' home, and the date the girl had been left there by her mother. Welch checked the home and learned the girl had been named Ilona. So he started hunting up gals named Ilona."

"Ilona?" Carol said gently. "Isn't that odd?"

"The odd part is that you asked me about Ilona Cabot earlier. And I didn't ever tell you that the homely Ilona in my office was named Cabot. I did foolishly admit to you this morning that I was looking for her husband; and you must have heard me talking to Missing Persons on the phone about a missing John *Cabot*. I mean when you came into my office with that spur-of-the-moment story about thinking it was Dr. Forrest's. I suppose you put one and one together and tonight asked me about Ilona Cabot to make sure that was, in fact, her married name."

Carol didn't say anything. I went on, "Well, to continue, nobody around the late Mr. Grant even knew he had a daughter until the will was read. That's understandable, under the circumstances. Anyway, all his money was left to just three people. Two of them in Fresno—Grant's personal secretary, and his private nurse, both of whom had been with him for years. He had no other relatives, so half his estate went to those two. The other half was to go to his daughter. And that, of course, set up a kind of dangerous situation for this Ilona."

"Oh? I—don't understand," said Carol.

What she probably didn't understand was why I was still able to yak away, but I went on, "Nobody knew for sure if this Ilona was still alive. If found, she would inherit a couple million dollars. But if nobody found her—or if she were dead—according to the terms of the will the two million would then devolve upon the secretary and nurse. That's an extra million bucks apiece. There's a nice motive for murder—murder for a million. So it looks as if either Grant's secretary or his nurse tried to knock off Ilona. It's really too bad what the hunger for money will do to otherwise nice people."

Carol was looking at me strangely, in apparent puzzlement. I hadn't gasped and gurgled for quite a while, and probably she felt that I was taking a distressingly long time to die. So I went into my dying-horribly act.

Suddenly I gasped twice as loud and gurgled much more musically then anything I'd achieved yet. I sprang to my feet and straightened up, then bent forward like a man doing a jackknife, arms going around my stomach. I spun about, staggering, toppled forward almost at Carol's feet, and continued groaning while writhing on the carpet.

Carol didn't extend a helping hand, didn't say a word, didn't do a thing. In momentary glimpses that I got of her from my rolling eyes, I saw that she had merely put her arms across her breasts, hands clasping her shoulders, and was gently hugging herself. Her narrowed blue eyes were fixed on me, and that tight little smile twisted her soft red lips.

Finally I got to my hands and knees and raised my face so I could stare at her. "You!" I croaked. "You've croaked me!"

Her eyes were bright. She squinted at me, pressing against the divan as if to move farther from me. I said, "It was you, Carol. You killed Welch—and tried twice to kill Ilona."

She got to her feet and started to step around me. This wasn't the way I'd planned it. So, in what must have appeared my final burst of living, I struggled to my feet and staggered toward Carol.

Her eyes widened, a little fright showing in them at last. Because she must have thought I would by now be unable to move with much grace or speed, she spun around to run, too late. I jumped about six feet through the air and grabbed her, turned her to face me, and mashed her tightly against me. "Tell me the truth!" I shouted as we both toppled to the floor.

Her face was only about three inches from mine, and she really looked frightened now. "Yes," she half whimpered. "I did kill him. I couldn't let him tell where she was. And I tried to kill her–but I didn't, I didn't kill her. Let me go. Let me go!"

I just squeezed her tighter. We were lying on our sides on the thick shag nap of my carpet, and I couldn't very well have been holding her more tightly. Her breasts mashed against me, her thighs pressed mine, and she was after all a very delightfully fashioned female. She was moving a lot, too. And I wasn't really dying. In fact, I was living.

I said, "You tried to kill her with a car last Sunday, and then by lacing her milk with cyanide this morning. Didn't you?"

"Yes, yes!"

"And you were much surprised when Ilona came out of her house alive. So you followed her to my office this morning, right, love?"

She nodded. All of this wallowing about had sort of upped my blood pressure. After those last two words, Carol hadn't said anything else, but every second she was straining against me, moving frantically, squirming and trying to get away, and it was almost enough all by itself to kill a man. I'm only human. Pretty quick I even forgot what questions I'd been meaning to ask this gal.

And, inevitably, Carol finally got my message. Her face went through a startling array of expressions. First, a queer kind of amazement. A sort of "Can this be?" look, as though it were too soon for rigor mortis to be setting in. And then the expression of a person slowly, and with complete awareness of what was happening, experiencing apoplexy. And then, at last, Carol's much-used sexy look.

She had me pegged. Hell, I had her pegged, too. But she knew what old Shell Scott was interested in. She knew, all right. And she figured, I guess, that she could take advantage of my interest in hers. At any rate, she began speaking to me, softly.

"What if I did kill that detective, Shell? What difference does it make, really? We can have a lot of fun together, you and I. I'll be rich, Shell, rich. Millions, millions of dollars. For both of us... "

She was still squirming, wriggling round there on the carpet. But she wasn't trying to get away. "Once Ilona's taken care of," she said, "I'll have two million dollars–maybe even more later. We'll have to get rid of her husband, too. I didn't even know until this morning that she was married." She paused. "Shell, if we can get rid of both of them, there'll maybe be four million later. That's more money than I can imagine–but it was supposed all to be mine. Bill said once that it would all be mine."

For a second or two that "Bill" puzzled me, but then I realized she must have referred to Grant, William Grant as I knew him. Maybe she and Bill had played games on carpets, or had some less unusual arrangement. Carol's face wasn't frightened any longer, it was only an inch or two from mine, and she was smiling again. The smile, though, was still that pulled-muscle operation. She looked not quite all there, as if mentally she were absent, or at least tardy.

She went on, speaking softly, "I know you like me. I can tell when a man likes me."

"Welch, for example? He must have liked you pretty well. You were living with him at those Rancho cottages, weren't you?"

"For a little while, but I had to be close to him so I'd know when he found Ilona. If he found her."

"He didn't know you were Ann Wilson, did he?" I held my breath, but she answered without any hesitation.

"Of course not. I made up a name for him. I managed to meet him in a bar. It's a good thing. He'd even written up his report before he told me he'd finished what he'd been hired to do. That he'd found the girl he was looking for. After I–after he died, I burned the report. That's how I learned where Ilona was."

"And were you the one who shot at me earlier tonight?"

"Shot at you? I don't know what you're talking about."

I believed her. She was quiet for seconds, then she put her cheek against mine and said, in a pleased voice that was almost laughing, "You do like me a lot, I know. And we will have fun together, won't we? You won't tell anybody about me, will you, Shell?"

"Baby, we are off to the clink."

It didn't penetrate for a few moments. Then she pulled back her head and stared at me. "What? What did you say?"

"Honey, that second drink you made me earlier–the one you mixed all by yourself in the kitchenette–had enough poison in it to kill me for sure. I was just another Welch who might upset your plans. Luckily I had only a small sip of the drink, but even so, it affected me a little after I'd left here. I just can't afford to do any more drinking with you. You must have brought eight pounds of cyanide down here from Fresno."

"Oh, you're imagining things, Shell." Yeah, she was nuts, all right. "I wouldn't do anything to hurt you." Man, she was squirming and wobbling around like crazy.

"No, of course not," I said pleasantly. "I didn't realize quite what was wrong until I saw Welch's body, and the blue tinge of cyanosis on his face. That told me what was wrong with me, my love, and who was responsible for it all. That was the dead giveaway. No, love, I'm afraid I'll have to take you to jail."

And this time she believed me. She hauled off and hit me with everything she had—that is, everything she hadn't already hit me with. Arms, elbows, head, knees and so on. She even tried to bite me. I finally had to tie her arms and legs with electrical cord from one of the living-room lamps.

11

The police had taken Ann Wilson, alias Carol Austin, away from my apartment an hour before, and I was just knocking at the door of apartment 12 in the Franklin. While waiting for the police to arrive, the Franklin's desk clerk had phoned to earn his twenty bucks, and report the arrival of Cabot and his wife. So I had come straight here as soon as I could; this would wrap the case up. But I hated the thought of what the truth was going to do to Ilona. Johnny wasn't going to be happy, either, so I took out my .38 Colt and held it in my hand as I waited.

Footsteps sounded inside, then the door opened part way. Johnny Cabot blinked sleepily at me and began to speak. But then his eyes snapped open, he started to slam the door as a swear word burst from his throat.

"Hold it, Cabot!" I shoved the gun toward his sharp nose, and he froze. He stared at the gun, inches from his face, and I said, "Ask me in, Cabot. The party's over."

"What the hell's the idea? I've had about—"

"Shut up. You going to ask me in?"

He glanced again at my coat pocket, then stepped back. I walked in and looked around. The door into the next room, the bedroom, was ajar. From the bedroom Ilona's voice called, "What is it, Johnny?"

"I'll—be right in," he said, then looked at me.

I spoke softly, "Get her and bring her out here, Cabot. I'll do this much for you, though I don't know why—you can tell her if you want to; or I will. You can have your choice."

He licked his lips. "Tell her what?"

"Come off it. You're washed up. I know all about William Grant, your bride's inheritance, the works."

He sighed, then shrugged. "Well," he said finally, "you can't blame me for trying. You–uh, you better tell her, Scott. She is pretty much of a mess, but–well, I don't want to tell her."

"I didn't think anything would bother you, Cabot." He shrugged, and I said, "Tell her to come out. But you keep in my sight. I'd hate for you to come back with that forty-five in your mitt."

"What forty-five?"

"The one you shot at me with earlier tonight."

He started to deny it, but then walked to the door and told Ilona to put on some clothes and come out. Then he shut the door, walked over and said to me, "I guess there's no point in trying to make it work now. Sure, I shot at you–or at your car. Don't kid yourself, mister. If I'd wanted to plug you, I wouldn't have missed by three or four feet. I just wanted to scare you off me and Ilona." He paused. "Maybe I should have shot you–but I'm not a murderer."

This time I believed him. I put the .38 in my coat pocket but kept my hand on it and said, "I figured you were for a while, Cabot. I found Welch's body tonight–"

"He's dead?" Honest surprise was in his voice.

"Several days. Poisoned. I thought you might have done it, but under the circumstance you'd have been nuts to kill him. You wanted him alive–at least long enough to report to Fresno that he'd found Ilona. But because you'd told me at the Westlander you wouldn't use cyanide to kill somebody, I figured you must've slipped the cyanide into your wife's milk."

"You're way off," he said. "The minute after you talked to me at the Westlander I called Ilona, asked her what the score was. She told me about bringing the milk to your office, cyanide and all. She told me."

"Uh-huh. That's the way it figured to me."

"Welch's been dead several days? You mean they don't know Ilona's here in L.A." He grinned wryly. "Not that it makes any difference to *me* now."

He was almost likeable for a second there. Cabot talked freely enough, now that he knew the game was over. As I had guessed, he'd first talked to Welch on the 15th when the detective came into the Westlander Theater to check on Ilona the Hungarian Hurricane. Cabot had learned enough from Ilona and Welch himself that he stuck to Welch like a leech. They'd visited the Grotto, where Welch had interviewed Neptuna–and Cabot had got an eyeful that almost knocked him off his feet.

He and Welch had planned to have dinner the next night, but Welch had phoned to say he'd found the girl he was looking for and thus couldn't make it.

I said, "How much did Welch tell you? Did he actually say the Ilona he'd found was going to inherit a couple of million? Did he tell you where she lived?"

Cabot shrugged. "No, he just said she was going to get some money from the estate of a guy named William J. Grant–he didn't tell Ilona that; his job was only to find her. I knew Welch was from Fresno, checked recent Fresno papers and learned this Grant had been loaded. The next day when Welch phoned me, I asked him where he'd found the girl and he said in an insurance office on Hill. I didn't ask him to narrow it down. The rest of it was just a little checking here and with Fresno." He shrugged again. "A couple million bucks was worth a good try."

"What I can't understand is why you took off Monday night and didn't come back."

"Well, you've seen my... wife. And you've seen Ilona Betun. I thought I could get away with it."

That was a good enough answer. Cabot told me that he'd kept his job at the burlesque house because he wasn't supposed to know his Ilona was going to inherit any money, and it would later have looked funny if he had quit his job as soon as they'd met. Besides, he added dully, they really did need the money.

The door opened then and Ilona Cabot came in. Wearing her husband's robe, and with no makeup, her hair almost straight, she didn't look good at all. Not pretty, at least. She still had that air of mousy sweetness about her.

Her face brightened with a smile when she saw me. "Mr. Scott. What are you doing here?"

"Hello, Mrs. Cabot. You'd better sit down."

We all found seats, me in a chair and Ilona with Johnny on the couch. She grabbed his hand and held it. Johnny was starting to look very uncomfortable.

Just to be positive, I asked her if she'd spent the first half dozen years of her life in the Bunting Orphanage, and if a detective named Welch had talked to her a couple weeks ago about that. After a little hesitation she admitted it, but expressed her puzzlement.

I said, "Well, Mrs. Cabot, you're an heiress. I mean, you'll soon inherit about two million dollars."

It went right by her. If I was talking about two million dollars,

I couldn't possibly be talking about her. It took me five minutes to partially convince her that she was actually going to get money, and explain enough so she could believe it. When she finally got it through her head, all she did was turn to Cabot and say, "Johnny, isn't it wonderful?"

I broke in quickly, "Wait a minute. That's not all of what I've got to tell you. The other part is about your husband. About Johnny."

She smiled. "Yes?" She looked at Johnny Cabot. She beamed at him.

I remembered how she had lit up in my office when I'd asked her to describe her husband. This was the same kind of look. A bright, happy, everything's-wonderful look. It wasn't a very new expression, not original, just the look of a woman in love.

But it was, of course, new for Ilona.

I hated to think of how she was going to look when she knew that Johnny Cabot had found out about her from Welch, learned from Welch about her inheritance, found her and rushed her and married her, just for whatever part he could grab of that two million bucks. I didn't like the thought of what was going to happen to her already plain and homely face.

I said, "You see, Mrs. Cabot, this detective, Welch, who talked to you—well, he talked to some other Ilonas first, before he found you. During his search for you. Two million dollars is an awful lot of money, and... " I stopped. It was difficult to find the right words. It was going to hurt enough no matter how it was told, but I wanted to find the gentlest way to break it to her, if I could.

But then Cabot said slowly, "Let it go, Scott. This is something I... Well, maybe I better tell her." He chewed on his lip for a moment, then turned to her. "Honey, it's like this. When I met you, I–well, I–"

Ilona was looking up at him, sort of smiling. And it seemed to me that she didn't look plain and almost ugly–not when she was looking at her husband. Her face seemed to get bright and warm, as if it were lighted from happiness welling up inside her, and I thought that all the hunger and trampled-down love and affection she must have been saving for years was right there on her face. It was there in the brightness of her eyes, and in the curve of her lips. It was so frank and honest and open that it didn't seem quite right for me to be looking at her then.

Johnny had taken a deep breath, and now he said, rapidly, not looking at her, "Honey, when I met you I told you I was crazy about you, you remember, but the real reason I bumped into you was because I knew all about–"

"Wait a minute. Hold it, just a minute."

I was on my feet and the words had popped out of me almost involuntarily. All I knew was that I didn't want to see Ilona's face change from the expression it now wore to one of hurt and disillusionment. Or maybe I was just out of my mind.

But, anyway, I went on in a rush, "I can't sit around her all night listening to you two gab away. This is probably the same thing your husband said to me just a little while ago when I told him about the money you're inheriting. He said he was afraid you might not feel the same toward him, now that you're a millionaire."

"Johnny!" she cried. She was shocked.

I went on, "What I wanted to tell you about was the other half of the job you hired me for. Somebody really was trying to kill you, Mrs. Cabot. It was a woman named Ann Wilson. She was scheduled to inherit a million herself, but that wasn't enough for her, so she tried to knock you off. I think she's a little cracked–anyway, the cops have her in the hoosegow now, so all your troubles are over. Funny, you'll probably inherit half of the million she would have gotten."

"All my troubles are over," she said softly. "I just can't understand it–all this at once."

Neither could Cabot. He was gaping at me, his mouth half open. I walked to the door and out into the hall, then I jerked my head at him. "I'd like to have a last word with you, Cabot."

He came outside and shut the door. "What the hell?" he said, bewildered. "What happened just now?"

"I had a cerebral hemorrhage. Shut up and listen. That little girl in there must be crazier than Ann Wilson, because she thinks you're the end. Well, I think you're the other end, but maybe you could be real nice to this Ilona-with-two-million-dollars, if you tried. And I've got a hunch you're going to try."

He nodded slowly. "Yeah. You're making sense." He paused. "I didn't think you were flipping your lid in there for me."

I said, "I can still tell her, you know. I can still prove it. I'd hate to tear apart two people so much in love, though."

"You know," he said quietly, "She's really prettier now than when I met her. Not pretty–but less horrible."

"Wait'll she gets that inheritance. She'll be beautiful."

I was being sarcastic, in a way, but somehow I had a hunch that Ilona–with a lot more love, and a little more money–just might work her way up to not-half-bad. Well, time would tell.

I nodded at Johnny Cabot and said, "Tell your wife I'll be sending her a bill for my fee. My *big* fee."

I walked down the hall. Before I reached the elevator I heard the door shut behind me. When I looked around, the door was closed and Johnny Cabot was again alone with his wife...

Because I kept wondering about Johnny and his Ilona even after I got in the Cad and started home, I was well out Beverly Boulevard and actually passing the Grotto before I remembered the other Ilona. Neptuna. *My* Ilona.

I slammed on the breaks so suddenly that the car skidded to a stop in the middle of the street. A quick glance at the dash clock showed me it was three a.m. What was it Ilona Betun had said? She'd asked me to come back if I could, and said she would wait around a little while after closing. After two a.m. Well, it was only an hour after two. Maybe she'd still be here.

I swung into the parking lot, parked the car and trotted to the club's rear entrance. With mild surprise I discovered that I was grinning. My Ilona had also said, I remembered, that sometimes she had a little swim all by herself here after everybody else had gone.

I paused before the Grotto's rear door to catch my breath, then put my hand on the knob. It turned easily and the door opened. Inside, the club was dark. I could see nothing but blackness beyond the door. But the fact that this door had been unlocked was encouraging, I thought.

Either the club was being burglarized, or Ilona was waiting. I went in, shut the door behind me, and walked ahead, still grinning, through the darkness.

JOSEPH HANSEN
(b.1923)

Surf
(Dave Brandstetter)

Lieutenant Ken Barker of the LAPD shared a gray-green office with too many other men, too many gray-green metal desks and file cabinets, too many phones that kept crying for attention like new life in a sad maternity ward. He had a broken nose. Under his eyes were bruises. He wore beard stubble. His teeth were smoky. He scowled across a sprawl of papers and spent styrofoam cups. He said: "Yes, Robinson was murdered. On the deck of his apartment. In that slum by the sea called Surf. Shot clean through the head. He went over the rail, was dead when he hit the sand. There's nothing wrong with the case. The DA is happy. What do you want to mess it up for?"

"I don't." Dave shed a wet trenchcoat, hung it over a chairback, sat on another chair. "I just want to know why Robinson made Bruce K. Shevel the beneficiary of his life insurance policy. Didn't he have a wife, a mother, a girlfriend?"

"He had a boyfriend, and the boyfriend killed him. Edward Earl Lily, by name. With a deer rifle, a thirty-thirty. Probably Robinson's. He owned one." Barker blinked. "It's weird, Dave. I mean, what have you got–an instinct for this kind of case?"

"Coincidence," Dave said. "What does probably mean–Robinson was 'probably' killed with his own gun."

Barker found a bent cigarette. "Haven't located it."

"Where does Lily say it is?"

"Claims he never saw it." Barker shuffled papers, hunting a match. "But it'll be in the surf someplace along there. Or buried in the sand. We're raking for it." Dave leaned forward and snapped a thin steel gas lighter. Barker said thanks and asked through smoke, "You don't like it? Why not? What's wrong with it?"

Dave put the lighter away. "Ten years ago, Bruce K. Shevel jacked up his car on one of those trails in Topanga Canyon to change a tire, and the car rolled over on him and cost him the use of his legs. He was insured with us. We paid. We still pay. Total disability. I'd forgotten him. But I remembered him today when I checked Robinson's policy. Shevel looked to me like someone who'd tried self-mutilation to collect on his accident policy."

"Happens, doesn't it?" Barker said.

"People won't do anything for money." Dave's smile was thin. "But they will hack off a foot or a hand for it. I sized Shevel up for one of those. His business was in trouble. The policy was a fat one. I don't think paralysis was in his plans. But it paid better. The son of a bitch grinned at me from that hospital bed. He knew I knew and there was no way to prove it."

"And there still isn't," Barker said. "Otherwise you could stop paying and put him in the slams. And it pisses you off that he took you. And now you see a chance to get him." Barker looked into one of the empty plastic cups, made a face, stood up. "You'd like him to have killed Robinson."

He edged between desks to a coffee urn at the window end of the room, the glass wall end. Dave followed. Through vertical metal sun slats outside, gray rain showed itself like movie grief. "I'd like Robinson to have died peacefully in bed of advanced old age." Dave pulled a cup from a chrome tube bolted to a window strut and held the cup while Barker filled it. "And since he didn't, I'd sure as hell like him to have left his money to someone else."

"We interviewed Shevel." Next to the hot plate that held the coffee urn was cream substitute in a widemouth brown bottle and sugar in little cellophane packets. Barker used a yellow plastic spoon to stir some of each into his coffee. "We interviewed everybody in Robinson's little black book." He led the way back to his desk, sat down, twisted out his cigarette in a big glass ashtray glutted with butts. "And Shevel is a wheelchair case."

Dave tasted his coffee. Weak and tepid. "A wheelchair case can shoot a gun."

Barker snorted. "Have you seen where Robinson lived?"

"I'll go look. But first tell me about Lily." Dave sat down, then eyed the desk. "Or do I need to take your time? Shall I just read the file?"

"My time? I'd only waste it sleeping. And I'm out of practice. I wouldn't do it well." Barker glanced sourly at the folders, forms, photographs on his desk, then hung another cigarette from his mouth and leaned forward so Dave could light it. "Lily is a trick Robinson picked up at the Billy Budd. You know the place?"

Dave nodded. "Ocean Front Walk."

"Robinson tended bar there. The kid's a hustler but way out of Robinson's league. A hundred bucks a night and/or a part in your next TV segment, sir. But somehow Robinson managed to keep him. Eight, ten weeks, anyway–" The phone on Barker's desk jangled. He lifted the receiver, listened, grunted, cradled the receiver. "–Till he was dead. Lily ran, but not far and not clever. He was better at crying. You know the type. Muscles, but a real girl. Kept sobbing that he loved Robinson and why would he kill him?"

"And why would he?" Dave lit a cigarette.

Barker shrugged. "Probably hysteria. Toward the end they were fighting a lot. About money. Robinson had bought him fancy clothes, an Omega watch, a custom surf board. They'd been pricing Porsches and Aston-Martins on the lots. But Robinson was broke. He'd hocked his stereo, camera, projector. He was borrowing from friends."

"What friends?" Dave asked. "Shevel?"

"Among others," Barker said. "Which kind of louses up your theory, doesn't it? Shevel didn't need to shoot anybody for their insurance money. He's loaded."

The boy who opened the door had dressed fast. He still hadn't buttoned his white coverall with L A *Marina* stitched on the pocket. Under the coverall his jockeys were on inside out and backward. Below the nick of navel in his flat brown belly a label read *Pilgrim*. He was chicano and wore his hair long. He looked confused. "He thought it would be the layouts."

"It isn't," Dave said. "Brandstetter is my name. Death claims investigator, Medallion Life. I'm looking for Bruce K. Shevel. Is he here?"

"Brand–what?" the boy said.

At his back a dense jungle of philodendrons climbed a trellis to the ceiling. From beyond it a voice said, "Wait a minute, Manuel." A pair of chrome spoked wheels glittered into view, a pair of wasted legs under a lap robe, a pair of no color eyes that had never forgiven anyone anything. "I remember you. What do you want?"

"Arthur Thomas Robinson is dead," Dave said.

"I've already told the police what I know."

"Not all of it." Wind blew cold rain across the back of Dave's neck. He turned up the trench coat collar. "You left out the part that interests me–that you're the beneficiary of his life insurance."

Shevel stared. There was no way for his face to grow any paler. It was parchment. But his jaw dropped. When he shut it, his dentures clicked. "You must be joking. There's got to be some mistake."

"There's not." Dave glanced at the rain. "Can I come in and talk about it?"

Shevel's mouth twitched. "Did you bring the check?"

Dave shook his head. "Murder has a way of slowing down the routine."

"Then there's nothing to talk about." The wheelchair was motorized. It started to turn away.

"Why would he name you?" Dave asked.

Shrug. "We were old friends."

Dave studied the Chicano boy who was watching them with something frantic in his eyes. "Friends?"

"Oh, come in, come in," Shevel snarled, and wheeled out of sight. Dave stepped onto deep beige carpeting and the door closed behind him. But when he turned to hand the trenchcoat over, there was no one to take it. Manuel had buttoned up and left. Dave laid the coat over his arm and went around the leafy screen. A long, handsome room stretched to sliding glass doors at its far end that looked down on a marina where little white boats waited row on row like children's coffins in the rain. Shevel rattled ice and glasses at a low bar. "I met Robbie in the hospital," he said, "ten years ago." He came wheeling at Dave, holding out a squat studded glass in which dark whiskey islanded an ice cube. "Just as I met you." His smile was crooked. "He worked there. An orderly."

"And you brought him along to look after you when the hospital let you go." Dave took the drink. "Thanks."

"Robbie had good hands." Shevel aimed the chair at the planter. From under it somewhere he took a small green plastic watering can. He tilted it carefully into the mulch under the climbing vines. "And patience."

"Who took his place?"

"No one. No one could. This apartment is arranged so that I don't need day to day help." Shevel set the watering can back. "The market sends in food and liquor." He drank from his glass. "I can cook my own meals. I'm able to bathe myself and so on. A cleaning woman comes in twice a week. I have a masseur on call."

"Manuel?" Dave wondered.

"Not Manuel," Shevel said shortly and drank again.

"You publish a lot of magazines," Dave said. "How do you get to your office? Specially equipped car?"

"No car," Shevel said. "Cars are the enemy." He purred past Dave and touched a wall switch. A panel slid back. Beyond gleamed white wet-look furniture, a highgloss white desk stacked with papers, a white electric typewriter, a photocopy machine. Blowup color photos of naked girls muraled the walls. "I don't go to the office. My work comes to me. And there's the telephone." He swallowed more whiskey. "You remember the telephone?" He touched the switch and the panel slid closed.

Dave asked, "When did Robinson quit you?"

"Eight months, two weeks and six days ago," Shevel said. He said it grimly with a kind of inverse satisfaction, like counting notches in a gun butt.

"Did he give a reason?"

"Reason?" Shevel snorted and worked on his drink again. "He felt old age creeping up on him. He was all of thirty-two. He decided he wanted to be the one who was looked after, for a change."

"No quarrels? No hard feelings?"

"Just boredom." Shevel looked at his glass but it was empty. Except for the ice cube. It still looked new. He wheeled abruptly back to the bar and worked the bottle again. Watching him, Dave tried his drink for the first time. Shevel bought good Bourbon with Medallion's money. Shevel asked, "If there'd been hard feelings, would he have come back to borrow money?"

"That might depend on how much he needed it," Dave said. "Or thought he did. I hear he was desperate."

Shevel's eyes narrowed. "What does that mean?"

"Trying to keep a champagne boy on a beer income."

"Exactly." Shevel's mouth tightened like a drawstring purse. "He never had any common sense."

"So you didn't lend him anything," Dave said.

"I told him not to be a fool. Fortynine percent of the world's population is male." Shevel's chair buzzed. He steered it back, stopped it, tilted his glass, swallowed half the new drink. He looked toward the windows where the rain was gray. His voice was suddenly bleak. "I'm sorry he's dead. He was life to me for a long time."

"I'll go." Dave walked to the bar, set down his glass, began shrugging into the trenchcoat. "Just two more questions. Manuel. Does he take you deer hunting?"

Shevel looked blank.

Dave said, "Your thirty-thirty. When did you use it last?"

Shevel squinted. "What are you talking about?"

"A deer rifle. Winchester. Remington."

"Sorry." His bony fingers teased his white wig. He simpered like a skid row barroom floozy. "I've always preferred indoor sports." He was suddenly drunk. He looked Dave up and down hungrily. "Next question."

"Those magazines of yours," Dave said. "The new Supreme Court decision on obscenity. You're going to have to do some retooling– right?"

Shevel's eyes got their old hardness back. "It's been on the draw-ingboards for months. A whole new line. Home crafts. Dune buggies. Crossword puzzles. And if you're suggesting I shot Robbie with his rifle in order to get the money to finance the change-over, then you don't know much about publishing costs. Ten thousand dollars wouldn't buy the staples."

"But you do know how much the policy paid."

The crooked smile came back. "Naturally. I bought it for him. Years ago." The smile went away. "How typical of him to have forgotten to take my name off it."

"And the thirty-thirty. Did you buy that too?"

"I paid for it, of course. He had no money."

"I'll just bet he didn't," Dave said.

The development may have looked sharp to start with but it had gone shabby fast. It was on the coast road at the north end of Surf, which had gone shabby a long time ago. You couldn't see the development from the coast road. You had to park between angled white lines on the tarmacked shoulder and walk to a cliff where an iron pipe railing was slipping, its cement footings too near the crumbling edge.

Below, along a narrow rock and sand curve of shore stood apart-ment buildings. The tinwork vents on the roofs were rusting. Var-nish peeled from rafter ends and wooden decks. The stucco had been laid on thin. It was webbed with cracks. Chunks had broken out at corners showing tarpaper and chickenwire underneath.

Dave saw what Ken Barker had meant. The only access to the place was down cement steps, three long flights against the cliff face. There'd been too much sand in the cement. Edges had crumbled. Today rain washed dirt and pebbles across the treads and made them treacherous. No–no wheelchair case could get down there. He was about to turn back when, the way it will sometimes for a second, the surf stopped booming. It charged and fell heavily today, like a big, tired army under one of those generals that never gives up. But it breathed.

And in the sudden silence he heard from below a voice, raised in argument, protest, complaint. He went on down. The iron rail was scabby with corrosion. His hand came away rusty. He left cement for a boardwalk over parts of which sand had drifted, sand now dark and sodden with rain. He passed the backs of buildings, slope-top metal trash modules, the half open doors of laundry rooms. The voice kept on. He turned between two buildings to walk for the beach front.

The voice came from halfway up wooden steps to a second story deck. A small man stood there under a clear plastic umbrella. He was arguing up at the legs of a young black police officer above him on the second story deck. The officer wore a clear plastic slicker.

The little man shouted, "But I'm the God damn owner of the God damn place. A taxpayer. It's not Chief Gates that pays you–it's me. You know what the taxes are here? No–well, I'm not going to tell you because I hate to see a strong man cry. But they got to be paid, friend, if I rent it or don't rent it. And have you looked at it? I was screwed by the contractor. It's falling apart. Nineteen months old and falling apart. I'm suing the son of a bitch but the lawyers are breaking me. Not to mention the mortgage. A storm like this, carpets get soaked, plaster falls down. Could be happening in there right now. Why do you want to make things worse for me?"

Dave climbed the steps. When he'd come up to the little man, the officer said, "Mr. Brandstetter. That make three. This one. Robinson's ex-boss. Now you." His grin was very white. "This a real popular spot this morning."

"Turning people away, right?" Dave said. "Because the apartment's sealed, waiting for the DA?" He looked past the little man. Up the beach, a clutch of slickered cops was using a drag with deep teeth on the sand. Plastic wrapped their caps, their shoes. Nothing about them looked happy. It was work for tractors. But there was no way to get tractors down here.

The black officer said, "DA been and gone."

"Yeah." The little man goggled at Dave through big horn rims. "They talk about human rights. What happened to property rights? I own the place but I get treated like a thief. I can't get in till Robinson's brother comes and collects his stuff." His nose was red. And not from sunburn. There hadn't been any sun this month. "You're not his brother, are you?"

"Not the way you mean," Dave said. And to the officer, "Flag me when he comes, will you?" He went down the stairs and down the rain-runnelled beach. The sergeant he talked to wore plain clothes and no hat. His name was Slocum. Rain plastered strands of pale red hair to his freckled scalp. Dave said, "What about the surf?"

"Running too high. You can't work a launch on it. Not close in where we have to look. Keep washing you up all the time." He glanced bitterly at the muddy sky. "Storm doesn't quit, we'll never find it."

"The storm could be your friend," Dave said. "Ought to wash anything ashore–all that power." And fifty yards off a cop yelled in the rain, bent in the rain, picked something out of the muddy surf, came with it at a trot, waving it above his head, like a movie Apache who'd got the wrong room at Western Costume. "See?" Dave said.

"No wonder you're rich," Slocum said. It was a rifle. The cop offered it. Slocum shook his head. "You've got gloves, I don't. You hold it. Let me just look at it." He just looked at it while the cop turned it over and it dripped. "Thirty-thirty Remington," Slocum said. "Eight years old but like new. Won't act like new–not unless they get the seawater out of it right away."

"Sea water doesn't erase prints," Dave said and turned back toward the apartments because he heard his name called above the slam of surf, the hiss of rain. The black officer was waving an arm from the deck. A bulky man was with him. Dave jogged back. The landlord was yammering to a girl with ragged short hair in a Kobe coat at the foot of the stairs but there wasn't any hope in his voice now. Dave went up the stairs.

"Reverend Merwin Robinson," the black officer said. "Mr. Brandstetter. Insurance."

"Something wrong with the insurance?" The reverend had a hoarse voice. The kind you get from shouting at baseball games or congregations. A thick man, red-faced. A big crooked vein bulged at one temple.

"What's wrong with it is the beneficiary," Dave said.

Robinson stiffened, glared. "I don't understand."

"Not you," Dave said. "Bruce K. Shevel."

Robinson blinked. "You must be mistaken."

"That's what Shevel said," Dave said.

"But I'm Arthur's only living relative. Neither of us has anyone else. And he'd left Shevel. Said he never wanted to see him again."

"He saw him again," Dave said. "Tried to borrow money from him. I gather he saw you too."

The minister's mouth twitched. "Never at my invitation. And years would go by. He knew my stand. On how he lived. The same saintly mother raised us. He knew what the Bible says about him and his kind."

"But lately he tried to borrow money," Dave said.

"He did." The black officer had opened the glass wall panel that was the apartment door. Robinson saw, grunted, went in. Dave followed. The room was white shag carpet, long low fake-fur couches, swag lamps in red and blue pebbled glass. "Of course I refused. My living comes from collection plates. For the glory of God and His beloved Son. Not to buy fast automobiles for descendents of the brothels of Sodom."

"I don't think they had descendents," Dave said. "Anyway, did you have that kind of money?"

"My church is seventy years old. We've had half a dozen fires from faulty wiring. The neighborhood the church serves is just as old and just as poor." Robinson glanced at a shiny kitchenette where a plaster Michaelangelo David stood on a counter with plastic ferns. He went on to an alcove at the room's end, opened and quickly closed again a door to a bathroom papered with color photos of naked men from *Playgirl*, and went into a room where the ceiling was squares of gold-veined mirror above a round, tufted bed.

Dave watched him open drawers, scoop out the contents, dump them on the bed. Not a lot of clothes. A few papers. He slid back closet doors. Little hung inside. He took down what there was, spilling coat hangers, clumsily stooped, pushed the papers into a pocket, then bundled all the clothes into his arms and turned to face Dave. "That ten thousand dollars would have meant a lot to my church—new wiring, shingles, paint, new flooring to replace what's rotted–" He broke off, a man used to having dreams cancelled. He came at the door with his bundle of dead man's clothes and Dave made way for him. "Well, at least these will keep a few needy souls warm for the winter." He lumbered off down the length of the apartment, on to the deck and out of sight.

Dave looked after him. The view was clear from this room to the deck–maybe forty feet. Lily could have stood here with the 30-30. At that distance the bullet hole wouldn't be too messy. Dave went for the door where cold, damp air came in. Also the little man who owned the place. He collided with Dave.

"Your turn," Dave said.

"It rents furnished," the little man said. "A preacher, for God sake! Crookeder than a politician. Did you see? Did he take kitchen stuff? I saw that bundle. Anything could have been in it. All the kitchen stuff stays with the place. Sheets, towels? All that's mine." He rattled open kitchen drawers, cupboards, slammed them shut again, dodged into the bathroom, banged around in there–"Jesus, look what that fag did to the walls!"–shot out of the bathroom and into the bedroom. Merwin Robinson had left the chest drawers hanging. From the doorway Dave could see their total emptiness. The little man stopped in front of them. His shoulders sagged. In relief or disappointment?

"All okay?" Dave asked.

"What? Oh, yeah. Looks like it." He didn't sound convinced.

Downstairs Dave pressed a buzzer next to a glass panel like the one directly above that had opened into Arthur Thomas Robinson's apartment. While he'd talked to the dead man's brother and the black officer he'd looked past their wet shoes through the slats in the deck and seen the short-haired girl go into this apartment. She came toward him now with *Daily Variety* in her hand, looking as if she didn't want to be bothered. She still wore the Kobe coat but her hair wasn't short any more. She had on a blond wig out of an Arthur Rackham illustration–big and fuzzy. She slid the door. A smell of fresh coffee came out.

"Were you at home when Robinson was killed?"

She studied him. Without makeup she looked like a ten year old boy dressed up as the dandelion fairy. "You a cop?"

He told her who he was, gave her a card. "The police like to think Lily killed him because it's easy, it will save the taxpayers money. I'm not so sure."

She tilted her head, "Whose money will that save?"

"Not Medallion's," he said. "I'd just like to see it go to somebody else."

"Than?" She shivered. "Look–come in." He did that and she slid the door to and put the weather outside where it belonged. "Coffee?" Dropping *Variety* on a couch like the ones upstairs, she led him to the kitchenette, talking. "Who did Robbie leave his money to?" She filled pottery mugs from a glass urn. "It's funny, thinking of him having money to leave when he was hitting on me and everybody else for twenty here, twenty there." She came around the counter, pushed a tall, flower-cushioned bar stool at Dave and perched on one herself. "He was really sick."

"Sick?" Dave tried the coffee. Rich and good.

"Over that Eddie. Nothing–beautiful junk. Like this pad. Robbie was nice, a really nice, gentle, sweet, warm human being. Of all things to happen to him!" She took a mouthful of coffee, froze with the cup halfway to the countertop, stared, swallowed. "You don't mean Robbie left Ed Lily that money?"

"That would be too easy," Dave said. "No–he left it to Bruce K. Shevel."

"You're kidding," she said.

Dave twitched an eyebrow, sighed, got out cigarettes. "That's what everybody thinks. Including Shevel." He held the pack for her to take one, took one himself, lit both. He dropped the lighter into his pocket. "Was Shevel ever down here?"

"How? He was a wheelchair case. Robbie told me about him. It was one of the reasons he chose this place. So Shevel couldn't get to him. The stairs. Why would he leave Shevel his money?"

"An oversight, I expect. After all, what was he–thirty-two? At that age, glimmerings of mortality are still dim. Plenty of time to make changes. Or maybe because Shevel had bought him the policy, he thought he owed him something."

"Robbie owed him? That's a laugh. He used him like a slave for ten years. If anything, it was the other way around. Shevel owed him. But he wouldn't shell out a dime when Robbie asked for it."

"So I hear," Dave said. "Tell me about Lily."

She shrugged. "You know the type. Dime a dozen in this town. They drift in on their thumbs, all body, no brains. If they even get as far as a producer, they end up with their face in his pillow. Then it's back to Texas or Tennessee to pump gas for the rest of their lives. Only Eddie was just a little different. Show business he could live without. Hustling was surer and steadier. He always asked for parts in pictures but he settled for cash. A born whore. Loved it.

"I tried to tell Robbie. He wouldn't listen. Couldn't hear. Gone on the little shit, really gone. You want to know something? Eddie hadn't been here a week when he tried to get me into the sack." Her mouth twitched a half grin. "I told him, 'I don't go to bed with fags.' 'I'm not a fag,' was all he said. As if I and every other woman in the place didn't know that. Woman. Man. Everybody–except Robbie." She turned her head to look down the room at the glass front wall, the gray rain beyond it, the deserted beach, the muddy slop of surf. "Poor Robbie! What happens to people?" She turned back for an answer.

"In his case," Dave said, "murder."

"Yeah." She rolled her cigarette morosely against a little black ashtray. "And he never said a wrong word to Eddie. Never. Eddie was all over him all the time–I want this, I want that. You promised to introduce me to so-and-so. Take me here, take me there."

Dave looked at the ceiling. "Soundproofing another thing they cheated the owner on?"

"I got pretty familiar with Robbie's record collection. Sure, I could hear damn near every word. And a lot that wasn't words. The bedroom's right over mine too."

"Was that where the shot came from?" Dave asked.

"I wasn't here. Didn't I tell you? I was on location in Montana. Up to my elbows in flour in a tumble-down ranch house with little kids tugging at my skirts and my hair hanging over one eye. Twenty seconds on film. All that way on Airwest for twenty seconds."

"Too bad," Dave said. "Were you ever up there?"

"Robbie's? Yeah, for drinks. Now and then."

"Ever see a rifle?"

"They found it, didn't they?" She jerked the big fuzzy wig toward the beach. "Talking to Dieterle, I saw the cop fish it out of the kelp and run to you with it. You brought them luck. They were raking for it all day yesterday too."

"But did you ever see it in the apartment?"

She shrugged. "It was probably in a closet." She drank some coffee and frowned. "Wait a minute. I helped Robbie move in. No, I didn't know him. I parked up at the cliff edge and there he was with all this stuff to carry. I just naturally offered to help. And I hung around helping him settle in and we had a drink."

"Easy to know," Dave said.

"A bartender," she said. "Had been since he was a kid, except for that period with Shevel. Easy friendliness is part of a bartender's stock in trade—right? Only he didn't fake it. He honestly liked people. Those old aunties Lauder and White fell all over themselves to get him back. Business has doubled since he took over. If he owned his own place he'd make a bundle." She remembered he was dead and sadness happened in her face. "Except for one thing."

Dave worked on his coffee. "Which was?"

"He also trusted people. And that's for losers."

"About the rifle?" he prompted her.

"He didn't own one," she said flatly. "I'd have seen it while we were putting away his stuff. No rifle. But I can tell you one thing. If there'd been one, Eddie could have used it. He used to talk about hunting rabbits when he was a kid back in Oklahoma."

"Thanks." Dave tilted up the mug, drained it, set it on the counter, got off the stool. "And for the coffee." He checked his watch. "But now it's out into the cold rain and the mean streets again."

"Aw," she said.

Climbing the gritty stairs up the cliff face, he still heard the surf. But as he neared the top there was the wet tire sibilance of traffic on the the coast road and the whine of a car engine that didn't want to start. At the railing, the little landlord, Dieterle, sat in a faded old Triumph, swearing. Dave walked over and wondered in a shout if he could help. Dieterle, with a sour twist of his mouth, gave up.

"Ah, it'll catch, it'll catch. Son of a bitch knows I'm in a hurry. Always acts like this." Rain had misted the big round lenses of his glasses. He peered up at Dave through them. "You're some kind of cop, no? I saw you with them on the beach. I heard you tell Bambi

O'Mara you didn't think Lily killed Robinson." Dieterle cocked his head. "You think Bambi did it?"

"Why would I think that?"

"Hell, she was in love with Robinson. And I mean, off the deep end. Weird, a smart chick like that. Not to mention her looks. You know she was a *Playboy* centerfold?"

"It's raining and I'm getting wet," Dave said. "Tell me why she'd kill Robinson so I can go get Slocum to put cuffs on her."

Dieterle's mouth fell open. "Ah, now, wait. I didn't mean to get her in trouble. I figured you knew." He blinked anxious through the glasses. "Anybody around here could have told you. She made a spectacle of herself." Maybe the word reminded him. He took off the horn-rims, poked in the dash for a Kleenex, wiped the rain off the lenses. "I mean, what chance did she have?" He dropped the tissues on the floor and put the glasses back on. "Robinson was a fag, worked in a fag bar. It didn't faze her. So many chicks like that–figure one good lay with them and a flit will forget all about boys. Except Bambi never got the lay. And Robinson got Ed Lily. And did she hate Lily! Hoo!"

"And so she shot Robinson dead." Dave straightened, looked away to where rain glazed cars hissed past against the rain curtained background of another cliff. "Hell hath no fury, etcetera?"

"And framed Lily for it. You follow?"

"Thanks," Dave said. "I'll check her out."

"Any time." Dieterle reached and turned the key and the engine started with a snarl. "What'd I tell you?" he yelled. The car backed, scattering wet gravel, swung in a bucking U, and headed down the highway toward Surf. Fast. Dave watched. Being in a chronic hurry must be rough on a man who couldn't stop talking.

Nobody ate at The Big Cup because it was an openfront place and rain was lashing its white Formica. It faced a broad belt of cement that marked off the seedy shops and scabby apartment buildings of Venice from the beach where red dune fences leaned. Dave got coffee in an outsize cup and took it into a phone booth. After a swallow of coffee, he lit a cigarette and dialled people he knew in the television business. He didn't learn anything but they'd be able to tell him later.

He returned the empty mug to the empty counter and hiked a block among puddles to the Billy Budd whose neon sign buzzed and sputtered as if rain had leaked into it. He checked his watch. Twenty minutes ago it had been noon. A yellowed card tacked to the black door said in faded felt pen that the hours were 12 noon to 2 A.M.

But the door was padlocked. He put on reading glasses and bent to look for an emergency number on the card and a voice back of him said:

"Excuse me."

The voice belonged to a bony man, a boy of fifty, in an expensive raincoat and expensive cologne. He was out of breath, pale, and when he used a key on the padlock, his hands shook. He pushed open the door and bad air came out–stale cigarette smoke, last night's spilled whiskey. He kicked a rubber wedge under the door to hold it open and went inside.

Dave followed. The place was dark but he found the bar that had a padded leather bevel for the elbows and padded leather stools that sighed. Somewhere at the back, a door opened and fell shut. Fluorescent tubing winked on behind the bar, slicking mirrors, glinting on rows of bottles, stacks of glasses. A motor whined, fan blades clattered, air began to blow along the room. The man came out without his raincoat, without his suitcoat. The shirt was expensive too. But he'd sweated it.

"Weather, right? What can I get you?"

"Just the answer to a question," Dave said. "What did you want at Arthur Thomas Robinson's apartment in Surf this morning?"

The man narrowed his lovely eyes. "Who are you?"

Dave told him. "There are details the police haven't time for. I've got time. Can I have your answer?"

"Will you leave without it? No–I didn't think so." The man turned away to drop ice into glasses. He tilted in whiskey, edged in water. He set a glass in front of Dave, held one himself. The shaking of his hand made the ice tinkle. The sound wasn't Christmasy. "All right," he said. "Let's see if I can shock you. Ten years ago, Arthur Thomas Robinson and I were lovers."

"You don't shock me," Dave said. "But it's not responsive to my question."

"I wrote him letters. I wanted those letters back before his oh-so-righteous brother got his hands on them. I didn't know how to go about it. I simply drove over to Robbie's. I mean–I never see television. What do I know about police procedure?"

"Ten years ago," Dave said. "Does that mean Robinson left you for Bruce K. Shevel?"

"That evil mummy," the man said.

"Clear up something for me." Dave tried the whiskey. Rich and smooth. They didn't serve this out of the well. "Shevel said he'd met Robinson in the hospital. Robinson was an orderly. A neighbor named Bambi O'Mara says Robinson was a bar-keep all his life."

The man nodded. "I taught him all he knew. He was eighteen when he drifted in here." The man's eyes grew wet. He turned away and lit a cigarette. "He'd never had another job in his life. Orderly? Be serious! He fainted at the sight of blood. No, one sinister night Bruce Shevel walked in here, slumming. And that was the beginning of the end. An *old* man. He was, even then. He must be all glamour by now."

"You know that Robinson kept your letters?"

"Yes. He was always promising to return them but he didn't get around to it. Now he never will." The man's voice broke and he took a long swallow from his drink. "That damn brother will probably have apoplexy when he reads them. And of course he'll read them. His type are always snooping after sin. Claim it revolts them but they can't get enough. And of course, he hated me. Always claimed I'd perverted his baby brother. We had some pretty ugly dialogs when he found out Robbie and I were sleeping together. I wouldn't put it past him to go to the liquor board with those letters. You've got to have unimpeachable morals to run a bar, you know. It could be the end of me."

"I don't think he's that kind of hater," Dave said. "Are you Lauder?"

"I'm White, Wilbur White. Bob Lauder and I have been partners since we got out of the Army—World War II. We've had bars all over L.A. County. Fifteen years here in Venice."

"Where is he now?"

"Bob? He'll be in at six. Today's my long day. His was yesterday. It's getting exhausting. We haven't replaced Robbie yet." He tried for a wan smile. "Of course we never will. But we'll hire somebody."

"You live in Venice?" Dave asked.

"Oh, heavens, no. Malibu."

It was a handsome new place on the beach. Raw cedar planking. An Alfa Romeo stood in the carport. Dave pulled the company car into the empty space beside it. The house door was a slab at the far end of a walk under a flat roof overhang. He worked a bell push. Bob Lauder was a time getting to the door. When he opened it he was in a bathrobe and a bad mood. He was as squat and pudgy as his partner was the opposite. His scant hair was tousled, his eyes were pouchy. He winced at the daylight, what there was of it.

"Sorry to bother you," Dave said. "But I'm death claims investigator for Medallion Life. Arthur Robinson was insured with us. He worked for you. Can I ask you a few questions?"

"The police asked questions yesterday," Lauder said.

"The police don't care about my company's ten thousand dollars,"

Dave said. "I do."

"Come in, stay out, I don't give a damn." Lauder flopped a hand and turned away. "All I want is sleep."

It was Dave's day for livingrooms facing the Pacific. Lauder dropped onto a couch and leaned forward, head in hands, moaning quietly to himself.

"I've heard," Dave said, "that Robinson was good for business, that you were happy to get him back."

"He was good for business," Lauder droned.

"But you weren't happy to get him back?"

"Wilbur was happy." Lauder looked up, red-eyed. "Wilbur was overjoyed. Wilbur came un-God-dam–glued."

"To the extent of letting Robinson take what he wanted from the till?"

"How did you know? We didn't tell the police."

Dave shrugged. "He was hurting for money."

"Yeah. Wilbur tried to cover for him. I let him think it worked. But I knew." He rose and tottered off. "I need some coffee."

Dave went after him, leaned in a kitchen doorway and watched him heat a pottery urn of left-over coffee on a bricked-in burner deck. "How long have you and Wilbur been together?"

"Thirty years"–Lauder reached down a mug from a hook–"since you ask."

"Because you didn't let the Arthur Thomas Robinsons of this world break it up, right? There were others, weren't there?"

"You don't look it, you don't sound it, but you have got to be gay. Nobody straight could guess that." Lauder peered into the mouth of the pot, hoping for steam. "Yes. It wasn't easy but it was worth it. To me. If you met Wilbur, you'd see why."

Dave didn't. "Do you own a hunting rifle? Say a thirty-thirty?"

Lauder turned and squinted. "What does that mean? Look, I was working in the bar when Robbie got it. I did not get jealous and kill him, if that's what you're thinking. Or did I do it to stop him skimming fifty bucks an evening off the take?"

"I'm trying to find out what to think," Dave said.

"Try someplace else." Lauder forgot to wait for the steam. He set the mug down hard and sloshed coffee into it. "Try now. Get out of here."

"If you bought a rifle in the past five-six years," Dave said, "there'll be a Federal registration record."

"We own a little pistol," Lauder said. "We keep it at the bar. Unloaded. To scare unruly trade."

Where Los Santos canyon did a crooked fall out of tree-green hills at the coast road was a cluster of Tudor style buildings whose 1930 stucco fronts looked mushy in the rain. Between a shop that sold snorkles and swim-fins and a hamburger place Dave remembered from his childhood, lurked three telephone booths. Two were occupied by women in flowered plastic raincoats and hair curlers, trying to let somebody useful know their cars had stalled. He took the third booth and dialled the television people again.

While he learned that Bambi O'Mara had definitely been in Bear Paw, Montana at the time a bullet made a clean hole through the skull of the man she loved, Dave noticed a scabby sign across the street above a door with long black iron hinges. L. DIETERLE REAL ESTATE. He glanced along the street for the battered Triumph. It wasn't in sight but it could be back of the building. He'd see later. Now he phoned Lieutenant Ken Barker.

He was at his desk. Still. Or again. "Dave?"

"Shevel is lying. He wouldn't lie for no reason."

"Your grammar shocks me," Barker said.

"He claims he met Robinson when he was in the hospital. *After* his so-called accident. Says Robinson was an orderly. But at the Sea Shanty they say Shevel *walked* in one night and met Robinson. According to a girlfriend, Robinson was never anything but a bartender. You want to check Junipero Hospital's employment records?"

"For two reasons," Barker said. "First, that rifle didn't have any prints on it and it was bought long before Congress ordered hunting guns registered. Second, an hour ago the Coast Guard rescued a kid in a power boat getting battered on the rocks off Point Placentia. It wasn't his power boat. It's registered to one Bruce K. Shevel. The kid works at the Marina. My bet is he was heading for Mexico."

"Even money," Dave said. "His name is Manuel–right? Five foot six, a hundred twenty pounds, long hair? Somewhere around twenty?"

"You left out something," Barker said. "He's scared to death. He won't say why, but it's not just about what happened to the boat. I'll call Junipero."

"Thanks," Dave said. "I'll get back to you."

He left the booth and dodged rain-bright bumpers to the opposite curb. He took a worn step up and pushed the real estate office door. Glossy eight by tens of used Los Santos and Surf side street bungalows curled on the walls. A scarred desk was piled with phone directories. They slumped against a finger smeared telephone. A nameplate by the telephone said *L. Dieterle.* But the little man wasn't in the chair back of the desk.

The room wasn't big to start with but a Masonite partition halved it and behind this a typewriter rattled. A lumberyard bargain door was shut at the end of the partition. Tacked to the door was a pasteboard dimestore sign NOTARY and under it a business card. *Verna Marie Casper, Public Stenographer.* He rapped the door and a tin voice told him to come in.

She'd used henna on her hair for a lot of years. Her makeup too was like Raggedy Ann's. Including the yarn eyelashes. She was sixty but the dress was off the Young Misses rack at Grant's. Glass diamonds sparked at her ears, her scrawny throat, her wrists, the bony hands that worked a Selectric with a finish like a Negev tank. She wasn't going to, but he said anyway:

"Don't let me interrupt you. I just want to know when Mr. Dieterle will be back."

"Can't say," she said above the fast clatter of the type ball. "He's in and out. A nervous man, very nervous. You didn't miss him by long. He was shaking today. That's a new one."

"He thinks the storm is going to knock down his apartments in Surf," Dave said. "Will you take a message for him?"

"What I write down I get paid for," she said. "He was going through phone books. So frantic he tore pages. Really. Look"– suddenly she stopped typing and stared at Dave–"I just sublet this space. We're not in business together. He looks after his business. I look after mine. I'm self-sufficient."

"Get a lot of work, do you?"

"I'm part of this community," she said and began typing again. "A valued part. They gave me a testimonial dinner at the Chamber of Commerce last fall. Forty years of loyal public service."

"I believe it," Dave said. "Ever do anything for a man named Robinson? Recently, say–the last two weeks or so? Arthur Thomas Robinson?"

She broke off typing again and eyed him fiercely. "Are you a police officer? Are you authorized to have such information?"

"He wanted you to write out an affidavit for him, didn't he?" Dave said. "And to notarize it?"

"Now, see here! You know I can't–"

"I'm not asking what was in it. I think I know. I also think it's what got him killed."

"Killed!" She went white under the circles of rouge. "But he only did it to clear his conscience! He said–" She clapped a hand to her mouth and glared at Dave. "You! You're trying to trick me. Well, it won't work. What I'm told is strictly confidential."

Dave swung away. His knuckles rapped the Masonite as he went out of her cubbyhole. "Not with this partition," he said. "With Dieterle on the other side."

Past batting windshield wipers, he saw the steeple down the block above the dark greenery of old acacia trees. Merwin Robinson had told the truth about the neighborhood. Old one story frame houses with weedy front yards where broken down autos turned to rust. Stray dogs ran cracked sidewalks in the rain. An old woman in man's shoes and hat dragged a coaster wagon through puddles.

CHURCH OF GOD'S ABUNDANCE was what the weathered signboard said. God's neglect was what showed. Dave tried the front doors from which the yellow varnish was peeling. They were loose in their frame but locked. A hollow echo came back from the rattling he gave them. He followed a narrow strip of cement that led along the shingled side of the church to a shingle-sided bungalow at the rear. The paint flaking off it was the same as what flaked off the church, white turning yellow. There was even a cloverleaf of stained glass in the door. *Rev. Merwin Robinson* in time dimmed ink was in a little brass frame above a bell push.

But the buzz pushing it made at the back of the house brought nobody. A dented gray and blue sedan with fifties tail fins stood at the end of the porch. Its trunk was open. Some of Arthur Thomas Robinson's clothes were getting rained on. Dave tried the tongue latch of the house door and it opened. He put his head inside, called for the preacher. It was dusky in the house. No lights anywhere. Dave stepped inside onto a threadbare carpet held down by overstuffed chairs covered in faded chintz.

"Reverend Robinson?"

No answer. He moved past a room divider of built-in bookcases with diamond-pane glass doors. There was a round golden oak diningroom table under a chain-suspended stained-glass light fixture. Robinson evidently used the table as a desk. Books were stacked on it. A loose leaf binder lay open, a page half filled with writing in ballpoint. *Am I my brother's keeper?* Sermon topic. But not for this week. Not for any week now.

Because on the far side of the table, by a kitchen swing door his head had pushed ajar when he fell, Merwin Robinson lay on his back and stared at Dave with the amazed eyes of the dead. One of his hands clutched something white. Dave knelt. It was an envelope, torn open, empty. But the stamp hadn't been cancelled. He put on his glasses, flicked his lighter to read the the address. *City Attorney, 200 Spring St., Los Angeles, CA.* Neatly typed on an electric machine with carbon ribbon. Probably the battered IBM in Verna Casper's office.

Which meant there wasn't time to hunt up the rectory phone in the gloom, to report, to explain. It didn't matter. Merwin Robinson wouldn't be any deader an hour from now. But somebody else might be, unless Dave got back to the beach. Fast.

Wind lashed rain across the expensive decks of the apartments facing the Marina. It made the wet trenchcoat clumsy, flapping around his legs. Then he quit running because he saw the door. He took the last yards in careful, soundless steps. The door was shut. That would be reflex even for a man in a chronic hurry–to shut out the storm. And that man had to be here. The Triumph was in the lot.

Dave put a hand to the cold, wet brass knob. It turned. He leaned gently against the door. It opened. He edged in and softly shut it. The same yammering voice he'd heard earlier today in Surf above the wash of rain and tide, yammered now someplace beyond the climbing vines.

"–That you got him to help you try to rip off an insurance company–accident and injury. By knocking your car off the jack while one wheel was stripped and your foot was under it. And he told you he was going to spill the whole story unless you paid out."

"I'm supposed to believe it's on that paper?" Shevel's voice came from just the other side of the philodendrons. "That Robbie actually–"

"Yeah, right–he dictated it to the old hag that's a notary public, splits my office space with me. I heard it all. He told her he'd give you twenty-four hours to cop out too, then he'd mail it. But I didn't think it was a clear conscience he was after. He was after money–for a sportscar for that hustler he was keeping."

"I'm surprised at Robbie," Shevel said. "He often threatened to do things. He rarely did them."

"He did this. And you knew he would. Only how did you waste him? You can't get out of that chair."

"I had two plans. The other was complicated–a bomb in his car. Happily, the simpler plan worked out. It was a lovely evening. The storm building up off the coast made for a handsome sunset. The sea was calm–long, slow swells. I decided to take an hour's cruise in my launch. I have a young friend who skippers it for me."

"You shot him from out there?"

"The draft is shallow. Manuel was able to steer quite close in. It can't have been a hundred fifty yards. Robbie was on the deck as I'd expected. It was warm, and he adored sunsets with his martinis. Manuel's a fine marksman. Twenty four months in Viet Nam sharpened his natural skills. And the gun was serviceable." Shevel's voice went hard. "This gun is not, but you're too close to miss. Hand over that paper. No, don't try anything. I warn you–"

Dave stepped around the screen of vines and chopped at Shevel's wrist. The gun went off with a slapping sound. The rug furrowed at Dieterle's feet. Shevel screamed rage, struggled in the wheelchair, clawed at Dave's eyes. Dieterle tried to run past. Dave put a foot in his way. He sprawled. Dave wrenched the .22 out of Shevel's grip, leveled it at them, backed to a white telephone, cranked zero and asked an operator to get him the police.

Ken Barker had managed a shower and a shave. He still looked wearier than this morning. But he worked up a kind of smile. "Neat," he said. "You think like a machine–a machine that gets the company's money back."

"Shevel's solvent but not that solvent," Dave said. "Hell, we paid out a hundred thousand initially. I don't remember what the monthly payments were. We'll be lucky to get half. And we'll have to sue for that." He frowned at a paper in his hands, typing on a police form, signed in shaky ballpoint–*Manuel Sanchez*. It said Shevel had done the shooting. He, Manuel, had only run the boat. "Be sure this kid gets a good lawyer."

"The best in the Public Defender's office."

"No." Dave rose, flapped into the trenchcoat. "Not good enough. Medallion will foot the bill. I'll send Abe Greenglass. Tomorrow morning."

"Jesus." Barker blinked. "Remind me never to cross you."

Dave grinned, worked the coat's wet leather buttons, quit grinning. "I'm sorry about Robinson's brother. If I'd just been a little quicker–"

"It was natural causes," Barker said. "Don't blame yourself. Can't even blame Dieterle–or Wilbur White."

"The bar owner? You mean he was there?"

"Slocum checked him out. He had the letters."

"Yup." Dave fastened the coat belt. "Twenty minutes late to work. White, sweaty, shaking. It figures. Hell, he even talked about apoplexy, how the Reverend hated him for perverting his brother."

"The man had horrible blood pressure," Barker said. "We talked to his doctor. He'd warned him. The least excitement and"–Barker snapped his fingers–"cerebral hemorrhage. Told him to retire. Robinson refused. They needed him–the people at that run-down church."

"It figures," Dave said. "He didn't make it easy, but he was the only one in this mess I could like. A little."

"Not Bambi O'Mara?" Barker went and snagged a topcoat from a rack. "She looked great in those magazine spreads." He took Dave's arm, steered him between gray-green desks toward a gray-green door.

"I want to hear all about her. I'll buy you a drink."

But the phone rang and called him back. And Dave walked alone out of the beautiful, bright glass building into the rain that looked as if it would never stop falling.

MICHAEL COLLINS
(b.1924)

A Reason to Die
(Dan Fortune)

There are many kinds of courage. Maybe the hardest is doing what you have to do. No matter how it looks to other people or what happens in the end.

Irish Johnny's Tavern is a gray frame house near the railroad tracks in Syracuse, New York. A beacon of red and blue neon through the mounded old snow in the dusk of another cold winter day too far from Chelsea. My missing left arm hurt in the cold, and one of the people I was meeting was a killer.

I'd been in Irish Johnny's before, on my first day in Syracuse looking for why Alma Jean Brant was dead. Her mother had sent me.

"You go to Irish Johnny's, Mr. Fortune," Sada Patterson said. "They'll tell you about my Alma Jean."

"What can they tell me, Mrs. Patterson?" I said. I'd read the Syracuse Police Department's report, made my voice as gentle as I could in the winter light of my office-apartment loft above Eighth Avenue.

"They can tell you my girl wasn't walkin' streets without she got a reason, and whatever that there reason was it got to be what killed her."

"Every girl on the streets has a reason, Mrs. Patterson," I said.

"I don't mean no reason everyone got. I means a special reason.

Somethin' made her do what she never would do," Sada Patterson said.

"Mrs. Patterson, listen—"

"No! You listen here to me." She held her old black plastic handbag in both hands on the lap of her starched print dress and fixed me across the desk with unflinching eyes. "I did my time hookin' when I was a girl. My man he couldn't get no work, so one day he ain't there no more, and I got two kids, and I hooked. A man got no work, he goes. A woman got no man, she hooks. But a woman got a man at home, she don't go on no streets. Not a good woman like my Alma Jean. She been married to that Indian ten years, and she don't turn no tricks 'less she got a powerful reason."

"What do you want me to do. Mrs. Patterson?"

Ramrod straight, as thin and rock hard as any Yankee farmer, Sada Patterson studied me with her black eyes as if she could see every thought I'd ever had. She probably could. The ravages of sixty years of North Carolina dirt farms, the Syracuse ghetto, and New York sweatshops had left her nothing but bones and tendon, the flesh fossilized over the endless years.

"You go on up there 'n' find out who killed my Alma Jean. I can pay. I got the money. You go to Irish Johnny's and ask 'bout my Alma Jean. She ain't been inside the place in ten years, or any place like it. You tell 'em Sada sent you and they talk to you even if you is a honkie."

"It's a police job, Mrs. Patterson. Save your money."

"No cop's gonna worry hard 'bout the killin' of no black hooker. You go up there, Fortune. You find out." She stood up, the worn plastic handbag in both hands out in front of her like a shield. A grandmother in a print dress. Until you looked at her eyes. "She was my last—Alma Jean. She come when we had some money, lived in a house up there. She almos' got to finish grade school. I always dressed her so good. Like a real doll, you know? A little doll."

Inside, Irish Johnny's is a single large room with a bandstand at the far end. The bar is along the left wall, backed by bottles and fronted by red plastic stools. Tables fill the room around a small dance floor. Behind the bar and the rows of bottles is a long mirror. The rear wall over the bandstand is bare, except when it is hung with a banner proclaiming the band or *artiste* to perform that night.

On the remaining two walls there is a large mural in the manner of Orozco or maybe Rivera. Full of violent, struggling ghetto figures, it was painted long ago by some forgotten radical student from the university on the hill above the tavern.

The crowd had not yet arrived, only a few tables occupied as I came in. The professor and his wife sat at a table close to the dance floor. I crossed the empty room under the lost eyes of the red, blue, and yellow people in the mural.

I knew who the killer was, but I didn't know how I was going to prove it. Someone was going to have to help me before I made the call to the police.

The police are always the first stop in a new town. Lieutenant Derrida of the Syracuse Police Department was an older man. He remembered Sada Patterson.

"Best-looking hooker ever walked a street in Syracuse." His thin eyes were bright and sad at the same time, as if he wished he and Sada Patterson could be back there when she had been the best-looking hooker in Syracuse, but knew it was too late for both of them.

"What made Alma Jean go to the streets, Lieutenant?"

He shrugged. "What makes any of 'em?"

"What does?" I said.

"Don't shit me, Fortune. A new car or a fur coat. Suburbs to Saskatchewan. It just happens more in the slums where the bucks ain't so big or easy."

"Sada says no way unless the girl had a large reason," I said. "She didn't mean a fur coat or a watch."

"Sada Patterson's a mother," Derrida said.

"She's also a client. Can I earn my fee?"

He opened a desk drawer, took out a skinny file. "Alma Jean was found a week ago below a street bridge over the tracks. Some kids going to school spotted her. The fall killed her. She died somewhere between midnight and four A.M., the snow and cold made it hard to be sure. It stopped snowing about two A.M., there was no snow on top of her, so she died after that."

Derrida swiveled in his chair, looked out his single window at the gray sky and grayer city. "She could have fallen, jumped, or been pushed. There was no sign of a struggle, but she was a small woman; one push would have knocked her over that low parapet. M.E. says a bruise on her jaw could have come from a blow or from hitting a rock. No suicide note, but the snow showed someone had climbed up on the parapet. Only whoever it was didn't get near the edge, held to a light pole, jumped off the other way back onto the street."

"What's her pimp say?"

"Looks like she was trying to work independent."

I must have stared. Derrida nodded.

"I know," he said, "we sweated the pimp in the neighborhood.

Black as my captain, but tells everyone he's a Polack. He says he didn't even know Alma Jean, and we can't prove he did or place him around her."

"Who do you place around her?"

"That night, no one. She was out in the snow all by herself. No one saw her, heard her, or smelled her. If she turned any tricks that night, she used doorways; no johns are talking. No cash in her handbag. A bad night."

"What about other nights?"

"The husband, Joey Brant. He's a Mohawk, works high steel like most Indians. They married ten years ago, no kids and lived good. High steel pays. With her hooking he was *numero uno* suspect, only he was drinking in Cherry Valley Tavern from nine till closing with fifty witnesses. Later, the bartender, him, and ten others sobered up in a sweat lodge until dawn."

"Anyone else?"

"*Mister* Walter Ellis. Owns the numbers, runs a big book. He was an old boyfriend of Sada's, seems to have had eyes for the daughter. She was seen visiting him a couple of times recently. Just friendly calls, he says, but he got no alibi."

"That's it?"

Derrida swiveled. "No, we got a college professor named Margon and his wife. Margon was doing 'research' with Alma Jean. Maybe the wrong kind of research. Maybe the wife got mad."

I took a chair at the table with the Margons. In Irish Johnny's anyone who opened a book in the university above the ghetto was a "professor." Fred Margon was a thin, dark-haired young man in his midtwenties. His wife, Dorothy, was a beauty-contest blonde with restless eyes.

"A temple," Fred Margon said as I sat down. "The bartenders are the priests, that mural is the holy icon painted by a wandering disciple, the liquor is God."

"I think I'll scream," Dorothy Margon said. "Or is that too undignified for the wife of a scholar, a pure artist?"

Fred Margon drank his beer, looked unhappy.

"Booze is their god," Dorothy Margon said. "That's very good. Isn't that good, Mr. Fortune? You really are bright, Fred. I wonder what you ever saw in me? Just the bod, right? You like female bods at least. You like them a lot when you've got time."

"You want to leave?" Fred said.

"No, tell us why drink is their god. Go one tell us."

"No other god ever helped them."

"Clever," Dorothy said. "Isn't he clever, Mr. Fortune? Going to do great scholarly research, teach three classes, and finish his novel all at the same time. Or maybe he makes time for that."

"We'll leave," Fred said.

"All day every day: scholar, teacher, novelist. For twenty whole thousand dollars a year!"

"We manage," Fred Margon said.

"Never mind," Dorothy said. "Just never mind."

I met him in a coffee shop on South Crouse after a class. He looked tired. We had coffee, and he told me about Alma Jean.

"I found her in an Indian bar six months ago. I like to walk through the city, meet the real people." He drank his coffee. "She had a way of speaking full of metaphors. I wrote my doctoral dissertation on the poetry of totally untrained people, got a grant to continue the research. I met her as often as I could. In the bars and in her home. To listen and record her speech. She was highly intelligent. Her insights were remarkable for someone without an education, and her way of expressing her thoughts was pure uneducated poetry."

"You liked her?"

He nodded. "She was real, alive."

"How much did you like her, professor?"

"Make it Fred, okay? I'm only a bottom-step assistant professor, and sometimes I want to drop the whole thing, live a real life, make some money." He drank his coffee, looked out the cafe window. He knew what I was asking. "My wife isn't happy. Mr. Fortune. When she's unhappy, she has the classic female method of showing it. Perhaps in time I would have tried with Alma Jean, but I didn't. She really wasn't interested, you know? In me or any other man. Only her husband."

"You know her husband?"

"I've met him. Mostly at her house, sometimes in a bar. He seems to drink a lot. I asked her about that. She said it was part of being an Indian, a 'brave.' Work hard and drink hard. He always seemed angry. At her, at his bosses, at everything. He didn't like me, or my being there, as if it were an insult to him, but he just sat in the living room, drinking and looking out a window at the tall buildings downtown. Sometimes he talked about working on those buildings. He was proud of that. Alma Jean said that was the culture; a 'man' did brave work, daring."

"When was the last time you saw her?"

"The day she died." He shrugged as he drank his coffee. "The police know. I had a session with her early in the day at her house.

Her husband wasn't there, and she seemed tired, worried. She'd been
unhappy for months, I think, but it was always hard to tell with her.
Always cheerful and determined. I told her there was a book in her
life, but she only scorned the idea. Life was to be lived, not written
about. When there were troubles, you did something."

"What troubles sent her out on the streets?"

He shook his head. "She never told me. A few weeks ago she asked
me to pay her for making the tapes. She needed money. I couldn't
pay her much on my grant, but I gave her what I could. I know it
wasn't anywhere near enough. I heard her talking on the telephone,
asking about the cost of something."

"You don't know what?"

"No." He drank coffee. "But whoever she was talking to offered
to pay for whatever it was. She turned him down."

"You're sure it was a him?"

"No, I'm not sure."

"Who killed her, professor?"

Outside, the students crunched through the snow in the gray light.
He watched them as if he wished he were still one of them, his future
unknown. "I don't know who killed her. Mr. Fortune. I know she
didn't commit suicide, and I doubt that she fell off that bridge. I never
saw her drunk. When her husband drank, she never did, as if she
had to be sober to take care of him."

"Where were you that night?"

"At home," he said, looked up at me. "But I couldn't sleep, another
argument with my wife. So I went out walking in the snow. Didn't
get back until two A.M. or so."

"Was it still snowing?"

"It had just stopped when I got home."

"Did you see anyone while you were out?"

"Not Alma Jean, if that's what you want to know. I did see that
older friend of hers. What's his name? Walter Ellis?"

"Where?"

"Just driving around. That pink Caddy of his is easy to remember.
Especially in the snow, so few cars driving."

"And all you were doing with her was recording her speech?"

He finished his coffee. "That's all, Mr. Fortune."

After he left, I paid for the coffee. He was an unhappy man, and
not just about money or work.

The scar-faced man stood just inside the door. Snow dripped from
his dirty raincoat into a pool around his black boots. A broad, power-
fully built man with a fresh bandage on his face. Dark stains covered

the front of his raincoat. The raincoat and his black shirt were open at the throat. He wore a large silver cross bedded in the hair of his chest.

"Now there's something you can write about," Dorothy Margon said. "Real local color. Who is he? What is he? Why don't you make notes. You didn't forget your notebook, did you, Fred?"

"His name is Duke," Fred Margon said. "He's a pimp, and this is his territory. A small-time pimp, only three girls on the street now. He takes 80 percent of what they make to protect them, lets them support him with most of the rest. But the competition is fierce, and business is bad this season. He gives students a cut rate; professors pay full price."

"Of course," Dorothy said. "Part of your 'research' into 'ordinary' people. All for art and scholarship." She looked at the man at the entrance. "I wonder what his girls are like. Are they young or old? Do they admire him? I suppose they all love him, Of course they do. All three of them in love with him."

"In love with him and afraid of him," I said.

"Love and fear," Fred Margon said. "Their world."

"Do I hear a story?" Dorothy said. "Is everything a story? Nothing real? With results? Change? A future?"

I watched him come across the dance floor toward our table. Duke Wiltkowski, the pimp in the streets where Alma Jean had been found dead.

The pimp's office was a cellar room with a single bare bulb, a table for a desk, some battered armchairs, a kerosene heater, and water from melted snow pooled in a dark corner. Times had been better for Duke Wiltkowski.

"You sayin' I killed her? You sayin' that, man?" His black face almost hidden in the shadows of the cellar room, the light of the bare bulb barely reaching where he sat behind the table.

"Someone did," I said. "You had a motive."

"You say I kill that chippie, you got trouble, man. I got me a good lawyer. He sue you for everythin' you got!"

"The police say she was in your territory."

"The police is lyin'! The police say I kill that chippie, they lyin'!" His voice was high and thin, almost hysterical. It's a narrow world of fear, his world. On the edge. Death on one side, prison on the other, hunger and pain in between.

"She was free-lance in your territory. You can't let her do that. Not and survive. Let her do that, and you're out of business."

He sat in the gloom of the cold basement room, unmoving in the half shadows. The sweat shone on his face liked polished ebony. The face of a rat with his back to the wall, cornered. Protesting.

"I never see that chippie. Not me. How I know she was working my turf? You tell the cops that, okay? You tell the cops Duke Wiltkowski never nowhere near that chippie."

He sweated in the cold cellar room. A depth in his wide eyes almost of pleading. Go away, leave him alone. Go away before he told what he couldn't tell. Wanted to tell but couldn't. Not yet.

"Where were you that night?"

"Right here. An' with one o' my pigs. All night. Milly-O. Me 'n' Milly-O we was makin' it most all night. You asks her."

One of his prostitutes who would say anything he told her to say, to the police or to God himself. That desperate. An alibi he knew was no alibi. Sweated. Licked his lips.

"That Injun husband she got, maybe he done it. Hey, they all crazy, them Injuns! That there professor hangs in Irish Johnny's. Hey, he got to of been playin' pussy with her. I mean, a big-shot white guy down there. Hey, that there professor he got a wife. Maybe she don't like that chippie, right?"

"How about Walter Ellis? He was out in the snow that night."

The fear on his face became sheer terror. "I don' know nothin' 'bout Mr. Ellis! You hears, Fortune! Nothin'!"

Now he walked into Irish Johnny's with the exaggerated swing and lightness of a dancer. Out in public, the big man. His face in the light a mass of crisscross scars. The new bandage dark with dried blood. He smiled a mouthful of broken yellow teeth.

"Saw it was you, professor. That your lady?" He clicked his heels, bowed to Dorothy Margon. A Prussian officer. "Duke Wiltkowski. My old man was Polack." He nodded to me, cool and casual, expansive. An image to keep up and no immediate fear in sight. "Hey, Fortune. How's the snoopin'?"

"Slow," I said, smiled. "But getting there."

"Yeh." The quick lick of the lips, and sat down at the table, legs out in his Prussian boots. The silver cross at his throat reflected the bright tavern light. He surveyed the room with a cool, imperious eye. Looked at Dorothy Margon. "You been holdin' out on the Duke, professor. You could do real business with that one."

The Duke admired Dorothy's long blonde hair, the low-cut black velvet dress that looked too expensive for an assistant professor's wife, her breasts rising out of the velvet.

"It's not what I do," Fred Margon said.

Dorothy Margon tore a cardboard coaster into small pieces, dropped the pieces onto the table. She began to build the debris into a pyramid. She worked on her pyramid, watched the Duke.

The people were filling the tavern now. I watched them come out of the silence and cold of the winter night into the light and noise of the tavern. They shed old coats and worn jackets, wool hats and muddy galoshes, to emerge in suits and dresses the colors of the rainbow. Saturday night.

The Duke sneered. "Works their asses a whole motherin' year for the rags they got on their backs." He waved imperiously to a waiter. "Set 'em up for my man the professor 'n' his frau. Fortune there too. Rye for me."

Dorothy Margon built her pyramid of torn pieces of coaster. "What happened to your face?"

"Injuns." The Duke touched the bandage on his face, his eyes fierce. "The fuckers ganged me. I get 'em."

"Alma Jean's husband?" I said. "The Cherry Valley bar?"

The Cherry Valley Tavern was a low-ceilinged room with posts and tables and a long bar with high stools. As full of dark Iroquois faces as the massacre that had given it its name. All turned to look at me as I entered. I order a beer.

The bartender brought me the beer. "Maybe you'd like it better downtown, mister. Nothing personal."

"I'm looking for Joey Brant."

He mopped the bar. "You're not a cop."

"Private. Hired by his mother-in-law."

He went on mopping the bar.

"She wants to know who killed her daughter."

"Brant was in here all night."

"They told me. What time do you close?"

"Two."

"When the snow stopped," I said.

"We went to the sweat lodge. Brant too."

"Good way to sober up on a cold night. Maybe Brant has some ideas about who did kill her."

"Down the end of the bar."

He was a small man alone on the last bar stool. He sat hunched, a glass in both hands. An empty glass. Brooding into the glass or staring up at himself in the bar mirror. I stood behind him. He didn't notice, waved at the bartender, violent and arrogant.

"You had enough, Joey."

"I says when I got enough." He scowled at the bartender. The bartender did nothing, Brant looked down at his empty glass. "I got no woman, Crow. She's dead, Crow. My woman. How I'm gonna live my woman's dead?"

"You get another woman," the bartender, Crow, said.

Brant stared at his empty glass, remembered what he wanted. "C'mon, Crow."

"You ain't got two paychecks now."

Brant swung his head from side to side as if caught in the mesh of a net, thrashing in the net. "Lemme see the stuff."

The bartender opened a drawer behind the bar, took out a napkin, opened it on the bar. Various pieces of silver and turquoise Indian jewelry lay on the towel. There were small red circles of paper attached to most pieces. Rings, bracelets, pendants, pins, a silver cross. Joey Brant picked up a narrow turquoise ring. It was one of the last pieces without a red tag.

"Two bottles," Crow said.

"It's real stuff, Crow. Four?"

"Two."

I thought Brant was going to cry, but he only nodded. Crow took an unopened bottle of cheap rye blend from under the bar, wrote on it. Close, Brant's shoulders were thickly muscled, his arms powerful, his neck like a bull. A flyweight bodybuilder. Aware of his body, his image. I sat on the stool beside him. He stared at my empty sleeve. Crow put a shot glass and a small beer on the bar, opened the marked bottle of rye.

"On me," I said. "Both of us."

Crow stared at me, then closed the marked bottle, poured from a bar bottle. He brought my beer and a chaser beer, walked away. The small, muscular Indian looked at the whisky, at me.

"Why was Alma Jean on the street, Joey?" I said.

He looked down at the whisky. His hand seemed to wait an inch from the shot glass. Then he touched it, moved it next to the beer chaser.

"How the hell I know? The bitch."

"Her mother says she had to have a big reason."

"Fuck her mother." He glared at my missing arm. "You no cop. Cops don't hire no cripples."

"Dan Fortune. Private detective. Sada Patterson hired me to find out who murdered Alma Jean. Any ideas?"

He stared into the shot glass of cheap rye as if it held all the beauty of the universe. "She think I don' know? Stupid bitch an' her black whoremaster! I knows he give her stuff. I get him, you watch. Make him talk. Black bastard, he done it sure. I get him." He drank, went on staring into the bottom of the glass as if it were a crystal ball. "Fuckin' around with that white damn professor. Think she fool Joey

Brant? Him an' that hot-bitch wife he got. Business, she says; old
friends, she says. Joey knows, yessir. Joey knows.''

"You knew," I said, "so you killed her."

There was a low rumble through the room. The bartender, Crow,
stopped pouring to watch me. They didn't love Brant, but he was
one of them, and they would defend him against the white man. Any
white man, black or white.

Brant shook his head. "With my friends. Not worth killin'. Nossir.
Joey Brant takes care of hisself." He drained the shot, finished the
beer chaser, and laid his head on the bar.

The bartender came and removed the glasses, watched me finish
my beer. When I did, he made no move to serve another.

"He was in here all night; fifty guys saw him. We went to the reservation and sweated. Me and ten other guys and Brant."

"Sure," I said.

I felt their eyes all the way out. They didn't like him, even despised
him, but they would all defend him, lie for him.

The band burst into sound. Dancers packed into a mass on the floor.
A thick mass of bodies that moved as one, the colors and shapes of
the mural on the wall, a single beast with a hundred legs and arms.
Shrill tenor sax, electronic guitar, keyboard, and trumpet blaring.
Drums.

"Or did Brant find you?" I said.

The Duke scowled at the dancers on the floor. "Heard he was
lookin' to talk to the Duke, so I goes to the Cherry Valley. He all
shit and bad booze. He never know me, 'n' I never knows him. I
tells him I hear he talkin' 'bout me 'n' from now on all I wants to
hear is sweet nothin'.''

"You're a tough man," I said. "I'll bet you scared him."

He licked his lips. I watched the sweat on his brow, the violent
swinging of his booted foot. He was hiding *something*.

"I tell him I never even heard o' his broad. What I know about
no Injun's broad? I tell him iffen she goes out on the tricks, it got
to be he put her out. Happens all the time. Some ol' man he needs
the scratch, so he puts the ol' woman out on the hustle." The swinging foot in its black boot seemed to grow more agitated. His eyes
searched restlessly around the packed room, the crowded dance floor.
"I seen it all times, all ways. They comes out on the streets, nice
chicks should oughta be home watchin' the kids, puttin' the groceries
on the table. I seen 'em, scared 'n' no way knows what they s'posed
to do. All 'cause some dude he ain't got what it takes."

Restless, he sweated. The silver cross reflected the tavern light where it lay on his thick chest hair above the black shirt. Talked. But what was he telling me?

"Is that when he jumped you? Pulled a knife?"

The Duke sneered. "Not him. He too drunk. All of 'em, they ganged me. He pull his blade, sure, but he ain't sober 'nuff he can cut cheese. It was them others ganged me. I got some of 'em, got out o' there."

"Did you see him out on the street that night, Duke? Is that what you really told him? Why they ganged on you?"

He jerked back as if snakebitten. "I ain't seen no one that there night! I ain't on the street that there night. I–"

He stared toward the door. As if he saw a demon.

Joey Brant stood inside the tavern entrance blinking at the noise and crowd. Walter Ellis stood beside Brant. Which one was the Duke's demon?

It was a big house by Syracuse-ghetto standards. A two-story, three-bedroom, cinder-block box painted yellow and green, with a spiked wrought-iron fence, a swimming pool that took up most of the postage-stamp side yard. Concrete paths wound among birdbaths and fountains and the American flag on a pole and naked plaster copies of the Venus de Milo and Michelangelo's David.

Walter Ellis met me on his front steps. "The cops send you to me, Fortune?"

He was a tall, slim man with snow-white hair and a young face. He looked dangerous. Quick eyes that smiled now. Simple gray flannel slacks, a white shirt open at the throat, and a red cashmere sweater that gave a vigorous tint to his face. Only the rings on both pinkies and both index fingers, diamonds and rubies and gold, showed his money and his power.

"They said you knew Alma Jean Brant," I said.

"Her and her mother. Come on in. Drink?"

"Beer if you have it."

He laughed. "Now you know I got beer. What kind of rackets boss wouldn't have a extra refrigerator full of beer? Beck's? Stroh's? Bud?"

"Beck's, thanks."

"Sure. A New York loner."

We were in a small, cluttered, overstuffed living room all lace and velvet and cushions. Ellis pressed a button somewhere. A tall, handsome black man in full suit and tie materialized, not the hint of a bulge anywhere under the suit, was told to bring two Beck's.

"Not that I'm much of a racket boss like in the movies, eh? A small-town gambler. Maybe a little border stuff if the price is right." He laughed again, sat down in what had to be his private easy chair, worn and comfortable with a footstool, waved me to an overstuffed couch. I sank into it. He lit a cigar, eyed me over it. "But you didn't come about my business, right? Sada sent you up to find out what happened to Alma Jean."

"What did happen to her?"

"I wish I knew."

The immaculate black returned with two Beck's and two glasses on an ornate silver tray. A silver bowl of bar peanuts. Ellis raised his glass. We drank. He ate peanuts and smoked.

"You liked her?" I said. "Alma Jean?"

He savored the cigar. "I liked her. She was married. That's all. Not my age or anything else. She didn't cheat on her husband. A wife supports her husband."

"But she went on the streets."

"Prostitution isn't cheating, Fortune. Not in the ghetto, not down here where it hurts. It's the only way a woman has of making money when she got no education or skills. It's what our women do to help in a crisis."

"And the men accept that?"

He smoked, drank, fingered peanuts. "Some do, some don't."

"Which are you?"

"I never cottoned to white slaving."

"You were out that night. In your car. On the streets down near Irish Johnny's."

He drank, licked foam from his lips. "Who says?"

"Professor Fred Margon saw you. I think Duke Wiltkowski did too. He's scared, sweating, and hiding something."

His eyes were steady over the glass, the peanuts he ate one by one. "I like a drive, a nice walk in the snow. I saw the Duke and Margon. I didn't see no one else. But a couple of times I saw that wife of Margon's tailing Alma Jean."

"Was it snowing when you got home?"

He smiled.

I watched Walter Ellis steer Joey Brant to a table on the far side of the dance floor. Brant was already drunk, but his startled eyes were wary, almost alert. This wasn't one of his taverns. The Duke watched Walter Ellis.

I said, "It's okay; we know he was out that night. He saw you, knows you saw him, and it's okay. Who else did you see?"

The Duke licked his lips, looked at Fred Margon.

"You writes, yeh, professor?"

He looked back across the dance floor to Ellis and Joey Brant.

"I means," the Duke said, "like stories 'n' books 'n' all that there?"

"God, does he write!" Dorothy Margon said. "Writes, studies, teaches. All day, every day. Tell the Duke about your art, Fred. Tell the Duke what you *do*. All day, every damn day."

"Like," the Duke said, "poetry stuff?" He watched only Fred Margon now. "Words they got the same sound 'n' all?"

"I write poetry," Fred said. "Sometimes it rhymes."

"You likes poetry, yeh?"

"Yes, I like poetry. I read it."

"Oh, but it's so hard!" Dorothy said. "Tell the Duke how hard poetry is, Fred. Tell him how hard all *real* writing is. Tell him how you can learn most careers in a few years but it takes a lifetime to learn to write well."

"We better go," Fred said.

I watched the people packed body to body on the dance floor, flushed and excited, desperate for Saturday night. On the far side Walter Ellis ordered drinks. Joey Brant saw us: the Duke, me, Fred and Dorothy Margon. I watched him turn on Ellis. The racket boss only smiled, shook his head.

Dorothy smiled at the Duke. "I'm a bitch, right? I wasn't once. Do your women talk to you like that, Duke? No, they wouldn't, would they? They wouldn't dare. They wouldn't want to. Tell me about the Indians? How many were there? Did they all have knives? Do they still wear feathers? How many did you knock out? Kill?"

The Duke watched Fred Margon. "You writes good, professor?"

"You see," Dorothy said, "we're going to stay at the university three more years. We may even stay forever. Isn't that grand news? I can stay here and do nothing forever."

The Duke said to Fred, "They puts what you writes in books?"

Dorothy said, "Did you ever want something, wait for something, think you have it at last, and then suddenly it's so far away again you can't even see it anymore?"

"I'm a writer," Fred said. "A writer and a teacher. I can't go to New York and write lies for money."

Dorothy stood up. "Dance with me, Duke. I want to dance. I want to dance right now."

She opened the apartment door my second day in Syracuse, looked at my duffel coat, beret, and missing arm.

"He's out. Go find him in one of your literary bars!"

"Mrs. Margon?" I said.

She cocked her head, suspicious yet coy, blonde and flirtatious.

"You want me?"

"Would it do me any good?"

She laughed. "Do we know each other, Mr.-?"

"Fortune," I said. "No."

She eyed me. "Then what do you want to talk to me about?"

"Alma Jean Brant," I said.

She started to close the door. "Go and find my husband."

I held the door with my foot. "No, I want you. Both ways."

She laughed again, neither flirtatious nor amused this time. Self-mocking, a little bitter. "You can probably have me. Both ways." But stepped back, held the door open. "Come in."

It was a small apartment: a main room, bedroom, kitchenette, and bathroom. All small, cramped. The furniture had to have been rented with the apartment. They don't pay assistant professors too well, and the future of a writer is at best a gamble, so without children they saved their money, scrimped, did without. She lit a cigarette, didn't offer me one.

"What about that Alma Jean woman?"

"What can you tell me about her?"

"Nothing. That's Fred's territory. Ask him."

"About her murder?"

She smoked. "I thought it was an accident. Or suicide. Drunk and fell over that bridge wall, or jumped. Isn't that what the police think?"

"The police don't think anything one way or the other. I think it was murder."

"What do you want, Mr. Fortune? A confession?"

"Do you want to make one?"

"Yes, that I'm a nasty bitch who wants more than she's got. Just more. You understand that, Mr. Fortune."

"It's a modern disease," I said, "but what's it got to do with Alma Jean Brant?"

She smoked. "You wouldn't be here if someone hadn't seen me around her."

"Her husband," I said. "And Walter Ellis."

The couch creaked under her as if it had rusty springs. "I was jealous. Or maybe just suspicious. He's so involved in his work, I'm so bored, our sex life is about zero. We never do anything! We talk, read, think, discuss, but we never *do*! I make his life miserable, I admit it. But he promised we would stay here only five years or until he published a novel. We would go down to New York, he'd make money, we'd have some life! I counted on that. Now he wants to get tenure, stay here!"

"So he can teach and write?" I said. "That's all? No other reason for wanting to stay here?"

She nodded. "When he started going out all the time, I wondered too. Research for his work, he said, but I heard about Alma Jean. So I followed him and found where she lived. Then I followed her to see if she'd meet him somewhere else. That's all. I just watched her house, followed her a few times. I never saw him do a damn thing that could be close to cheating. At her house that husband of hers was around all the time. He must work nights."

"Did you see her do anything?"

She smoked. "I saw her visit the same house three or four times. I got real suspicious then. I hadn't seen Fred go in, but after she left the last time, I went up and rang the bell. A guy answered, but it wasn't Fred, so I made some excuse and got out of there. She was meeting someone all right, but not Fred."

"Any idea who?"

She shook her head. "He wasn't an Indian, I can say that."

"What was he?"

"Black, Mr. Fortune. One big black man."

Through the mass of sound and movement, bodies and faces that glistened with sweat and gaudy color and melted into the bright colors and tortured figures of the mural on the walls, I watched Joey Brant across the dance floor drinking and talking to Walter Ellis, who only listened.

I watched Dorothy Margon move lightly through the shuffle of the massed dancers. Her slender body loose and supple, her eyes closed, her lips parted, her face turned up to the Duke. I could see a man she denied turn to someone else. A man who could not give her what she wanted turning to someone who wanted less.

Her hips moved a beat behind the band; her long blonde hair swung free against the black velvet of her dress and the scarred face of the Duke. I could see her, restless and rejecting, but still not wanting her man to go anywhere else.

"I can't tell the dancers from the people in the mural," Fred Margon said. "I can't be sure which woman is my wife with the Duke and which is the woman chained in the mural."

He was talking about himself: a man who could not tell which was real and which was only an image. He could not decide, be certain, which was real to him, image or reality.

"Which man is the Duke on the dance floor with my wife," Fred Margon said, "and which is the blue man with the bare chest and hammer in the mural? Am I the man at the ringside table with a glass of beer in a pale, indoor hand watching the Duke dance with his wife, or the thin scarecrow in the mural with his wrists chained and his starving face turned up to an empty sky?"

He was trying to understand something, and across the dance floor Joey Brant was talking and talking to Walter Ellis. Ellis only listened and watched the Duke and Dorothy Margon on the dance floor. The Duke sweated, and Dorothy Margon danced with her eyes closed, her body moving as if by itself.

Walter Ellis sat alone in the back of his pink Cadillac. I leaned in the window.

"A black man, she said. A big black man Alma Jean visited in a house in the ghetto."

"A lot of big black men in the ghetto, Fortune."

"What was the crisis?" I said. "You said going on the streets was what ghetto women did in a crisis."

"I don't know."

"You offered to pay for whatever she needed money for."

"She only told me she needed something that cost a lot of money."

"Needed what?"

"A psychiatrist. I sent her to the best."

"A black? Big? Lives near here? Expensive?"

"All that."

"Can we go and talk to him?"

"Anytime."

"And you didn't give her the money to pay him?"

"She wouldn't take it. Said she would know what it was really for even if it was only in my mind."

The Duke said, "There was this here chippie. I mean, she's workin' my street 'n' I don' work her, see? I mean, it's snowin' bad 'n' there ain't no action goin' down, my three pigs're holed up warmin' their pussy, but this chippie she's out workin' on my turf. Hey, that don't go down, you know? I mean, that's no scene, right? So I moves in to tell her to fly her pussy off'n my streets or sign up with the Duke."

I said, "The last time it snowed was the night Alma Jean died."

Dorothy Margon built another pyramid of torn coasters on the tavern table and watched the Saturday night dancers. Fred Margon and I watched the Duke. The Duke mopped his face with a dirty handkerchief, a kind of desperation in his voice that rose higher, faster, as if he could not stop himself, had to talk while Fred Margon was there.

"I *knows* that there fox. I mean, I gets up close to tell her do a fade and I remembers that chippie in the snow."

I said, "It was Alma Jean."

He sweated in that hot room with its pounding music and packed bodies swirling and rubbing. It was what he had been hiding, holding back. What he had wanted to tell from the start. What he had to tell.

"Back when I was jus' a punk kid stealin' dogs, my ol' man beatin' my ass to go to school, that there chippie out in the snow was in that school. I remembers. Smart 'n' clean 'n' got a momma dresses her up real good. I remembers, you know? Like, I had eyes for that pretty little kid back then."

The band stopped. The dancers drifted off the floor, sat down. A silence like a blow from a hammer in the hands of the big blue man in the mural.

"I walks off. I mean, when I remembers that little girl, I walks me away from that there chippie. I remembers how good her momma fixes her up, so I walks off 'n' lets her work, 'n' I got the blues, you know. I got the blues then, 'n' I got 'em now."

"Everybody got the blues," Dorothy said. "We should write a song. Fred should write a poem."

"It was Alma Jean, Duke," I said.

Walter Ellis stopped to say a few low words to the tall, handsome doctor, while I walked down the steps of his modest house and out to the ghetto street. The numbers boss caught up with me before I reached his Cadillac.

"Does that tell you who killed her?" Ellis said.

"I think so. All I have to do is find a way to prove it."

He nodded. We both got into the back of the pink car. It purred away from the curb. The silent driver in the immaculate suit drove slowly, sedately, parading Ellis through his domain where the people could see him.

"Any ideas?" Ellis said.

"Watch and hope for a break. They've all got something on their minds; maybe it'll get too heavy."

He watched the street ahead. "That include me?"

"It includes you," I said. "You were out that night."

"You know what I've got on my mind?"

"I've got a hunch," I said. "I'm going to meet the Margons in Irish Johnny's tonight. Why don't you come around and bring Brant, friend of the family."

We drove on to my motel.

"The Duke hangs out in Irish Johnny's," Ellis said.

"I know," I said.

"I writes me a poem," the Duke said. "'Bout that there chippie. I go home 'n' writes me a poem."

The scarred black face of the Duke seemed to watch the empty dance floor as he told about the poem he had written. Fred Margon looked at him. All through the long room the Saturday night people waited for the music to begin again. Across the floor Walter Ellis talked to those who came to him one by one to pay their respects. Joey Brant drank, stared into his glass, looked toward me and the Margons and the Duke.

"Do you have it with you?" Fred said.

The Duke's eyes flickered above the scars on his face and the new bandage. Looked right and left.

"Did you bring it to show me?" Fred Margon said.

The Duke sweated in the hot room. Nodded.

"All right," Fred said. "But don't just show it to me, read it. Out loud. Poetry should be read aloud. While the band is still off, get up and read your poem. This is your tavern; they all know you in here. Tell them why you wrote it, how it came to you, and read it to them."

The Duke stared. "You fuckin' with me, man?"

"Fred?" Dorothy Margon said.

"You wrote it, didn't you? You felt it. If you feel something and write it, you have to believe in it. You have to show it to the world, make the world hear."

"You a crazy man," the Duke said.

Dorothy tore another coaster. Across the room Joey Brant and Walter Ellis watched our table. I waited.

"Give it to me," Fred said.

The Duke sat there for some time, the sweat beaded on his face, his booted foot swinging, while the people all through the room waited for Saturday night to return.

"What happened to Alma Jean, Duke?" I said.

Fred Margon said, "You wrote it; give it to me."

The Duke reached into his filthy raincoat and handed a torn piece of lined notebook paper to Fred Margon. Fred stood up. On the other side of the dance floor Joey Brant held his glass without drinking as Fred Margon walked to the bandstand, jumped up to the microphone.

"Ladies and gentlemen!"

In the long room, ice loud in the glasses and voices in the rumble of conversation, the people who waited only for the music to begin again, Saturday night to return, turned toward the bandstand. Fred

Margon told them about the Duke and the chippie working his territory without his permission. The Duke alone in the night with the snow and the chippie.

"The Duke remembered that girl. He let her work, went home and wrote a poem. I'm going to read that poem."

There were some snickers, a murmur of protest or two, the steady clink of indifferent glasses. Fred called for silence. Waited. Until the room silenced. Then he read the poem.

> *Once I was pure*
> *as a snow but I fell,*
> *fell like a snowflake*
> *from heaven to hell.*
>
> *Fell to be scuffed,*
> *to be spit on and beat,*
> *fell to be like*
> *the filth in the street.*
>
> *Pleading and cursing*
> *and dreading to die*
> *to the fellow I know*
> *up there in the sky.*
>
> *The fellow his cross*
> *I got on this chain*
> *I give it to her*
> *she gets clean again.*
>
> *Dear God up there,*
> *have I fell so low,*
> *and yet to be once*
> *like the beautiful snow.*

Through the smoke haze of the crowded tavern room they shifted their feet. They stirred their drinks. The musicians, ready to return, stood in the wings. A woman giggled. The bartenders hid grins. Some men suddenly laughed. A murmur of laughter rippled through the room. The Duke stood up, stepped toward the bandstand. Fred came across the empty dance floor.

"I like it," Fred Margon said. "It's not a good poem; you're not a poet. But it's real and I like it. I like anything that says what you really feel, says it openly and honestly. It's what you had to do."

The Duke's eyes were black above the scars and the bandage. The Duke watched only Fred, his fists clenched, his eyes wide.

"It's you," Fred said. "Go up and read it yourself. Make them see what you saw out there in the snow when you remembered Alma Jean, the girl whose mother dressed her so well. To hell with anyone who laughs. They're laughing at themselves. The way they would have laughed if Alma Jean had told them what she was going to do. They're afraid, so they laugh. They're afraid to know what they feel. They're afraid to feel. Help them face themselves. Read your poem again. And again."

The Duke stood in Irish Johnny's Tavern, five new stitches in his scarred face under the bandage, and read his poem to the people who only wanted Saturday night to start again with the loud blare of the music and the heavy mass of the dancing and a kind of oblivion. He read without stumbling over the words, not reading but hearing it in the smoke of the gaudy tavern room. Hearing it as it had come to him when he stood in the snow and remembered the girl whose mother had always dressed her so well.

There was no laughter now. The Duke was doing what he had to do. Fred and Dorothy Margon were listening, and no one wanted to look stupid. Walter Ellis and Joey Brant were listening, and no one wanted to offend Mr. Ellis. So they sat, and the band waited to come back and start Saturday night again, and I went to the telephone and called Lieutenant Derrida.

Walter Ellis moved his chair, and I faced Joey Brant across the tavern table. "High steel pays good money, but you haven't been making good money in a long time. You were home whenever Professor Margon went to talk to Alma Jean. You were home when Dorothy Margon watched Alma Jean. You haven't been working high steel for over a year. That's why she went out on the streets. You even had to sell Alma Jean's jewelry to buy whisky at Cherry Valley Tavern. One of those pieces wasn't hers, though, and that was a mistake. It was the cross the Duke gave her the night she was killed, the one he wrote about in his poem. You knew someone else had given it to her, but you didn't know the Duke had given it to her that night, and it proves you killed her. You grabbed it from her neck before you knocked her off that bridge."

Lieutenant Derrida stood over the table. The room was watching now. The Duke with his poem in his hand, Walter Ellis sad, Fred and Dorothy Margon holding hands but not looking at each other. Derrida said, "It's the cross the Duke gave her that night, has his

initials inside. Your boss says you haven't worked high steel in over
a year, just low-pay ground jobs when you show up at all. When the
bartender, Crow, saw we had proof and motive, he talked. You left
the tavern when it closed, didn't get to the sweat lodge until pushing
3:30 A.M. You brought the jewelry to Crow after she was dead."

Joey Brant drained his whisky, looked at us all with rage in his
dark eyes. "She didn't got to go on no streets. We was makin' it all
right. She got no cause playin' with white guys, sellin' it to old men,
working for black whoremasters. I cut him good, that black bastard,
'n' I knocked her off that there bridge when she was out selling her
ass so she could live high and rich with her white friends and her
gamblers and her black pimps! Sure, I hit her. I never meant to kill
her, but I saw that cross on her neck 'n' I never give her no cross
'n' I hit her and she went on over."

I said, "Her mother said she would only go on the streets for a
big reason. You know what that was, Brant? You know why she went
back on the streets?"

"I know, mister. Money, that's why! 'Cause I ain't bringing home
the big bucks like the gambler 'n' the professor 'n' the black pimp!"

"She wanted to hire a psychiatrist," I said. "You know what that
is, Joey. A man who makes a sick mind get better."

"Psychiatrist?" Joey Brant said.

"A healer, Joey. For a scared man who sat at home all day and
drank too much. An expensive healer, so she had to go out on the
streets to make the money she couldn't make any other way."

"Shut up, you hear? Shut up!" His dark face almost white.

I shook my head. "We know, Joey. We talked to the psychiatrist
and your boss. You're afraid of heights, Joey. You couldn't even go
to the edge of that bridge parapet and see where she had fallen. You
can't go up high on the steel anymore, where the big money is. Where
a brave goes. Up there with the real men. You became afraid and
it was killing you and that was killing her and she had to try to help
you, save you, so she wanted money to take you to a psychiatrist who
would cure you, help you go up the steel again where you could feel
like a man!"

'Psychiatrist?" Joey Brant said.

"That's right, Joey. Her big, special reason to make big money the
only way she knew how."

Joey Brant sat there for a long time looking at all of us, at the floor,
at his hands, at his empty whisky glass. Just sat while Lieutenant
Derrida waited and everyone drifted away, and at last he put his head
down on the table and began to cry.

Derrida had taken Joey Brant away. The Duke had stopped reading his poem to anyone who would listen. I sat at the floor-side table with Fred and Dorothy Margon. Out on the floor the Saturday night people clung and twined and held each other in their fine shimmering clothes, while in the mural the silent yellow women and bent blue men frozen in the red and yellow sky watched and waited.

"Dance with me, Fred," Dorothy Margon said.

"I'm a bad dancer," Fred Margon said. "I always have been a bad dancer. I always will be a bad dancer."

"I know," Dorothy said. "Just dance with me now."

They danced among the faceless crowd, two more bodies that would soon go their separate ways. I knew that and so did they. Fred would teach and write and go on examining life for what he must write about. Dorothy would go to New York or Los Angeles to find more out of life than an assistant professor, a would-be writer. What they had to do.

The Duke has one kind of courage and Fred Margon has another. Joey Brant lost his. Fred Margon's kind will cost him his wife. Alma Jean's courage killed her. The courage to do what she had to do to help her man, even though she knew he would not understand. He would hate her, but she had to do it anyway. Courage has its risks, and we don't always win.

In my New York office-apartment Sada Patterson listened in silence, her worn plastic handbag on her skinny lap, the ramrod back so straight it barely touched my chair.

"I knew she had a big reason," she said. "That was my Alma Jean. To help her man find hisself again." She nodded, almost satisfied, "I'm sorry for him. He's a little man." She stood up. "I gonna miss her—Alma Jean. She was my last: I always dressed her real good."

She paid me. I took the money. She had her courage too. And her pride. She'd go on living, fierce and independent, even if she couldn't really tell herself why.

ED MCBAIN
(b.1926)

Death Flight
(Milt Davis)

Squak Mountain was cold at this time of the year. The wind groaned around Davis, and the trees trembled bare limbs, and even at this distance he could hear the low rumble of planes letting down at Boeing and Renton. He found the tree about a half-mile east of the summit. The DC-4 had struck the tree and then continued flying. He looked at the jagged, splintered wood and then his eyes covered the surrounding terrain. Parts of the DC-4 were scattered all over the ridge in a fifteen-hundred-foot radius. He saw the upper portion of the plane's verticle fin, the number-two propeller, and a major portion of the rudder. He examined these very briefly, and then he began walking toward the canyon into which the plane had finally dropped.

Davis turned his head sharply once, thinking he had heard a sound. He stood stock-still, listening, but the only sounds that came to him were the sullen moan of the wind and the muted hum of aircraft in the distant sky.

He continued walking.

When he found the plane, it made him a little sick. The Civil Aeronautics Board report had told him that the plane was demolished by fire. The crash was what had obviously caused the real demolition. But the report had only been typed words. He saw *impact* now, and *causing fire*, and even though the plane had been moved by the investigating board, he could imagine something of what had happened.

It had been in nearly vertical position when it struck the ground, and the engines and cockpit had bedded deep in soft, muddy loam. Wreckage had been scattered like shrapnel from a handgrenade burst, and fire had consumed most of the plane, leaving a ghostlike skeleton that confronted him mutely. He stood watching it for a time, then made his way down to the charred ruins.

The landing gear was fully retracted, as the report said. The wings flaps were in the twenty-five-degree down position.

He studied these briefly and then climbed up to the cockpit. The plane still stank of scorched skin and blistered paint. When he entered the cockpit, he was faced with complete havoc. It was impossible to obtain a control setting or an instrument reading from the demolished instrument panel. The seats were twisted and tangled. Metal jutted into the cockpit and cabin at grotesque angles. The windshield had shattered into a million jagged shards.

He shook his head and continued looking through the plane, the stench becoming more overpowering. He was silently grateful that he had not been here when the bodies were still in the plane, and he still wondered what he was doing here anyway, even now.

He knew that the report had proved indication of an explosion prior to the crash. There had been no structural failure or malfunctioning of the aircraft itself. The explosion had occurred in the cabin, and the remnants of the bomb had shown it to be a home-made job. He'd learned all this in the past few days, with the co-operation of the CAB. He also knew that the Federal Bureau of Investigation and the Military Police were investigating the accident, and the knowledge had convinced him that this was not a job for him. Yet here he was.

Five people had been killed. Three pilots, the stewardess, and Janet Carruthers, the married daughter of his client, George Ellison. It could not have been a pleasant death.

Davis climbed out of the plane and started toward the ridge. The sun was high on the mountain, and it cast a feeble, pale yellow tint on the white pine and spruce. There was a hard gray winter sky overhead. He walked swiftly, with his head bent against the wind.

When the shots came, they were hard and brittle, shattering the stillness as effectively as twin-mortar explosions.

He dropped to the ground, wriggling sideways toward a high outcropping of quartz. The echo of the shots hung on the air and then the wind carried it toward the canyon and he waited and listened, with his own breathing the loudest sound on the mountain.

I'm out of my league, he thought. *I'm way out of my league. I'm just a small-time detective, and this is something big . . .*

The third shot came abruptly. It came from some high-powered rifle, and he heard the sharp *twannng* of the bullet when it struck the quartz and ricocheted into the trees.

He pressed his cheek to the ground, and he kept very still, and he could feel the hammering of his heart against the hard earth. His hands trembled as he waited for the next shot.

The next shot never came. He waited for a half-hour, and then he bundled his coat and thrust it up over the rock, hoping to draw fire if the sniper was still with him. He waited for several minutes after that, and then he backed away from the rock on his stomach, not venturing to get to his feet until he was well into the trees.

Slowly, he made his way down the mountain.

"You say you want to know more about the accident?" asked Arthur Porchek. "I thought it was all covered in the CAB report."

"It was," Davis said. "I'm checking further. I'm trying to find out who set that bomb."

Porchek drew in on his cigarette. He leaned against the wall and the busy hum of radios in Seattle Approach Control was loud around them. "I've only told this story a dozen times already."

"I'd appreciate it if you could tell it once more," Davis said.

"Well," Porchek said heavily, "it was about twenty-thirty-six or so." He paused. "All our time is based on a twenty-four-hour check, like the Army."

"Go ahead."

"The flight had been cleared to maintain seven thousand feet. When they contacted us, we told them to make a standard range approach to Boeing Field and requested that they report leaving each one-thousand-foot level during the decent. That's standard, you know."

"Were you doing all the talking to the plane?" Davis asked.

"Yes."

"All right, what happened?"

"First I gave them the weather."

"And what was that?"

Porchek shrugged, a man weary of repeating information over and over again. "Boeing Field," he said by rote. "Eighteen hundred scattered, twenty-two hundred overcast, eight-miles, wind south-southeast, gusts to thirty, altimeter twenty-nine, twenty-five; Seattle-Tacoma - measured nineteen hundred broken with thirty-one hundred overcast."

"Did the flight acknowledge?" Davis asked.

"Yes, it did. And it reported leaving seven thousand feet at twenty-forty. About two minutes later, it reported being over the outer marker and leaving the six-thousand-foot level."

"Go on," Davis said.

"Well, it didn't report leaving five thousand and then at twenty-forty-five, it reported leaving four thousand feet. I acknowledged that and told them what to do. I said, "If you're not VFR by the time you reach the range you can shuttle on the northwest course at two thousand feet. It's possible you'll break out in the vicinity of Boeing Field for a south landing."

"What's VFR?" Davis asked, feeling his inadequacy to cope with the job once more.

"Visual Flight Rules. You see, it was overcast at twenty-two hundred feet. The flight was on instruments above that. They've got to report to us whether they're on IFR or VFR."

"I see. What happened next?"

"The aircraft reported at twenty-fifty that it was leaving three thousand feet, and I told them they were to contact Boeing Tower on one eighteen, point three for landing instructions. They acknowledged with 'Roger,' and that's the last I heard of them."

"Did you hear the explosion?"

"I heard something, but I figured it for static. Ground witnesses heard it, though."

"But everything was normal and routine before the explosion. Is that right?"

Porchek nodded his head emphatically. "Yes, sir. A routine letdown."

"Almost," Davis said. He thanked Porchek for his time, and then left.

He called George Ellison from a pay phone. When the old man came on the line, Davis said, "This is Milt Davis, Mr. Ellison."

Ellison's voice sounded gruff and heavy, even over the phone. "Hello, Davis," he said. "How are you going?"

"I'll be honest with you, Mr. Ellison. I'd like out."

"Why?" He could feel the old man's hackles rising.

"Because the FBI and the MPs are already onto this one. They'll crack it for you, and it'll probably turn out to be some nut with a grudge against the government. Either that, or a plain case of sabotage. This really doesn't call for a private investigation."

"Look, Davis," Ellison said, "I'll decide whether this calls for . . ."

"All right, you'll decide. I'm just trying to be frank with you. This kind of stuff is way out of my line. I'm used to trailing wayward husbands, or skip tracing, or an occasional bodyguard stint. When you drag in bombed planes, I'm in over my head."

"I heard you were a good man," Ellison said. "You stick with it. I'm satisfied you'll do a good job."

Davis sighed. "Whatever you say," he said. "Incidentally, did you tell anyone you'd hired me?"

"Yes, I did. As a matter of fact..."

"Who'd you tell?"

"Several of my employees. The word got to a local reporter somehow, though, and he came to my home yesterday. I gave him the story. I didn't think it would do any harm."

"Has it reached print yet?"

"Yes," Ellison said. "It was in this morning's paper. A small item. Why?"

"I was shot at today, Mr. Ellison. At the scene of the crash. Three times."

There was a dead silence on the line. Then Ellison said, "I'm sorry, Davis, I should have realized." It was a hard thing for a man like Ellison to say.

"That's all right," Davis assured him. "They missed."

"Do you think - do you think whoever set the bomb shot at you?"

"Possibly. I'm not going to start worrying about it now."

Ellison digested this and then said, "Where are you going now, Davis?"

"To visit your son-in-law, Nicholas Carruthers. I'll call in again."

"Fine, Davis."

Davis hung up, jotting down the cost of the call, and then made reservations on the next plane to Burbank. Nicholas Carruthers was chief pilot of Insuperable Aircraft's Burbank Division. The fatal flight had been made in two segments; the first from Burbank to San Francisco, and the second from Frisco to Seattle. The DC-4 was to let down at Boeing, with Seattle-Tacoma designated as an alternate field. It was a simple ferry flight, and the plane was to pick up military personnel in Seattle, in accordance with the company's contract with the Department of National Defense.

Quite curiously, Carruthers had been along the Burbank-to-Frisco segment of the hop, as company observer. He'd disembarked at Frisco, and his wife, Janet, had boarded the plane there as a non-revenue passenger. She was bound for a cabin up in Washington, or so old man Ellison had told Davis. He'd also said that Janet had been looking forward to the trip for a long time.

When Davis found Captain Nicholas Carruthers in the airport restaurant, he was sitting with a blonde in a black cocktail dress, and he had his arm around her waist. They lifted their martini glasses and clinked them together, the girl laughing. Davis studied the pair from the doorway and reflected that the case was turning into something he knew a little more about.

He hesitated inside the doorway for just a moment and then walked directly to the bar, taking the stool on Carruthers' left. He waited until Carruthers had drained his glass and then he said, "Captain Carruthers?"

Carruthers turned abruptly, a frown distorting his features. He was a man of thirty-eight or so, with prematurely graying temples and sharp gray eyes. He had thin lips and a thin, straight nose which divided his face like an immaculate stone wall. He wore civilian clothing.

"Yes," he said curtly.

"Milton Davis. Your father-in-law has hired me to look into the DC-4 accident. "Davis showed his identification. "I wonder if I might ask you a few questions?"

Carruthers hesitated, and then glanced at the blonde, apparently realizing the situation was slightly compromising. The blonde leaned over, pressing her breasts against the bar top, looking past Carruthers to Davis.

"Take a walk, Beth," Carruthers said.

The blonde drained her martini glass, pouted, lifted her purse from the bar, and slid off the stool. Davis watched the exaggerated swing of her hips across the room and then said, "I'm sorry if. . ."

"Ask your questions," Carruthers said.

Davis studied him for a moment. "All right, Captain," he said mildly. "I understand you were aboard the crashed DC-4 on the flight segment from Burbank to San Francisco. Is that right?"

"That' right," Carruthers said. "I was aboard as observer."

"Did you notice anything out of the ordinary on the trip?"

"If you mean did I see anyone with a goddamn bomb, no."

"I didn't–"

"And if you're referring to the false alarm, Mister Whatever-the-Hell-Your-Name-Is, you can just start asking your questions straight. You know all about the false alarm."

Davis felt his fists tighten on the bar top. "You tell me about it again."

"Sure," Carruthers said testily. "Shortly after take-off from Burbank, we observed a fire-warning signal in the cockpit. From number three engine."

"I'm listening," Davis said.

"As it turned out, it was a false warning. When we got to Frisco, the mechanics there checked and found no evidence of a fire having occurred. Mason told the mechanics–"

"Was Mason pilot in command?"

"Yes." A little of Carruthers' anger seemed to be wearing off.

"Mason told the mechanics he was satisfied from the inspection that no danger of fire was present. He did not delay the flight."

"Were *you* satisfied with the inspection?" Davis asked.

"It was Mason's command."

"Yes, but your wife boarded the plane in Frisco. Were you satisfied there was no danger of fire?"

"Yes, I was."

"Did your wife seem worried about it?" Davis asked.

"I didn't get a chance to talk to Janet in Frisco," Carruthers said. Davis was silent for a moment. Then he asked, "How come?"

"I had to take another pilot up almost the moment I arrived."

"I don't understand."

"For a hood test. I had to check him out. I'm chief pilot, you know. That's one of my jobs."

"And there wasn't even enough time to stop and say hello to your wife?"

"No. We were a little ahead of schedule. Janet wasn't there when we landed."

"I see."

"I hung around while the mechanics checked the fire-warning system, and Janet still hadn't arrived. This other pilot was waiting to go up, so I left."

"Then you didn't see your wife at all," said Davis.

"Well, that's not what I meant. I meant I hadn't spoken to her. As we were taxiing for take-off, I saw her come onto the field."

"Alone?"

"No," Carruthers said. "She was with a man." The announcement did not seem to disturb him.

"Do you know who he was?"

"No. They were rather far from me, and I was in a moving ship. I recognized Janet's red hair immediately, of course, but I couldn't make out the man with her. I waved, but I guess she didn't see me."

"She didn't wave back?"

"No. She went directly to the DC-4. The man helped her aboard, and then the plane was behind us and I couldn't see any more."

"What do you mean, helped her abroad?"

"Took her elbow, you know. Helped her up the ladder."

"I see. Was she carrying luggage?"

"A suitcase, yes. She was bound for our cabin, you know."

"Yes," Davis said. "I understand she was on a company pass. What does that mean exactly, Captain?"

"We ride for a buck and a half," Carruthers said. 'Normally, any pilot applies to his chief pilot for written permission for his wife to ride and then presents the permission at the ticket window. He then pays one-fifty for the ticket. Since I'm chief pilot, I simply got the ticket for Janet when she told me she was going up to the cabin."

"Mmm," Davis said. "Did you know all the pilots on the ship?"

"I knew one of them. Mason. The other two were new on the route. That's why I was along as observer."

"Did you know Mason socially?"

"No. Just business."

"And the stewardess?"

"yes, I knew her. Business, of course."

"Of course," Davis said, remembering the blonde in the cocktail dress. He stood up and moved his jacket cuff of his wristwatch. "Well, I've got to catch a plane, Captain. Thanks for your help."

"Not at all," Carruthers said. "When you report in to Dad, give him my regards, won't you."

"I'll do that," Davis said. He thanked Carruthers again, and then went out to catch his return plane.

He got five thousand dollars' worth of insurance for a quarter from one of the machines in the waiting room, and then got aboard the plane at about five minutes before take-off. He browsed through the magazine he'd picked up at the news-stand, and when the fat fellow plopped down into the seat beside him, he just glanced up and then turned back to his magazine again.

The plane left the ground and began climbing, and Davis looked back through the window and saw the field drop away below him.

"First time flying?" the fellow asked.

Davis looked up from the magazine into a pair of smiling green eyes. The eyes were imbedded deep in soft, ruddy flesh. The man owned a nose like the handle of a machete, and a mouth with thick, blubbery lips. He wore an orange sports shirt against which the color of his complexion seemed even more fiery.

"No," Davis said. "I've been off the ground before."

"Always gives me a thrill," the man said. "No matter how many times I do it." He chuckled and added, "An airplane ride is just like a woman. Lots of ups and downs, and not always too smooth - but guaranteed to keep a man up in the air."

Davis smiled politely, and the fat man chuckled a bit more and then thrust a beefy hand at Davis. "MacGregor," he said. "Charlie or Chuck or just plain Mac, if you like."

Davis took his hand and said, "Milt Davis."

"Glad to know you, Milt," MacGregor said. "You down here on business?"

"Yes," he said briefly.

"Me, too," MacGregor said. "Business mostly." He grinned slyly. "'Course, what the wife don't know won't hurt her, eh?"

"I'm not married," Davis told him.

"A wonderful institution," MacGregor said. He laughed aloud, and then added, "But who likes being in an institution?"

Davis hoped he hadn't winced. He wondered if he was to be treated to MacGregor's full repertoire of wornout gags before the trip was over. To discourage any further attempts at misdirected wit, he turned back to the magazine as politely as he could, smiling once to let MacGregor know he wasn't being purposely rude.

"Go right ahead," MacGregor said genially. "Don't mind me."

That was easy, Davis thought. *If it lasts.*

He was surprised that it did last. MacGregor stretched out in the seat beside him, closing his eyes.

He did not speak again until the plane was ten minutes out of San Francisco.

"Let's walk to the john, eh, Milt?" he said.

Davis lifted his head and smiled. "Thanks, but–"

"This is a .38 here under my overcoat, Milt," MacGregor said softly.

For a second, Davis thought it was another of the fat man's tired jokes. He turned to look at MacGregor's lap. The overcoat was folded over his chunky left arm, and Davis could barely see the blunt muzzle of a pistol poking from beneath the folds.

He lifted his eyebrows a little. "What are you going to do after you shoot me, MacGregor? Vanish into thin air?"

MacGregor smiled. "Now who mentioned anything about shooting, Milt? Eh? Let's go back, shall we, boy?"

Davis rose and moved past MacGregor into the aisle. MacGregor stood up behind him, the coat over his arm, the gun completely hidden now. Together, they began walking toward the rear of the plane, past the food buffet on their right, and past the twin facing seats behind the buffet. An emergency window was set in the cabin wall there, and Davis sighed in relief when he saw that the seats were occupied.

When they reached the men's room, MacGregor flipped open the door and nudged Davis inside. Then he crowded in behind him, putting his wide back to the door. He reached up with one heavy fist and rammed Davis against the sink, then ran is free hand over Davis' body.

"Well," he said pleasantly. "No gun."

"My name is Davis, not Spade," Davis told him.

MacGregor lifted the .38, pointing it at Davis' throat. "All right,

Milt, now give a listen. I want you to forget all about that crashed DC-4. I want you to forget there are even such things as airplanes, Miltie. Now, I know you're a smart boy, and so I'm not even going to mark you up, Miltie. I could mark you up nice with the sight and butt of this thing." He hefted the .38 in his hand. "I'm not going to do that. Not now. I'm just telling you, nice-like, to lay off. Just lay off and go back to skip-tracing, Miltie boy, or you're going to get hurt. Next time, I'm not going to be so considerate."

"Look . . ." Davis started.

"So let's not have a next time, Miltie. Let's call it off now. You give your client a ring and tell him you're dropping it, Miltie boy. Have you got that?"

Davis didn't answer.

"Fine," MacGregor said. He reached up suddenly with his left hand, almost as if he were reaching up for a light cord. At the same time, he grasped Davis' shoulder with his right hand and spun him around, bringing the hand with the gun down in a fast motion, flipping it butt-end up.

The walnut stock caught Davis at the base of his skull. He stumbled forward, his hands grasping the sink in front of him. He felt the second blow at the back of his head, and then his hands dropped from the sink, and the aluminum deck of the plane came up to meet him suddenly, all too fast . . .

Someone said, "He's coming around now," and he idly thought, *Coming around where?*

"How do you feel, Mr. Davis?" a second voice asked.

He looked up at the ring of faces. He did not recognize any of them. "Where am I?" he asked.

"San Francisco," the second voice said. The voice belonged to a tall man with a salt-and-pepper mustache and friendly blue eyes. MacGregor had owned friendly green eyes, Davis remembered.

"We found you in the men's room after all the passengers had disembarked," the voice went on. 'You've had a nasty fall, Mr. Davis. Nothing serious, however. I've dressed the cut, and I'm sure there'll be no complications."

"Thank you," Davis said. "I wonder . . . did you say all the passengers have already gone?"

"Why, yes."

"I wonder if I might see the passenger list? There was a fellow aboard I promised to look up, and I'm darned if I haven't forgotten his name."

"I'll ask the stewardess," the man said. "By the way, my name is Doctor Burke."

"How do you do?" Davis said. He reached for a cigarette and lighted it. When the stewardess brought the passenger list, he scanned it hurriedly.

There was no MacGregor listed, Charles or otherwise. This fact did not surprise him greatly. He looked down the list to see if there were any names with the initials C. M., knowing that when a person assumes an alias, he will usually choose a name with the same initials as his real name. There were no C. M.s on the list, either.

"Does that help?" the stewardess asked.

"Oh, yes. Thank you. I'll find him now."

The doctor shook Davis' hand, and then asked if he'd sign a release stating he had received medical treatment and absolving the airline. Davis felt the back of his head, and then signed the paper.

He walked outside and leaned against the building, puffing idly on his cigarette. The night was a nest of lights. He watched the lights and listened to the hum of aircraft all around him. It wasn't until he had finished his cigarette that he remembered he was in San Francisco.

He dropped the cigarette to the concrete and ground it out beneath his heel. Quite curiously, he found himself ignoring MacGregor's warning. He was a little surprised at himself, but he was also pleased. And more curious, he found himself wishing that he and MacGregor would meet again.

He walked briskly to the cyclone fence that hemmed in the runway area. Quickly, he showed the uniformed guard at the gate his credentials and then asked where he could find the hangars belonging to Insuperable Aircraft. The guard pointed them out.

Davis walked through the gate and toward the hangars the guard had indicated, stopping at the first one. Two mechanics in greasy coveralls were leaning against a work bench, chatting idly. One was smoking, and the other tilted a Coke bottle to his lips, draining half of it in one pull. Davis walked over to them.

"I'm looking for the mechanics who serviced the DC-4 that crashed up in Seattle," he said.

They looked at him blankly for a few seconds, and then the one with the Coke bottle asked, "You from the CAB?"

"No," Davis said. "I'm investigating privately."

The mechanic with the bottle was short, with black hair curling over his forehead, and quick brown eyes that silently appraised Davis now. "If you're thinking about that fire warning," he said, "it had nothing to do with the crash. There was a bomb aboard."

"I know," Davis said. "Were you one of the mechanics?"

"I was one of them," he said.

"Good." Davis smiled and said, "I didn't catch your name."

"Jerry," the man said. "Mangione." His black brows pulled together suspiciously. "Who you investigating for?"

"A private client. The father of the girl who was a passenger."

"Oh. Carruthers' wife, huh?"

"Yes. Did you know her?"

"No. I just heard it was his wife. He's chief pilot down Burbank, ain't he?"

"Yes," Davis said.

Mangione paused and studied Davis intently. "What'd you want to know?"

"First, was the fire-warning system okay?"

"Yeah. We checked it out. Just one of those things, you know. False alarm."

"Did you go into the plane?"

"Yeah, sure. I had to check the signal in the cockpit. Why?"

"I'm just asking."

"You don't think I put that damn bomb in the plane, do you?"

"Somebody did," Davis said.

"That's for sure. But not me. There were a lot of people on that plane, mister. Any one of 'em could've done it."

"Be a little silly to bring a bomb onto a plane you were going to fly."

"I guess so. But don't drag me into this. I just checked the fire-warning system, that's all."

"Were you around when Mrs. Carruthers boarded the plane?"

"The redhead? Yeah, I was there."

"What'd she look like?"

Mangione shrugged. "A broad, just like any other broad. Red hair."

"Was she pretty?"

"The red hair was the only thing gave her any flash. In fact, I was a little surprised."

"Surprised? What about?"

"That Tony would bother, you know."

"Who? Who would bother?"

"Tony. Tony Radner. He brought her out to the plane."

"What!" Davis said.

"Yeah, Tony. He used to sell tickets inside. He brought her out to the plane and helped her get aboard."

"Are you sure about that? Sure you know who the man with her was?"

Mangione made an exasperated gesture with his hairy hands. "Hell, ain't I been working here for three years? Don't I know Tony when

I see him? It was him, all right. He took the broad right to her seat. Listen, it was him, all right. I guess maybe . . . well, I was surprised, anyway."

"Why?"

"Tony's a good-looking guy. And this Mrs. Carruthers, well, she wasn't much. I'm surprised he went out of his way. But I guess maybe she wasn't feeling so hot. Tony's a gent that way."

"Wasn't feeling so hot?"

"Well, I don't like to talk about anybody's dead, but she looked like she had a snootful to me. Either that, or she was pretty damn sick."

"What makes you say that?"

"Hell, Tony had to help her up the ladder, and he practically carried her to her seat. Yeah, she musta been looped."

"You said Radner used to work here. Has he quit?"

"Yeah, he quit."

"Do you know where I can find him?"

Mangione shrugged. "Maybe you can get his address from the office in the morning. But, mister, I wouldn't bother him right now, if I was you."

"Why not?"

Mangione smiled. "Because he's on his honeymoon," he said.

He slept the night through and when he awoke in the morning, the back of his head hardly hurt at all. He shaved and washed quickly, downed a breakfast of orange juice and coffee, and then went to the San Francisco office of Insuperable Aircraft.

Radner, they told him, was no longer with them. But they did have his last address, and they parted with it willingly. He grabbed a cab, and then sat back while the driver fought with the California traffic. When he reached Radner's address, he paid and tipped the cabbie, and listed the expenditure in his book.

The rooming house was not in a good section of the city. It was red brick, with a brown front stoop. There was an old-fashioned bell pull set in the wide, wooden door jamb. He pulled this and heard the sound inside, and then he waited for footsteps. They came sooner than he expected.

The woman who opened the door couldn't have been more than fifty. Her face was still greasy with cold cream, and her hair was tied up in rags. "Yes?"

"I'm looking for Tony Radner," Davis said. "I'm an old friend of his, knew him in the Army. I went out to Insuperable, but they told me he doesn't work for them any more. I wonder if you know where I can reach him."

The landlady regarded him suspiciously for a moment. "He doesn't live here any more," she said.

"Darn," Davis said. He shook his head and assumed a false smile. "Isn't that always the way? I came all the way from New York, and now I can't locate him."

"That's too bad," the landlady agreed.

"Did he leave any forwarding address?" Davis asked.

"No. He left because he was getting married."

"Married!" Davis said. "Well, I'll be darned! Old Tony getting married!"

The landlady continued to watch Davis, her small eyes staring fixedly.

"You wouldn't know who he married, would you?"

"Yes," she said guardedly. "I guess I would."

"Who?" he asked.

"Trimble," the landlady said. "A girl named Alice Trimble."

"Alice Trimble," Davis said reflectively. "You wouldn't have her phone number, would you?"

"Come on in," the landlady said, finally accepting Davis at face value. She led him into the foyer of the house, and Davis followed her to the pay phone on the wall.

"They all scribble numbers here," she said. "I keep washing them off, but they keep putting them back again."

"Shame," Davis said sympathetically.

"Hers is up there, too. You just wait a second, and I'll tell you which one." She stepped close to the phone and examined the scribbled numbers on the wall. She stood very close to the wall, moving her head whenever she wanted to move her eyes. She stepped back at last and placed a long white finger on one of the numbers. "This one. This is the one he always called."

Davis jotted down the number hastily, and then said, "Well, gee, thanks a million. You don't know how much I appreciate this."

"I hope you find him," the landlady said. "Nice fellow, Mr. Radner?"

"One of the best," Davis said.

He called the number from the first pay phone he found. He listened to the phone ring four times on the other end, and then a voice said, "Hello?"

"Hello," he said. "May I speak to Miss Trimble, please?"

"This is Miss Trimble," the voice said.

"My name is Davis," he said. "I'm an old friend of Tony Radner's. He asked me to look him up if I ever was in town . . ." He paused and forced himself to laugh in embarrassment. "Trouble is, I can't seem to find him. His landlady said you and Tony..."

"Oh," the girl said. "You must want my sister. This is *Anne* Trimble."

"Oh," he said. "I'm sorry. I didn't realize...." He paused. "Is your sister there?"

"No, she doesn't live with me any more. She and Tony got married."

"Well, now, that's wonderful," Davis said. "Know where I can find them?"

"They're still on their honeymoon."

"Oh, that's too bad." He thought for a few seconds, and then said, "I've got to catch a plane back tonight. I wonder... I wonder if I might come over and...well, you could fill me in on what Tony's been doing and all. Hate like the devil to go back without knowing *something* about him."

The girl hesitated, and he could sense her reluctance.

"I promise I'll make it a very short visit. I've still got some business to attend to here. Besides...well, Tony loaned me a little money once, and I thought...well, if you don't mind, I'd like to leave it with you."

"I–I suppose it would be all right," she said.

"Fine. May I have the address?"

She gave it to him, and he told her he'd be out in about an hour, if that was all right with her. Then he went to the coffee counter, ordered coffee and a toasted English, and browsed over them until it was time to go. He bought a plain white envelope on the way out, slipped twenty dollars into it, and sealed it. Then he hailed a cab.

He found the mailbox marked *A. Trimble*, and he realized the initial sufficed for both Alice and Anne. He walked up two flights, stopped outside apartment 22, and thumbed the ivory stud in the door jamb. A series of chimes floated from beyond the door, and then the peephole flap was thrown back.

"I'm Mr. Davis," he said to the flap. "I called about–"

"Oh, yes," Anne Trimble said. The flap descended, and the door swung wide.

She was a tall brunette, and her costume emphasized her height. She was wearing tightly tailored toreador slacks. A starched white blouse with a wide collar and long sleeves was tucked firmly into the band of the slacks. A bird in flight, captured in sterling, rested on the blouse just below the left breast pocket.

"Come in," she said, "won't you?" She had green eyes, and she smiled pleasantly now, lifting her black brows.

Davis stepped into the cool apartment, and she closed the door behind him.

"I'm sorry if I seemed rude when you called me," she said. "I'm afraid you woke me."

"Then I should be the one to apologize," Davis said.

He followed her into a sunken living room furnished in Swedish modern. She walked to a long, low coffee table and took a cigarette from a box there, offering the box to him first. Davis shook his head and watched her as she lighted the cigarette. Her hair was cut close to her head, ringing her face with ebony wisps. She wore only lipstick, and Davis reflected that this was the first truly beautiful woman he had ever met. Two large, silver hoop earrings hung from her ears. She lifted her head, and the earrings caught the rays of the sun streaming through the blinds.

"Now," she said. "You're a friend of Tony's, are you?"

"Yes," he answered. He reached into his jacket pocket and took out the sealed envelope. "First, let me get this off my mind. Please tell Tony I sincerely appreciate the loan, won't you?"

She took the envelope without comment, dropping it on the coffee table.

This is a very cool one, Davis thought.

"I was really surprised to learn that Tony was married," he said.

"It was a little sudden, yes," she said.

"Oh? Hadn't he known your sister long?"

"Three months, four months."

Davis shook his head. "I still can't get over it. How'd he happen to meet your sister?"

"Like that," Anne said. "How do people meet? A concert, a club, a soda fountain." She shrugged. "You know, people meet."

"Don't you like Tony?" he asked suddenly.

She seemed surprised. "Me? Yes, as a matter of fact, I do. I think he'll be very good for Alice. He has a strong personality, and she needs someone like him. Yes, I like Tony."

"Well, that's good," Davis said.

"When we came to Frisco, you see, Alice was sort of at loose ends. We'd lived in L.A. all our lives, and Alice depended on Mom a good deal, I suppose. When Mom passed away, and this job opening came for me...well, the change affected her. Moving and all. It was a good thing Tony came along."

"You live here alone then, just the two of you?"

Anne Trimble smiled and sucked in a deep cloud of smoke. "Just two little gals from Little Rock," she said.

Davis smiled with her. "L.A., you mean."

"The same thing. We're all alone in the world. Just Alice and me. Dad died when we were both little girls. Now, of course, Alice is married. Don't misunderstand me. I'm very happy for her."

"When were they married?"

"January 6th," she answered. "It's been a long honeymoon."

January 6th, Davis thought. *The day the DC-4 crashed.*

"Where are they now?" he asked.

"Las Vegas."

"Where in Las Vegas?"

Anne Trimble smiled again. "You're not planning on visiting a pair of honeymooners, are you, Mr. Davis?"

"God, no," he said. "I'm just curious."

"Fact is," Anne said, "I don't know where they're staying. I've only had a wire from them since they were married. I don't imagine they're thinking much of me. Not on their honeymoon."

"No, I guess not," Davis said. "I understand Tony left his job. Is that right?"

"Yes. It didn't pay much, and Tony is really a brilliant person. He and Alice said they'd look around after the honeymoon and settle wherever he could get located."

"When did he quit?"

"A few days before they were married, I think. No, wait, it was on New Year's Eve, that's right. He quit then."

"Then he wasn't selling tickets on the day of..."

Anne looked at him strangely. "The day of what?"

"The day he was married," Davis said quickly.

"No, he wasn't." She continued looking at him, and then asked, "How do you happen to know Tony, Mr. Davis?"

"Oh, the Army," Davis said. "The last war, you know."

"That's quite a feat," Anne said.

"Huh?" Davis looked up.

"Tony was in the Navy."

Once again, he felt like a damn fool. He cursed the crashed plane, and he cursed George Ellison, and he cursed the stupidity that had led him to take the job in the first place. He sighed deeply.

"Well," he said, "I guess I pulled a bloomer."

Anne Trimble stared at him coldly. "Maybe you'd better get out, Mr. Davis. If that's your name."

"It's my name. Look," he said, "I'm a private eye. I'm investigating the crash for my client. I thought..."

"*What* crash?"

'A DC-4 took a dive in Seattle. My client's daughter was aboard her when she went down. There was also a bomb aboard."

"Is this another one of your stories?"

Davis lifted his right hand. "God's truth, s'help. I'm trying to find whoever put the bomb aboard."

"And you think Tony did?"

"No, I didn't say that. But I've got to investigate all the possibilities."

Anne suddenly smiled. "Are you new at this business?"

"No, I've been at it a long time now. This case is a little out of my usual line."

"You called yourself a private eye. Do private eyes really call themselves that? I thought that was just for the paperback trade."

"I'm afraid we really do," Davis said. "Private Investigator, shortened to Private I, and then naturally to private eye."

"It must be exciting."

"Well, I'm afraid it's usually deadly dull." He rose and said, "Thanks very much for your time, Miss Trimble. I'm sorry I got to see you on a ruse, but..."

"You should have just asked. I'm always willing to help the cause of justice." She smiled. "And I think you'd better take this money back."

"Well, thanks again," he said, taking the envelope.

"Not at all," she said. She led him to the door and shook his hand, and her grip was firm and warm. "Good luck."

The door whispered shut behind him. He stood in the hallway for a few moments, sighed, and then made his way down to the courtyard and the street.

The time has come, he thought, *to replenish the bank account. If Ellison expects me to chase hither and yon, then Ellison should also realize that I'm a poor boy, raised by the side of a railroad car. And if a trip to Vegas is in the offing...* the time has come to replenish the bank account.

He thought no more about it. He hailed a cab for which Ellison would pay, and headed for the old man's estate.

The butler opened the door and announced, "Mr. Davis, sir."

Davis smiled at the butler and entered the room. It was full of plates and pitchers and cups and saucers and mugs and jugs and platters. For a moment Davis thought he'd wandered into the pantry by error, but then he saw Ellison seated behind a large desk.

Ellison did not look old, even though Davis knew he was somewhere in his seventies. He had led an easy life, and the rich are expert at conserving their youth. The only signs of age on Ellison were in his face. It was perhaps a bit too ruddy for good health, and it reminded him of MacGregor's complexion–but Ellison was not a fat man. He had steel gray hair cropped close to his head. His brows were black, in direct contrast to the hair on his head, and his eyes were a penetrating pale blue. Davis wondered from whom Janet had inherited her red hair, then let the thought drop when Ellison rose and extended his hand.

"Ah, Davis, come in, come in."

Davis walked to the desk, and Ellison took his hand in a tight grip.

"Hope you don't mind talking in here," he said. "I've got a new piece of porcelain, and I wanted to mount it."

"Not at all," Davis said.

"Know anything about porcelain?" Ellison asked.

"Not a thing, sir."

"Pity. Volkstedt wouldn't mean anything to you then, would it?"

"No, sir."

"Or Rudolstadt? It's more generally known as that."

"I'm afraid not, sir," Davis said.

"Here now," Ellison said. "Look at this sauce boat."

Davis looked.

"This dates back to 1783, Davis. Here, look." He turned over the sauce boat, but he did not let it out of his hands. "See the crossed hayforks. That's the mark, you know, shows it's genuine stuff. Funny thing about this. The mark so resembles the Meissen crossed swords . . ." He seemed suddenly to remember that he was not talking to a fellow connoisseur. He put the sauce boat down swiftly but gently. "Have you learned anything yet, Davis?"

"A little, Mr. Ellison. I'm here mainly for money."

Ellison looked up sharply and then began chuckling. "You're a frank young man, aren't you?"

"I try to be," Davis said. "When it concerns money."

"How much will you need?"

"A few hundred or so. I'll probably be flying to Vegas and back, and I may have to spread little money for information while I'm there."

Ellison nodded briefly. "I'll give you a check before you leave. What progress have you made, Davis?"

"Not very much. Do you know a Tony Radner, Mr. Ellison?"

Ellison looked up swiftly. "Why?"

"He put your daughter on the DC-4, sir. Do you know him?"

Ellison's mouth lengthened, and he tightened his fists on the desk top. "Has that son of a bitch got something to do with this?" he asked.

"Do you know him, sir?"

"Of course I do! How do you know he put Janet on that plane?"

"An eyewitness, sir."

"I'll kill that bastard!" Ellison shouted. "If he had anything to do with . . ."

"How do you know him, Mr. Ellison?"

Ellison's rage subsided for a moment. "Janet was seeing him," he said.

"What do you mean, seeing him?"

"She fancied herself to be in love with him," Ellison said. "He's a no-good, Davis, a plain . . ."

"You mean she wanted to marry him, rather than Carruthers?"

"No, that's not what I mean. I mean she was seeing Radner. *After* she and Nick were married. She . . . she had the supreme gall to tell me she wanted a divorce from Nick." Ellison clenched his hands and then relaxed them again. "You don't know Nick, Davis. He's a fine boy, one of the best. I feel toward him the way I'd feel toward my own son. I never had any boys, Davis, and Janet wasn't much of a daughter." He paused, then said, "I'm grateful I've still got Nick."

"Your daughter wanted to divorce Carruthers?"

"Yes," Ellison said.

"Did she tell Carruthers?"

"Yes, she did. But I told *her* I'd cut her off without a penny if she did any such damn-fool thing. She changed her mind mighty fast after that. Janet was used to money, Davis. The idea of marrying a ticket seller didn't appeal to her when she knew she'd have to do without it."

"So she broke it off with him?"

"On the spot."

"When was this?"

"About six months ago," Ellison said.

"And she hadn't seen him since?"

"Not that I knew of. Now you tell me he put her on that plane. I don't know what to think."

Davis nodded. "It *is* a little confusing."

"Do you suppose she was going to keep a rendezvous in Washington with Radner?" Ellison shook his head.

"Damnit, I wouldn't put it past her."

"I don't think so. At least . . . well, I should think they'd have left together if that were the case."

"Not if she didn't want to be seen. She was traveling on a company pass, you know."

"That seems odd," Davis said. "I mean—"

"You mean, with all my money, why should she travel on a pass?" Ellison smiled. "I like to help Nick out, Davis. I keep him living well; did it when Janet was alive, and still do it. But he's a proud boy, and I've got to be careful with my methods of seeing to his welfare. Getting Janet her ticket was one of the things that kept his pride going."

"I see." Davis washed his hand over his face. "Well, I'll talk to Radner. Did you know he was married now?"

"No, I didn't."

"Yes. On the day of the crash."

"On the day...then what on earth was he doing with Janet?"

"That's a good question," Davis said. He paused, and then added, "Can I have that check now?"

It was not until after supper that evening that Nicholas Carruthers showed up. Davis had eaten lightly, and after a hasty cigarette he had begun packing a small bag for the Vegas trip. When the knock sounded on the door to his apartment, he dropped a pair of shorts into the suitcase and called, "Who is it?"

"Me. Carruthers."

"Second," Davis said. He went to the door rapidly, wondering what had occasioned this visit from the pilot. He threw back the night latch, and then unlocked the door.

Carruthers was in uniform this time. He wore a white shirt and black tie, together with the pale blue trousers and jacket of the airline, and a peaked cap.

"Surprised to see you, Carruthers," Davis said. "Come on in."

"Thanks," Carruthers said. He glanced around the simply furnished apartment noncommittally, then stepped inside and took off his cap, keeping it in his hands.

"Something to drink?" Davis asked. "Bourbon?"

"Please," Carruthers replied.

Davis poured, and when Carruthers had downed the drink, he refilled the glass. "What's on your mind, Carruthers?"

Carruthers looked into the depths of his glass, sipped a bit of the bourbon, and then looked up. "Janet," he said.

"What about her?"

"Let it lie. Tell the old man you're dropping it. Let it lie."

"Why?"

"How much is the old man paying you?" Carruthers asked, avoiding Davis' question.

"That's between the old man and myself."

"I'll match it," Carruthers said. "And then some. Just let's drop the whole damn thing."

Davis thought back to the genial Mr. MacGregor. "You remind

me of someone else I know," he said.

Carruthers did not seem interested. "Look, Davis, what does this mean to you, anyway? Nothing. You're getting paid for a job. All right, I'm willing to pay you what you would have made. So why are you being difficult?"

"Am I being difficult? I didn't say I *wouldn't* drop it, did I?"

"Will you?"

"It depends. I'd like to know why you want it dropped."

"Let's just say I'd like it better if the whole thing were forgotten."

"A lot of people would like it better that way. Including the person who put that bomb on the plane."

Carruthers opened his eyes wide. "You don't think I did that, do you?"

"You were aboard the plane. You could have."

"Why would I do a thing like that?"

"I can think of several reasons," Davis said.

"Like what?" Carruthers sipped at the bourbon again.

"Maybe you didn't like the idea of Janet playing around with Tony Radner."

Carruthers laughed a short, brittle laugh. "You think that bothered me? That two-bit punk? Don't be ridiculous." He drank some more bourbon and then said, "I was used to Janet's excursions, Davis. Radner didn't bother me at all."

"You mean there were others?"

"Others? Janet collected them, Davis, the way the old man collects porcelain. A hobby, you know."

"Did the old man know this?"

"I doubt it. He knew his daughter was a bitch, but I think Radner was the first time it came into the open. He quelched that pretty damn fast, you can bet."

"But you knew about it? And it didn't bother you?"

"Not in the least. I'm no angel myself, Davis. If Janet wanted to roam, fine. If she thought of leaving me, that was another thing."

"That you didn't like," Davis said.

"That I didn't like at all." Carruthers paused. "Look, Davis, I like money. The old man has a lot of it. Janet was my wife, and the old man saw to it that we lived in style. I could have left the airline any time I wanted to, and he'd have set me up for life. Fact is, I like flying, so I stayed on. But I sure as hell wasn't going to let my meal ticket walk out."

"That's not the way I heard it," Davis said.

"What do you mean?"

"Janet's gone, and the old man is still feeding the kitty."

"Sure, but I didn't know it would work that way."

"Didn't you?"

Carruthers swallowed the remainder of his bourbon. "I don't get you, Davis."

"Look at it this way, Carruthers. Janet's a handy thing to have around. She comes and goes, and you come and go, and the old man sees to it that you come and go in Cadillacs. A smart man may begin wondering why he needs Janet at all. If he can be subsidized even after she's gone, why not get rid of her? Why not give her a bomb to play with?"

"Why not?" Carruthers asked. "But I didn't!"

"That's what they all say," Davis told him. "Right up to the gas chamber."

"You're forgetting that I didn't know what the old man's reactions would be. Still don't know. It's early in the game yet, and he's still crossing my palm, but that may change. Look, Davis, when a man takes out accident insurance, it's not because he hopes he'll get into an accident. The same thing with Janet. I needed her. She was my insurance. As long as she was around, my father-in-law saw to it that I wasn't needing." Carruthers shook his head. "No, Davis, I couldn't take a chance on my insurance lapsing."

"Perhaps not. Why do you want me to drop the case?"

"Because I want a status quo. The memory of Janet is fresh in the old man's mind. I'm coupled with the memory. That means he keeps my Cadillac full of gas. Suppose you crack this damned thing? Suppose you find out who set that bomb? It becomes something that's resolved. There's a conclusion, and the old man can file it away like a piece of rare porcelain. He loses interest–and maybe my Cadillac stops running."

"You're a pretty scurvy bastard, aren't you, Carruthers?"

Carruthers smiled. "Why? Because I'm trying to protect an investment? Because I don't give a damn that Janet is gone? Look, Davis, let's get this thing straight. We hated each other's guts. I stayed with her because I like the old man's money. And she stayed with the me because she knew she'd be cut off penniless if she didn't. A very simple arrangement." He paused. "What do you say, Davis?"

"I say get the hell out of here."

"Be sensible, Davis. Look at it . . ."

"Take a walk, Carruthers. Take a long walk and don't come back."

Carruthers stared at Davis for a long time. He said nothing, and there was no enmity in his eyes. At last he rose and settled his cap on his head.

At the door, he turned and said, "You're not being smart, Davis."

Davis didn't answer him.

Perhaps he was not being smart at all. Perhaps Carruthers was right.

It would have been easier to have said no, right from the start. *No, Mr. Ellison, I'm sorry. I won't take the case. Sorry.*

That would have been the easy way. He had not taken the easy way. The money had appealed to him, yes, and so he'd stepped into something that was really far too big for him. He had no right. You don't call in a druggist to perform an appendectomy.

But he was in now, and someone had shot at him a good long while ago. And MacGregor had dented the back of his head, and now Carruthers had been around, too—everyone calling on the dimwitted investigator, everyone suddenly interested in a guy whose life had been routine and commonplace up to now.

If I wait long enough, he thought, everyone will be around, either with money or automatics in their fists.

At first, he thought it was sabotage, plain and simple. The DC-4, after all, had been headed for Seattle to pick up military personnel.

The shots on the mountain had changed his mind. Carruthers—that was another thing again. Carruthers *could* have put that bomb aboard. So could Mangione, the mechanic. And so could Radner. Or perhaps Janet had been a suicide, had brought the bomb aboard herself.

No, he could not buy that one. Janet Carruthers, from what he had heard about her, did not strike him as the sort of person who takes her own life.

But if someone other than Janet had brought the bomb aboard, there had to be a damn good reason for it. Nobody kills five people without having a reason.

Carruthers? He had a reason, all right. If he got rid of Janet, he'd still have Ellison's money, and he wouldn't have the annoyance of being saddled with a woman he hated.

Mangione? That was a tough one. He'd been aboard the plane before the takeoff, but he hardly seemed like a murderer. Besides, what was his motive?

Radner? He had put her aboard the plane, and God knew how he'd finagled that on the day of his wedding. But he *had* put her aboard, and she had dumped him six months previously, and some people don't like the idea of being thrown over.

MacGregor? A hood, probably. A cheap gunsel who'd been hired to put a scare into Davis. Davis wouldn't be surprised if MacGregor had been the sniper on the mountain, too.

But a bomb is an awfully elaborate way of killing someone, assuming the death of Janet Carruthers was the reason for the bomb. It would have been so much easier to have used a knife, or a gun, or a rope, or poison.

Unless the destruction of the plane was an important factor in the killing.

Did the killer have a grudge against the airline as well?

Carruthers worked for the airline, but he was apparently well satisfied with his job. Liked flying, he'd said. Besides, to hear him tell it, he'd never even considered killing his wife. Sort of killing the goose, you know. She was too valuable to him. She was—what had he alluded to? insurance, yes, insurance.

Which, in a way, was true. Carruthers had no way of knowing how Ellison would react to his daughter's death. He could just as easily have washed his hands of Carruthers, and a man couldn't take a chance on...

"I'll be goddamned!" Davis said aloud.

He glanced at his watch quickly. It was too late now. He would have to wait until morning.

"I'll be goddamned," he said again.

It would be a long night.

Mr. Schlemmer was a balding man in his early fifties. A pair of rimless glasses perched on his nose, and his blue eyes were genial behind them.

"I can only speak for Aircraft Insurance Association of America, you understand," he said. "Other companies may operate on a different basis, though I think it unlikely."

"I understand," Davis said.

"First, you wanted to know how much insurance can be obtained from our machines at the San Francisco airport." Schlemmer paused. "We sell it at five cents a thousand dollars. For a quarter, you get a five-thousand-dollar coverage. For five quarters, you're covered for twenty-five thousand."

"And what's the maximum insurance for any one person?"

"Fifty thousand," Schlemmer said. "The premium is two dollars and fifty cents."

"Is there anything in your policy that excludes a woman traveling on a company pass?" Davis asked.

"No," Schlemmer said. "Our airline trip policy states 'traveling on ticket or pass.' No, this woman would not be excluded."

"Suppose the plane's accident occurred because of a bomb explosion aboard the plane while it was in flight? Would that invalidate a beneficiary's claim?"

"I should hardly think so. Just a moment, I'll read you the exclusions." He dug into his desk drawer and came out with a policy which he placed on the desk top, leafing through it rapidly. "No," he said.

"The exclusions are disease, suicide, war, and, of course, we will not insure the pilot or any active member of the crew."

"I see," Davis said. "Can I get down to brass tacks now?"

"By all means, do," Schlemmer said.

"How long does it take to pay?"

"Well, the claim must be filed within twenty days after the occurrence. Upon receipt of the claim, and within fifteen days, we must supply proof-of-loss forms to the claimant. As soon as these are completed and presented to us, we pay. We've paid within hours on some occasions. Sometimes it takes days, and sometimes weeks. It depends on how rapidly the claim is made, the proof of loss submitted—all that. You understand?"

"Yes," Davis said. He took a deep breath. "A DC-4 crashed near Seattle on January 6th. Was anyone on that plane insured with your company?"

Schlemmer smiled, and a knowing look crossed his face. "I had a suspicion you were driving at that, Mr. Davis. That was the reason for your 'bomb' question, wasn't it?"

"Yes. Was anyone insured?"

"There was only one passenger," Schlemmer said. "We would not, of course, insure the crew."

"The passenger was Janet Carruthers," Davis said. "Was she insured?"

"Yes."

"For how much?"

Schlemmer paused. "Fifty thousand dollars, Mr. Davis." He wiped his lips and said, "You know how it works, of course. You purchase your insurance from a machine at the airport. An envelope is supplied for the policy, and you mail this directly to your beneficiary or beneficiaries as the case may be, before you board the flight.

"Yes, I've taken insurance," Davis said.

"A simple matter," Schlemmer assured him, "and well worth the investment. In this case, the beneficiaries have already received a check for fifty thousand dollars."

"They have?"

"Yes. The claim was made almost instantly, proof of loss filed, the entire works. We paid at once."

"I see," Davis said. "I wonder...could you tell me...you mentioned suicide in your excluding clause. Was there any thought about Mrs. Carruthers' death being suicide?"

"We considered it," Schlemmer said. "But quite frankly, it seemed a bit absurd. An accident like this one is hardly conceivable as suicide. I mean, a person would have to be seriously unbalanced to take a plane and its crew with her when she chose to kill herself. Mrs. Carruthers' medical history showed no signs of mental instability. In fact, she was in amazingly good health all through her life. No, suicide was out. We paid."

Davis nodded. "Can you tell me who the beneficiaries were?" he asked.

"Certainly," Schlemmer said. "Mr. and Mrs. Anthony Radner."

He asked her to meet him in front of DiAngelo's and they lingered on the wharf a while, watching the small boats before entering the restaurant. When they were seated, Anne Trimble asked, "Have you ever been here before?"

"I followed a delinquent husband as far as the door once," he answered.

"Then it's your first time."

"Yes."

"Mine, too." She rounded her mouth in mock surprise. "Goodness, we're sharing a first."

"That calls for a drink," he said.

She ordered a daiquiri, and he settled for scotch on the rocks, and he sipped his drink slowly, thinking. *I wish I didn't suspect her sister of complicity in murder.*

They made small talk while they ate, and Davis felt he'd known her for a long time, and that made his job even harder. When they were on their coffee, she said, "I'm a silly girl, I know. But not silly enough to believe this is strictly social."

"I'm an honest man," he said. "It isn't."

She laughed. "Well, what is it then?"

"I want to know more about your sister."

"Alice? For heaven's sake, why?" Her brow furrowed, and she said, "I really should be offended, you know. You take me out and then want to know more about my sister."

"You've no cause for worry," he said very softly. He was not even sure she heard him. She lifted her coffee cup, and her eyes were wide over the brim.

"Will you tell me about her?" he asked.

"Do you think she put the bomb on the plane?"

He was not prepared for the question. He blinked his eyes in confusion.

"Do you?" she repeated. "Remember, you're an honest man."

"Maybe she did," he said.

Anne considered this, and then took another sip of coffee. "What do you want to know?" she asked.

"I want to..."

"Understand, Mr. Davis..."

"Milt," he corrected.

"All right. Understand that I don't go along with you, not at all. Not knowing my sister. But I'll answer any of your questions because that's the only way you'll see she had nothing to do with it."

"That's fair enough," he said.

"All right, Milt. Fire away."

"First, what kind of a girl is she?"

"A simple girl. Shy, often awkward. Honest, Milt, very honest. Innocent. I think Tony Radner is the first man she ever kissed."

"Do you come from a wealthy family, Anne?"

"No."

"How does your sister feel about—"

"About not having a tremendous amount of money?" Anne shrugged. "All right, I suppose. We weren't destitute, even after Dad died. We always got along very nicely, and I don't think she ever yearned for anything. What are you driving at, Milt?"

"Would fifty thousand dollars seem like a lot of money to Alice?"

"Yes," Anne answered without hesitation. "Fifty thousand would seem like a lot of money to anyone."

"Is she easily persuaded? Can she be talked into doing things?"

"Perhaps. I know damn well she couldn't be talked into putting a bomb on a plane, though."

"No. But could she be talked into sharing fifty thousand that was come by through devious means?"

"Why all this concentration on fifty thousand dollars? Is that an arbitrary sum, or has a bank been robbed in addition to the plane crash?"

"Could she be talked," Davis persisted, "into drugging another woman?"

"No," Anne said firmly.

"Could she be talked into forging another woman's signature on an insurance policy?"

"Alice wouldn't do anything like that. Not in a million years."

"But she married Radner. A man without money, a man without a job. Doesn't that seem like a shaky foundation upon which to build a marriage?"

"Not if the two people are in love."

"Or unless the two people were going to come into a lot of money shortly."

Anne said, "You're making me angry. And just when I was beginning to like you."

"Then please don't be angry. I'm just digging, believe me."

"Well, dig a little more gently, please."

"What does your sister look like?"

"Fairly pretty, I suppose. Well, not really. I suppose she isn't pretty, in fact. I never appraised her looks."

"Do you have a picture of her?"

"Yes, yes, I do."

She put her purse on the table and unclasped it. She pulled out a red leather wallet, unsnapped it, and then removed one of the pictures from the gatefold. "It's not a good shot," she apologized.

The girl was not what Davis would have termed pretty. He was surprised, in fact, that she could be Anne's sister. He studied the black-and-white photograph of a fair-haired girl with a wide forehead, her nose a bit too long, her lips thin. He studied the eyes, but they held the vacuous smile common to all posed snapshots.

"She doesn't look like your sister," he said.

"Don't you think so?"

"No, not at all. You're much prettier."

Anne screwed up her eyebrows and studied Davis seriously. "You have blundered upon my secret, Mr. Davis," she said with mock exaggeration.

"You wear a mask, Miss Trimble," he said, pointing his finger at her like a prosecuting attorney.

"Almost, but not quite. I visit a remarkable magician known as Antoine. He operates a beauty salon and fender-repair shop. He is responsible for the midnight of my hair and the ripe apple of my lips. He made me what I am today, and now you won't love me any more." She brushed away an imaginary tear.

"I'd love you if you were bald and had green lips," he said, hoping his voice sounded light enough.

"Goodness!" she said, and then she laughed suddenly, a rich, full laugh he enjoyed hearing. "I may very well be bald after a few more tinting sessions with Antoine."

"May I keep the picture?" he asked.

"Certainly," she said. "Why?"

"I'm going up to Vegas. I want to find your sister and Radner."

"Then you're serious about all this," she said softly.

"Yes, I am. At least, until I'm convinced otherwise. Anne..."

"Yes?"

"It's just a job. I..."

"I'm not really worried, you understand. I know you're wrong about Alice, and Tony, too. So I won't worry."

"Good," he said. "I hope I *am* wrong."

She lifted one raven brow, and there was no coyness or archness in the motion. "Will you call me when you get back?"

"Yes," he said. "Definitely."

"If I'm out when you call, you can call my next-door neighbor, Freida. She'll take the message." She scribbled the number on a sheet of paper. "You will call, won't you, Milt?"

He covered her hand with his and said, "Try and stop me."

He went to City Hall right after he left her. He checked on marriage certificates issued on January 6th, and he was not surprised to find that one had been issued to Anthony Louis Radner and Alice May Trimble. He left there and went directly to the airport, making a reservation on the next plane for Las Vegas. Then he headed back for his apartment to pick up his bag.

The door was locked, just as he had left it. He put his key into the lock, twisted it, and then swung the door wide.

"Close it," MacGregor said.

MacGregor was sitting in the armchair to the left of the door. One hand rested across his wide middle and the other held the familiar .38, and this time it was pointed at Davis' head. Davis closed the door, and MacGregor said, "Better lock it, Miltie."

"You're a bad penny, MacGregor," Davis said, locking the door.

MacGregor chuckled. "Ain't it the truth, Miltie?"

"Why are you back, MacGregor? Three strikes and I'm out, is that it?"

"Three..." MacGregor cut himself short, and then grinned broadly. "So you figured the mountain, huh Miltie?"

"I figured it."

"I wasn't aiming at you, you know. I just wanted to scare you off. You don't scare too easy, Milt."

"Who's paying you, MacGregor?"

"Now, now" MacGregor said chidingly, waving the gun like an extended forefinger. "That's a secret now, ain't it?" Davis watched the way MacGregor moved the gun, and he wondered if he'd repeat the gesture again. It might be worth remembering, for later.

"So what do we do?" he asked.

"We take a little ride, Miltie."

"Like in the movies, huh? Real melodrama."

MacGregor scratched his head. "Is a pleasant little ride melodrama?"

"Come on, MacGregor, who hired you?" He poised himself on the balls of his feet, ready to jump the moment MacGregor started wagging the gun again. MacGregor's hand did not move.

"Don't let's be silly, Miltie boy," he said.

"Do you know *why* you were hired?"

"I was told to see that you dropped the case. That's enough instructions for me."

"Do you know that fifty grand is involved? How much are you getting for handling the sloppy end of the stick?"

MacGregor lifted his eyebrows and then nodded his head. "Fifty grand, huh?"

"Sure. Do you know there's a murder involved, MacGregor? Five murders, if you want to get technical. Do you know what it means to be accessory after?"

"Can it, Davis. I've been in the game longer than you're walking."

"Then you know the score. And you know I can go down to R and I, and identify you from a mug shot. Think about that, MacGregor. It adds up to rock-chopping."

"Maybe you'll never get to see a mug shot."

"Maybe not. But that adds another murder to it. Are they paying you enough for a homicide rap, MacGregor?"

"Little Miltie, we've talked enough."

"Maybe we haven't talked enough yet. Maybe you don't know that the Feds are in on this thing, and that the Army..."

"Oh, come on, Miltie. Come on now, boy. You're reaching."

"Am I? Check around, MacGregor. Find out what happens when sabotage is suspected, especially on a plane headed to pick up military personnel. Find out if J. Edgar isn't on the scene. And find out what happens when a bigtime fools with the Federal government."

"I never done a state pen," MacGregor said, seemingly hurt. "Don't call me a big-time."

"Then why are you juggling a potato as hot as this one? Do you yearn for Quentin, MacGregor? Wise up, friend. You've been conned. The gravy is all on the other end of the line. You're getting all the cold beans, and when it comes time to hang a frame, guess who'll be it. Give a good guess, MacGregor."

MacGregor said seriously. "You're a fast talker."

"I listen to 'Dragnet'," Davis told him. "What do you say, MacGregor? How do you feel, playing the boob in a big ante deal? How much are you getting?"

"Four bills," Macgregor said. "Plus."

"Plus what?"

MacGregor smiled the age-old smile of a man who has known a woman and is reluctant to admit. "Just plus," he said.

"All right, keep the dough and forget you were hired. You've already had the 'plus', and you can keep that as a memory."

"I've only been paid half the dough," MacGregor said.

"When's the rest due?"

"When you drop the case."

"I can't match it, MacGregor, but I'll give you fifty for your trouble. You're getting off easy, believe me. If I don't crack this, the Feds will, and then you'll really be in hot water."

"Yeah," MacGregor said, nodding.

"You'll forget it then?"

"Where's the fifty?"

Davis reached for his wallet on the dresser. "Who hired you, MacGregor?" He looked up, and MacGregor's smile had widened now.

"I'll take it all, Miltie."

"Huh?"

"All of it." MacGregor waved the gun. "Everything in the wallet. Come on."

"You *are* a jackass, aren't you?" Davis said. He fanned out the money in the wallet, and then held it out to MacGregor. MacGregor reached for it, and Davis loosened his grip, and the bills began fluttering toward the floor.

MacGregor grabbed for them with his free hand, turning sideways at the same time, taking the gun off Davis.

It had to be then, and it had to be right, because the talking game was over and MacGregor wasn't buying anything.

Davis leaped, ramming his shoulder against the fat man's chest. MacGregor staggered back, and then swung his arm around just as Davis' fingers clamped on his wrist. He did not fire, and Davis knew he probably didn't want to bring the apartment house down around his ears.

They staggered across the room in a clumsy embrace, like partners at a dance school for beginners. Davis had both hands on MacGregor's gun wrist now, and the fat man swung his arm violently, trying to shake the grip. They didn't speak or curse. MacGregor grunted loudly each time he swung his arm, and Davis' breath was audible as it rushed through his parted lips. He did not loosen his grip. He forced MacGregor across the room, and when the fat man's back was against the wall Davis began methodically smashing the gun hand against the plaster.

"Drop it," he said through clenched teeth. "Drop it."

He hit the wall with MacGregor's hand again, and this time the fingers opened and the gun clattered to the floor. Davis stepped back for just an instant, kicking the gun across the room, and then rushed forward with his fist clenched.

He felt his fist sink into the flesh around MacGregor's middle. The fat man's face went white, and then he buckled over, his arms embracing his stomach. Davis dropped his fist and then brought it up from his shoelaces, catching MacGregor on the point of his jaw. MacGregor lurched backward, slamming into the wall, knocking a picture to the floor. Davis hit him once more, and MacGregor pitched forward onto his face. He wriggled once, and was still.

Davis stood over him, breathing hard. He waited until he caught his breath, and then he glanced at his watch.

Quickly, he picked up the .38 from where it lay on the floor. He broke it open, checked the load, and then brought it to his suitcase, laying it on top of his shirts.

He snapped the suitcase shut, called the police to tell them he'd just subdued a burglar in his apartment, and then left to catch his Las Vegas plane.

He started with the hotels. He started with the biggest ones.

"Mr. and Mrs. Anthony Radner," he said. "Are they registered here?"

The clerks all looked the same.

"Radner, Radner. The name doesn't sound familiar, but I'll check, sir."

Then the shifting of the ledger, the turning of pages, the signatures, largely scrawled, and usually illegible.

"No, sir, I'm sorry. No Radner."

"Perhaps you'd recognize the woman, if I showed you her picture?"

"Well . . ." The apologetic cough. "Well, we get an awful lot of guests, sir."

And the fair-haired girl emerging from the wallet. The black and white, stereotyped photograph of Alice Trimble, and the explanation, "She's a newlywed–with her husband."

"We get a lot of newlyweds, sir."

The careful scrutiny of the head shot, the tilting of one eyebrow, the picture held at arm's length, then closer.

"No, I'm sorry. I don't recognize her. Why don't you try ..?"

He tried them all, all the hotels, and then all the rooming houses, and then all the motor courts. They were all very sorry. They had no Radners registered, and couldn't identify the photograph.

So he started making the rounds then. He lingered at the machines, feeding quarters into the slots, watching the oranges and lemons and cherries whirl before his eyes, but never watching them too closely, always watching the place instead, looking for the elusive woman named Alice Trimble Radner.

Or he sat at the bars, nursing along endless scotches, his eyes fastened to the mirrors that commanded the entrance doorways. He was bored, and he was tired, but he kept watching, and he began making the rounds again as dusk tinted the sky, and the lights of the city flicked their siren song on the air.

He picked up the newspaper by chance. He flipped through it idly, and he almost turned the page, even after he'd read the small head: FATAL ACCIDENT.

The item was a very small one. It told of a 1964 Pontiac convertible with defective brakes which had crashed through the guard rail on the highway, killing its occupant instantly. The occupant's name was Anthony Radner. There was no mention of Alice in the article.

Little Alice Trimble, Davis thought. A simple girl. Shy, often awkward. Honest.

Murder is a simple thing. All it involves is killing another person or persons. You can be shy and awkward, and even honest–but that doesn't mean you can't be a murderer besides. So what is it that takes a simple girl like Alice Trimble and transforms her into a murderess?

Figure it this way. Figure a louse named Tony Radner who sees a way of striking back at the girl who jilted him and coming into a goodly chunk of dough besides. Figure a lot of secret conversations, a pile of carefully planned moves. Figure a wedding, planned to coincide with the day of the plotted murder, so the murderers can be far away when the bomb they planted explodes.

Radner gets to see Janet Carruthers on the same pretext, perhaps a farewell drink to show there are no hard feelings. This is his wedding day, and he introduces her to his bride, Alice Trimble. They share a drink, perhaps, but the drink is loaded and Janet suddenly feels very woozy. They help her to the airport, and they stow the bomb in her valise. None of the pilots know Radner. The only bad piece of luck is the fact that the fire-warning system is acting up, and a mechanic named Mangione recognizes him. But that's part of the game.

He helps her aboard and then goes back to his loving wife, Alice. They hop the next plane for Vegas, and when the bomb explodes they're far, far away. They get the news from the papers, file claim, and come into fifty thousand.

Just like falling off Pier 8.

Except that it begins to get sour about there. Except that maybe Alice Trimble likes the big time now. Fifty Gs is a nice little pile. Why share it?

So Tony Radner meets with an accident. If he's not insured, the fifty grand is still Alice's. If he is insured, there's more for her.

The little girl has made her debut. The shy, awkward thing has emerged.

Portrait of a killer.

Davis went back to the news-stand, and he bought copies of all the local newspapers and then went back to the hotel.

When he was in his room, he called room service and asked for a tall scotch, easy on the ice. He took off his shoes and threw himself on the bed.

The drink came, and he went back to the bed again.

The easy part was over, of course. The hard part was still ahead. He still had to tell Anne about it, and he'd give his right arm not to have that task ahead of him. Alice Trimble? The police would find her. She'd probably left Vegas the moment Radner piled up the Pontiac. She was an amateur, and it wouldn't be too hard to find her. But telling Anne, that was the difficult thing.

Davis sat upright, took a long swallow of the scotch, and then swung his stockinged feet to the floor. He walked to the pile of newspapers on the dresser, picked them up with one hand, and carried them back to the bed.

He thumbed through the first one until he found the item about Radner's accident. It was a small notice, and it was basically the same as the one he'd read. It did add that Alice Trimble was on her honeymoon, and that she had come from San Francisco where she lived with her sister.

He leafed through the second newspaper, scanning the story quickly. Again, basically the same facts. Radner had taken the car for a spin. Alice hadn't gone along because of a headache. The accident had been attributed to faulty brakes, and there was speculation that Alice might have grounds for suit, if she cared to press charges, against the dealer who'd sold them the car.

The third newspaper really did a bang-up job. They treated the accident as a human-interest piece, playing up the newly-wed angle. They gave it the tearful head, "FATE CHEATS BRIDE," and then went on to wring the incident dry. There was also a picture of Alice Trimble leaving the coroner's office. She was raising her hand to cover her face when the picture had been taken. It was a good shot, close up, clear. The caption read: *Tearful Alice Radner, leaving the coroner's office after identifying the body of her husband, Anthony Radner.*

Davis did not notice any tears on Alice Trimble's face.

He looked at the photograph again.

He sat erect and took a long gulp of his scotch, and then he brought the newspaper closer to his face and stared at the picture for a long time.

And he suddenly remembered something important he'd forgotten to ask Anne about her sister. Something damned important. So important he nearly broke his neck getting to the phone.

He asked long distance for Anne's number, and then let the phone ring fifteen minutes before he gave up. He remembered the alternate number she'd given him then, the one belonging to Freida, the girl next door. He fished the scrap of paper out of his wallet, studying the number in Anne's handwriting, recalling their conversation in the restaurant. He got long distance to work again, and the phone was picked up on the fourth ring.

"Hello?"

"Hello. Freida?"

"Yes?"

"My name is Milt Davis. You don't know me, but Anne said I could leave a message here if . . ."

"Oh, yes. Anne's told me all about you, Mr. Davis."

"Well, good, good. I just tried to phone her, and there was no answer. I wonder if you know where I can reach her?"

"Why, yes." Freida said. "She's in Las Vegas."

'What!"

"Yes. Her brother-in-law was killed in a car crash there. She . . ."

"You mean she's here? Now?"

"Well, I suppose so. She caught a plane early this evening. Yes, I'm sure she's there by now. Her sister called, you see. Alice. She called and asked Anne to come right away. Terrible thing, her husband getting killed like . . ."

"Oh, Christ!" Davis said. He thought for a second and then asked, "Did she say where I could reach her?"

"Yes. Just a moment."

Freida put the phone down with a clatter, and Davis waited impatiently. By the time she returned, he was ready to start chewing the mouthpiece.

"What's the address?" he asked.

"It's outside of Las Vegas. A private party. Alice and Tony were lucky to get such a nice .."

"Please, the address!"

"Well, all right," Freida said, a little miffed. She read off the address and Davis scribbled it quickly. He said goodbye, and hung up immediately. There was no time for checking plane schedules now. No time for finding out which plane Anne caught out of Frisco, nor for finding out what time it arrived in Vegas.

There was only time to tuck MacGregor's .38 into the waistband of his trousers and then run like hell down to the street. He caught a cab and reeled off the address, and then sat on the edge of his seat while the lights of Vegas dimmed behind him.

A private party, Freida had said. That was good because you don't go around shooting people in private houses. And Anne was sure as hell going to be shot the way he figured it.

When the cabbie pulled up in front of the clapboard structure, he gave him a fiver and then leaped out of the car. He ran up the front steps and pulled the door pull, listening to steps approaching inside. A white-haired woman opened the door, and Davis said, "Alice Radner. Where?"

"Upstairs, but who...?"

Davis shoved the woman aside and started up the flight of steps, not looking back. There was a door at the top of the stair well, and he rapped on it loudly. When he received no answer, he shouted, "I know you're in there! Open the goddamn door."

The door opened instantly, and Davis found himself looking into the bore of a .22.

"Come in," a woman's voice said softly.

He didn't need an invitation to do that. He stepped into the room, and the woman bolted the door behind him, the gun pointed at his gut.

"Where is she?" he asked.

"Anne Trimble? In the bedroom. I had to tie her and gag her, I'm afraid. She raised a bit of a fuss when she got here."

Davis ran into the bedroom. Anne was lying on the bed, her hands tied behind her, a scarf stuffed in her mouth. He made a move toward her and the voice came from the doorway, cool and crisp.

"Leave her alone."

"Why?" Davis said. "It's all over now, anyway. You know that, don't you?"

"You're Davis, aren't you?" the woman said. She smiled, but there was no mirth on her mouth. "You should have stayed out of it. From the very beginning."

"Everybody's been telling me that," Davis said. "Right from go."

"You should have paid more attention to them, Mr. Davis. All this might have been avoided then."

"All what?"

She did not answer. She moved out of the room quickly, walking to the door through which Davis had entered. She opened the door and called, "It's all right, Mrs. Mulready. He's a friend of mine." Then she slammed the door and bolted it, walking back to the bedroom quickly.

"That takes care of her," she said, the .22 steady in her hand. She was a beautiful woman with a pale complexion and blue eyes set against the ivory of her skin. She stared at Davis solemnly.

"It all seemed out of whack," Davis said, "but I didn't know just where. It all pointed to Tony Radner and Alice Trimble, but I couldn't conceive of her as a murderess. Sure, I figured Tony led her into it. A woman in love can be talked into anything. But when I learned about Tony's accident here, a new Alice Trimble took shape. Not the gal who was talked into anything, and not the gal who'd do anything for love. This new Alice Trimble was a cold-blooded killer, a murderess who..."

Davis saw Anne's eyes widen. She struggled to speak.

"Anne," he said, "tell me something. Was your sister a redhead?"

Anne nodded dumbly, and he saw the confused look that stabbed her eyes. It was then that he realized he'd unconsciously used the past tense in talking about her sister.

"I'm sorry," he said. "I'm sorry as hell, Anne." He paused and drew a deep breath. "Alice is dead, Anne."

It was almost as if he'd struck her. She flinched, and then a strangled cry tried to shove its way past the gag.

"Believe me," he said, "I'm sorry. I..." He wiped his hand across his lips and then said, "I never thought to ask. About her hair, I mean. Hell, I had her picture and that was all I needed to identify her. I'm... I'm sorry, Anne."

He saw the tears spring into her eyes, and he went to her in spite of the .22 that was still pointed at him. He ripped the gag from her mouth, and she said, "I don't understand. I...what...what do you mean?"

"Alice left you on the sixth," he said, "to meet Tony Radner, allegedly to marry him. She didn't know about the trap that had been planned by Tony and Janet Carruthers."

Anne took her eyes from Davis and looked at the .22 in the woman's hand. "Is...is that who..."

"Janet Carruthers," Davis said, "who wanted to be free of her husband more than anything else in the world. But not at the expense of cutting herself off without a cent. So she and Tony figured it all out, and they started looking for a redhead who would take the hook. Your sister came along, starry-eyed and innocent, and Radner led her to the chopping block."

Davis paused and turned to the redhead with the gun. "I can fill it in, if you like. A lot of guessing, but I think I'm right."

"Go ahead," Janet said. "Fill it in."

"Sure. Alice met Tony as scheduled on the day they were to be married. He probably suggested a drink in celebration, drugged her, and then took her some place to get her into some of your clothes. He drove her to the airport then, where you were waiting. You had to go to the airport because your signature was necessary on the insurance policy. You insured Alice, who was now in Janet Carruthers' clothing, with Janet Carruthers' identification in case anything was left of her after the crash, for fifty thousand dollars. And Janet Carruthers' beneficiaries were Mr. and Mrs. Anthony Radner. You knew that Nick would be on the DC-4, but outside of him, no one else on the plane knew what you looked like. It would be simple to substitute Alice for you. You left the airport, probably to go directly to City Hall to wait for Tony. Tony waited until Nick took a pilot up on a test, and then he brought Alice to the plane, dumped her into her seat, with the bomb in her suitcase, and left to meet you. You got married shortly after the DC-4 took off. You used Alice Trimble's name, and most likely the identification—if it was needed—that Tony had taken from her. The switch had been completed, and you were now Mrs. Radner. You flew together to Las Vegas, and as soon as the DC-4 crashed, you made your claim for the fifty Gs."

"You're right except for the drug, Mr. Davis. That would have been overdoing it a bit."

"All right, granted. What'd Tony do, just get her too damned drunk to walk or know what was going on?"

"Exactly. Her wedding day, you know. It wasn't difficult."

Davis heard a sob catch in Anne's throat. He glanced at her briefly and then said to Janet, "Did Tony know he was going to be driving into a pile of rocks?"

Janet smiled. "Poor Tony. No. I'm afraid he didn't know. That part was all my idea. Even down to stripping the brakes. Tony never knew what hit him."

"Neither did all the people on that DC-4. It was a long way to go for a lousy hunk of cash," Davis said. "Was Tony insured, too?"

"Yes," Janet said, "but not for much." She smiled. "Enough, though."

Davis nodded. "One after the other, right down the line. And then you sent for Anne because she was the only living person who could know you were *not* Alice Trimble. And it had to be fast, especially after that picture appeared in the Las Vegas paper."

"Was that how you found out?" she asked.

"Exactly how. The picture was captioned *Alice Radner*—but the girl didn't match the one in the photo I had. Then I began thinking about the color of Alice's hair, which I knew was light, and got clear as a bell." He shook his head sadly. "I still don't know how you hoped to swing it. You obviously sent for Anne because you were afraid someone would recognize you in Frisco. Hell, someone would have recognized you sooner or later, anyway."

"In Mexico?" Janet asked. "Or South America? I doubt it. Fifth thousand can do a lot outside of this country, Mr. Davis. Plus what I'll get on Tony's death. I'll manage nicely, don't you worry." She smiled pleasantly.

Davis smiled back. "Go ahead," he said. "Shoot. And then try to explain the shots to your landlady."

Janet Carruthers walked to the dresser, keeping the gun on Davis. "I hadn't wanted to do it here," she said, shrugging. "I was going to take Miss Trimble away after everyone was asleep. You're forcing my hand, though." She opened a drawer and came out with a long, narrow cylinder. The cylinder had holes punched into its sides, and Davis knew a silencer when he saw one. He was Janet fitting the silencer to the end of the .22 and he saw the dull gleam in her eyes and knew it was time to move. He threw back his coat and reached for the .38 in his waistband. The .22 went off with a sharp *pouff*, and he felt the small bullet rip into his shoulder. But he'd squeezed the trigger of the .38 and he saw her arm jerk as his larger bullet tore flesh and bone. Her fingers opened, and the silenced gun fell to the floor.

Her face twisted in pain. She closed her eyes, and he kicked the gun away, and then she began swearing. She kept swearing when he took her good arm and twisted it behind her back.

He heard footsteps rushing up the stairs, and then the landlady shouted, "What is it? *What is it?*"

"Get the police!" he yelled through the closed door. "Get them fast."

"You don't know what you're doing," Janet said. "This will kill my father."

Davis looked over to where Anne sat sobbing on the bed, her face buried in her hands. He wanted to go to her and clasp her into his arms, but there would be time for that later.

"My father..." Janet started.

"Your father still has Nick," Davis said, "and his porcelain." His shoulder ached, and the trickle of blood down his jacket front was not pleasant to watch. He paused and lifted his eyes to Janet's. "That's all your father ever had."

STEPHEN MARLOWE
(b.1928)

Wanted—Dead and Alive
(Chester Drum)

I was drinking an ouzo-and-water on the aft deck of the car-ferry *Hellas* and watching the lights of Brindisi fade into the Mediteranean darkness when a stocky figure came toward me, lurching slightly with the ship's roll.

"What the hell are you doing aboard?" I said.

"Did I ever say I wouldn't be?"

"Wife see you yet?" I asked.

"In the lounge. A real touching scene. She was looped. As usual."

That made two of them, I thought. Sabastian Spinner's lurch hadn't been all ship's roll. He was gripping the rail hard with both hands to keep the deck from tilting.

"What about the hired gun?"

"Christ, no. If he's aboard, I haven't made him." Spinner sighed ruefully. "Provided I remember what the sonofabitch looks like." A foghorn tooted in the bay, sounding derisive.

Sebastian Spinner was producer-director of *Lucrezia Borgia*, which was being filmed on location all over Italy. Twenty-five million bucks, not Spinner's money, had been pumped into it so far. The studio was near bankruptcy, the picture still wasn't finished and never would be if Spinner's wife kept wandering all over the map, with or without whatever stud struck her fancy at the moment.

It seemed even less likely that the picture would be finished if

Spinner's wife, Carole Frazer, who was playing La Lucrezia, wound up dead on the twenty-six hour steamer trip between Brindisi, Italy, and Patras, Greece. Neither Spinner nor I would make book that she wouldn't. Spinner had hired a Neapolitan killer to hit her in the head.

I'd first bumped into Sebastian Spinner in Rome a couple of weeks ago, when I'd blown myself to a vacation after the Axel Spade case. It was a party, the kind they throw in Cinecita or Hollywood, where somebody dressed to the earlobes always gets tossed into the pool, where an unknown starlet named Simonetta or something like that peels to the waist to prove her astonishing abundancy and where guys like me, if their luck is running bad, get hired by guys like Sebastian Spinner.

"Drum?" he'd said, scooping a couple of martinis off a tray and handing me one. "That wouldn't be Chester Drum?"

I admitted my guilt.

"The private dick?"

"Not very private if you keep shouting it like that."

Spinner laughed phlegmily and clamped my arm with a small, soft hand. He was a stocky bald man, and his face and pate were shiny with sweat.

"They say you're the best in the business," he said, and added modestly: "I'm the best in my business. Sweetheart, if we get together it could be you're gonna save my life. Though sometimes I ain't to sure it's worth the trouble." Spinner was alternately egotistic and self-deprecating, a typical Hollywood type who made me glad I usually worked out of Washington, D.C.

He steered me outside and we drove off into the hot Roman night in his low-slung Facel Vega. He said nothing until we'd parked on the Via Veneto and took a curb-side table at Doney's.

"Somebody's gonna hit my wife in the head," he said then. "Christ, they kill her and there goes *Lucrezia Borgia*, not to mention twenty-five million bucks of Worldwide Studio money. If that happens, they wouldn't give me a job sweeping out the latrine of the second unit of one of those goddam grade Z epics made with the Yugoslav army."

I asked: "How do you know somebody's going to kill your wife, Mr. Spinner?" I asked it politely, the way you do with a loquacious drunk.

Spinner recognized my point of view and didn't like it. "On account of I hired the guy," he said indignantly, and then I was all ears.

A few days before, while they were shooting on location outside of Naples, Spinner had gone up to Vomero on a bat. You couldn't blame him. His wife was sleeping with Philip Stanley, her leading man, and everybody knew it.

"I was sitting in this trattoria in Vomero," Spinner said. "I was gassed to the eyeballs, and all of a sudden it was like that Hitchcock gimmick where two guys meet on a train and... You remember the film, don't you?

"Well, I met me a mafiosa type and we started in to talking. I ain't usually the jealous type. Merde, I been married six times, what's an extra-curricular roll in the hay more or less matter, it's a free country, I get yens too. But Carole's been spreading it around and her middle name ain't exactly discretion and this Stanley bastard practically rubs my face in it. No dame's gonna make Sebastian Spinner wear neon horns.

"That's what I tell the mafiosa type, and he nods his head and listens, and pretty soon, like, I'm foaming at the mouth, and finally I shut up. That's when he says, 'For five thousand dollars American I will kill her,' and that's when I say, 'For five thousand dollars American you got yourself a deal,' and he swifty cons me into giving him half of it in advance walks out of the trattoria after I tell him when the best time to hit Carole in the head would be."

"When would it be?"

He told me about her up-coming trip to Greece. "On the boat," he said. "They got a ferry that runs from Brindisi to Patras. Carole hates to fly."

I watched the traffic swarming along the Via Veneto and being swallowed by the Pinciana Gate. "I take it you sort of changed your mind."

"You bet your sweet life I did. What goes with *Lucrezia Borgia* if Carole gets hit in the head? You tell me that, pal."

"Okay, call your gun off. What do you need me for?"

"I can't call him off."

That got a raised eyebrow from me.

"I don't even know his goddam name, I'm not sure what trattoria in Vomero it was and he had a face like all the other little swifties who'll sell their own sisters for a thousand lira in Naples. Kee-rist, I need a drink."

"Maybe he just let you talk yourself out of twenty-five hundred bucks," I suggested. "What makes you so sure he intends to go through with it?"

"Nothing, sweetheart," Spinner admitted with a slightly sick smile. "Nothing at all. Maybe he *is* laughing up his sleeve down in Vomero. Don't you think I know that?"

"So?"

"So maybe on the other hand he ain't."

I went down to Naples for a few days and prowled all the dives in Vomero without any luck. I got to Brindisi half an hour before the *Hellas* sailed. Now, on the aft deck of the car ferry, I told Spinner: "Look. Sober up and stay that way. I'll watch your wife, but if the guy's abroad maybe you'll recognize him."

A voice, not Spinner's, said: "I say, old man, don't you feel a bit of a horse's ass following us?" and a man joined us at the rail. In the light streaming through the portholes of the lounge, I recognized Philip Stanley. He was a big guy, about my size, in a navy blue blazer with gold buttons and a pair of gray flannel slacks. He had a hard, handsome face going a little heavy in the jowls, and his eyes held that look of smug, inbred self-satisfaction they seem to give out along with the diplomas at Eton and Harrow and the other public schools that turn out the members of the British Establishment. Actually, he had grown up in a Birmingham slum, and it had taken him all his life to cultivate that look of supercilious disdain.

"Sweetheart," Spinner said, "I never dreamed Carole would pack her playmate for the trip. Maybe she's slipping if she don't think she can do better in Greece. A lot better. They're pretty torrid in the sack, those Greeks, what I hear."

Stanley laughed. "Better than you she can always do, at any rate. But tell me, old boy," he asked dryly, "would you be speaking about those Greeks from personal experience?"

Spinner took a drunken, clumsy swing at him. Evading it easily, Stanley grabbed his wrist and levered the plump man a few staggering steps along the deck before letting go. Spinner fell down and leaped up again as if he had springs in his shoes.

I got between them, and Spinner said gratefully, "Hold me back, Drum. Hold me back, sweetheart. Every mark I put on his face'll cost Worldwide half a million bucks."

Stanley snickered, and neatly turned his broad back, and walked away along the rail. Spinner shuffled toward the door to the lounge. I lit a cigarette and followed the Englishman. A few more minutes away from Carole Frazer wouldn't hurt. Spinner would have the sense to keep an eye on her until I showed up.

"Got a few minutes?" I asked Stanley.

"Twenty-five hours to Patras," he said, leaning both elbows on the rail and staring down at the frothy white wake. "But just who are you?"

"Drum," I said crisply. "Worldwide front office."

"I never heard of you."

"You're not supposed to—until I land on you with both feet."

"Meaning?"

"Meaning if I can't get some assurance *Lucrezia* 'll be in the cutter's room inside of six months, the front office is half-inclined to chuck the whole works."

Stanley straightened and turned suddenly in my direction. He looked worried. "Are you serious?"

"Sure I am," I said. Though with his rugged Anglo-Saxon good looks Philip Stanley was about as far from a hungry little Neapolitan killer as you could get, the more I knew about the principals in the case the better I'd be able to handle whatever developed. "The director's been throwing a bat all the way from the Italian Alps to Callabria and between takes the stars go hop-scotching from bed to bed all over Europe. You think maybe Worldwide's wild about that?"

"I'll admit I've slept with Carole," Stanley said, "but–"

"Admit it? Hell, everybody knows it."

"But I had hoped to keep her somewhat closer to the set by doing it."

"That's what I like about you box-office big-shots. Your modesty."

"I am afraid you misunderstand," Stanley said, and a tortoni wouldn't have melted in his mouth. "Naturally I've gotten a certain amount of publicity as Carole's leading man, but I am not, as you put it, a box-office big-shot. I will be, if we ever finish *Lucrezia*. Otherwise I'll just be another not-quite-matinee-idol knocking at the back doors of Cinecita for work."

Him and Sebastian Spinner both, I thought. The only one who didn't seem to mind was Carole Frazer.

"Damn it all," he went on, "why d'you think we're languishing a year behind schedule? Because I've slept with Carole? That's nonsense, old boy. I don't have to tell you the woman's a nymphomaniac, if a lovely one. But if it isn't me then it's someone else, and that's only the half of it. Carole was rushed to London three times for emergency medical treatment, and each time as I also don't have to tell you it was some psychosomatic foolishness. Why, she's only appeared in half a dozen crucial scenes so far, close-ups, and virtually every far shot's been done by her stand-in. We have a great deal more footage of the stand-in than we do of Carole. If you doubt my word, ask Spinner. And Dawn Sibley's no mere double, she's a fine actress in her own right. Sometimes I think it would be simpler all around if we were to chuck Carole and let Dawn do *Lucrezia*. I don't stand alone. Ask around, old boy, and then tell *that* to the front office. Most of us want to see this film completed as much as you do. But unfortunately it was conceived as a vehicle for Carole."

After that long tirade, he had nothing else to say. I watched him walk across the deck and inside. For a little while I listened to the rush of water under the hull-plates. Brindisi was a faint and distant line of light. Overhead a gull, nailed in silhouette against the starlit sky, screamed and flapped its wings once. When I looked again, only a glow remained on the horizon in the direction of Brindisi. I carried my empty ouzo glass to the lounge.

At a big table near the bar, Carole Frazer was holding court. She was wearing black tapered slacks and a paisley blouse that fondled her high breasts without hugging them lasciviously. A casual lock of her blond hair had fallen across her right eye and right cheek. A languid smile that did not quite part her moist red lips was the reward her suitors got.

There were about a dozen of them, most of them dark and slender Italians and Greeks with intense eyes and gleaming teeth. Any one of them, I realized, could have been Sebastian Spinner's little swifty from Vomero. He'd be as easy to single out as a fingerling in a fish hatchery.

"Ouzo," I told the barman, and he poured the anis-flavored liquor and added enough water to turn it milky. His hand was not steady on the carafe, and he sloshed a little water on the bar. In the world that Hollywood made, Carole Frazer was an institution. He was staring at her bugeyed. I couldn't blame him. Seen close, her blond beauty was really scorching.

Spinner sat alone at a table nearby. He was drinking Scotch and darting small, anxious glances at the men clustered around his wife. Each time he'd shake his head slightly, and his eyes would flick on like a snake's tongue. He had trouble keeping his head off the table. He was very drunk.

I went over to him and sat down. "Any luck?"

"Nope. Maybe he's here. Maybe not. I can't tell them apart, bunch a goddam Chinamen."

"Lay off the sauce," I suggested, "and you won't see double."

Carole Frazer called across to us in her throaty purr of a voice. "Mister, if you can make him do that, you're a better man than his psychiatrist. Who are you?"

"I'm his new psychiatrist," I said, and she laughed, and then she lost interest in us as the dark heads bobbed and the white teeth flashed all around her. She lapped up male adulation the way a thirsty kitten laps up milk.

Pretty soon Spinner told me, "Gonna hit the sack. It's no use. You'll keep an eye on her?"

I said that was why I was here, and he lurched across the lounge toward the companionway that led to the *Hellas* de luxe staterooms. A while later Carole Frazer got up and stretched like a cat, every muscle of her lithe body getting into the act. The Italians and Greeks went pop-eyed, watching. She patted the nearest dark head, said, "Down, boy," and, "Arrivederci" and went in the direction her husband had gone. But that didn't necessarily mean she was going to find him. After all, her leading man Philip Stanley was aboard too.

Finishing my ouzo, I went in search of the purser's office. It was located in the first class entrance foyer. A kid in a white uniform sat there reading a letter and sighing.

"What's the number of Carole Frazer's stateroom?" I asked him.

"Kyros," he said smoothly, "the next time you see the lady, why not ask her?"

He smiled. I smiled and studied half a dozen travel brochures spread out on the counter. I picked one of them up. In English, French and Italian it described the delights of a motor trip that could be made from Athens to Delphi and back in a day.

"How much?" I asked.

"Depending on whether you wish a chauffeur or a self-drive car, kyros–"

"No. I mean the brochure."

"That is free, kyros, compliments of the Adriatic Line."

I pocketed the folder and dropped a fifty drachma note on the counter. "Fifty?" I said. "That seems fair enough."

"But I just–" he began, and then his eyes narrowed and his lips just missed smiling. "De Luxe Three, starboard side," he said without moving his mouth, and returned to his letter.

The starboard de luxe companionway ended at a flight of metal stairs going up. At the top was a door and beyond that a narrow deck above the boat-deck, with three doors numbered one, two and three spaced evenly along it. There were wide windows rather than portholes, all of them curtained and two of them dark. Faint light seaped through the third. It was Carole Frazer's cabin.

Looking at it, I liked the setup. Door and window both outside, on this deck. If I spent the night here, nobody could reach Carole Frazer without me knowing it. I listened to the throb of the ship's engines and looked at my watch. It was a quarter to one. I sat down between the door and the window of Carole Frazer's stateroom. The bulk of the Magnum .44 in its clam-shell rig under my left arm was uncomfortable. I shifted the holster around a little, but that didn't help. No one has ever invented a shoulder holster that is comfortable, just as no one has ever invented any other way of wearing a revolver the size of a Magnum and hiding it when what else you are wearing is a light-weight seersucker suit.

For about an hour I kept a silent vigil. Nobody screamed, no Vomero swifty came stalking up stairs, nothing happened except that the *Hellas* covered another twenty-five miles of Adriatic Sea.

And then I heard voices. The only thing that wasn't de luxe about the half-dozen de luxe state rooms aboard the *Hellas* was the sound-proofing. Well, you couldn't have everything.

"Awake?" a man asked.

"Uh-huh."

"Like another drink?"

"My head's spinning right now."

"Just one more? With me?"

"All right."

Silence while Philip Stanley and Carole Frazer had a post-nightcap nightcap. Like any private dick, I'd been called a peeper more than once. Like any private dick, I'd never liked it. I'd done my share of peeping–or anyway listening–but never outside a woman's bedroom. The one kind of work I don't do is divorce work. But if the hired gun was going to make his move, it figured to be during the night. "Peeper," I muttered sourly under my breath, and remained where I was.

"Oh, Phil," Carole Frazer said, and her voice was more throaty than it had been in the lounge. "When you do that–"

"What's wrong, don't you like it?"

"You know I do. I love it. But I'm so–drunky. Head going around and 'round."

Another silence. Then he laughed, and she laughed and said: "Phil, you amaze me." She called him a brief Angle-Saxon word that is usually not a term of endearment, but her voice made it sound endear-ing. Then she laughed again, deep in her throat, and then she said, "You keep this up, you're going to screw yourself right into the wall," and then after that there was silence for a long time.

I must have half-dozed. I blinked suddenly and realized that the night had grown cooler and I had grown stiff from sitting in one posi-tion for so long. I glanced at the luminous dial of my watch. After three o'clock. It would be dawn before long, and still no sign of the Vomero swifty.

There was a faint click, and the stateroom door opened enough for Philip Stanley to poke his head out and take a quick look to left and right. The one way he didn't look was down, where I was sit-ting. His head popped back inside, and the door shut softly. I remained where I was.

The door opened again. This time Stanley came out. He was car-rying a suitcase, and from the way his shoulder slumped it looked heavy. He took it to the rail, set it down and placed a coil of rope on top of it. I froze, absolutely still. If he turned right on his way back to the stateroom he would see me. If he turned left, he wouldn't.

He turned left and went inside again. What the hell was he up to?

In a few seconds he reappeared with Carole Frazer cradled in his arms. He was fully dressed. She wasn't dressed any way at all. She mumbled against his ear. He set her down, gently, next to the suitcase. For a while longer I sat there like someone who had walked in on the middle of a movie and didn't know what the hell was happening on the screen or why. Stanley tied the rope to the handle of the suitcase, uncoiled the rest of it, took two turns around the suitcase, passed the rope through the handle once more, took four or five turns around Carole Frazer's body under the arms, passed the rope through the handle a third time and knotted it.

Carole Frazer mumbled again, faintly complaining. She was as drunk as Bacchus. He ignored her until she said, "It's cold out here. I'm cold. What's the matter with you? I don't–"

He clipped her once, behind the left ear, with his fist, just as I started to get up in a hurry. I had the Magnum in my hand.

"Need some help with your package?" I said. "Kind of heavy for one man to get over the rail."

The gun meant nothing to him. He cried out once, hoarsely, and came for me. The big Magnum could have ripped a hole the size of a saucer in him, but I didn't fire. When you get trigger happy you're not long for my line of work, despite any evidence to the contrary on TV.

Stanley lunged as a bull lunges, horns and head down, going for the muleta. I took his head in chancery under my arm, and his weight slammed us both against the wall. I jarred him loose. I was stiff from my long vigil, and he was fighting for his life. What I'd seen was attempted murder, and he knew it. He butted me. My teeth clicked and my head jolted the wall a second time. He stepped back, almost gracefully, and kicked me in the gut. Right around there I began to wish I had used the gun.

But by then it was too late. We hit the deck together, Stanley on top, me trying my best to remember how to breathe and Stanley clamping a hand like a Stilson wrench on my right wrist so I couldn't use the Magnum. I cuffed his head, somewhat indolently, with my left hand. He cuffed mine, harder, with his right. I tasted blood in my mouth. At least I had begun to breathe again, and that was something.

All of a sudden the Magnum went off. The big slug hit the window of Carole Frazer's stateroom, and glass crashed down all around us. I judo-chopped the side of Stanley's neck. His weight left me as he went over sideways. I got up before he did, but not by much. His eyes were wild. He knew that shot was going to bring company.

He swung a right that sailed past my ear, and I hooked a left that hit bone somewhere on his face. He dropped to his knees and got up and dropped to them again.

I heard footsteps pounding up the metal staircase . Stanley heard them too. Two faces and two white, black-visored caps appeared. Stanley did not try to get up again right away. There was a dark and glistening stain on the deck below him. He stared down at it, fascinated. He touched his throat. Blood pumped, welling through his fingers.

The two ship's officers saw the gun in my hand and remained where they were.

A shard of flying glass had hit Stanley in the throat. The way the blood pumped, an artery had to be severed.

"There a doctor aboard?" I said, going to Stanley. "This man needs help in a hurry."

But he got to his feet and backed away from me. Who knows what a guy will do when he's little drunk, and half-crazy with fear, and in danger of bleeding to death?

"Keep away from me," he said.

"You crazy? You won't last ten minutes bleeding like that."

Smiling faintly he said, "I'm afraid I wouldn't come on very well as a convict, old boy."

Then he took a single step to the rail and went over.

They stopped the ship. They always do, but it rarely helps. We covered another mile, and turned sharp to port, and came back. Three life-preservers were floating in the water, where the ship's officers had thrown them. But Philip Stanley was gone.

On deck after lunch and after I'd made and signed a deposition for the *Hellas'* captain, Spinner said: "I don't get it. You think I'm nuts or something? There was this little swifty in Vomero. I know there was."

"Sure," I said. "Stanley hired him, but his job ended in Vomero."

"Stanley hired him?"

"To make you think you'd hired yourself a killer. If your wife had disappeared during the crossing, you'd have kept your mouth shut about the possibility of foul play if you thought your own man had done it."

"Why did Stanley want her dead?" Skinner squealed.

"Because the picture was more important to him. He got scared they'd never finish it, the way Carole was carrying on." I lit a cigarette. "Hell, he told me last night how he wanted Carole's understudy to take over. She almost did."

Carole Frazer joined us on deck. She was wearing a bikini and stretched out languidly in the bright, hot sun. She didn't look at all like a girl who'd almost been murdered a few hours ago.

"Watch the sun," Spinner warned her. "La Lucrezia's pale, baby." He sighed. "That is, if you're gonna do the picture after what you been through."

"Do it?" Carole asked sleepily. "But of course I'll do it, darling. The publicity will be marvelous."

It was, and after our night aboard the *Hellas*, Carole Frazer settled down to work. They made *Lucrezia Borgia* with a new leading man. Carole Frazer's up for an Oscar.

EDWARD D. HOCH
(b.1930)

The Other Eye
(Al Darlan)

The day started poorly with the arrival of the morning mail. The only first-class letter was a reminder from my landlord that the office rent was overdue. I was wondering what to do about it when Mike Trapper walked through the partly open doorway.

"Pardon me, are you Al Darlan?"

He was tall and blond and young–young enough to be my son. "That's me," I admitted. "Al Darlan Investigations, just like the sign says. What can I do for you?"

"I'm looking for a job. I want to learn the private detective business."

"Afraid I'm not taking on any help this week, kid."

He sat down without being asked, and slipped off his sports jacket. The office was muggy with late July heat. "Look, I'm just out of college, and I've got a little money saved up. I don't want a job. I'm looking for a small business I can buy into."

"Buy into?" I frowned and thought of the letter from my landlord. "What's your name, kid?"

"Mike Trapper." He stuck out his hand and I shook it. "I've had four years at Cornell, including a lot of pre-law courses. I was going to enter law school like my dad, but I decided I couldn't take another couple years of classes and books. I'm twenty-two and I want to get started with my life."

"What makes you think you want to be a private investigator?"

"I figure it's the closest thing to the law. You do a lot of work for lawyers, don't you?"

"Occasionally," I admitted. "But there's nothing glamorous about this work. If you've been stuffing your head with books about California private eyes, let me tell you—"

"I know."

"It's not even messy divorce cases anymore. Nobody needs a private detective to win a divorce case in this state. It's staking out department stores to catch some employee going out the back door with a camera or a couple of shirts. It's chasing after some kid who's been kidnapped by its father after the mother won custody in a divorce case. It's maybe even doing an illegal telephone tap for some guy who doesn't trust his business partner."

"I know," he repeated.

"And you still want to do it?"

"Sure."

"I've got a small operation here."

"That's why I picked it. I can't afford to start big."

"There's not even a secretary right now. I had to let her go."

"How much would it cost me to buy in for, say, a third of the business?"

"I'd have to think about that. I can't rush into this."

"Ten thousand is all the money I could afford to invest."

"Where'd a college kid manage to save ten thousand?"

"Here and there. My dad said he'd stake me to part of it."

I sighed and scratched my head. "Look, Mike, I've got to level with you. There's not even enough business here to keep one person busy. The one-man private agency is a thing of the past. I outlived my profession. Go down to one of the big outfits and start out working on insurance cases. They always need smart young kids like you."

"I don't want that, Mr. Darlan. I want a place like this."

"There's no liquor in the desk drawer. And I keep my gun in that big iron safe most of the time. I just turned fifty years old—"

"Ten thousand dollars, Mr. Darlan. Will it buy me a third of the business?"

I looked over at the dirty window and the dusty bookshelves and wondered what the hell I was letting myself in for. Was I just going to pull this kid into bankruptcy with me?

"Maybe a quarter of the business," I said quietly.

And so it happened.

A week later he moved in, and I had a sign painter change the lettering on the door to read *Darlan & Trapper, Investigations.*

"Looks good, doesn't it?" he asked, seeing it for the first time.

"Not bad," I admitted. "I used some of your money to spruce up the office a bit, and to get you a good used desk. And I took out a small announcement ad on the business page of the morning newspaper. That might bring us in something."

He looked over the desk and tried the chair. "I guess I'll need a typewriter too, for letters and reports."

I was about to suggest he could use mine, but that didn't seem right on his first day. "I'll rent you one for a month, till we can find a good one to buy."

"Swell."

"Your dad coming by to see the office?" I asked casually.

"Uh, no—not right away. He wanted to, but I thought he should wait awhile till we get settled."

"That's probably best," I agreed.

I set to work on the telephone trying to drum up business then, because I couldn't have the two of us sitting around doing nothing all day. I got lucky on the third phone call, to one of the big agencies. Some of their people were on vacation, and they were farming out a few routine insurance jobs. I told them my new partner Mike Trapper would be right over.

He was gone all afternoon and hadn't returned by the time I locked up the office a little before six. At the bar around the corner where I often stopped for a drink, I ran into Sergeant O'Keefe from Headquarters. We'd been casual friends for years, and as he slipped on to the stool next to me he said, "I hear you got yourself a partner, Al."

"Yeah, kid just out of college. Wants to learn the business. I was down yesterday and got him a license."

"Who in hell'd want to be a private eye these days? Does he think he'll get rich?"

"Family's got money. Maybe the pay doesn't matter to him."

"What's his name?"

I took a sip of Scotch. "Mike Trapper. You'll probably see a request for a gun permit come through for him."

O'Keefe patted my shoulder. "Hell, Al, maybe it's a good thing. Maybe it's like having a son to carry on the business."

"Yeah."

The next morning I had to wind up some business on a shoplifting case. After that, on my way down to the office, I stopped by a gun shop and picked out a fiveshot Smith & Wesson caliber .38 Terrier.

I told the clerk to put it aside, that we'd be in with the permit in a day or two. I figured if the kid invested ten grand in my business I could afford to buy him his first gun.

When I reached the office I was surprised to see the door standing open. Mike Trapper was inside at his desk, over in the opposite corner from mine. But he wasn't alone. A tall white-haired man occupied the visitor's chair. Mike jumped up as I entered.

"Al, we have a client! This is Craig Winton; Al Darlan. I met Mr. Winton over at the insurance office. He has a perplexing problem and he thinks we can help him."

Craig Winton's handshake was firm, and his eyes reflected a shrewd intelligence I'd often noticed in successful middle-aged businessmen. "A pleasure to meet you, Mr. Darlan. Your young partner here impressed me at the office this morning. I decided your firm might be able to help me with an annoying situation." He glanced around at the big single room as he spoke, and I feared for a moment that the kid had oversold us.

"We're hoping to move to larger quarters soon," I explained. "My secretary is on vacation, but when she returns we'll be moving to a suite of offices on the fifth floor."

His cool eyes studied me and he smiled slightly. "I chose your agency because I wanted a small outfit. Our insurance firm deals routinely with the larger agencies in fraud investigations. I know those people, and I don't want them involved in my personal affairs. It wouldn't be good for our future business relationship."

"I understand completely," I said. "What's the nature of your problem, Mr. Winton?"

"I explained it to Mike on the way over. Someone seems to be impersonating me. It started about three months ago when I flew to Las Vegas for a convention. The clerk at the hotel insisted I'd arrived a day earlier, stayed one night, and then checked out that morning. I considered it a foolish mix-up, and didn't think too much about it. But a month later there was a similar occurrence. This imposter or double actually showed up at a meeting where I was to speak. Several people saw him, but he disappeared just before the time of my arrival."

"Have you reported this to the police?" I asked.

"There's been nothing to report. The imposter has committed no crime, and in fact has shown no attempt to harm me in any way. And yet—"

"There must have been more recent instances," I said. "The last one you mentioned was two months ago. What caused you to act now?"

"I suppose it's that the appearances of this phantom double are becoming more personal all the time. Last month, while I was out of the office for lunch, he actually walked past my secretary, entered my private office, and remained there for five minutes. When I returned from lunch she asked me what I'd come back for. Believe me, I was prepared to call the police that time! But though no my desk had been disturbed, nothing was missing."

"What did you tell your secretary?"

"I insisted it hadn't been me. She dropped the subject, probably thinking I'd had too many luncheon martinis."

"And the latest appearance?"

Craig Winton gave me another of his tired smiles. "Yes, there was one just yesterday. You may have guessed that's why I'm acting today. My wife saw him in our garage yesterday morning, after I'd left for the office. She thought it was me."

"Did he speak to her?"

"Yes. He muttered something about forgetting his briefcase. Then he left before she could get a good look at him. She phoned me later at the office and asked if I was all right."

"And you told her about this double?"

"I told her the whole story last night for the first time. She insisted I go to the police with it. We finally compromised, and I agreed to hire a private detective."

Mike Trapper shook his head. "Weird, isn't it, Al?"

"Strange," I agreed. "And just a bit menacing. You're aware of the pattern in all this, of course."

"Pattern?" the kid asked, but Craig Winton gave a little nod. He knew what I meant.

"Yes. The first time he appeared, the double was seen only by a hotel clerk who didn't know me. The second time he was seen by some casual business associates who knew me slightly. The third time my secretary saw him. And the fourth time my wife saw him."

"It's leading up to the grand finale," I said. "The next time you'll see him."

"I read a story in college about a doppelganger," Mike said. "That's German for a sort of ghostly double. When someone sees his own doppelganger it's supposed to kill him."

I picked up a pad and started making some notes. "Do you have a weak heart, Mr. Winton?"

He shook his head. "Strong as an ox. I have a checkup every year."

"So we can assume no one's trying to scare you to death. What about a twin? Do you have any brothers?"

"Only a sister living out west. You can be sure there's no secret twin hiding someplace."

I turned to the kid. "You want to work on this, Mike?"

"I sure do!"

"All right." I pulled a figure out of the air and told Winton how much we charged per day, plus expenses. He didn't bat an eye, and I wished I'd made it higher. "I want you to give Mike here a schedule of everything you'll be doing for the next week. Every business meeting, every luncheon or dinner engagement, even social events with your wife. Mike's going to be one step ahead of you, and sometimes one step behind you. Meanwhile, I'll do some investigating on my own."

Craig Winton got to his feet and shook hands once more. "I believe I'm in competent hands. You've taken a load off my mind already."

"We'll want to speak with Mrs. Winton, and possibly with your secretary as well."

"Go right ahead."

After he'd gone, Mike Trapper was beaming with pleasure. "I got us a client, Al! The first real client for Darlan and Trapper!"

"That was good work. I couldn't have done better myself." I meant it, yet I was puzzled as to why a man like Winton would have chosen a kid he'd never met before. I'd listened to his explanation about wanting a small agency and it made sense. And yet—

"You don't really think it's a ghost, do you? A doppelganger sort of thing?"

"I stopped believing in ghosts a long time ago. For one thing, they've got no money to pay my bills."

In the morning we drove out to the suburbs and visited Rina Winton. Somehow I wasn't surprised when she turned out to be a curly-haired blond at least twenty years younger than her husband. Divorce and remarriage to a younger woman seemed to go with success in the executive suite these days.

"What can you tell us about this man who impersonated your husband, Mrs. Winton?"

Though I asked the question, her eyes were all over Mike, like she was undressing him while we talked. "Frankly, Mr. Darlan, I don't know what to think. We only have one car right now and we're not planning to get a second one till fall, so I'm pretty much tied down to the house when Craig is at work. The other morning after Craig drove off to the office I heard a noise in the garage. I went out there and saw someone I thought was Craig."

"Did he speak to you?"

"He muttered something about forgetting his briefcase and then went out again. But our car wasn't in the driveway. He simply walked down the road. I phoned his office later and he said it wasn't him. You know the rest. I insisted he hire a detective."

"Was Craig married before?"

"Yes. He was divorced five years ago."

"Any chance his first wife bears a grudge?"

"Why should she? He certainly made a generous settlement!"

"Is she here in the city?"

"No, she moved to Arizona after the divorce. There were no children." Her eyes kept shifting to Mike, and she asked him, "Don't you have any questions for me?"

He blushed and said, "Al is handling it pretty well."

As she saw us to the door she asked, "Is my husband in danger?"

"Possibly. We're checking out every angle."

We left her standing in the doorway of the fashionable ranch home and drove back to the city. "She seems quite nice," Mike commented.

"Watch yourself, kid. That kind could eat you alive."

"I just meant—"

"I know. Look, I've got a surprise for you on the way back."

"What sort of surprise?"

"You'll see."

I took him to the gun shop and produced the permit he'd signed for the police. The clerk handed over the .38 Terrier and I thought Mike's eyes would pop out of his head. "This is mine?" he asked.

"Yeah. A little gift. Do you want a shoulder or belt holster for it?"

"I don't know. What do you think?"

"A belt holster's a lot cooler in the summer."

"Sounds good to me."

"I've arranged with Sergeant O'Keefe for you to use the police pistol range for practice."

As we left the gun shop he said, "We make a pretty good team, don't we?"

"Not bad. I'll tell you better when we see what happens with the Winton case."

Later that afternoon I took him to the bar around the corner for a drink. "You ever been married, Al?" he asked me.

"Yeah, when I was a kid about your age."

"What happened?"

I shrugged. "Nothing. I guess kids today are smarter to live together. One day we just decided to call it quits."

"Have you got any family?"

"Parents are both dead. I've got a sister who sends me Christmas cards."

"Isn't it sort of lonely? Didn't you ever want to get married again?"

"Sure, kid." I gave him a smile. "Maybe I will some day."

"What about the Winton case? What should I do?"

I pulled out a copy of Craig Winton's schedule. "Cover him like we discussed. Look for anyone who resembles him and is dressed like him. Meanwhile I'll go talk to his secretary."

I did that the next day but I didn't learn much. Winton was a middle-level executive with the insurance company and she was a middle-level secretary. Her name was Milly Scorese and she was a fortyish redhead, a bit overweight. When I mentioned it, she remembered the month-old incident. "Oh, yes. Mr. Winton seemed quite disturbed by it."

"Did the man speak to you at all?"

"No. He entered through that private door and went right into Mr. Winton's office."

"So no one else saw him?"

"No."

"Did you get a good look at him?"

"Well," she admitted, "more at his clothes than at him. He went by my desk so fast I just got a glimpse of the pink sports jacket Mr. Winton was wearing that day. But I certainly thought it was him. When he left a few minutes later it looked like him from the rear. But he didn't speak."

I gave her a smile. "Thanks, Milly. Look, here's my card. If anything unusual like that happens again, call me right away."

"I'll help any way I can. Mr. Winton told me to cooperate."

On my way out of the office I thought I saw Winton ahead of me, getting on the elevator. I hurried to catch up, but it wasn't him. I decided there were a lot of tall white-haired men in the business world.

The case dragged on for a couple of weeks without noticeable progress. I saw Mike Trapper only during the hours when Winton was safely in his office with no plans to leave. The rest of the time Mike was watching the Winton home, or shadowing him at business meetings. Once, when Winton flew to New York, the kid went ahead on an earlier flight and was at the airport to pick up the trail when our client landed.

But there was no sign of the double.

"Maybe only Winton can see him," Mike speculated one evening after he'd trailed him home.

"You're back to your doppelgangers again."

"I just like to consider all the possibilities." He had a sudden thought. "Hey, my dad's in town tonight and I'm meeting him for a late dinner. Come along with us! I know he's been wanting to meet you."

"Well, it's sort of short notice," I replied.

"Come on! He'll love it!"

James Trapper was a stout friendly man who wore thick glasses and a checked vest. "I never imagined Mike would end up the partner in a detective agency," he admitted. "How's he doing, Mr. Darlan?"

"He's learning."

"Had any good murder cases yet?"

I laughed. "I haven't had a case involving murder in four years. They don't come along every week, despite what you see on TV."

Dinner was pleasant, and somehow they made me feel like part of the family. It was a good feeling. At one point James Trapper said, "Mike's always had an eye for the ladies. You've probably noticed that already."

"I've noticed they have an eye for him," I said, remembering our client's wife. "But I keep him pretty busy."

As we were leaving the restaurant Mike asked me, "How long we going to keep on with this Winton case?"

"As long as he pays us. Speaking of Winton, I have an appointment to meet with one of the vice-presidents at his insurance company tomorrow morning. I'll let you know if I learn anything. What's Winton's schedule?"

"Routine during the day, but he has a Civic Club meeting in the evening, out at the Expressway Motel."

I nodded. "I'll check with you tomorrow. It's been better than two weeks. The double might be getting ready to show himself again."

James Trapper shook my hand at the car. "It's been a pleasure, Mr. Darlan."

"Please call me Al."

"I know my son is in good hands, Al."

"I hope so."

The next morning I met with Isaac Rath in the executive suite of Winton's company. He was a balding man in his sixties, with brown spots on the backs of his hands. He frowned at me and said, "I don't quite understand the reason for this meeting, Mr. Darlan."

"Craig Winton has hired me about a personal matter. I'd be interested in anything you could tell me about him."

Isaac Rath touched the tips of his fingers together. "Craig is one of the finest executives. He runs our investments division and has full authority over a good share of company funds."

"I know that much already. I guess what I'm getting at is this. Would it be possible for someone impersonating Winton to get his hands on any large amount of company money?"

"Impersonating–? I don't understand."

I tried to make it simple. "Could Craig Winton, or someone pretending to be Craig Winton, steal any money from this company?"

"Well, of course! He could divert investments into phoney accounts. He could–"

"Thank you, Mr. Rath. That's all I wanted to know."

I went back to the office and waited for the kid to call in. I waited all afternoon and never heard from him. Finally I went home to my apartment, hoping nothing was wrong. It was after dark, around ten o'clock, when the phone finally rang.

"Al?"

"Mike! Where in hell are you?"

"At the Expressway Motel." His voice sounded awful. "Al, could you get out here fast? Craig Winton's dead. Somebody shot him in the parking lot."

"OK, kid. Are the cops there?"

"I just called them."

"I'll be along."

I had to drive through downtown anyway, so I went up to the office for just a minute. I got my revolver out of the old iron safe.

A ring of police cars had their spotlights trained on the body as I walked up. The police photograper was snapping pictures and Sergeant O'Keefe was standing off to one side. I got near enough to see that Winton had been shot at least once in the center of the chest. Then I went over to O'Keefe.

"That was your client?" he asked, looking up from his notebook. "His wife's driving down to make an official identification."

"Yeah. Where's the kid?"

"Trapper? Inside with one of my boys. His story is that he was waiting in his car for Winton to leave the meeting. Apparently Winton decided to leave early, before the meeting broke up. Trapper didn't see him, but he heard a shot. He found Winton dead between a couple of parked cars, with no one else around."

"I want to see him," I said. "Now."

O'Keefe led me into the motel. Mike was seated in a corner of the lobby with one of the detectives. He looked terrible. O'Keefe motioned his man away and let me have a few words alone with the kid.

"Look," I said, "first of all, it's not your fault. There's nothing you could have done."

He looked like he was going to cry. "I bungled it, Al. And now he's dead!"

"Tell me everything that happened, right from the beginning.

When's the last time you saw him alive?"

"When he drove his car up to the motel and went inside."

"How come you didn't check in with me this afternoon?"

He looked edgy. "I was out at Winton's house for a while, seeing if his wife had any new information."

"All right," I said with a sigh. "What happened tonight?"

"I scouted the area before Winton drove up. There was no sign of a double or anything else out of whack. He parked the car and went into his meeting. I already knew it wouldn't be over till ten o'clock so I sat in the car playing the radio. Once the meeting started I didn't notice anyone else in the parking lot at all. Winton had gone in the motel's front entrance and I figured he'd come out the same way. But he came out the side door instead. The first thing I knew, I heard a shot. I got out of the car and ran over and found him lying out there between the cars."

"There was no sign of anyone else?"

He shook his head. "I called the police, and then I phoned you. I didn't know what to do."

I had an empty feeling in the pit of my stomach. "Kid," I said quietly, "let me have your gun."

"What?"

"If you didn't see Winton before he was shot, how'd you know he came out the side door?"

"I—"

"Come on, give me your gun."

He froze then, staring at me with that terrible expression on his face, and I wondered what I would do if he resisted. My fingers were only inches from my gun, but I knew I couldn't shoot him any more than I could have shot my own son.

His shoulders slumped and he pulled the revolver from its belt holster. I took it and opened the cylinder. All five chambers were loaded but I could catch the unmistakable scent of gunpowder in the barrel. It had been fired recently. "You killed him, didn't you, kid?"

He couldn't meet my eyes. "Yeah," he said huskily, close to tears. "I killed him."

I put my hand on his shoulder. "Was it that wife of his, Mike?"

He raised his head then. "Is that what you think? She had nothing to do with it! I was watching for the double and Winton came out the wrong door, a half hour early. I called to him and he acted funny, started going the other way. When I went after him he pulled out something that looked like a gun. I panicked and shot him."

"Why didn't you tell the police that?"

"Because I was scared when I saw that I'd killed the real Winton.

The police didn't find any weapon by the body and I knew I'd made a terrible mistake. Don't you realize that?"

I realized it. I realized I'd have to phone his dad and tell him what had happened. He'd been too fast to pull a trigger, and we were both going to pay for it.

I walked over and handed the gun to O'Keefe. "Here's your murder weapon," I said. "The kid's ready to tell the truth now. For God's sake, go easy on him."

I didn't go home that night. Instead I went back to the office and sat in my swivel chair staring out at the city. I wanted to go down to Headquarters just to be near him, but I knew there was nothing I could do for him now. After a long time I fell asleep in my chair, and when I woke up it was morning.

I drove through the streets only beginning to come awake, not knowing at first just where I was headed. I passed out of downtown, away from the jail where they'd be holding Mike until his dad came up with the bail money. I just drove.

After a while it came to me where I was headed. Maybe I'd known all along. The suburban traffic was all headed into the city as the morning rush hour began, and I made good time going against the stream. It was just eight o'clock when I pulled into the driveway of the Winton ranch home. Craig Winton's car was in the garage.

It took me five minutes of ringing the doorbell before she'd answer. When she finally came she was wearing a rumpled T-shirt and faded jeans, looking like she was dead instead of her husband.

"God, what is it? What do you want? Haven't you done enough to us already?"

"I'd like to come in, Mrs. Winton. It's very important."

She seemed ready to bar my way, but finally she stepped aside. "You'll have to forgive me," she said, passing a hand over her eyes. "I took a sleeping pill and I just woke up."

"I'm sorry about what happened to your husband."

"Is it true that Mike Trapper killed him?"

"I'm afraid so."

"He was just here yesterday asking more questions. He was really trying to help us. How could he have killed Craig?"

"I drove out here to ask the same question." I'd followed her into the kitchen and taken a chair across the table from her.

"Do you want some coffee?"

"That would be fine." She rose to make it and I continued, "Your husband's death still leaves the problem of the double unresolved."

"It hardly matters now. Just send me your bill."

"It's not as simple as that."

"Why not?"

"There wasn't any double, was there, Mrs. Winton? It was Craig Winton all the time."

She turned from the coffee percolator. "I don't know what you're talking about."

"It was a scheme of Craig's to embezzle money from his company, and a clever scheme at that. He created a double who made a few appearances. He even hired a two-bit private detective agency to find the double. Last night was to be a key element of his plan. Mike Trapper would testify to having seen the double. He'd know it wasn't our client because the double would run from him and even draw a gun. Unfortunately for Craig Winton, he didn't know that a nervous kid like Mike, investigating his first case, would shoot and kill him."

"That's guesswork." She poured two cups of coffee.

"Not entirely," I said. "Craig's secretary, Milly, told me the double didn't speak to her. At first this made sense but then I remembered the supposed double had spoken to you in the garage here. If his voice could fool you it could certainly fool his secretary. Yet he hurried in and out of the office, giving Milly only a glimpse. It didn't sound like a true impersonation to me. It sounded like someone trying to fake an impersonation. The same goes for the two earlier events. Craig made a fuss at the hotel and at the meeting just so the incidents would be remembered."

"It still could have been a double."

"Then consider this. That day at the office Milly saw the supposed double wearing a pink sports jacket like Craig's. And obviously he was wearing the same clothes as Craig that day in the garage. Duplicating those clothes–the correct clothes for each day–would be next to impossible, unless you believe in the supernatural. Either the double had prior knowledge of each day's costume, or there was no double. Either way Craig had to be involved in the plot."

"I don't know a thing about that," she insisted.

"I believe you do, Mrs. Winton. You were there last night when Mike shot your husband in the parking lot."

"What? That's insane!"

"Is it? The first time I spoke to you I learned the two of you had only one car, and didn't plan to buy another one till fall. Mike saw Winton drive up to the motel in that car last night, yet the police made no mention of the car later. O'Keefe even told me you were driving over to identify the body. And the car is sitting in your garage right now. How did it get from the motel parking lot back to this house before the police called, unless you were there to drive it back?"

"I–"

"Mike said he saw a gun in Winton's hand, yet by the time the police arrived there was no sign of one. That's one reason the kid tried to lie about the shooting. I think you saw it all from nearby. When Mike ran into the motel to phone the police and me, you hurried over to the body, picked up the gun, and drove the car home. You didn't want the police finding the gun and guessing this double business had been part of an embezzlement scheme. And you had to take the car because you couldn't risk a cab driver identifying you later. And you had to be home before the police called."

"All right," she said quietly. The fight had gone out of her.

"You admit you took the gun?"

"It was only a starter's pistol. Craig wasn't going to harm anyone. He simply wanted your partner's testimony that a double existed. He'd been manipulating his company's money for years, ever since that big divorce settlement took all his cash. He tried to create a double who could be blamed for unauthorized bank withdrawals and other shady business. It was a far-fetched scheme, but it would have been enough to raise a reasonable doubt in any jury's mind."

"What about the car?"

"I took a cab to the motel hours earlier for just that purpose. After Mike saw him Craig planned to jump in a cab and get away. While Mike was chasing him I was to drive the car home, as if Craig had come out of his meeting and left with it. When Mike returned to the lot and found Craig's car gone, it would be extra proof there must be two Craig Wintons."

I finished my coffee. "Mike's in jail and you're the only one who can get him out. I want you to come with me and tell all this to the police."

"Is he that important to you?"

"I guess he is. I want him out."

Our eyes met for just an instant. She may have been trying to tell me something, to offer me something, but we both knew it was useless.

She picked up her purse and I followed her out to the car.

STUART M. KAMINSKY
(b.1934)

Busted Blossoms
(Toby Peters)

Darkness. I couldn't see, but I could hear someone shouting at me about Adolf Hitler. I opened my eyes. I still couldn't see. Panic set in before memory told me where I was. I pushed away the jacket covering my head. After a good breath of stale air, I realized where I was, who I was, and what I was doing there.

It was 1938, February, a cool Sunday night in Los Angeles, and I was Toby Peters, a private investigator who had been hired to keep an eye on a washed-up movie director who had come in from out of town and picked up a few death threats. I was getting fifteen dollars a day, for which I was expected to stay near the target and put myself in harm's way if trouble came up. I was not being paid to fall asleep.

My mouth tasted like ragweed pollen. I reached over to turn off the radio. When I had put my head back to rest on the bed and pulled my suede zipped jacket over me, Jeanette MacDonald had been singing about Southern moons. I woke up to the news that Reichsführer Hitler had proclaimed himself chief of national defense and had promoted Hermann Wilhelm Göring, minister of aviation, to field marshal. I was just standing when the door opened and D. W. Griffith walked in.

"Mr. Peters," he said, his voice deep, his back straight, and, even across the room, his breath dispensing the Kentucky fumes of bourbon.

"I was on my way down," I said. "I was listening to the news."

Griffith eyed me from over his massive hawk of a nose. He was about five-ten, maybe an inch or so taller than me, though I guessed he weighed about 180, maybe twenty pounds more than I did. We both seemed to be in about the same shape, which says something good for him or bad for me. I was forty-one, and he was over sixty. He was wearing a black suit over a white shirt and thin black tie.

"I have something to tell you," Griffith said.

So, I was canned. It had happened before, and I had a double sawbuck in my wallet.

"I really was coming down," I said, trying to get some feeling in my tongue.

"You were not," Griffith said emphatically. "But that is of little consequence. A man has been murdered."

"Murdered?" I repeated.

I am not the most sophisticated sight even when I'm combed, shaved, and operating on a full stomach. My face is dark and my nose mush, not from business contacts, but from an older brother who every once in a while thought I needed redefinition. I sold that tough look to people who wanted a bodyguard. Most of my work was for second-rate clothing stores that had too much shoplifting, hard-working bookies whose wives had gone for Chiclets and never came back, and old ladies who had lost their cats, who were always named Sheiba. That's what I usually did, but once in a while I spent a night or a few days protecting movie people who got themselves threatened or were afraid of getting crushed in a crowd. D.W. had no such fears. No one was looking for his autograph anymore. No one was hiring him. He seemed to have plenty of money and a lot of hope; that was why he had driven up from Louisville. He hoped someone would pick up the phone and call him to direct a movie, but in the week I had worked for him, no one had called, except the guy who threatened to lynch him with a Ku Klux Klan robe. D.W. had explained that such threats had not been unusual during the past two decades since the release of *Birth of a Nation*, which had presented the glories of the Ku Klux Klan. D.W. had tried to cover his prejudice with *Intolerance* and a few more films, but the racism of *Birth* wouldn't wash away.

"Mr. Peters." He tried again, his voice now loud enough to be heard clearly in the back row if we were in a Loews theater. "You must rouse yourself. A man has been murdered downstairs."

"Call the police," I said brilliantly.

"We are , you may recall, quite a distance from town," he reminded me. "A call has been placed, but it will be some time before the constabulary arrives."

Constabulary. I was in a time warp. But that was the way I had felt since meeting Griffith, who now touched his gray sideburns as if he were about to be photographed for *Click* magazine.

"Who's dead?" I asked.

"Almost everyone of consequence since the dawn of time," Griffith said, opening the door. "In this case, the victim is Jason Sikes. He is sitting at the dinner table with a knife in his neck."

"Who did it?" I began.

"That, I fear, is a mystery," Griffith said. "Now let us get back to the scene."

I walked out the door feeling that I was being ushered from act one to act two. I didn't like the casting. Griffith was directing the whole thing, and I had the feeling he wanted to cast me as the detective. I wanted to tell him that I had been hired to protect his back, not find killers. I get double time for finding killers. But one just didn't argue with Dave Griffith. I slouched ahead of him, scratched an itch on my right arm, and slung my suede jacket over my shoulder so I could at least straighten the wrinkled striped tie I was wearing.

What did I know? That I was in a big house just off the California coast about thirty miles north of San Diego. The house belonged to a producer named Korites, who Griffith hoped would give him a directing job. Korites had gathered his two potential stars, a comic character actor, and a potential backer, Sikes, to meet the great director. I had come as Griffith's "associate." D.W. had left his young wife back at the Roosevelt Hotel in Los Angeles, and we had stopped for drinks twice on the way in his chauffeur-driven Mercedes. In the car Griffith had talked about Kentucky, his father, his mother, who had never seen one of his films–"She did not approve of the stage," he explained–and about his comeback. He had gone on about his youthful adventures as an actor, playwright, boxer, reporter, and construction worker. Then, about ten minutes before we arrived, he had clammed up, closed his eyes, and hadn't said another word.

Now we were going silently down the stairs of the house of Marty Korites, stepping into a dining room, and facing five well-dressed diners, one of whom lay with his face in a plate of Waldorf salad with a knife in his back.

The diners looked up when we came in. Korites, a bald, jowly man with Harold Lloyd glasses, was about fifty and looked every bit of it and more. His eyes had been resting angrily on the dead guest, but they shot up to us as we entered the room. On one side of the dead guy was a woman, Denise Giles, skinny as ticker tape, pretty, dark, who knows what age. I couldn't even tell from the freckles on her bare shoulders. On the other side of the dead guy was an actor named James Vann, who looked like the lead in a road-show musical, blond, young, starched, and confused. He needed someone to feed him lines. Griffith was staring at the corpse. The great director looked puzzled. The last guest sat opposite the dead man. I knew him, too, Lew Dollard, a frizzy-haired comedian turned character actor who was Marty Korites' top name, which gives you an idea of how small an operator Marty was and what little hope Griffith had if he had traveled all the way here in the hope of getting a job from him.

"Mr. Griffith says you're a detective, not a film guy," Korites said, his eyes moving from the body to me for an instant and then back to the body. I guessed he didn't want the dead guy to get away when he wasn't looking.

"Yeah, I'm a detective," I said. "But I don't do windows and I don't do corpses."

Dollard, the roly-poly New York street comic in a rumpled suit, looked up at me.

"A comedy writer," he said with a smile showing big teeth. I had seen one of Dollard's movies. He wasn't funny.

"Someone killed Sikes," Korites said with irritation.

"Before the main course was served, too," I said. "Some people have no sense of timing. Look. Why don't we just sit still, have a drink or two, and wait till the police get here. We can pass the time by your telling me how someone can get killed at the dinner table and all of you not know who did it. That must have been some chicken liver appetizer."

"It was," said Griffith, holding his open palm toward the dead man, "like a moment of filmic chicanery, a magic moment from Méliès. I was sipping an aperitif and had turned to Miss Giles to answer a question. And then, a sound, a groan. I turned, and there sat Mr. Sikes."

We all looked at Sikes, His face was still in the salad.

"Who saw what happened?" I asked.

They all looked up from the corpse and at each other. Then they looked at me. Dollard had a cheek full of something and a silly grin on his face. He shrugged.

"A man gets murdered with the lights on with all of you at the table and no one knows who did it?" I asked. "That's a little hard to believe. Who was standing up?"

"No one," said Vann, looking at me unblinking.

"No one," agreed Griffith.

There was no window behind the body. One door to the room was facing the dead man. The other door was to his right. The knife

couldn't have been thrown from either door and landed in his back.
The hell with it. I was getting paid to protect Griffith, not find killers.
I'd go through the motions till the real cops got there. I had been
a cop back in Glendale before I went to work for Warner Brothers
as a guard and then went into business on my own. I knew the routine.

"Why don't we go into the living room?" Korites said, starting
to get up and glancing at the corpse. "I could have Mrs. Windless–"

"Sit down," I said. "Mrs. Windless is...?"

"Housekeeper," Korites said. "Cook."

"Was she in here when Sikes was killed?"

I looked around. All heads shook no.

"Anyone leave the room before or after Sikes was killed?" I went on.

"Just Mr. Griffith," said Vann. The woman still hadn't said
anything.

"We stay right here till the police arrive. Anyone needs the toilet,
I go with them, even the dragon lady," I said, trying to get a rise
out of Denise Giles. I got none.

"What about you?" said Dollard, rolling his eyes and gurgling in
a lousy imitation of Bert Lahr.

"I wasn't in the room when Sikes took his dive into the salad,"
I said. "Look, you want to forget the whole thing and talk about
sports? Fine. You hear that Glenn Cunningham won the Wanamaker
mile for the fifth time yesterday?"

"With a time of 4:11," said Denise Giles, taking a small sip of wine
from a thin little glass.

I looked at her with new respect. Griffith had sat down at the end
of the table, the seat he had obviously been in when murder interrupted the game. Something was on his mind.

"Who was Sikes?" I asked, reaching down for a celery stick.

"A man of means," said Griffith, downing a slug of bourbon.

"A backer," said Korites. "He was thinking of bankrolling a movie
D.W. would direct and I would produce."

"With Vann here and Miss Giles as stars?" I said.

"Right," said Korites.

"Never," said Griffith emphatically.

"You've got no choice here," Korites shouted back. "You take the
project the way we give it to you or we get someone else. Your name's
got some curiosity value, right, but it doesn't bring in any golden
spikes."

"A man of tender compassion," sighed Griffith, looking at me for
understanding. "It was my impression that the late Mr. Sikes had
no intention of supplying any capital. On the contrary, I had the
distinct impression that he felt he was in less than friendly waters

and had only been lured here with the promise of meeting me, the wretched director who had once held the industry in his hand, had once turned pieces of factory-produced celluloid into art. As I recall, Sikes also talked about some financial debt he expected to be paid tonight."

"You recall?" Korites said with sarcasm, shaking his head. "You dreamed it up. You're still back in the damn nineteenth century. Your movies were old-fashioned when you made them. You don't work anymore because you're an anachronism."

"Old-fashioned?" said Griffith with a smile. "Yes, old-fashioned, a romantic, one who respects the past. I would rather die with my Charles Dickens than live with your Hemingway."

Dollard finished whatever he had in his mouth and said, "You think it would be sacrilegious to have the main course? Life goes on."

"Have a celery stick," I suggested.

"I don't want to eat a celery stick," he whined.

"I wasn't suggesting that you put it in your mouth," I said.

This was too much for Dollard. He stood up, pushing the chair back.

"I'm the comic here," he said. "Tell him."

He looked around for someone to tell me. The most sympathetic person was Sikes, and he was dead.

"So that's the way it is," Dollard said, looking around the room. "You want me to play second banana."

"This is a murder scene," shouted Korites, taking his glasses off, "not a night club, Lew. Try to remember that." His jowls rumbled as he spoke. He was the boss, but not mine.

"Someone in this room murdered the guy in the salad," I reminded them.

"My father," said Griffith.

"Your father killed Sikes?" I asked, turning to the great director. Griffith's huge nose was at the rim of his almost empty glass. His dark eyes were looking into the remaining amber liquid for an answer.

"My father," he said without looking up, "would have known how to cope with this puzzle. He was a resourceful man, a gentleman, a soldier."

"Mine was a grocer," I said.

"This is ridiculous," said Denise Giles throwing down her napkin.

"Not to Sikes," I said. Just then the door behind me swung open. I turned to see a rail of a woman dressed in black.

"Are you ready for the roast?" she asked.

"Yes," said Dollard.

"No," said Korites, "we're not having any more food."

"I have rights here," Dollard insisted.

Now I had it. This was an Alice in Wonderland nightmare and I was Alice at the Mad Hatter's tea party. We'd all change places in a few seconds and the Dormouse, Sikes, would have to be carried.

"What," demanded Mrs. Windless, "am I to do with the roast?"

"You want the punch line or can I have it?" Dollard said to me.

"Sikes already got the punch line," I reminded him.

Mrs. Windless looked over at Sikes for the first time.

"Oh my God," she screamed. "That man is dead."

"Really?" shouted Dollard leaping up. "Which one?"

"Goddamn it," shouted Korites. "This is serious." His glasses were back on now. He didn't seem to know what to do with them.

Griffith got up and poured himself another drink.

"We know he's dead, Mrs. Windless," Korites said. "The police are on the way. You'll just have to stick all the food in the refrigerator and wait."

"What happened?" Mrs. Windless asked, her voice high, her eyes riveted on Sikes. "Who did this? I don't want anything to do with murder."

"You don't?" said Dollard. "Why didn't you tell us that before we killed him? We did it for you." He crossed his eyes but didn't close them in time to block out the wine thrown in his face by the slinky Denise.

Dollard stood up sputtering and groped for a napkin to wipe his face. Purple tears rolled down his cheeks.

"Damn it," he screamed. "What the hell? What the hell?"

His hand found a napkin. He wiped his eyes. The stains were gone, but there was now a piece of apple from the Waldorf salad on his face.

"Mrs. Windless," said D.W., standing and pointing at the door. "You will depart and tell my driver, Mr. Reynolds, that Mr. Peters and I will be delayed. Mr. Dollard. You will sit down and clean your face. Miss Giles, you will refrain from outbursts, and Mr. Vann, you will attempt to show some animation. It is difficult to tell you from Mr. Sikes. Mr. Peters will continue the inquiry."

Vann stood up now, kicking back his chair. Griffith rose to meet him. They were standing face to face, toe to toe. Vann was about thirty years younger, but Griffith didn't back away.

"You can't tell us what to do. You can't tell anyone what to do. You're washed up," Vann hissed.

"As Bluebeard is rumored to have said," whispered Griffith, "I'm merely between engagements."

"See, see," grouched Dollard, pointing with his fork at the two antagonists. "Everyone's a comic. I ask you."

I sighed and stood up again.

"Sit down," I shouted at Vann and Griffith. The room went silent. The mood was ruined by my stomach growling. But they sat and Mrs. Windless left the room. "Who called the police?"

"I did," said Korites.

"I thought no one left the room but Griffith?" I said.

"Phone is just outside the door, everyone could see me call. I left the door open," Korites said. He pushed his dirty plate away from him and then pulled it back. "What's the difference?"

"Why didn't you all start yelling, panic, accuse each other?" I asked.

"We thought it was one of Jason's practical jokes," said Denise Giles. "He was fond of practical jokes."

"Rubber teeth, joy buzzers, ink in the soup," sighed Dollard. "A real amateur, a putz. Once pretended he was poisoned at a lunch in..."

"Lew," shouted Korites. "Just shut up."

"All right you people," I said. "None of you liked Sikes, is that right?"

"Right," Korites said, "but that's a far cry from one of us..."

"How about hate?" I tried. "Would hate be a good word to apply to your feelings about the late dinner guest?"

"Maybe," said Korites, "there was no secret about that among our friends. I doubt if anyone who knew Jason did anything less than hate him. But none of us murdered him. We couldn't have."

"And yet," Griffith said, "one of you had to have done the deed. In *The Birth of a Nation*–"

"This is death, not birth," hissed Vann. "This isn't a damn movie."

Griffith drew his head back and examined Vann over his beak of a nose.

"Better," said Griffith. "Given time I could possibly motivate you into a passable performance. Even Richard Barthelmess had something to learn from my humble direction."

There was a radio in the corner. Dollard had stood up and turned it on. I didn't stop him. We listened to the radio and watched Sikes and each other while I tried to think. Griffith was drawing something on the white tablecloth with his fork.

Dollard found the news, and we learned that Hirohito had a cold but was getting better, King Farouk of Egypt had just gotten married, Leopold Stokowski was on his way to Italy under an assumed name, probably to visit Greta Garbo, and a guy named Albert Burroughs had been found semi-conscious in a hotel room in Bloomington, Illinois. The room was littered with open cans of peas. Burroughs managed to whisper to the ambulance driver that he had lived on peas for nine days even though he had $77,000 in cash in the room.

I got up and turned off the radio.

"You tell a story like that in a movie," said Korites, "and they say it isn't real."

"If you tell it well, they will believe anything," said Griffith, again doodling on the cloth.

The dinner mess, not to mention Sikes' corpse, was beginning to ruin the party.

"Things are different," Griffith said, looking down at what he had drawn. He lifted a long-fingered hand to wipe out the identations in the tablecloth.

"Things?" I asked, wondering if he was going to tell us tales about his career, his father, or the state of the universe.

"I am an artist of images," he explained, looking up, his eyes moving from me to each of the people around the table. "I kept the entire script of my films, sometimes 1,500 shots, all within my head." He pointed to his head in case we had forgotten where it was located.

"This scene," he went on, "has changed. When I left this room to find Mr. Peters, Mr. Sikes had a knife in his neck, not his back, and it was a somewhat different knife."

"You've had three too many D.W.," Dollard said with a smile.

I got up and examined Sikes. There was no hole in his neck or anywhere else on his body that I could find.

"No cuts, bruises, marks..." I began, and then it hit me. My eyes met Giffith's. I think it hit him at the same moment.

"We'll just wait for the police," Korites said, removing his glasses again.

"Go on Mr. G.," I said. "Let's hear your script."

Griffith stood again, put down his glass, and smiled. He was doing either Abe Lincoln or Sherlock Holmes.

"This scene was played for me," he said. "I was not the director. I was the audience. My ego is not fragile, at least not too fragile to realize that I have witnessed an act. I can see each of you playing your roles, even the late Mr. Sikes. Each of you in an iris, laughing, silently enigmatic, attentive. And then the moment arrives. The audience is distracted by a pretty face in close-up. Then a cut to body, or supposed body, for Sikes was not dead when I left this room to find Mr. Peters."

"Come on..." laughed Dollard.

"Of all..." sighed Denise Giles.

"You're mad..." counterpointed Vann.

But Korites sat silent.

"He wasn't dead," I said again, picking up for Griffith, who seemed to have ended his monologue. All he needed was applause. He looked good, but he had carried the scene as far as he could. It was mine now.

"Let's try this scenario," I said. "Sikes was a practical joker, right?"

"Right," Dollard agreed, "but–"

"What if you all agreed to play a little joke on D.W.? Sikes pretends to be dead with a knife in his neck when Denise distracts Griffith. Sikes can't stick the fake knife in his back. He can't reach his own back. He attaches it to his neck. Then you all discover the body, Griffith comes for me, Sikes laughs. You all laugh, then one of you, probably Korites, moves behind him and uses a real knife to turn the joke into fact. You're all covered. Someone did it. The police would have a hell of a time figuring out which one, and meanwhile, it would make a hell of a news story. Griffith a witness. All of you suspects. Probably wind up with a backer who'd cash in on your morbid celebrity."

"Ridiculous," laughed Korites.

"I was the audience," Griffith repeated with a rueful laugh.

"Even if this were true," said Denise Giles, "you could never prove it."

"Props," I said. "You didn't have time to get rid of that fake knife, at least not to get it hidden too well. D.W. was with me for only a minute or two, and you didn't want to get too far from this room in case we came running back here. No, if we're right, that prop knife is nearby, where it can be found, somewhere in this room or not far from it."

"This is ridiculous," said Vann, standing up. "I'm not staying here for any more of this charade." He took a step toward the door behind Griffith, giving me a good idea of where to start looking for the prop knife, but the director was out of his chair and barring his way.

"Move," shouted Vann.

"Never," cried Griffith.

Vann threw a punch, but Griffith caught it with his left and came back with a right. Vann went down. Korites started to rise, looked at my face, and sat down again.

"We can work something out here," he said, his face going white.

A siren blasted somewhere outside.

"Hell of a practical joke," Dollard said, dropping the radish in his fingers. "Hell of a joke."

No one moved while we waited for the police. We just sat there, Vann on the floor, Griffith standing. I imagined a round iris closing in on the scene, and then a slow fade to black.

LAWRENCE BLOCK
(b.1938)

Out of the Window
(Matt Scudder)

There was nothing special about her last day. She seemed a little jittery, preoccupied with something or with nothing at all. But this was nothing new for Paula.

She was never much of a waitress in the three months she spent at Armstrong's. She'd forget some orders and mix up others, and when you wanted the check or another round of drinks you could go crazy trying to attract her attention. There were days when she walked through her shift like a ghost through walls, and it was as though she had perfected some arcane technique of astral projection, sending her mind out for a walk while her long lean body went on serving food and drinks and wiping down empty tables.

She did make an effort, though. She damn well tried. She could always manage a smile. Sometimes it was the brave smile of the walking wounded and other times it was a tight-jawed, brittle grin with a couple tabs of amphetamine behind it, but you take what you can to get through the days and any smile is better than none at all. She knew most of Armstrong's regulars by name and her greeting always made you feel as though you'd come home. When that's all the home you have, you tend to appreciate that sort of thing.

And if the career wasn't perfect for her, well, it certainly hadn't been what she'd had in mind when she came to New York in the first place. You no more set out to be a waitress in a Ninth Avenue gin mill than you intentionally become an ex-cop coasting through the months on bourbon and coffee. We have that sort of greatness thrust upon us. When you're as young as Paula Wittlauer you hang in there, knowing things are going to get better. When you're my age you just hope they don't get too much worse.

She worked the early shift, noon to eight, Tuesday through Saturday. Trina came on at six so there were two girls on the floor during the dinner rush. At eight Paula would go wherever she went and Trina would keep on bringing cups of coffee and glasses of bourbon for another six hours or so.

Paula's last day was a Thursday in late September. The heat of the summer was starting to break up. There was a cooling rain that morning and the sun never did show its face. I wandered in around four in the afternoon with a copy of the *Post* and read through it while I had my first drink of the day. At eight o'clock I was talking with a couple of nurses from Roosevelt Hospital who wanted to grouse about a resident surgeon with a Messiah complex. I was making sympathetic noises when Paula swept past our table and told me to have a good evening.

I said, "You too, kid." Did I look up? Did we smile at each other? Hell, I don't remember.

"See you tomorrow, Matt."

"Right," I said. "God willing."

But He evidently wasn't. Around three Justin closed up and I went around the block to my hotel. It didn't take long for the coffee and bourbon to cancel each other out. I got into bed and slept.

My hotel is on Fifty-seventh Street between Eighth and Ninth. It's on the uptown side of the block and my window is on the street side looking south. I can see the World Trade Center at the tip of Manhattan from my window.

I can also see Paula's building. It's on the other side of Fifty-seventh Street a hundred yards or so to the east, a towering high-rise that, had it been directly across from me, would have blocked my view of the trade center.

She lived on the seventeenth floor. Sometime after four she went out a high window. She swung out past the sidewalk and landed in the street a few feet from the curb, touching down between a couple of parked cars.

In high school physics they teach you that falling bodies accelerate at a speed of thirty-two feet per second. So she would have fallen thirty-two feet in the first second, another sixty-four feet the next second, then ninety-six feet in the third. Since she fell something like two hundred feet, I don't suppose she could have spent more than four seconds in the actual act of falling.

It must have seemed a lot longer than that.

I got up around ten, ten-thirty. When I stopped at the desk for my mail Vinnie told me they'd had a jumper across the street during the night. "A dame," he said, which is a word you don't hear much anymore. "She went out without a stitch on. You could catch your death that way."

I looked at him.

"Landed in the street, just missed somebody's Caddy. How'd you like to find something like that for a hood ornament? I wonder if your insurance would cover that. What do you call it, act of God?" He came out from behind the desk and walked with me to the door. "Over there," he said, pointing. "The florist's van there is covering the spot where she flopped. Nothing to see anyway. They scooped her up with a spatula and a sponge and then they hosed it all down. By the time I came on duty there wasn't a trace left."

"Who was she?"

"Who knows?"

I had things to do that morning, and as I did them I thought from time to time of the jumper. They're not that rare and they usually do the deed in the hours before dawn. They say it's always darkest then.

Sometime in the early afternoon I was passing Armstrong's and stopped in for a short one. I stood at the bar and looked around to say hello to Paula but she wasn't there. A doughy redhead named Rita was taking her shift.

Dean was behind the bar. I asked him where Paula was. "She skipping school today?"

"You didn't hear?"

"Jimmy fired her?"

He shook his head, and before I could venture any further guesses he told me.

I drank my drink. I had an appointment to see somebody about something, but suddenly it ceased to seem important. I put a dime in the phone and cancelled my appointment and came back and had another drink. My hand was trembling slightly when I picked up the glass. It was a little steadier when I set it down.

I crossed Ninth Avenue and sat in St. Paul's for a while. Ten, twenty minutes. Something like that. I lit a candle for Paula and a few other candles for a few other corpses, and I sat there and thought about life and death and high windows. Around the time I left the

police force I discovered that churches were very good places for thinking about that sort of thing.

After a while I walked over to her building and stood on the pavement in front of it. The florist's truck had moved on and I examined
the street where she'd landed. There was, as Vinnie had assured me,
no trace of what had happened. I tilted my head back and looked
up, wondering what window she might have fallen from, and then
I looked down at the pavement and then up again, and a sudden rush
of vertigo made my head spin. In the course of all this I managed
to attract the attention of the building's doorman and he came out
to the curb anxious to talk about the former tenant. He was a black
man about my age and he looked as proud of his uniform as the guy
in the Marine Corps recruiting poster. It was a good-looking uniform,
shades of brown, epaulets, gleaming brass buttons.

"Terrible thing," he said. "A young girl like that with her whole
life ahead of her."

"Did you know her well?"

He shook his head. "She would give me a smile, always say hello,
always call me by name. Always in a hurry, rushing in, rushing out
again. You wouldn't think she had a care in the world. But you never
know."

"You never do."

"She lived on the seventeenth floor. I wouldn't live that high above
the ground if you gave me the place rent-free."

"Heights bother you?"

I don't know if he heard the question. "I live up one flight of stairs.
That's just fine for me. No elevator and no, no high window." His
brow clouded and he looked on the verge of saying something else,
but then someone started to enter his building's lobby and he moved
to intercept him. I looked up again, trying to count windows to the
seventeenth floor, but the vertigo returned and I gave it up.

"Are you Matthew Scudder?"

I looked up. The girl who'd asked the question was very young,
with long straight brown hair and enormous light brown eyes. Her
face was open and defenseless and her lower lip was quivering. I said
I was Matthew Scudder and pointed at the chair opposite mine. She
remained on her feet.

"I'm Ruth Wittlauer," she said.

The name didn't register until she said, "Paula's sister." Then I
nodded and studied her face for signs of a family resemblance. If they
were there I couldn't find them. It was ten in the evening and Paula
Wittlauer had been dead for eighteen hours and her sister was standing

expectantly before me, her face a curious blend of determination and uncertainty.

I said, "I'm sorry. Won't you sit down? And will you have something to drink?"

"I don't drink."

"Coffee?"

"I've been drinking coffee all day. I'm shaky from all the damn coffee. Do I *have* to order something?"

She was on the edge, all right. I said, "No, of course not. You don't have to order anything." And I caught Trina's eye and warned her off and she nodded shortly and let us alone. I sipped my own coffee and watched Ruth Wittlauer over the brim of the cup.

"You knew my sister, Mr. Scudder."

"In a superficial way, as a customer knows a waitress."

"The police say she killed herself."

"And you don't think so?"

"I know she didn't."

I watched her eyes while she spoke and I was willing to believe she meant what she said. She didn't believe that Paula went out the window of her own accord, not for a moment. Of course, that didn't mean she was right.

"What do you think happened?"

"She was murdered." She made the statement quite matter-of-factly. "I know she was murdered. I think I know who did it."

"Who?"

"Cary McCloud."

"I don't know him."

"But it may have been somebody else," she went on. She lit a cigarette, smoked for a few moments in silence. "I'm pretty sure it was Cary," she said.

"Why?"

"They were living together." She frowned, as if in recognition of the fact that cohabitation was small evidence of murder. "He could do it," she said carefully. "That's why I think he did. I don't think just anyone could commit murder. In the heat of the moment, sure, I guess people fly off the handle, but to do it deliberately and throw someone out of a, out of a, to just deliberately throw someone out of a—"

I put my hand on top of hers. She had long small-boned hands and her skin was cool and dry to the touch. I thought she was going to cry or break or something but she didn't. It was just not going to be possible for her to say the word *window* and she would stall every time she came to it.

"What do the police say?"

"Suicide. They say she killed herself." She drew on the cigarette. "But they don't know her, they never knew her. If Paula wanted to kill herself she would have taken pills. She liked pills."

"I figured she took ups."

"Ups, tranquilizers, ludes, barbiturates. And she liked grass and she liked to drink." She lowered her eyes. My hand was still on top of hers and she looked at our two hands and I removed mine. "I don't do any of those things. I drink coffee, that's my one vice, and I don't even do that much because it makes me jittery. It's the coffee that's making me nervous tonight. Not...all of this."

"Okay."

"She was twenty-four. I'm twenty. Baby sister, square baby sister, except that was always how she *wanted* me to be. She did all these things and at the same time she told me not to do them, that it was a bad scene. I think she kept me straight. I really do. Not so much because of what she was saying as that I looked at the way she was living and what it was doing to her and I didn't want that for myself. I thought it was crazy, what she was doing to herself, but at the same time I guess I worshipped her, she was always my heroine. I loved her, God, I really did, I'm just starting to realize how much, and she's dead and he killed her, I *know* he killed her, I just know it."

After a while I asked her what she wanted me to do.

"You're a detective."

"Not in an official sense. I used to be a cop."

"Could you...find out what happened?"

"I don't know."

"I tried talking to the police. It was like talking to the wall. I can't just turn around and do nothing. Do you understand me?"

"I think so. Suppose I look into it and it still looks like suicide?"

"She didn't kill herself."

"Well, suppose I wind up thinking that she did."

She thought it over. "I still wouldn't have to believe it."

"No," I agreed. "We get to choose what we believe."

"I have some money." She put her purse on the table. "I'm the straight sister, I have an office job, I save money. I have five hundred dollars with me."

"That's too much to carry in this neighborhood."

"Is it enough to hire you?"

I didn't want to take her money. She had five hundred dollars and a dead sister, and parting with one wouldn't bring the other back to life. I'd have worked for nothing but that wouldn't have been good because neither of us would have taken it seriously enough.

And I have rent to pay and two sons to support, and Armstrong's charges for the coffee and the bourbon. I took four fifty-dollar bills from her and told her I'd do my best to earn them.

After Paula Wittlauer hit the pavement, a black-and-white from the Eighteenth Precinct caught the squeal and took charge of the case. One of the cops in the car was a guy named Guzik. I hadn't known him when I was on the force but we'd met since then. I didn't like him and I don't think he cared for me either, but he was reasonably honest and had struck me as competent. I got him on the phone the next morning and offered to buy him a lunch.

We met at an Italian place on Fifty-sixth Street. He had veal and peppers and a couple glasses of red wine. I wasn't hungry but I made myself eat a small steak.

Between bites of veal he said, "The kid sister, huh? I talked to her, you know. She's so clean and so pretty it could break your heart if you let it. And of course she don't want to believe sis did the Dutch act. I asked is she Catholic because then there's the religious angle but that wasn't it. Anyway your average priest'll stretch a point. They're the best lawyers going, the hell, two thousand years of practice, they oughta be good. I took that attitude myself. I said, 'Look, there's all these pills. Let's say your sister had herself some pills and drank a little wine and smoked a little pot and then she went to the window for some fresh air. So she got a little dizzy and maybe she blacked out and most likely she never knew what was happening.' Because there's no question of insurance, Matt, so if she wants to think it's an accident I'm not gonna shout suicide in her ear. But that's what it says in the file."

"You close it out?"

"Sure. No question."

"She thinks murder."

He nodded. "Tell me something I don't know. She says this McCloud killed sis. McCloud's the boyfriend. Thing is he was at an after-hours club at Fifty-third and Twelfth about the time sis was going skydiving."

"You confirm that?"

He shrugged. "It ain't airtight. He was in and out of the place, he coulda doubled back and all, but there was the whole business with the door."

"What business?"

"She didn't tell you? Paula Wittlauer's apartment was locked and the chain bolt was on. The super unlocked the door for us but we had to send him back to the basement for a bolt cutter so's we could get through the chain bolt. You can only fasten the chain bolt from inside and you can only open the door a few inches with it on, so either Wittlauer launched her own self out the window or she was shoved out by Plastic Man, and then he went and slithered out the door without unhooking the chain bolt."

"Or the killer never left the apartment."

"Huh?"

"Did you search the apartment after the super came back and cut the chain for you?"

"We looked around, of course. There was an open window, there was a pile of clothes next to it. You know she went out naked, don't you?"

"Uh-huh."

"There was no burly killer crouching in the shrubbery, if that's what you're getting at."

"You checked the place carefully?"

"We did our job."

"Uh-huh. Look under the bed?"

"It was a platform bed. No crawl space under it."

"Closets?"

He drank some wine, put the glass down hard, glared at me. "What the hell are you getting at? You got reason to believe there was somebody in the apartment when we went in there?"

"Just exploring the possibilities."

"Jesus. You honestly think somebody's gonna be stupid enough to stay in the apartment after shoving her out of it? She musta been on the street ten minutes before we hit the building. If somebody did kill her, which never happened, but if they did they coulda been halfway to Texas by the time we hit the door, and don't that make more sense than jumping in the closet and hiding behind the coats?"

"Unless the killer didn't want to pass the doorman."

"So he's still got the whole building to hide in. Just the one man on the front door is the only security the building's got, anyway, and what does he amount to? And suppose he hides in the apartment and we happen to spot him. Then where is he? With his neck in the noose, that's where he is."

"Except you didn't spot him."

"Because he wasn't there, and when I start seeing little men who aren't there is when I put in my papers and quit the department."

There was an unvoiced challenge in his words. I had quit the department, but not because I'd seen little men. One night some years ago I broke up a bar holdup and went into the street after the pair who'd killed the bartender. One of my shots went wide and a little girl died, and after that I didn't see little men or hear voices, not exactly, but I did leave my wife and kids and quit the force and start drinking on a more serious level. But maybe it all would have happened just that way even if I'd never killed Estrellita Rivera. People go through changes and life does the damnedest things to us all.

"It was just a thought," I said. "The sister thinks it's murder so I was looking for a way for her to be right."

"Forget it."

"I suppose. I wonder why she did it."

"Do they even need a reason? I went in the bathroom and she had a medicine cabinet like a drugstore. Ups, downs, sideways. Maybe she was so stoned she thought she could fly. That would explain her being naked. You don't fly with your clothes on. Everybody knows that."

I nodded. "They find drugs in her system?"

"Drugs in her . . . oh, Jesus, Matt. She came down seventeen flights and she came down fast."

"Under four seconds."

"Huh?"

"Nothing," I said; I didn't bother telling him about high school physics and falling bodies. "No autopsy?"

"Of course not. You've seen jumpers. You were in the department a lot of years, you know what a person looks like after a drop like that. You want to be technical, there coulda been a bullet in her and nobody was gonna go and look for it. Cause of death was falling from a great height. That's what it says and that's what is was, and don't ask me was she stoned or was she pregnant or any of those questions because who the hell knows and who the hell cares, right?"

"How'd you even know it was her?"

"We got a positive ID from the sister."

I shook my head. "I mean how did you know what apartment to go to? She was naked so she didn't have any identification on her. Did the doorman recognize her?"

"You kidding? He wouldn't go close enough to look. He was alongside the building throwing up a few pints of cheap wine. He couldn't have identified his own ass."

"Then how'd you know who she was?"

"The window." I looked at him. "Hers was the only window that was open more than a couple of inches, Matt. Plus her lights were on. That made it easy."

"I didn't think of that."

"Yeah, well, I was there, and we just looked up and there was an open window and a light behind it, and that was the first place we went to. You'da thought of it if you were there."

"I suppose."

He finished his wine, burped delicately against the back of his hand. "It's suicide," he said. "You can tell the sister as much."

"I will. Okay if I look at the apartment?"

"Wittlauer's apartment? We didn't seal it, if that's what you mean. You oughta be able to con the super out of a key."

"Ruth Wittlauer gave me a key."

"Then there you go. There's no department seal on the door. You want to look around?"

"So I can tell the sister I was there."

"Yeah. Maybe you'll come across a suicide note. That's what I was looking for, a note. You turn up something like that and it clears up doubts for the friends and relatives. If it was up to me I'd get a law passed. No suicide without a note."

"Be hard to enforce."

"Simple," he said. "If you don't leave a note you gotta come back and be alive again." He laughed. "That'd start 'em scribbling away. Count on it."

The doorman was the same man I'd talked to the day before. It never occurred to him to ask me my business. I rode up in the elevator and walked along the corridor to 17G. The key Ruth Wittlauer had given me opened the door. There was just the one lock. That's the way it usually is in high-rises. A doorman, however slipshod he may be, endows tenants with a sense of security. The residents of unserviced walk-ups affix three or four extra locks to their doors and still cower behind them.

The apartment had an unfinished air about it, and I sensed that Paula had lived there for a few months without ever making the place her own. There were no rugs on the wood parquet floor. The walls were decorated with a few unframed posters held up by scraps of red Mystik tape. The apartment was an L-shaped studio with a platform bed occupying the foot of the L. There were newspapers and magazines scattered around the place but no books. I noticed copies of Variety and Rolling Stone and People and the Village Voice.

The television set was a tiny Sony perched on top of a chest of drawers. There was no stereo, but there were a few dozen records, mostly classical with a sprinkling of folk music, Pete Seeger and Joan Baez and Dave Van Ronk. There was a dustfree rectangle on top of the dresser next to the Sony.

I looked through the drawers and closets. A lot of Paula's clothes. I recognized some of the outfits, or thought I did.

Someone had closed the window. There were two windows that opened, one in the sleeping alcove, the other in the living room section, but a row of undisturbed potted plants in front of the bedroom window made it evident she'd gone out of the other one. I wondered why anyone had bothered to close it. In case of rain, I supposed. That was only sensible. But I suspect the gesture must have been less calculated than that, a reflexive act akin to tugging a sheet over the face of a corpse.

I went into the bathroom. A killer could have hidden in the stall shower. If there'd been a killer.

Why was I still thinking in terms of a killer?

I checked the medicine cabinet. There were little tubes and vials of cosmetics, though only a handful compared with the array on one of the bedside tables. Here were containers of aspirin and other headache remedies, a tube of antibiotic ointment, several prescriptions and nonprescription hay fever preparations, a cardboard packet of Band-aids, a roll of adhesive tape, a box of gauze pads. Some Q-tips, a hairbrush, a couple of combs. A toothbrush in the holder.

There were no footprints on the floor of the stall shower. Of course he could have been barefoot. Or he could have run water and washed away the traces of his presence before he left.

I went over and examined the window sill. I hadn't asked Guzik if they'd dusted for prints and I was reasonably certain no one had bothered. I wouldn't have taken the trouble in their position. I couldn't learn anything looking at the sill. I opened the window a foot or so and stuck my head out, but when I looked down the vertigo was extremely unpleasant and I drew my head back inside at once. I left the window open, though. The room could stand a change of air.

There were four folding chairs in the room, two of them closed and leaning against a wall, one near the bed, the fourth alongside the window. They were royal blue and made of high-impact plastic. The one by the window had her clothes piled on it. I went through the stack. She'd placed them deliberately on the chair but hadn't bothered folding them.

You never know what suicides will do. One man will put on a tuxedo before blowing his brains out. Another one will take off everything. Naked I came into the world and naked will I go out of it, something like that. A skirt. Beneath it a pair of panty hose. Then a blouse, and under it a bra with two small, lightly padded cups, I put the clothing back as I had found it, feeling like a violator of the dead.

The bed was unmade. I sat on the edge of it and looked across the room at a poster of Mick Jagger. I don't know how long I sat there. Ten minutes, maybe.

On the way out I looked at the chain bolt. I hadn't even noticed it when I came in. The chain had been neatly severed. Half of it was still in the slot on the door while the other half hung from its mounting on the jamb. I closed the door and fitted the two halves together, then released them and let them dangle. Then I touched their ends together again. I unhooked the end of the chain from the slot and went to the bathroom for the roll of adhesive tape. I brought the tape back with me, tore off a piece and used it to fasten the chain back together again. Then I let myself out of the apartment and tried to engage the chain bolt from outside, but the tape slipped whenever I put any pressure on it.

I went inside again and studied the chain bolt. I decided I was behaving erratically, that Paula Wittlauer had gone out the window of her own accord. I looked at the window sill again. The light dusting of soot didn't tell me anything one way or the other. New York's air filthy and the accumulation of soot could have been deposited in a couple of hours, even with the window shut. It didn't mean anything.

I looked at the heap of clothes on the chair, and I looked again at the chain bolt, and I rode the elevator to the basement and found either the superintendent or one of his assistants. I asked to borrow a screwdriver. He gave me a long screwdriver with an amber plastic grip. He didn't ask me who I was or what I wanted it for.

I returned to Paula Wittlauer's apartment and removed the chain bolt from its moorings on the door and jamb. I left the building and walked around the corner to a hardware store on Ninth Avenue. They had a good selection of chain bolts but I wanted one identical to the one I'd removed and I had to walk down Ninth Avenue as far as Fiftieth Street and check four stores before I found what I was looking for.

Back in Paula's apartment I mounted the new chain bolt, using the holes in which the original had been mounted. I tightened the screws with the super's screwdriver and stood out in the corridor and played with the chain. My hands are large and not terribly skillful, but even so I was able to lock and unlock the chain bolt from outside the apartment.

I don't know who put it up, Paula or a previous tenant or someone on the building staff, but that chain bolt had been as much protection as the Sanitized wrapper on a motel toilet seat. As evidence that Paula'd been alone when she went out the window, well, it wasn't worth a thing.

I replaced the original chain bolt, put the new one in my pocket, returned to the elevator and gave back the screwdriver. The man I returned it to seemed surprised to get it back.

It took me a couple of hours to find Cary McCloud. I'd learned that he tended bar evenings at a club in the West Village called The Spider's Web. I got down there around five. The guy behind the bar had knobby wrists and an underslung jaw and he wasn't Cary McCloud. "He don't come on till eight," he told me, "and he's off tonight anyway." I asked where I could find McCloud. "Sometimes he's here afternoons but he ain't been in today. As far as where you could look for him, that I couldn't tell you."

A lot of people couldn't tell me but eventually I ran across someone who could. You can quit the police force but you can't stop looking and sounding like a cop, and while that's hindrance in some situations it's a help in others. Ultimately I found a man in a bar down the block from The Spider's Web who'd learned it was best to cooperate with the police if it didn't cost you anything. He gave me an address on Barrow Street and told me which bell to ring.

I went to the building but I rang several other bells until somebody buzzed me through the downstairs door. I didn't want Cary to know he had company coming. I climbed two flights of stairs to the apartment he was supposed to be occupying. The bell downstairs hadn't had his name on it. It hadn't had any name at all.

Loud rock music was coming through his door. I stood in front of it for a minute, then hammered on it loud enough to make myself heard over the electric guitars. After a moment the music dropped in volume. I pounded on the door again and a male voice asked who I was.

I said, "Police. Open up." That's misdemeanor but I didn't expect to get in trouble for it.

"What's it about?"

"Open up, McCloud."

"Oh, Jesus," he said. He sound tired, aggravated. "How did you find me, anyway? Give me a minute, huh? I want to put some clothes on."

Sometimes that's what they say while they're putting a clip into an automatic. Then they pump a handful of shots through the door and into you if you're still standing behind it. But his voice didn't have that kind of edge to it and I couldn't summon up enough anxiety to get out of the way. Instead I put my ear against the door and heard whispering within. I couldn't make out what they were whispering about or get any sense of the person who was with him. The music was down in volume but there was still enough of it to cover their conversation.

The door opened. He was tall and thin, with hollow cheeks and prominent eyebrows and a worn, wasted look to him. He must have been in his early thirties and he didn't really look much older than that but you sensed that in another ten years he'd look twenty years older. If he lived that long. He wore patched jeans and a T-shirt with The Spider's Web silkscreened on it. Beneath the legend there was a sketch of a web. A macho spider stood at one end of it, grinning, extending two of his eight arms to welcome a hesitant girlish fly.

He noticed me noticing the shirt and managed a grin. "Place where I work," he said.

"I know."

"So come into my parlor. It ain't much but it's home."

I followed him inside, drew the door shut after me. The room was about fifteen feet square and held nothing you could call furniture. There was a mattress on the floor in one corner and a couple of cardboard cartons alongside it. The music was coming from a stereo, turntable and turner and two speakers all in a row along the far wall. There was a closed door over on the right. I figured it led to the bathroom, and that there was a woman on the other side of it.

"I guess this is about Paula," he said. I nodded. "I been over this with you guys," he said. "I was nowhere near there when it happened. The last I saw her was five, six hours before she killed herself. I was working at the Web and she came down and sat at the bar. I gave her a couple of drinks and she split."

"And you went on working."

"Until I closed up. I kicked everybody out a little after three and it was close to four by the time I had the place swept up and the garbage on the street and the window gates locked. Then I came over here and picked up Sunny and we went up to the place on Fifty-third."

"And you got there when?"

"Hell, I don't know. I wear a watch but I don't look at it every damn minute. I suppose it took five minutes to walk here and then Sunny and I hopped right in a cab and we were at Patsy's in ten minutes at the outside, that's the after-hours place. I told you people all of this, I really wish you would talk to each other and leave me the hell alone."

"Why doesn't Sunny come out and tell me about it?" I nodded at the bathroom door. "Maybe she can remember the time a little more clearly."

"Sunny? She stepped out a little while ago."

"She's not in the bathroom?"

"Nope. Nobody's in the bathroom."

"Mind if I see for myself?"

"Not if you can show me a warrant."

We looked at each other. I told him I figured I could take his word for it. He said he could always be trusted to tell the truth. I said I sensed as much about him.

He said, "What's the hassle, huh? I know you guys got forms to fill out, but why not give me a break? She killed herself and I wasn't anywhere near her when it happened."

He could have been. The times were vague, and whoever Sunny turned out to be, the odds were good that she'd have no more time sense than a koala bear. There were any number of ways he could have found a few minutes to go up to Fifty-seventh Street and heave Paula out a window, but it didn't add up that way and he just didn't feel like a killer to me. I knew what Ruth meant and I agreed with her that he was capable of murder but I don't think he'd been capable of this particular murder.

I said, "When did you go back to the apartment?"

"Who said I did?"

"You picked up your clothes, Cary."

"That was yesterday afternoon. The hell, I needed my clothes and stuff."

"How long were you living there?"

He hedged. "I wasn't exactly living there."

"Where were you exactly living?"

"I wasn't exactly living anywhere. I kept most of my stuff at Paula's place and I stayed with her most of the time but it wasn't as serious as actual living together. We were both too loose for anything like that. Anyway, the thing with Paula, it was pretty much winding itself down. She was a little too crazy for me." He smiled with his mouth. "They have to be a little crazy," he said, "but when they're too crazy it gets to be too much of a hassle."

Oh, he could have killed her. He could kill anyone if he had to, if someone was making too much of a hassle. But if he were to kill cleverly, faking the suicide in such an artful fashion, fastening the chain bolt on his way out, he'd pick a time when he had a solid alibi. He was not the sort to be so precise and so slipshod all at the same time.

"So you went and picked up your stuff."

"Right."

"Including the stereo and records."

"The stereo was mine. The records, I left the folk music and the classical shit because that belonged to Paula. I just took my records."

"And the stereo."

"Right."

"You got a bill of sale for it, I suppose."

"Who keeps that crap?"

"What if I said Paula kept the bill of sale? What if I said it was in with her papers and cancelled checks?"

"You're fishing."

"You sure of that?"

"Nope. But if you did say that, I suppose I'd say the stereo was a gift from her to me. You're not really gonna charge me with stealing a stereo, are you?"

"Why should I? Robbing the dead's a sacred tradition. You took drugs, too, didn't you? Her medicine cabinet used to look like a drugstore but there was nothing stronger than Excedrin when I took a look. That's why Sunny's in the bathroom. If I hit the door all the pretty little pills go down the toilet."

"I guess you can think that if you want."

"And I can come back with a warrant if I want."

"That's the idea."

"I ought to rap on the door just to do you out of the drugs but it doesn't seem worth the trouble. That's Paula Wittlauer's stereo. I suppose its' worth a couple hundred dollars. And you're not her heir. Unplug that thing and wrap it up, McCloud. I'm taking it with me."

"The hell you are."

"The hell I'm not."

"You want to take anything but your own ass out of here, you come back with a warrant. Then we'll talk about it."

"I don't need a warrant."

"You can't–"

"I don't need a warrant because I'm not a cop. I'm a detective. McCloud, I'm private, and I'm working for Ruth Wittlauer, and that's who's getting the stereo. I don't know if she wants it or not, but that's her problem. She doesn't want Paula's pills so you can pop them yourself or give them to your girl friend. You can shove 'em up your ass for all I care. But I'm walking out of here with that stereo and I'll walk through you if I have to, and don't think I wouldn't enjoy it."

"You're not even a cop."

"Right."

"You got no authority at all." He spoke in tones of wonder. "You said you were a cop."

"You can always sue me."

"You can't take that stereo. You can't even be in this room."

"That's right." I was itching for him. I could feel my blood in my veins. "I'm bigger than you," I said, "and I'm a whole lot harder, and I'd get a certain amount of satisfaction in beating the crap out of you. I don't like you. It bothers me that you didn't kill her because somebody did and it would be a pleasure to hang it on you. But you didn't do it. Unplug the stereo and pack it up so I can carry it or I'm going to take you apart."

I meant it and he realized as much. He thought about taking a shot at me and he decided it wasn't worth it. Maybe it wasn't all that much of a stereo. While he was unhooking it I dumped a carton of his clothes on the floor and we packed the stereo in it. On my way out the door he said he could always go to the cops and tell them what I'd done.

"I don't think you want to do that," I said.

"You said somebody killed her."

"That's right."

"You just making noise?"

"No."

"You're serious?" I nodded. "She didn't kill herself? I thought it was open and shut, from what the cops said. It's interesting. In a way, I guess you could say it's a load off my mind."

"How do you figure that?"

He shrugged. "I thought, you know, maybe she was upset it wasn't working out between us. At the Web the vibes were on the heavy side, if you follow me. Our thing was falling apart and I was seeing Sunny and she was seeing other guys and I thought maybe that was what did it for her. I suppose I blamed myself, like."

"I can see it was eating away at you."

"I just said it was on my mind."

I didn't say anything.

"Man," he said, "*nothing* eats away at me. You let things get to you that way and it's death."

I shouldered the carton and headed on down the stairs.

Ruth Wittlauer had supplied me with an Irving Place address and a GRamercy 5 telephone number. I called the number and didn't get an answer, so I walked over to Hudson and caught a northbound cab. There were no messages for me at the hotel desk. I put Paula's stereo in my room, tried Ruth's number again, then walked over to the Eighteenth Precinct. Guzik had gone off duty but the desk man told me to try a restaurant around the corner, and I found him there drinking draft Heinekens with another cop named Birnbaum. I sat at their table and ordered bourbon for myself and another round for the two of them.

I said, "I have a favor to ask. I'd like you to seal Paula Wittlauer's apartment."

"We closed that out," Guzik reminded me.

"I know, and the boyfriend closed out the deal girl's stereo." I told him how I'd reclaimed the unit from Cary McCloud. "I'm working for Ruth, Paula's sister. The least I can do is make sure she gets what's coming to her. She's not up to cleaning out the apartment now and it's rented through the first of October. McCloud's got a key and God knows how many other people have keys. If you slap a seal on the door it'd keep the grave robbers away."

"I guess we can do that. Tomorrow all right?"

"Tonight would be better."

"What's there to steal? You got the stereo out of there and I didn't see anything else around that was worth much."

"Things have a sentimental value."

He eyed me, frowned. "I'll make a phone call," he said. He went to the booth in the back and I jawed with Birnbaum until he came back and told me it was all taken care of.

I said, "Another thing I was wondering. You must have had a photographer on the scene. Somebody to take pictures of the body and all that."

"Sure. That's routine."

"Did he go up to the apartment while he was at it? Take a roll of interior shots?"

"Yeah. Why?"

"I thought maybe I could have a look at them."

"What for?"

"You never know. The reason I knew it was Paula's stereo in McCloud's apartment was I could see the pattern in the dust on top of the dresser where it had been. If you've got interior pictures maybe I'll see something else that's not there anymore and I can lean on McCloud a little and recover it for my client."

"And that's why you'd like to see the pictures."

"Right."

He gave me a look. "That door was bolted from the inside, Matt. With a chain bolt."

'I know."

"And there was no one in the apartment when we went in there."

"I know that, too."

"You're still barking up the murder tree, aren't you? Jesus, the case is closed and the reason it's closed is the ditzy broad killed herself. What are you making waves for?"

"I'm not. I just wanted to see the pictures."

"To see if somebody stole her diaphragm or something."

"Something like that." I drank what remained of my drink. "You need a new hat anyway, Guzik. The weather's turning and a fellow like you needs a hat for fall."

"If I had the price of a hat, maybe I'd go out and get one."

"You got it," I said.

He nodded and we told Birnbaum we wouldn't be long. I walked with Guzik around the corner to the Eighteenth. On the way I palmed him two tens and a five, twenty-five dollars, the price of a hat in police parlance. He made the bills disappear.

I waited at his desk while he pulled the Paula Wittlauer file. There were about a dozen black-and-white prints, eight by tens, high-contrast glossies. Perhaps half of them showed Paula's corpse from various angles. I had no interest in these but I made myself look at them as a sort of reinforcement, so I wouldn't forget what I was doing on the case.

The other pictures were interior shots of the L-shaped apartment. I noted the wide-open window, the dresser with the stereo sitting on it, the chair with her clothing piled haphazardly upon it. I separated the interior pictures from the ones showing the corpse and told Guzik I wanted to keep them for the time being. He didn't mind.

He cocked his head and looked at me. "You got something, Matt?"

"Nothing worth talking about."

"If you ever do, I'll want to hear about it."

"Sure."

"You like the life you're leading? Working private, scuffling around?"

"It seems to suit me."

He thought it over, nodded. Then he started for the stairs and I followed after him.

Later that evening I managed to reach Ruth Wittlauer. I bundled the stereo into a cab and took it to her place. She lived in a well-kept brownstone a block and a half from Gramercy Park. Her apartment was inexpensively furnished but the pieces looked to have been chosen with care. The place was clean and neat. Her clock radio was tuned to an FM station that was playing chamber music. She had coffee made and I accepted a cup and sipped it while I told her about recovering the stereo from Cary McCloud.

"I wasn't sure whether you could use it," I said, "but I couldn't see any reason why he should keep it. You can always sell it."

"No, I'll keep it. I just have a twenty-dollar record player that I bought on Fourteenth Street. Paula's stereo cost a couple of hundred dollars." She managed a smile. "So you've already more than earned what I gave you. Did he kill her?"

"No."

"You're sure of that?"

I nodded. "He'd kill if he had a reason but I don't think he did. And if he did kill her he'd never have taken the stereo or the drugs, and he wouldn't have acted the way he did. There was never a moment when I had the feeling that he'd killed her. And you have to follow your instincts in this kind of situation. Once they point things out to you, then you can usually find the facts to go with them."

"And you're sure my sister killed herself?"

"No. I'm pretty sure someone gave her a hand."

Her eyes widened.

I said, "It's mostly intuition. But there are a few facts to support it." I told her about the chain bolt, how it had proved to the police that Paula'd killed herself, how my experiment had shown it could have been fastened from the corridor. Ruth got very excited at this but I explained that it didn't prove anything in and of itself, only that suicide remained a theoretical possibility.

Then I showed her the pictures I'd obtained from Guzik. I selected one shot which showed the chair with Paula's clothing without showing too much of the window. I didn't want to make Ruth look at the window.

"The chair," I said, pointing to it. "I noticed this when I was in your sister's apartment. I wanted to see a photograph taken at the time to make sure things hadn't been rearranged by the cops or McCloud or somebody else. But that clothing's exactly the way it was when I saw it."

"I don't understand."

"The supposition is that Paula got undressed, put her clothes on the chair, then went to the window and jumped." Her lip was trembling but she was holding herself together and I went right on talking. "Or she'd taken her clothes off earlier and maybe she took a shower or a nap and then came back and jumped. But look at the chair. She didn't fold her clothes neatly, she didn't put them away. And she didn't just drop them on the floor, either. I'm no authority on the way women get undressed but I don't think many people would do it that way."

Ruth nodded. Her face was thoughtful.

"That wouldn't mean very much by itself. If she were upset or stoned or confused she might have thrown things on the chair as she took them off. But that's not what happened. The order of the clothing is all wrong. The bra's underneath the blouse, the panty hose is underneath the skirt. She took her bra off after she took her blouse off, obviously, so it should have wound up on top of the blouse, not under it."

"Of course."

I held up a hand. 'It's nothing like proof, Ruth. There are any number of other explanations. Maybe she knocked the stuff onto the floor and then picked it up and the order of the garments got switched around. Maybe one of the cops went through the clothing before the photographer came around with his camera. I don't really have anything terribly strong to go on."

"But you think she was murdered."

"Yes, I guess I do."

"That's what I thought all along. Of course I had a reason to think so."

"Maybe I've got one, too. I don't know."

"What are you going to do now?"

"I think I'll poke around a little. I don't know much about Paula's life. I'll have to learn more if I'm going to find out who killed her. But it's up to you to decide whether you want me to stay with it."

"Of course I do. Why wouldn't I?"

"Because it probably won't lead anywhere. Suppose she was upset after her conversation with McCloud and she picked up a stranger and took him home with her and he killed her. If that's the case we'll never know who he was."

"You're going to stay with it, aren't you?"

"I suppose I want to."

"It'll be complicated, though. It'll take you some time. I suppose you'll want more money." Her gaze was very direct. "I gave you two hundred dollars. I have three hundred more that I can afford to pay. I don't mind paying it, Mr. Scudder. I already got... I got my money's worth for the first two hundred, didn't I? The stereo. When the three hundred runs out, well, you can tell me if you think it's worth staying with the case. I couldn't afford more cash right away, but I could arrange to pay you later on or something like that."

I shook my head. "It won't come to more than that," I said. "No matter how much time I spend on it. And you keep the three hundred for the time being, all right? I'll take it from you later on. If I need it, and if I've earned it."

"That doesn't seem right."

"It seems right to me," I said. "And don't make the mistake of thinking I'm being charitable."

"But your time's valuable."

I shook my head. "Not to me it isn't."

I spent the next five days picking the scabs off Paula Wittlauer's life. It kept turning out to be a waste of time but the time's always gone before you realize you've wasted it. And I'd been telling the truth when I said my time wasn't valuable. I had nothing better to do, and my peeks into the corners of Paula's world kept me busy.

Her life involved more than a saloon on Ninth Avenue and an apartment on Fifty-seventh Street, more than serving drinks and sharing a bed with Cary McCloud. She did other things. She went one evening a week to group therapy on West Seventy-ninth Street. She took voice lessons every Tuesday morning on Amsterdam Avenue. She had an ex-boyfriend she saw once in a while. She hung out in a couple of bars in the neighborhood and a couple of others in the Village. She did this, she did that, she went here, she went there, and I kept busy dragging myself around town and talking to all sorts of people, and I managed to learn quite a bit about the person she'd been and the life she'd led without learning anything at all about the person who'd put her on the pavement.

At the same time, I tried to track her movements on the final night of her life. She'd evidently gone more or less directly to The Spider's Web after finishing her shift at Armstrong's. Maybe she'd stopped at her apartment for a shower and a change of clothes, but without further ado she'd headed downtown. Somewhere around ten she left the Web, and I traced her from there to a couple of other Village bars. She hadn't stayed at either of them long, taking a quick drink or two and moving on. She'd left alone as far as anyone seemed to remember. This didn't prove a thing because she could have stopped elsewhere before continuing uptown, or she could have picked someone up on the street, which I'd learned was something she'd done more than once in her young life. She could have found her killer loitering on a street corner or she could have phoned him and arranged to meet him at her apartment.

Her apartment. The doormen changed off at midnight, but it was impossible to determine whether she'd returned before or after the changing of the guard. She'd lived there, she was a regular tenant, and when she entered or left the building it was not a noteworthy occasion. It was something she did every night, so when she came home for the final time the man at the door had no reason to know it was the final time and thus no reason to take mental notes.

Had she come in alone or with a companion? No one could say, which did suggest she'd come in alone. If she'd been with someone her entrance would have been a shade more memorable. But this also proved nothing, because I stood on the other side of Fifty-seventh Street one night and watched the doorway of her building, and the

doorman didn't take the pride in his position that the afternoon doorman had shown. He was away from the door almost as often as he
was on it. She could have walked in flanked by six Turkish sailors
and there was a chance no one would have seen her.

The doorman who'd been on duty when she went out the window
was a rheumy-eyed Irishman with liver-spotted hands. He hadn't
actually seen her land. He'd been in the lobby, keeping himself out
of the wind, and then he came rushing out when he heard the impact
of the body on the street.

He couldn't get over the sound she made.

"All of a sudden there was this noise," he said. "Just out of the
blue there was this noise and it must be it's my imagination but I
swear I felt it in my feet, I swear she shook the earth. I had no idea
what it was, and then I came rushing out, and Jesus God, there she
was."

"Didn't you hear a scream?"

"Street was empty just then. This side, anyway. Nobody around
to scream."

"Didn't *she* scream on the way down?"

"Did somebody say she screamed? I never heard it."

Do people scream as they fall? They generally do in films and on
television. During my days on the force I saw several of them after
they jumped, and by the time I got to them there were no screams
echoing in the air. And a few times I'd been on hand while they talked
someone in off a ledge, but in each instance the talking was successful
and I didn't have to watch a falling body accelerate according to the
immutable laws of physics.

Could you get much of a scream out in four seconds?

I stood in the street where she'd fallen and I looked up toward her
window. I counted off four seconds in my mind. A voice shrieked
in my brain. It was Thursday night, actually Friday morning, one
o'clock. Time I got myself around the corner to Armstrong's, because
in another couple of hours Justin would be closing for the night and
I'd want to be drunk enough to sleep.

And an hour or so after that she'd be one week dead.

I'd worked myself into a reasonably bleak mood by the time I got
to Armstrong's. I skipped the coffee and crawled straight into the
bourbon bottle, and before long it began to do what it was supposed
to do. It blurred the corners of the mind so I couldn't see the bad
dark things that lurked there.

When Trina finished for the night she joined me and I bought her
a couple of drinks. I don't remember what we talked about. Some
but by no means all of our conversation touched upon Paula Wittlauer.

Trina hadn't known Paula terribly well—their contact had been largely limited to the two hours a day when their shifts overlapped—but she knew a little about the sort of life Paula had been leading. There'd been a year or two when her own life had not been terribly different from Paula's. Now she had things more or less under control, and maybe there would have come a time when Paula would have taken charge of her life, but that was something we'd never know now.

I suppose it was close to three when I walked Trina home. Our conversation had turned thoughtful and reflective. On the street she said it was a lousy night for being alone. I thought of high windows and evil shapes in dark corners and took her hand in mine.

She lives on Fifty-sixth between Ninth and Tenth. While we waited for the light to change at Fifty-seventh Street I looked over at Paula's building. We were far enough away to look at the high floors. Only a couple of windows were lighted.

That was when I got it.

I've never understood how people think of things, how little perceptions trigger greater insights. Thoughts just seem to come to me. I had it now, and something clicked within me and a source of tension unwound itself.

I said something to that effect to Trina.

"You know who killed her?"

"Not exactly," I said. "But I know how to find out. And it can wait until tomorrow."

The light changed and we crossed the street.

She was still sleeping when I left. I got out of bed and dressed in silence, then let myself out of her apartment. I had some coffee and a toasted English muffin at the Red Flame. Then I went across the street to Paula's building. I started on the tenth floor and worked my way up, checking the three or four possible apartments on each floor. A lot of people weren't home. I worked my way clear to the top floor, the twenty-fourth, and by the time I was done I had three possibles listed in my notebook and a list of over a dozen apartments I'd have to check that evening.

At eight-thirty that night I rang the bell of Apartment 21G. It was directly in line with Paula's apartment and four flights above it. The man who answered the bell wore a pair of Lee corduroy slacks and a shirt with a blue vertical stripe on a white background. His socks were dark blue and he wasn't wearing shoes.

I said, "I want to talk with you about Paula Wittlauer."

His face fell apart and I forgot my three possibles forever because he was the man I wanted. He just stood there. I pushed the door open and stepped forward and he moved back automatically to make room for me. I drew the door shut after me and walked around him, crossing the room to the window. There wasn't a speck of dust or soot on the sill. It was immaculate, as well-scrubbed as Lady Macbeth's hands.

I turned to him. His name was Lane Posmantur and I suppose he was around forty, thickening at the waist, his dark hair starting to go thin on top. His glasses were thick and it was hard to read his eyes through them but it didn't matter. I didn't need to see his eyes.

"She went out this window," I said. "Didn't she?"

"I don't know what you're talking about."

"Do you want to know what triggered it for me, Mr. Posmantur? I was thinking of all the things nobody noticed. No one saw her enter the building. Neither doorman remembered it because it wasn't something they'd be likely to remember. Nobody saw her go out the window. The cops had to look for an open window in order to know who the hell she was. They backtracked her from the window she fell out of.

"And nobody saw the killer leave the building. Now that's the one thing that would have been noticed, and that's the point that occurred to me. It wasn't that significant by itself but it made me dig a little deeper. The doorman was alert once her body hit the street. He'd remember who went in or out of the building from that point on. So it occurred to me that maybe the killer was still inside the building, and then I got the idea that she was killed by someone who *lived* in the building, and from that point on it was just a question of finding you because all of a sudden it all made sense."

I told him about the clothes on the chair. "She didn't take them off and pile them up like that. Her killer put her clothes like that, and he dumped them on the chair so that it would looks though she undressed in her apartment, and so that it would be assumed she'd gone out of her own window.

"But she went out of your window, didn't she?"

He looked at me. After a moment he said he thought he'd better sit down. He went to an armchair and sat in it. I stayed on my feet.

I said, "She came here. I guess she took off her clothes and you went to bed with her. Is that right?"

He hesitated, then nodded.

"What made you decide to kill her?"

"I didn't.

I looked at him. He looked away, then met my gaze, then avoided my eyes again. "Tell me about it," I suggested. He looked away again and a minute went by and then he started to talk.

It was about what I'd figured. She was living with Cary McCloud but she and Lane Posmantur would get together now and then for a quickie. He was a lab technician at Roosevelt and he brought home drugs from time to time and perhaps that was part of his attraction for her. She'd turned up that night a little after two and they went to bed. She was really flying, he said, and he'd been taking pills himself, it was something he'd begun doing lately, maybe seeing her had something to do with it.

They went to bed and did the dirty deed, and then maybe they slept for an hour, something like that, and then she was awake and coming unglued, getting really hysterical, and he tried to settle her down and he gave her a couple of slaps to bring her around, except they didn't bring her around, and she was staggering and she tripped over the coffee table and fell funny, and by the time he sorted himself out and went to her she was lying with her head at a crazy angle and he knew her neck was broken and when he tried for a pulse there was no pulse to be found.

"All I could think of was she was dead in my apartment and full of drugs and I was in trouble."

"So you put her out the window."

"I was going to take her back to her own apartment. I started to dress her but it was impossible. And even with her clothes on I couldn't risk running into somebody in the hallway or on the elevator. It was crazy.

"I left her here and went to her apartment. I thought maybe Cary would help me. I rang the bell and nobody answered and I used her key and the chain bolt was on. Then I remembered she used to fasten it from outside. She'd showed me how she could do that. I tried with mine but it was installed properly and there's not enough play in the chain. I unhooked her bolt and went inside.

"Then I got the idea. I went back to my apartment and got her clothes and I rushed back and put them on her chair. I opened her window wide. On my way out the door I put her lights on and hooked the chain bolt again.

"I came back here to my own apartment. I took her pulse again and she was dead, she hadn't moved or anything, and I couldn't do anything for her, all I could do was stay out of it, and I, I turned off the lights here, and I opened my own window and dragged her body over to it, and, oh, God in heaven, God, I almost couldn't make myself do it but it was an accident that she was dead and I was so damned *afraid*–"

"And you dropped her out and closed the window." He nodded. "And if her neck was broken it was something that happened in the fall. And whatever drugs were in her system was just something she'd taken by herself, and they'd never do an autopsy anyway. And you were home free."

"I didn't hurt her," he said. "I was just protecting myself."

"Do you really believe that, Lane?"

"What do you mean?"

"You're not a doctor. Maybe she was dead when you threw her out the window. Maybe she wasn't."

"There was no pulse!"

"You couldn't find a pulse. That doesn't mean there wasn't any. Did you try artificial respiration? Do you know if there was any brain activity? No, of course not. All you know was that you looked for a pulse and you couldn't find one."

"Her neck was broken."

"Maybe. How many broken necks have you had occasion to diagnose? And people sometimes break their necks and live anyway. The point is that you couldn't have known she was dead and you were too worried about your own skin to do what you should have done. You should have phoned for an ambulance. You know that's what you should have done and you knew it at the time but you wanted to stay out of it. I've known junkies who left their buddies to die of overdoses because they didn't want to get involved. You went them one better. You put her out a window and let her fall twenty-one stories so that you wouldn't get involved, and for all you know she was alive when you let go of her."

"No," he said. "No. She was dead."

I'd told Ruth Wittlauer she could wind up believing whatever she wanted. People believe what they want to believe. It was just as true for Lane Posmantur.

"Maybe she was dead," I said. "Maybe that's your fault, too."

"What do you mean?"

"You said you slapped her to bring her around. What kind of a slap, Lane?"

"I just tapped her on the face."

"Just a brisk slap to straighten her out."

"That's right."

"Oh, hell, Lane. Who knows how hard you hit her? Who knows whether you may not have given her a shove? She wasn't the only one on pills. You said she was flying. Well, I think maybe you were doing a little flying yourself. And you'd been sleepy and you were groggy and she was buzzing around the room and being a general pain in the ass, and you gave her a slap and a shove and another slap and another shove and—"

"No!"

"And she fell down."

"It was an accident."

"It always is."

"I didn't hurt her. I liked her, She was a good kid, we got on fine, I didn't hurt her, I–"

"Put your shoes on, Lane."

"What for?"

"I'm taking you to the police station. It's a few blocks from here, not very far at all."

"Am I under arrest?"

"I'm not a policeman." I'd never gotten around to saying who I was and he'd never thought to ask. "My name's Scudder, I'm working for Paula's sister. I suppose you're under citizen's arrest. I want you to come to the precinct house with me. There's a cop named Guzik there and you can talk to him."

"I don't have to say anything," he said. He thought for a moment. "You're not a cop."

"No."

"What I said to you doesn't mean a thing." He took a breath, straightened up a little in his chair. "You can't prove a thing," he said. "Not a thing."

"Maybe I can and maybe I can't. You probably left prints in Paula's apartment. I had them seal the place a while ago and maybe they'll find traces of your presence. I don't know if Paula left any prints here or not. You probably scrubbed them up. But there may be neighbors who know you were sleeping with her, and someone may have noticed you scampering back and forth between the apartments that night, and it's even possible a neighbor heard the two of you struggling in here just before she went out the window. When the cops know what to look for, Lane, they usually find it sooner or later. It's knowing what you're after that's the hard part.

"But that's not even the point. Put your shoes on, Lane. That's right. Now we're going to go see Guzik, that's his name, and he's going to advise you of your rights. He'll tell you that you have aright to remain silent, and that's the truth, Lane, that's a right that you have. And if you remain silent and if you get a decent lawyer and do what he tells you I think you can beat this charge, Lane. I really do."

"Why are you telling me this?"

"Why?" I was starting to feel tired, drained, but I kept on with it. "Because the worst thing you could do is remain silent, Lane . Believe me, that's the worst thing you could do. If you're smart you'll tell Guzik everything you remember. You'll make a complete voluntary statement and you'll read it over when they type it up and you'll sign your name on the bottom.

"Because you're not really a killer, Lane. It doesn't come easily to you. If Cary McCloud had killer her he'd never lose a night's sleep over it. But you're not a psychopath. You were drugged and half-crazy and terrified and you did something wrong and it's eating you up. Your face fell apart the minute I walked in here tonight. You could play it cute and beat this charge, Lane, but all you'd wind up doing is beating yourself.

"Because you live in a high floor, Lane, and the ground's only four seconds away. And if you squirm off the hook you'll never get it out of your head, you'll never be able to mark it Paid in Full, and one day or night you'll open the window and you'll go out of it, Lane. You'll remember the sound her body made when she hit the street—"

"No!"

I took his arm. "Come on," I said. "We'll go see Guzik."

JOHN LUTZ
(b.1939)

Ride the Lighting
(Alo Nudger)

A slanted sheet of rain swept like a scythe across Placid Cove Trailer Park. For an instant, an intricate web of lightning illumined the park. The rows of mobile homes loomed square and still and pale against the night, reminding Nudger of tombs with awnings and TV antennas. He held his umbrella at a sharp angle to the wind as he walked, putting a hand in his pocket to pull out a scrap of paper and double-check the address he was trying to find in the maze of trailers. Finally, at the end of Tranquility Lane, he found Number 307 and knocked on its metal door.

"I'm Nudger," he said when the door opened.

For several seconds the woman in the doorway stood staring out at him, rain blowing in beneath the metal awning to spot her cornflower-colored dress and ruffle her straw blond hair. She was tall but very thin, fragile-looking, and appeared at first glance to be about twelve years old. Second glance revealed her to be in her mid-twenties. She had slight crow's feet at the corners of her luminous blue eyes when she winced as a raindrop struck her face, a knowing cast to her oversized, girlish, full-lipped mouth, and slightly buck teeth. Her looks were hers alone. There was no one who could look much like her, no middle ground with her; men would consider her scrawny and homely, or they would see her as uniquely sensuous. Nudger liked coltish girl-women; he catalogued her as attractive.

"Whoeee!" she said at last, as if seeing for the first time beyond Nudger. "Ain't it raining something terrible?"

"It is," Nudger agreed. "And on me."

Her entire thin body gave a quick, nervous kind of jerk as she smiled apologetically. "I'm Holly Ann Adams, Mr. Nudger. And you are getting wet, all right. Come on in."

She moved aside and Nudger stepped up into the trailer. He expected it to be surprisingly spacious; he'd once lived in a trailer and remembered them as such. This one was cramped and confining. The furniture was cheap and its upholstery was threadbare; a portable black and white TV on a tiny table near the Scotch-plaid sofa was blaring shouts of ecstasy emitted by "The Price is Right" contestants. The air was thick with the smell of something greasy that had been fried too long.

Holly Ann cleared a stack of *People* magazines from a vinyl chair and motioned for Nudger to sit down. He folded his umbrella, left it by the door, and sat. Holly Ann started to say something, then jerked her body in that peculiar way of hers, almost a twitch, as if she'd just remembered something not only with her mind but with her blood and muscle, and walked over and switched off the noisy television. In the abrupt silence, the rain seemed to beat on the metal roof with added fury. "Now we can talk," Holly Ann proclaimed, sitting opposite Nudger on the undersized sofa. "You a sure-enough private investigator?"

"I'm that," Nudger said. "Did someone recommend me to you, Miss Adams?"

"Gotcha out of the Yellow Pages. And if you're gonna work for me, it might as well be Holly Ann without the Adams."

"Except on the check," Nudger said.

She grinned a devilish twelve-year-old's grin. "Oh, sure, don't worry none about that. I wrote you out a check already, just gotta fill in the amount. That is, if you agree to take the job. You might not."

"Why not?"

"It has to do with my fiancé, Curtis Colt."

Nudger listened for a few seconds to the rain crashing on the roof. "The Curtis Colt who's going to be executed next week?"

"That's the one. Only he didn't kill that liquor store woman; I know it for a fact. It ain't right he should have to ride the lightning."

"Ride the lightning?"

"That's what convicts call dying in the electric chair, Mr. Nudger. They call that chair lotsa things: Old Sparky . . . The Lord's Frying Pan. But Curtis don't belong sitting in it wired up, and I can prove it."

"It's a little late for that kind of talk," Nudger said. "Or did you testify for Curtis in court?"

"Nope. Couldn't testify. You'll see why. All them lawyers and the judge and jury don't even know about me. Curtis didn't want them to know, so he never told them." She crossed her legs and swung her right calf jauntily. She was smiling as if trying to flirt him into wanting to know more about the job so he could free Curtis Colt by a governor's reprieve at the last minute, as in an old movie.

Nudger looked at her gauntly pretty, country-girl face and said, "Tell me about Curtis Colt, Holly Ann."

"You mean you didn't read about him in the newspapers or see him on the television?"

"I only scan the media for misinformation. Give me the details."

"Well, they say Curtis was inside the liquor store, sticking it up—him and his partner had done three other places that night, all of 'em gas stations, though—when the old man that owned the place came out of a back room and seen his wife there behind the counter with her hands up and Curtis holding the gun on her. So the old man lost his head and ran at Curtis, and Curtis had to shoot him. Then the woman got mad when she seen that and ran at Curtis, and Curtis shot her. She's the one that died. The old man, he'll live, but he can't talk nor think nor even feed himself."

Nudger remembered more about the case now. Curtis Colt had been found guilty of first degree murder, and because of a debate in the legislature over the merits of cyanide gas versus electricity, the state was breaking out the electric chair to make him its first killer executed by electricity in over a quarter of a century. Those of the back-to-basics school considered that progress.

"They're gonna shoot Curtis full of electricity next Saturday, Mr. Nudger," Holly Ann said plaintively. She sounded like a little girl complaining that the grade on her report card wasn't fair.

"I know," Nudger said. "But I don't see how I can help you. Or, more specifically, help Curtis."

"You know what they say thoughts really are, Mr. Nudger?" Holly Ann said, ignoring his professed helplessness. Her wide blue eyes were vague as she searched for words. "Thoughts ain't really nothing but tiny electrical impulses in the brain. I read that somewheres or other. What I can't help wondering is, when they shoot all that electricity into Curtis, what's it gonna be like to his thinking? How long will it seem like to him before he finally dies? Will there be a big burst of crazy thoughts along with the pain? I know it sounds loony, but I can't help laying awake nights thinking about that, and I feel I just gotta do whatever's left to try and help Curtis."

There was a sort of checkout-line tabloid logic in that, Nudger conceded; if thoughts were actually weak electrical impulses, then high-voltage electrical impulses could become exaggerated, horrible thoughts. Anyway, try to disprove it to Holly Ann.

"They never did catch Curtis's buddy, the driver who sped away and left him in that service station, did they?" Nudger asked.

"Nope. Curtis never told who the driver was, neither, no matter how much he was threatened. Curtis is a stubborn man."

Nudger was getting the idea.

"But you know who was driving the car."

"Yep. And he told me him and Curtis was miles away from that liquor store at the time it was robbed. When he seen the police closing in on Curtis in that gas station where Curtis was buying cigarettes, he hit the accelerator and got out of the parking lot before they could catch him. The police didn't even get the car's license plate number."

Nudger rubbed a hand across his chin, watching Holly Ann swing her leg as if it were a shapely metronome. She was barefoot and wearing no nylon hose. "The jury thought Curtis not only was at the liquor store, but that he shot the old man and woman in cold blood."

"That ain't true, though. Not according to–" she caught herself before uttering the man's name.

"Curtis's friend," Nudger finished.

"That's right. And he ought to know," Holly Ann said righteously, as if that piece of information were the trump card and the argument was over.

"None of this means anything unless the driver comes forward and substantiates that he was with Curtis somewhere other than at the liquor store when it was robbed."

Holly Ann nodded and stopped swinging her leg. "I know. But he won't. He can't. That's where you come in."

"My profession might enjoy a reputation a notch lower than dognapper," Nudger said, "but I don't hire out to do anything illegal."

"What I want you to do is legal," Holly Ann said in a hurt little voice. Nudger looked past her into the dollhouse kitchen and saw an empty gin bottle. He wondered if she might be slightly drunk. "It's the eyewitness accounts that got Curtis convicted," she went on. "And those people are wrong. I want you to figure out some way to convince them it wasn't Curtis they saw that night."

"Four people, two of them customers in the store, picked Curtis out of a police lineup."

"So what? Ain't eyewitnesses often mistaken?"

Nudger had to admit that they were, though he didn't see how they could be in this case. There were, after all, four of them. And yet,

Holly Ann was right; it was amazing how people could sometimes be so certain that the wrong man had committed a crime just five feet in front of them.

"I want you to talk to them witnesses," Holly Ann said. "Find out *why* they think Curtis was the killer. Then show them how they might be wrong and get them to change what they said. We got the truth on our side, Mr. Nudger. At least one witness will change his story when he's made to think about it, because Curtis wasn't where they said he was."

"Curtis has exhausted all his appeals," Nudger said. "Even if all the witnesses changed their stories, it wouldn't necessarily mean he'd get a new trial."

"Maybe not, but I betcha they wouldn't kill him. They couldn't stand the publicity if enough witnesses said they was wrong, it was somebody else killed the old woman. Then, just maybe, eventually, he'd get another trial and get out of prison."

Nudger was awed. Here was foolish optimism that transcended even his own. He had to admire Holly Ann.

The leg started pumping again beneath the cornflower-colored dress. When Nudger lowered his gaze to stare at it, Holly Ann said, "So will you help me, Mr. Nudger?"

"Sure. It sounds easy."

"Why should I worry about it anymore?" Randy Gantner asked Nudger, leaning on his shovel. He didn't mind talking to Nudger; it meant a break from his construction job on the new Interstate 170 cloverleaf. "Colt's been found guilty and he's going to the chair, ain't he?"

The afternoon sun was hammering down on Nudger, warming the back of his neck and making his stomach queasy. He thumbed an antacid tablet off the roll he kept in his shirt pocket and popped one of the white disks into his mouth. With his other hand, he was holding up a photograph of Curtis Colt for Gantner to see. It was a snapshot Holly Ann had given him of the wiry, shirtless Colt leaning on a fence post and holding a beer can high in a mock toast: this one's for Death!

"This is a photograph you never saw in court. I just want you to look at it closely and tell me again if you're sure the man you saw in the liquor store was Colt. Even if it makes no difference in whether he's executed, it will help ease the mind of somebody who loves him."

"I'd be a fool to change my story about what happened now that the trial's over," Gantner said logically.

"You'd be a murderer if you really weren't sure."

Gantner sighed, dragged a dirty red handkerchief from his jeans pocket, and wiped his beefy, perspiring face. He peered at the photo, then shrugged. "It's him, Colt, the guy I seen shoot the man and woman when I was standing in the back aisle of the liquor store. If he'd known me and Sanders was back there, he'd have probably zapped us along with them old folks."

"You're positive it's the same man?"

Gantner spat off to the side and frowned; Nudger was becoming a pest, and the foreman was staring. "I said it to the police and the jury, Nudger; that little twerp Colt did the old lady in. Ask me, he deserves what he's gonna get."

"Did you actually see the shots fired?"

"Nope. Me and Sanders was in the back aisle looking for some reasonable-priced bourbon when we heard the shots, then looked around to see Curtis Colt back away, turn, and run out to the car. Looked like a black or dark green old Ford. Colt fired another shot as it drove away."

"Did you see the driver?"

"Sort of. Skinny dude with curly black hair and a mustache. That's what I told the cops. That's all I seen. That's all I know."

And that was the end of the conversation. The foreman was walking toward them, glaring. *Thunk!* Gantner's shovel sliced deep into the earth, speeding the day when there'd be another place for traffic to get backed up. Nudger thanked him and advised him not to work too hard in the hot sun.

"You wanna help?" Gantner asked, grinning sweatily.

"I'm already doing some digging of my own," Nudger said, walking away before the foreman arrived.

The other witnesses also stood by their identifications. The fourth and last one Nudger talked with, an elderly woman named Iris Langeneckert, who had been walking her dog near the liquor store and had seen Curtis Colt dash out the door and into the getaway car, said something that Gantner had touched on. When she'd described the getaway car driver, like Gantner she said he was a thin man with curly black hair and a beard or mustache, then she had added, "Like Curtis Colt's hair and mustache."

Nudger looked again at the snapshot Holly Ann had given him. Curtis Colt was about five foot nine, skinny, and mean-looking, with a broad bandito mustache and a mop of curly, greasy black hair. Nudger wondered if it was possible that the getaway car driver had been Curtis Colt himself, and his accomplice had killed the shopkeeper. Even Nudger found that one hard to believe.

He drove to his second-floor office in the near suburb of Maplewood and sat behind his desk in the blast of cold air from the window unit, sipping the complimentary paper cup of iced tea he'd brought up from Danny's Donuts directly below. The sweet smell of the doughnuts was heavier than usual in the office; Nudger had never quite gotten used to it and what it did to his sensitive stomach.

When he was cool enough to think clearly again, he decided he needed more information on the holdup, and on Curtis Colt, from more objective source than Holly Ann Adams. He phoned Lieutenant Jack Hammersmith at home and was told by Hammersmith's son Jed that Hammersmith had just driven away to go to work on the afternoon shift, so it would be awhile before he got to his office.

Nudger checked his answering machine, proving that hope did indeed spring eternal in a fool's breast. There was a terse message from his former wife Eileen demanding last month's alimony payment; a solemn-voiced young man reading an address where Nudger could send a check to help pay to form a watchdog committee that would stop the utilities from continually raising their rates; and a cheerful man informing Nudger that with the labels from ten packages of a brand name hot dog he could get a Cardinal's ballgame ticket at half price. (That meant eating over eighty hot dogs. Nudger calculated that baseball season would be over by the time he did that.) Everyone seemed to want some of Nudger's money. No one wanted to pay Nudger any money. Except for Holly Ann Adams. Nudger decided he'd better step up his efforts on the Curtis Colt case.

He titled back his head, downed the last dribble of iced tea, then tried to eat what was left of the crushed ice. But the ice clung stubbornly to the bottom of the cup, taunting him. Nudger's life was like that.

He crumpled up the paper cup and tossed it, ice and all, into the wastebasket. Then he went downstairs where his Volkswagen was parked in the shade behind the building and drove east on Manchester, toward downtown and the Third District station house.

Police Lieutenant Jack Hammersmith was in his Third District office, sleek, obese, and cool-looking behind his wide metal desk. He was pounds and years away from the handsome cop who'd been Nudger's partner a decade ago in a two-man patrol car. Nudger could still see traces of a dashing quality in the flesh-upholstered Hammersmith, but he wondered if that was only because he'd known Hammersmith ten years ago.

"Sit down, Nudge," Hammersmith invited, his lips smiling but his slate gray, cop's eyes unreadable. If eyes were the windows to the soul, his shades were always down.

Nudger sat in one of the straight-backed chairs in front of Hammersmith's desk. "I need some help," he said.

"Sure," Hammersmith said, "you never come see me just to trade recipes or to sit and rock." Hammersmith was partial to irony; it was a good thing, in his line of work.

"I need to know more about Curtis Colt," Nudger said.

Hammersmith got one of his vile greenish cigars out of his shirt pocket and stared intently at it, as if its paper ring label might reveal some secret of life and death. "Colt, eh? The guy who's going to ride the lightning?"

"That's the second time in the past few days I've heard that expression. The first time was from Colt's fiancée. She thinks he's innocent."

"Fiancées think along those lines. Is she your client?"

Nudger nodded but didn't volunteer Holly Ann's name.

"Gullibility makes the world go round." Hammersmith said. "I was in charge of the Homicide investigation on that one. There's not a chance Colt is innocent, Nudge."

"Four eyewitness I.D.'s is compelling evidence," Nudger admitted. "What about the getaway car driver? His description is a lot like Colt's. Maybe he's the one who did the shooting and Colt was the driver."

"Colt's lawyer hit on that. The jury didn't buy it. Neither do I. The man is guilty, Nudge."

"You know how inaccurate eyewitness accounts are," Nudger persisted.

That seemed to get Hammersmith mad. He lit the cigar. The office immediately fogged up.

Nudger made his tone more amicable. "Mind if I look at the file on the Colt case?"

Hammersmith gazed thoughtfully at Nudger through a dense greenish haze. He inhaled, exhaled; the haze became a cloud. "How come this fiancée didn't turn up at the trial to testify for Colt? She could have at least lied and said he was with her that night."

"Colt apparently didn't want her subjected to taking the stand."

"How noble," Hammersmith said. "What makes this fiancée think her prince charming is innocent?"

"She knows he was somewhere else when the shopkeepers were shot."

"But not with her?"

"Nope."

"Well, that's refreshing."

Maybe it was refreshing enough to make up Hammersmith's mind. He picked up the phone and asked for the Colt file. Nudger could barely make out what he was saying around the fat cigar, but apparently everyone at the Third was used to Hammersmith and could interpret cigarese.

The file didn't reveal much that Nudger didn't know. Fifteen minutes after the liquor store shooting, officers from a two-man patrol car, acting on the broadcast description of the gunman, approached Curtis Colt inside a service station where he was buying a pack of cigarettes from a vending machine. A car that had been parked near the end of the dimly lighted lot had sped away as they'd entered the station office. The officers had gotten only a glimpse of a dark green old Ford; they hadn't made out the license plate number but thought it might start with the letter "L."

Colt had surrendered without a struggle, and that night at the Third District Station the four eyewitnesses had picked him out of a lineup. Their description of the getaway car matched that of the car the police had seen speeding from the service station. The loot from the holdup, and several gas station holdups committed earlier that night, wasn't on Colt, but probably it was in the car.

"Colt's innocence just jumps out of the file at you, doesn't it, Nudge?" Hammersmith said. He was grinning a fat grin around the fat cigar.

"What about the murder weapon?"

"Colt was unarmed when we picked him up."

"Seems odd."

"Not really," Hammersmith said. "He was planning to pay for the cigarettes. And maybe the gun was still too hot to touch so he left it in the car. Maybe it's still hot; it got a lot of use for one night."

Closing the file folder and laying it on a corner of Hammersmith's desk, Nudger stood up. "Thanks, Jack. I'll keep you tapped in if I learn anything interesting."

"Don't bother keeping me informed on this one, Nudge. It's over. I don't see how even a fiancée can doubt Colt's guilt."

Nudger shrugged, trying not to breathe too deeply in the smoke-hazed office. "Maybe it's an emotional thing. She thinks that because thought waves are tiny electrical impulses, Colt might experience time warp and all sorts of grotesque thoughts when all that voltage shoots through him. She has bad dreams."

"I'll bet she does," Hammersmith said. "I'll bet Colt has bad dreams, too. Only he deserves his. And maybe she's right."

"About what?"

"About all that voltage distorting thought and time. Who's to say?"

"Not Curtis Colt," Nudger said. "Not after they throw the switch."

"It's a nice theory, though," Hammersmith said. "I'll remember it. It might be a comforting thing to tell the murder victim's family."

"Sometimes," Nudger said, "you think just like a cop who's seen too much."

"Any of it's too much, Nudge," Hammersmith said with surprising sadness. He let more greenish smoke drift from his nostrils and the corners of his mouth; he looked like a stone Buddha seated behind the desk, one in which incense burned.

Nudger coughed and said goodbye.

"Only two eyewitnesses are needed to convict," Nudger said to Holly Ann the next day in her trailer, "and in this case there are four. None of them is at all in doubt about their identification of Curtis Colt as the killer. I have to be honest; it's time you should face the fact that Colt is guilty and that you're wasting your money on my services."

"All them witnesses know what's going to happen to Curtis," Holly Ann said. "They'd never want to live with the notion they might have made a mistake, killed an innocent man, so they've got themselves convinced that they're positive it was Curtis they saw that night."

"Your observation on human psychology is sound," Nudger said, "but I don't think it will help us. The witnesses were just as certain three months ago at the trial. I took the time to read the court transcript; the jury had no choice but to find Colt guilty, and the evidence hasn't changed."

Holly Ann drew her legs up and clasped her knees to her chest with both arms. Her little-girl posture matched her little-girl faith in her lover's innocence. She believed the white knight must arrive at any moment and snatch Curtis Colt from the electrical jaws of death. She believed hard. Nudger could almost hear his armor clank when he walked.

She wanted him to believe just as hard. "I see you need to be convinced of Curtis innocence," she said wistfully. There was no doubt he'd forced her into some kind of corner. "If you come here tonight at eight, Mr. Nudger, I'll convince you."

"How?"

"I can't say. You'll understand why tonight."

"Why do we have to wait till tonight?"

"Oh, you'll see."

Nudger looked at the waiflike creature curled in the corner of the sofa. He felt as if they were playing childhood guessing game while Curtis Colt waited his turn in the electric chair. Nudger had never seen an execution; he'd heard it took longer than most people thought for the condemned to die. His stomach actually twitched.

"Can't we do this now with twenty questions?" he asked.

Holly Ann shook her head. "No, Mr. Nudger."

Nudger sighed and stood up, feeling as if he were about to bump his head on the trailer's low ceiling even though he was barely six feet tall.

"Make sure you're on time tonight, Mr. Nudger," Holly Ann said as he went out the door. "It's important."

At eight on the nose that evening Nudger was sitting at the tiny table in Holly Ann's kitchenette. Across from him was a thin, nervous man in his late twenties or early thirties, dressed in a longsleeved shirt despite the heat, and wearing sunglasses with silver mirror lenses. Holly Ann introduced the man as "Len, but that's not his real name," and said he was Curtis Colt's accomplice and the driver of their getaway car on the night of the murder.

"But me and Curtis was nowhere near the liquor store when them folks got shot," Len said vehemently.

Nudger assumed the sunglasses were so he couldn't effectively identify Len if it came to a showdown in court. Len had lank, dark brown hair that fell to below his shoulders, and when he moved his arm Nudger caught sight of something blue and red on his briefly exposed wrist. A tattoo. Which explained the longsleeved shirt.

"You can understand why Len couldn't come forth and testify for Curtis in court," Holly Ann said.

Nudger said he could understand that. Len would have had to incriminate himself.

"We was way on the other side of town," Len said, "casing another service station, when that liquor store killing went down. Heck, we never help up nothing but service stations. They was our specialty."

Which was true, Nudger had to admit. Colt had done time for armed robbery six years ago after sticking up half a dozen service stations within a week. And all the other holdups he'd been tied to this time around were of service stations. The liquor store was definitely a departure in his M.O., one not noted in court during Curtis Colt's rush to judgment.

"Your hair is in your favor," Nudger said to Len.

"Huh?"

"Your hair didn't grow that long in the three months since the liquor store killing. The witnesses described the getaway car driver as having shorter, curlier hair, like Colt's, and a mustache."

Len shrugged. "I'll be honest with you–it don't help at all. Me and Curtis was kinda the same type. So to confuse any witnesses,

in case we got caught, we made each other look even more alike. I'd
tuck up my long hair and wear a wig that looked like Curtis's hair.
My mustache was real, like Curtis's. I shaved it off a month ago.
We did look alike at a glance; sorta like brothers."

Nudger bought that explanation; it wasn't uncommon for a team
of holdup men to play tricks to confuse witnesses and the police. Too
many lawyers had gotten in the game; the robbers, like the cops, were
taking the advice of their attorneys and thinking about a potential
trial even before the crime was committed.

"Is there any way, then, to prove you were across town at the time
of the murder?" Nudger asked, looking at the two small Nudgers
staring back at him from the mirror lenses.

"There's just my word," Len said, rather haughtily.

Nudger didn't bother telling him what that was worth. Why
antagonize him?

"I just want you to believe Curtis is innocent," Len said with
desperation. "Because he is! And so am I!"

And Nudger understood why Len was here, taking the risk. If Colt
was guilty of murder, Len was guilty of being an accessory to the
crime. Once Curtis Colt had ridden the lightning, Len would have
hanging over him the possibility of an almost certain life sentence,
and perhaps even his own ride on the lightning, if he were ever caught.
It wasn't necessary to actually squeeze the trigger to be convicted
of murder.

"I need for you to try extra hard to prove Curtis is innocent," Len
said. His thin lips quivered; he was near tears.

"Are you giving Holly Ann the money to pay me?" Nudger asked.

"Some of it, yeah. From what Curtis and me stole. And I gave
Curtis's share to Holly Ann, too. Me and her are fifty-fifty on this."

Dirty money, Nudger thought. Dirty job. Still, if Curtis Colt happened to be innocent, trying against the clock to prove it was a job
that needed to be done.

"Okay. I'll stay on the case."

"Thanks," Len said. His narrow hand moved impulsively across
the table and squeezed Nudger's arm in gratitude. Len had the look
of an addict; Nudger wondered if the longsleeved shirt was to hide
needle tracks as well as the tattoo.

Len stood up. "Stay here with Holly Ann for ten minutes while
I make myself scarce. I gotta know I wasn't followed. You understand it ain't that I don't trust you; a man in my position has gotta
be sure, is all."

"I understand. Go."

Len gave a spooked smile and went out the door. Nudger heard his running footfalls on the gravel outside the trailer. Nudger was forty-three years old and ten pounds overweight; lean and speedy Len needed a ten minute head start like Sinatra needed singing lessons.

"Is Len a user?" Nudger asked Holly Ann.

"Sometimes. But my Curtis never touched no dope."

"You know I have to tell the police about this conversation, don't you?"

Holly Ann nodded. "That's why we arranged it this way. They won't be any closer to Len than before."

"They might want to talk to you, Holly Ann."

She shrugged. "It don't matter. I don't know where Len is, nor even his real name nor how to get in touch with him. He'll find out all he needs to know about Curtis by reading the papers."

"You have a deceptively devious mind," Nudger told her, "considering that you look like Barbie Doll's country kid cousin."

Holly Ann smiled, surprised and pleased. "Do you find me attractive, Mr. Nudger?"

"Yes. And painfully young."

For just a moment Nudger almost thought of Curtis Colt as a lucky man. Then he looked at his watch, saw that his ten minutes were about up, and said goodbye. If Barbie had a kid cousin, Ken probably had one somewhere, too. And time was something you couldn't deny. Ask Curtis Colt.

"It doesn't wash with me," Hammersmith said from behind his desk, puffing angrily on his cigar. Angrily because it did wash a little bit; he didn't like the possibility, however remote, of sending an innocent man to his death. That was every good homicide cop's nightmare. "This Len character is just trying to keep himself in the clear on a murder charge."

"You could read it that way," Nudger admitted.

"It would help if you gave us a better description of Len," Hammersmith said gruffly, as if Nudger were to blame for Curtis Colt's accomplice still walking around free.

"I gave you what I could," Nudger said. "Len didn't give me much to pass on. He's streetwise and scared and knows what's at stake."

Hammersmith nodded, his fit of pique past. But the glint of weary frustration remained in his eyes.

"Are you going to question Holly Ann?" Nudger said.

"Sure, but it won't do any good. She's probably telling the truth. Len would figure we'd talk to her; he wouldn't tell her how to find him."

"You could stake out her trailer,"

"Do you think Holly Ann and Len might be lovers?"

"No."

Hammersmith shook his head. "Then they'll probably never see each other again. Watching her trailer would be a waste of manpower."

Nudger knew Hammersmith was right. He stood up to go.

"What are you going to do now?" Hammersmith asked.

"I'll talk to the witnesses again. I'll read the court transcript again. And I'd like to talk with Curtis Colt."

"They don't allow visitors on Death Row, Nudge, only temporary boarders."

"This case is an exception," Nudger said. "Will you try to arrange it?"

Hammersmith chewed thoughtfully on his cigar. Since he'd been the officer in charge of the murder investigation, he'd been the one who'd nailed Curtis Colt. That carried an obligation.

"I'll phone you soon," he said, "let you know."

Nudger thanked Hammersmith and walked down the hall into the clear, breathable air of the booking area.

That day he managed to talk again to all four eyewitnesses. Two of them got mad at Nudger for badgering them. They all stuck to their stories. Nudger reported this to Holly Ann at the Right-Steer Steakhouse, where she worked as a waitress. Several customers that afternoon got tears with their baked potatoes.

Hammersmith phoned Nudger that evening.

"I managed to get permission for you to talk to Colt," he said, "but don't get excited. Colt won't talk to you. He won't talk to anyone, not even a clergyman. He'll change his mind about the clergyman, but not about you."

"Did you tell him I was working for Holly Ann?"

"I had that information conveyed to him. He wasn't impressed. He's one of the stoic ones on Death Row."

Nudger's stomach kicked up, growled something that sounded like a hopeless obscenity. If even Curtis Colt wouldn't cooperate, how could he be helped? Absently Nudger peeled back the aluminum foil on a roll of antacid tablets and slipped two chalky white disks into his mouth. Hammersmith knew about his nervous stomach and must have heard him chomping the tablets. "Take it easy, Nudge. This isn't your fault."

"Then why do I feel like it is?"

"Because you feel too much of everything. That's why you had to quit the department."

"We've got another day before the execution," Nudger said. "I'm going to go through it all again. I'm going to talk to each of those witnesses even if they try to run when they see me coming. Maybe somebody will say something that will let in some light."

"There's no light out there, Nudge. You're wasting your time. Give up on this one and move on."

"Not yet," Nudger said. "There's something elusive here that I can't quite grab."

"And never will," Hammersmith said. "Forget it, Nudge. Live your life and let Curtis Colt lose his."

Hammersmith was right. Nothing Nudger did helped Curtis Colt in the slightest. At eight o'clock Saturday morning, while Nudger was preparing breakfast in his apartment, Colt was put to death in the electric chair. He'd offered no last words before two thousand volts had turned him from something into nothing.

Nudger heard the news of Colt's death on his kitchen radio. He went ahead and ate his eggs, but he skipped the toast.

That afternoon he consoled a numbed and frequently sobbing Holly Ann and apologized for being powerless to stop her true love's execution. She was polite, trying to be brave. She preferred to suffer alone. Her boss at the Right-Steer gave her the rest of the day off, and Nudger drove her home.

Nudger slept a total of four hours during the next two nights. On Monday, he felt compelled to attend Curtis Colt's funeral. There were about a dozen people clustered around the grave, including the state-appointed clergyman and pall-bearers. Nudger stood off to one side during the brief service. Holly Ann, looking like a child playing dress-up in black, stood well off to the other side. They didn't exchange words, only glances.

As the coffin was lowered into the earth, Nudger watched Holly Ann walk to where a taxi was waiting by a weathered stone angel. The cab wound its way slowly along the snaking narrow cemetery road to tall iron gates and the busy street. Holly Ann never looked back.

That night Nudger realized what was bothering him, and for the first time since Curtis Colt's death, he slept well.

In the morning he began watching Holly Ann's trailer.

At seven-thirty she emerged, dressed in her yellow waitress uniform, and got into another taxi. Nudger followed in his battered Volkswagen Beetle as the cab drove her the four miles to her job at the Right-Steer Steakhouse. She didn't look around as she paid the driver and walked inside through the molded plastic Old-West-saloon swinging doors.

At six that evening another cab drove her home, making a brief stop at a grocery store.

It went that way for the rest of the week, trailer to work to trailer. Holly Ann had no visitors other than the plain brown paper bag she took home every night.

The temperature got up to around ninety-five and the humidity rose right along with it. It was one of St. Louis's legendary summer heat waves. Sitting melting in the Volkswagen, Nudger wondered if what he was doing was really worthwhile. Curtis Colt was, after all, dead, and had never been his client. Still, there were responsibilities that went beyond the job. Or perhaps they were actually the essence of the job.

The next Monday, after Holly Ann had left for work, Nudger used his Visa card to slip the flimsy lock on her trailer door, and let himself in.

It took him over an hour to find what he was searching for. It had been well hidden, in a cardboard box inside the access panel to the bathroom plumbing. After looking at the box's contents–almost seven hundred dollars in loot from Curtis Colt's brief life of crime, and another object Nudger wasn't surprised to see–Nudger resealed the box and replaced the access panel.

He continued to watch and follow Holly Ann, more confident now.

Two weeks after the funeral, when she left work one evening, she didn't go home.

Instead her taxi turned the opposite way and drove east on Watson Road. Nudger followed the cab along a series of side streets in South St. Louis, then part way down a dead-end alley to a large garage, above the door of which was lettered "Clifford's Auto Body."

Nudger backed out quickly onto the street, then parked the Volkswagen near the mouth of the alley. A few minutes later the cab drove by without a passenger. Within ten minutes, Holly Ann drove past in a shiny red Ford. Its license plate number began with an L.

When Nudger reached Placid Cove Trailer Park, he saw the Ford nosed in next to Holly Ann's trailer.

On the way to the trailer door, he paused and scratched the Ford's hood with a key. Even in the lowering evening light he could see that beneath the new red paint the car's color was dark green.

Holly Ann answered the door right away when he knocked. She tried a smile when she saw it was him, but she couldn't quite manage her facial muscles, as if they'd become rigid and uncoordinated. She appeared ten years older. The little-girl look had deserted her; now she was an emaciated, grief-eroded woman, a country Barbie doll whose features some evil child had lined with dark crayon. The shaded crescents beneath her eyes completely took away their innocence. She was holding a glass that had once been a jelly jar. In it were two fingers of a clear liquid. Behind her on the table was a crumpled brown paper bag and a half-empty bottle of gin.

"I figured it out," Nudger told her.

Now she did smile, but it was fleeting, a sickly bluish shadow crossing her taut features. "You're like a dog with a rag, Mr. Nudger. You surely don't know when to let go." She stepped back and he followed her into the trailer. It was warm in there; something was wrong with the air conditioner. "Hot as hell, ain't it," Holly Ann commented. Nudger thought that was apropos.

He sat down across from her at the tiny Formica table, just as he and Len had sat facing each other two weeks ago. She offered him a drink. He declined. She downed the contents of the jelly jar glass and poured herself another, clumsily striking the neck of the bottle on the glass. It made a sharp, flinty sound, as if sparks might fly.

"Now, what's this you've got figured out, Mr. Nudger?" She didn't want to, but she had to hear it. Had to share it.

"It's almost four miles to the Right-Steer Steakhouse," Nudger told her. "The waitresses there make little more than minimum wage, so cab fare to and from work has to eat a big hole in your salary. But then you seem to go everywhere by cab."

"My car's been in the shop."

"I figured it might be, after I found the money and the wig."

She bowed her head slightly and took a sip of gin. "Wig?"

"In the cardboard box inside the bathroom wall."

"You been snooping, Mr. Nudger." There was more resignation than outrage in her voice.

"You're sort of skinny, but not a short girl," Nudger went on. "With a dark curly wig and a fake mustache, sitting in a car, you'd resemble Curtis Colt enough to fool a dozen eyewitnesses who just caught a glimpse of you. It was a smart precaution for the two of you to take."

Holly Ann looked astounded.

"Are you saying I was driving the getaway car at the liquor store holdup?"

"Maybe. Then maybe you hired someone to play Len and convince me he was Colt's accomplice and that they were far away from the murder scene when the trigger was pulled. After I found the wig, I talked to some of your neighbors, who told me that until recently you'd driven a green Ford sedan."

Holly Ann ran her tongue along the edges of her protruding teeth.

"So Curtis and Len used my car for their holdups."

"I doubt if Len ever met Curtis. He's somebody you paid in stolen money or drugs to sit there where you're sitting now and lie to me."

"If I was driving that getaway car, Mr. Nudger, and *knew* Curtis was guilty, why would I have hired a private investigator to try to find a hole in the eyewitnesses' stories?"

"That's what bothered me at first," Nudger said, "until I realized you weren't interested in clearing Curtis. What you were really worried about was Curtis Colt talking in prison. You didn't want those witnesses' stories changed, you wanted them verified. And you wanted the police to learn about not-his-right-name Len."

Holly Ann raised her head to look directly at him with eyes that begged and dreaded. She asked simply, "Why would I want that?"

"Because you were Curtis Colt's accomplice in all of his robberies. And when you hit the liquor store, he stayed in the car to drive. You fired the shot that killed the old woman. He was the one who fired the wild shot from the speeding car. Colt kept quiet about it because he loved you. He never talked, not to the police, not to his lawyer, not even to a priest. Now that he's dead you can trust him forever, but I have a feeling you could have anyway. He loved you more than you loved him, and you'll have to live knowing he didn't deserve to die."

She looked down into her glass as if for answers and didn't say anything for a long time. Nudger felt a bead of perspiration trickle crazily down the back of his neck. Then she said, "I didn't want to shoot that old man, but he didn't leave me no choice. Then the old woman came to me." She looked up at Nudger and smiled ever so slightly. It was a smile Nudger hadn't seen on her before, one he didn't like. "God help me, Mr. Nudger, I can't quit thinking about shooting that old woman."

"You murdered her," Nudger said, "and you murdered Curtis Colt by keeping silent and letting him die for you."

"You can't prove nothing," Holly Ann said, still with her ancient-eyed, eerie smile that had nothing to do with amusement.

"You're right," Nudger told her, "I can't. But I don't think legally proving it is necessary, Holly Ann. You said it: thoughts are actually tiny electrical impulses in the brain. Curtis Colt rode the lightning all at once. With you, it will take years, but the destination is the same. I think you'll come to agree that his way was easier."

She sat very still. She didn't answer. Wasn't going to.

Nudger stood up and wiped his damp forehead with the back of his hand. He felt sticky, dirty, confined by the low ceiling and near walls of the tiny, stifling trailer. He had to get out of there to escape the sensation of being trapped.

He didn't say goodbye to Holly Ann when he walked out. She didn't say goodbye to him. The last sound Nudger heard as he left the trailer was the clink of the bottle on the glass.

SUE GRAFTON
(b.1940)

She Didn't Come Home
(Kinsey Millhone)

September in Santa Teresa. I've never known anyone yet who doesn't suffer a certain restlessness when autumn rolls around. It's the season of new school clothes, fresh notebooks, and finely sharpened pencils without any teeth marks in the wood. We're all eight years old again and anything is possible. The new year should never begin on January 1. It begins in the fall and continues as long as our saddle oxfords remain unscuffed and our lunch boxes have no dents.

My name is Kinsey Millhone. I'm female, thirty-two, twice divorced, "doing business" as Kinsey Millhone Investigations in a little town ninety-five miles north of Los Angeles. Mine isn't a walk-in trade like a beauty salon. Most of my clients find themselves in a bind and then seek my services, hoping I can offer a solution for a mere thirty bucks an hour, plus expenses. Robert Ackerman's message was waiting on my answering machine that Monday morning at nine when I got in.

"Hello. My name is Robert Ackerman and I wonder if you could give me a call. My wife is missing and I'm worried sick. I was hoping you could help me out." In the background, I could hear whiney children, my favorite kind. He repeated his name and gave me a telephone number. I made a pot of coffee before I called him back.

A little person answered the phone. There was a murmured child-size hello and then I heard a lot of heavy breathing close to the mouthpiece.

"Hi," I said, "can I speak to your daddy?"

"Yes." Long silence.

"Today?" I asked.

The receiver was clunked down on a tabletop and I could hear the clatter of footsteps in a room that sounded as if it didn't have any carpeting. In due course, Robert Ackerman picked up the phone. "Lucy?"

"It's Kinsey Millhone, Mr. Ackerman. I just got your message on my answering machine. Can you tell me what's going on?"

"Oh wow, yeah..."

He was interrupted by a piercing shriek that sounded like one of those policeman's whistles you use to discourage obscene phone callers. I didn't jerk back quite in time. "Shit, that hurt."

I listened patiently while he dealt with the errant child.

"Sorry," he said when he came back on the line. "Look, is there any way you could come out to the house? I've got my hands full and I just can't get away."

I took his address and brief directions, then headed out to my car.

Robert and the missing Mrs. Ackerman lived in a housing tract that looked like it was built in the forties before anyone ever dreamed up the notion of family rooms, country kitchens, and his 'n' hers solar spas. What we had here was a basic drywall box; cramped living room with a dinning L, a kitchen and one bathroom sandwiched between two nine-by-twelve-foot bedrooms. When Robert answered the door I could just about see the whole place at a glance. The only thing the builders had been lavish with was the hardwood floors, which, in this case, was unfortunate. Little children had banged and scraped these floors and had brought in some kind of foot grit that I sensed before I was even asked to step inside.

Robert, though harried, had a boyish appeal; a man in his early thirties perhaps, lean and handsome, with dark eyes and dark hair that came to a pixie point in the middle of his forehead. He was wearing chinos and a plain white T-shirt. He had a baby, maybe eight months old, propped on his hip like a grocery bag. Another child clung to his right leg, while a third rode his tricycle at various walls and doorways, making quite loud sounds with his mouth.

"Hi, come on in," Robert said. "We can talk out in the backyard while the kids play." His smile was sweet.

I followed him through the tiny disorganized house and out to the backyard, where he set the baby down in a sandpile framed with two-by-fours. The second child held on to Robert's belt loops and stuck a thumb in its mouth, staring at me while the tricycle child tried to ride off the edge of the porch. I'm not fond of children. I'm really not. Especially the kind who wear hard brown shoes. Like dogs, these infants sensed my distaste and kept their distance, eyeing me with a mixture of rancor and disdain.

The backyard was scruffy, fenced in, and littered with the fifty-pound sacks the sand had come in. Robert gave the children homemade-style cookies out of a cardboard box and shooed them away. In fifteen minutes the sugar would probably turn them into lunatics. I gave my watch a quick glance, hoping to be gone by then.

"You want a lawn chair?"

"No, this is fine," I said and settled on the grass. There wasn't a lawn chair in sight, but the offer was nice anyway.

He perched on the edge of the sandbox and ran a distracted hand across his head. "God, I'm sorry everything is such a mess, but Lucy hasn't been here for two days. She didn't come home from work on Friday and I've been a wreck ever since."

"I take it you notified the police."

"Sure. Friday night. She never showed up at the babysitter's house to pick the kids up. I finally got a call here at seven asking where she was. I figured she'd just stopped off at the grocery story or something, so I went ahead and picked 'em up and brought 'em home. By ten o'clock when I hadn't heard from her, I knew something was wrong. I called her boss at home and he said as far as he knew she'd left work at five as usual, so that's when I called the police."

"You filed a missing persons report?"

"I can do that today. With an adult, you have to wait seventy-two hours, and even then, there's not much they can do."

"What else did they suggest?"

"The usual stuff, I guess. I mean, I called everyone we know. I talked to her mom in Bakersfield and this friend of hers at work. Nobody has any idea where she is. I'm scared something's happened to her."

"You've checked with hospitals in the area, I take it."

"Sure. That's the first thing I did."

"Did she give you any indication that anything was wrong?"

"Not a word."

"Was she depressed or behaving oddly?"

"Well, she was kind of restless the past couple of months. She always seemed to get excited around this time of year. She said it reminded her of her old elementary school days." He shrugged. "I hated mine."

"But she's never disappeared like this before."

"Oh, heck no. I just mentioned her mood because you asked. I don't think it amounted to anything."

"Does she have any problem with alcohol or drugs?"

"Lucy isn't really like that," he said. "She's petite and kind of quiet. A homebody, I guess you'd say."

"What about your relationship? Do the two of you get along okay?"

"As far as I'm concerned, we do. I mean, once in a while we get into it but never anything serious."

"What are your disagreements about?"

He smiled ruefully. "Money, mostly. With three kids, we never seem to have enough. I mean, I'm crazy about big families, but it's tough financially. I always wanted four or five, but she says three is plenty, especially with the oldest not in school yet. We fight about that some . . . having more kids."

"You both work?"

"We have to. Just to make ends meet. She has a job in an escrow company downtown, and I work for the phone company."

"Doing what?"

"Installer," he said.

"Has there been any hint of someone else in her life?"

He sighed, plucking at the grass between his feet. "In a way, I wish I could say yes. I'd like to think maybe she just got fed up or something and checked into a motel for the weekend. Something like that."

"But you don't think she did."

"Unh-uh and I'm going crazy with anxiety. Somebody's got to find out where she is."

"Mr. Ackerman . . ."

"You can call me Rob," he said.

Clients always say that. I mean, unless their names are something else.

"Rob," I said, "the police are truly your best bet in a situation like this. I'm just one person. They've got a vast machinery they can put to work and it won't cost you a cent."

"You charge a lot, huh?"

"Thirty bucks an hour plus expenses."

He thought about that for a moment, then gave me a searching look. "Could you maybe put in ten hours? I got three hundred bucks we were saving for a trip to the San Diego Zoo."

I pretended to think about it, but the truth was, I knew I couldn't say no to that boyish face. Anyway, the kids were starting to whine and I wanted to get out of there. I waived the retainer and said I'd send him an itemized bill when the ten hours were up. I figured I could put a contract in the mail and reduce my contact with the short persons who were crowding around him now, begging for more sweets. I asked for a recent photograph of Lucy, but all he could come up with was a two-year-old snapshot of her with the two older kids. She looked beleaguered even then, and that was before the third baby came along. I thought about quiet little Lucy Ackerman whose three strapping sons had legs the size of my arms. If I were she, I knew where I'd be. Long gone.

Lucy Ackerman was employed as an escrow officer for a small company on State Street not far from my office. It was a modest establishment of white walls, rust and brown plaid furniture with burnt orange carpeting. There were Gauguin reproductions all around and a live plant on every desk. I introduced myself first to the office manager, a Mrs. Merriman, who was in her sixties, had tall hair, and wore lace-up boots with stiletto heels. She looked like a woman who'd trade all her pension monies for a head-to-toe body tuck.

I said, "Robert Ackerman has asked me to see if I can locate his wife."

"Well, the poor man. I heard about that," she said with her mouth. Her eyes said, "Fat chance!"

"Do you have any idea where she might be?"

"I think you'd better talk to Mr. Sotherland." She had turned all prim and officious, but my guess was she knew something and was dying to be asked. I intended to accommodate her as soon as I'd talked to him. The protocol in small offices, I've found, is ironclad.

Gavin Sotherland got up from his swivel chair and stretched a big hand across the desk to shake mine. The other member of the office force, Barbara Hemdahl, the bookkeeper, got up from her chair simultaneously and excused herself. Mr. Sotherland watched her depart and then motioned me into the same seat. I sank into leather still hot from Barbara Hemdahl's backside, a curiously intimate effect. I made a mental note to find out what she knew, and then I looked, with interest, at the company vice president. I picked up all these names and job titles because his was cast in stand-up bronze letters on his desk, and the two women both had white plastic name tags affixed to their breasts, like nurses. As nearly as I could tell, there were only four of them in the office, including Lucy Ackerman, and I couldn't understand how they could fail to identify each other on sight. Maybe all the badges were for clients who couldn't be trusted to tell one from the other without the proper ID's.

Gavin Sotherland was large, an ex-jock to all appearances, maybe forty-five years old, with a heavy head of blond hair thinning slightly at the crown. He had a slight paunch, a slight stoop to his shoulders, and a grip that was damp with sweat. He had his coat off, and his

once-starched white shirt was limp and wrinkled, his beige gabardine pants heavily creased across the lap. Altogether, he looked like
a man who'd just crossed a continent by rail. Still, I was forced to
credit him with good looks, even if he had let himself go to seed.

"Nice to meet you, Miss Millhone. I'm so glad you're here." His
voice was deep and rumbling, with confidence-inspiring undertones.
On the other hand, I didn't like the look in his eyes. He could have
been a con man, for all I knew. "I understand Mrs. Ackerman never
got home Friday night," he said.

"That's what I'm told," I replied. "Can you tell me anything about
her day here?"

He studied me briefly. "Well, now I'm going to have to be honest
with you. Our bookkeeper has come across some discrepancies in the
accounts. It looks like Lucy Ackerman has just walked off with half
a million dollars entrusted to us."

"How'd she manage that?"

I was picturing Lucy Ackerman, free of those truck-busting kids,
lying on a beach in Rio, slurping some kind of rum drink out of a
coconut.

Mr. Sotherland looked pained. "In the most straightforward manner imaginable," he said. "It looks like she opened a new bank account
at a branch in Montebello and deposited ten checks that should have
gone into other accounts. Last Friday, she withdrew over five hundred thousand dollars in cash, claiming we were closing out a big
real estate deal. We found the passbook in her bottom drawer." He
tossed the booklet across the desk to me and I picked it up. The word
VOID had been punched into the pages in a series of holes. A quick
glance showed ten deposits at intervals dating back over the past three
months and a zero balance as of last Friday's date.

"Didn't anybody else double-check this stuff?"

"We'd just undergone our annual audit in June. Everything was
fine. We trusted this woman implicitly and had every reason to."

"You discovered the loss this morning?"

"Yes, ma'am, but I'll admit I was suspicious Friday night when
Robert Ackerman called me at home. It was completely unlike that
woman to disappear without a word. She's worked here eight years,
and she's been punctual and conscientious since the day she walked
in."

"Well, punctual at any rate," I said. "Have you notified the police?"

"I was just about to do that. I'll have to alert the Department of
Corporations, too. God, I can't believe she did this to us. I'll be fired.
They'll probably shut this entire office down."

"Would you mind if I had a quick look around?"

"To what end?"

"There's always a chance we can figure out where she went. If we move fast enough, maybe we can catch her before she gets away with it."

"Well, I doubt that," he said. "The last anybody saw her was Friday afternoon. That's two full days. She could be anywhere by now."

"Mr. Sotherland, her husband has already authorized three hundred dollars' worth of my time. Why not take advantage of it?"

He stared at me. "Won't the police object?"

"Probably. But I don't intend to get in anybody's way, and whatever I find out, I'll turn over to them. They may not be able to get a fraud detective out here until late morning anyway. If I get a line on her, it'll make you look good to the company *and* to the cops."

He gave a sigh of resignation and waved his hand. "Hell, I don't care. Do what you want."

When I left his office, he was putting the call through to the police department.

I sat briefly at Lucy's desk, which was neat and well organized. Her drawers contained the usual office supplies; no personal items at all. There was a calendar on her desktop, one of those loose-leaf affairs with a page for each day. I checked back through the past couple of months. The only personal notation was for an appointment at the Women's Health Center August 2, and a second visit last Friday afternoon. It must have been a busy day for Lucy, what with a doctor's appointment and ripping off her company for half a million bucks. I made a note of the address she'd penciled in at the time of her first visit. The other two women in the office were keeping an eye on me, I noticed, though both pretended to be occupied with paperwork.

When I finished my search, I got up and crossed the room to Mrs. Merriman's desk. "Is there any way I can make a copy of the passbook for that account Mrs. Ackerman opened?"

"Well, yes, if Mr. Sotherland approves," she said.

"I'm also wondering where she kept her coat and purse during the day."

"In the back. We each have a locker in the storage room."

"I'd like to take a look at that, too."

I waited patiently while she cleared both matters with her boss, and then I accompanied her to the rear. There was a door that opened onto the parking lot. To the left of it was a small rest room and, on the right, there was a storage room that housed four connecting upright metal lockers, the copy machine, and numerous shelves neatly stacked with office supplies. Each shoulder-high locker was marked with a name. Lucy Ackerman's was still securely padlocked. There was something about the blank look of that locker that seemed ominous somehow. I looked at the lock, fairly itching to have a crack at it with my little set of key picks, but I didn't want to push my luck with the cops on the way.

"I'd like for someone to let me know what's in that locker when it's finally opened," I remarked while Mrs. Merriman ran off the copy of the passbook pages for me.

"This, too," I said, handing her a carbon of the withdrawal slip Lucy'd been required to sign in receipt of the cash. It had been folded and tucked into the back of the booklet. "You have any theories about where she went?"

Mrs. Merriman's mouth pursed piously, as though she were debating with herself about how much she might say.

"I wouldn't want to be accused of talking out of school," she ventured.

"Mrs. Merriman, it does look like a crime's been committed," I suggested. "The police are going to ask you the same thing when they get here."

"Oh. Well, in that case, I suppose it's all right. I mean, I don't have the faintest idea where she is, but I do think she's been acting oddly the past few months."

"Like what?"

"She seemed secretive. Smug. Like she knew something the rest of us didn't know about."

"That certainly turned out to be the case," I said.

"Oh, I didn't mean it was related to that," she said hesitantly. "I think she was having an affair."

That got my attention. "An affair? With whom?"

She paused for a moment, touching at one of the hairpins that supported her ornate hairdo. She allowed her gaze to stray back toward Mr. Sotherland's office. I turned and looked in that direction, too.

"Really?" I said. "No wonder he was in a sweat," I thought.

"I couldn't swear to it," she murmured, "But his marriage has been rocky for years, and I gather she hasn't been that happy herself. She has those beastly little boys, you know, and a husband who seems determined to spawn more. She and Mr. Sotherland...Gavie, she calls him...have...well, I'm sure they've been together. Whether it's connected to this matter of the missing money, I wouldn't presume to guess." Having said as much, she was suddenly uneasy. "You won't repeat what I've said to the police, I hope."

"Absolutely not," I said. "Unless they ask, of course."

"Oh. Of course."

"By the way, is there a company travel agent?"

"Right next door," she replied.

I had a brief chat with the bookkeeper, who added nothing to the general picture of Lucy Ackerman's last few days at work. I retrieved my VW from the parking lot and headed over to the health center eight blocks away, wondering what Lucy had been up to. I was guessing birth control and probably the permanent sort. If she were having an affair (and determined not to get pregnant again in any event), it would seem logical, but I hadn't any idea how to verify the fact. Medical personnel are notoriously stingy with information like that.

I parked in front of the clinic and grabbed my clipboard from the backseat. I have a supply of all-purpose forms for occasions like this. They look like a cross between a job application and an insurance claim. I filled one out now in Lucy's name and forged her signature at the bottom where it said "authorization to release information." As a model, I used the Xerox copy of the withdrawal slip she'd tucked in her passbook. I'll admit my methods would be considered unorthodox, nay illegal, in the eyes of law-enforcement officers everywhere, but I reasoned that the information I was seeking would never actually be used in court, and therefore it couldn't matter *that* much how it was obtained.

I went into the clinic, noting gratefully the near-empty waiting room. I approached the counter and took out my wallet with my California Fidelity ID. I do occasional insurance investigations for CF in exchange for office space. They once made the mistake of issuing me a company identification card with my picture right on it that I've been flashing around quite shamelessly ever since.

I had a choice of three female clerks and, after a brief assessment, I made eye contact with the oldest of them. In places like this, the younger employees usually have no authority at all and are, thus, impossible to con. People without authority will often simply stand there, reciting the rules like mynah birds. Having no power, they also seem to take a vicious satisfaction in forcing others to comply.

The woman approached the counter on her side, looking at me expectantly. I showed my CF ID and made the form on the clipboard conspicuous, as though I had nothing to hide.

"Hi. My name is Kinsey Millhone," I said. "I wonder if you can give me some help. Your name is what?"

She seemed wary of the request, as though her name had magical powers that might be taken from her by force. "Lillian Vincent," she said reluctantly. "What sort of help did you need?"

"Lucy Ackerman has applied for some insurance benefits and we need verification of the claim. You'll want a copy of the release form for your files, of course."

I passed the forged paper to her and then busied myself with my clipboard as though it were all perfectly matter-of-fact.

She was instantly alert. "What is this?"

I gave her a look. 'Oh, sorry. She's applying for maternity leave and we need her due date."

"Maternity leave?"

"Isn't she a patient here?"

Lillian Vincent looked at me. "Just a moment," she said, and moved away from the desk with the form in hand. She went to a file cabinet and extracted a chart, returning to the counter. She pushed it over to me. "The woman has had a tubal ligation," she said, her manner crisp.

I blinked, smiling slightly as though she were making a joke. "There must be some mistake."

"Lucy Ackerman must have made it then if she thinks she can pull this off." She opened the chart and tapped significantly at the August 2 date. "She was just in here Friday for a final checkup and a medical release. She's sterile."

I looked at the chart. Sure enough, that's what it said. I raised my eyebrows and then shook my head slightly. "God. Well. I guess I better have a copy of that."

"I should think so," the woman said and ran one off for me on the desktop dry copier. She placed it on the counter and watched as I tucked it onto my clipboard.

She said, "I don't know how they think they can get away with it."

"People love to cheat," I replied.

It was nearly noon by the time I got back to the travel agency next door to the place where Lucy Ackerman had worked. It didn't take any time at all to unearth the reservations she'd made two weeks before. Buenos Aires, first class on Pan Am. For one. She'd picked up the ticket Friday afternoon just before the agency closed for the weekend.

The travel agent rested his elbows on the counter and looked at me with interest, hoping to hear all the gory details, I'm sure. "I heard about that business next door," he said. He was young, maybe twenty-four, with a pug nose, auburn hair and a gap between his teeth. He'd make the perfect co-star on a wholesome family TV show.

"How'd she pay for the tickets?"

"Cash," he said. "I mean, who'd have thunk?"

"Did she say anything in particular at the time?"

"Not really. She seemed jazzed and we joked some about Montezuma's revenge and stuff like that. I knew she was married, and I was asking her all about who was keeping the kids and what her old man was going to do while she was gone. God, I never in a million *years* guessed she was pulling off a scam like that, you know?"

"Did you ask why she was going to Argentina by herself?"

"Well, yeah, and she said it was a surprise." He shrugged. "It didn't really make sense, but she was laughing like a kid, and I thought I just didn't get the joke."

I asked for a copy of the itinerary, such as it was. She had paid for a round-trip ticket, but there were no reservations coming back. Maybe she intended to cash in the return ticket once she got down there. I tucked the travel docs onto my clipboard along with the copy of her medical forms. Something about this whole deal had begun to chafe, but I couldn't figure out quite why.

"Thanks for your help," I said, heading toward the door.

"No problem. I guess the other guy didn't get it either," he remarked.

I paused, midstride, turning back. "Get what?"

"The joke. I heard 'em next door and they were fighting like cats and dogs. He was pissed."

"Really?" I asked. I stared at him. "What time was this?"

"Five-fifteen. Something like that. They were closed and so were we, but Dad wanted me to stick around for a while until the cleaning crew got here. He owns this place, which is how I got in the business myself. These new guys were starting and he wanted me to make sure they understood what to do."

"Are you going to be here for a while?"

"Sure."

"Good. The police may want to hear about this."

I went back into the escrow office with mental alarm bells clanging away like crazy. Both Barbara Hemdahl and Mrs. Merriman had opted to eat lunch in. Or maybe the cops had ordered them to stay where they were. The bookkeeper sat at her desk with a sandwich, apple, and a carton of milk neatly arranged in front of her, while Mrs. Merriman picked at something in a plastic container she must have brought in from a fast-food place.

"How's it going?" I asked.

Barbara Hemdahl spoke up from her side of the room. "The detectives went off for a search warrant so they can get in all the lockers back there, collecting evidence."

"Only one of 'em is locked," I pointed out.

She shrugged. "I guess they can't even peek without the paperwork."

Mrs. Merriman spoke up then, her expression tinged with guilt. "Actually, they asked the rest of us if we'd open our lockers voluntarily, so of course we did."

Mrs. Merriman and Barbara Hemdahl exchanged a look.

"And?"

Mrs. Merriman colored slightly. "There was an overnight case in Mr. Sotherland's locker, and I guess the things in it were hers."

"Is it still back there?"

"Well, yes, but they left a uniformed officer on guard so nobody'd walk off with it. They've got everything spread out on the copy machine."

I went through the rear of the office, peering into the storage room. I knew the guy on duty and he didn't object to my doing a visual survey of the items, as long as I didn't touch anything. The overnight case had been packed with all the personal belongings women like to keep on hand in case the rest of the luggage gets sent to Mexicali by mistake. I spotted a toothbrush and toothpaste, slippers, a filmy nightie, prescription drugs, hairbrush, extra eyeglasses in a case. Tucked under a change of underwear, I spotted a round plastic container, slightly convex, about the size of a compact.

Gavin Sotherland was still sitting at his desk when I stopped by his office. His skin tone was gray and his shirt was hanging out, big rings of sweat under each arm. He was smoking a cigarette with the air of a man who's quit the habit and has taken it up again under duress. A second uniformed officer was standing just inside the door to my right.

I leaned against the frame, but Gavin scarcely looked up.

I said, "You knew what she was doing, but you thought she'd take you with her when she left."

His smile was bitter. "Life is full of surprises," he said.

I was going to have to tell Robert Ackerman what I'd discovered, and I dreaded it. As a stalling manoeuver, just to demonstrate what a good girl I was, I drove over to the police station first and dropped off the data I'd collected, filling them in on the theory I'd come up with. They didn't exactly pin a medal on me, but they weren't as pissed off as I thought they'd be, given the number of civil codes I'd violated in the process. They were even moderately courteous, which is unusual in their treatment of me. Unfortunately, none of it took that long and before I knew it, I was standing at the Ackermans' front door again.

I rang the bell and waited, bad jokes running through my head. Well, there's good news and bad news, Robert. The good news is we've wrapped it up with hours to spare so you won't have to pay me the full three hundred dollars we agreed to. The bad news is your wife's a thief, she's probably dead, and we're just getting out a warrant now, because we think we know where the body's stashed.

The door opened and Robert was standing there with a finger to his lips. "The kids are down for their naps," he whispered.

I nodded elaborately, pantomiming my understanding, as though the silence he'd imposed required this special behavior on my part.

He motioned me in and together we tiptoed through the house and out to the backyard, where we continued to talk in low tones. I wasn't sure which bedroom the little rugrats slept in, and I didn't want to be responsible for waking them.

Half a day of playing papa to the boys had left Robert looking disheveled and sorely in need of relief.

"I didn't expect you back this soon," he whispered.

I found myself whispering too, feeling anxious at the sense of secrecy. It reminded me of grade school somehow: the smell of autumn hanging in the air, the two of us perched on the edge of the sandbox like little kids, conspiring. I didn't want to break his heart, but what I was to do?

"I think we've got it wrapped up," I said.

He looked at me for a moment, apparently guessing from my expression that the news wasn't good. "Is she okay?"

"We don't think so," I said. And then I told him what I'd learned, starting with the embezzlement and the relationship with Gavin, taking it right through to the quarrel the travel agent had heard. Robert was way ahead of me.

"She's dead, isn't she?"

"We don't know it for a fact, but we suspect as much."

He nodded, tears welling up. He wrapped his arms around his knees and propped his chin on his fists. He looked so young, I wanted to reach out and touch him. "She was really having an affair?" he asked plaintively.

"You must have suspected as much," I said. "You said she was restless and excited for months. Didn't that give you a clue?"

He shrugged one shoulder, using the sleeve of his T-shirt to dash at the tears trickling down his cheeks. 'I don't know," he said. "I guess."

"And then you stopped by the office Friday afternoon and found her getting ready to leave the country. That's when you killed her, isn't it?"

He froze, staring at me. At first, I thought he'd deny it, but maybe he realized there wasn't any point. He nodded mutely.

"And then you hired me to make it look good, right?"

He made a kind of squeaking sound in the back of his throat and sobbed once, his voice reduced to a whisper again. "She shouldn't have done it...betrayed us like that. We loved her so much..."

"Have you got the money here?"

He nodded, looking miserable. "I wasn't going to pay your fee out of that," he said incongruously. "We really did have a little fund so we could go to San Diego one day."

"I'm sorry things didn't work out," I said.

"I didn't do so bad, though, did I? I mean, I could have gotten away with it, don't you think?"

I'd been talking about the trip to the zoo. He thought I was referring to his murdering his wife. Talk about poor communication. God.

"Well, you nearly pulled it off," I said. Shit, I was sitting there trying to make the guy *feel* good.

He looked at me piteously, eyes red and flooded, his mouth trembling. "But where did I slip up? What did I do wrong?"

"You put her diaphragm in the overnight case you packed. You thought you'd shift suspicion onto Gavin Sotherland, but you didn't realize she'd had her tubes tied."

A momentary rage flashed through his eyes and then flickered out. I suspected that her voluntary sterilization was more insulting to him than the affair with her boss.

"Jesus, I don't know what she saw in him," he breathed. "He was such a pig."

"Well," I said, "if it's any comfort to you, she wasn't going to take *him* with her, either. She just wanted freedom, you know?"

He pulled out a handkerchief and blew his nose, trying to compose himself. He mopped his eyes, shivering with tension. "How can you prove it, though, without a body? Do you know where she is?"

"I think we do," I said softly. "The sandbox, Robert. Right under us."

He seemed to shrink. "Oh, God," he whispered, "Oh, God, don't turn me in. I'll give you the money, I don't give a damn. Just let me stay here with my kids. The little guys need me. I did it for them. I swear I did. You don't have to tell the cops, do you?"

I shook my head and opened my shirt collar, showing him the mike. "I don't have to tell a soul, I'm wired for sound," I said, and then I looked over toward the side yard.

For once, I was glad to see Lieutenant Dolan amble into view.

EDWARD GORMAN
(b.1941)

The Reason Why
(Jack Dwyer)

"**I**'m, scared."

"This was your idea, Karen."

"You scared?"

"No."

"You bastard."

"Because I'm not scared I'm a bastard?"

"You not being scared means you don't believe me."

"Well."

"See. I knew it."

"What?"

"Just the way you said 'Well.' You bastard."

I sighed and looked out at the big red brick building that sprawled over a quarter mile of spring grass turned silver by a fat June moon. Twenty-five years ago a 1950 Ford fastback had sat in the adjacent parking lot. Mine for two summers of grocery store work.

We were sitting in her car, a Volvo she'd cadged from her last marriage settlement, number four if you're interested, and sharing a pint of bourbon the way we used to in high school when we'd been more than friends but never quite lovers.

The occasion tonight was our twenty-fifth class reunion. But there was another occasion, too. In our senior year a boy named Michael Brandon had jumped off a steep clay cliff called Pierce Point to his death on the winding river road below. Suicide. That, anyway, had been the official version.

A month ago Karen Lane (she had gone back to her maiden name these days, the Karen Lane-Cummings-Todd-Browne-LeMay getting a tad too long) had called to see if I wanted to go to dinner and I said yes, if I could bring Donna along, but then Donna surprised me by saying she didn't care to go along, that by now we should be at the point in our relationship where we trusted each other ("God, Dwyer, I don't even look at other men, not for very long anyway, you know?"), and Karen and I had had dinner and she'd had many drinks, enough that I saw she had a problem, and then she'd told me about something that had troubled for her a long time...

In senior year she'd gone to a party and gotten sick on wine and stumbled out to somebody's backyard to throw up and it was there she'd overheard the three boys talking. They were earnestly discussing what had happened to Michael Brandon the previous week and they were even more earnestly discussing what would happen to them if "anybody ever really found out the truth."

"It's bothered me all these years," she'd said over dinner a month earlier. "They murdered him and they got away with it."

"Why didn't you tell the police?"

"I didn't think they'd believe me."

"Why not?"

She shrugged and put her lovely little face down, dark hair covering her features. Whenever she put her face down that way it meant that she didn't want to tell you a lie so she'd just as soon talk about something else.

"Why not, Karen?"

"Because of where we came from. The Highlands."

The Highlands is an area that used to ring the iron foundries and factories of this city. Way before pollution became a fashionable concern, you could stand on your front porch and see a peculiarly beautiful orange haze on the sky every dusk. The Highlands had bars where men lost ears, eyes, and fingers in just garden-variety fights, and streets where nobody sane ever walked after dark, not even cops unless they were in pairs. But it wasn't the physical violence you remembered so much as the emotional violence of poverty. You get tired of hearing your mother scream because there isn't enough money for food and hearing your father scream back because there's nothing he can do about it. Nothing.

Karen Lane and I had come from the Highlands, but we were smarter and, in her case, better looking than most of the people from the area, so when we went to Wilson High School—one of those nightmare conglomerates that shoves the poorest kids in a city in with the richest–we didn't do badly for ourselves. By senior year we found ourselves hanging out with the sons and daughters of bankers and doctors and city officials and lawyers and riding around in new Impala convertibles and attending an occasional party where you saw an actual maid. But wherever we went, we'd manage for at least a few minutes to get away from our dates and talk to each other. What we were doing, of course, was trying to comfort ourselves. We shared terrible and confusing feelings–pride that we were acceptable to those we saw as glamorous, shame that we felt disgrace for being from the Highlands and having fathers who worked in factories and mothers who went to Mass as often as nuns and brothers and sisters who were doomed to punching the clock and yelling at ragged kids in the cold factory dusk. (You never realize what a toll such shame takes till you see your father's waxen face there in the years-later casket.)

That was the big secret we shared, of course, Karen and I, that we were going to get out, leave the place once and for all. And her brown eyes never sparkled more Christmas-morning bright than at those moments when it all was ahead of us, money, sex, endless thrills, immortality. She had the kind of clean good looks brought out best by a blue cardigan with a line of white button-down shirt at the top and a brown suede car coat over her slender shoulders and moderately tight jeans displaying her quietly artful ass. Nothing splashy about her. She had the sort of face that snuck up on you. You had the impression you were talking to a pretty but in no way spectacular girl, and then all of a sudden you saw how the eyes burned with sad humor and how wry the mouth got at certain times and how absolutely perfect that straight little nose was and how the freckles enhanced rather than detracted from her beauty and by then of course you were hopelessly entangled. Hopelessly.

This wasn't just my opinion, either. I mentioned four divorce settlements. True facts. Karen was one of those prizes that powerful and rich men like to collect with the understanding that it's only something you hold in trust, like a yachting cup. So, in her time, she'd been an ornament for a professional football player (her college beau), an orthodontist ("I think he used to have sexual fantasies about Barry Goldwater"), the owner of a large commuter airline ("I slept with half his pilots; it was kind of a company benefit"), and a sixty-nine-year-old millionaire who was dying of heart disease ("He used to have me sit next to his beside and just hold his hand–the weird thing was that of all of them, I loved him, I really did–and his eyes would be closed and then every once in a while tears would start streaming down his cheeks as if he was remembering something that really filled him with remorse; he was really a sweetie, but then cancer got him before the heart disease and I never did find out what he regretted so much, I mean if it was about his son or his wife or what"), and now she was comfortably fixed for the rest of her life and if the crow's feet were a little more pronounced around eyes and mouth and if the slenderness was just a trifle too slender (she weighed, at five-three, maybe ninety pounds and kept a variety of diet books in her big sunny kitchen), she was a damn good-looking woman nonetheless, the world's absurdity catalogued and evaluated in a gaze that managed to be both weary and impish, with a laugh that was knowing without being cynical.

So now she wanted to play detective.

I had some more bourbon from the pint–it burned beautifully– and said, "If I had your money, you know what I'd do?"

"Buy yourself a new shirt?"

"You don't like my shirt?"

"I didn't know you had this thing about Hawaii."

"If I had your money, I'd just forget about all this."

"I thought cops were sworn to uphold the right and the true."

"I'm an ex-cop."

"You wear a uniform."

"That's for the American Security Agency."

She sighed. "So I shouldn't have sent the letters?"

"No."

"Well, if they're guilty, they'll show up at Pierce Point tonight."

"Not necessarily."

"Why?"

"Maybe they'll know it's a trap. And not do anything."

She nodded to the school. "You hear that?"

"What?"

"The song."

It was Bobby Vinton's "Roses Are Red."

"I remember one party when we both hated our dates and we ended up dancing to that over and over again. Somebody's basement. You remember?"

"Sort of, I guess," I said.

"Good. Let's go in the gym and then we can dance to it again."

Donna, my lady friend, was out of town attending an advertising convention. I hoped she wasn't going to dance with anybody else because it would sure make me mad.

I started to open the door and she said, "I want to ask you a question."

"What?" I sensed what it was going to be so I kept my eyes on the parking lot.

"Turn around and look at me."

I turned around and looked at her. "Okay."

"Since the time we had dinner a month or so ago I've started receiving brochures from Alcoholics Anonymous in the mail. If you were having them sent to me, would you be honest enough to tell me?"

"Yes, I would."

"Are you having them sent to me?"

"Yes, I am."

"You think I'm a lush?"

"Don't you?"

"I asked you first."

So we went into the gym and danced.

Crepe of red and white, the school colors, draped the ceiling; the stage was a cave of white light on which stood four balding fat guys with spit curls and shimmery gold lamé dinner jackets (could these be the illegitmate sons of Bill Haley?) playing guitars, drum, and saxophone; on the dance floor couples who'd lost hair, teeth, jaw lines, courage, and energy (everything, it seemed, but weight)danced to lame cover versions of "Breaking Up Is Hard To Do" and "Sheila," "Runaround Sue" and "Running Scared" (tonight's lead singer sensibly not even trying Roy Orbison's beautiful falsetto) and then, while I got Karen and myself some no-alcohol punch, they broke into a medley of dance tunes–everything from "Locomotion" to "The Peppermint Twist"–and the place went a little crazy, and I went right along with it.

"Come on," I said.

"Great."

We went out there and we burned ass. We'd both agreed not to dress up for the occasion so we were ready for this. I wore the Hawaiian shirt she found so despicable plus a blue blazer, white socks and cordovan penny-loafers. She wore a salmon-colored Merikani shirt belted at the waist and tan cotton fatigue pants and, sweet Christ, she was so adorable half the guys in the place did the kind of doubletakes usually reserved for somebody outrageous or famous.

Over the blasting music, I shouted, "Everybody's watching you!"

She shouted right back, "I know! Isn't it wonderful?"

The medley went twenty minutes and could easily have been confused with an aerobics session. By the end I was sopping and wishing I was carrying ten or fifteen pounds less and sometimes feeling guilty because I was having too much fun (I just hoped Donna, probably having too much fun, too, was feeling equally guilty), and then finally it ended and mate fell into the arms of mate, hanging on to stave off sheer collapse.

Then the head Bill Haley clone said, "Okay, now we're going to do a ballad medley," so then we got everybody from Johnny Mathis to Connie Francis and we couldn't resist that, so I moved her around the floor with clumsy pleasure and she moved me right back with equally clumsy pleasure. "You know something?" I said.

"We're both shitty dancers?"

"Right."

But we kept on, of course, laughing and whirling a few times, and then coming tighter together and just holding each other silently for a time, two human beings getting older and scared about getting older, remembering some things and trying to forget others and trying to make sense of an existence that ultimately made sense to nobody, and then she said, "There's one of them."

I didn't have to ask her what "them" referred to. Until now she'd refused to identify any of the three people she'd sent the letters to.

At first I didn't recognize him. He had almost white hair and a tan so dark it looked fake. He wore a black dinner jacket with a lacy shirt and a black bow tie. He didn't seem to have put on a pound in the quarter century since I'd last seen him.

"Ted Forester?"

"Forester," she said. "He's president of the same savings and loan his father was president of."

"Who are the other two?"

"Why don't we get some punch?"

"The kiddie kind?"

"You could really make me mad with all this lecturing about alcoholism."

"If you're not really a lush then you won't mind getting the kiddie kind."

"My friend, Sigmund Fraud."

We had a couple of pink punches and caught our respective breaths and squinted in the gloom at name tags to see who we were saying hello to and realized all the terrible things you realize at high school reunions, namely that people who thought they were better than you still think that way, and that all the sad little people you feared for- the ones with blackheads and low IQs and lame left legs and walleyes and lisps and every other sort of unfair infirmity people get stuck with–generally turned out to be deserving of your fear, for there was a sadness in their eyes tonight that spoke of failures of every sort, and you wanted to go up and say something to them (I wanted to go up to nervous Karl Carberry, who used to twitch–his whole body twitched–and throw my arm around him and tell him what a neat guy he was, tell him there was no reason whatsoever for his twitching, grant him peace and self-esteem and at least a modicum of hope; if he needed a woman, get him a woman, too), but of course you didn't do that, you didn't go up, you just made edgy jokes and nodded a lot and drifted on to the next piece of human carnage.

"There's number two," Karen whispered.

This one I remembered. And despised. The six-three blond movie-star looks had grown only slightly older. His blue dinner jacket just seemed to enhance his air of malicious superiority. Larry Price. His wife Sally was still perfect, too, though you could see in the lacquered blond hair and maybe a hint of face lift that she'd had to work at it a little harder. A year out of high school, at a bar that took teenage IDs checked by a guy who must have been legally blind, I'd gotten drunk and told Larry that he was essentially an asshole for beating up a friend of mine who hadn't had a chance against him. I had the street boy's secret belief that I could take anybody whose father was a surgeon and whose house included a swimming pool. I had hatred, bitterness, and rage going, right? Well, Larry and I went out into the parking lot, ringed by a lot of drunken spectators, and before I got off a single punch, Larry hit me with a shot that stood me straight up, giving him a great opportunity to hit me again. He hit me three times before I found his face and sent him a shot hard enough to push him back for a time. Before we could go at it again, the guy who checked IDs got himself between us. He was madder than either Larry or me. He ended the fight by taking us both by the ears (he must have trained with nuns) and dragging us out to the curb and telling neither of us to come back.

"You remember the night you fought him?"

"Yeah."

"You could have taken him, Dwyer. Those three punches he got in were just lucky."

"Yeah, that was my impression, too. Lucky."

She laughed. "I was afraid he was going to kill you."

I was going to say something smart, but then a new group of people came up and we gushed through a little social dance of nostalgia and lies and self-justifications. We talked success (at high school reunions, everybody sounds like Amway representatives at a pep rally) and the old days (nobody seems to remember all the kids who got treated like shit for reasons they had no control over) and didn't so-and-so look great (usually this meant they'd managed to keep their toupees on straight) and introducing new spouses (we all had to explain what happened to our original mates; I said mine had been eaten by alligators in the Amazon, but nobody seemed to find that especially believeable) and in the midst of all this, Karen tugged my sleeve and said, "There's the third one."

Him I recognized, too. David Haskins. He didn't look any happier than he ever had. Parent trouble was always the explanation you got for his grief back in high school. His parents had been rich, truly so, his father an importer of some kind, and their arguments so violent that they were as eagerly discussed as who was or who was not pregnant. Apparently David's parents weren't getting along any better today because although the features of his face were open and friendly enough, there was still the sense of some terrible secret stooping his shoulders and keeping his smiles to furtive wretched imitations. He was a paunchy balding little man who might have been a church usher with a sour stomach.

"The Duke of Earl" started up then and there was no way we were going to let that pass so we got out on the floor; but by now, of course, we both watched the three people she'd sent letters to. Her instructions had been to meet the anonymous letter writer at nine-thirty at Pierce Point. If they were going to be there on time, they'd be leaving soon.

"You think they're going to go?"

"I doubt it, Karen."

"You still don't believe that's what I heard them say that night?"

"It was a long time ago and you were drunk."

"It's a good thing I like you because otherwise you'd be a distinct pain in the ass."

Which is when I saw all three of them go stand under one of the glowing red EXIT signs and open a fire door that led to the parking lot.

"They're going!" she said.

"Maybe they're just having a cigarette."

"You know better, Dwyer. You know better."

Her car was in the lot on the opposite side of the gym.

"Well, it's worth a drive even if they don't show up. Pierce Point should be nice tonight."

She squeezed against me and said, "Thanks, Dwyer. Really."

So we went and got her Volvo and went out to Pierce Point where twenty-five years ago a shy kid named Michael Brandon had fallen or been pushed to his death.

Apparently we were about to find out which.

The river road wound along a high wall of clay cliffs on the left and a wide expanse of water on the right. The spring night was impossibly beautiful, one of those moments so rich with sweet odor and even sweeter sight you wanted to take your clothes off and run around in some kind of crazed animal circles out of sheer joy.

"You still like jazz," she said, nodding to the radio.

"I hope you didn't mind my turning the station."

"I'm kind of into Country."

"I didn't get the impression you were listening."

She looked over at me. "Actually, I wasn't. I was thinking about you sending me all those AA pamphlets."

"It was arrogant and presumptuous and I apologize."

"No, it wasn't. It was sweet and I appreciate it."

The rest of the ride, I leaned my head back and smelled flowers and grass and river water and watched moonglow through the elms and oaks and birches of this new spring. There was a Dakota Staton song, "Street of Dreams," and I wondered as always where she was and what she was doing, she'd been so fine, maybe the most underappreciated jazz singer of the entire fifties.

Then we were going up a long, twisting gravel road. We pulled up next to a big park pavillion and got out and stood in the wet grass, and she came over and slid her arm around my waist and sort of hugged me in a half-serious way. "This is all probably crazy, isn't it?"

I sort of hugged her back in a half-serious way. "Yeah, but it's a nice night for a walk so what the hell."

"You ready?"

"Yep."

"Let's go then."

So we went up the hill to the Point itself, and first we looked out at the far side of the river where white birches glowed in the gloom and where beyond you could see the horseshoe shape of the city lights. Then we looked down, straight down the drop of two hundred feet, to the road where Michael Brandon had died.

When I heard the car starting up the road to the east, I said, "Let's get in those bushes over there."

A thick line of shrubs and second-growth timber would give us a place to hide, to watch them.

By the time we were in place, ducked down behind a wide elm and a mulberry bush, a new yellow Mercedes sedan swung into sight and stopped several yards from the edge of the Point.

A car radio played loud in the night. A Top 40 song. Three men got out. Dignified Forester, matinee-idol Price, anxiety-tight Haskins.

Forester leaned back into the car and snapped the radio off. But he left the headlights on. Forester and Price each had cans of beer. Haskins bit his nails.

They looked around in the gloom. The headlights made the

darkness beyond seem much darker and the grass in its illumination much greener. Price said harshly, "I told you this was just some god-damn prank. Nobody knows squat."

"He's right, he's probably right," Haskins said to Forester. Obviously he was hoping that was the case.

Forester said, "If somebody didn't know something, we would never have gotten those letters."

She moved then and I hadn't expected her to move at all. I'd been under the impression we would just sit there and listen and let them ramble and maybe in so doing reveal something useful.

But she had other ideas.

She pushed through the undergrowth and stumbled a little and got to her feet again and then walked right up to them.

"Karen!" Haskins said.

"So you did kill Michael," she said.

Price moved toward her abruptly, his hand raised. He was drunk and apparently hitting women was something he did without much trouble.

Then I stepped out from our hiding place and said, "Put your hand down, Price."

Forester said, "Dwyer."

"So," Price said, lowering his hand, "I was right, wasn't I?" He was speaking to Forester.

Forester shook his silver head. He seemed genuinely saddened. "Yes, Price, for once your cynicism is justified."

Price said, "Well, you two aren't getting a goddamned penny, do you know that?"

He lunged toward me, still a bully. But I was ready for him, wanted it. I also had the advantage of being sober. When he was two steps away, I hit him just once and very hard in his solar plexus. He backed away, eyes startled, and then he turned abruptly away.

We all stood looking at one another, pretending not to hear the sounds of violent vomiting on the other side of the splendid new Mercedes.

Forester said, "When I saw you there, Karen. I wondered if you could do it alone."

"Do what?"

"What?" Forester said. "What? Let's at least stop the games. You two want money."

"Christ," I said to Karen, who looked perplexed, "they think we're trying to shake them down."

"Shake them down?"

"Blackmail them."

"Exactly," Forester said.

Price had come back around. He was wiping his mouth with the back of his hand. In his other hand he carried a silver-plated .45, the sort of weapon professional gamblers favor.

Haskins said, "Larry, Jesus, what is that?"

"What does it look like?"

"Larry, that's how people get killed." Haskins sounded like Price's mother.

Price's eyes were on me. "Yeah, it would be terrible if Dwyer here got killed, wouldn't it?" He waved the gun at me. I didn't really think he'd shoot, but I sure was afraid he'd trip and the damn thing would go off accidentally. "You've been waiting since senior year to do that to me, haven't you, Dwyer?"

I shrugged. "I guess so, yeah."

"Well, why don't I give Forester here the gun and then you and I can try it again."

"Fine with me."

He handed Forester the .45. Forester took it all right, but what he did was toss it somewhere into the gloom surrounding the car. "Larry, if you don't straighten up here, I'll fight you myself. Do you understand me?" Forester had a certain dignity and when he spoke, his voice carried an easy authority. "There will be no more fighting, do you both understand that?"

"I agree with Ted." Karen said.

Forester, like a teacher tired of naughty children, decided to get on with the real business. "You wrote those letters, Dwyer?"

"No."

"No?"

"No. Karen wrote them."

A curious glance was exchanged by Forester and Karen. "I guess I should have known that," Forester said.

"Jesus, Ted," Karen said, "I'm not trying to blackmail you, no matter what you think."

"Then just what exactly are you trying to do?"

She shook her lovely little head. I sensed she regretted ever writing the letters, stirring it all up again. "I just want the truth to come out about what really happened to Michael Brandon that night."

"The truth," Price said. "Isn't that goddamn touching?"

"Shut up, Larry," Haskins said.

Forester said, "You know what happened to Michael Brandon?"

"I've got a good idea," Karen said. "I overheard you three talking at a party one night."

"What did we say?"

"What?"

"What did you overhear us say?"

Karen said, "You said that you hoped nobody looked into what really happened to Michael that night."

A smile touched Forester's lips. "So on that basis you concluded that we murdered him?"

"There wasn't much else to conclude."

Price said, weaving still, leaning on the fender for support, "I don't goddamn believe this."

Forester nodded to me. "Dwyer, I'd like to have a talk with Price and Haskins here, if you don't mind. Just a few minutes." He pointed to the darkness beyond the car. "We'll walk over there. You know we won't try to get away because you'll have our car. All right?"

I looked at Karen.

She shrugged.

They left, back into the gloom, voices receding and fading into the sounds of crickets and a barn owl and a distant roaring train.

"You think they're up to something?"

"I don't know," I said.

We stood with our shoes getting soaked and looked at the green green grass in the headlights.

"What do you think they're doing?" Karen asked.

"Deciding what they want to tell us."

"You're used to this kind of thing, aren't you?"

"I guess."

"It's sort of sad, isn't it?"

"Yeah. It is."

"Except for you getting the chance to punch out Larry Price after all these years."

"Christ, you really think I'm that petty?"

"I know you are. I know you are."

Then we both turned to look back to where they were. There'd been a cry and Forester shouted, "You hit him again, Larry, and I'll break your goddamn jaw." They were arguing about something and it had turned vicious.

I leaned back against the car. She leaned back against me. "You think we'll ever go to bed?"

"I'd sure like to, Karen, but I can't."

"Donna?"

"Yeah. I'm really trying to learn how to be faithful."

"That been a problem?"

"It cost me a marriage."

"Maybe I'll learn how someday, too."

Then they were back. Somebody, presumably Forester, had torn Price's nice lacy shirt into shreds. Haskins looked miserable.

Forester said, "I'm going to tell you what happened that night."

I nodded.

"I've got some beer in the back seat. Would either of you like one?"

Karen said, "Yes, we would."

So he went and got a six pack of Michelob and we all had a beer and just before he started talking he and Karen shared another one of those peculiar glances and then he said, "The four of us—myself, Price, Haskins, and Michael Brandon—had done something we were very ashamed of."

"Afraid of," Haskins said.

"Afraid that, if it came out, our lives would be ruined. Forever," Forester said.

Price said, "Just say it, Forester." He glared at me. "We raped a girl, the four of us."

"Brandon spent two months afterward seeing the girl, bringing her flowers, apologizing to her over and over again, telling her how sorry we were, that we'd been drunk and it wasn't like us to do that and—" Forester sighed, put his eyes to the ground. "In fact we had been drunk; in fact it wasn't like us to do such a thing—"

Haskins said, "It really wasn't. It really wasn't."

For a time there was just the barn owl and the crickets again, no talk, and then gently I said, "What happened to Brandon that night?"

"We were out as we usually were, drinking beer, talking about it, afraid the girl would finally turn us into the police, still trying to figure out why we'd ever done such a thing—"

The hatred was gone from Price's eyes. For the first time the matinee idol looked as melancholy as his friends. "No matter what you think of me, Dwyer, I don't rape women. But that night—" He shrugged, looked away.

"Brandon," I said. "you were going to tell me about Brandon."

"We came up here, had a case of beer or something, and talked about it some more, and that night," Forester said, "that night Brandon just snapped. He couldn't handle how ashamed he was or how afraid he was of being turned in. Right in the middle of talking—"

Haskins took over. "Right in the middle, he just got up and ran out to the Point." He indicated the cliff behind us. "And before we could stop him, he jumped."

"Jesus," Price said, "I can't forget his screaming on the way down. I can't ever forget it."

I looked at Karen. "So what she heard you three talking about outside the party that night was not that you'd killed Brandon but that you were afraid a serious investigation into his suicide might turn up the rape?"

Forester said, "Exactly." He stared at Karen. "We didn't kill Michael, Karen. We loved him. He was our friend."

But by then, complete without warning, she had started to cry and then she began literally sobbing, her entire body shaking with some grief I could neither understand nor assuage.

I nodded to Forester to get back in his car and leave. They stood and watched us a moment and then they got into the Mercedes and went away, taking the burden of years and guilt with them.

This time I drove. I went far out the river road, miles out, where you pick up the piney hills and the deer standing by the side of the road.

From the glove compartment she took a pint of J&B, and I knew better than to try and stop her.

I said, "You were the girl they raped, weren't you?"

"Yes."

"Why didn't you tell the police?"

She smiled at me. "The police weren't exactly going to believe a girl from the Highlands about the sons of rich men."

I sighed. She was right.

"Then Michael started coming around to see me. I can't say I ever forgave him, but I started to feel sorry for him. His fear–" She shook her head, looked out the window. She said, almost to herself, "But I had to write those letters, get them there tonight, know for sure if they killed him." She paused. "you believe them?"

"That they didn't kill him?"

"Right."

"Yes, I believe them."

"So do I."

Then she went back to staring out the window, her small face childlike there in silhouette against the moonsilver river. "Can I ask you a question, Dwyer?"

"Sure."

"You think we're ever going to get out of the Highlands?"

"No," I said, and drove on faster in her fine new expensive car. "No, I don't."

STEPHEN GREENLEAF
(b.1942)

Iris
(John Marshall Tanner)

The Buick trudged toward the summit, each step slower than the last, the automatic gearing slipping ever-lower as the air thinned and the grade steepened and the trucks were rendered snails. At the top the road leveled, and the Buick spent a brief sigh of relief before coasting thankfully down the other side, atop stiff gray strap that was Interstate 5. As it passed from Oregon to California the car seemed cheered. Its driver shared the mood, though only momentarily.

He blinked his eyes and shrugged his shoulders and twisted his head. He straightened his leg and shook it. He turned up the volume of the radio, causing a song to be sung more loudly than it merited. But the acid fog lay still behind his eyes, eating at them. As he approached a roadside rest area he decided to give both the Buick and himself a break.

During the previous week he had chased a wild goose in the shape of a rumor all the way to Seattle, with tantalizing stops in Eugene and Portland along the way. Eight hours earlier, when he had finally recognized the goose for what it was, he had headed home, hoping to make it in one day but realizing as he slowed for the rest area that he couldn't reach San Francisco that evening without risking more than was sensible in the way of vehicular manslaughter.

He took the exit, dropped swiftly to the bank of the Klamath River and pulled into a parking slot in the Randolph Collier safety rest area.

After making use of the facilities, he pulled out his map and considered where to spend the night. Redding looked like the logical place, out of the mountains, at the head of the soporific valley that separated him from home. He was reviewing what he knew about Redding when a voice, aggressively gay and musical, greeted him from somewhere near the car. He glanced to his side, sat up straight and rolled down the window. "Hi," the thin voice said again.

"Hi."

She was blond, her long straight tresses misbehaving in the wind that tumbled through the river canyon. Her narrow face was white and seamless, as though it lacked flesh, was only skull. Her eyes were blue and tardy. She wore a loose green blouse gathered at the neck and wrists and a long skirt of faded calico, fringed in white ruffles. Her boots were leather and well-worm, their tops disappearing under her skirt the way the tops of the mountains at her back disappeared into a disc of cloud.

He pegged her for a hitchhiker, one who perpetually roams the roads and provokes either pity or disapproval in those who pass her by. He glanced around to see if she was fronting for a partner, but the only thing he saw besides the picnic and toilet facilities and travelers like himself was a large bundle resting atop a picnic table at the far end of the parking lot. Her worldly possessions, he guessed; her only aids to life. He looked at her again and considered whether he wanted to share some driving time and possibly a motel room with a girl who looked a little spacy and a little sexy and a lot heedless of the world that delivered him his living.

"My name's Iris," She said, wrapping her arms across her chest, shifting her weight from foot to foot, shivering in the autumn chill.

"Mine's Marsh."

"You look tired." Her concern seemed genuine, his common symptoms for some reason alarming to her.

"I am," he admitted.

"Been on the road long?"

"From Seattle."

"How far is that about?" The question came immediately, as though she habitually erased her ignorance.

"Four hundred miles. Maybe a little more."

She nodded as though the numbers made him wise. "I've been to Seattle."

"Good."

"I've been lots of places."

"Good."

She unwrapped her arms and placed them on the car door and

leaned toward him. Her musk was unadulterated. Her blouse dropped open to reveal breasts sharpened to twin points by the mountain air. "Where you headed, Marsh?"

"South."

"L.A.?"

He shook his head. "San Francisco."

"Good. Perfect."

He expected it right then, the flirting pitch for a lift, but her request was slightly different. "Could you take something down there for me?"

He frowned and thought of the package on the picnic table. Drugs? "What?" he asked.

"I'll show you in a sec. Do you think you could, though?"

He shook his head. "I don't think so. I mean, I'm kind of on a tight schedule, and..."

She wasn't listening. "It goes to..." She pulled a scrap of paper from the pocket of her skirt and uncrumpled it. "It goes to 95 Albosa Drive, in Hurley City. That's near Frisco, isn't it? Marvin said it was."

He nodded. "But I don't..."

She put up a hand. "Hold still. I'll be right back."

She skipped twice, her long skirt hopping high above her boots to show a shaft of gypsum thigh, then trotted to the picnic table and picked up the bundle. Halfway back to the car she proffered it like a prize soufflé.

"Is this what you want me to take?" he asked as she approached.

She nodded, then looked down at the package and frowned. "I don't like this one," she said, her voice dropping to a dismissive rasp.

"Why not?"

"Because it isn't happy. It's from the B Box, so it can't help it, I guess, but all the same it should go back, I don't care *what* Marvin says."

"What is it? A puppy?"

She thrust the package through the window. He grasped it reflexively, to keep it from dropping to his lap. As he secured his grip the girl ran off. "Hey! Wait a minute," he called after her. "I can't take this thing. You'll have to..."

He thought the package moved. He slid one hand beneath it and with the other peeled back the cotton strips that swaddled it. A baby—not canine but human—glared at him and screamed. He looked frantically for the girl and saw her climbing into a gray Volkswagen bug that was soon scooting out of the rest area and climbing toward the freeway.

He swore, then rocked the baby awkwardly for an instant, trying to quiet the screams it formed with every muscle. When that didn't work, placed the child on the seat beside him, started the car and backed out. As he started forward he had to stop to avoid another car, and then to reach out wildly to keep the child from rolling off the seat.

He moved the gear to park and gathered the seat belt on the passenger side and tried to wrap it around the baby in a way that would be more safe than throttling. The result was not reassuring. He unhooked the belt and put the baby on the floor beneath his legs, put the car in gear and set out after the little gray VW that had disappeared with the child's presumptive mother. He caught it only after several frantic miles, when he reached the final slope that descended to the grassy plain that separated the Siskiyou range from the lordly aspect of Mt. Shasta.

The VW buzzed toward the mammoth mountain like a mad mouse assaulting an elephant. He considered overtaking the car, forcing Iris to stop, returning the baby, then getting the hell away from her as fast as the Buick would take him. But something in his memory of her look words and made him keep his distance, made him keep Iris in sight while he waited for her to make a turn toward home.

The highway flattened, then crossed the high meadow that nurtured sheep and cattle and horses below the lumps of the southern Cascades and the Trinity Alps. Traffic was light, the sun low above the western peaks, the air a steady splash of autumn. He checked his gas gauge. If Iris didn't off in the next fifty miles he would either have to force her to stop or let her go. The piercing baby sounds that rose from beneath his knees made the latter choice impossible.

They reached Yreka, and he closed to within a hundred yards of the bug, but Iris ignored his plea that the little city be her goal. Thirty minutes later, after he had decided she was nowhere near her destination, Iris abruptly left the interstate, at the first exit to a village that was hand-maiden to the mountain, a town reputed to house an odd collection of spiritual seekers and religious zealots.

The mountain itself, volcanic, abrupt, spectacular, had been held by the Indians to be holy, and the area surrounding it was replete with hot springs and mud baths and other prehistoric marvels. Modern mystics had accepted the mantle of the mountain, and the crazy girl and her silly bug fit with what he knew about the place and those who gathered there. What didn't fit was the baby she had foisted on him.

He slowed and glanced at his charge once again and failed to receive anything resembling contentment in return. Fat little arms escaped the blanket and pulled the air like taffy. Spittle dribbled down its chin. A translucent bubble appeared at a tiny nostril, then broke silently and vanished.

The bug darted through the north end of town, left, then right, then left again, quickly, as though it sensed pursuit. He lagged behind, hoping Iris was confident she had ditched him. He looked at the baby again, marvelling that it could cry so loud, could for so long expend the major portion of its strength in unrequited pleas. When he looked at the road again the bug had disappeared.

He swore and slowed and looked at driveways, then began to plan what to do if he had lost her. Houses dwindled, the street became dirt, then flanked the log decks and lumber stacks and wigwam burners of a sawmill. A road sign declared it unlawful to sleigh, toboggan or ski on a county road. He had gasped the first breaths of panic when he saw the VW nestled next to a ramshackle cabin on the back edge of town, empty, as though it had been there always.

A pair of firs sheltered the cabin and the car, made the dwindling day seem night. The driveway was mud, the yard bordered by a falling wormwood fence. He drove to the next block and stopped his car, the cabin now invisible.

He knew he couldn't keep the baby much longer. He had no idea what to do, for it or with it, had no idea what it wanted, no idea what awaited it in Hurley City, had only a sense that the girl, Iris, was goofy, perhaps pathologically so, and that he should not abet her plan.

Impossibly, the child cried louder. He had some snacks in the car—crackers, cookies, some cheese—but he was afraid the baby was too young for solids. He considered buying milk, and a bottle, and playing parent. The baby cried again, gasped and sputtered, then repeated its protest.

He reached down and picked it up. The little red face inflated, contorted, mimicked a steam machine that continuously whistled. The puffy cheeks, the tiny blue eyes, the round pug nose, all were engorged in scarlet fury. He cradled the baby in his arms as best he could and rocked it. The crying dimmed momentarily, then began again.

His mind ran the gauntlet of childhood scares—diphtheria, smallpox, measles, mumps, croup, even a pressing need to burp. God knew what ailed it. He patted its forehead and felt the sticky heat of fever.

Shifting position, he felt something hard within the blanket, felt for it, finally drew it out. A nippled baby bottle, half-filled, body-warm. He shook it and presented the nipple to the baby, who sucked it as its due. Giddy at his feat, he unwrapped his package further, enough to tell him he was holding a little girl and that she seemed whole and healthy except for her rage and fever. When she was feeding steadily he put her back on the floor and got out of the car.

The stream of smoke it emitted into the evening dusk made the cabin seem dangled from a string. Beneath the firs the ground was moist, a spongy mat of rotting twigs and needles. The air was cold and damp and smelled of burning wood. He walked slowly up the drive, courting silence, alert for the menace implied by the hand-lettered sign, nailed to the nearest tree, that ordered him to KEEP OUT.

The cabin was dark but for the variable light at a single window. The porch was piled high with firewood, both logs and kindling. A maul and wedge leaned against a stack of fruitwood piled next to the door. He walked to the far side of the cabin and looked beyond it for signs of Marvin.

A tool shed and a broken-down school bus filled the rear yard. Between the two a tethered nanny goat grazed beneath a line of drying clothes, silent but for her neck bell, the swollen udder oscillating easily beneath her, the teats extended like accusing fingers. Beyond the yard a thicket of berry bushes served as a fence, and beyond the bushes a stand of pines blocked further vision. He felt alien, isolated, exposed, threatened, as Marvin doubtlessly hoped all strangers would.

He thought about the baby, wondered if it was all right, wondered if babies could drink so much they got sick or even choked. A twinge of fear sent him trotting back to the car. The baby was fine, the bottle empty on the floor beside it, its noises not wails but only muffled whimpers. He returned to the cabin and went onto the porch and knocked at the door and waited.

Iris wore the same blouse and skirt and boots, the same eyes too shallow to hold her soul. She didn't recognize him; her face pinched only with uncertainty.

He stepped toward her and she backed away and asked him what he wanted. The room behind her was a warren of vague shapes, the only source of light far in the back by a curtain that spanned the room.

"I want to give you your baby back," he said.

She looked at him more closely, then opened her mouth in silent exclamation, then slowly smiled. "How'd you know where I lived?"

"I followed you."

"Why? Did something happen to it already?"

"No, but I don't want to take it with me."

She seemed truly puzzled. "Why not? It's on your way, isn't't? Almost?"

He ignored the question. "I want to know some more about the baby."

"Like what?"

"Like whose is it? Yours?"

Iris frowned and nibbled her lower lip. "Sort of."

"What do you mean," 'sort of?' Did you give birth to it?"

"Not exactly." Iris combed her hair with her fingers, then shook it off her face with an irritated twitch. "What are you asking all these questions for?"

"Because you asked me to do you a favor and I think I have the right to know what I'm getting into. That's only fair, isn't it?"

She paused. Her pout was dubious. "I guess."

"So where did you get the baby?" he asked again.

"Marvin got it."

"From whom?"

"Those people in Hurley City. So I don't know why you won't take it back, seeing as how it's theirs and all."

"But why..."

His question was obliterated by a high glissando, brief and piercing. He looked at Iris, then at the shadowy interior of the cabin.

There was no sign of life, no sign of anything but the leavings of neglect and a spartan bent. A fat gray cat hopped off a shelf and sauntered toward the back of the cabin and disappeared behind the blanket that was draped on the rope that spanned the rear of the room. The cry echoed once again. "What's that?" he asked her.

Iris giggled. "What does it sound like?"

"Another baby?"

Iris nodded.

"Can I see it?"

"Why?"

"Because I like babies."

"If you like them, why won't you take the one I gave you down to Hurley City?"

"Maybe I'm changing my mind. Can I see this one?"

"I'm not supposed to let anyone in here."

"It'll be okay. Really. Marvin isn't here, is he?"

She shook her head. "But he'll be back any time. He just went to town."

He summoned reasonableness and geniality. "Just let me see your baby for a second, Iris. Please? Then I'll go. And take the other baby with me. I promise."

She pursed her lips, then nodded and stepped back. "I got more than one," she suddenly bragged. "Let me show you." She turned and walked quickly toward the rear of the cabin and disappeared behind the blanket.

When he followed he found himself in a space that was half-kitchen and half-nursery. Opposite the electric stove and Frigidaire, along the wall between the wood stove and the rear door, was a row of wooden boxes, seven of them, old orange crates, dividers removed, painted different colors and labelled A to G. Faint names of orchards and renderings of fruits rose through the paint on the stub ends of the crates. Inside boxes C through G were babies, buried deep in nests of rags and scraps of blanket. One of them was crying. The others slept soundly, warm and toasty, healthy and happy from all the evidence he had.

"My God." he said.

"Aren't they beautiful? They're just the best little things in the whole world. Yes they are. Just the best little babies in the whole wide world. And Iris loves them all a bunch. Yes, she does. Doesn't she?"

Beaming, Iris cooed to the babies for another moment, then her face darkened. "The one I gave you, she wasn't happy here. That's because she was a B Box baby. My B babies are always sad, I don't know why. I treat them all the same, but the B babies are just contrary. That's why the one I gave you should go back. Where is it, anyway?"

"In the car."

"By itself?"

He nodded.

"You shouldn't leave her there like that," Iris chided. "She's pouty enough already."

"What about these others?" he asked, looking at the boxes. "Do they stay here forever?"

Her whole aspect solidified. "They stay till Marvin needs them. Till he does, I give them everything they want. Everything they need. No one could be nicer to my babies than me. *No* one."

The fire in the stove lit her eyes like ice in sunlight. She gazed raptly at the boxes, one by one, and received something he sensed was sexual in return. Her breaths were rapid and shallow, her fists clenched at her sides. "Where'd you get these babies?" he asked softly.

"Marvin gets them." She was only half-listening.

"Where?"

"All over. We had one from Nevada one time, and two from Idaho I think. Most are from California, though. And Oregon. I think that C Box baby's from Spokane. That's Oregon, isn't it?"

He didn't correct her. "Have there been more besides these?"

"Some."

"How many?"

"Oh, maybe ten. No, more than that. I've had three of all the babies except G babies."

"And Marvin got them all for you?"

She nodded and went to the stove and turned on a burner. "You want some tea? It's herbal. Peppermint."

He shook his head. "What happened to the other babies? The ones that aren't here any more?"

"Marvin took them." Iris sipped her tea.

"Where?"

"To someone that wanted to love them." The declaration was as close as she would come to gospel.

The air in the cabin seemed suddenly befouled, not breathable. "Is that what this is all about, Iris? Giving babies to people that want them?"

"That want them and will *love* them. See, Marvin gets these babies from people that *don't* want them, and gives them to people that *do*. It's his business."

"Does he get paid for it?"

She shrugged absently. "A little, I think."

"Do you go with Marvin when he picks them up?"

"Sometimes. When it's far."

"And where does he take them? To Idaho and Nevada, or just around here?"

She shrugged again. "He doesn't tell me where they go. He says he doesn't want me to try and get them back." She smiled peacefully. "He knows how I am about my babies."

"How long have you and Marvin been doing this?"

"I been with Marvin about three years."

"And you're been trading in babies all that time?"

"Just about."

She poured some more tea into a ceramic cup and sipped it. She gave no sign of guile or guilt, no sign that what he suspected could possibly be true.

"Do you have any children of your own, Iris?"

Her hand shook enough to spill her tea. "I *almost* had one once."

"What do you mean?"

She made a face. "I got pregnant, but nobody wanted me to keep it so I didn't."

"Did you put it up for adoption?"

She shook her head.

"Abortion?"

Iris nodded, apparently in pain, and mumbled something. He asked her what she'd said. "I did it myself," she repeated. "That's what

I can't live with. I scraped it out of there myself. I passed out. I . . ."

She felt silent. He looked back at the row of boxes that held her penance. When she saw him look she began to sing a song. "Aren't they just perfect?" she said when she was through. "Aren't they all just perfect?"

"How do you know where the baby you gave me belongs?" he asked quietly.

"Marvin's got a book that keeps track. I sneaked a look at it one time when he was stoned."

"Where's he keep it?"

"In the van. At least that's where I found it." Iris put her hands on his chest and pushed. "You better go before Marvin gets back. You'll take the baby, won't you? It just don't belong here with the others. It fusses all the time and I can't love it like I should."

He looked at Iris' face, at the firelight washing across it, making it alive. "Where are you from, Iris?"

"Me? Minnesota."

"Did you come to California with Marvin?"

She shook her head. "I come with another guy. I was tricking for him when I got knocked up. After the abortion I told him I wouldn't trick no more so he ditched me. Then I did a lot of drugs for a while, till I met Marvin at a commune down by Mendocino."

"What's Marvin's last name?"

"Hessel. Now you got to go. Really. Marvin's liable to do something crazy if he finds you here." She walked toward him and he retreated.

"Okay, Iris. Just one thing. Could you give me something for the baby to eat? She's real hungry."

Iris frowned. "She only likes goat's milk, is the problem, and I haven't milked today." She walked to the Frigidaire and returned with a bottle. "This is all I got. Now, git."

He nodded, took the bottle from her, then retreated to his car.

He opened the door on the stinging smell of ammonia. The baby greeted him with screams. He picked it up, rocked it, talked to it, hummed a tune, finally gave it the second bottle, which was the only thing it wanted.

As it sucked its sustenance he started the car and let the engine warm, and a minute later flipped the heater switch. When it seemed prudent, he unwrapped the child and unpinned her soggy diaper and patted her dumplinged bottom dry with a tissue from the glove compartment. After covering her with her blanket he got out of the car, pulled his suitcase from the trunk and took out his last clean T-shirt, then returned to the car and fashioned a bulky diaper out of the cotton-shirt and affixed it to the child, pricking his finger in the process, spotting both the garment and the baby with his blood. Then he sat for a time, considering his obligations to the children that had suddenly littered his life.

He should go to the police, but Marvin might return before they responded and might learn of Iris' deed and harm the children or flee with them. He could call the police and wait in place for them to come, but he doubted his ability to convey his precise suspicions over the phone. As he searched for other options, headlights ricocheted off his mirror and into his eyes, then veered off. When his vision was re-established he reached into the glove compartment for his revolver. Shoving it into his pocket, he got out of the car and walked back to the driveway and disobeyed the sign again.

A new shape had joined the scene, rectangular and dark. Marvin's van, creaking as it cooled. He waited, listened, and when he sensed no other presence he approached it. A converted bread truck, painted Navy blue, with sliding doors into the driver's cabin and hinged doors at the back. The right fender was dented, the rear bumper wired in place. A knobby-tired motorcycle was strapped to a rack on the top. The door on the driver's side was open, so he climbed in.

The high seat was rotted through, its stuffing erupting like white weeds through the dirty vinyl. The floorboards were littered with food wrappers and beer cans and cigarette butts. He activated his pencil flash and pawed through the refuse, pausing at the only pristine object in the van–a business card, white with black engraving, taped to a corner of the dash: 'J. Arnold Rasker, Attorney at Law. Practice in all Courts. Initial Consultation Free. Phone day or night.'

He looked through the cab for another minute, found nothing resembling Marvin's notebook and nothing else of interest. After listening for Marvin's return and hearing nothing he went through the narrow doorway behind the driver's seat into the cargo area in the rear, the yellow ball that dangled from his flash bouncing playfully before him.

The entire area had been carpeted, ceiling included, in a matted pink plush that was stained in unlikely places and coming unglued in others. A roundish window had been cut into one wall by hand, then covered with plasticine kept in place with tape. Two upholstered chairs were bolted to the floor on one side of the van, and an Army cot stretched out along the other. Two orange crates similar to those in the cabin, though empty, lay between the chairs. Above the cot a picture of John Lennon was tacked to the carpeted wall with a rusty nail. A small propane bottle was strapped into one corner, an Igloo cooler in another. Next to the Lennon poster a lever-action rifle rested in two leather slings. The smells were of gasoline and marijuana and unwashed flesh. Again he found no notebook.

He switched off his light and backed out of the van and walked to the cabin, pausing on the porch. Music pulsed from the interior, heavy metal, obliterating all noises including his own. He walked to the window and peered inside.

Iris, carrying and feeding a baby, paced the room, eyes closed, mumbling, seemingly deranged. Alone momentarily, she was soon joined by a wide and woolly man, wearing cowboy boots and Levi's, a plaid shirt, full beard, hair to his shoulders. A light film of grease coated flesh and clothes alike, as though he had just been dipped. Marvin strode through the room without speaking, his black eyes angry, his shoulders tipping to the frenetic music as he sucked the final puffs of a joint held in an oddly dainty clip.

Both Marvin and Iris were lost in their tasks. When their paths crossed they backed away as though they feared each other. He watched them for five long minutes. When they disappeared behind the curtain in the back he hurried to the door and went inside the cabin.

The music paused, then began again, the new piece indistinguishable from the old. The heavy fog of dope washed into his lungs and lightened his head and braked his brain. Murmurs from behind the curtain erupted into a swift male curse. A pan clattered on the stove; wood scraped against wood. He drew his gun and moved to the edge of the room and sidled toward the curtain and peered around its edge.

Marvin sat in a chair at a small table, gripping a bottle of beer. Iris was at the stove, her back to Marvin, opening a can of soup. Marvin guzzled half the bottle, banged it on the table, and swore again. "How could you be so fucking stupid?"

"Don't, Marvin. Please?"

"Just tell me who you gave it to. That's all I want to know. It was your buddy Gretel, wasn't it? Had to be, she's the only one around here as looney as you."

"It wasn't anyone you know. Really. It was just a guy."

"What guy?"

"Just a *guy*. I went out to a rest area way up by Oregon, and I talked to him and he said he was going to Frisco so I gave it to him and told him where to take it. You *know* it didn't belong here, Marvin. You know how puny it was."

Marvin stood up, knocking his chair to the floor. "You stupid bitch." His hand raised high, Marvin advanced on Iris with beer dribbling from his chin. "I'll break your jaw, woman. I swear I will."

"Don't hit me, Marvin. Please don't hit me again."

"Who was it? I want a name."

"I don't *know*, I told you. Just some guy going to Frisco. His name was Mark, I think."

"And he took the kid?"

Iris nodded. "He was real nice."

"You bring him here? Huh? Did you bring the son-of-a-bitch to the cabin? Did you tell him about the others?"

"No, Marvin. No. I swear. You know I'd never do that."

"Lying bitch."

Marvin grabbed Iris by the hair and dragged her away from the stove and slapped her across the face. She screamed and cowered. Marvin raised his hand to strike again.

Sucking a breath, he raised his gun and stepped from behind the curtain. "Hold it," he told Marvin. "Don't move."

Marvin froze, twisted his head, took in the gun and released his grip on Iris and backed away from her, his black eyes glistening. A slow smile exposed dark and crooked teeth. "Well, now," Marvin drawled. "Just who might you be besides a fucking trespasser? Don't tell me; let me guess. You're the nice man Iris gave a baby to. The one she swore she didn't bring out here. Right?"

"She didn't bring me. I followed her."

Both men glanced at Iris. Her hand was at her mouth and she was nibbling a knuckle. "I thought you went to Frisco," was all she said.

"Not yet."

"What do you want?" Her question assumed a fearsome answer.

Marvin laughed. "You stupid bitch. He wants the *rest* of them. Then he wants to throw us in jail. He wants to be a hero, Iris. And to be a hero he has to put you and me behind bars for the rest of our fucking lives." Marvin took a step forward.

"Don't be dumb." He raised the gun to Marvin's eyes.

Marvin stopped, frowned, then grinned again. "You look like you used that piece before."

"One or twice."

"What's your gig?"

"Detective. Private."

Marvin's lips parted around his crusted teeth. "You must be kidding. Iris flags down some bastard on the freeway and he turns out to be a private cop?"

"That's about it."

Marvin shook his head. "Judas H. Priest. And here you are. A professional hero, just like I said."

He captured Marvin's eyes. "I want the book."

"What book?" Marvin burlesqued ignorance.

"The book with the list of babies and where you got them and where you took them."

Marvin looked at Iris, stuck her with his stare. "You're dead meat, you know that? You bring the bastard here and tell him all about it and expect him to just take off and not try to *stop* us? You're too fucking dumb to breathe, Iris. I got to put you out of your misery."

"I'm sorry, Marvin."

"He's going to take them *back*, Iris. Get it? He's going to take those sweet babies away from you and give them back to the assholes that don't want them. And then he's going to the cops and they're going to say you *kidnapped* those babies, Iris, and that you were bad to them and should go to jail because of what you did. Don't you see that, you brain-fried bitch? *Don't you see what he's going to do?*"

"I . . ." Iris stopped, overwhelmed by Marvin's incantation. "Are you?" she asked, finally looking away from Marvin.

"I'm going to do what's best for the babies, Iris. That's all."

"What's best for them is with me and Marvin."

"Not any more," he told her. "Marvin's been shucking you, Iris. He steals those babies. Takes them from their parents, parents who love them. He roams up and down the coast stealing children and then he sells them, Iris. Either back to the people he took them from or to people desperate to adopt. I think he's hooked up with a lawyer named Rasker, who arranges private adoptions for big money and splits the take with Marvin. He's not interested in who loves those kids, Iris. He's only interested in how much he can sell them for."

Something had finally activated Iris' eyes. "Marvin? Is that true?"

"No, baby. The guy's blowing smoke. He's trying to take the babies away from you and then get people to believe you did something bad, just like that time with the abortion. He's trying to say you did bad things to babies again, Iris. We can't let him do that."

He spoke quickly, to erase Marvin's words. "People don't give away babies, Iris. Not to guys like Marvin. There are agencies that arrange that kind of thing, that check to make sure the new home is in the best interests of the child. Marvin just swipes them and sells them to the highest bidder, Iris. That's all he's in it for."

"I don't believe you."

"It doesn't matter. Just give me Marvin's notebook and we can check it out, contact the parents and see what they say about their kids. Ask if they wanted to be rid of them. That's fair, isn't it?"

"I don't know. I guess."

"Iris?"

"What, Marvin?"

"I want you to pick up that pan and knock this guy on the head. Hard. Go on, Iris. He won't shoot you, you know that. Hit him on the head so he can't put us in jail."

He glanced at Iris, then as quickly to Marvin and to Iris once again, "Don't do it, Iris. Marvin's trouble. I think you know that now." He looked away from Iris and gestured at her partner. "Where's the book?"

"Iris?"

Iris began to cry. "I can't Marvin. I can't do that."

"The book," he said to Marvin again. "Where is it?"

Marvin laughed. "You'll never know, detective."

"Okay. We'll do it your way. On the floor. Hands behind your head. Legs spread. Now."

Marvin didn't move. When he spoke the words were languid. "You don't look much like a killer, detective, and I've known a few, believe me. So I figure if you're not gonna shoot me I don't got to do what you say. I figure I'll just take that piece away from you and feed it to you inch by inch. Huh? Why don't I do just that?"

He took two quick steps to Marvin's side and sliced open Marvin's cheek with a quick swipe of the gun barrel. "Want some more?"

Marvin pawed at his cheek with a grimy hand, then examined his bloody fingers. "You bastard. Okay. I'll get the book. It's under here."

Marvin bent toward the floor, twisting away from him, sliding his hands toward the darkness below the stove. He couldn't tell what Marvin was doing, so he squinted, then moved closer. When Marvin began to stand he jumped back, but Marvin wasn't attacking, Marvin was holding a baby, not a book, holding a baby by the throat.

"Okay, pal." Marvin said through his grin. "Now, you want to see this kid die before your eyes, you just keep hold of that gun. You want to see it breathe some more, you drop it."

He froze, his eyes on Marvin's fingers, which inched further around the baby's neck and began to squeeze.

The baby gurgled, gasped, twitched, was silent. Its face reddened; its eyes bulged. The tendons in Marvin's hand stretched taut. Between grimy gritted teeth, Marvin wheezed in rapid streams of glee.

He dropped his gun. Marvin told Iris to pick it up. She did, and exchanged the gun for the child. Her eyes lapped Marvin's face, as though to renew its acquaintance. Abruptly, she turned and ran around the curtain and disappeared.

"Well, now." Marvin's words slid easily. "Looks like the worm has turned, detective. What's your name, anyhow?"

"Tanner."

"Well, Tanner, your ass is mine. No more John Wayne stunts for you. You can kiss this world good-bye."

Marvin fished in the pocket of his jeans, then drew out a small spiral notebook and flashed it. "It's all in here, Tanner. Where they came from; where they went. Now watch."

Gun in one hand, notebook in the other, Marvin went to the wood stove and flipped open the heavy door. The fire made shadows dance.

"Don't."

"Watch, bastard."

Marvin tossed the notebook into the glowing coals, fished in the box beside the stove for a stick of kindling, then tossed it in after the notebook and closed the iron door. "Bye-bye babies." Marvin's laugh was quick and cruel. "Now turn around. We're going out back."

He did as he was told, walking toward the door, hearing only a silent shuffle at his back. As he passed her he glanced at Iris. She hugged the baby Marvin had threatened, crying, not looking at him. "Remember the one in my car," he said to her. She nodded silently, then turned away.

Marvin prodded him in the back and he moved to the door. Hand on the knob, he paused, hoping for a magical deliverance, but none came. Marvin prodded him again and he moved outside, onto the porch then into the yard. "Around back," Marvin ordered. "Get in the bus."

He staggered, tripping over weeds, stumbling over rocks, until he reached the rusting bus. The moon and stars had disappeared; the night was black and still but for the whistling wind, clearly Marvin's ally. The nanny goat laughed at them, then trotted out of reach. He glanced back at Marvin. In one hand was a pistol, in the other a blanket. "Go on in. Just pry the door open."

He fit his finger between the rubber edges of the bus door and opened it. The first step was higher than he thought, and he tripped and almost fell. "Watch it. I almost blasted you right then."

He couldn't suppress a giggle. For reasons of his own, Marvin matched his laugh. "Head on back, Tanner. Pretend you're on a field trip to the zoo."

He walked down the aisle between the broken seats, smelling rot and rust and the lingering scent of skunk. "Why here?" he asked as he reached the rear.

"Because you'll keep in here just fine till I get time to dig a hole out back and open that emergency door and dump you in. Plus it's quiet. I figure with the bus and the blanket no one will hear a thing. Sit."

He sat. Marvin draped the blanket across the arm that held the gun, then extended the shrouded weapon toward his chest. He had no doubt that Marvin would shoot without a thought or fear. "Any last words, Tanner? Any parting thoughts?"

"Just that you forgot something."

"What?"

"You left the door open."

Marvin glanced quickly toward the door in the front of the bus. He dove for Marvin's legs, sweeping at the gun with his left hand as he did so, hoping to dislodge it into the folds of the blanket where it would lie useless and unattainable.

"Cocksucker."

Marvin wrested the gun from his grasp and raised it high, tossing off the blanket in the process. He twisted frantically to protect against the blow he knew was coming, but Marvin was too heavy and strong, retained the upper hand by kneeling on his chest. The revolver glinted in the darkness, a missile poised to descend.

Sound split the air, a piercing scream of agony from the cabin or somewhere near it. "What the hell?" Marvin swore, started to retreat, then almost thoughtlessly clubbed him with the gun, once, then again. After a flash of pain a broad black creature held him down for a length of time he couldn't calculate.

When he was aware again he was alone in the bus, lying in the aisle. His head felt crushed to pulp. He put a hand to his temple and felt blood. Midst throbbing pain he struggled to his feet and made his way outside and stood leaning against the bus while the night air struggled to clear his head.

He took a step, staggered, took another and gained an equilibrium, then lost it and sat down. Back on his feet, he trudged toward the porch and opened the door. Behind him, the nanny laughed again.

The cabin was dark, the only light the faint flicker from the stove behind the curtain. He walked carefully, trying to avoid the litter on the floor, the shapes in the room. Halfway to the back his foot struck something soft. As he bent to shove it out of his way it made a human sound. He knelt, saw that it was Iris, then found a lamp and turned it on.

She was crumpled, face down, in the center of the room, arms and legs folded under her, her body curled to avoid assault. He knelt again, heard her groan once more, and saw that what he'd thought was a piece of skirt was in fact a pool of blood and what he'd thought was shadow was a broad wet trail of the selfsame substance leading toward the rear of the cabin.

He ran his hands down her body, feeling for wounds. Finding none, he rolled Iris to her side, then to her back. Blood bubbled from a point beneath her sternum. Her eyelids fluttered, open, closed, then open again. "He shot me," she said. "It hurt so bad I couldn't stop crying so he shot me."

"I know. Don't try to talk."

"Did he shoot the babies, too? I thought I heard..."

"I don't know."

"Would you look? Please?"

He nodded, stood up, fought a siege of vertigo, then went behind the curtain, then returned to Iris. "They're all right."

She tried to smile her thanks. "Something scared him off. I think some people were walking by outside and heard the shot and went for help. I heard them yelling."

"Where would he go, Iris?"

"Up in the woods. On his dirt bike. He knows lots of people up there. They grow dope, live off the land. The cops'll never find him." Iris moaned again. "I'm dying, aren't I?"

"I don't know. Is there a phone here?"

She shook her head. "Down at the end of the street. By the market."

"I'm going down and call an ambulance. And the cops. How long ago did Marvin leave?"

She closed her eyes. "I blacked out. Oh, God. It's real bad now, Mr. Tanner. Real bad."

"I know, Iris. You hang on. I'll be back in a second. Try to hold this in place." He took out his handkerchief and folded it into a square and placed in on her wound. "Press as hard as you can." He took her left hand and placed it on the compress, then stood up.

"Wait. I have to..."

He spoke above her words. "You have to get to a hospital. I'll be back in a minute and we can talk some more."

"But..."

"Hang on."

He ran from the cabin and down the drive, spotted the lights of the convenience market down the street and ran to the phone booth and placed his calls. The police said they'd already been notified and a car was on the way. The ambulance said it would be six minutes. As fast as he could he ran back to the cabin, hoping it would be fast enough.

Iris had moved. Her body was straightened, her right arm outstretched toward the door, the gesture of a supplicant. The sleeve of her blouse was tattered, burned to a ragged edge above her elbow. Below the sleeve her arm was red in spots, blistered in others, dappled like burned food. The hand at its end was charred and curled into a crusty fist that was dusted with gray ash. Within the fingers was an object, blackened, burned, and treasured.

He pried it from her grasp. The cover was burned away, and the edges of the pages were curled and singed, but they remained decipherable, the written scrawl preserved. The list of names and places was organized to match the gaily painted boxes in the back. Carson City. Boise. Grant's Pass. San Bernardino. Modesto. On and on, a gazetteer of crime.

"I saved it," Iris mumbled. "I saved it for my babies."

He raised her head to his lap and held it till she died. Then he went to his car and retrieved his B Box baby and placed her in her appointed crib. For the first time since he'd known her the baby made only happy sounds, an irony that was lost on the five dead children at her flank and on the just dead woman who had feared it all.

BILL PRONZINI
(b.1943)

Skeleton Rattle Your Mouldy Leg
(Nameless Detective)

He was one of the oddest people I had ever met. Sixty years old, under five and a half feet tall, slight, with great bony knobs for elbows and knees, with bat-winged ears and a bent nose and eyes that danced left and right, left and right, and had sparkly little lights in them. He wore baggy clothes–sweaters and jeans, mostly, crusted with patches–and a baseball cap turned around so that the bill poked out from the back of his head. In his back pocket he carried a whisk broom, and if he knew you, or wanted to, he would come up and say, "I know you–you've got a speck on your coat," and he would brush it off with the broom. Then he would talk, or maybe recite or even sing a little: a gnarled old harlequin cast up from another age.

These things were odd enough, but the oddest of all was his obsession with skeletons.

His name was Nick Damiano and he lived in the building adjacent to the one where Eberhardt and I had our new office–lived in a little room in the basement. Worked there, too, as a janitor and general handyman; the place was a small residence hotel for senior citizens, mostly male, called the Medford. So it didn't take long for our paths to cross. A week or so after Eb and I moved in, I was coming up the street one morning and Nick popped out of the alley that separated our two buildings.

He said, "I know you–you've got a speck on your coat," and out came the whisk broom. Industriously he brushed away the imaginary speck. Then he grinned and said, "Skeleton rattle your mouldy leg."

"Huh?"

"That's poetry," he said. "From *archy and mehitabel*. You know archy and mehitabel?"

"No," I said, "I don't."

"They're lower case; they don't have capitals like we do. Archy's cockroach and mehitabel's a cat and they were both poets in another life. A fellow named don marquis created them a long time ago. He's lower case too."

"Uh . . . I see."

"One time mehitabel went to Paris," he said, "and took up with a tom cat named francy who was once the poet Francois Villon, and they used to go to the catacombs late at night. They'd caper and dance and sing among those old bones."

And he began to recite:

> *prince if you pipe and plead and beg*
> *you may yet be crowned with a grisly kiss*
> *skeleton rattle your mouldy leg*
> *all mens lovers come to this*

That was my first meeting with Nick Damiano; there were others over the next four months, none of which lasted more than five minutes. Skeletons came into all of them, in one way or another. Once he sang half a dozen verses of the old spiritual, "Dry Bones," in a pretty good baritone. Another time he quoted, "'The Knight's bones are dust/And his good sword rust-/ His Soul is with the saints, I trust.'" Later I looked it up and it was a rhyme from an obscure work by Coleridge. On other days he made sly little comments: "Why hello there, I knew it was you coming-I heard your bones chattering and clacking all the way down the street." And "Cleaned out your closet lately? Might be skeletons hiding in there." And "Sure is hot today. Sure would be fine to take off our skins and just sit around in our bones."

I asked one of the Medford's other residents, a guy named Irv Feinberg, why Nick seemed to have such a passion for skeletons. Feinberg didn't know; nobody knew, he said, because Nick wouldn't discuss it. He told me that Nick even owned a genuine skeleton, liberated from some medical facility, and that he kept it wired to the wall of his room and burned candles in its skull.

A screwball, this Nick Damiano-sure. But he did his work and did it well, and he was always cheerful and friendly, and he never gave anybody any trouble. Harmless old Nick. A happy whack, marching to the rhythm of dry old bones chattering and clacking together inside his head. Everybody in the neighborhood found him amusing, including me: San Francisco has always been proud of its characters, its kooks. Yeah, everyone liked old Nick.

Except that somebody *didn't* like him, after all.

Somebody took hold of a blunt instrument one raw November night, in that little basement room with the skeleton leering on from the wall, and beat Nick Damiano to death.

It was four days after the murder that Irv Feinberg came to see me. He was a rotund little guy in his sixties, very energetic, a retired plumber who wore loud sports coats and spent most of his time doping out the races at Golden Gate Fields and a variety of other tracks. He had known Nick as well as anyone could, had called him his friend.

I was alone in the office when Feinberg walked in; Eberhardt was down at the Hall of Justice, trying to coerce some of his former cop pals into giving him background information on a missing-person case he was working. Feinberg said by way of greeting, "Nice office you got here," which was a lie, and came over and plopped himself into one of the clients' chairs. "You busy? Or you got a few minutes we can talk?"

"What can I do for you, Mr. Feinberg?"

"The cops have quit on Nick's murder," he said. "They don't come around anymore, they don't talk to anybody in the hotel. I called down to the Hall of Justice, I wanted to know what's happening, I got the big runaround."

"The police don't quit a homicide investigation–"

"The hell they don't. A guy like Nick Damiano? It's no big deal to them. They figure it was somebody looking for easy money, a drug addict from over in the Tenderloin. On account of Dan Cady, he's the night clerk, found the door to the alley unlocked just after he found Nick's body."

"That sounds like a reasonable theory," I said.

"Reasonable, hell. The door wasn't tampered with or anything; it was just unlocked. So how'd the drug addict get in? Nick wouldn't have left that door unlocked; he was real careful about things like that. And he wouldn't have let a stranger in, not at that time of night."

"Well, maybe the assailant came in through the front entrance and went out through the alley door . . ."

"No way," Feinberg said. "Front door's on a night security lock from eight o'clock on; you got to buzz the desk from outside and Dan Cady'll come see who you are. If he don't know you, you don't get in."

"All right, maybe the assailant wasn't a stranger. Maybe he's somebody Nick knew."

"Sure, that's what I think. But not somebody outside the hotel. Nick never let people in at night, not anybody, not even somebody lives there; you had to go around to the front door and buzz the desk. Besides, he didn't have any outside friends that came to see him. He didn't go out himself either. He had to tend to the heat, for one thing, do other chores, so he stayed put. I know all that because I spent plenty of evenings with him, shooting craps for pennies... Nick liked to shoot craps, he called it 'rolling dem bones.'"

Skeletons, I thought. I said, "What do you think then, Mr. Feinberg? That somebody from the hotel killed Nick?"

"That's what I think," he said. "I don't like it, most of those people are my friends, but that's how it looks to me."

"You have anybody specific in mind?"

"No. Whoever it was, he was in there arguing with Nick before he killed him."

"Oh? How do you know that?"

"George Weaver heard them. He's our newest tenant, George is, moved in three weeks ago. Used to be a bricklayer in Chicago, came out here to be with his daughter when he retired, only she had a heart attack and died last month. His other daughter died young and his wife died of cancer; now he's all alone." Feinberg shook his head. "It's a hell of a thing to be old and alone."

I agreed that it must be.

"Anyhow, George was in the basement getting something out of his storage bin and he heard the argument. Told Charley Slattery a while later that it didn't sound violent or he'd have gone over and banged on Nick's door. As it was, he just went back upstairs."

"Who's Charley Slattery?"

"Charley lives at the Medford and works over at Monahan's Gym on Turk Street. Used to be a small-time fighter; now he just hangs around doing odd jobs. Not too bright, but he's okay."

"Weaver didn't recognize the other voice in the argument?"

"No. Couldn't make out what it was all about either."

"What time was that?"

"Few minutes before eleven, George says."

"Did anyone else overhear the argument?"

"Nobody else around at the time."

"When was the last anybody saw Nick alive?"

"Eight o'clock. Nick came up to the lobby to fix one of the lamps wasn't working. Dan Cady talked to him a while when he was done."

"Cady found Nick's body around two a.m., wasn't it?"

"Two-fifteen."

"How did he happen to find it? That wasn't in the papers."

"Well, the furnace was still on. Nick always shut it off by midnight or it got to be too hot upstairs. So Dan went down to find out why and there was Nick lying on the floor of his room with his head all beat in."

"What kind of guy is Cady?"

"Quiet, keeps to himself, spends most of his free time reading library books. He was a college history teacher once, up in Oregon. But he got in some kind of trouble with a woman–this was back in the forties, teachers had to watch their morals–and the college fired him and he couldn't get another teaching job. He fell into the booze for a lot of years afterward. But he's all right now. Belongs to AA."

I was silent for a time. Then I asked, "The police didn't find anything that made them suspect one of the other residents?"

"No, but that don't mean much." Feinberg made a disgusted noise through his nose. "Cops. They don't even know what it was bashed in Nick's skull, what kind of weapon. Couldn't find it anywhere. They figure the killer took it away through that unlocked alley door and got rid of it. *I* figure the killer unlocked the door to make it look like an outside job, then went upstairs and hid the weapon somewhere til next day."

"Let's suppose you're right. Who might have a motive to've killed Nick?"

"Well...nobody, far as I know. But *somebody's* got one, you can bet on that."

"Did Nick get along with everybody at the Medford?"

"Sure," Feinberg said. Then he frowned a little and said, "Except Wesley Thane, I guess. But I can't see Wes beating anybody's head in. He pretends to be tough but he's a wimp. And a goddamn snob."

"Oh?"

"He's an actor. Little theater stuff these days, but once he was a bit player down in Hollywood, made a lot of crappy B movies where he was one of the minor bad guys. Hear him tell it, he was Clark Gable's best friend back in the forties. A windbag who thinks he's better than the rest of us. He treated Nick like a freak."

"Was there ever any trouble between them?"

"Well, he hit Nick once, just after he moved in five years ago and Nick tried to brush off his coat. I was there and I saw it."

"Hit him with what?"

"His hand. A kind of slap. Nick shied away from him after that."

"How about recent trouble?"

"Not that I know about. I didn't even have to noodge him into kicking in twenty bucks to the fund. But hell, everybody in the building kicked in something except old lady Howsam; she's bedridden and can barely make ends meet on her pension, so I didn't even ask her."

I said, "Fund?"

Feinberg reached inside his gaudy sport jacket and produced a bulky envelope. He put the envelope on my desk and pushed it toward me with the tips of his fingers. "There's two hundred bucks in there," he said. "What'll that hire you for? Three-four days?"

I stared at him. "Wait a minute, Mr. Feinberg. Hire me to do what?"

"Find out who killed Nick. What do you think we been talking about here?"

"I thought it was only talk you came for. A private detective can't investigate a homicide in this state, not without police permission . . ."

"So get permission," Feinberg said. "I told you, the cops have quit on it. Why should they try to keep you from investigating?"

"Even if I did get permission, I doubt if there's much I could do that the police haven't already–"

"Listen, don't go modest on me. You're a good detective, I see your name in the papers all the time. I got confidence in you; we all do. Except maybe the guy who killed Nick."

There was no arguing him out of it; his mind was made up, and he'd convinced the others in the Medford to go along with him. So I quit trying finally and said all right, I would call the Hall of Justice and see if I could get clearance to conduct a private investigation. And if I could, then I'd come over later and see him and take a look around and start talking to people. That satisfied him. But when I pushed the envelope back across the desk, he wouldn't take it.

"No," he said, "that's yours, you just go ahead and earn it." And he was on his feet and gone before I could do anything more than make a verbal protest.

I put the money away in the lock-box in my desk and telephoned the Hall. Eberhardt was still hanging around, talking to one of his old cronies in General Works, and I told him about Feinberg and what he wanted. Eb said he'd talk to the homicide inspector in charge of the Nick Damiano case and see what was what; he didn't seem to think there'd be any problem getting clearance. There were problems, he said, only when private eyes tried to horn in on big-money and/or VIP cases, the kind that got heavy media attention.

He used to be a homicide lieutenant so he knew what he was talking about. When he called back a half hour later he said, "You got your clearance. Feinberg had it pegged: the case is already in the Inactive

File for lack of leads and evidence. I'll see if I can finagle a copy of the report for you."

Some job, I thought as I hung up. In a way it was ghoulish, like poking around in a fresh grave. And wasn't that an appropriate image; I could almost hear Nick's sly laughter.

Skeleton rattle your mouldy leg.

The basement of the Medford Hotel was dimly lighted and too warm: a big, old-fashioned oil furnace rattled and roared in one corner, giving off shimmers of heat. Much of the floor space was taken up with fifty-gallon trash receptacles, some full and some empty and one each under a pair of garbage chutes from the upper floor. Over against the far wall, and throughout a small connecting room beyond, were rows of narrow storage cubicles made out of wood and heavy wire, with padlocks on each of the doors.

Nick's room was at the rear, opposite the furnace and alongside the room that housed the hot-water heaters. But Feinberg didn't take me there directly; he said something I didn't catch, mopping his face with a big green handkerchief, and detoured over to the furnace and fiddled with the controls and got it shut down.

"Damn thing," he said. "Owner's too cheap to replace it with a modern unit that runs off a thermostat. Now we got some young snot he hired to take Nick's job, don't live here and don't stick around all day and leaves the furnace turned on too long. It's like a goddamn sauna in here."

There had been a police seal on the door to Nick's room, but it had been officially removed. Feinberg had the key; he was a sort of building mayor, by virtue of seniority–he'd lived at the Medford for more than fifteen years–and he had got custody of the key from the owner. He opened the lock, swung the thick metal door open, and clicked on the lights.

The first thing I saw was the skeleton. It hung from several pieces of shiny wire on the wall opposite the door, and it was a grisly damned thing streaked with blobs of red and green and orange candle wax. The top of the skull had been cut off and a fat red candle jutted up from the hollow inside, like some sort of ugly growth. Melted wax rimmed and dribbled from the grinning mouth, giving it a bloody look.

"Cute, ain't it?" Feinberg said. "Nick and his frigging skeletons."

I moved inside. It was just a single room with a bathroom alcove, not more than fifteen feet square. Cluttered, but in a way that suggested everything had been assigned a place. Army cot against one wall, a small table, two chairs, one of those little waist-high refrigerators with a hot plate on top, a standing cupboard full of pots and dishes; stacks of newspapers and magazines, some well-used books–volumes of poetry, an anatomical text, two popular histories about ghouls and grave-robbers, a dozen novels with either "skeleton" or "bones" in the title; a broken wooden wagon, a Victrola without its ear-trumpet amplifier, an ancient Olivetti typewriter, a collection of oddball tools, a scabrous ironbound steamer trunk, an open box full of assorted pairs of dice, and a lot of other stuff, most of which appeared to be junk.

A thick fiber mat covered the floor. On it, next to the table, was the chalked outline of Nick's body and some dark stains. My stomach kicked a little when I looked at the stains; I had seen corpses of bludgeon victims and I knew what those stains looked like when they were fresh. I went around the table on the other side and took a closer look at the wax-caked skeleton. Feinberg tagged along at my heels.

"Nick used to talk to that thing," he said. "Ask it questions, how it was feeling, could he get it anything to eat or drink. Gave me the willies at first. He even put his arm around it once and kissed it, I swear to God. I can still see him do it."

"He got it from a medical facility?"

"One that was part of some small college he worked at before he came to San Francisco. He mentioned that once."

"Did he say where the college was?"

"No."

"Where did Nick come from? Around here?"

Feinberg shook his head. "Midwest somewhere, that's all I could get out of him."

"How long had he been in San Francisco?"

"Ten years. Worked here the last eight; before that, he helped out at a big apartment house over on Geary."

"Why did he come to the city? Did he have relatives here or what?"

"No, no relatives, he was all alone. Just him and his bones–he said that once."

I poked around among the clutter of things in the room, but if there had been anything here relevant to the murder, the police would have found it and probably removed it and it would be mentioned in their report. So would anything found among Nick's effects that determined his background. Eberhardt would have a copy of the report for me to look at later; when he said he'd try to do something he usually did it.

When I finished with the room we went out and Feinberg locked the door. We took the elevator up to the lobby. It was dim up there, too–and a little depressing. There was a lot of plaster and wood and imitation marble, and some antique furniture and dusty potted plants, and it smelled of dust and faintly of decay. A sense of age permeated the place: you felt it and you smelled it and you saw it in the surroundings, in the half-dozen men and one woman sitting on the sagging chairs, reading or staring out through the windows at O'Farrell Street, people with nothing to do and nobody to do it with, waiting like doomed prisoners for the sentence of death to be carried out. Dry witherings and an aura of hopelessness–that was the impression I would carry away with me and that would linger in my mind.

I thought: I'm fifty-four, another few years and I could be stuck in here too. But that wouldn't happen. I had work I could do pretty much to the end and I had Kerry–Kerry Wade, my lady–and I had some money in the bank and a collection of 6500 pulp magazines that were worth plenty on the collectors' market. No, this kind of place wouldn't happen to me. In a society that ignored and showed little respect for its elderly, I was one of the lucky ones.

Feinberg led me to the desk and introduced me to the day clerk, a sixtyish barrel of a man named Bert Norris. If there was anything he could do to help, Norris said, he'd be glad to oblige; he sounded eager, as if nobody had needed his help in a long time. The fact that Feinberg had primed everyone here about my investigation made things easier in one respect and more difficult in another. If the person who had killed Nick Damiano *was* a resident of the Medford, I was not likely to catch him off guard.

When Norris moved away to answer a switchboard call, Feinberg asked me, "Who're you planning to talk to now?"

"Whoever's available," I said.

"Dan Cady? He lives here–two-eighteen. Goes to the library every morning after he gets off, but he's always back by noon. You can probably catch him before he turns in."

"All right, good."

"You want me to come along?"

"That's not necessary, Mr. Feinberg."

"Yeah, I get it. I used to hate that kind of thing too when I was out on a plumbing job."

"What kind of thing?"

"Somebody hanging over my shoulder, watching me work. Who needs crap like that? You want me, I'll be in my room with the scratch sheets for today's races."

Dan Cady was a thin, sandy-haired man in his mid-sixties, with cheeks and nose roadmapped by ruptured blood vessels–the badge of the alcoholic, practicing or reformed. He wore thick glasses, and behind them his eyes had a strained, tired look, as if from too much reading.

"Well, I'll be glad to talk to you," he said, "but I'm afraid I'm not very clear-headed right now. I was just getting ready for bed."

"I won't take up much of your time, Mr. Cady."

He let me in. His room was small and strewn with library books, most of which appeared to deal with American history; a couple of big maps, an old one of the United States and an even older parchment map of Asia, adorned the walls, and there were plaster busts of historical figures I didn't recognize, a huge globe on a wooden stand. There was only one chair; he let me have that and perched himself on the bed.

I asked him about Sunday night, and his account of how he'd come to find Nick Damiano's body coincided with what Feinberg had told me. "It was a frightening experience," he said. "I'd never seen anyone dead by violence before. His head . . . well, it was awful."

"Were there signs of a struggle in the room?"

"Yes, some things were knocked about. But I'd say it was a brief struggle–there wasn't much damage."

"Is there anything unusual you noticed? Something that should have been there but wasn't, for instance?"

"No. I was too shaken to notice anything like that."

"Was Nick's door open when you got there?"

"Wide open."

"How about the door to the alley?"

"No. Closed."

"How did you happen to check it, then?"

"Well, I'm not sure," Cady said. He seemed faintly embarrassed; his eyes didn't quite meet mine. "I was stunned and frightened; it occurred to me that the murderer might still be around somewhere. I took a quick look around the basement and then opened the alley door and looked out there . . . I wasn't thinking very clearly. It was only when I shut the door again that I realized it had been unlocked."

"Did you see or hear anything inside or out?"

"Nothing. I left the door unlocked and went back to the lobby to call the police."

"When you saw Nick earlier that night, Mr. Cady, how did he seem to you?"

"Seem? Well, he was cheerful; he usually was. He said he'd have come up sooner to fix the lamp but his old bones wouldn't allow it. That was the way he talked . . ."

"Yes, I know. Do you have any idea who he might have argued with that night, who might have killed him?"

"None," Cady said. "He was such a gentle soul . . . I still can't believe a thing like that could happen to him."

Down in the lobby again, I asked Bert Norris if Wesley Thane, George Weaver, and Charley Slattery were on the premises. Thane was, he said, Room 315; Slattery was at Monahan's Gym and would be until six o'clock. He started to tell me that Weaver was out, but then his eyes shifted past me and he said, "No, there he is now. Just coming in."

I turned. A heavy-set, stooped man of about seventy had just entered from the street, walking with the aid of a hickory cane; but he seemed to get along pretty good. He was carrying a grocery sack in his free hand and a folded newspaper under his arm.

I intercepted him halfway to the elevator and told him who I was. He looked me over for about ten seconds, out of alert blue eyes that had gone a little rheumy, before he said, "Irv Feinberg said you'd be around." His voice was surprisingly strong and clear for a man his age. "But I can't help you much. Don't know much."

"Should we talk down here or in your room?"

"Down here's all right with me."

We crossed to a deserted corner of the lobby and took chairs in front of a fireplace that had been boarded up and painted over. Weaver got a stubby little pipe out of his coat pocket and began to load up.

I said, "About Sunday night, Mr. Weaver. I understand you went down to the basement to get something out of your storage locker..."

"My old radio," he said. "New one I bought a while back quit playing and I like to listen to the eleven o'clock news before I got to sleep. When I got down there I heard Damiano and some fella arguing."

"Just Nick and one other man?"

"Sounded that way."

"Was the voice at all familiar to you?"

"Didn't sound familiar. But I couldn't hear it too well; I was over by the lockers. Couldn't make out what they were saying either."

"How long were you in the basement?"

"Three or four minutes, is all."

"Did the argument get louder, more violent, while you were there?"

"Didn't seem to. No." He struck a kitchen match and put the flame to the bowl of his pipe. "If it had I guess I'd've gone over and banged on the door, announced myself. I'm as curious as the next man when it comes to that."

"But as it was you went straight back to your room?"

"That's right. Ran into Charley Slattery when I got out of the elevator; his room's just down from mine on the third floor."

"What was his reaction when you told him what you'd heard?"

"Didn't seem to worry him much," Weaver said. "So I figured it was nothing for me to worry about either."

"Slattery didn't happen to go down to the basement himself, did he?"

"Never said anything about it if he did."

I don't know what I expected Wesley Thane to be like–the Raymond Massey or John Carradine type, maybe, something along those shabbily aristocratic and vaguely sinister lines–but the man who opened the door to Room 315 looked about as much like an actor as I do. He was a smallish guy in his late sixties, he was bald, and he had a nondescript face except for mean little eyes under thick black brows that had no doubt contributed to his career as a B-movie villain. He looked somewhat familiar, but even though I like old movies and watch them whenever I can, I couldn't have named a single film he had appeared in.

He said, "Yes? What is it?" in a gravelly, staccato voice. That was familiar, too, but again I couldn't place it in any particular context.

I identified myself and asked if I could talk to him about Nick Damiano. "That cretin," he said, and for a moment I thought he was going to shut the door in my face. But then he said, "Oh, all right, come in. If I don't talk to you, you'll probably think I had something to do with the poor fool's murder."

He turned and moved off into the room, leaving me to shut the door. The room was larger than Dan Cady's and jammed with stage and screen memorabilia: framed photographs, playbills, film posters, blown-up black-and-white stills; and a variety of salvaged props, among them the plumed helmet off a suit of armor and a Napoleonic uniform displayed on a dressmaker's dummy.

Thane stopped near a lumpy-looking couch and did a theatrical about-face. The scowl he wore had a practiced look, and it occurred to me that under it he might be enjoying himself. "Well?" he said.

I said, "You didn't like Nick Damiano, did you, Mr. Thane," making it a statement instead of a question.

"No, I didn't like him. And no, I didn't kill him, if that's your next question."

"Why didn't you like him?"

"He was a cretin. A gibbering moron. All that nonsense about skeletons–he ought to have been locked up long ago."

"You have any idea who did kill him?"

"No. The police seem to think it was a drug addict."

"That's one theory," I said. "Irv Feinberg has another: he thinks the killer is a resident of this hotel."

"I know what Irv Feinberg thinks. He's a dammed meddler who doesn't know when to keep his mouth shut."

"You don't agree with him then?"

"I don't care one way or another."

Thane sat down and crossed his legs and adopted a sufferer's pose; now he was playing the martyr. I grinned at him, because it was something he wasn't expecting, and went to look at some of the stuff on the walls. One of the black-and-white stills depicted Thane in Western garb, with a smoking sixgun in his hand. The largest of the photographs was of Clark Gable, with an ink inscription that read, "For my good friend, Wes."

Behind me Thane said impatiently, "I'm waiting."

I let him wait a while longer. Then I moved back near the couch and grinned at him again and said, "Did you see Nick Damiano the night he was murdered?"

"I did not."

"Talk to him at all that day?"

"No."

"When was the last you had trouble with him?"

"Trouble? What do you mean, trouble?"

"Irv Feinberg told me you hit Nick once, when he tried to brush off your coat."

"My God," Thane said, "that was years ago. And it was only a slap. I had no problems with him after that. He avoided me and I ignored him; we spoke only when it was necessary." He paused, and his eyes got bright with something that might have been malice. "If you're looking for someone who had trouble with Damiano recently, talk to Charley Slattery."

"What kind of trouble did Slattery have with Nick?"

"Ask him. It's none of my business."

"Why did you bring it up then?"

He didn't say anything. His eyes were still bright.

"All right, I'll ask Slattery," I said. "Tell me, what did you think when you heard about Nick? Were you pleased?"

"Of course not. I was shocked. I've played many violent roles in my career, but violence in real life always shocks me."

"The shock must have worn off pretty fast. You told me a couple of minutes ago you don't care who killed him."

"Why should I, as long as no one else is harmed?"

"So why did you kick in the twenty dollars?"

"What?"

"Feinberg's fund to hire me. Why did you contribute?"

"If I hadn't it would have made me look suspicious to the others.

I have to live with these people; I don't need that sort of stigma." He gave me a smug look. "And if you repeat that to anyone, I'll deny it."

"Must be tough on you," I said.

"I beg your pardon?"

"Having to live in a place like this, with a bunch of broken-down old nobodies who don't have your intelligence or compassion or great professional skill."

That got to him; he winced, and for a moment the actor's mask slipper and I had a glimpse of the real Wesley Thane–a defeated old man with faded dreams of glory, a never-was with a small and mediocre talent, clinging to the tattered fringes of a business that couldn't care less. Then he got the mask in place again and said with genuine anger, "Get out of here. I don't have to take abuse from a cheap gumshoe."

"You're dating yourself, Mr Thane; nobody uses the word 'gumshoe' any more. It's forties B-movie dialogue."

He bounced up off the couch, pinch-faced and glaring. "Get out, I said. "Get out!"

I got out. And I was on my way to the elevator when I realized why Thane hadn't liked Nick Damiano. It was because Nick had taken attention away from him–upstaged him. Thane was an actor, but there wasn't any act he could put on that was more compelling than the real-life performance of Nick and his skeleton.

Monahan's Gym was one of those tough, men-only places that catered to ex-pugs and oldtimers in the fight game, the kind of place you used to see a lot of in the forties and fifties but that have become an anachronism in this day of chic health clubs, fancy spas, and dwindling interest in the art of prizefighting. It smelled of sweat and steam and old leather, and it resonated with the grunts of weightlifters, the smack and thud of gloves against leather bags, the profane talk of men at liberty from a more or less polite society.

I found Charley Slattery in the locker room, working there as an attendant. He was a short, beefy guy, probably a light-heavyweight in his boxing days, gone to fat around the middle in his old age; white-haired, with a face as seamed and time-eroded as a chunk of desert sandstone. One of his eyes had a glassy look; his nose and mouth were lumpy with scar tissue. A game fighter in his day, I thought, but not a very good one. A guy who had never quite learned how to cover up against the big punches, the hammerblows that put you down and out.

"Sure, I been expectin you," he said when I told him who I was. "Irv Feinberg, he said you'd be around. You findin out anything the cops dint?"

"It's too soon to tell, Mr. Slattery."

"Charley," he said, "I hate that Mr. Slattery crap."

"All right, Charley."

"Well, I wish I could tell you somethin would help you, but I can't think of nothin. I dint even see Nick for two-three days before he was murdered."

"Any idea who might have killed him?"

"Well, some punk off the street, I guess. Guy Nick was arguin with that night—George Weaver, he told you about that, dint he? What he heard?"

"Yes. He also said he met you upstairs just afterward."

Slattery nodded. "I was headin down the lobby for a Coke, they got a machine down there, and George, he come out of the elevator with his cane and this little radio unner his arm. He looked kind of funny and I ast him what's the matter and that's when he told me about the argument."

"What did you do then?"

"What'd I do? Went down to get my Coke."

"You didn't go to the basement?"

"Nah, damn it. George, he said it was just a argument Nick was having with somebody. I never figured it was nothin, you know, violent. If I had—Yeah, Eddie? You need somethin?"

A muscular black man in his mid-thirties, naked except for a pair of silver-blue boxing trunks, had come up. He said, "Towel and some soap, Charley. No soap in the showers again."

"Goddamn. I catch the guy keeps swipin it," Slattery said, "I'll kick his ass." He went and got a clean towel and a bar of soap, and the black man moved off with them to a back row of lockers. Slattery watched him go; then he said to me, "That's Eddie Jordan. Pretty fair welterweight once, but he never trained right, never had the right manager. He could of been good, that boy, if—" He broke off, frowning. "I shouldn't ought to call him that, I guess. 'Boy.' Blacks, they don't like to be called that nowadays."

"No," I said, "they don't."

"But I don't mean nothin by it. I mean, we always called em 'boy,' it was just somethin we called em. 'Nigger,' too, same thing. It wasn't nothing personal, you know?"

I knew, all right, but it was not something I wanted to or ever could explain to Charley Slattery. Race relations, the whole question of race, was too complex an issue. In his simple world, 'nigger' and 'boy' were just words, meaningless words without a couple of centuries of hatred and malice behind them, and it really wasn't anything personal.

"Let's get back to Nick," I said. "You liked him, didn't you, Charley?"

"Sure I did. He was goofy, him and his skeletons, but he worked hard and he never bothered anybody."

"I had a talk with Wesley Thane a while ago. He told me you had some trouble with Nick not long ago."

Slattery's eroded face arranged itself into a scowl. "That damn actor, he don't know what he's talkin about. Why don't he mind his own damn business? I never had no trouble with Nick."

"Not even a little? A disagreement of some kind, maybe?"

He hesitated. Then he shrugged and said, "Well, yeah, I guess we had that. A kind of disagreement."

"When was this?"

"I dunno. Couple of weeks ago."

"What was it about?"

"Garbage," Slattery said.

"Garbage?"

"Nick, he didn't like nobody touchin the cans in the basement. But hell, I was down there one night and the cans unner the chutes was full, so I switched em for empties. Well, Nick come around and yelled at me, and I wasn't feelin too good so I yelled back at him. Next thing, I got sore and kicked over one of the cans and spilled out some garbage. Dan Cady, he heard the noise clear up in the lobby and come down and that son of a bitch Wes Thane was with him. Dan, he got Nick and me calmed down. That's all there was to it."

"How were things between you and Nick after that?"

"Okay. He forgot it and so did I. It dint mean nothin. It was just one of them things."

"Did Nick have problems with any other people in the hotel?" I asked.

"Nah. I don't think so."

"What about Wes Thane? He admitted he and Nick didn't get along very well."

"I never heard about them havin no fight or anythin like that."

"How about trouble Nick might have had with somebody outside the Medford?"

"Nah," Slattery said. "Nick, he got along with everybody, you know? Everybody liked Nick, even if he was goofy."

Yeah, I thought, everybody liked Nick, even if he was goofy. Then why is he dead? *Why?*

I went back to the Medford and talked with three more residents, none of whom could offer any new information or any possible answers to that question of motive. It was almost five when I gave it up for the day and went next door to the office.

Eberhardt was there, but I didn't see him at first because he was on his hands and kness behind his desk. He poked his head up as I came inside and shut the door.

"Fine thing," I said, "you down on your knees like that. What if I'd been a prospective client?"

"So? I wouldn't let somebody like you hire me."

"What're you doing down there anyway?"

"I was cleaning my pipe and I dropped the damn bit." He disappeared again for a few seconds, muttered, "Here it is," reappeared, and hoisted himself to his feet.

There were pipe ashes all over the front of his tie and his white shirt; he'd even managed to get a smear of ash across his jowly chin. He was something of a slob, Eberhardt was, which gave us one of several common bonds: I was something of a slob myself. We had been friends for more then thirty years, and we'd been through some hard times together—some very hard times in the recent past. I hadn't been sure at first that taking him in as a partner after his retirement was a good idea, for a variety of reasons; but it had worked out so far. Much better than I'd expected, in fact.

He sat down and began brushing pipe dottle off his desk; he must have dropped a bowlful on it as well as on himself. He said as I hung up my coat, "How goes the Nick Damiano investigation?"

"Not too good. Did you manage to get a copy of the police report?"

"On your desk. But I don't think it'll tell you much."

The report was in an unmarked manila envelope; I read it standing up. Eberhardt was right that it didn't enlighten me much. Nick Damiano had been struck on the head at least three times by a heavy blunt instrument and had died of a brain hemorrhage, probably within seconds of the first blow. The wounds were "consistent with" a length of three-quarter-inch steel pipe, but the weapon hadn't been positively identified because no trace of it had been found. As for Nick's background, nothing had been found there either. No items of personal history among his effects, no hint of relatives or even of his city of origin. They'd run a check on his fingerprints through the FBI computer, with negative results: he had never been arrested on a felony charge, never been in military service or applied for a civil service job, never been fingerprinted at all.

When I put the report down Eberhardt said, "Anything?"

"Doesn't look like it." I sat in my chair and looked out the window for a time, at heavy rainclouds massing above the Federal

Building down the hill. "There's just nothing to go on in this thing, Eb–no real leads or suspects, no apparent motive."

"So maybe it's random. A street-killing, drug-related, like the report speculates."

"Maybe."

"You don't think so?"

"Our client doesn't think so."

"You want to talk over the details?"

"Sure. But let's do it over a couple of beers and some food."

"I thought you were on a diet."

"I am. Whenever Kerry's around. But she's working late tonight–new ad campaign she's writing. A couple of beers won't hurt me. And we'll have something nonfattening to eat."

"Sure we will," Eberhardt said.

We went to an Italian place out on Clement at 25th Avenue and had four beers apiece and plates of fettucine Alfredo and half a loaf of garlic bread. But the talking we did got us nowhere. If one of the residents of the Medford had killed Nick Damiano, what was the damn motive? A broken-down old actor's petulant jealousy? A mindless dispute over garbage cans? Just what *was* that argument all about that George Weaver had overheard?

Eberhardt and I split up early and I drove home to my flat on Pacific Heights. The place had a lonely feel; after spending most of the day in and around the Medford, I needed some laughter and *bonhomie* to cheer me up–I needed Kerry. I thought about calling her at Bates and Carpenter, her ad agency, but she didn't like to be disturbed while she was working. And she'd said she expected to be there most of the evening.

I settled instead for cuddling up to my collection of pulp magazines–browsing here and there, finding something to read. On nights like this the pulps weren't much of a substitute for human companionship in general and Kerry in particular, but at least they kept my mind occupied. I found a 1943 issue of *Dime Detective* that looked interesting, took it into the bathtub, and lingered there reading until I got drowsy. Then I went to bed, went right to sleep for a change–

–and woke up at three A.M. by the luminous dial of the nightstand clock, because the clouds had finally opened up and unleashed a wailing torrent of wind-blown rain: the sound of it on the roof and on the rainspouts outside the window was loud enough to wake up a deaf man. I lay there half groggy, listening to the storm and thinking about how the weather had gone all screwy lately and maybe it was time somebody started making plans for another ark.

And then all of a sudden I was thinking about something else, and I wasn't groggy anymore. I sat up in bed, wide awake. And inside of five minutes, without much effort now that I had been primed, I knew what it was the police had overlooked and I was reasonably sure I knew who had murdered Nick Damiano.

But I still didn't know why; I didn't even have an inkling of why. That was what kept me awake until dawn–that, and the unceasing racket of the storm.

The Medford's front door was still on its night security lock when I got there at a quarter to eight. Dan Cady let me in. I asked him a couple of questions about Nick's janitorial habits, and the answers he gave me pretty much confirmed my suspicions. To make absolutely sure, I went down to the basement and spent ten minutes poking around in its hot and noisy gloom.

Now the hard part, the part I never liked. I took the elevator to the third floor and knocked on the door to Room 304. He was there; not more than five seconds passed before he called out, "Door's not locked." I opened it and stepped inside.

He was sitting in a faded armchair near the window, staring out at the rain and the wet streets below. He turned his head briefly to look at me, then turned it back again to the window. The stubby little pipe was between his teeth and the overheated air smelled of his tobacco, a kind of dry, sweet scent, like withered roses.

"More questions?" he said.

"Not exactly, Mr. Weaver. You mind if I sit down?"

"Bed's all there is."

I sat on the bottom edge of the bed, a few feet away from him. The room was small, neat–not much furniture, not much of anything; old patterned wallpaper and a threadbare carpet, both of which had a patina of gray. Maybe it was my mood and the rain-dull day outside, but the entire room seemed gray, full of that aura of age and hopelessness.

"Hot in here," I said. "Furnace is going full blast down in the basement."

"I don't mind it hot."

"Nick Damiano did a better job of regulating the heat, I understand. He'd turn it on for a few hours in the morning, leave it off most of the day, turn it back on in the evenings, and then shut it down again by midnight. The night he died, though, he didn't have time to shut it down."

Weaver didn't say anything.

"It's pretty noisy in the basement when that furnace is on," I said.

"You can hardly hold a normal conversation with somebody standing right next to you. It'd be almost impossible to hear anything, even raised voices, from a distance. So you couldn't have heard an argument inside Nick's room, not from back by the storage lockers. And probably not even if you stood right next to the door, because the door's thick and made of metal."

He still didn't stir, didn't speak.

"You made up the argument because you ran into Charley Slattery, didn't you? He might have told the police he saw you come out of the elevator around the time Nick was killed, and that you seemed upset; so you had to protect yourself. Just like you protected yourself by unlocking the alley door after the murder."

More silence.

"You murdered Nick, all right. Beat him to death with your cane—hickory like that is as thick and hard as three-quarter-inch steel pipe. Charley told me you had it under your arm when you got off the elevator. Why under your arm? Why weren't you walking with it like you usually do? Has to be that you didn't want your fingers around the handle, the part you clubbed Nick with, even if you did wipe off most of the blood and gore."

He was looking at me now, without expression—just a dull steady waiting look.

"How did you clean the cane once you were here in your room? Soap and water? Cleaning fluid of some kind? It doesn't matter, you know. There'll still be minute traces of blood on it that the police lab can match up to Nick's."

He put an end to his silence then; he said in a clear, toneless voice, "All right. I done it," and that made it a little easier on both of us. The truth is always easier, no matter how painful it might be.

I said, "Do you want to tell me about it, Mr. Weaver?"

"Not much to tell," he said, "I went to the basement to get my other radio, like I told you before. He was fixing the door to one of the storage bins near mine. I looked at him up close, and I knew he was the one. I'd had a feeling he was ever since I moved in, but that night, up close like that, I knew it for sure."

He paused to take the pipe out of his mouth and lay it carefully on the table next to his chair. Then he said, "I accused him point blank. He put his hands over his ears like a woman, like he couldn't stand to hear it, and ran to his room. I went after him. Got inside before he could shut the door. He started babbling, crazy things about skeletons, and I saw that skeleton of his grinning across the room, and I . . . I don't know, I don't remember that part too good. He pushed me, I think, and I hit him with my cane . . . I kept hitting him . . ."

His voice trailed off and he sat there stiffly, with his big gnarled hands clenched in his lap.

"*Why*, Mr. Weaver? You said he was the one, that you accused him—accused him of what?"

He didn't seem to hear me. He said, "After I come to my senses, I couldn't breathe. Thought I was having a heart attack. God, it was hot in there . . . hot as hell. I opened the alley door to get some air and I guess I must have left it unlocked. I never did that on purpose. Only the story about the argument."

"Why did you kill Nick Damiano?"

No answer for a few seconds; I thought he still wasn't listening and I was about to ask the question again. But then he said. "My Bible's over on the desk. Look inside the front cover."

The Bible was a well-used Gideon and inside the front cover was a yellowed newspaper clipping. I opened the clipping. It was from the Chicago *Sun-Times*, dated June 23, 1957—a news story, with an accompanying photograph, that bore the headline: FLOWER SHOP BOMBER IDENTIFIED.

I took it back to the bed and sat again to read it. It said that the person responsible for a homemade bomb that had exploded in a crowded florist shop the day before, killing seven people, was a handyman named Nicholas Donato. One of the dead was Marjorie Donato, the bomber's estranged wife and an employee of the shop; another victim was the shop's owner, Arthur Cullen, with whom Mrs. Donato had apparently been having an affair. According to friends, Nicholas Donato had been despondent over the estrangement and the affair, had taken to drinking heavily, and had threatened "to do something drastic" if his wife didn't move back in with him. He had disappeared the morning of the explosion and had not been apprehended at the time the news story was printed. His evident intention had been to blow up only his wife and her lover; but Mrs. Donato had opened the package containing the bomb immediately after it was brought by messenger, in the presence of several customers, and the result had been mass slaughter.

I studied the photograph of Nicholas Donato. It was a head-and-shoulders shot, of not very good quality, and I had to took at it closely for a time to see the likeness. But it was there: Nicholas Donato and Nick Damiano had been the same man.

Weaver had been watching me read. When I looked up from the clipping he said, "They never caught him. Traced him to Indianapolis, but then he disappeared for good. All these years, twenty-seven years, and I come across him here in San Francisco.

Coincidence. Or maybe it was supposed to happen that way. The hand of the Lord guides us all, and we don't always understand the whys and wherefores."

"Mr. Weaver, what did that bombing massacre have to do with you?"

"One of the people he blew up was my youngest daughter. Twenty-two that year. Went to that flower shop to pick out an arrangement for her wedding. I saw her after it happened, I saw what his bomb did to her . . ."

He broke off again; his strong voice trembled a little now. But his eyes were dry. He'd cried once, he'd cried many times, but that had been long ago. There were no tears left any more.

I got slowly to my feet. The heat and the sweetish tobacco scent were making me feel sick to my stomach. And the grayness, the aura of age and hopelessness and tragedy were like an oppressive weight.

I said, "I'll be going now."

"Going?" he said. "Telephone's right out in the hall."

"I won't be calling the police, Mr. Weaver. From here or from anywhere else."

"What's that? But . . . you know I killed him . . ."

"I don't know anything," I said. "I don't even remember coming here today."

I left him quickly, before he could say anything else, and went downstairs and out to O'Farrell Street. Wind-hurled rain buffeted me, icy and stinging, but the feel and smell of it was a relief. I pulled up the collar on my overcoat and hurried next door.

Upstairs in the office I took Irv Feinberg's two hundred dollars out of the lock-box in the desk and slipped the envelope into my coat pocket. He wouldn't like getting it back; he wouldn't like my calling it quits on the investigation, just as the police had done. But that didn't matter. Let the dead lie still, and the dying find what little peace they had left. The judgment was out of human hands anyway.

I tried not to think about Nick Damiano any more, but it was too soon and I couldn't blot him out yet. Harmless old Nick, the happy whack. Jesus Christ. Seven people–he had slaughtered seven people that day in 1957. And for what? For a lost woman; for a lost love. No wonder he'd gone batty and developed an obsession for skeletons. He had lived with them, seven of them, all those years, heard them clattering and clacking all those thousands of nights. And now, pretty soon, he would be one himself.

Skeleton rattle your mouldy leg.

All men's lovers come to this.

MARCIA MULLER
(b.1944)

The Broken Men
(Sharon McCone)

Dawn was breaking when I returned to the Diablo Valley Pavilion. The softly rounded hills that encircled the amphitheatre were edged with pinkish gold, but their slopes were still dark and forbidding. They reminded me of a herd of humpbacked creatures huddling together while they waited for the warmth of the morning sun; I could imagine them stretching and sighing with relief when its rays finally touched them.

I would have given a lot to have daylight bring me that same sense of relief, but I doubted that would happen. It had been a long, anxious night since I'd arrived here the first time, over twelve hours before. Returning was a last-ditch measure, and a long shot at best.

I drove up the blacktop road to where it was blocked by a row of posts and got out of the car. The air was chill; I could see my breath. Somewhere in the distance a lone bird called, and there was a faint, monotonous whine that must have had something to do with the security lights that topped the chain link fence at intervals, but the overall silence was heavy, oppressive. I stuffed my hands into the pockets of my too-light suede jacket and started toward the main entrance next to the box office.

As I reached the fence, a stocky, dark-haired man stepped out of the adjacent security shack and began unlocking the gate. Roy Canfield, night supervisor for the pavilion. He'd been dubious about what

I'd suggested when I'd called him from San Francisco three quarters of an hour ago, but had said he'd be glad to cooperate if I came back out here. Canfield swung the gate open and motioned me through one of the turnstiles that had admitted thousands to the Diablo Valley Clown Festival the night before.

He said, "You made good time from the city."

"There's no traffic at five a.m. I could set my own speed limit."

The security man's eyes moved over me appraisingly, reminding me of how rumpled and tired I must look. Canfield himself seemed as fresh and alert as when I'd met him before last night's performance. But then, *be* hadn't been chasing over half the Bay Area all night, hunting for a missing client.

"Of course," I added, "I was anxious to get here and see if Gary Fitzgerald might still be somewhere on the premises. Shall we take a look around?"

Canfield looked as dubious as he'd sounded on the phone. He shrugged and said, "Sure we can, but I don't think you'll find him. We check every inch of the place after the crowd leaves. No way anybody could still be inside when we lock up."

There had been a note of reproach in his words, as if he thought I was questioning his ability to do his job. Quickly I said, "It's not that I don't believe you, Mr. Canfield. I just don't have any place else left to look."

He merely grunted and motioned for me to proceed up the wide concrete steps. They led uphill from the entrance to a promenade whose arms curved out in opposite directions around the edge of the amphitheater. As I recalled from the night before, from the promenade the lawn sloped gently down to the starkly modernistic concert shell. Its stage was wide–roughly ninety degrees of the circle–with wings and dressing rooms built back into the hill behind it. The concrete roof, held aloft by two giant pillars, was a curving slab shaped like a warped arrowhead, its tip pointing to the northeast, slightly off center. Formal seating was limited to a few dozen rows in a semi-circle in front of the stage; the pavilion had been designed mainly for the casual type of concert-goer who prefers to lounge on a blanket on the lawn.

I reached the top of the steps and crossed the promenade to the edge of the bowl, then stopped in surprise.

The formerly pristine lawn was now mounded with trash. Paper bags, cups and plates, beer cans and wine bottles, wrappers and crumpled programs and other indefinable debris were scattered in a crazy-quilt pattern. Trash receptacles placed at strategic intervals along the promenade had overflowed, their contents cascading to the ground. On the low wall between the formal seating and the lawn stood a monumental pyramid of Budweiser cans. In some places the debris was only thinly scattered, but in others it lay deep, like dirty drifted snow.

Canfield came up behind me, breathing heavily from the climb. "A mess, isn't it?" he said.

"Yes, Is it always like this after a performance?"

"Depends. Shows like last night, where you get a lot of young people, families, picnickers, it gets pretty bad. A symphony concert, that's different."

"And your maintenance crew doesn't come on until morning?" I tried not to sound disapproving, but allowing such debris to lie there all night was faintly scandalous to a person like me, who had been raised to believe that not washing the supper dishes before going to bed just might constitute a cardinal sin.

"Cheaper that way—we'd have to pay overtime otherwise. And the job's easier when it's light anyhow."

As if in response to Canfield's words, daylight—more gold than pink now—spilled over the hills in the distance, slightly to the left of the stage. It disturbed the shadows on the lawn below us, making them assume different, distorted forms. Black became gray, gray became white; short shapes elongated, others were truncated; fuzzy lines came into sharp focus. And with the light a cold wind came gusting across the promenade.

I pulled my jacket closer, shivering. The wind rattled the fall-dry leaves of the young poplar trees—little more than saplings—planted along the edge of the promenade. It stirred the trash heaped around the receptacles, then swept down the lawn, scattering debris in its wake. Plastic bags and wads of paper rose in an eerie dance, settled again as the breeze passed. I watched the undulation—a paper wave upon a paper sea—as it rolled toward the windbreak of cypress trees to the east.

Somewhere in the roiling refuse down by the barrier between the lawn and the formal seating I spotted a splash of yellow. I leaned forward, peering toward it. Again I saw the yellow, then a blur of blue and then a flicker of white. The colors were there, then gone as the trash settled.

Had my eyes been playing tricks on me in the half-light? I didn't think so, because while I couldn't be sure of the colors, I was distinctly aware of a shape that the wind's passage had uncovered—long, angular, solid-looking. The debris had fallen in a way that didn't completely obscure it.

The dread that I had held in check all night spread through me.

After a frozen moment, I began to scramble down the slope toward the spot I'd been staring at. Behind me, Canfield called out, but I ignored him.

The trash was deep down by the barrier, almost to my knees. I waded through bottles, cans, and papers, pushing their insubstantial mass aside, shoveling with my hands to clear a path. Shoveled until my fingers encountered something more solid...

I dropped to my knees and scooped up the last few layers of debris, hurling it over my shoulder.

He lay on his back, wrapped in his bright yellow cape, his baggy blue plaid pants and black patent leather shoes sticking out from underneath it. His black beret was pulled halfway down over his white clown's face hiding his eyes. I couldn't see the red vest that made up the rest of the costume because the cape covered it, but there were faint red stains on the irridescent fabric that draped across his chest.

I yanked the cape aside and touched the vest. It felt sticky, and when I pulled my hand away it was red too. I stared at it, wiped it off on a scrap of newspaper. Then I felt for a pulse in his carotid artery, knowing all the time what a futile exercise it was.

"Oh, Jesus!" I said. For a moment my vision blurred and there was a faint buzzing in my ears.

Roy Canfield came thrashing up behind me, puffing with exertion. "What... Oh, my God!"

I continued staring down at the clown; he looked broken, an object that had been used up and tossed on a trash heap. After a moment, I touched my thumb to his cold cheek, brushed at the white makeup. I pushed the beret back, looked at the theatrically blackened eyes. Then I tugged off the flaxen wig. Finally I pulled the fake bulbous nose away.

"Gary Fitzgerald?" Canfield asked.

I looked up at him. His moonlike face creased in concern. Apparently the shock and bewilderment I was experiencing showed.

"Mr. Canfield," I said, "this man is wearing Gary's costume, but it's not him. I've never seen him before in my life."

2

The man I *was* looking for was half of an internationally famous clown act, Fitzgerald and Tilby. The world of clowning, like any other artistic realm, has its various levels–from the lowly rodeo clown whose chief function is to keep bull riders from being stomped on, to circus clowns such as Emmett Kelly and universally acclaimed mimes like Marcel Marceau. Fitzgerald and Tilby were not far below Kelly and Marceau in that hierarchy and gaining on them every day. Instead of merely employing the mute body language of the typical clown, the two Britishers combined it with a subtle and sophisticated verbal comedy routine. Their fame had spread beyond aficionados of clowning in the late seventies when they had made a series of artful and entertaining television commercials for one of the Japanese auto makers, and subsequent ads for, among others, a major U.S. airline, one of the big insurance companies, and a computer firm had assured them of a place in the hearts of humor-loving Americans.

My involvement with Fitzgerald and Tilby came about when they agreed to perform at the Diablo Valley Clown Festival, a charity benefit co-sponsored by the Contra Costa County Chamber of Commerce and KSUN, the radio station where my friend Don Del Boccio works as a disc jockey. The team's manager, Wayne Kabalka, had stipulated only two conditions to their performing for free: that they be given star billing, and that they be provided with a bodyguard. Since Don was to be emcee of the show, he was in on all the planning, and when he heard of Kabalka's second stipulation, he suggested me for the job.

As had been the case ever since I'd bought a house near the Glen Park district of San Francisco the spring before, I was short of money at the time. And All Souls Legal Cooperative, where I am staff investigator, had no qualms about me moonlighting provided it didn't interfere with any of the co-op's cases. Since things had been slack at All Souls during September, I felt free to accept. Bodyguarding isn't my idea of challenging work, but I had always enjoyed Fitzgerald and Tilby, and the idea of meeting them intrigued me. Besides, I'd be part of the festival and get paid for my time, rather than attending on the free pass Don had promised me.

So on that hot Friday afternoon in late September, I met with Wayne Kabalka in the lounge at KSUN's San Francisco studios. As radio stations go, KSUN is a casual operation, and the lounge gives full expression to this orientation. It is full of mismatched Salvation Army reject furniture, the posters on the walls are torn and tattered, and the big coffee table is always littered with rumpled newspapers, empty Coke cans and coffee cups, and overflowing ashtrays. On this particular occasion, it was also graced with someone's half-eaten Big Mac.

When Don and I came in, Wayne Kabalka was seated on the very edge of one of the lumpy chairs, looking as if he were afraid it might

have fleas. He saw us and jumped as if one had just bitten him. *His*
orientation was anything but casual: in spite of the heat, he wore a
tan three-piece suit that almost matched his mane of tawny hair, and
a brown striped tie peeked over the V of his vest. Kabalka and his
clients might be based in L.A., but he sported none of the usual
Hollywoodish accoutrements–gold chains, diamond rings, or Adidas
running shoes. Perhaps his very correct appearance was designed to
be in keeping with his clients, Englishmen with rumored connections to the aristocracy.

Don introduced us and we all sat down, Kabalka again doing his
balancing act on the edge of his chair. Ignoring me, he said to Don,
"I didn't realize the bodyguard you promised would be female."

Don shot me a look, his shaggy black eyebrows raised a fraction
of an inch.

I said, "Please don't let my gender worry you, Mr. Kabalka. I've
been a private investigator for nine years, and before that I worked
for a security firm. I'm fully qualified for the job."

To Don he said, "But has she done this kind of work before?"
Again Don looked at me.

I said, "Bodyguarding is only one of any number of types of
assignments I've carried out. And one of the most routine."

Kabalka continued looking at Don. "Is she licensed to carry
firearms?"

Don ran his fingers over his thick black mustache, trying to hide
the beginnings of a grin. "I think," he said, "that I'd better let the
two of you talk alone."

Kabalka put out a hand as if to stay his departure, but Don stood.
"I'll be in the editing room if you need me."

I watched him walk down the hall, his gait surprisingly graceful
for such a tall, stocky man. Then I turned back to Kabalka. "To
answer your question, sir, yes, I'm firearms qualified."

He made a sound halfway between clearing his throat and a grunt.
"Uh...then you have no objection to carrying a gun on this assignment?"

"Not if it's necessary. But before I can agree to that, I'll have to
know why you feel your clients require an armed bodyguard."

"I'm sorry?"

"Is there some threat to them that indicates the guard should be
armed?"

"Threat. Oh...no."

"Extraordinary circumstances, then?"

"Extraordinary circumstances. Well, they're quite famous, you
know. The TV commercials–you've seen them?"

I nodded.

"Then you know what a gold mine we have here. We're due to sign for three more within the month. Bank of America, no less. General Foods is getting into the act. Mobil Oil is hedging, but they'll sign. Fitzgerald and Tilby are important properties; they must be protected."

Properties, I thought, not people. "That still doesn't tell me what I need to know."

Kabalka laced his well-manicured fingers together, flexing them rhythmically. Beads of perspiration stood out on his high forehead; no wonder, wearing that suit in this heat. Finally he said, "In the past couple of years we've experienced difficulty with fans when the boys have been on tour. In a few instances, the crowds got a little too rough."

"Why haven't you hired a permanent bodyguard, then? Put one on staff?"

"The boys were opposed to that. In spite of their aristocratic connections, they're men of the people. They didn't want to put any more distance between them and their public than necessary."

The words rang false. I suspected the truth of the matter was that Kabalka was too cheap to hire a permanent guard. "In a place like the Diablo Valley Pavilion, the security is excellent, and I'm sure that's been explained to you. It hardly seems necessary to hire an armed guard when the pavilion personnel–"

He made a gesture of impatience. "Their security force will have dozens of performers to protect, including a number who will be wandering throughout the audience during the show. My clients need extra protection."

I was silent, watching him. He shifted his gaze from mine, looking around with disproportionate interest at the tattered wall posters. Finally I said, "Mr. Kabalka, I don't feel you're being quite frank with me. And I'm afraid I can't take on this assignment unless you are."

He looked back at me. His eyes were a pale blue, washed out–and worried. "The people here at the station speak highly of you," he said after a moment.

"I hope so. They–especially Mr. Del Boccio–know me well." Especially Don; we'd been lovers for more than six months now.

"When they told me they had a bodyguard lined up, all they said was that you were a first-rate investigator. If I was rude earlier because I was surprised by your being a woman, I apologize."

"Apology accepted."

"I assume by first-rate, one of the things they mean is that you are discreet."

"I don't talk about my cases, if that's what you want to know."

He nodded. "All right, I'm going to entrust you with some information. It's not common knowledge, and you're not to pass it on, gossip about it to your friends–"

Kabalka was beginning to annoy me. "Get on with it, Mr. Kabalka. Or find yourself another bodyguard." Not easy to do, when the performers needed to arrive at the pavilion in about three hours.

His face reddened, and he started to retort, but bit back the words. He looked down at his fingers, still laced together and pressing against one another in a feverish rhythm. "All right. Once again I apologize. In my profession you get used to dealing with such scum-bags that you lose perspective–"

"You were about to tell me...?"

He looked up, squared his shoulders as if he were about to deliver a state secret to an enemy agent. "All right. There *is* a reason why my clients require special security precautions at the Diablo Valley Pavilion. They–Gary Fitzgerald and John Tilby–are originally from Contra Costa County."

"What? I thought they were British."

"Yes, of course you did. And so does almost everyone else. It's part of the mystique, the selling power."

"I don't understand."

"When I discovered the young men in the early seventies, they were performing in a cheap club in San Bernardino, in the valley east of L.A. They were cousins, fresh off the farm–the ranch, in their case. Tilby's father was a dairy rancher in the Contra Costa hills, near Clayton; he raised both boys–Gary's parents had died. When old Tilby died, the ranch was sold and the boys ran off to seek fortune and fame. Old story. And they'd found the glitter doesn't come easy. Another old story. But when I spotted them in that club, I could see they were good. Damned good. So I took them on and made them stars."

"The oldest story of all."

"Perhaps. But now and then it does come true."

"Why the British background?"

"It was the early seventies. The mystique still surrounded such singing groups as the Rolling Stones and the Beatles. What could be better than a British clown act with aristocratic origins? Besides, they were already doing the British bit in their act when I discovered them, and it worked."

I nodded, amused by the machinations of show business. "So you're afraid someone who once knew them might get too close out at the pavilion tonight and recognize them?"

"Yes."

"Don't you think it's a long shot–after all these years?"

"They left there in sixty-nine. People don't change all that much in sixteen years."

That depended, but I wasn't about to debate the point with him. "But what about makeup? Won't that disguise them?" Fitzgerald and Tilby wore traditional clown white-face.

"They can't apply the makeup until they're about to go on–in other circumstances, it might be possible to put it on earlier, but not in this heat."

I nodded. It all made sense. But why did I feel there was something Kabalka wasn't telling me about his need for an armed guard? Perhaps it was the way his eyes had once again shifted from mine to the posters on the walls. Perhaps it was the nervous pressing of his laced fingers. Or maybe it was only that sixth sense that sometimes worked for me: what I called a detective's instinct and others–usually men–labeled woman's intuition.

"All right, Mr. Kabalka," I said, "I'll take the job."

3

I checked in with Don to find out when I should be back at the studios, then went home to change clothing. We would arrive at the pavilion around four; the show–an early one because of its appeal for children– would begin at six. And I was certain that the high temperature– sure to have topped 100 in the Diablo Valley–would not drop until long after dark. Chambray pants and an abbreviated tank top, with my suede jacket to put on in case of a late evening chill were all I would need. That, and my .38 special, tucked in the outer compart- ment of my leather shoulderbag.

By three o'clock I was back at the KSUN studios. Don met me in the lobby and ushered me to the lounge where Kabalka, Gary Fit- zgerald, and John Tilby waited.

The two clowns were about my age–a little over thirty. Their British accents might once have been a put-on, but they sounded as natural now as if they'd been born and raised in London. Gary Fitzgerald was tall and lanky, with straight dark hair, angular features that stop- ped just short of being homely, and a direct way of meeting one's eye. John Tilby was shorter, sandy haired–the type we used to refer to in high school as "cute." His shy demeanor was in sharp contrast to his cousin's straightforward greeting and handshake. They didn't really seem like relatives, but then neither do I in comparison to my four siblings and numerous cousins. All of them resemble one another–typical Scotch-Irish towheads–but I have inherited all the characteristics of our one-eighth Shoshone Indian blood. And none of us are similar in personality or outlook, save for the fact we care a great deal about one another.

Wayne Kabalka hovered in the background while the introductions were made. The first thing he said to me was, "Did you bring your gun?"

"Yes, I did. Everything's under control."

Kabalka wrung his hands together as if he only wished it were true. Then he said, "Do you have a car, Ms. McCone?"

"Yes."

"Then I suggest we take both yours and mine. I have to swing by the hotel and pick up my wife and John's girlfriend."

"All right. I have room for one passenger in mine. Don, what about you? How are you getting out there?"

"I'm going in the Wonder Bus."

I rolled my eyes. The Wonder Bus was a KSUN publicity ploy–a former schoolbus painted in rainbow hues and emblazoned with the station call letters. It traveled to all KSUN-sponsored events, plus to anything else where management deemed its presence might be beneficial. As far as I was concerned, it was the most outrageous in a panoply of the station's brazen efforts at self-promotion, and I took every opportunity to expound this viewpoint to Don. Surprisingly, Don–a quiet classical musician who hated rock-and-roll and the notoriety that went with being a D.J.–never cringed at riding the Wonder Bus. If anything, he took an almost perverse pleasure in the motorized monstrosity.

Secretly, I had a shameful desire to hitch a ride on the Wonder Bus myself.

Wayne Kabalka looked somewhat puzzled at Don's statement. "Wonder Bus?" he said to himself. Then, "Well, if everyone's ready, let's go."

I turned to Don and smiled in a superior fashion. "Enjoy your ride."

We trooped out into the parking lot. Heat shimmered off the concrete paving. Kabalka pulled a handkerchief from his pocket and wiped his brow. "Is it always this hot here in September?"

"This is the month we have our true summer in the city, but no, this is unusual." I went over and placed my bag carefully behind the driver's seat of my MG convertible.

When John Tilby saw the car, his eyes brightened; he came over to it, running a hand along one of its battle-scarred flanks as if it were a brand new Porsche. "I used to have one of these."

"I'll bet it was in better shape than this one."

"Not really." A shadow passed over his face and he continued to caress the car in spite of the fact that the metal must be burning hot to the touch.

"Look," I said, "if you want to drive it out to the pavilion, I wouldn't mind being a passenger for a change."

He hesitated, then said wistfully, "That's nice of you, but I can't . . . I don't drive. But I'd like to ride along–"

"John!" Kabalka's voice was impatient behind us. "Come on, we're keeping Corinne and Nicole waiting."

Tilby gave the car a last longing glance, then shrugged. "I guess I'd better ride out with Wayne and the girls." He turned and walked off to Kabalka's new-looking Seville that was parked at the other side of the lot.

Gary Fitzgerald appeared next to me, a small canvas bag in one hand, garment bag in the other. "I guess you're stuck with me," he said, smiling easily.

"That's not such a bad deal."

He glanced back at Tilby and Kabalka, who were climbing into the Cadillac. "Wayne's right to make John go with him. Nicole would be jealous if she saw him drive up with another woman." His tone was slightly resentful. Of Nicole? I wondered. Perhaps the girlfriend has caused dissension between the cousins.

"Corinne is Wayne's wife?" I asked as we got into the MG.

"Yes. You'll meet both of them at the performance; they're never very far away." Again I heard the under-tone of annoyance.

We got onto the freeway and crossed the Bay Bridge. Commute traffic out of the city was already getting heavy; people left their offices early on hot Fridays in September. I wheeled the little car in and out from lane to lane, bypassing trucks and A.C. Transit buses. Fitzgerald didn't speak. I glanced at him a couple of times to see if my maneuvering bothered him, but he sat slumped against the door, his almost-homely features shadowed with thought. Pre-performance nerves, possibly.

From the bridge, I took Highway 24 east toward Walnut Creek. We passed through the outskirts of Oakland, smog-hazed and sprawling–ugly duckling of the Bay Area. Sophisticates from San Francisco scorned Oakland, repeating Gertrude Stein's overused phrase, "There is no there there," but lately there had been a current of unease in their mockery. Oakland's thriving port had stolen much of the shipping business from her sister city across the Bay; her politics were alive and spirited; and on the site of former slums, sleek new buildings had been put up. Oakland was at last shedding her pinfeathers, and it made many of my fellow San Franciscans nervous.

From there we began the long ascent through the Berkeley Hills to the Caldecott Tunnel. The MG's aged engine strained as we passed lumbering trucks and slower cars, and when we reached the tunnel–three tunnels, actually, two of them now open to accommodate the eastbound commuter rush–I shot into the far lane. At the top of the grade midway through the tunnel, I shifted into neutral to give the engine a rest. Arid heat assailed us as we emerged; the temperature in San Francisco had been nothing compared to this.

The freeway continued to descend, past brown sun-baked hills covered with live oak and eucalyptus. Then houses began to appear, tucked back among the trees. The air was scented with dry leaves and grass and dust. Fire danger, I thought. One spark and those houses become tinderboxes.

The town of Orinda appeared on the right. On the left, in the center of the freeway, a BART train was pulling out of the station. I accelerated and tried to outrace it, giving up when my speedometer hit eighty and waving at some schoolkids who were watching from the train. Then I dropped back to sixty and glanced at Fitzgerald, suddenly embarrassed by my childish display. He was sitting up straighter and grinning.

I said, "The temptation was overwhelming."

"I know the feeling."

Feeling more comfortable now that he seemed willing to talk, I said, "Did Mr. Kabalka tell you that he let me in on where you're really from?"

For a moment he looked startled, then nodded.

"Is this the first time you've been back here in Contra Costa County?"

"Yes."

"You'll find it changed."

"I guess so."

"Mainly there are more people. Places like Walnut Creek and Concord have grown by leaps and bounds in the last ten years."

The county stretched east from the ridge of hills we'd just passed over, toward Mount Diablo, a nearly 4,000-foot peak which had been developed into a 15,000-acre state park. On the north side of the county was the Carquinez Strait, with its oil refineries, Suisun Bay, and the San Joaquin River which separated Contra Costa from

Sacramento County and the Delta. The city of Richmond and environs, to the west, were also part of the county, and their inclusion had always struck me as odd. Besides being geographically separated by the expanse of Tilden Regional Park and San Pablo Reservoir, the mostly black industrial city was culturally light years away from the rest of the suburban, upwardly mobile county. With the exception of a few towns like Pittsburgh or Antioch, this was affluent, fast-developing land; I supposed one day even those north-county backwaters would fall victim to expensive residential tracts and shopping centers full of upscale boutiques.

When Fitzgerald didn't comment, I said, "Does it look different to you?"

"Not really."

"Wait till we get to Walnut Creek. The area around the BART station is all highrise buildings now. They're predicting it will become an urban center that will eventually rival San Francisco."

He grunted in disapproval.

"About the only thing they've managed to preserve out here is the area around Mount Diablo. I suppose you know it from when you were a kid."

"Yes."

"I went hiking in the park last spring, during wildflower season. It was really beautiful that time of year. They say if you climb high enough you can see thirty-five counties from the mountain."

"This pavilion," Fitzgerald said, "is it part of the state park?"

For a moment I was surprised, then realized the pavilion hadn't been in existence in 1969, when he'd left home. "No, but near it. The land around it is relatively unspoiled. Horse and cattle ranches, mostly. They built it about eight years ago, after the Concord Pavilion became such a success. I guess that's one index of how this part of the Bay Area has grown, that it can support two concert pavilions."

He nodded. "Do they ever have concerts going at the same time at both?"

"Sure."

"It must really echo off these hills."

"I imagine you can hear it all the way to Port Chicago." Port Chicago was where the Naval Weapons Station was located, on the edge of Suisun Bay.

"Well, maybe not all the way to Chicago."

I smiled at the feeble joke, thinking that for a clown, Fitzgerald really didn't have much of a sense of humor, then allowed him to lapse back into his moody silence.

4

When we arrived at the pavilion, the parking lot was already crowded, the gates having opened early so people could picnic before the show started. An orange-jacketed attendant directed us to a far corner of the lot which had been cordoned off for official parking near the performers' gate. Fitzgerald and I waited in the car for about fifteen minutes, the late afternoon sun beating down on us, until Wayne Kabalka's Seville pulled up alongside. With the manager and John Tilby were two women: a chic, fortyish redhead, and a small, dark-haired woman in her twenties. Fitzgerald and I got out and went to greet them.

The redhead was Corinne Kabalka; her strong handshake and level gaze made me like her immediately. I was less sure about Nicole Leland; the younger woman was beautiful, with short black hair sculpted close to her head and exotic features, but her manner was very cold. She nodded curtly when introduced to me, then took Tilby's arm and led him off toward the performer's gate. The rest of us trailed behind.

Security was tight at the gate. We met Roy Canfield, who was personally superintending the check-in, and each of us was issued a pass. No one, Canfield told us, would be permitted backstage or through the gate without showing his pass. Security personnel would also be stationed in the audience to protect those clowns who, as part of the show, would be performing out on the lawn.

We were then shown to a large dressing room equipped with a couch, a folding card table and chairs. After everyone was settled there I took Kabalka aside and asked him if he would take charge of the group for about fifteen minutes while I checked the layout of the pavilion. He nodded distractedly and I went out front.

Stage personnel were scurrying around, setting up sound equipment and checking the lights. Don had already arrived, but he was conferring with one of the other KSUN jocks and didn't look as if he could be disturbed. The formal seating was empty, but the lawn was already crowded. People lounged on blankets, passing around food, drink and an occasional joint. Some of the picnics were elaborate–fine china, crystal wineglasses, ice buckets, and in once case, a set of lighted silver candelabra; others were of the paper-plate and plastic-cup variety. I spotted the familiar logos of Kentucky Fried Chicken and Jack-in-the-Box here and there. People called to friends, climbed up and down the hill to the restroom and refreshment facilities, dropped by other groups' blankets to see what goodies they had to trade. Children ran through the crowd, an occasional frisbee sailed through the air. I noticed a wafting trail of irridescent soap bubbles, and my eyes followed it to a young woman in a red halter top who was blowing them, her face aglow with childlike pleasure.

For a moment I felt a stab of envy, realizing that if I hadn't taken on this job I could be out front, courtesy of the free pass Don had promised me. I could have packed a picnic, perhaps brought along a woman friend, and Don could have dropped by to join us when he had time. But instead, I was bodyguarding a pair of clowns who–given the pavilion's elaborate security measures–probably didn't need me. And in addition to Fitzgerald and Tilby, I seemed to be responsible for an entire group. I could see why Kabalka might want to stick close to his clients, but why did the wife and girlfriend have to crowd into what was already a stuffy, hot dressing room? Why couldn't they go out front and enjoy the performance? It complicated my assignment, having to contend with an entourage, and the thought of those complications made me grumpy.

The grumpiness was probably due to the heat, I decided. Shrugging it off, I familiarized myself with the layout of the stage and the points at which someone could gain access. Satisfied that pavilion security could deal with any problems that might arise there, I made my way through the crowd–turning down two beers, a glass of wine, and a pretzel–and climbed to the promenade. From there I studied the stage once more, then raised my eyes to the sun-scorched hills to the east.

The slopes were barren, save for an occasional outcropping of rock and live oak trees, and on them a number or horses with riders stood. They clustered together in groups of two, four, six and even at this distance, I sensed they shared the same camaraderie as the people on the lawn. They leaned toward one another, gestured, and occasionally passed objects–perhaps they were picnicking too–back and forth.

What a great way to enjoy a free concert, I thought. The sound, in this natural echo chamber, would easily carry to where the watchers were stationed. How much more peaceful it must be on the hill, free of crowds and security measures. Visibility, however, would not be very good . . .

And then I saw a flare of reddish light and glanced over to where a lone horseman stood under the sheltering branches of a live oak. The light flashed again, and I realized he was holding binoculars which had caught the setting sun. Of course–with binoculars or opera glasses, visibility would not be bad at all. In fact, from such a high vantage point it might even be better than from many points on the lawn. My grumpiness returned; I'd have loved to be mounted on a horse on that hillside.

Reminding myself that I was here on business that would pay for part of the new bathroom tile, I turned back toward the stage, then started when I saw Gary Fitzgerald. He was standing on the lawn not more than six feet from me, looking around with one hand forming a visor over his eyes. When he saw me he started too, and then waved.

I rushed over to him and grabbed his arm. "What are you doing out here? You're supposed to stay backstage!"

"I just wanted to see what the place looks like."

"Are you out of your mind? Your manager is paying good money for me to see that people stay away from you. And here you are, wandering through the crowd–"

He looked away, at a family on a blanket next to us. The father was wiping catsup from the smallest child's hands. "No one's bothering me."

"That's not the point." Still gripping his arm, I began steering him toward the stage. "Someone might recognize you, and that's precisely what Kabalka hired me to prevent."

"Oh, Wayne's just being a worrywart about that. No one's going to recognize anybody after all this time. Besides, it's common knowledge in the trade that we're not what we're made out to be."

"In the trade, yes. But your manager's worried about the public." We got to the stage, showed our passes to the security guard, and went back to the dressing room.

At the door Fitzgerald stopped. "Sharon, would you mind not mentioning my going out there to Wayne?"

"Why shouldn't I?"

"Because it would only upset him, and he's nervous enough before a performance. Nothing happened–except that I was guilty of using bad judgment."

His smile was disarming, and I took the words as an apology. "All right. But you'd better to get into costume. There's only half an hour before the grand procession begins."

5

The next few hours were uneventful. The grand procession–a parade through the crowd in which all the performers participated–went off smoothly. After they returned to the dressing room, Fitzgerald and Tilby removed their makeup–which was already running in the intense heat–and the Kabalkas fetched supper from the car–deli food packed in hampers by their hotel. There was a great deal of grumbling about the quality of the meal, which was not what one would have expected of the St. Francis, and Fitzgerald teased the others because he was staying at a small bed-and-breakfast establishment in the Haight-Ashbury which had better food at half the price.

Nicole said, "Yes, but your hotel probably has bed-bugs."

Fitzgerald glared at her, and I was reminded of the disapproving tone of voice in which he'd first spoken of her. "Don't be ignorant. Urban chic has come to the Haight-Ashbury."

"Making it difficult for you to recapture your mis-spent youth there, no doubt."

"Nicole," Kabalka said.

"That *was* your intention in separating from the rest of us, wasn't it, Gary?" Nicole added.

Fitzgerald was silent.

"Well, Gary?"

He glanced at me. "You'll have to excuse us for letting our hostilities show."

Nicole smiled nastily. "Yes, when a man gets to a certain age, he must try to recapture–"

"Shut up, Nicole," Kabalka said.

She looked at him in surprise, then picked up her sandwich and nibbled daintily at it. I could understand why she had backed off; there was something in Kabalka's tone that said he would put up with no more from her.

After the remains of supper were packed up, everyone settled down. None of them displayed the slightest inclination to go out front and watch the show. Kabalka read–one of those slim volumes that claim you can make a financial killing in spite of the world economic crisis. Corinne crocheted–granny squares. Fitzgerald brooded. Tilby played solitaire. Nicole fidgeted. And while they engaged in these activities, they also seemed to be watching one another. The covert vigilant atmosphere puzzled me; after a while I concluded that maybe the reason they all stuck together was that each was afraid to leave the others alone. But why?

Time crawled. Outside, the show was going on; I could hear music, laughter, and–occasionally–Don's enthusiastic voice as he introduced the acts. Once more I began to regret taking this job.

After a while Tilby reshuffled the cards and slapped them on the table. "Sharon, do you play gin rummy?"

"Yes."

"Good. Let's have a few hands."

Nicole frowned and made a small sound of protest.

Tilby said to her, "I offered to teach you. It's not my fault you refused."

I moved my chair over to the table and we played in silence for a while. Tilby was good, but I was better. After about half an hour, there was a roar from the crowd and Tilby raised his head. "Casey O'Connell must be going on."

"Who?" I said.

"One of our more famous circus clowns."

"There really is quite a variety among the performers in your profession, isn't there?"

"Yes, and quite a history: clowning is an old and honored art. They had clowns back in ancient Greece. Wandering entertainers, actually, who'd show up at a wealthy household and tell jokes, do acrobatics, or juggle for the price of a meal. Then in the Middle Ages, mimes appeared on the scene."

"That long ago?"

"Uh-huh. They were the cream of the crop back then. Most of the humor in the Middle Ages was kind of basic; they loved buffoons, jesters, simpletons, that sort of thing. But they served the purpose of making people see how silly we really are."

I took the deuce he'd just discarded, then lay down my hand to show I had gin. Tilby frowned and slapped down his cards; nothing matched. Then he grinned. "See what I mean–I'm silly to take this game so seriously."

I swept the cards together and began to shuffle. "You seem to know a good bit about the history of clowning."

"Well, I've done some reading along those lines. You've heard the term *commedia dell'arte?*"

"Yes."

"It appeared in the late 1500s, an Italian brand of the traveling comedy troupe. The comedians always played the same role–a Harlequin or a Pulcinella or a Pantalone. Easy for the audience to recognize."

"I know what a Harlequin is, but what are the other two?"

"Pantalone is a personification of the overbearing father figure. A stubborn, temperamental old geezer. Pulcinella was costumed all in white, usually with a dunce's cap; he assumed various roles in the comedy–lawyer, doctor, servant, whatever–and was usually greedy, sometimes pretty coarse. One of his favorite tricks was urinating onstage."

"Good Lord!"

"Fortunately we've become more refined since then. The British contributed a lot, further developing the Harlequin, creating the Punch and Judy shows. And of course, the French had their Figaro. The Indians created the *vidushaka*-a form of court jester. The entertainers at the Chinese court were known as *Chous*, after the dynasty in which they originated. And Japan has a huge range of comic figures appearing in their *Kyogen* plays-the humorous counterpart of the *Noh* play."

"You really have done your homework."

"Well, clowning's my profession. Don't you know about the history of yours?"

"What I know is mostly fictional; private investigation is more interesting in books than in real life, I'm afraid."

"Gin." Tilby spread his cards on the table. "Your deal. But back to what I was saying, it's the more contemporary clowns that interest me. And I use the term 'clown' loosely."

"How so?"

"Well, do you think of Will Rogers as a clown?"

"No."

"I do. And Laurel and Hardy, Flip Wilson, Mae West, Woody Allen, Lucille Ball. As well as the more traditional figures like Emmett Kelly, Charlie Chaplin, and Marceau. There's a common denominator among all those people: they're funny and, more important, they all make the audience take a look at humanity's foibles. They're as much descended from those historical clowns as the white-face circus performer."

"The whiteface is the typical circus clown, right?"

"Well, there are three basic types. Whiteface is your basic slaphappy fellow. The Auguste-who was created almost simultaneously in Germany and France-usually wears pink or blackface and is the one you see falling all over himself in the ring, often sopping wet from having buckets of water thrown at him. The Grotesque is usually a midget or a dwarf, or has some other distorted feature. And there are performers whom you can't classify because they've created something unique, such as Kelly's Weary Willie, or Russia's Popov, who is such an artist that he doesn't even need to wear makeup."

"It's fascinating. I never realized there was such variety. Or artistry."

"Most people don't. They think clowning is easy, but a lot of the time it's just plain hard work. Especially when you have to go on when you aren't feeling particularly funny." Tilby's mouth drooped as he spoke, and I wondered if tonight was one of those occasions for him.

I picked up a trey and said, "Gin," then tossed my hand on the table and watched as he shuffled and dealt. We fell silent once more. The sounds of the show went on, but the only noise in the dressing room was the slap of the cards on the table. It was still uncomfortably hot. Moths fluttered around the glaring bare bulbs of the dressing tables. At about ten-thirty, Fitzgerald stood up.

"Where are you going?" Kabalka said.

"The men's room. Do you mind?"

I said, "I'll go with you."

Fitzgerald smiled faintly. "Really, Sharon, that's above and beyond the call of duty."

"I mean, just to the door."

He started to protest, then shrugged and picked up his canvas bag.

Kabalka said, "Why are you taking that?"

"There's something in it I need."

"What?"

"For Christ's sake, Wayne!" He snatched up his yellow cape, flung it over one shoulder.

Kabalka hesitated. "All right, go. But Sharon goes with you."

Fitzgerald went out into the hall and I followed. Behind me, Nicole said, "Probably Maalox or something like that for his queasy stomach. You can always count on Gary to puke at least once before a performance."

Kabalka said, "Shut up, Nicole."

Fitzgerald started off, muttering, "Yes, we're one big happy family."

I followed him and took up a position next to the men's room door. It was ten minutes before I realized he was taking too long a time, and when I did I asked one of the security guards to go in after him. Fitzgerald had vanished, apparently through an open window high off the floor—a trash receptacle had been moved beneath it, which would have allowed him to climb up there. The window opened onto the pavilion grounds rather than outside of the fence, but from there he could have gone in any one of a number of directions—including out the performers' gate.

From then on, all was confusion. I told Kabalka what had happened and again left him in charge of the others. With the help of the security personnel, I combed the backstage area—questioning the performers, stage personnel, Don, and the other people from KSUN. No one had seen Fitzgerald. The guards in the audience were alerted, but no one in baggy plaid pants, a red vest, and a yellow cape was spotted. The security man on the performers' gate knew nothing; he'd only come on minutes ago, and the man he had relieved had left the grounds on a break.

Fitzgerald and Tilby were to be the last act to go on—at midnight, as the star attraction. As the hour approached, the others in their party grew frantic and Don and the KSUN people grew grim. I continued to search systematically. Finally I returned to the performers' gate; the guard had returned from his break and Kabalka had buttonholed him. I took over the questioning. Yes, he remembered Gary Fitzgerald. He'd left at about ten thirty, carrying his yellow cape and a small canvas bag. But wait—hadn't he returned just a few minutes ago, before Kabalka had come up and started asking questions? But maybe that wasn't the same man, there had been something different . . .

Kabalka was on the edge of hysterical collapse. He yelled at the guard and only confused him further. Maybe the man who had just come in had been wearing a red cape . . . maybe the pants were green rather than blue . . . no, it wasn't the same man after all . . .

Kabalka yelled louder, until one of the stage personnel told him to shut up, he could be heard out front. Corinne appeared and momentarily succeeded in quieting her husband. I left her to deal with him and went back to the dressing room. Tilby and Nicole were there. His face was pinched, white around the mouth. Nicole was pale and –oddly enough–had been crying. I told them what the security guard had said, cautioned them not to leave the dressing room.

As I turned to go, Tilby said, "Sharon, will you ask Wayne to come in here?"

"I don't think he's in any shape–"

"Please, it's important."

"All right. But why?"

Tilby looked at Nicole. She turned her tear-streaked face away toward the wall.

He said, "We have a decision to make about the act."

"I hardly think so. It's pretty clear cut. If Gary doesn't turn up, you simply can't go on."

He stared bleakly at me. "Just ask Wayne to come in here."

Of course the act didn't go on. The audience was disappointed, the KSUN people were irate, and the Fitzgerald and Tilby entourage were grim–a grimness that held a faint undercurrent of tightly-reined panic. No one could shed any light on where Fitzgerald might have gone, or why–at least, if anyone had suspicions, he was keeping it to himself. The one thing everyone agreed on was that his disappearance wasn't my fault; I hadn't been hired to prevent treachery within the ranks. I myself wasn't so sure of my lack of culpability.

So I'd spent the night chasing around, trying to find a trace of him. I'd gone to San Francisco: to Fitzgerald's hotel in the Haight-Ashbury, to the St. Francis where the rest of the party were staying, even to the KSUN studios. Finally I went back to the Haight, to a number of the after-hours places I knew of, in the hopes Fitzgerald was there recapturing his youth, as Nicole had termed it earlier. And I still hadn't found a single clue to his whereabouts.

Until now. I hadn't located Gary Fitzgerald, but I'd found his clown costume. On another man. A dead man.

6

After the county sheriff's men had finished questioning me and said I could go, I decided to return to the St. Francis and talk to my clients once more. I wasn't sure if Kabalka would want me to keep searching for Fitzgerald now, but he—and the others—deserved to hear from me about the dead man in Gary's costume, before the authorities contacted them. Besides, there were things bothering me about Fitzgerald's disappearance, some of them obvious, some vague. I hoped talking to Kabalka and company once more would help me bring the vague ones into more clear focus.

It was after seven by the time I had parked under Union Square and entered the hotel's elegant, dark-paneled lobby. The few early risers who clustered there seemed to be tourists, equipped with cameras and anxious to get on with the day's adventures. A dissipated-looking couple in evening clothes stood waiting for an elevator, and a few yards away in front of the first row of expensive shops, a maid in the hotel uniform was pushing a vacuum cleaner with desultory strokes. When the elevator came, the couple and I rode up in silence; they got off at the floor before I did.

Corinne Kabalka answered my knock on the door of the suite almost immediately. Her eyes were deeply shadowed, she wore the same white linen pantsuit—now severely rumpled—that she'd had on the night before, and in her hand she clutched her crocheting. When she saw me, her face registered disappointment.

"Oh," she said, "I thought . . ."

"You hoped it would be Gary."

"Yes. Well, any of them, really."

"Them? Are you alone?"

She nodded and crossed the sitting room to a couch under the heavily-draped windows, dropping onto it with a sigh and setting down the crocheting.

"Where did they go?"

"Wayne's out looking for Gary. He refuses to believe he's just...vanished. I don't know where John is, but I suspect he's looking for Nicole."

"And Nicole?"

Anger flashed in her tired eyes. "Who knows?"

I was about to ask her more about Tilby's unpleasant girlfriend when a key rattled in the lock, and John and Nicole came in. His face was pulled into taut lines, reflecting a rage more sustained than Corinne's brief flare-up. Nicole looked haughty, tight-lipped, and a little defensive.

Corinne stood. "Where have you two been?"

Tilby said, "*I* was looking for Nicole. It occurred to me that we didn't want to lose another member of this happy party."

Corinne turned to Nicole. "And you?"

The younger woman sat on a spindly chair, studiously examining her plum-colored fingernails. "I was having breakfast."

"Breakfast?"

"I was hungry, after that disgusting supper last night. So I went around the corner to a coffee shop–"

"You could have ordered from room service. Or eaten downstairs where John could have found you more easily."

"I needed some air."

Now Corinne drew herself erect. "Always thinking of Nicole, aren't you?"

"Well, what of it? Someone around here has to act sensibly."

In their heated bickering, they all seemed to have forgotten I was there. I remained silent, taking advantage of the situation; one could learn very instructive things by listening to people's unguarded conversations.

Tilby said, "Nicole's right, Corinne. We can't all run around like Wayne, looking for Gary when we have no idea where to start."

"Yes, *you* would say that. You never did give a damn about him, or anyone. Look how you stole Nicole from your own cousin–"

"Good God, Corinne! You can't *steal* one person from another."

"You did. You stole her and then you wrecked–"

"Let's not go into this, Corinne. Especially in front of an outsider." Tilby motioned at me.

Corinne glanced my way and colored. "I'm sorry, Sharon. This must be embarrassing for you."

On the contrary, I wished they would go on. After all, if John had taken Nicole from his cousin, Gary would have had reason to resent him--perhaps even to want to destroy their act.

I said to Tilby, "Is that the reason Gary was staying at a different hotel--because of you and Nicole?"

He looked startled.

"How long have you two been together?" I asked.

"Long enough." He turned to Corinne. "Wayne hasn't come back or called, I take it?"

"I've heard nothing. He was terribly worried about Gary when he left."

Nicole said, "He's terribly worried about the TV commercials and his cut of them."

"Nicole!" Corinne whirled on her.

Nicole looked up, her delicate little face all innocence. "You know it's true. All Wayne cares about is money. I don't know why he's worried, though. He can always get someone to replace Gary, Wayne's good at doing that sort of thing--"

Corinne stepped forward and her hand lashed out at Nicole's face, connecting with a loud smack. Nicole put a hand to the reddening stain on her cheekbone, eyes widening; then she got up and ran from the room. Corinne watched her go, satisfaction spreading over her handsome features. When I glanced at Tilby, I was surprised to see he was smiling.

"Round one to Corinne," he said.

"She had it coming." The older woman went back to the couch and sat, smoothing her rumpled pantsuit. "Well, Sharon, once more you must excuse us. I assume you came here for a reason?"

"Yes." I sat down in the chair Nicole had vacated and told them about the dead man at the pavilion. As I spoke, the two exchanged glances that were at first puzzled, then worried, and finally panicky.

When I had finished, Corinne said, "But who on earth can the man in Gary's costume be?" The words sounded theatrical, false.

"The sheriff's department is trying to make an identification. Probably his fingerprints will be on file somewhere. In the meantime, there are a few distinctive things about him which may mean something to you or John."

John sat down next to Corinne. "Such as?"

"The man had been crippled, probably a number of years ago, according to the man from the medical examiner's office. One arm was bent badly, and he wore a lift to compensate for a shortened leg. He would have walked with a limp."

The two of them looked at each other, and then Tilby said--too quickly–"I don't know anyone like that."

Corinne also shook her head, but she didn't meet my eyes.

I said, "Are you sure?"

"Of course we're sure." There was an edge of annoyance in Tilby's voice.

I hesitated, then went on, "The sheriff's man who examined the body theorizes that the dead man may have been from the countryside around there, because he had fragments of madrone and chapparal leaves caught in his shoes, as well as foxtails in the weave of his pants. Perhaps he's someone you knew when you lived in the area?"

"No, I don't remember anyone like that."

"He was about Gary's height and age, but with sandy hair. He must have been handsome once, in an elfin way, but his face was badly scarred."

"I said, I don't know who he is."

I was fairly certain he was lying, but accusing him would get me nowhere.

Corinne said, "Are you sure the costume was Gary's? Maybe this man was one of the other clowns and dressed similarly."

"That's what I suggested to the sheriff's man, but the dead man had Gary's pass in his vest pocket. We all signed our passes, remember?"

There was a long silence. "So what you're saying," Tilby finally said, "is that Gary *gave* his pass and costume to this man."

"It seems so."

"But why?"

"I don't know. I'd hoped you could provide me with some insight."

They both stared at me. I noticed Corinne's face had gone quite blank. Tilby was as white-lipped as when I'd come upon him and Nicole in the dressing room shortly after Fitzgerald's disappearance.

I said to Tilby, "I assume you each have more than one change of costume."

It was Corinne who answered. "We brought three on this tour. But I had the other two sent out to the cleaner when we arrived here in San Francisco... Oh!"

"What is it?"

"I just remembered. Gary asked me about the other costumes yesterday morning. He called from that hotel where he was staying. And he was very upset when I told him they would be at the cleaner until this afternoon."

"So he planned it all along. Probably he hoped to give his extra costume to the man, and when he found he couldn't, he decided to make a switch." I remembered Fitzgerald's odd behavior immediately after we'd arrived at the pavilion–his sneaking off into the audience when he'd been told to stay backstage. Had he had a confederate out there? Someone to hand the things to? No. He couldn't have turned over either the costume or the pass to anyone, because the clothing was still backstage, and he'd needed his pass when we returned to the dressing room.

Tilby suddenly stood up. "The son of a bitch! After all we've done–"

"John!" Corinne touched his elbow with her hand.

"John," I said, "why was your cousin staying at the hotel in the Haight?"

He looked at me blankly for a moment. "What? Oh, I don't know. He claimed he wanted to see how it had changed since he'd lived there."

"I thought you grew up together on your father's ranch near Clayton and then went to Los Angeles."

"We did. Gary lived in the Haight before we left the Bay Area."

"I see. Now, you say he 'claimed' that was the reason. Was there something else?"

Tilby was silent, then looked at Corinne. She shrugged.

"I guess," he said finally, "he'd had about all he could take of us. As you may have noticed, we're not exactly a congenial group lately."

"Why is that?"

"Why is what?"

"That you're all at odds? It hasn't always been this way, has it?"

This time Tilby shrugged. Corinne was silent, looking down at her clasped hands.

I sighed, silently empathizing with Fitzgerald's desire to get away from these people. I myself was sick of their bickering, lies, backbiting, and evasions. And I knew I would get nowhere with them–at least not now. Better to wait until I could talk with Kabalka, see if he were willing to keep on employing me. Then, if he was, I could start fresh.

I stood up, saying, "The Contra Costa authorities will be contacting you. I'd advise you to be as frank as possible with them."

To Corinne, I added, "Wayne will want a personal report from me when he comes back; ask him to call me at home." I took out a card with both my All Souls and home number, lay it on the coffee table, and started for the door.

As I let myself out, I glanced back at them. Tilby stood with his arms folded across his chest, looking down at Corinne. They were still as statues, their eyes locked, their expressions bleak and helpless.

7

Of course, by the time I got home to my brown-shingled cottage the desire to sleep had left me. It was always that way when I harbored nagging unanswered questions. Instead of going to bed and forcing myself to rest, I made coffee and took a cup of it out on the back porch to think.

It was a sunny, clear morning and already getting hot. The neighborhood was Saturday noisy: to one side, my neighbors, the Halls, were doing something to their backyard shed that involved a lot of hammering; on the other side, the Curleys' dog was barking excitedly. Probably, I thought, my cat was deviling the dog by prancing along the top of the fence, just out of his reach. It was Watney's favorite game lately.

Sure enough, in a few minutes there was a thump as Wat dropped down from the fence onto an upturned half barrel I'd been meaning to make into a planter. His black-and-white spotted fur was full of foxtails; undoubtedly he'd been prowling around in the weeds at the back of the Curleys' lot.

"Come here, you," I said to him. He stared at me, tail swishing back and forth. "Come here!" He hesitated, then galloped up. I managed to pull one of the foxtails from the ruff of fur over his collar before he trotted off again, his belly swaying pendulously, a great big horse of a cat...

I sat staring at the foxtail, rolling it between my thumb and forefinger, not really seeing it. Instead, I pictured the hills surrounding the pavilion as I'd seen them the night before. The hills that were dotted with oak and madrone and chapparal ... that were sprinkled with people on horses... where a lone horseman had stood under the sheltering branches of a tree, his binoculars like a signal flare in the setting sun...

I got up and went inside to the phone. First I called the Contra Costa sheriff's deputy who had been in charge of the crime scene at the pavilion. No, he told me, the dead man hadn't been identified yet; the only personal item he had been carrying was a bus ticket–issued yesterday–from San Francisco to Concord which had been tucked into his shoe. While this indicated he was not a resident of the area, it told them nothing else. They were still hoping to get an identification on his finger-prints, however.

Next I called the pavilion and got the home phone number of Jim Hayes, the guard who had been on the performers' gate when

Fitzgerald had vanished. When Hayes answered my call, he sounded as if I'd woken him, but he was willing to answer a few questions.

"When Fitzgerald left he was wearing his costume, right?" I asked.

"Yes."

"What about makeup?"

"No. I'd have noticed that; it would have seemed strange, him leaving with his face all painted."

"Now, last night you said you thought he'd come back in a few minutes after you returned from your break. Did he show you his pass?"

"Yes, everyone had to show one. But–"

"Did you look at the name on it?"

"Not closely. I just checked to see if it was valid for that date. Now I wish I *had* looked, because I'm not sure it was Fitzgerald. The costume seemed the same, but I just don't know."

"Why?"

"Well, there was something different about the man who came in. He walked funny. The guy you found murdered, he was crippled."

So that observation might or might not be valid. The idea that the man walked "funny" could have been planted in Hayes' mind by his knowing the dead man was a cripple. "Anything else?"

He hesitated. "I think...yes. You asked if Gary Fitzgerald was wearing makeup when he left. And he wasn't. But the guy who came in, he *was* made up. That's why I don't think it was Fitzgerald."

"Thank you, Mr. Hayes. That's all I need to know."

I hung up the phone, grabbed my bag and car keys, and drove back out to the pavilion in record time.

The heat-hazed parking lots were empty today, save for a couple of trucks that I assumed belonged to the maintenance crew. The gates were locked, the box office windows shuttered, and I could see no one. That didn't matter, however. What I was interested in lay outside the chain-link fence. I parked the MG near the trucks and went around the perimeter of the amphitheater to the area: near the performers' gate, then looked up at the hill to the east. There was a fire break cut through the high wheat-colored grass, and I started up it.

Halfway to the top, I stopped, wiping sweat from my forehead and looking down at the pavilion. Visibility was good from here. Pivoting, I surveyed the surrounding area. To the west lay a monotonous grid-like pattern of tracts and shopping centers, broken here and there by hills and the upthrusting skyline of Walnut Creek. To the north I could see smoke billowing from the stacks of the paper plant at Antioch, and the bridge spanning the river toward the Sacramento Delta. Further east, the majestic bulk of Mount Diablo rose; between it and this foothill were more hills and hollows–ranch country.

The hill on which I stood was only lightly wooded, but there was an outcropping of rock surrounded by madrone and live oak about a hundred yards to the south, on a direct line from the tree where the lone horseman with the signal-like binoculars had stood. I left the relatively easy footing of the fire break and waded through the dry grass toward it. It was cool and deeply shadowed under the branches of the trees, and the air smelled of vegetation gone dry and brittle. I stood still for a moment, wiping the sweat away once more, then began to look around. What I was searching for was wedged behind a low rock that formed a sort of table: a couple of tissues smeared with makeup. Black and red and white greasepaint–the theatrical makeup of a clown.

The dead man had probably used this rock as a dressing table, applying what Fitzgerald had brought him in the canvas bag. I remembered Gary's insistence on taking the bag with him to the men's room; of course he needed it; the makeup was a necessary prop to their plan. While Fitzgerald could leave the pavilion without his greasepaint, the other man couldn't enter un-madeup; there was too much of a risk that the guard might notice the face didn't match the costume or the name on the pass.

I looked down at the dry leaves beneath my feet. Oak, and madrone, and brittle needles of chapparal. And the foxtails would have been acquired while pushing through the high grass between here and the bottom of the hills. That told me the route the dead man had taken, but not what had happened to Fitzgerald. In order to find that out, I'd have to learn where one could rent a horse.

I stopped at a feed store in the little village of Hill-side, nestled in a wooded hollow southeast of the pavilion. It was all you could expect of a country store, with wood floors and big sacks and bins of feed. The weatherbeaten old man in overalls who looked up from the saddle he was polishing completed the rustic picture.

He said, "Help you with something?"

I took a closer look at the saddle, then glanced around at the hand-tooled leather goods hanging from the hooks on the far wall. "That's beautiful work. Do you do it yourself?"

"Sure do."

"How much does a saddle like that go for these days?" My experience with horses had ended with the lessons I'd taken in junior high school.

"Custom job like this, five hundred, thereabouts."

"Five hundred! That's more than I could get for my car."

"Well . . ." He glanced through the door at the MG.

"I know. You don't have to say another word."

"It runs, don't it?"

"Usually." Rapport established, I got down to business. "What I need is some information. I'm looking for a stable that rents horses."

"You want to set up a party or something?"

"I might."

"Well, there's MacMillan's, on the south side of town. I wouldn't recommend them, though. They've got some mean horses. This would be for a bunch of city folks?"

"I wasn't aware it showed."

"Doesn't, all that much. But I'm good at figuring out about folks. You don't look like a suburban lady, and you don't look country either." He beamed at me, and I nodded and smiled to compliment his deductive ability. "No," he went on, "I wouldn't recommend MacMillan's if you'll have folks along who maybe don't ride so good. Some of those horses are mean enough to kick a person from here to San Jose. The place to go is Wheeler's; they got some fine mounts."

"Where is Wheeler's?"

"South too, a couple of miles beyond MacMillan's. You'll know it by the sign."

I thanked him and started out. "Hey!" he called after me. "When you have your party, bring your city friends by. I got a nice selection of handtooled belts and wallets."

I said I would, and waved at him as I drove off.

About a mile down the road on the south side of the little hamlet stood a tumble-down stable with a hand-lettered sign advertising horses for rent. The poorly recommended MacMillan's, no doubt. There wasn't an animal, mean or otherwise, in sight, but a large, jowly woman who resembled a bulldog greeted me, pitchfork in hand.

I told her the story that I'd hastily made up on the drive: a friend of mine had rented a horse the night before to ride up on the hill and watch the show at the Diablo Valley Pavilion. He had been impressed with the horse and the stable it had come from, but couldn't remember the name of the place. Had she, by any chance, rented to him? As I spoke, the woman began to frown, looking more and more like a pugnacious canine every minute.

"It's not honest," she said.

"I'm sorry?"

"It's not honest, people riding up there and watching for free. Stealing's stealing, no matter what name you put on it. Your Bible tells you that."

"Oh." I couldn't think of any reply to that, although she was probably right.

She eyed me severely, as if she suspected me of pagan practices. "In answer to your question, no, I didn't rent to your friend. I wouldn't let a person near one of my horses if he was going to ride up there and watch."

"Well, I don't suppose my friend admitted what he planned to do–"

"Any decent person would be too ashamed to admit to a thing like that." She motioned aggressively with the pitchfork.

I took a step backwards. "But maybe you rented to him not knowing–"

"You going to do the same thing?"

"What?"

"Are you going to ride up there for tonight's concert?"

"Me? No, ma'am. I don't even ride all that well. I just wanted to find out if my friend had rented his horse from–"

"Well, he didn't get the horse from here. We aren't open evenings, don't want our horses out in the dark with people like you who can't ride. Besides, even if people don't plan it, those concerts are an awful temptation. And I can't sanction that sort of thing. I'm a born-again Christian, and I won't help people go against the Lord's word."

"You know," I said hastily, "I agree with you. And I'm going to talk with my friend about his behavior. But I still want to know where he got that horse. Are there any other stables around here besides yours?"

The woman looked somewhat mollified. "There's only Wheeler's. They do a big business–trail trips on Mount Diablo, hayrides in the fall. And, of course, folks who want to sneak up to that pavilion. They'd rent to a person who was going to rob a bank on horseback if there was enough money in it."

Stifling a grin, I started for my car. "Thanks for the information."

"You're welcome to it. But you remember to talk to your friend, tell him to mend his ways."

I smiled and got out of there in a hurry.

Next to MacMillan's, Wheeler's Riding Stables looked prosperous and attractive. The red barn was freshly painted, and a couple of dozen healthy, sleek horses grazed within white rail fences. I rumbled down a dirt driveway and over a little bridge that spanned a gully, and parked in front of a door labeled OFFICE. Inside, a blond-haired man in faded Levi's and a T-shirt lounged in a canvas chair behind the counter, reading a copy of *Playboy*. He put it aside reluctantly when I came in.

I was tired of my manufactured story, and this man looked like someone I could be straightforward with. I showed him the photostat of my license and said, "I'm cooperating with the county sheriff's department on the death at the Diablo Valley Pavilion last night. You've heard about it?"

"Yes, it made the morning news."

"I've got reason to believe that the dead man may have rented a horse prior to the show last night."

The man raised a sun-bleached eyebrow and waited, as economical with his words as the woman at MacMillan's had been spendthrift.

"Did you rent any horses last night?"

"Five. Four to a party, another later on."

"Who rented the single horse?"

"Tall, thin guy. Wore jeans and a plaid shirt. At first I thought I knew him."

"Why?"

"He looked familiar, like someone who used to live near here. But then I realized it couldn't be. His face was disfigured, his arm crippled up, and he limped. Had trouble getting on the horse, but once he was mounted, I could tell he was a good rider."

I felt a flash of excitement, the kind you get when things start coming together the way you've hoped they would. "That's the man who was killed."

"Well, that explains it."

"Explains what?"

"Horse came back this morning, riderless."

"What time?"

"Oh, around five, five-thirty."

That didn't fit the way I wanted it to. "Do you keep a record of who you rent the horses to?"

"Name and address. And we take a deposit that's returned when they bring the horses back."

"Can you look up the man's name?"

He grinned and reached under the counter for a looseleaf notebook. "I can, but I don't think it will help you identify him. I noted it at the time–Tom Smith. Sounded like a phony."

"But you still rented to him?"

"Sure. I just asked for double the deposit. He didn't look too prosperous, so I figured he'd be back. Besides, none of our horses are so terrific that anyone would trouble to steal one."

I stood there for a few seconds, tapping my fingers on the counter. "You said you thought he was someone you used to know."

"At first, but the guy I knew wasn't crippled. Must have been just a chance resemblance."

"Who was he?"

"Fellow who lived on a ranch near here back in the late sixties. Gary Fitzgerald."

I stared at him.

"But like I said, Gary Fitzgerald wasn't crippled."

"Did this Gary have a cousin?" I asked.

"Yeah, John Tilby. Tilby's dad owned a dairy ranch. Gary lived with them."

"When did Gary leave here?"

"After the old man died. The ranch was sold to pay the debts and both Gary and John took off. For southern California." He grinned again. "Probably had some cock-eyed idea about getting into show business."

"By any chance, do you know who was starring on the bill at the pavilion last night?"

"Don't recall, no. It was some kind of kid show, wasn't it?"

"A clown festival."

"Oh." He shrugged. "Clowns don't interest me. Why?"

"No reason." Things definitely weren't fitting together the way I'd wanted them to. "You say the cousins took off together after John Tilby's father died."

"Yes."

"And went to Southern California."

"That's what I heard."

"Did Gary Fitzgerald ever live in the Haight-Ashbury?"

He hesitated. "Not unless they went there instead of L.A. But I can't see Gary in the Haight, especially back then. He was just a country boy, if you know what I mean. But what's all this about him and John? I thought–"

"How much to rent a horse?"

The man's curiosity was easily sidetracked by business. "Ten an hour. Twenty for the deposit."

"Do you have a gentle one?"

"You mean for you? Now?"

"Yes."

"Got all kinds, gentle or lively."

I took out my wallet and checked it. Luckily, I had a little under forty dollars. "I'll take the gentlest one."

The man pushed the looseleaf notebook at me, looking faintly surprised. "You sign the book, and then I'll go saddle up Whitefoot."

9

Once our transaction was completed, the stable man pointed out the bridle trail that led toward the pavilion, wished me a good ride, and left me atop one of the gentlest horses I'd ever encountered. Whitefoot–a roan who did indeed have one white fetlock–was so placid I was afraid he'd go to sleep. Recalling my few riding lessons, which had taken place sometime in my early teens, I made some encouraging clicking sounds and tapped his flanks with my heels. Whitefoot put his head down and began munching a clump of dry grass.

"Come on, big fellow," I said. Whitefoot continued to munch.

I shook the reins–gently, but with authority.

No response. I stared disgustedly down the incline of his neck, which made me feel I was sitting at the top of a long slide. Then I repeated the clicking and tapping process. The horse ignored me.

"Look, you lazy bastard," I said in a low, menacing tone, "get a move on!"

The horse raised his head and shook it, glancing back at me with one sullen eye. Then he started down the bridle trail in a swaying, lumbering walk. I sat up straighter in correct horsewoman's posture, feeling smug.

The trail wound through a grove of eucalyptus, then began climbing uphill through grassland. The terrain was rough, full of rocky outcroppings and eroded gullies, and I was thankful for both the well-traveled path and Whitefoot's slovenly gait. After a few minutes I began to feel secure enough in the saddle to take stock of my surroundings, and when we reached the top of a rise, I stopped the horse and looked around.

To one side lay grazing land dotted with brown-and-white cattle. In the distance, I spotted a barn and a corral with horses. To the other side, the vegetation was thicker, giving onto a canyon choked with manzanita, scrub oak, and bay laurel. This was the type of terrain I was looking for–the kind where a man can easily become disoriented and lost. Still, there must be dozens of such canyons in the surrounding hills; to explore all of them would take days.

I had decided to ride a little further before plunging into rougher territory, when I noticed a movement under the leafy overhang at the edge of the canyon. Peering intently at the spot, I made out a tall figure in light-colored clothing. Before I could identify it as male or female, it slipped back into the shadows and disappeared from view.

Afraid that the person would see me, I reined the horse to one side, behind a large sandstone boulder a few yards away. Then I slipped from the saddle and peered around the rock toward the canyon. Nothing moved there. I glanced at Whitefoot and decided he would stay where he was without being tethered; true to form, he had lowered his head and was munching contentedly. After patting him once for reassurance, I crept through the tall grass to the underbrush. The air there was chill and pungent with the scent of bay laurel— more reminiscent of curry powder than of the bay leaf I kept in a jar in my kitchen. I crouched behind the billowy bright green mat of a chaparral bush while my eyes became accustomed to the gloom. Still nothing stirred; it was as if the figure had been a creature of my imagination.

Ahead of me, the canyon narrowed between high rock walls. Moss coated them, and stunted trees grew out of their cracks. I came out of my shelter and started that way, over ground that was sloping and uneven. From my right came a trickling sound; I peered through the under-brush and saw a tiny stream of water falling over the outcropping. A mere dribble now, it would be a full cascade in the wet season.

The ground became even rougher, and at times I had difficulty finding a foothold. At a point where the mossy walls almost converged, I stopped, leaning against one of them, and listened. A sound, as if someone were trashing through thick vegetation, came from the other side of the narrow space. I squeezed between the rocks and saw a heavily forested area. A tree branch a few feet from me looked as if it had recently been broken.

I started through the vegetation, following the sounds ahead of me. Pine boughs brushed at my face, and chaparral needles scratched my bare arms. After a few minutes, the thrashing sounds stopped. I stood still, wondering if the person I was following had heard me.

Everything was silent. Not even a bird stirred in the trees above me. I had no idea where I was in relation to either the pavilion or the stables. I wasn't even sure if I could find my way back to where I'd left the horse. Foolishly I realized the magnitude of the task I'd undertaken; such a search would better be accomplished with a helicopter than on horseback.

And then I heard the voices.

They came from the right, past a heavy screen of scrub oak. They were male, and from their rhythm I could tell they were angry. But I couldn't identify them or make out what they were saying. I edged around a clump of manzanita and started through the trees, trying to make as little sound as possible.

On the other side of the trees was an outcropping that formed a flat rock shelf that appeared to drop off sharply after about twenty feet. I clambered up on it and flattened onto my stomach, then crept forward. The voices were louder now, coming from straight ahead and below. I identified one as belonging to the man I knew as Gary Fitzgerald.

". . . didn't know he intended to blackmail anyone. I thought he just wanted to see John, make it up with him." The words were labored, twisted with pain.

"If that were the case, he could have come to the hotel." The second man was Wayne Kabalka. "He didn't have to go through all those elaborate machinations of sneaking into the pavilion."

"He told me he wanted to reconcile. After all, he was John's own cousin–"

"Come on, Elliott. You knew he had threatened us. You knew all about the pressure he'd put on us the past few weeks, ever since he found out the act would be coming to San Francisco."

I started at the strange name, even though I had known the missing man wasn't really Gary Fitzgerald. Elliott. Elliott who?

Elliott was silent.

I continued creeping forward, the mossy rock cold through my clothing. When I reached the edge of the shelf, I kept my head down until Kabalka spoke again. "You knew we were all afraid of Gary. That's why I hired the McCone woman; in case he tried anything, I wanted an armed guard there. I never counted on you playing the Judas."

Again Elliott was silent. I risked a look over the ledge.

There was a sheer drop of some fifteen or twenty feet to a gully full of jagged rocks. The man I'd known as Gary Fitzgerald lay at its bottom, propped into a sitting position, his right leg twisted at an unnatural angle. He was wearing a plaid shirt and jeans–the same clothing the man at the stables had described the dead man as having on. Kabalka stood in front of him, perhaps two yards from where I lay, his back to me. For a minute, I was afraid Elliott would see my head, but then I realized his eyes were glazed half blind with pain.

"What happened between John and Gary?" he asked.

Kabalka shifted his weight and put one arm behind his back, sliding his hand into his belt.

"Wayne, what happened?"

"Gary was found dead at the pavilion this morning. Stabbed. None of this would have happened if you hadn't connived to switch clothing so he could sneak backstage and threaten John."

Elliott's hand twitched, as if he wanted to cover his eyes but was too weak to lift it. "Dead." He paused. "I was afraid something awful had happened when he didn't come back to where I was waiting with the horse."

"Of course you were afraid. You knew what would happen."

"No..."

"You planned this for weeks, didn't you? The thing about staying at the fleabag in the Haight was a ploy, so you could turn over one of your costumes to Gary. But it didn't work, because Corinne had sent all but one to the cleaner. When did you come up with the scheme of sneaking out and trading places?"

Elliott didn't answer.

"I suppose it doesn't matter when. But why, Elliott? For God's sake, *why?*"

When he finally answered, Elliott's voice was weary. "Maybe I was sick of what you'd done to him. What we'd *all* done. He was so pathetic when he called me in L.A. And when I saw him... I thought maybe that if John saw him too, he might persuade you to help Gary."

"And instead he killed him."

"No. I can't believe that."

"And why not?"

"John loved Gary."

"John loved Gary so much he took Nicole away from him. And then he got into a drunken quarrel with him and crashed the car they were riding in and crippled him for life."

"Yes, but John's genuinely guilty over the accident. And he hates you for sending Gary away and replacing him with me. What a fraud we've all perpetrated—"

Kabalka's body tensed and he began balancing aggressively on the balls of his feet. "That fraud had made us a lot of money. Would have made us more until you pulled this stunt. Sooner or later they'll identify Gary's body and then it will all come out. John will be tried for the murder—"

"I still don't believe he killed him. I want to ask him about it."

Slowly Kabalka slipped his hand from his belt—and I saw the knife. He held it behind his back in his clenched fingers and took a step toward Elliott.

I pushed up with my palms against the rock. The motion caught Elliott's eye and he looked around in alarm. Kabalka must have taken the look to be aimed at him because he brought the knife up.

I didn't hesitate. I jumped off the ledge. For what seemed like an eternity I was falling toward the jagged rocks below. Then I landed heavily—directly on top of Kabalka.

As he hit the ground, I heard the distinctive sound of cracking bone. He went limp, and I rolled off of him—unhurt, because his body had cushioned my fall. Kabalka lay unconscious, his head against a rock.

When I looked at Elliott, I saw he had passed out from pain and shock.

10

The room at John Muir Hospital in Walnut Creek was antiseptic white, with bright touches of red and blue in the curtains and a colorful spray of fall flowers on the bureau. Elliott Larson–I'd found out that was his full name–lay on the bed with his right leg in traction. John Tilby stood by the door, his hands clasped formally behind his back, looking shy and afraid to come any further into the room. I sat on a chair by the bed, sharing a split of smuggled-in wine with Elliott.

I'd arrived at the same time as Tilby, who had brought the flowers. He'd seemed unsure of a welcome, and even though Elliott had acted glad to see him, he was still keeping his distance. But after a few awkward minutes, he had agreed to answer some questions and had told me about the drunken auto accident five years ago in which he had been thrown clear of his MG and the real Gary Fitzgerald had been crippled. And about how Wayne Kabalka had sent Gary away with what the manager had termed an "ample settlement"–and which would have been except for Gary's mounting medical expenses, which eventually ate up all his funds and forced him to live on welfare in a cheap San Francisco hotel. Determined not to lose the bright financial future the comedy team had promised him, Kabalka had looked around for a replacement for Gary and found Elliott performing in a seedy Haight-Ashbury club. He'd put him into the act, never telling the advertisers who were clamoring for Fitzgerald and Tilby's services that one of the men in the whiteface was not the clown they had contracted with. And he'd insisted Elliott totally assume Gary's identity.

"At first," Elliott said, "it wasn't so bad. When Wayne found me, I was on a downslide. I was heavy into drugs, and I'd been kicked out of my place in the Haight and was crashing with whatever friends would let me. At first it was great mulling all that money, but after a while I began to realize I'd never be anything more than the shadow of a broken man."

"And then." I said, "Gary reappeared."

"Yes. He needed some sort of operation and he contacted Wayne in L.A. Over the years Wayne had been sending him money–hush money, I guess you could call it–but it was barely enough to cover his minimum expenses. Gary had been seeing all the ads on TV, reading about how well we were doing, and he was angry and demanding a cut."

"And rightly so," Tilby added. "I'd always thought Gary was well provided for, because Wayne took part of my earnings and said he was sending it to him. Now I know most of it was going into Wayne's pocket."

"Did Wayne refuse to give Gary the money for the operation?" I asked.

Tilby nodded. "There was a time when Gary would merely have crept back into the woodwork when Wayne refused him. But by then his anger and hurt had festered, and he wasn't taking no for an answer. He threatened Wayne, and continued to make daily threats by phone. We were all on edge, afraid of what he might do. Corinne kept urging Wayne to give him the money, especially because we had contracted to come to San Francisco, where Gary was, for the clown festival. But Wayne was too stubborn to give in."

Thinking of Corinne, I said, "How's she taking it, anyway?"

"Badly," Tilby said. "But she's a tough lady. She'll pull through."

"And Nicole?"

"Nicole has vanished. Was packed and gone by the time I went back to the hotel after Wayne's arrest." He seemed unconcerned; five years with Nicole had probably been enough.

I said, "I talked to the sheriff's department. Wayne hasn't confessed." After I'd revived Elliott out there in the canyon, I'd given him my gun and made my way back to where I'd left the horse. Then I'd ridden–the most energetic ride of old Whitefoot's life–back to the stables and summoned the sheriff's men. When we'd arrived at the gully, Wayne had regained consciousness and was attempting to buy Elliott off. Elliott seemed to be enjoying bargaining and then refusing.

Remembering the conversation I'd overheard between the two men, I said to Elliott, "Did Wayne have it right about you intending to loan Gary one of your spare costumes?"

"Yes. When I found I didn't have an extra costume to give him, Gary came up with the plan of signaling me from a horse on the hill. He knew the area from when he lived there and had seen a piece in the paper about how people would ride up on the hill to watch the concerts. You guessed about the signal?"

"I saw it happen. I just didn't put it together until later, when I thought about the fragments of leaves and needles they found in Gary's clothing." No need to explain about the catalyst to my thought process–the horse of a cat named Watney.

"Well," Elliott said, "that was how it worked. The signal with the field glasses was to tell me Gary had been able to get a horse and show me where he'd be waiting. At the prearranged time, I made the excuse about going to the men's room, climbed out the window, and left the pavilion. Gary changed and got himself into white face in a clump of trees with the aid of a flashlight. I put on his clothes and took the horse and waited, but he never came back. Finally the crowd was streaming out of the pavilion, and then the lights went out; I tried to ride down there, but I'm not a very good horseman, and I got turned around in the dark. Then something scared the horse and it threw me into that ravine and bolted. As soon as I hit the rocks I knew my leg was broken."

"And you lay there all night."

"Yes, half frozen. And in the morning I heard Wayne thrashing through the underbrush. I don't know if he intended to kill me at first, or if he planned to try to convince me that John had killed Gary and we should cover it up."

"Probably the latter, at least initially." I turned to Tilby. "What happened at the pavilion with Gary?"

"He came into the dressing room. Right off I knew it was him, by the limp. He was angry, wanted money. I told him I was willing to give him whatever he needed, but that Wayne would have to arrange for it. Gary hid in the dressing room closet and when you came in there, I asked you to get Wayne. He took Gary away, out into the audience, and when he came back, he said he'd fixed everything." He paused, lips twisting bitterly. "And he certainly had."

We were silent for a moment. Then Elliott said to me, "Were you surprised to find out I wasn't really Gary Fitzgerald?"

"Yes and no. I had a funny feeling about you all along."

"Why?"

"Well, first there was the fact you and John just didn't look like you were related. And then when we were driving through Contra Costa County, you didn't display much interest in it—not the kind of curiosity a man would have when returning home after so many years. And there was one other thing."

"What?"

"I said something about sound from the two pavilions being audible all the way to Port Chicago. That's the place where the Naval Weapons Station is, up on the Strait. And you said, 'Not all the way to Chicago.' You didn't know what Port Chicago was, but I took it to mean you were making a joke. I remember thinking that for a clown, you didn't have much of a sense of humor."

"Thanks a lot." But he grinned, unoffended.

I stood up. "So now what? Even if Wayne never confesses, they've got a solid case against him. You're out a manager, so you'll have to handle your own future plans."

They shrugged almost simultaneously.

"You've got a terrific act," I said. "There'll be some adverse publicity, but you can probably weather it."

Tilby said, "A couple of advertisers have already called to withdraw their offers."

"Others will be calling with new ones."

He moved hesitantly toward the chair I'd vacated. "Maybe."

"You can count on it. A squeaky clean reputation isn't always an asset in show business; your notoriety will hurt you in some ways, but help you in others." I picked up my bag and squeezed Elliott's arm, went toward the door, touching Tilby briefly on the shoulder. "At least think about keeping the act going."

As I went out, I looked back at them. Tilby had sat down in the chair. His posture was rigid, tentative, as if he might flee at any moment. Elliott looked uncertain, but hopeful.

What was it, I thought, that John had said to me about clowns when we were playing gin in the dressing room at the pavilion? Something to the effect that they were all funny but, more important, that they all made people take a look at their own foibles. John Tilby and Elliott Larson–in a sense both broken men like Gary Fitzgerald had been– knew more about those foibles than most people. Maybe there was a way they could continue to turn that sad knowledge into laughter.

ARTHUR LYONS
(b.1946)

Trouble in Paradise
(Jacob Asch)

"That whore did it," John Anixter proclaimed angrily. "I know she did. I want you to prove it."

He was a tall and gristly forty-odd, with a long, rectangular face and brown hair that was deciding to be gray. His eyes were pale blue and had a no-nonsense expression in them. Hid dress was no-nonsense, too; a gray worsted suit, a white shirt, and a gray and blue striped tie. His hands were jewelryless except for an inexpensive Seiko watch. All in all, he looked no more than a fairly prosperous businessman; I would have had no idea he was worth $8 million if Harry Scranton hadn't told me.

Harry was an attorney for whose firm I occasionally did investigative work and the one who had recommended me to Anixter. All that he had told me about the man, except for how much money he had, was that he had made it dabbling in the commodities market before starting up his own successful commodities brokerage firm, and that he was a hell of a nice guy. Oh yeah, he also told me that the man's son had recently died in an accident, which was why he wanted to see me.

"What whore is that, Mr. Anixter?"

His face flushed. "The one Chip married. He couldn't see what she was, but it was obvious to me the first time I laid eyes on her."

"Chip was your son?"

He nodded, then turned and looked out the window. The office was plush, with elm burl walls adorned by deco light sconces and furnished with big, cushy chairs with great wide arms. "When I cut Chip off," Anixter said, looking down the fourteen floors to the streets of Century City, "I thought for sure she would take the hint and leave, but she found another way to work it."

He was trucking now and I was peddling slowly behind on my bicycle. I peddled harder, trying to catch up. "Work what?"

He turned and gave me solemn look. "Three months ago, my son took out a life insurance policy worth $300,000, with her as the beneficiary. Two months later, Chip died under mysterious circumstances while scuba diving in the Caribbean. The authorities in St. Maarten have declared it an accident, but I'm certain that woman had something to do with it. Chip was an experienced diver and a super athlete. Scuba was one of his passions. She probably worked some sort of deal with the scuba instructor to do away with Chip and split the money."

"Was an autopsy performed?"

"You have to have a body to perform an autopsy."

"They never found his body?"

He shook his head. "All they found was his diving gear and swim trunks. Both were pretty chewed up."

"Sharks?"

He shrugged.

One thing I have found with parents whose children have died unnaturally, murder is always a preferable alternative to suicide or accidental death. With the former comes a truckload of guilt and with the latter comes a capricious and uncaring universe.

"The insurance company has to have investigators on it, Mr. Anixter–"

He waved a hand in exasperation and sat back down at the desks. "There's nothing they can do. Chip's death is officially an accident. In the absence of new evidence, they're going to have to pay off." Two knots of muscle rose on his jawline, just below his ears. "I'll see that bitch in hell before I let her collect a bounty on my son's life."

"How long were they married?"

"Five months." He leaned back in his chair, and his brow furrowed. "My son was a screw-up, Mr. Asch."

"The only thing he ever showed any interest in was fast cars and faster women. A lot if it was my fault, probably. I wasn't the best father in the world. My wife–Chip's mother–died when he was only nine and I was too busy trying to keep the business going to give him the supervision he needed. When he was a teenager, I had to get him out of one scrape after another. I always thought he would straighten up, even after he quit college and drifted from one job to another. I offered him a position with my company, but he said he had to 'find himself,'' whatever that means. But when he came to me and said he intended to marry that tramp, that was the last straw.''

He paused, but he wasn't through yet. He came forward and rested his forearm on the desk.

"I've worked my butt off my whole life, Mr. Asch. I came up from nothing and struggled to put something together. Too damned hard to sit back and watch it squandered on some fortune-hunting hooker. I told Chip if he wanted to marry the girl, fine, but he could support her on his own, because he wouldn't get one more dime from me, before or after I died. We both said things we shouldn't have. That was the last time I saw him." Coldness in the blue eyes softened; guilt tugged at his features. "You called the woman a hooker," I said. "Did you mean that literally?" He gave a look of distaste. "They all hook in places like that."

"Places like what?"

"The Paradise," he said, folding his hands on the desk top. "It's a topless bar on Beverly Boulevard. She was dancing there when Chip met her."

I wrote it down. "What's her first name?"

"Rhonda," he said, as if he did not like the sound of the word.

"Where is she living now?"

"In Chip's apartment." He recited the address, then looked at me appraisingly as if I were a pork belly for which he was trying to guess tomorrow's market value. "Harry says you're good."

Never one to deal well with flattery, I said nothing.

"That bitch took away my only son," he said through pursed lips. "I don't care how much money it takes, I want her nailed for it."

It sounded as if he had lost his son years ago and wanted me to help him pin his guilt on the woman. For two hundred a day plus expenses, I was willing to at least try.

"I'll see what I can do," I said.

Chip and Rhonda Anixter had gotten married in September, in Westwood, and I obtained a copy of the marriage license from the Hall of Records downtown. Her maiden name was Rhonda Jo Banks, and she was twenty-eight, two years older than Chip. She had been born in Arizona, had completed high school, and listed her occupation as "dancer." I figured that was as good a place to start as any.

The Paradise was on Beverly Boulevard, on the edge of the Silver Lake district, in the middle of a fatigued city block of laundromats and seedy-looking Mexican and Vietnamese restaurants. From the outsides, it looked like a dirty plywood and plaster box, covered with cartoon paintings of leggy, scantily-clad girls. Inside, it was a dirty plywood and plaster box with real girls instead of cartoons. The cartoons looked better.

The place was built like a dog pit, with tables set around the perimeters of the sunken dance floor, where an anemic-looking redhead in nothing but a G-string was gyrating listlessly to a Michael Jackson tune. "Flashdance" it wasn't.

Afternoon trade was sparse and I had no trouble securing a table. Passing myself off as an old acquaintance of Rhonda's, it took one hour, five beers and twenty-eight dollars in "tips" spread between the bartender and a bovine brunette named Noreen to find out Rhonda had not been around much since she'd gotten married. Noreen was particularly talkative, especially after I picked up some latent hostility from her and assumed the role of one of Rhonda's jilted ex-boyfriends.

"Don't feel like the Lone Ranger," she said in a snide tone, the hostility becoming less latent as she talked. "You're in some good company. She was going out with the owner of the club, Arnie Phalen, when she met that rich kid. The minute she found the kid had bucks, she dumped Arnie on his ass. Strutted around here bragging how she was going to set herself up for life with that score. I guess the joke was on her."

"Why is that?"

The corners of her mouth turned up in a self-satisfied leer. "She came back in a few months ago, crying to Arnie about how the kid was broke. The kid's old man was the one with the money and he'd cut them off on account of her I guess. He had about as much use for her as a case of herpes."

"She been back in since then?" I asked, sipping my beer.

"Naw," she said, waving a hand disparagingly. "She's too good for this place. All she did when she worked here was bitch her whole shift about what a dive this place was and how she was gonna make a score and get out. She must have thought she was Grace Fucking Kelly or something, the way she acted."

"Arnie around now?" I asked casually.

She shook her dark, ratted hair. "He doesn't come in till around seven." She looked down at the blond dancing in the pit and said, "I'm up." I took out my wallet. "Thanks for the conversation, Noreen," I said, and left her an extra five as a tip, just for public relations in case I needed to talk to her again.

Her changebox snapped up the bill and she smiled warmly. She had a live one now. "My shift is over at six," she said. "Stop back then and maybe we can have a drink or something."

"Maybe I'll do that."

When I left, she was moving her big body to Bob Seger's "Fire Down Below," and she threw me a few hip-pumps and breast-flops as I went out the door.

The Anixter's ex-connubial love nest was in a new, two-story, vanilla-colored apartment building on a tree-lined street of apartments scissored out of the same nondescript mold. After making sure that the red Porsche Carrera John Anixter had bought his son for his twenty-first birthday was in its slot in the garage, I went back around front, and through the glass doors. At the edge of the swimming-pool courtyard, I stopped.

A lone woman was sunning herself in one of the deck chairs by the pool, and I knew instinctively it was Rhonda. She had on a tiny string bikini, and her tanned body glistened with oil. She had a hard, flat stomach and long, slim legs, and maybe a little too much in the chest department, but being the magnanimous person that I was, I figured I could live with that. Her face, although not as spectacular as her body, was a solid 8, framed by mane of ash blond hair. She shifted languorously onto her stomach and I wiped a hand across my chin and checked for drool. I could see why Chip had ignored his father's advice.

Figuring that if she intended to go out anywhere it wouldn't be for a while, I went back to the car and drove to Carl's Jr., where I grabbed a quick infusion of cholesterol with cheese, and was back in place across the street within half an hour. I found a jazz station and settled back with my styrofoam cup of coffee. Shadows lengthened, cars went by, cars pulled in and out of the driveway to the apartment building, but she was not in any of them. It was almost dark when a black Corvette cruised by slowly, and parked in a space a few cars up.

There was something about the man who got out of the Vette that attracted my attention. Maybe part of it was the shades he was still wearing, despite the thickening dusk; the sun is always shining when you're cool. He was short and weaselly-looking, with a thin, olive-complected face and oily black hair slicked straight back from his high forehead. To go with the shades, he wore a gray sports jacket over a black shirt, jeans and white tennis shoes. He didn't notice me watching him across the street; he was a man on a mission.

I waited until he was through the glass doors of the building before I got out of the car and followed. By the time I got to the mailboxes, he was on the other side of the pool, disappearing through a door into the building. The door opened into a corridor and he was standing in front of a door halfway down it. He glanced at me as I went past him, pretending to be looking at apartment numbers, and then Rhonda Anixter's door opened and he went inside.

I hurried back outside. The Corvette was locked, so I contented myself with taking down the plate number, and went back to my car. At two-fifteen, I was rudely awakened by the sound of an engine starting. I slouched down while the Corvette flipped a U and roared up the block toward Overland. I pulled out with my lights off and drove that way until we picked up some traffic. He got on the freeway at Overland and headed north to the Wilshire exit, where he got off. At Barrington he made a right and half a dozen blocks up, turned into the driveway of a single-roofed, ranch-style house with a lot of trees in the front yard.

He had taken off his shades and was locking up the Corvette when I drove past. The house was dark and there was a yellow compact of some sort parked in front of the Vette. Up the block, I stopped and jotted down the address, counted to one thousand, then went back on foot.

At the neighbor's hedge, I crouched down and peeked into the front yard of the house. There was no sign of Mr. Cool, and I assumed from the faint glow behind the curtains of the living room window that he had gone inside. I stood up and sauntered by as if it were perfectly normal to be out for a casual stroll at three in the morning, then went into a crouch on the other side of the driveway and used the body of the Corvette as a cover to reach the yellow car.

It was a Nissan. I took down the plate number, then duck-walked to the door on the passenger side. It was locked, of course. My flash located the registration attached to the sun visor in a leather-framed case. I leaned close to the window to get a look.

>   Barbara Phalen
>   777 Barrington
>   Brentwood, CA.

Barbara Phalen. Arnie Phalen's wife? Maybe Phalen was making a comeback, now that Chip was out of the picture. Maybe he had never left.

I snapped off the flash and something hard and small and cold pressed against the back of my head. The hammer clicking back sounded like a sonic boom.

"Just straighten up nice and easy, asshole," a voice said quietly.

I did as I was told. I didn't know what caliber the gun was, but at that range, a pellet gun would have muddled some of my fondest

ARTHUR LYONS

memories.

"If you're thinking of getting cute," the voice said, "you'll never think again." A hand slammed me into the car and the gun moved down to poke me in the kidney.

"Easy." I said, the pain straightening me up.

"Fuck you. Stand back and spread your feet and put your hands on the top of the car."

I did it and his free hand patted me down. It brushed my wallet and plucked it from my inside pocket. The pressure of the gun went away as he stepped back to inspect it. "Turn around," he said after a moment.

Without the shades he lost some of his weaselly look. He was not bad looking, in fact, in a greasy kind of way. His eyes were dark and deeply set. In the dim light from the house, they were devoid of any emotion except for a mildly contemptuous curiosity. "All right, peeper, what the hell are you doing sneaking around here?" The corner of his mouth twitched.

"I'm on a case."

"What case?"

I considered that for a moment. "A little girl hired me to track down her lost Lhasa Apso. Named 'Button,' as in 'cute as a?' Maybe you've seen him. About a foot tall, blond hair, brown eyes–"

The twitch stopped and tightened into an angry line. He pointed the gun at my head again. "You know who you're fucking with, asshole? I could have you made into an ashtray if I wanted to. Now, I'm gonna ask you again: What case?"

I pointed at the gun. "Why don't you put that thing down? I have trouble talking when I'm nervous." I was sweating; he seemed to like that.

One side of his mouth lifted into a lopsided, self-confident sneer. "You'll find a way."

I had nothing to lose, so I threw out a guess. "Your wife hired me to find out where you go when you're supposed to be watching tits bounce up and down. I wonder what she's going to say when I tell her you're watching them okay, but the wrong set?"

The confidence on his face dried up and flaked off like a month-old Christmas tree. "You're a liar."

It was my turn to smile. "Let's get her out here and ask her."

He shot a troubled look at the house, then back at me.

"Of course, I'm always open for a better offer."

"What kind of an offer?" he asked in a clipped voice.

"That's open for discussion."

The porch light above the front door went on and his head snapped around. A woman's voice called out from the crack in the door: "Arnie?"

I looked at Phalen's panicked face. He was the one who was sweating now. "Well?"

"Get out of here," he whispered, his voice thick with hate.

I held out my hand. "My wallet."

He hesitated, and Barbara Phalen called out again: "Arnie?"

"Coming, hon," he called back, and tossed the wallet at me. In a hoarse whisper, he said: "Move your ass out of here. Quick."

"I'll be in touch," I told him, and hurried down the driveway. At the sidewalk, I turned left and used the other side of the street to circle back to my car so she wouldn't see me.

All the way home, I chewed myself out for my carelessness. But it was more than just the fact that Phalen and Rhonda now knew they were being watched that bothered me; it was Phalen himself. The man was bad news, I could feel it. Maybe it was the comfortable way he handled a .38 or the dead eyes and the hard sneer, or the silent, deadly way he'd pounced on me. And now he knew who I was. I figured I'd better find out who he was before he made good on his threat and I would up a receptacle for some Mustache Pete's cigar.

I got up at nine, nor wanting to. I'd spent a fitful night being pursued by various people and things, and although I didn't remember exactly who they were or why they were pursuing me, there had been a lot of running and jumping done, and I woke up exhausted. Figuring that if I was going to be chased around in my sleep I should probably know by whom, I went into the kitchen and made a pot of coffee and drank half of it before calling Sheriff's Homicide.

Al Herrera sounded chipper when he picked up the phone. I was glad to hear that; the last few times we'd talked he had sounded as if he were ripe for a stress disability.

Al and I went way back to my reporting days at the *Chronicle*, and if I had changed a lot since then, he hadn't. He was still the same thick-skinned, straight-shooting, 100 percent cop, which was probably to his detriment. He took the job too seriously and had nearly suffered a couple of emotional and marital breakdowns because of it. "Jake boy, where you been keeping yourself?"

"On my knees, Al, looking through keyholes. How are things with you?"

"Great, if you like being up to your ass in dead bodies."

After the obligatory small talk–how's the wife and kids, that sort of thing–I sprung it. "Al, I need a favor–"

"Of course. Why else would you call?"

I told him that for a Mexican, he did a passable imitation of a Jewish mother, then gave him all the information I had on Phalen and Rhonda Anixter and asked him to run them for priors.

"And you need it done yesterday, right?"

"Today would be all right."

He said he would be in the field until four or so and to call back then and I hung up and thought about my next step. Deciding a little soft-shoe might be appropriate, I dropped another quarter and dialled Rhonda Anixter's number. Her voice was as sultry as her body–husky and vaporous.

"Mrs. Rhonda Anixter?"

"Yes?"

"This is Bob Exley at the Collection Department of Pacific Bell. I'm calling to inform you, Mrs. Anixter, that unless we receive immediate payment for last month's bill, your phone will be disconnected on the first–"

The huskiness turned into a growl. "What the hell are you talking about? I paid that bill two weeks ago."

"What was the date and number of the check and at what bank do you have your checking account?"

"Security National, West L.A. Pico branch," she said in a vexed voice. "I'll have to look up the number."

"Just a minute, Mrs. Anixter, that may not be necessary. Running this through again, I see that the computer posted your check late, for some reason. I'm very sorry to have bothered you."

"Sure you are," she said in a nasty tone, and hung up.

I called Troy Wilcox. Troy was chief loan officer at L.A. First Federal, and two years ago, while working on an entirely different matter, I'd saved his ass when I tumbled onto a man who had skipped on a $75,000 bank loan Troy had okayed for him. Ever since, Troy had always been pleased to help me out with a favor when I needed one. And just as he would be pleased to do me a favor, the people at Security National would be pleased to do him one. There is no such thing as privileged information in the banking fraternity.

I was batting a thousand today; Troy was in a good mood, too. I gave him Rhonda Anixter's name and told him I needed to know if she had written any checks for sizeable amounts in the past two months, and if so, to whom. He told me to get back to him a little before three, that he should have the information by then.

Since there didn't seem to be anything else to do until that time, I went home to pack.

Both Al and Troy were ready for me when I got back to them that afternoon, and on the red-eye to Miami, I mulled over what they had given me.

Chip and Rhonda's joint account at Security National showed a balance of $746.98. Only two checks of any sizeable amount had been written by either of them in the past two months, one on September 1 to Wynee World Travel for $3500, which would have been for the Caribbean trip, and another a week later to "Cash," for $2000, which was more than likely for vacation spending money. I hadn't really expected Troy to come up with anything incriminating; if Rhonda Anixter had paid someone to kill her husband and make it look like an accident. she wouldn't have been likely to write him a check from their joint account.

Al's stuff was more interesting. Rhonda had no record in California, but the Vice boys knew all about Phalen. Besides being the owner on record of the Paradise, Phalen was part-owner and front man for two other topless bars that were suspected of being laundries for mob money; he was also the main man at New Eros, a distributor of hard-core porn films and magazines. He had been popped three times–for extortion, pandering, and burning with intent to defraud an insurer–but never convicted. That last one particularly interested me. The arrest report had been filed by the Sheriff's Office, and I asked Al if he could pull it for me. After three-and-a-half minutes of bitching and moaning about how busy he was, he finally agreed, but said it would take a couple of days. I told him I'd be in touch, threw my bag in the car, and drove out to LAX.

My flight didn't leave until eleven-ten, and the three double-vodkas I absorbed in the airport terminal bar and the two more I ingested on the plane allowed me to sleep straight through to Miami. After a two-hour layover there and another three hours on an Eastern 727, I was sober, awake, and buckling up for a landing in St. Maarten.

From the air, one side of the island didn't look any different from the other–it just looked like one tiny green teardrop surrounded by a blue-green sea that seemed to change color on a whim–but according to the Caribbean guidebook I'd picked up in the Miami airport gift shop, St. Maarten/St. Martin had the distinction of being the smallest island in the world with two sovereignties. The French and Dutch both settled the island in the early 1600s, and legend had it that instead of fighting for possession, they'd decided to divvy it up by a walking contest. One man from each side walked around the island in opposite directions, and where they met determined the border. I hoped the resolution of my current case would be as peaceful.

I checked in at the Sheraton near the airport and caught a cab into

Philipsburg, the Dutch capital. It was a cloudless, balmy day in the small, dusty town strung out along a sandbar that ran between the sea and a large salt marsh. Front Street, the main drag, was narrow and congested with cars and people, and the cab seemed to make about four feet an hour.

I tried to get into the laid-back Caribbean mentality by sightseeing out the window.

The town had an electric ambiance to it, which was a nice way of saying it was a mish-mash of architectural styles. Modern glass-sheeted shopping malls were stuck between old, pastel painted, colonial-style buildings and slat wood, front-porched houses. No matter how different the buildings were in appearance, they all had the same function–to sell to the shorts-clad, window-gaping army of tourists laden with cameras and chicly imprinted shopping bags as they thronged the sun-drenched sidewalks.

The police station was one of the older colonial buildings, at the end of Front Street. After identifying myself to the desk sergeant, I was turned over to a surly black cop named Cribbs who had handled the Anixter investigation. His attitude thawed a bit when I assured him I had not come all this way to question his competence, rather to consult his expertise.

Chip Anixter's diving equipment was in a storage room in back. There was a weight belt, an air tank with the regulator still attached, and what was left of a pair of trunks. The trunks were shredded but the eight or nine cuts in the weight belt looked too clean to have been made by any fish. When I mentioned that to Cribbs, he just shrugged, and said in his West Indian accent, "You ever see a shark's teeth? They are as sharp as razor blades." There didn't seem to be any point in arguing with him. Besides the lacerations in the weight belt and the fact that the tank was empty of air when it was found, the equipment checked out okay and did not seem to have been tampered with in any way.

The diving instructor Chip had gone down with, Stuart Murphy, was a California transplant who had come to St. Maarten eight years ago and started Mako Water Sports, an operation specializing in recreational dives. Except for Chip, the company had a perfect safety record, and Cribbs considered Murphy beyond suspicion. As for Rhonda Anixter, Cribbs thought her "cold" considering what had happened, but that was no crime. She couldn't have had anything to do with the accident, because she had never left the boat during the dive. The entire incident was an unfortunate accident, but that was all it was. I thanked him and left.

Mako Water Sports was in a small wooden building that sat at the edge of a yacht marina. The desk inside was surrounded by racks of life vests, regulators, and air tanks. The man sitting behind it was a rangy, freckled, beachy type with a bleached-out mustache and pink splotches on his prematurely balding head where the skin had sunburned and peeled off. He wore swim trunks and a short-sleeved shirt covered with red hibiscus.

"I'm looking for Stu Murphy."

"You've found him," he said, smiling broadly. He had a lot of nice, white teeth.

"My name is Asch." I handed him a card. "I'm down here working on the Anixter case. I'd like to ask you a few questions, if you could spare a little time—"

He looked at the card and frowned. "I'm afraid I can't. I'm very busy."

I looked around the room. There didn't seem to be too much happening in it.

"I told everything I know to the police," he said, picking up my skeptical look. "Why don't you talk to them?"

"I did. They absolved you of all guilt in the matter. That's not why I'm here. There is a lot of insurance money involved and Chip's father is concerned that his son's death might have been the result of foul play. Was there anything that struck you as peculiar about his disappearance?"

"Yeah," he said sourly. "The whole damned thing. Believe it or not, mister, I'm not used to having my clients disappear on me."

"That wasn't what I was implying."

He made a face and let out a breath. "Look, I don't mean to sound rude. But all I want is to put this thing behind me." He waved a hand at the room. "It wasn't exactly the greatest publicity for my business, as you can see."

I took out my wallet, extracted a fifty-dollar bill, and laid it on the desk in front of him. "Would that cover a quick run out to where Chip disappeared? No equipment. We wouldn't even have to break the surface."

"What do you expect to see from the surface?"

"I don't know," I said, truthfully.

He looked at the money, bit his lip thoughtfully, then put his hand over the bill and slid it toward him. He stood and went over to the rack of life vests, selected one, and tossed it at me. "You'd better put this on. If I lose one more client, I might as well close this place up and go back to the States."

The trade winds were kicking up a good chop and my clothes were soaked by the time Murphy killed the engine of the speedboat and dropped anchor. "This is it," he said.

We were two or three miles offshore and the water was dark blue, not green as it was in the sandy shallows closer to the island. The sunlight was clean and hard and glinted white off the surface of the sea. I looked down.

"How can you tell this is the exact spot?"

He smiled cryptically. "It's my business."

I let it go at that. "You two went down alone?"

He nodded. "He didn't want to out with a group. Wanted a more personal dive, he said."

"What kind of a diver was he? Good?"

The welcome warmth of the sun seeped through my wet clothes, taking the chill off.

"So he said. He was certified."

"So what happened?"

"Good question. One minute, he was behind me, the next, he wasn't. The only thing I can think of is that he got absorbed in something and got carried away by the current without realizing. It's pretty strong here."

"If the current is so strong, why did you pick this spot to dive?"

"I didn't," he said. "He did."

"When was that?"

"The day before, when he came into the office. He said a friend of his wife who dove around here all the time recommended it."

A mill wheel in my mind turned a notch and caught. "A friend of his wife?"

"That's what he said."

"Did he mention a name?"

"I don't think so. I would've remembered if it was anybody local. Anybody local would've known there are better places to dive around here."

The boat rocked in the waves and I put a hand on the windshield to steady myself. "Which way does the current run here?"

He waved a hand toward the green mountains of St. Maarten.

"Where did you find his gear?"

Again, he waved toward the island. "About four hundred yards from here."

"I saw the stuff," I said. "Cribbs seems to think a shark did the damage."

"That's possible," he said. "They're around."

"Did you see one hanging around that day?"

"No, but that doesn't mean anything. I've seen them materialize like ghosts, out of nowhere."

"The cuts in the weight belt looked more like they'd been made by a knife–"

"That's possible, too. Anixter had a knife and he was out of air. The buckle on the belt was still fastened when I found it. Maybe it got stuck and he panicked and tried to cut it off. I've seen divers do screwier things in situations like that."

"He cut off his trunks, too?"

He said nothing to that, just shrugged.

"Was that his own equipment?"

"No. It was mine."

"How about his wife? Was she certified too?"

"No. She said she'd been down a couple of times, but didn't like it. She just went along for the ride."

"And she never left the boat the entire time you were under?"

"That's one thing I'm positive about."

"Did you see any other boats in the area?"

"Not that I remember."

"You say the current is strong here. Strong enough to carry a man to shore?"

I went on with the train of thought. "Say a diver had been dropped off here earlier. Would it have been possible for him to have been waiting down there without you seeing him?"

"Maybe, if he was careful, and didn't breathe a lot." His eyes widened as the idea crystalized in his mind. "You think that's what happened? You think somebody was waiting down there?"

"I'm just looking at all the possibilities."

"Then what happened to the body?"

"If there were signs of violence on it, knife wounds, for instance, they would have to keep it from being found," I speculated. "Who else knew where you were going to dive?"

"My parents, Sonny. But he had a group out that afternoon–"

"Don't worry, I don't consider him a suspect."

He shrugged. "As far as I know, only the four of us knew."

"How did Mrs. Anixter act when you told her you couldn't find her husband?"

He looked at me strangely. "That was something that always bothered me."

"Why?"

"When I came up with his equipment, she got hysterical. Cried and wailed all the way back to shore. She only stopped long enough to ask one question."

"What was that?"

"She wanted to know what the waiting period was before someone is declared legally dead."

The entire flight back to L.A. my thoughts drifted as unrelentingly toward the solution as that St. Maarten current ran toward shore. No matter how hard I tried to swim in other directions, I wound up heading the same way.

It was almost ten in the evening when I pulled into my parking slot in front of my apartment, dog-tired and suffering from an intense case of heartburn from the catered cardboard the Eastern stewardess had jokingly referred to as "dinner." All I wanted was to make myself a strong drink and crawl into bed. I was definitely not in the mood for company; especially the two movie-extra heavies who detached themselves from the shadows and materialized on each side of my car.

They yanked open the doors and the one on the passenger's side stuck a .45 Browning automatic in my face. He was big and beefy and had a wide, loose face that gravity had gone to work on. The face didn't smile. "He'll drive," was all he said.

The one on the driver's side nudged me, and I moved over to keep from being sat on. They wedged me in firmly between them and the driver backed my car out of the driveway. The gun was jammed up under my rib cage, making it hard to breathe. The driver turned right onto Pacific and headed toward the Marina. He was slimmer than the other one, with a bony brow and a nose that someone had rearranged onto the side of his face, then decided it looked better where it had been, and moved it back again.

"Where are we going?" I asked, trying to sound calm. I wasn't calm. I was scared. Very scared. Nobody answered.

He got onto Washington. Longingly, I watched the tall, lighted office buildings of Marina del Rey passing outside the window. I thought about the couples and swinging singles out there in their favorite watering holes, drinking and dancing and performing their bird-like courtship rituals, trying to get the magic going for a night. They weren't exactly my kind of joints, but I wasn't so narrow-minded that I wasn't willing to bend a rule for an evening. "You guys want to pick up some chicks? I know a great place right over here–"

The gun barrel tried to find the seat behind my back and I sucked in some air and shut up. We got onto Lincoln and crossed Ballona Creek and the buildings were gone as we headed into the barren brown hills. The driver turned off onto a dirt road and we churned up dust for a short distance until he pulled up and stopped in front of a fence at the edge of the runway of a private industrial airport. They opened the doors and got out; the driver had a gun now too, a .38. "Out," the sagging-faced man said.

There were no stars, just a limitless blackness. The red lights bordering the runway blinked in sequence, away from us, beckoning planes from the dark and lonely sky.

"Okay," Saggy Face asked. "Who are you working for?"

"Truth, justice, and the American way," I said, I don't know why.

Nose Job stepped in fast and brought a hook from somewhere south of Tierra del Fuego that sent me to my knees, gasping for air like a sick guppy. He bent down and grabbed me under the arms, hoisted me up easily and leaned me against the car. Saggy Face leaned close, his breath hot and moist in my face. He was chewing a mint; I guess there's always something to be thankful for, if you just look for it.

He jammed his gun in my crotch. That didn't feel too good, either, but I couldn't work up enough breath to tell him. "Now listen, shit-for-brains," he said, "we can dance all night if you want, but we've all got better things to do, including you, I imagine. Now, I'm gonna ask you one more time: Who are you working for?"

I had to admit, he was a hell of a debater. "John Anixter," I gasped, barely.

He nodded and smiled and stepped back. He nodded at Nose Job, who put away his gun and grabbed my wrist before I had a chance to resist. He yanked my hand out and held it on the hood of my car while Saggy Face brought the barrel of the .45 down on it. I screamed as the pain shot halfway up my arm to my elbow, then I slid down the side of the car.

All I could do was cradle the hand and rock back and forth in the dirt as Saggy Face hovered over me and said: "The nuns used to do that to me in school when I did something I shouldn'ta. You been doing something you shouldn'ta, Asch. You been sticking your nose in other people's private business. I think we both know who I mean. Now if you keep it up, we're gonna have to come back and visit, and if we do, it ain't gonna be a slap on the wrist, it's gonna be traction-time. You get where I'm coming from?"

I might have said yes, I'm not sure. My hand felt as if it were full of broken glass.

"We'll leave your car back at your apartment," he said, and they got into the car and drove away, leaving me there.

I watched my taillights recede down the road and stood up. A cold, damp fog had begun to roll in from the ocean, chilling the sweat on my face and making me shiver. Maybe it would numb my swelling hand. I took a deep breath and started off. It was going to be a long, cold walk home, but I didn't mind. I kind of enjoyed being by myself.

I woke up groggy from the pain pills the E.R. doctor had given me.

I also had a headache, which got worse when I reached up and smacked myself with the cast I'd forgotten about that was holding my two broken metacarpals in place. I swore and rubbed my head with my good hand, then got up and made coffee. I made extra noise doing that, thinking about how I owed those guys and how I would more than likely never get the chance to repay them.

After three cups, I'd cleared enough cobwebs to call Al. He had Phalen's arrest report. I thought about telling him about my dance partners last night, but rejected the idea. He would have just wanted me to waste a lot of time looking at mug shots, and I wasn't in the mood. It wouldn't have done any good, anyway. Even if I could have identified them, they would have had six witnesses who had been playing poker with them last night, my car was outside where they had thoughtfully dropped it, and there was no way to prove that my hand had not been stepped on when I'd bent down to pick up a quarter from the sidewalk. My blood pressure went up ten points when I thought about it, but I kept my mouth shut and took down what Al gave me.

Phalen had been arrested after the fire department had found evidence of arson in the grease fire that completely destroyed his Encino restaurant, Arnie's Greenhouse. Traces of accelerants, possibly gasoline, had been found in the kitchen area where the fire had started, but Phalen claimed that those were possibly cleaning solvents which had been kept in a closet there. The case was weak, but it had been filed, anyway.

I thanked Al and called a friend of mine at Hooper Holms. The Hooper Holms Casualty Index in Morristown, New Jersey, contains the names of more than six million individuals and lists their insurance histories. The purpose is to spot insurance fraud. They had Phalen's name. Before moving to California, Phalen had owned two buildings in Baltimore that had mysteriously gone up in flames. No legal charges had ever been brought against him in those cases and the insurance claims had been paid.

Arnie the Torch. With three fires to his credit in the past ten years, one more business going up in smoke would certainly bring him more heat than just the combustible kind. Maybe he figured it was time to humanize his claim base.

I called Anixter and gave him a report. When I told him about my welcome home committee, he sounded shocked. "My God. Are you all right?"

"A broken hand. They were just administering an object lesson. They let me know that next time, the damage would be more extensive."

"You think they were working for this Phalen character?"

"Yeah, I think. And now he knows I'm working for you, not his wife."

"Have you told the police?"

"It wouldn't do any good–"

"But if he and Rhonda have been carrying on an affair all this time, and he's the kind of man you say he is, they could have plotted Chip's death from the beginning. He could have targeted Chip as a mark and sent her after him."

That thought had crossed my mind. Phalen certainly had the connections and the experience, and his mind seemed to run in those directions. "It's possible," I said, more to keep him from running off on that track than anything. "Did Chip own his own scuba gear, Mr. Anixter?"

"Huh? Yes."

"You're sure?"

"I should be. I paid enough for it. Why?"

I bypassed the question. "I'd like to put a twenty-four hour surveillance on both the woman and Phalen, Mr. Anixter, but that would run into some money–"

"I told you I don't care what it costs," he snapped.

My kind of client. I told him I'd keep in touch, then called Transcontinental Life. The agent handling the Anixter claim was named Manning and I repeated what I'd learned to him, then asked if he could send an investigator over to Rhonda Anixter's apartment and on some pretext ask to see Chip's diving gear. When he asked what I was looking for, I told him I basically wanted an inventory of what was there. He said it should be no problem, and promised to get right on it.

I called some people I knew and arranged for round-the-clock surveillance on both Rhonda and Phalen, warning them to be careful, then called the phone company. I told the service rep that my name was Chip Anixter and that I'd just gotten my phone bill and noticed I'd been billed for a call to Fort Lauderdale I'd never made. I gave her Rhonda's number and she came back on the line and said she could find no record of any such call billed to that number. Indignantly, I asked what calls had been made in the past month that she *did* have a record for, and she read off a list. I took them down and hung up.

Out of the sixteen toll calls Rhonda had made, two were to a number in Yuma, Arizona, seven were to a number in Los Angeles, and four to a Hollywood number. I started dialing. The Hollywood number, as I suspected, was the paradise; all the calls had been made since she had returned from the Caribbean. The Los Angeles number belonged to the law firm of Sadler, Bacon, and Pitts, Rhonda's attorneys. A woman named Zelda Banks answered the Yuma number when I called and it took a four-second scam to find out she was Rhonda's mother.

Manning called back after lunch. "There's nothing there," he said. "She told my guy that she trashed the stuff after the accident. Too painful for her to keep, she said."

I couldn't help grinning.

"Another little item of note," he went on. "She's got a new attorney. A young, Beverly Hills fire-breather named Cohen. We've come up against him before in a couple of questionable fire claims. He's already talking a five-figure lawsuit for damages unless we can show good cause why her claim shouldn't be paid."

"When did this happen?"

"We were notified of the change of counsel this morning, right after I talked to you."

"How long would a lawsuit take to settle?"

"Months, years, who knows?"

"Tell them they're going to have to sue. Tell them there's new evidence to dispute the validity of the claim."

"But there isn't, really–"

"They don't know that. Besides, there might be, if we can drag this thing out."

"I don't know if the company will go for it–"

"Do what you can do."

He promised to try. I sat there, thinking about it, then went down to my car and drove downtown. Arnie Phalen's arson case was listed in the index of the Superior Court. I took down the number and gave it to the clerk, who came back with a file. There wasn't much in the file. The case had been dropped in preliminary for lack of evidence. Harold Cohen must have done a good job representing his client.

Phalen must have thought Rhonda's attorney was a little weak and put his own man in to push a little harder. I couldn't blame him, really; he was merely protecting his investment. Just as he had been protecting it when he'd sent his goons to break my hand.

There wasn't much to do now but wait, so I went home, took a pain pill, made myself a drink, and started.

The waiting ran into a week. Harold Cohen screamed and threatened, but Transcontinental stood firm. Phalen stayed away from Rhonda, but he visited Cohen's office twice during the week.

I was taking the Monday morning shift at Rhonda Anixter's

apartment when the Porsche pulled out of the driveway and headed down the street. I put the glazed doughnut I was eating down on the front seat and followed her to I-10, where she headed east. She drove fast and it was hard to keep up in my old Dodge, but I managed to keep her in sight all the way to the Harbor freeway. She lost me there, but I had a pretty good idea where she was going. I confirmed it when I pulled up across from the Paradise and saw the Porsche parked in the lot.

Twenty minutes later, she came through the front door and headed to her car. She was wearing big sun-glasses and had her hair up, but even without makeup she made me drool. It made me sad that this was as close as I would ever get to her, playing Peeping Tom, but then I guess we all have our roles to play in life. Maybe I should brown-nose the Director more...

She turned right out of the driveway and headed toward Vermont, but two blocks up she suddenly pulled over to the curb, so I had to drive past her and park in the next block. I watched through my rear window as she got out of the Porsche and went to the curbside mailbox. Her body looked spectacular in a red tube top and tightfitting jeans, but my eyes were on the business-sized envelope she pulled out of her purse and dropped into the box.

She got back into her car and I waited until she had turned on Vermont before I got the fifteen colored blotters from the trunk of my car and walked back to the mailbox.

The pickup time marked on the box was 4:15, two hours away. I opened the mailbox, dropped in the blotters and went back to my car. I stopped at a nearby greasy spoon and killed some time downing a tuna fish sandwich and four cups of coffee, and was back at the mailbox by quarter to four.

The mail truck pulled up at 4:21, by my watch, but then my watch may have been a little fast. The mailman was opening the box when I trotted up, wearing my most worried expression. "Excuse me–"

He looked up, startled. "Huh?"

He was young, with shoulder-length dark hair and a beard. I hoped his attitude matched his appearance. What I needed was a little hang-loose flexibility, someone who would be willing to bend the rules a little to help out a fellow human being in distress.

I pointed up the street, and tried to put urgency in my voice. "I just live up the street here at 1015. I mailed a letter this afternoon and I'm sure I sent it to the wrong address. It's a check, and Jesus Christ, if it gets into the wrong hands and gets cashed, I'd be up shit's creek."

He shrugged. "I don't know what I can do about it–"

"If I could just take a look at the letter and see, I'd know whether to cancel the check or not–"

He frowned, his mouth following the lines of his mustache. "I can't go looking through all this mail–"

"You won't have to," I assured him. "After I mailed it and realized what I'd done, I took some blotters and dropped them in the box. The letter should be right below them."

He looked doubtful. "I don't know. . .

"Look, I don't have to touch anything. I know that's probably against the postal regulations. You can read me the address. I don't want the letter back or anything. I just want to know whether I should call the bank and cancel the check. I mean, if the check gets into the wrong hands, man, I'll really be screwed."

He bit his lip and made a sloughing motion with his shoulders. "I guess it'd be okay."

"I really appreciate this," I said truthfully.

The blotters were near the top of the pile of mail. He took the letter directly below them and picked it up, holding it away from me so I couldn't see it. "Charles Albertson?"

That was probably. For some reason, they always seemed to use their own first names or the same initials. The lack of imagination of the typical criminal mind never ceased to depress me. "That's the one."

"Two thirty-four Montvue Road," he read. "Old Towne, Montserrat."

"That takes a load off my mind, thanks," I said. "That's the right address." He handed me back my blotters and I thanked him again and jotted down the address in my notebook on the way to the car. I called my travel agent from a pay phone down the street and booked the first fight out of Miami, with connections to Antigua and Montserrat. Then I called Barbara Phalen and filled her in about her husband's affair with Rhonda Anixter. I figured I might as well have something nice to think about on the plane.

Montserrat was a green and rugged island paradise of forested mountains, manicured fields, and black sand beaches. Old Towne was a collection of affluent hillside houses overlooking a golf course and the sea. Two thirty-four Montvue was a pink house with a white shingle roof, surrounded by a white wrought iron fence festooned with flowers. I told my cab driver to wait for me and went up the walk to the front door.

The day was hot and sunny and the front door was wide open to let in the cool breeze that blew steadily from the ocean. I stepped inside and called out: "Hello?"

I heard his thongs slapping the tile floor before he appeared around the corner dressed in a pair of swim trunks. He had the unintelligent good looks and the lean, tanned body of a kid who surfed a lot and played volleyball on the beach and little else. His curly blond hair was wet.

"Hello, Chip." I looked around the place. It was light and airy, with whitewashed walls and rattan furniture. A swimming pool was visible out back through the open louvered doors. No wonder he needed money. "I can say one thing for you; you set yourself up well. What's the rent like?"

He stared at me, open-mouthed. The words were barely audible. "Who are you?"

"A detective hired by your father."

His expression turned to disgust and he threw both hands into the air and let them fall to his sides. "Shit. Dear old Dad. He even had to fuck this up–"

He was reverting to form–a whiner. "You're lucky he did. Rhonda had no intention of bringing that $300,000 to you. Why should she when she could have it all? You're legally dead and if you suddenly turned up alive, you'd be prosecuted for insurance fraud. By that time, she'd be long gone. She only agreed to send you money because she wanted to keep you placated and underground."

"How did you know about the money?" he asked, surprised.

"I got a look at the envelope it's being sent in. I knew that if the insurance settlement was held up long enough, you'd more than likely run out of money and have to send for some." I paused. I wanted to savor the look on his face when I told him. "She got it from Arnie Phalen."

His eyes widened. "Phalen?"

"He's in for a piece now. He found out what the scam was and cut himself in. She's even using his attorney. They've been having a good time together since you've been gone, by the way."

His hands clenched into fists and he stepped toward me. "You're a liar–"

I wasn't going to stand for any of that stuff; I figured I could handle him one-handed if I had to. I side-stepped him and put my good hand on his chest and shoved him back, hard. His foot hit the bottom of one of the rattan chairs and he lost his balance and sat down. I moved forward so that he couldn't get up without being hit. He didn't try.

"Don't be stupid," I said. "You were had, boy, from the moment she set her sights on you. Your old man was right. She was only after the money."

He stared up at me hatefully, like a beaten dog.

"Shit."

"That's what you're in." I turned and started toward the door.

"Hey!" he shouted after me. "Where are you going?"

I stopped and turned around. "To find a beach somewhere. I've been in the Caribbean twice in a week, and I don't even have a tan."

He jumped up out of the chair and his hand jerked up. "Wait. What about me?"

I shrugged. "I was hired to find out what happened to you, not babysit. I don't think I'd care for that job." I held up my cast. "You're not my favorite person, boy. It's because of you I have this."

I started to go, then turned back.

"My advice to you would be to get your tail back to 'dear old Dad' as fast as you can and start doing some serious brown-nosing, because you're going to need his money to pay for your lawyer. If you lay it out for the insurance company now, you might just get off with probation."

I left him standing there and took the cab to the airport, where I called John Anixter. The phone connection was lousy, but it was good enough to get the message across. He sounded very happy at first to learn his son was alive, then he just got plain mad. He told me to "let the snot-nosed little sonofabitch find his own way back," and informed me I could expect a bonus when I got back.

I caught a LIAT puddle-jumper back to Antigua and checked into a quaint, two-hundred-year-old hotel in Nelson's dockyard on the isolated side of the island and spent the next four days soaking up some serious sun and a lot of rum punches and listening to the gentle lilt of steel bands. If there was trouble in paradise, it wasn't going to find me.

MAX ALLAN COLLINS
(b.1948)

The Strawberry Teardrop
(Nate Heller)

In a garbage dump on East Ninth near Shore Street Drive, in Cleveland, Ohio, on August 17, 1938, a woman's body was discovered by a cop walking his morning beat.

I got there before anything much had been moved. Not that I was a plainclothes dick–I used to be, but not in Cleveland; I was just along for the ride. I'd been sitting in the office of Cleveland's Public Safety Director, having coffee, when the call came through. The Safety Director was in charge of both the police and fire department, and one would think that a routine murder wouldn't rate a call to such a high muckey-muck.

One would be wrong.

Because this was the latest in a series of anything-but-routine, brutal murders–the unlucky thirteenth, to be exact, not that the thirteenth victim would seem any more unlucky than the preceding twelve. The so-called "Mad Butcher of Kingsbury Run" had been exercising his ghastly art sporadically since the fall of '35, in Cleveland–or so I understood. I was an out-of-towner, myself.

So was the woman.

Or she used to be, before she became so many dismembered parts flung across this rock-and-garbage strewn dump. Her nude torso was slashed and the blood, splashed here, streaked there, was turning dark, almost black, though the sun caught scarlet glints and tossed them at us. Her head was gone, but maybe it would turn up. The Butcher wasn't known for that, though. The twelve preceding victims had been found headless, and had stayed that way. Somewhere in Cleveland, perhaps, a guy had a collection in his attic. In this weather it wouldn't smell too nice.

It's not a good sign when the Medical Examiner gets sick; and the half dozen cops, and the police photographer, were looking green around the gills themselves. Only my friend, the Safety Director, seemed in no danger of losing his breakfast. He was a ruddy-cheeked six-footer in a coat and tie and vest, despite the heat; hatless, his hair brushed back and pomaded, he still seemed–years after I'd met him– boyish. And he was only in his mid-thirties, just a few years older than me.

I'd met him in Chicago, seven or eight years ago, when I wasn't yet president (and everything else) of the A-l Detective Agency, but still a cop; and he was still a Prohibition Agent. Hell, *the* Prohibition agent. He'd considered me one of the more or less honest cops in Chicago–emphasis on the less, I guess–and I made a good contact for him, as a lot of the cops didn't like him much. Honesty doesn't go over real big in Chicago, you know.

Eliot Ness said, "Despite the slashing, there's a certain skill displayed, here."

"Yeah, right," I said. "A regular ballet dancer did this."

"No, really," he said, and bent over the headless torso, pointing. He seemed to be pointing at the gathering flies, but he wasn't. "There's an unmistakable precision about this. Maybe even indicating surgical training."

"Maybe," I said. "But I think the doctor lost this patient."

He stood and glanced at me and smiled, just a little; he understood me; he knew my wise-guy remarks were just my way of holding onto my own breakfast.

"You ought to come to Cleveland more often," he said.

"You know how to show a guy a good time, I'll give you that, Eliot."

He walked over and glanced at a forearm, which seemed to reach for an empty soap box, fingers stretched toward the Gold Dust twins. He knelt and studied it.

I wasn't here on a vacation, by any means. Cleveland didn't strike me as a vacation city, even before I heard about the Butcher of Kingsbury Run (so called because a number of the bodies, including the first several, were found on that Cleveland street). This was strictly business. I was here trying to trace the missing daughter of a guy in Evanston who owned a dozen diners around Chicago. He was one of those self-made men who started out in the greasy kitchen of his own first diner, fifteen or so years ago; and now he had a fancy brick house in Evanston and plenty of money, considering the times. But not much else. His wife had died four or five years ago, of consumption; and his daughter–who he claimed to be a good girl and by all other accounts was pretty wild–had wandered off a few months ago, with a taxi dancer from the Northside named Tony.

Well, I'd found Tony in Toledo–he was doing a floor show in a roadhouse with a dark-haired girl named Fifi; he'd grown a little pencil mustache and they did an apache routine–he was calling himself Antoine now. And Tony/Antoine said Ginger (which was the Evanston restaurateur's daughter's nickname) had taken up with somebody named Ray, who owned (get this) a diner in Cleveland.

I'd gotten here yesterday, and had talked to Ray, and without tipping I was looking for her, asked where was the pretty waitress, the one called Ginger, I think her name is. Ray, a skinny balding guy of about thirty with a silver front tooth, leered and winked and made it obvious that not only was Ginger working as a waitress here, she was also a side dish, where Ray was concerned. Further casual conversation revealed that it was Ginger's night off–she was at the movies with some girlfriends–and she'd be in tomorrow, around five.

I didn't push it further, figuring to catch up with her at the diner the next evening, after wasting a day seeing Cleveland and bothering my old friend Eliot. And now I was in a city dump with him, watching him study the severed forearm of a woman.

"Look at this," Eliot said, pointing at the outstretched fingers of the hand.

I went over to him and it. Not quickly, but I went over.

"What, Eliot? Do you want to challenge my powers of deduction, or just make me sick?"

"Just a lucky break," he said. "Most of the victims have gone unidentified; too mutilated. And a lot of 'em have been prostitutes or vagrants. But we've got a break, here. Two breaks, actually."

He pointed to the hand's little finger. To the small gold filigree band with a green stone.

"A nice specific piece of jewelry to try to trace," he said, with a dry smile. "And even better..."

He pointed to a strawberry birthmark, the shape of a teardrop, just below the wrist.

I took a close look; then stood. Put a hand on my stomach.

Walked away and dropped to my knees and lost my breakfast.

I felt Eliot's hand patting my back.

"Nate," he said. "What's the matter? You've seen homicides

before...even grisly ones like this...brace up, boy."

He eased me to my feet.

My tongue felt thick in my mouth, thick and restless.

"What is it?" he said.

"I think I just found my client's daughter," I said.

Both the strawberry birthmark and the filigree ring with the green stone had been part of my basic description of the girl; the photographs I had showed her to be a pretty but average-looking young woman–slim, brunette–who resembled every third girl you saw on the street. So I was counting on those two specifics to help me identify her. I hadn't counted on those specifics helping me in just this fashion.

I sat in Eliot's inner office in the Cleveland city hall; the mayor's office was next door. We were having coffee with some rum in it– Eliot kept a bottle in a bottom drawer of his rolltop desk. I promised him not to tell Capone.

"I think we should call the father," Eliot said. "Ask him to come and make the identification."

I thought about it. "I'd like to argue with you, but I don't see how I can. Maybe if we waited till...Christ. Till the head turns up..."

Eliot shrugged. "It isn't likely to. The ring and the birthmark are enough to warrant notifying the father."

"I can make the call."

"No. I'll let you talk to him when I'm done, but that's something I should do."

And he did. With quiet tact. After a few minutes he handed me the phone; if I'd thought him cold at the scene of the crime, I erased that thought when I saw the dampness in his gray eyes.

"Is it my little girl?" the deep voice said, sounding tinny out of the phone.

"I think so, Mr. Jensen. I'm afraid so."

I could hear him weeping.

Then he said: "Mr. Ness said her body was...dismembered. How can you say it's her? How...how cay you know it's her?"

And I told him of the ring and the strawberry teardrop.

"I should come there," he said.

"Maybe that won't be necessary." I covered the phone. "Eliot, will my identification be enough?"

He nodded. "We'll stretch it."

I had to argue with Jensen, but finally he agreed for his daughter's remains to be shipped back via train; I said I'd contact a funeral home this afternoon, and accompany her home.

I handed the phone to Eliot to hang up.

We looked at each other and Eliot, not given to swearing, said, "I'd give ten years of my life to nail that butchering bastard."

"How long will your people need the body?"

"I'll speak to the coroner's office. I'm sure we can send her home with you in a day or two. Where are you staying?"

"The Stadium Hotel."

"Not anymore. I've got an extra room for you. I'm a bachelor again, you know."

We hadn't gotten into that yet; I'd always considered Eliot's marriage an ideal one, and was shocked a few months back to hear it had broken up.

"I'm sorry, Eliot."

"Me too. But I am seeing somebody. Someone you may remember; another Chicagoan."

"Who?"

"Evie MacMillan."

"The fashion illustrator? Nice looking woman."

Eliot smiled slyly. "You'll see her tonight, at the Country Club...but I'll arrange some female companionship for you. I don't want you cutting my time."

"How can you say such a thing? Don't you trust me?"

"I learned a long time ago," he said, turning to his desk full of paperwork, "not to trust Chicago cops—even ex-ones."

Out on the Country Club terrace, the ten-piece band was playing Cole Porter and a balmy breeze from Lake Erie was playing with the women's hair. There were plenty of good-looking women, here—low-cut dresses, bare shoulders—and lots of men in evening clothes for them to dance with. But this was no party, and since some of the golfers were still here from late afternoon rounds, there were sports clothes and a few business suits (like mine) in the mix. Even some of the women were dressed casually, like the tall, slender blonde in pink shirt and pale green pleated skirt who sat down next to me at the little white metal table and asked me if I'd have a Bacardi with her. The smelled like a flower garden, and some of it was flowers, and some of it was her.

"I'd be glad to buy you a Bacardi," I said, clumsily.

"No," she said, touching my arm. She had eyes the color of jade. "You're a guest. I'll buy."

Eliot was dancing with his girl Evie, an attractive brunette in her mid-thirties; she'd always struck me as intelligent but sad, somehow. They smiled over at me.

The blonde in pink and pale green brought two Bacardis over, set one of them in front of me and smiled. "Yes," she said wickedly. "You've been set up. I'm the girl Eliot promised you. But if you were hoping for somebody in an evening gown, I'm not it. I just *had* to get an extra nine holes in."

"If you were looking for a guy in a tux," I said, "I'm not it. And I've never been on a golf course in my life. What else do we have in common?"

She had a nicely wry smile, which continued as she sipped the Bacardi. "Eliot, I suppose, If I have a few more of these, I may tell you a secret."

And after a few more, she did.

And it was a whopper.

"*You're* an undercover agent?" I said. A few sheets to the wind myself.

"Shhhh," she said, finger poised uncertainly before pretty lips. "It's a secret. But I haven't been doing it much lately."

"Haven't been doing what?"

"Well, undercover work. And there's a double-entendre there that I'd rather you didn't go looking for."

"I wouldn't think of looking under the covers for it."

The band began playing a tango.

I asked her how she got involved, working for Eliot. Which I didn't believe for a second, even in my cups.

But it turned out to be true (as Eliot admitted to me when he came over to see how Vivian and I were getting along, when Vivian–which was her name, incidentally–went to the powder room with Evie).

Vivian Chalmers was the daughter of a banker (a solvent one), a divorcee of thirty with no children and a lot of social pull. An expert trapshooter, golfer, tennis player and "all 'round sportswoman," with a sense of adventure. When Eliot called on her to case various of the gambling joints he planned to raid–as a socialite she could take a fling in any joint she chose, without raising any suspicion–she immediately said yes. And she'd been an active agent in the first few years of Eliot's ongoing battle against the so-called Mayfield Road Mob which controlled prostitution, gambling and the policy racket in the Cleveland environs.

"But things have slowed down," she said, nostalgically. "Eliot has pretty much cleaned up the place, and, besides, he doesn't want to use me anymore."

"An undercover agent can only be effective so long," I said. "Pretty soon the other side gets suspicious."

She shrugged, with resigned frustration, and let me buy the next round.

We took a walk in the dark, around the golf course, and ended up sitting on a green. The breeze felt nice. The flag on the pin--13--flapped.

"Thirteen," I said.

"Huh?"

"Victim thirteen."

"Oh. Eliot told me about that. Your 'luck' today, finding your client's missing daughter. Damn shame."

"Damn shame."

"A shame, too, they haven't found the son-of-a-bitch."

She was a little drunk, and so was I, but I was still shocked--well, amused--to hear a woman, particularly a "society" woman, speak that way.

"It must grate on Eliot, too," I said.

"Sure as hell does. It's the only mote in his eye. He's a hero around these parts, and he's kicked the Mayfield Mob in the seat of the pants, and done everything else from clean up a corrupt police department to throw labor racketeers in jail, to cut traffic deaths in half, to founding Boy's Town, to..."

"You're not in love with the guy, are you?"

She seemed taken aback for a minute, then her face wrinkled into a got-caught-with-my-pants-down grin. "Maybe a little. But he's got a girl."

"I don't."

"You might."

She leaned forward.

We kissed for a while, and she felt good in my arms; she was firm, almost muscular. But she smelled like flowers. And the sky was blue and scattered with stars above us, as we lay back on the golf-green to look up. It seemed like a nice world, at the moment.

Hard to imagine it had a Butcher in it.

I sat up talking with Eliot that night; he lived in a little converted boathouse on the lake. The furnishings were sparse, spartan; it was obvious his wife had taken most of the furniture with her and he'd had to all but start over.

I told him I thought Vivian was a terrific girl.

Leaning back in a comfy chair, feet on an ottoman, Eliot, tie loose around his neck, smiled in a melancholy way. "I thought you'd hit it off."

"Did you have an affair with her?"

He looked at me sharply; that was about as personal as I'd ever got with him.

He shook his head no, but I didn't quite buy it.

"You knew Evie MacMillan in Chicago," I said.

"Meaning what?"

"Meaning nothing."

"Meaning I knew her when I was still married."

"Meaning nothing."

"Nate, I'm sorry I'm not the Boy Scout you think I am."

"Hey, so you've slept with girls before. I'll learn to live with it."

There was a stone fireplace, in which some logs were trying to decide whether to burn any more or not; we watched them trying.

"I love Evie, Nate. I'm going to marry her."

"Congratulations."

We could hear the lake out there; could smell it some, too.

"I'd like that bastard's neck in my hands," Eliot said.

"What?"

"That Butcher. That goddamn Butcher."

"What made you think of him?"

"I don't know."

"Eliot, it's been over three years since he first struck, and you *still* don't have anything?"

"Nothing. A few months ago, last time he hit, we found some of the...body parts, bones and such...in a cardboard box in the Central Market area. There's a Hooverville over there, or what used to be a Hooverville...it's a shantytown, is more like it, genuine hobos as opposed to just good folks down on their luck. Most of the victims— before today—were either prostitutes or bums...and the bums from that shantytown were the Butcher's meat. So to speak."

The fire crackled.

Eliot continued: "I decided to make a clean sweep. I took twenty-five cops through there at one in the morning, and rousted out all the 'bo's and took 'em down and fingerprinted and questioned all of 'em."

"And it amounted to...?"

"It amounted to nothing. Except ridding Cleveland of that shantytown. I burned the place down that afternoon."

"Comes in handy, having all those firemen working for you. But what about those poor bastards whose 'city' you burned down?"

Sensing my disapproval, he glanced at me and gave me what tried to be a warm smile, but was just a weary one. "Nate, I turned them over to the Relief department, for relocation and, I hope, rehabilitation. But most of them were bums who just hopped a freight out. And I did 'em a favor by taking them off the potential victims list."

"And made room for Ginger Jensen."

Eliot looked away.

"That wasn't fair," I said. "I'm sorry I said that, Eliot."

"I know, Nate. I know."

But I could tell he'd been thinking the same thing.

I had lunch the next day with Vivian in a little outdoor restaurant in the shadow of Terminal Tower. We were served lemonade and little ham and cheese and lettuce and tomato sandwiches with the crusts trimmed off the toasted bread. The detective in me wondered what became of the crusts. "Thanks for having lunch with me," Vivian said. She had on a pale orange dress; she sat crossing her brown pretty legs.

"My pleasure," I said.

"Speaking of which...about last night..."

"We were both a little drunk. Forget it. Just don't ask *me* to."

She smiled as she nibbled her sandwich.

"I called and told Eliot something this morning," she said, "and he just ignored me."

"What was that?"

"That I have a possible lead on the Butcher murders."

"I can't imagine Eliot ignoring that...and it's not like it's just *anybody* approaching him—you *did* work for him..."

"Not lately. And he thinks I'm just..."

"Looking for an excuse to be around him?"

She nibbled at a little sandwich. Nodded.

"Did you resent him asking you to be with me as a blind date last night?"

"No," she said.

"Did...last night have anything to do with wanting to 'show' Eliot?"

If she weren't so sophisticated—or trying to be—she would've looked hurt; but her expression managed to get something else across: disappointment in me.

"Last night had to do with showing *you*," she said. "And...it had a little to do with Bacardi rum..."

"That it did. Tell me about your lead."

"Eliot has been harping on the 'professional' way the bodies have been dismembered. He's said again and again he sees a 'surgical' look to it."

I nodded.

"So it occurred to me that a doctor—anyway, somebody who'd at least been in medical school for a time—would be a likely candidate for the Butcher."

"Yes."

"And medical school's expensive, so, it stands to reason, the Butcher just might run in the same social circles as yours truly."

"Say, you *did* work for Eliot."

She liked that.

She went on: "I checked around with my friends, and heard about a guy whose family has money, plenty of it. Name of Watterson."

"Last name or first?"

"That's the family name. Big in these parts."

"Means nothing to me."

"Well, Lloyd Watterson used to be a medical student. He's a big man, very strong–the kind of strength it might take to do some of the things the Butcher has done. And he has a history of mental disturbances."

"What kind of mental disturbances?"

"He's been going to a psychiatrist since he was a schoolboy."

"Do you know this guy?"

"Just barely. But I've heard things about him."

"Such as?"

"I hear he likes boys."

Lloyd Watterson lived in a two-storey white house at the end of a dead-end street, a Victorian-looking miniature mansion among other such houses, where expansive lawns and towering hedges separated the world from the wealthy who lived within.

This wasn't the parental home, Vivian explained; Watterson lived here alone, apparently without servants. The grounds seemed well-tended, though, and there was nothing about this house that said anyone capable of mass murder might live here. No blood spattered on the white porch; no body parts scattered about the lawn.

It was mid-afternoon, and I was having second thoughts.

"I don't even have a goddamn gun," I said.

"I do," she said, and showed me a little .25 automatic from her purse.

"Great. If he has a dog, maybe we can use that to scare it."

"This'll do the trick. Besides, a gun won't even be necessary. You're just here to talk."

The game plan was for me to approach Watterson as a cop, flashing my private detective's badge quickly enough to fool him (and that almost always worked), and question him, simply get a feel for whether or not he was a legitimate suspect, worthy of lobbying Eliot for action against. My say-so, Vivian felt, would be enough to get Eliot off the dime.

And helping Eliot bring the Butcher in would be a nice wedding present for my old friend; with his unstated but obvious political ambitions, the capture of the Kingsbury Run maniac would offset the damage his divorce had done him in conservative, mostly Catholic Cleveland. He'd been the subject of near hero worship in the press here (Eliot was always good at getting press—Frank Nitti used to refer to him as "Eliot Press"); but the ongoing if sporadic slaughter of the Butcher was a major embarrassment for Cleveland's fabled Safety Director.

So, leaving Vivian behind in the roadster (Watterson might recognize her), I walked up the curved sidewalk and went up on the porch and rang the bell. In the dark hardwood door there was opaque glass through which I could barely make out movement, coming toward me.

The door opened, and a blond man about six-three with a baby-face and ice-blue eyes and shoulders that nearly filled the doorway looked out at me and grinned. A kid's grin, on one side of his face. He wore a polo shirt and short white pants; he seemed about to say, "Tennis, anyone?"

But he said nothing, as a matter of fact; he just appraised me with those ice-blue, somewhat vacant eyes. I now knew how it felt for a woman to be ogled—which is to say, not necessarily good.

I said, "I'm an officer of the court," which in Illinois wasn't exactly a lie, and I flashed him my badge, but before I could say anything else, his hand reached out and grabbed the front of my shirt, yanked me inside and slammed the door.

He tossed me like a horseshoe, and I smacked into something—the stairway to the second floor, I guess; I don't know exactly, because I blacked out. The only thing I remember is the musty smell of the place.

I woke up minutes later, and found myself tied in a chair in a dank, dark room. Support beams loomed out of a packed dirt floor. The basement.

I strained at the ropes, but they were snug; not so snug as to cut off my circulation, but snug enough. I glanced around the room. I was alone. I couldn't see much—just a shovel against one cement wall. The only light came from a window off to my right, and there were hedges in front of the window, so the light was filtered.

Feet came tromping down the open wooden stairs. I saw his legs first, white as pastry dough.

He was grinning. In his right hand was a cleaver. It shone, caught a glint of what little light there was.

"I'm no butcher," he said. His voice was soft, almost gentle. "Don't believe what you've heard..."

"Do you want to die?" I said.

"Of course not."

"Well then cut me loose. There's cops all over the place, and if you kill me, they'll shoot you down. You know what happens to cop killers, don't you?"

He thought that over, nodded.

Standing just to one side of me, displaying the cold polished steel of the cleaver, in which my face's frantic reflection looked back at me, he said, "I'm no butcher. This is a surgical tool. This is used for amputation, not butchery."

"Yeah. I can see that."

"I wondered when you people would come around."

"Do you want to be caught, Lloyd?"

"Of course not. I'm no different than you. I'm a public servant."

"How...how do you figure that, Lloyd?" My feet weren't tied to the chair; if he'd just step around in front of me...

"I only dispose of the flotsam. Not to mention jetsam."

"Not to mention that."

"Tramps. Whores. Weeding out the stock. Survival of the fittest. You know."

"That makes a lot of sense, Lloyd. But I'm not flotsam *or* jetsam. I'm a cop. You don't want to kill a cop. You don't want to kill a fellow public servant."

He thought about that.

"I think I have to, this time," he said.

He moved around the chair, stood in front of me, stroking his chin, the cleaver gripped tight in his right hand, held about breastbone high.

"I *do* like you," Lloyd said, thoughtfully.

"And I like you, Lloyd," I said, and kicked him in the balls.

Harder than any man tied to a chair should be able to kick; but you'd be surprised what you can do, under extreme circumstances. And things rarely get more extreme than being tied to a chair with a guy with a cleaver coming at you.

Only he wasn't coming at me, now: now, he was doubled over, and I stood, the chair strapped to my back; managed, even so, to kick him in the face.

He tumbled back, gripping his groin, his head leaning back, stretching, tears streaming down his cheeks, cords in his neck taut; my shoe had caught him on the side of the face and broken the skin. Flecks of blood, like little red tears, spattered his cheeks, mingling with the real tears.

That's when the window shattered, and Vivian squeezed down and through, pretty legs first.

And she gave me the little gun to hold on him while she untied me.

He was still on the dirt floor, moaning, when we went up the stairs and out into the sunny day, into a world that wasn't dank, onto earth that was grass-covered and didn't have God knows what buried under it.

We asked Eliot to meet us at his boathouse; we told him what had happened. He was livid; I never saw him angrier. But he held Vivian for a moment, and looked at her and said, "If anything had happened to you, I'd've killed you."

He poured all of us a drink; rum as usual. He handed me mine and said, "How could you get involved in something so harebrained?"

"I wanted to give my client something for his money," I said.

"You mean his daughter's killer."

"Why not?"

"I've been looking for the bastard three years, and you come to town and expect to find him in three days."

"Well, I did."

He smirked, shook his head. "I believe you did. But Watterson's family will bring in the highest-paid lawyers in the country and we'd be thrown out of court on our cans."

"What? The son of a bitch tried to cut me up with a cleaver!"

"Did he? Did he swing on you? Or did you enter his house under a false pretense, misrepresenting yourself as a law officer? And as far as that goes, *you* assaulted *him*. We have very little."

Vivian said, "You have the name of the Butcher."

Eliot nodded. "Probably. I'm going to make a phone call."

Eliot went into his den and came out fifteen minutes later.

"I spoke with Franklin Watterson, the father. He's agreed to submit his son for a lie detector test."

"To what end?"

"One step at a time," Eliot said.

Lloyd Watterson took the lie detector test twice–and on both instances denied committing the various Butcher slayings; his denials were, according to the machine, lies. The Watterson family attorney reminded Eliot that lie detector tests were not admissible as evidence. Eliot had a private discussion with Franklin Watterson.

Lloyd Watterson was committed, by his family, to an asylum for the insane. The Mad Butcher of Kingsbury Run–which to this day is marked "Unsolved" in the Cleveland police records–did not strike again.

At least not directly.

Eliot married Evie MacMillan a few months after my Cleveland visit, and from the start their marriage was disrupted by crank letters, postmarked from the same town as the asylum where Watterson had been committed. "Retribution will catch up with you one day," said one postcard, on the front of which was a drawing of an effeminate man grinning from behind prison bars. Mrs. Ness was especially unnerved by these continuing letters and cards.

Eliot's political fortunes waned, in the wake of the "unsolved" Butcher slayings. Known for his tough stance on traffic violators, he got mired in a scandal when one predawn morning in March of 1942, his car skidded into an oncoming car on the West Shoreway. Eliot and his wife, and two friends, had been drinking. The people report didn't identify Eliot by name, but his license number—EN-1, well-known to Cleveland citizens—was listed. And Eliot had left the scene of the accident.

Hit-and-run, the headlines said. Eliot's version was that his wife had been injured, and he'd raced her to a hospital—but not before stopping to check on the other driver, who confirmed this. The storm blew over, but the damage was done. Eliot's image in the Cleveland press was finally tarnished.

Two months later he resigned as Safety Director.

About that time, asylum inmate Lloyd Watterson managed to hang himself with a bed sheet, and the threatening mail stopped.

How much pressure those cards and letters put on the marriage I couldn't say; but in 1945 Eliot and Evie divorced, and Eliot married a third time a few months later. At the time he was serving as federal director of the program against venereal disease in the military. His attempt to run for Cleveland mayor in 1947 was a near disaster: Cleveland's one-time fairhaired boy was a has-been with a hit-run scandal and two divorces and three marriages going against him.

He would not have another public success until the publication of his autobiographical book, *The Untouchables*, but that success was posthumous; he died shortly before it was published, never knowing that television and Robert Stack would give him lasting fame.

I saw Eliot, now and then, over the years; but I never saw Vivian again.

I asked him about her, once, when I was visiting him in Pennsylvania, in the early '50s. He told me she'd been killed in a boating accident in 1943.

"She's been dead for years, then," I said, the shock of it hitting me like a blow.

"That's right. But shed a tear for her, now, if you like. Tears and prayers can never come too late, Nate."

Amen, Eliot.

AUTHOR'S NOTE: I wish to express my indebtedness to two non-fiction works, Four Against the Mob *by Oscar Fraley (Popular Library, 1961) and* Cleveland–The Best Kept Secret *by George E. Condon (Doubleday, 1967). Fact, speculation and fiction are freely mixed in the preceding story; with the exception of Eliot Ness, all characters–while in many cases having real-life counterparts–are fictional.*

ROBERT J. RANDISI
(b.1951)

The Nickel Derby
(Henry Po)

Kentucky Derby time is a special time of year for anyone involved in thoroughbred horse racing. The air crackles with excitement and tension as the big day approaches. My involvement with the Derby is usually as a non-betting spectator, but this year it had suddenly become a more substantial part of my life.

My boss, J. Howard Biel, president of the New York State Racing Club, had phoned me at home that morning, something which has customarily come to mean bad–or "serious"–news.

Invariably, every year there is a "Big Horse" from the east coast, and a "Big Horse" from the west coast. The Kentucky Derby is usually the first meeting between these two special thoroughbreds. This year, the west coast horse was a big, strapping colt named Dreamland, and the west coast entry was a sleek, rather smallish bundle of energy called Runamuck. So imposing were the credentials of these two horses that, to date, only five other horses had been named to run against them in the Derby. Of those, however, one had been felled by injury and another by illness, cutting the total field to five. This had caused this year's Run For The Roses to be dubbed by the media as "The Nickel Derby".

Arriving at Howard's office after his phone summons and accepting his offer of some of that mud he calls coffee, I took a seat while he started to tell me about it.

"I've had a meeting with officials from both California and Kentucky."

"About what?"

"There have been some threats against Dreamland and his camp."

"What sort of threats?"

"They've ranged from kidnapping to actually killing the horse."

"And the people on his camp?"

"They've been threatened with bodily harm, but no death threats as of yet."

"Well, that's all a real shame, Howard. But why would that cause you to have a meeting with the racing officials of two other states and then call me?"

He hesitated a moment, then said, "Because they don't have a team of special investigators, and I do."

He did have a team of investigators, for which he had fought long and hard with the Board of Directors of the NYSRC. They had finally agreed to give him a grant to hire *not* the twenty people he'd requested, but four. Take it or leave it, they told him, and he had taken it.

He took it and promptly contacted me because I had done some work for him before. I accepted the job, and helped find the other three people.

"Such as we are," I replied now.

"A poor lot, but mine own," he said, spreading his hands.

"So they want to borrow a man, is that it?"

"That's about the size of it. You'd be in charge of security for the animal while he's in California as well as when he's taken to Kentucky." He leaned forward and added, "Henry, if this horse were stolen or harmed, it would be a serious blow to all of thoroughbred racing. That's why I've decided it's important for us to work with these people."

"You mean you've decided that *I* should work with them."

He smiled grimly and said, "Yes, that's exactly what I mean."

"What about Runamuck?"

"No threats, no calls. Thank God."

"All right, Howard." I stood up. "I'll get going."

"I appreciate this, Henry," he said, opening his top drawer. He withdrew a brown envelope and held it out. "Here's your ticket, and some expense money."

"Think you know me pretty well, huh?" I asked, taking the envelope. "I'll need some background info on the people I'll be dealing with."

He reached down and brought an attache case out from behind his desk. "It's been prepared."

"Boy,"I said, taking that, too, "I really like being unpredictable."

"Good luck, Henry."

"I'll keep in touch."

On the plane, I went through the material in the attache case. It told me a little about the people in the Dreamland camp: Donald McCoy, his rider, who had ridden him in all of his previous races; his owner, Mrs. Emily Nixon, who had taken the stable over from her father when he died ten years ago and had not had a Derby winner since; and his trainer, Lew Hale, who had been hired by Mrs. Nixon at the time she took over the stable.

It sounded like there could be some pressure on Hale to come through with a Derby winner, so I decided he'd be a good place to start.

When I landed at LAX, I took a cab to a hotel, changed into some California duds, and then took another cab to the racetrack, where I sought and found Lew Hale.

It was early, and workouts were just concluding. I approached Hale as he was looking over a two year-old filly that was being galloped around the track, and introduced myself.

"Oh, you're the investigator from New York," he said, holding out his hand. "Glad to have you aboard, Mr. Po."

Deeply lined, be it from constant exposure to the weather, or otherwise, his face had character. His eyes were grey and his nose prominant. His mouth was what made him look ugly, though. His lips were heavy, and twisted, so that he always looked as if he had just sucked a lemon. He was taller than me by some four inches, which put him at least at six-two. He was in good shape for a man in his late fifties—hell, he was in good shape for a man my own age.

"I don't mind telling you, I've been plenty worried since those threats started."

"How long has that been?"

He thought a moment, then said, "A couple of weeks, I guess. First there was a note saying that Dreamland would never make it to the Derby."

"That sounds more like an opinion than a threat," I pointed out.

"Which was why we didn't react to it."

"Did you keep it?"

"I'm sorry, no. I threw it out. I never realized it was a threat until I got the phone call."

"Where did you receive the phone call?"

"Here, at the track."

"What time of day?"

"Early, before the day's racing began."

"Was the caller a man or a woman?"

"Uh, now that's hard to say. It could have been a woman with a deep voice..."

"I'm afraid so. It sounded sort of muffled, as if the person had their hand over the phone."

"What did they say?"

"That Dreamland was going to take a ride, but that it wouldn't be to Kentucky."

"How many other calls did you get after after that?"

"Two. The last one said that Dreamland would be dead before he could reach the finish line."

"What about the threats against you and his jock?"

"I don't scare, Mr. Po, but he sure did."

"What?"

"No, you wouldn't know about that yet," he said. "He quit yesterday. He got a call and wouldn't even tell me what was said. He just wanted out, and I let him go. I don't need a gutless jock."

"In what way were you threatened?"

"They told me I'd be dead if Dreamland won the Derby. Bullshit!"

"I wonder if I could see where you keep the colt now?"

"Of course. Just let me finish watching Miss Emily work."

"The filly?" I asked.

"Yeah"

"She looks like a beauty."

"Mrs. Nixon?"

He nodded. "She bid on the filly herself, and went for more bucks than I would have. But then, it's her money and I guess she knows what she's doing."

We watched the filly work until, apparently satisfied, Hale said, "Come on, let's go and see Dreamy. He's impressive as all hell just standing in his stall."

We walked out to a parking lot and got into a '73 Chevy that was covered with dust. We drove into the stable area on a dirt road, which explained the thick layers on the car. Most tracks have either dirt or gravel roads running through their stable areas.

Hale stopped the car in front of one of the larger stables and we got out. I could see a uniformed guard standing outside one of the stalls, so it wasn't hard to figure out where Dreamland was.

"I've had a guard on him day and night for three days now, since the last call," Hale explained.

When we reached the stall, the guard nodded at Hale but made no attempt to stop me or have me identify myself.

"This is Mr. Po." Hale told him. "He's from New York, and he will be in charge of security from now on."

"Yes, sir," the guard replied, and he nodded at me now that we'd been introduced.

"Are you private, or track security?" I asked the guard.

"Private, sir."

Hale said, "He's actually from the same company the track uses, but he's not assigned to the track permanently. Mrs. Nixon hired his company and they send us our own guards."

"Do you want to see my ID?" I asked the uniformed man.

"Uh, that won't be necessary, sir," he answered.

"Yes, it will," I said, taking out my ID and showing it to him. "I don't care whose company a stranger is in," I added, "I want his ID checked. Understand?"

The guard compressed his lips at the scolding and said, "Yes, sir, I understand."

I stepped past him, leaned on the stall door and peered in. Hale had been right; Dreamland was impressive. He picked up his head and looked me straight in the eye, wondering who the interloper was.

"Well, hello, your majesty," I greeted him.

"You get that feeling too, huh?" Hale asked. "He's regal-looking as all hell, eh?"

"That he is," I agreed.

"And he runs like all hell, too."

"How many shifts do you have the guards working on?"

"Three."

"When are you flying to Kentucky?"

"Day after tomorrow."

"Okay, until that time I want two guards on every shift. One here, and one moving about."

"I'll arrange it."

"It'll cost more."

"Lady Emily doesn't care about the cost," he assured me.

"Is that a nickname?"

"One of the milder ones," he answered, "and they're usually used behind her back."

"Has McCoy been around today?" I asked.

"Not today," he said. He turned his attention to the horse and said, "See you later, Dreamy." Dreamland gave him a sideways glance and then raised his head up high, as if ignoring us.

"Not very friendly," I commented.

"And that may be his only idiosyncrasy. But the way he runs, who cares? Come on, let's go to my office. If you can't locate McCoy around here, you might find him there, lickering his wounds."

"Why wouldn't I find him around here?" I asked. "He didn't quit riding altogether, did he?"

"When he quit me, he might as well have."

Hale gave me McCoy's address and phone number, and then I spent the better part of an hour trying to locate him on the track. When the day's racing began and I still hadn't found him, I gave up. None of the trainers I spoke to would admit that McCoy had been blackballed, but none of them were using him as a rider.

When I left the track, I grabbed a cab and gave the driver McCoy's home address, which turned to be an apartment building in a middle class neighborhood. Asking the driver to wait, I went into the lobby and rang McCoy' bell, but received no answer. I returned to the cab and had him take me back to my hotel, where I'd plan out my next move.

I checked in at the desk to see if there were any messages, not really expecting any, but when you're staying at a hotel you tend to do that. To my surprise, there was a message in my box. I controlled my curiousity until I got to my room. Once inside, I opened the envelope and took out a neatly typewritten note.

I read: "Mrs. Emily Nixon requests that you dine with her tonight. A car will come by your hotel to pick you up at seven sharp."

No signature.

It was some hell of a "request", but since I wanted to talk to the lady anyway, I wouldn't argue.

I read the note again, then put it down on a writing desk. Before showering, I dialed McCoy's number but got no answer. I showered, then tried again, still getting no response. I wanted very much to talk to McCoy and find out from him why he withdrew from a mount that very likely would have him a lot of money. Hale had told me his version, but Hale–and Emily Nixon–were management; and management always had their own ideas about how things should be.

I got dressed and was ready when "Miss Emily's" driver knocked on the door.

I didn't expect to find anyone else in the car, since I thought that the vehicle was being sent specifically to take me somewhere, but there she was. When I stuck my head in, the first thing I saw were a pair of shapely legs. The second thing I saw was the face of an extremely handsome woman, which at the moment was wearing an amused smile.

"Good evening, Mr. Po," she greeted.

"Mrs. Nixon."

"Please, step all the way in and take a seat."

When I stepped in, the driver slammed the door behind me, got behind the wheel and got under way.

"Let me say how grateful I am that you agreed to come to California and help us with our problem."

"I'm happy to be of help, Mrs. Nixon."

She had violet eyes that were very bright and intelligent. She appeared to be in her early forties, but was exceptionally attractive and radiated a youthful vitality.

"I hope you like expensive food, Mr. Po," she said then. "It's the only kind I ever eat."

"I only indulge when someone else is paying, Mrs. Nixon."

"Then you're in luck, aren't you?"

We spoke idly of racing until we reached our destination, an extremely expensive-looking Italian restaurant on Wilshire. When we entered we received the preferential treatment a woman of her station deserved–and craved–and were shown to "her" table.

After we had ordered dinner and had drinks in our hands, she said, "Well, what will your first step be in finding the man who has been making all these ghastly threats against us?"

"I think I should explain," I replied, "that my primary concern is not in finding the person making the threats, but to make sure that no harm comes to Dreamland or any of the people around him."

"I see," she said. "I'm afraid I misunderstood then. I was under the impression you were a special 'investigator' for the New York State Racing Club."

"I am," I assured her.

"Oh? Then what is it that a special investigator does?" she asked. "Investigate, no?"

"Under normal circumstances, yes," I said, trying not to lose my temper with her. "But not in this instance, I'm afraid."

"What have you done, then, to assure Dreamland's safety?" she asked. Her tone was considerably colder than what it had been to that point.

I explained that I had been to the track and had increased the security around Dreamland's stall. I also told her that I had spoken to Lew Hale, and was looking for McCoy.

"I don't want to talk about McCoy," she said vehemently. "How dare he do that to me!"

"You're talking about withdrawing from the mount?"

"Of course! What else!?" she shot back. "I cannot believe–" she stopped herself in midsentence, closed her eyes and said, "I do not want to talk about that little man."

"What about Hale?"

"Hale is fired if Dreamy doesn't win the Derby," she said. "I've given long enough."

"Ten years, isn't it?"

"Yes, ever since my father died. My father, George Gregg, had two Derby winners and three other horses who finished in the money. I have not had a horse accomplish any of that."

"Lew Hale seems fairly confident," I observed.

"We are all confident," she agreed, "but confidence does not win horse races."

Dinner came and I asked if she minded talking while we ate.

"Well, well, a gentleman," she said. "How nice. No, of course I don't mind. Thank you for asking."

As we cut into our food, I asked, "Will you be going to Kentucky with, uh, Dreamy?"

"No, but I'll be there later in the week, the day before the race," she answered. "I don't want to miss the Derby Eve festivities."

"Mrs. Nixon, about the threats. The notes, the calls—"

"One call," she said. "I received only one call."

"I understood there were more. And at least one note."

"The other calls, and the note, were received by Lew Hale."

"Did you see the note?"

"No, I did not. He told me about it, but said he threw it away."

"What about the call you did get?"

"A voice—"

"Male or female?"

That stopped her, as it had Hale, and she had to think about it.

"The voice was rather deep. I did not get the impression that I was speaking to a woman."

I put a lot of stock into her "impression"—or lack of one. I reasoned that a woman would know instinctively if she were speaking to another woman.

"Go on," I said.

"The voice said that if I made the trip to Kentucky, I'd be lucky as all hell to make it back."

This time I was the one who was stopped for a moment. Then I said, "Was that verbatim?"

"What?" she asked, hesitating over a forkful of linguini.

"The message you got on the phone, the way you gave it to me just now—was that word for word?"

She thought a moment, then said, "Yes. That's the way I remember it. Why?"

"Nothing," I said, not wanting to voice my thoughts at that

moment. It would take more than what I was thinking to build a case. I went on, "How much contact have you had with Lew Hale over your ten year association?"

"Actually, not all that much. Outside of the winner's circle–when we get there–I don't think I see him more than two or three times a year."

"Isn't that unusual?"

"Perhaps. But, unlike my father, I do *not* like the way horses smell. I don't spend that much time around the stables, and if I'm at the track it's either in the clubhouse or my private box."

"I see."

She put her fork down and said, "Why are you asking all these questions about the threats if you don't intend to investigate them?"

I was caught.

"Curiousity," I pleased, "an investigator's curiousity. A few questions can't hurt, and if I *can* find something out, I naturally will. But security is still my prime concern. I'll be satisfied just to see Dreamland run in the Derby."

"And win?" she asked.

I put my right hand out, palm down, and wiggled it back and forth a few times. "I'm like that about who wins, although I *am* an Easterner at heart," I confessed.

There was less tension between us after that, and at times I thought she might even be coming on to me. But I feigned ignorance.

When her driver arrived, we got up to leave and I asked if she minded if I made a phone call. She said she'd wait for me in the car.

I found a pay phone and dialed Don McCoy's number again and this time got a busy signal. I hung up, dialed again, got the same thing. On a hunch, I called the operator and had her check the line. She informed me there was no ongoing conversation and said the phone was either out of order or off the hook.

When I got back to Mrs. Nixon's car, I said, "Would you take me by Don McCoy's apartment?"

She compressed her lips and I thought she was going to refuse, but instead she said, "I'll have Arthur take me home, and then drive you over there."

"Thank you."

We dropped her at "one of" her residences, a ritzy apartment house near Beverly Hills, and then her driver took me to McCoy's less ostentatious residence.

"Mrs. Nixon instructed me to wait if you wanted," Arthur told me.

"I appreciate that," I said, "but I'll find my way back. Thanks."

He touched the tip of his cap, then drove off.

I went into the lobby of McCoy's building and rang his bell. There was no answer. I tried the oldest trick in the official Private Eye Handbook. I pushed a few of the other buttons and was buzzed in. With access to the elevators now, I rode up to McCoy's floor—the fifth—and found his apartment. I knocked and rang his buzzer and when I still didn't get an answer, I used my lock picks to get in.

The apartment was lit by a small lamp in the living room. On the desk next to the lamp was the phone, its receiver hanging by the cord, dangling just above the floor.

I went from room to room—there were only three—and finally found what I wasn't looking for in the bathroom.

Don McCoy was in the tub, but he wasn't taking a bath.

He was dead.

"How did you get in?" Lt. Taylor of the L.A.P.D. Homicide Squad asked me.

"The door was open," I lied.

"Is that so? If I searched you right now, Mr. Po, I wouldn't just happen to come up with a dandy little set of lock picks, would I?"

"You might," I admitted. "But that still wouldn't mean that I didn't find the door open."

He had to concede me that point, and he did so, grudgingly.

After getting over the shock of finding McCoy in the tub, with his blood running down the drain, I put the phone back on the hook and called for the police. A squad car had responded first, taken one look at the tub, and put in a call for Homicide, Forensics, and the M.E..

Homicide was Lt. Bryce Taylor, who reminded me a little of my sometime friend, sometime adversary on the N.Y.P.D., Detective James Diver. Taylor had a ruddy complexion and salt-and-pepper hair, and he also had a spare tire around his middle-aged middle. It didn't look so bad on him, though, because he was tall enough to carry it. Actually, at six-six or so, he was tall enough to carry almost anything.

The M.E., a Doctor Zetnor, came out of the bathroom and Taylor asked, "What can you tell me, Doc?"

Zetnor, a small, neat, precise-looking man of indeterminable ancestry—and his name didn't help—said, "He was shot twice, at close range. Either bullet looks like it could've done the trick, but I'll know more after I go inside."

"Report on my desk in the morning?" Taylor asked.

"As soon as I can," Zetnor promised. He supervised the removal of the body, and followed it out.

"You toss the place?" Taylor asked, turning to me. Before I could speak, he added, "Don't dummy up on me, Po. I won't come down on you if you level with me, but you're out of town talent. If you hold out on me I could cause you a lot of heartache."

He was tough, but didn't come on as tough as he could have, so I decided to level.

"I did look around," I said. "Just for something to do while I waited."

"What did you come up with that we'll eventually come up with anyway?"

"A note," I said.

"What kind of note?"

I explained to him my reason for being in town, and told him that McCoy had received a note that had caused him to withdraw from the mount of Dreamland.

"Horses," he said, shaking his head. "You know, even my wife makes a bet at Kentucky Derby time. Waste of money. Where's the note?"

"Top drawer of his dresser."

"Not in your pocket?"

"Lieutenant," I scolded.

"Sorry," he said, touching his forehead, "I don't know what came over me. Come on."

I followed him into the bedroom.

"You dust this dresser yet?" he asked one of the Forensics men.

"Yes, sir."

He opened the drawer, looked around and came up with an envelope.

"This it?" he asked me.

"That's it."

"Looks like a letter," he said. It was addressed to McCoy, with a stamp and a postmark, the date of which was earlier that week. He opened it, scanned it, and said, "Reads like a note."

"Read it out loud," I told him.

"What?"

"Humor me. I think I may be able to help you wrap this one up quick."

"I'm all for that," he said, and proceeded to read out loud.

When he'd finished, I said, "Let's check that note for prints, and I think I can tell you whose to check it against."

"If there *are* any prints," he said. "People who make death threats aren't usually that helpful."

"Why don't you give me a ride to my hotel," I suggested, "and

I'll tell you a story about a man and a slip of the tongue."

"All right, but you better have something worth the cab fare."

He drove me to my hotel, listened to what I had to say, and agreed to pick me up the next day. He admitted that I might have something, however slim a hook I was hanging it on.

"What did you get?" I asked as I got in his car the next morning.

"Enough to keep me going along," he said. "The man owes a bundle, his job is in danger, and we already had his prints on file from an old gambling bust. They matched the ones taken from the note."

"All right," I said. "Let me go in to talk to him first. Maybe I can get him to say something that will make your case easier."

"Okay," he said. "Here's the note."

"We going alone?"

"I'm short handed on my squad. That's the only reason I responded myself last night." He started the car, then added, "I'll have a unit meet us at the track."

"Quietly," I suggested.

"Natch."

I found Lew Hale watching the workouts and persuaded him to accompany me to his office. I told him I had some news about McCoy, and about the man making the threats.

"Man?" he asked me on the way. "So you've determined that it *was* a man?"

"Oh, yes," I said. "I'm dead sure it was a man."

When we got to his office, he sat down behind his desk and said, "Well, what about McCoy and the guy making the threats? You don't mean it was him, do you?"

I shook my head. "No, it wasn't him. McCoy's dead. According to the M.E.'s report, he was killed night before last."

"That's too bad," Hale said. "He was gutless, but that's not a reason for a man to have to die."

"My thoughts exactly, Mr. Hale," I said. "And yet, you *did* kill him."

"Me!?" he replied in surprise. "Are you crazy?"

"And there must have been more of a reason than the fact he was gutless."

"Have you got any proof of what you're saying?" he demanded.

"I think I do," I replied.

"Well, you'd better be sure as all hell that you do!"

"That's what first put me onto you, Hale," I told him. "That phrase you keep using. Most people say 'sure as hell' or 'fast as hell', but you always add the word 'all'. You said Dreamland was 'impressive as all hell', remember?"

"And that makes me guilty of murder?"

"Not necessarily, but that's what made me start to think you might be guilty of fabricating and making threats."

"Fabricating? Didn't Miss Emily tell you she got a call–"

"She did. She told me that the caller said she'd be 'lucky as all hell' to make it back from Kentucky."

"So?" he demanded, looking uncomfortable.

"And then there's this," I said, taking the envelope and note from my pocket.

"Now what's that?"

"A note Don McCoy received earlier this week, which probably caused him to withdraw from his mount on Dreamland. The note says he would be 'deader than hell' if he rode Dreamland in the Derby."

"I don't say–"

"Yes, you do, Hale. You don't notice it because it's become habit with you. But I noticed it right away. It didn't dawn on Mrs. Nixon because she didn't spend enough time around you that she would notice."

"This is ridiculous," he sputtered. "You have to have more proof than–"

"You owe a lot of money," I said, cutting him off. "Gambling debts. You stood to make plenty if Dreamland lost, but if he lost you also stood to lose your job."

"You're saying that I wanted him to run and lose, and that I didn't want him to run at all. You should make up your–"

"And then there are your prints on this piece of paper," I said.

"Prints?"

"Fingerprints. You probably had no way of knowing that McCoy would keep the note, and–not being a true criminal–it probably never occurred to you to wear gloves when you wrote it. Your prints are on file with the police because of an old gambling arrest, aren't they?"

He made a quick move, opening his top drawer and pulling out a .38.

"All right," he said, "all right." He was nervous, flexing his fingers around the gun, making me nervous. "I didn't mean to kill McCoy."

"Tell me about it," I said, sensing that he needed little prodding to do so.

"You were right, there were two ways I could go. I could allow Dreamland to run, hoping that he'd win and save my job, but that wouldn't pay my debts. Of course if he ran and lost, without my job I wouldn't be able to make any payments at all."

"Let me guess. First you scared McCoy, then you offered him a deal."

Hale nodded. "To pull the horse, throw the race. I'd make a bundle and the people I owe money to would make a bundle, too."

"What happened?"

"McCoy got irate, the little fool," he hissed. "He said he'd rather be scared off than bought off. When I showed him the gun, he jumped me. We struggled and it went off."

"Why were there no calls or threats for the past four days?" I asked.

"The people I owe found out what I was trying to do," he explained. "They said that keeping the horse from running so he wouldn't lose and cost me my job was small thinking. They said I'd lose my job anyway, sooner or later. They made me see that the only way to get square with them—and even make some money for myself—was to make sure Dreamland ran and lost. So I changed my plans." He flexed his fingers around the gun some more. "Now I've got to change my plans again."

"Did you find a jockey that could be bought?"

"There are enough of them," he said. "I'll give one of them the mount...but first I've got to take care of you."

"You're not going to kill me, Hale," I said. "Look at how nervous you are. You killed McCoy by accident. I don't think you can kill me in cold blood."

A drop of persperation rolled down his cheek to the corner of his mouth, where he licked it off.

"Besides," I went on, "the police are right outside listening to everything. Kill me, and you'll be a lot of worse off than you already are." I raised my voice and said, "Lieutenant?"

The door opened and Taylor walked in, followed by two uniform cops.

I took a step towards Hale, holding out my hand. "Let me have the gun, Hale. It's all over."

He hesitated long enough to scare me a little, but finally handed over the weapon.

"Okay," Taylor told his men, "take him out and read him his rights."

As they led the trainer from the office, Taylor walked over and relieved me of the .38.

"I guess he could look on the bright side," I said.

"What's that?"

"Maybe in prison he'll be safe from the people he owes money to."

"Maybe," the tall cop said, shaking his head, as if something were still eating at him.

"What's on your mind, Lieutenant?"

"Hm? Oh, nothing much," he said. "This is just the first time I've ever built a case around a slip of the tongue, that's all."

LOREN D. ESTLEMAN
(b.1952)

Greektown
(Amos Walker)

The restaurant was damp and dim and showed every indication of having been hollowed out of a massive stump, with floorboards scoured as white as wood grubs and tall booths separated from the stools at the counter by an aisle just wide enough for skinny waitresses like you never see in Greektown. It was Greektown, and the only waitress in sight looked like a garage door in a uniform. She caught me checking out the booths and trundled my way, turning stools with her left hip as she came.

"You are Amos Walker?" She had a husky accent and large, dark, pretty eyes set in the rye dough of her face. I said I was, and she told me Mr. Xanthes was delayed and sat me down in a booth halfway between the door and the narrow hallway leading to the restrooms in back. Somewhere a radio turned low was playing one of those frantic Mediterranean melodies that sound like hornets set loose in the string section.

The waitress was freshening my coffee when my host arrived, extending a small right hand and a smiling observation on downtown Detroit traffic. Constantine Xanthes was a wiry five feet and ninety pounds with deep laugh lines from his narrow eyes to his broad mouth and hair as black at fifty as mine was going gray at thirty-three. His light blue tailormade suit fit him like a sheen of water. He smiled a lot, but so does every other restaurateur, and none of them means it either. When he found out I hadn't eaten he ordered egg lemon soup, bread, feta cheese, roast lamb, and a bottle of ouzo for us both. I passed on the ouzo.

"Greektown used to be more than just fine places to eat," he sighed, poking a fork at his lamb. "When my parents came it was a little Athens, with markets and pretty girls in red and white dresses at festival time and noise like I can't describe to you. It took in Macomb, Randolph, and Monroe Streets, not just one block of Monroe like now. Now those colorful old men you see drinking retsina on the stoops get up and go home to the suburbs at dark."

I washed down the last of the strong cheese with coffee. "I'm a good P.I., Mr. Xanthes, but I'm not good enough to track down and bring back the old days. What else can I do to make your life easier?"

He refilled his glass with ouzo and I watched his Adam's apple bob twice as the syrupy liquid slid down his throat. Afterwards he was still smiling, but the vertical line that had appeared between his brows when he was talking about what had happened to his neighborhood had deepened.

"I have a half brother, Joseph," he began. "He's twenty-three years younger than I am; his mother was our father's second wife. She deserted him when he was six. When Father died, my wife and I took over the job of raising Joseph, but by then I was working sixty hours a week at General Motors and he was seventeen and too much for Grace to handle with two children of our own. He ran away. We didn't hear from him until last summer, when he walked into the house unannounced, all smiles and hugs, at least for me. He and Grace never got along. He congratulated me on my success in the restaurant business and said he'd been living in Iowa for the past nine years, where he'd married and divorced twice. His first wife left him without so much as a note and had a lawyer send him papers six weeks later. The second filed suit on grounds of brutality. It seems that during quarrels he took to beating her with the cord from an iron. He was proud of that.

"He's been here fourteen months, and in that time he's held more jobs than I can count. Some he quit, some he was fired from, always for the same reason. He can't work with or for a woman. I kept him on here as a busboy until he threw a stool at one of my waitresses. She'd asked him to get a can of coffee from the storeroom and forgot to say please. I had to let him go."

He paused, and I lit a Winston to keep from having to say anything. It was all beginning to sound familiar. I wondered why.

When he saw I wasn't going to comment he drew a folded clipping from an inside breast pocket and spread it out on the table with the reluctant care of a father getting ready to punish his child. It was from that morning's *Free Press*, and it was headed PSYCHIATRIST PROFILES FIVE O'CLOCK STRANGLER.

That was the name the press had hung on the nut who had stalked and murdered four women on their way home from work on the city's northwest side on four separate evenings over the past two weeks. The women were found strangled to death in public places around quitting time, or reported missing by their families from that time and discovered later. Their ages ranged from twenty to forty-six, they had had no connection with each other in life, and they were all WASPs. One was a nurse, two were secretaries, the fourth had been something mysterious in city government. None was raped. The *Freep* had dug up a shrink who claimed the killer was between twenty-five and forty, a member of an ethnic or racial minority group, and a hater of professional women, a man who had had experiences with such women unpleasant enough to unhinge him. It was the kind of article you usually find in the science section after someone's made off with the sports and the comics, only today it had run on page one because there hadn't been any murders in a couple of days to keep the story alive. I'd read it at breakfast. I knew now what had nagged me about Xanthes' story.

"Your brother's the Five O'Clock Strangler?" I tipped half an inch of ash into the tin tray on the table.

"Half brother," he corrected. "If I was sure of that, I wouldn't have called you. Joseph could have killed that waitress, Mr. Walker. As it was he nearly broke her arm with that stool, and I had to pay for X-rays and give her a bonus to keep her from pressing charges. This article says the strangler hates working women. Joseph hates *all* women, but working women especially. His mother was a licensed practical nurse and she abandoned him. His first wife was a legal secretary and *she* left him. He told me he started beating his second wife when she started talking about getting a job. The police say that because the killer strangles women with just his hands he has to be big and strong. That description fits my half brother; he's built more like you than me, and he works out regularly."

"Does he have anything against white Anglo-Saxon Protestants?"

"I don't know. But his mother was one and so was his first wife. The waitress he hurt was of Greek descent."

I burned some more tobacco. "Does he have an alibi for any of the times the women were killed?"

"I asked him, in a way that wouldn't make him think I suspected him. He said he was home alone." He shifted his weight on the bench. "I didn't want to press it, but I called him one of those nights and

he didn't answer. But it wasn't until I read this article that I really
started to worry. It could have been written about Joseph. That's
when I decided to call you. You once dug up an eyewitness to an
auto accident whose testimony saved a friend of mine a bundle. He
talks about you often."

"I have a license to stand in front of," I said. "If your half brother
is the strangler I'll have to send him over."

"I understand that. All I ask is that you call me before you call
the police. It's this not knowing, you know? And don't let him know
he's being investigated. There's no telling what he'll do if he finds
out I suspect him."

We took care of finances–in cash; you'll look in vain for a checkbook
in Greektown–and he slid over a wallet-sized photo of a darkly handsome man in his late twenties with glossy black hair like his half
brother's and big liquid eyes not at all like Xanthes's slits. "He goes
by Joe Santine. You'll find him working part-time at Butsukitis'
market on Brush." Joesph's home telephone number and an address
on Gratiot were written on the back of the picture. That was a long
way from the area where the bodies were found, but then the killer
hardly ever lives in the neighborhood where he works. Not that that
made any difference to the cops busy tossing every house and apartment on the northwest side.

He looked like his picture. After leaving the restaurant, I'd walked
around the corner to a building with a fruit and vegetable stand out
front and a faded canvas awning lettered BUTSUKITIS' FINE PRO-
DUCE. While a beefy bald man in his sixties with fat quilting his
chest under a white apron was dropping some onions into a paper
sack for me, a tall young man came out the front door lugging a crate
full of cabbages. He hoisted the crate onto a bare spot on the stand,
swept large shiny eyes over the milling crowd of tomato-squeezers
and melon-huggers, and went back inside swinging his broad
shoulders.

As the grocer was ringing up the sale, a blonde wearing a navy
blue business suit asked for help loading two bags of apples and cherries into her car. "Santine!" he bellowed.

The young man returned. Told to help the lady, he hesitated, then
slouched forward and snatched up the bags. He stashed them on the
front seat of a green Olds parked half a block down the street and
swung around and walked away while she was still rummaging in
her handbag for a tip. His swagger going back into the store was pronounced. I paid for my onions and left.

Back at the office I called Iowa information and got two numbers.

The first belonged to a private detective agency in Des Moines. I called them, fed them the dope I had on Santine and asked them to scrape up what they could. My next call was to the Des Moines *Express*, where a reporter held me up for fifty dollars for combing the morgue for stories about non-rape female assault and murder during the last two years Santine lived in the state. They both promised to wire the information to Barry Stackpole at the Detroit *News* and I hung up and dialed Barry's number and traded a case of scotch for his cooperation. The expenses on this one were going to eat up my fee. Finally I called John Alderdyce at police headquarters. "Who's working the Five O'Clock Strangler case?" I asked him.

"Why?"

I used the dead air counting how many times he'd asked me that and dividing it by how many times I'd answered.

"DeLong," he said then. "I could just hang up because I'm busy, but you'd probably just call again."

"Probably. Is he in?"

"He's in that lot off Lahser where they found the last body. With Michael Kurof."

"The psychic?"

"No, the plumber. They're stopping there on their way to fix DeLong's toilet." He broke the connection.

The last body had been found lying in a patch of weeds in a wooded lot off Lahser just south of West Grand River by a band student taking a shortcut home from practice. I parked next to the curb behind a blue-and-white and mingled with a group of uniforms and obvious plain-clothesmen watching Kurof walk around, with Inspector DeLong nipping along at his side like a spaniel trying to keep up with a Great Dane. DeLong was a razor-faced twenty-year cop with horns of pink scalp retreating along a mouse-colored widow's peak. Kurof, a Russian-born bear of a man, bushy-haired and blue of chin even when it was still wet from shaving, bobbed his big head in time with DeLong's mile-a-minute patter for a few moments, then raised a palm, cutting him off. After that they wandered the lot in silence.

"What they looking for, rattlesnakes?" muttered a grizzled fatty in a baggy brown suit.

"Vibes," someone answered. "Emanations, the Russky calls 'em."

Lardbottom snorted. "We ran fortune-tellers in when I was in uniform."

I was nudged by a young black uniform, who winked gravely and stooped to lay a gold pencil he had taken from his shirt pocket on the ground, then backed away from it. Kurof's back was turned.

Eventually he and DeLong made their way to the spot, where the psychic picked up the pencil, stroked it once between the first and second fingers of his right hand, and turned to the black cop with a broad smile, holding out the item. "You are having fun with me, officer," he announced in a deep burring voice. The uniform smiled stiffly back and accepted the pencil.

"Did you learn anything, Dr. Kurof?" DeLong wanted to know.

Kurof shook his great head slowly. "Nothing useful, I fear. Just a tangible hatred. The air is ugly everywhere here, but it is ugliest where we are standing. It crawls."

"We're standing precisely where the body was found." The inspector pushed aside a clump of thistles with his foot to expose a fresh yellow stake driven into the earth. He turned toward one of the watching uniforms. "Give our guest a lift home. Thank you, doctor. We'll be in touch when something else comes up." They shook hands and the Russian moved off slowly with his escort.

"Hatred," the fat detective growled. "Like we needed a gypsy to tell us that."

DeLong told him to shut up and go back to headquarters. As the knot of investigators loosened, I approached the inspector and introduced myself.

"Walker," he considered. "Sure, I've seen you jawing with Alderdyce. Who hired you, the family of one of the victims?"

"Just running an errand." Sometimes it's best to let a cop keep his notions. "What about what this psychiatrist said about the strangler in this morning's *Freep?* You agree with that?"

"Shrinks. Twenty years in school to tell us why some j.d. sapped an old lady and snatched her purse. I'll stick with guys like Kurof; at least he's not smug." He stuck a Tiparillo in his mouth and I lit it and a Winston for me. He sucked smoke. "My theory is the killer's unemployed and he sees all these women running out and getting themselves fulfilled by taking his job and something snaps. It isn't just coincidence that the statistics on crime against women have risen with their number in the work force."

"Is he a minority?"

"I hope so." He grinned quickly and without mirth. "No, I know what you mean. Maybe. Minorities outnumber the majority in this town in case you haven't noticed. Could be the victims are all WASPs because there are more women working who are WASPs. I'll ask him when we arrest him."

"Think you will?"

He glared at me, then he shrugged. "This is the third mass-murder case I've investigated. The one fear is that it'll just stop. I'm still hoping to wrap it up before famous criminologists start coming in from all over to give us a hand. I never liked circuses even when I was a kid."

"What are you holding back from the press on this one?"

"You expect me to answer that? Give up the one thing that'll help us differentiate between the original and all the copycats?"

"Call John Alderdyce. He'll tell you I sit on things till they hatch."

"Oh, hell." He dropped his little cigar half-smoked and crushed it out. "The guy clobbers his victims before he strangles them. One blow to the left cheek, probably with his right fist. Keeps 'em from struggling."

"Could he be a boxer?"

"Maybe. Someone used to using his dukes."

I thanked him for talking to me. He said, "I hope you are working for the family of a victim."

I got out of there without answering. Lying to a cop like DeLong can be like trying to smuggle a bicycle through customs.

It was coming up on two o'clock. If the killer was planning to strike that day, I had three hours. At the first telephone booth I came to, I excavated my notebook and called Constantine Xanthes' home number in Royal Oak. His wife answered. She had a mellow voice and no accent.

"Yes, Connie told me he was going to hire you. He's not home, though. Try the restaurant."

I explained she was the one I wanted to speak with and asked if I could come over. After a brief pause she agreed and gave me directions. I told her to expect me in half an hour.

It was a white frame house that would have been in the country when it was built, but now it was shouldered by two housing tracts with a third going up in the empty field across the street. The doorbell was answered by a tall woman on the far side of forty with black hair streaked blonde to cover the gray and a handsome oval face, the flesh shiny around the eyes and mouth from recent remodeling. She wore a dark knit dress that accentuated the slim lines of her torso and a long colored scarf to make you forget she was big enough to look down at the top of her husband's head without trying. We exchanged greetings and she let me in and hung up my hat and we walked into a dim living room furnished heavily in oak and dark leather. We sat down facing each other in a pair of horsehair-stuffed chairs.

"You're not Greek," I said.

"I hardly ever am." Her voice was just as mellow in person.

"Your husband was mourning the old Greektown at lunch and now

I find out he lives in the suburbs with a woman who isn't Greek."

"Connie's ethnic standards are very high for other people."

She was smiling when she said it, but I didn't press the point. "He says you and Joseph have never been friendly. In what ways weren't you friendly when he was living here?"

"I don't suppose it's ever easy bringing up someone else's son. His having been deserted didn't help. Lord save me if I suggested taking out the garbage."

"Was he sullen, abusive, what?"

"Sullen was his best mood. 'Abusive' hardly describes his reaction to the simplest request. The children were beginning to repeat his foul language. I was relieved when he ran away."

"Did you call the police?"

"Connie did. They never found him. By that time he was eighteen and technically an adult. He couldn't have been brought back without his consent anyway."

"Did he ever hit you?"

"He wouldn't dare. He worshiped Connie."

"Did he ever box?"

"You mean fight? I think so. Sometimes he came home from school with his clothes torn or a black eye, but he wouldn't talk about it. That was before he quit. Fighting is normal. We had some of the same problems with our son; he grew out of it."

I was coming to the short end. "Any scrapes with the law? Joseph, I mean."

She shook her head. Her eyes were warm and tawny. "You know, you're quite goodlooking. You have noble features."

"So does a German shepherd."

"I work in clay. I'd like to have you pose for me in my studio sometime." She waved long nails toward a door to the left. "I specialize in nudes."

"So do I. But not with clients' wives." I rose.

She lifted penciled eyebrows. "Was I that obvious?"

"Probably not, but I'm a detective." I thanked her and got my hat and let myself out.

Xanthes had told me his half brother got off at four. At ten to, I swung by the market and bought two quarts of strawberries. The beefy bald man, whom I'd pegged as Butsukitis, the owner, appeared glad to see me. Memories are long in Greektown. I said, "I just had an operation and the doc says I shouldn't lift any more than five pounds. Could your boy carry these to the car?"

"I let my boy leave early. Slow day. I will carry them."

He did, and I drove away stuck with two quarts of strawberries. They give me hives. Had Santine been around I'd planned to tail him after he punched out. Beating the steering wheel at red lights, I bucked and squirmed my way through late afternoon traffic to Gratiot, where my man kept an apartment on the second floor of a charred brick building that had housed a recording studio in the gravy days of Motown. I ditched my hat, jacket, and tie in the car and at Santine's door put on a pair of aviator's glasses in case he remembered me from the market. If he answered my knock, I was looking for another apartment. There was no answer. I considered slipping the latch and taking a look around inside, but it was too early in the round to play catch with my license. I went back down and made myself uncomfortable in my heap across the street from the entrance.

It was growing dark when a cab creaked its brakes in front of the building and Santine got out, wearing a blue wind-breaker over the clothes I'd seen him in earlier. He paid the driver and went inside. Since the window of his apartment looked out on Gratiot I let the cab go, noting its number, hit the starter, and wound my way to the company's headquarters on Woodward.

A puffy-faced black man in work clothes looked at me from behind a steel desk in an office smelling of oil. The floor tingled with the swallowed bellowing of engines in the garage below. I gave him a hinge at my investigator's photostat, placing my thumb over the "Private," and told him in an official voice I wanted information on the cab in question.

He looked back down at the ruled pink sheet he was scribbling on and said, "I been dispatcher here eleven years. You think I don't know a plastic badge when I see one?"

I licked a ten dollar bill across the sheet.

"That's Dillard," he said, watching the movement.

"He just dropped off a fare on Gratiot." I gave him the address. "I want to know where he picked him up and when."

He found the cab number on another ruled sheet attached to a clip-board on the wall and followed the line with his finger to some writing in another column. "Evergreen, between Schoolcraft and Kendall. Dillard logged it in at six twenty."

I handed him the bill without comment. The spot where Santine had entered the cab was an hour's easy walk from where the bodies of two of the murdered women had been found.

I swung past Joe Santine's apartment near Greektown on my way home. There was a light on. That night after supper I caught all the news reports on TV and looked for bulletins and wound up watching a succession of sitcoms full of single mothers shrieking at their kids about sex. There was nothing about any new stranglings. I went to bed. Eating breakfast next day I turned on the radio and read the *Free Press*. There was still nothing.

The name of the psychiatrist quoted in the last issue was Kornecki. I looked him up and called his office in the National Bank building. I expected a secretary, but I got him.

"I'd like to talk to you about someone I know," I said.

"Someone you know. I see." He spoke in Cathedral tones.

"It's not me. I have an entirely different set of neuroses."

"My consultation fee is one hundred dollars for forty minutes."

"I'll take twenty-five dollars' worth," I said.

"No, that's for forty minutes or any fraction thereof. I have a cancellation at eleven. Shall I have my secretary pencil you in when she returns from her break?"

I told him to do so, gave him my name, and rang off before I could say anything about his working out of a bank. The hundred went onto the expense sheet.

Kornecki's reception room was larger than my office by half. A redhead at a kidney-shaped desk smiled tightly at me and found my name on her calendar, and buzzed me through. The inner sanctum, pastel green with a blue carpet, dark green naugahyde couch, and a large glass-topped desk bare but for a telephone intercom, looked out on downtown through a window whose double panes swallowed the traffic noise. Behind the desk, a man about my age, wearing a blue pinstripe and steel-rimmed glasses, sat smiling at me with several thousand dollars' worth of dental work. He wore his sandy hair in bangs like Alfalfa.

We shook hands and I took charge of the customer's chair, a pedestal job unholstered in green vinyl to match the couch. I asked if I could smoke. He said whatever made me comfortable and indicated a smoking stand nearby. I lit up and laid out Santine's background without naming him. Kornecki listened.

"Is this guy capable of violence against strange women?" I finished.

He smiled again. "We all are, Mr. Walker. Every one of us men; it's our only advantage. You think your man is the strangler, is that it?"

"I guess I was absent the day they taught subtle."

"Oh, you were subtle. But you can't know how many people I've spoken with since that article appeared, wanting to be assured that their uncle or cousin or best friend isn't the killer. Hostility between the sexes is nothing new, but these last few confusing years have aggravated things. From what you've told me, though, I don't think you need to worry."

Those rich tones rumbling up from his slender chest made you want to look around to see who was talking. I waited, smoking.

"The powder is there," he went on. "But it needs a spark. If your man were to start murdering women, his second wife would have been his first victim. He wouldn't have stopped at beating her. My own theory is that the strangler suffered some real or imagined wrong at a woman's hand in his past, and that recently the wrong was repeated, either by a similar act committed by another woman, or by his coming into contact with the same woman."

"What sort of wrong?"

"It could be anything. Sexual domination is the worst because it means loss of self-esteem. Possibly she worked for a living, but it's just as likely that he equates women who work with her dominance. They would be a substitute; he would lack the courage to strike out at the actual source of his frustration."

"Suppose he ran into his mother or something like that."

He shook his head. "Too far back. I don't place as much importance on early childhood as many of my colleagues. Stale charges don't explode that easily."

"You've been a big help," I said, and we talked about sports and politics until my hundred dollars were up.

From there I went to the Detroit *News* and Barry Stackpole's cubicle, where he greeted me with the lopsided grin the silver plate in his head had left him with after some rough trade tried to blow him up in his car. He pointed to a stack of papers on his desk. I sat on one of the antique whisky crates he uses to file things in—there was a similar stack on the only other chair besides his—and went through the stuff. It had come over the wire that morning from the Des Moines agency and the *Express*, and none of it was for me. Santine had held six jobs in his last two years in Iowa, fetch-and-carry work, no brains need apply. His first wife had divorced him on grounds of marriage breakdown and he hadn't contested the action. His second had filed for extreme cruelty. The transcripts of that one were ugly but not uncommon. There were enough articles from the newspaper on violent crimes against women to make you think twice about moving there, but if there was a pattern it was lost on me. The telephone rang while I was reshuffling the papers. Barry barked his name into the receiver, paused, and held it out to me.

"I gave my service this number," I explained, accepting it.

"You bastard, you promised to call me before you called the police."

The voice belonged to Constantine Xanthes. I straightened. "Start again."

"Joseph just called me from police headquarters. They've arrested him for the stranglings."

I met Xanthes in Homicide. He was wearing the same light blue suit or one just like it and his face was pale beneath the olive pigment. "He's being interrogated now," he said stiffly. "My lawyer's with him."

"I didn't call the cops." I made my voice low. The room was alive with uniforms and detectives in shirtsleeves droning into telephones and comparing criminal anecdotes at the water cooler.

"I know. When I got here, Inspector DeLong told me that Joseph walked into some kind of trap."

On cue, DeLong entered the squad room from the hallway leading to Interrogation. His jacket was off and his shirt clung, transparent, to his narrow chest. When he saw me his eyes flamed. "You said you were representing a *victim's* family."

"I didn't," I corrected. "You did. What's this trap?"

He grinned to his molars. It's the kind of thing you do in these things when you did everything else. Sometimes it works. We had another strangling last night."

My stomach took a dive. "It wasn't on the news."

"We didn't release it. The body was jammed into a culvert on Schoolcraft. When we got the squeal we threw wraps over it, morgued the corpse–she was a teacher at Redford High–and stuck a department store dummy in its place. These nuts like publicity; when there isn't any they might check to see if the body is still there. So Santine climbs down the bank at half past noon and takes a look inside and three officers step out of the bushes and screw their service revolvers in his ears."

"Pretty thin," I said.

"How thick does it have to be with a full confession?"

Xanthes swayed. I grabbed his arm. I was still looking at DeLong.

"He's talking to a tape recorder now," he said, filling a Dixie cup at the cooler. "He knows the details on all five murders, including the blow to the cheek."

"I'd like to see him." Xanthes was still pale, but he wasn't needing me to hold him up now.

"It'll be a couple of hours."

"I'll wait."

The inspector shrugged, drained the cup, and headed back the way he'd come, side-arming the crumpled container at a steel wastebasket already bubbling over with them. Xanthes said, "He didn't do it."

"I think he probably did." I was somersaulting a Winston back and forth across the back of my hand. "Is your wife home?"

He started slightly. "Grace? She's shopping for art supplies in Southfield. I tried to reach her after the police called, but I couldn't."

"I wonder if I could have a look at her studio."

"Why?"

"I'll tell you in the car." When he hesitated: "It beats hanging around here."

He nodded. In my crate I said, "Your father was proud of his Greek heritage, wasn't he?"

"Fiercely. He was a stonecutter in the old country and he was built like Hercules. He taught me the importance of being a man and the sanctity of womanhood. That's why I can't understand . . ." He shook his head, watching the scenery glide past his window.

"I can. When a man who's been told all his life that a man should be strong lets himself be manipulated by a woman, it does things to him. If he's smart, he'll put distance between himself and the woman. If he's weak, he'll come back and it'll start all over again. And if the woman happens to be married to his half brother, whom he worships–"

I stopped, feeling the flinty chips of his eyes on me. "Who told you that?"

"Your wife, some of it. You, some more. The rest of it I got from a psychiatrist downtown. The women's movement has changed the lives of almost everyone but the women who have the most to lose by embracing it. Your wife's been cheating on you for years."

"Liar!" He lunged across the seat at me. I spun the wheel hard and we shrieked around a corner and he slammed back against the passenger's door. A big Mercury that had been close on our tail blatted its horn and sped past. Xanthes breathed heavily, glaring.

"She propositioned me like a pro yesterday." I corrected our course. We were entering his neighborhood now. "I think she's been doing that kind of thing a long time. I think that when he was living at your place Joseph found out and threatened to tell you. That would have meant divorce from a proud man like you, and your wife would have had to go to work to support herself and the children. So she bribed Joseph with the only thing she had to bribe him with. She's still attractive, but in those days she must have been a knockout; being weak, he took the bribe, and then she had leverage. She hedged her bet by making up those stories about his incorrigible behavior so that you wouldn't believe him if he did tell you. So he got out from under. But the experience had plundered him of his self-respect and tainted his relationships with women from then on.

"Even then he might have grown out of it, but he made the mistake of coming back. Seeing her again shook something loose. He walked into your house Joe Santine and came out the Five O'Clock Strangler, victimizing seemingly independent WASP women like Grace. Who taught him how to use his fists?"

"Our father, probably. He taught me. It was part of a man's training, he said, to know how to defend himself." His voice was as dead as last year's leaves.

We pulled into his driveway and he got out, moving very slowly. Inside the house we paused before the locked door to his wife's studio. I asked him if he had a key.

"No. I've never been inside the room. She's never invited me and I respect her privacy."

I didn't. I slipped the lock with the edge of my investigator's photostat and we entered Grace Xanthes' trophy room.

It had been a bedroom, but she had erected steel utility shelves and moved in a kiln and a long library table on which stood a turning pedestal supporting a lump of red clay that was starting to look like a naked man. The shelves were lined with nude male figure studies twelve to eighteen inches high, posed in various heroic attitudes. They were all of a type, athletically muscled and wide at the shoulders, physically large, all the things the artist's husband wasn't. He walked around the room in a kind of daze, staring at each in turn. It was clear he recognized some of them. I didn't know Joseph at first, but he did. He had filled out since seventeen.

I returned two days' worth of Xanthes' three-day retainer, less expenses, despite his insistence that I'd earned it. A few weeks later court-appointed psychiatrists declared Joe Santine mentally unfit to stand trial and he was remanded for treatment to the State Forensics Center at Ypsilanti. And I haven't had a bowl of egg lemon soup or a slice of feta cheese in months